THE LAST CAVALIER

ALEXANDRE DUMAS

THE LAST CAVALIER

Being the Adventures of
COUNT SAINTE-HERMINE
in the Age of Napoleon

TRANSLATED BY LAUREN YODER

PEGASUS BOOKS
NEW YORK

THE LAST CAVALIER

Pegasus Books LLC
45 Wall Street, Suite 1021
New York, NY 10005

ISBN-13: 978-0-7394-9373-1

Printed in the United States of America

The American edition of *The Last Cavalier*
is fondly dedicated to the Four Musketeers who
helped the book come to life:

Simon M. Sullivan, Michael Fusco, Phillip J. Gaskill,
and, most importantly, Peter Skutches

CONTENTS

A Note to the Reader

The Last Cavalier was originally published in France in 2005 under the title *Le Chevalier de Sainte-Hermine*.

A NOTE FROM THE EDITOR

Trumpeting the words *An unpublished work by Dumas has just been found!* is not the same thing as firing a cannon. The Great Alexandre, the most profligate spendthrift of his time, both with his creative energy and his money, had too many earthly needs to satisfy not to furnish at the slightest opportunity whatever texts publishers might ask for because they knew he was so willing. He wrote travel sketches, literary reflections, lectures, humorous essays on all sorts of topics, and recipes. Such pieces, often insignificant and printed in the columns of a hundred newspapers, were not always gathered together in book form; far from it. We are still finding some of them even today, and many of them have not yet been located.

But to proclaim the words *One of Dumas's great unpublished novels has just been discovered, and we had no idea that it even existed*—that is not simply lighting the powder to fire a cannon. It risks triggering a literary earthquake.

A few years ago, had those words been whispered to anyone who loved Dumas and knew anything about his work, that person would have smiled and said, "That is impossible!" And he would not have failed to support his opinion by asserting that even if we have not found the original versions of all the novels and tales that the writer first published in serial form in the contemporary press, surely all of his important narratives have been published in book form, thus escaping oblivion. Dumas needed money too badly not to take such precautions, for publishing his serialized novels as books allowed him to ensure that his work would last for centuries and also guaranteed that he would quickly double or triple his profits (the contracts he signed as a serial writer remind us that he was perfectly capable of demanding that he be allowed to publish his narratives in book form as quickly as possible).

So we can imagine Claude Schopp's astonishment and wonder when the universally respected scholar and premier specialist of Dumas's life and works discovered almost by chance (but is there really such a thing as chance?) a completely unknown Dumas text a few years ago. After he read the text and studied its background, he realized that it was the last of Dumas's great novels. "I imagine myself as fortunate as if I had discovered

El Dorado," Schopp writes today. We can easily believe that. For the novel in question, even though it was unfinished (and though unfinished, it is still a symphony of more than a thousand pages!), does not stand simply as our Alexandre's last conquest. It quickly proves to be the missing piece of the gigantic novelistic puzzle in which Alexandre the demiurge planned to include all of French history from the Renaissance up until his own day, from *La Reine Margot* up until *Le Comte de Monte-Cristo*. It is nothing less than the great novel of the Consulate and of the Empire, the same period that had seen the birth of our novelist and the death of his father, General Dumas, a brilliant officer who rose through the ranks during the Revolution and who was later broken by his rival Bonaparte.

All those knowledgeable about Dumas's work had noticed that this piece was missing and assumed that the writer had decided not to treat that era of history, perhaps because he was too closely associated with it. Some have proposed that Dumas gave the best part of his genius to illuminate history through his novels in order to avenge his father, who was a victim of history as much as anyone has been. So we shall not be surprised to see that Claude Schopp considers Le Chevalier de Sainte-Hermine to be a legacy novel.

One question remains. Even though this major text had been lost (which, after all, is not unique in literary history), how could it be that no one even suspected its existence? I could not help asking Claude Schopp that question the day that he told me about *Le Chevalier de Sainte-Hermine*, which he had been editing in secret for the past fifteen years, for Schopp had the reputation of knowing everything there was to know about Dumas. (Legend has it that during his long scholarly career Schopp has gathered enough documents about his hero Dumas to have in his own archives more than ten thousand biographical cards, each one corresponding to a single day in the writer's life from the time he was twenty years old until his death.)

Claude Schopp answered my question, but first he debunked his own legend somewhat. He said that he does not have a card for each day of Dumas's life (although it is true that for many days he has much more than one card). He pointed out that even though we know many details about how the energetic Alexandre spent his days, it is rarely possible to know exactly what he was working on when he shut himself up in his study. So, for the time period that corresponds to his writing *Le Chevalier de Sainte-Hermine,* the specialists know that he was writing a lot, even though he was ill. Sometimes he would cover the paper with his own large, beautiful penmanship, and sometimes he would dictate, if his hand trembled too much.

But he did not use ghostwriters on such occasions because they were expensive and the state of his finances did not allow it. As for the fruits of that late season, people only noticed those that had the opportunity to garner public praise, either because they appeared on stage or were published later in book form. Those works include *Le Grand Dictionnaire de cuisine,* a gigantic work that appeared only after his death; a five-act play drawn from his last novel, *Les Blancs et le bleus,* which enjoyed quite some success while he was still alive; and a novel he had set aside sixteen years earlier, *Création et rédemption*. He finished that novel in collaboration with his friend Alphonse Esquiros, though it appeared only after his death. He continued to make regular contributions to *Le D'Artagnan,* his final journalistic endeavor, and also wrote short notes and "chats" that people kept requesting. For a man near death, that is a lot. How can we imagine that he also had the time to launch (without any help, we must add) into a novel that would be longer than *Le Comte de Monte-Cristo,* even though Dumas had only about twenty months to live!

Claude Schopp explains how this final mammoth novel managed to see the light of day and how Dumas was interrupted by death before he finished it. He also provides today's reader the key for understanding the "Dumas mystery," for though Dumas seemed open and transparent, he knew better than most how to hide the shadowy parts of his own character. It took Claude Schopp fifteen years to study the ins and outs of that mystery. Season after season he worked to establish the novel's text from the serial segments that Dumas himself had never had the opportunity to edit.

For as we know, when Dumas took back his serialized texts to turn them into books, he took great care to correct the text and change any typographical errors, any inconsistencies, and any confusing sentences that had slipped by him when he wrote the first draft. No one better than Claude Schopp, of that we are sure, could complete such a Benedictine task. No one better than he could have presented the personal stakes that can be so clearly linked with the writer's final endeavor.

He proposed the following preface almost apologetically, because he thought it was probably too long. He asked me not to hesitate, if I thought it necessary, to cut it down. That was not necessary. What Claude Schopp discloses about his discovery and careful research shows that he is very much like a Sherlock Holmes, though perhaps a more modest Sherlock Holmes. As for the long quotations from Dumas that Schopp uses to support his ideas, they are often drawn from hard-to-find or unpublished sources, and they are fascinating (as when Alexandre puts in his place the bootlicker Henry d'Escamps, who panders to those in power and who dares lecture Dumas in the name of "History") and sometimes profoundly mov-ing (as when the writer, then only thirteen years old, sees Napoleon after his defeat at Waterloo).

Let us stop here. Claude Schopp's preface is indeed long, but so much the better. He has a great deal to tell us! Dumas is also long, much longer still, but his novel is more than a gift—it is pure happiness!

To some readers, though, the happiness will also bring sadness. For after the thousandth page, when we suddenly realize that the time for farewell is drawing near, we feel an unexpected lump rising in our throats.

A LOST LEGACY
Claude Schopp

❦

AN ARTIST'S LAST WORK, whether it be complete or only a sketch, whether it be a symphony, a painting, or a novel, carries *de facto* value as a legacy, as the artist's *ultima verba*.

On December 5, 1870, Alexandre Dumas passed away at his son's home in Puys, near Dieppe. Four days later, "on Friday, December 9, a Prussian column marched into the city . . . with music playing," we learn in *La Vigie de Dieppe*.

His sole legatee, Louis Charpillon, former notary in Saint-Bris (Yonne), justice of the peace in Gisors (Eure), a cautious man above all, had believed for a long time that Normandy would be "safe from Prussian incursions." Nonetheless, for fear that things might play out differently, he buried his most precious belongings.

"I am terribly sorry not to be able to send you the defeasance you request," he writes to Marie Dumas. "A week ago, I dug a hole in my cellar, and there I hid in a strongbox my most important papers, including the defeasance and my silver, etc.

"I am sending you a sketch of my cellar because my wife Jeanne and I are the only ones who know the hiding place. If we should happen to be killed, you, my dear friend, will be able to find what I hid for my children, along with your father's defeasance."[1]

Her father's defeasance, that is, Alexandre Dumas's testament, was buried-so the sketch indicates-in the second cellar, against one of the cross walls (near a circle, it is pointed out).

Once the war ended in debacle, Charpillon dug it up and placed it four months later, on January 21, 1871, with a notary in Rouen, Maître d'Été.

The writer's legacy novel, *Hector de Sainte-Hermine*,[2] lived a much longer

---

1 Autograph, BnF, n.a.fr. 24637. f. 96–97. L.a.s., Gisors, September 15, 1870.
2 The current editor and I, following a practice which would not have displeased Dumas, whose novel titles often changed as they moved from serial form to the editions they called reading room editions (*Une Famille corse* becomes *Les Frères corses*; *La Robe de noce* becomes

life underground than did the holograph testament—one hundred fifty years, in fact—before seeing the light of day again today. More than simply a book, it completes Dumas's work.

THE NOVEL REDISCOVERED

If perchance you find something you were not specifically seeking, it is because you have been looking fruitlessly for a long time. I was doing research in the Archives de la Seine near the end of the 1980s. I cannot be more precise than that. Though I am very careful about any dates relating to the life and works of Alexandre Dumas, I am much more casual about the dates marking my own life. The Archives were kept in the Hôtel de Maignan, a leaky old stone vessel, destined, it seemed, for early demolition. The reading room was dark and gloomy even on the loveliest summer days. We would feverishly skim through heavy file cards, which were dirty and crumpled, filed alphabetically, referring to acts from the Office of Public Records that had been reconstituted after fires during the time of the Communes. It was like wandering through an immense cemetery.

I no longer remember exactly what I was looking for. Certainly it was not the first time I had entered Alexandre Dumas's infinite dark forests with their thousands of twisting paths, but I had not yet examined all the dark corners of his work, which Victor Hugo called "sparkling, vast, multiple, astonishing, and felicitous in the light of day."[3] My ambition must have been limited to looking for the birth certificate of some illegitimate child or some document providing the exact identity of one of his mistresses or the mistress of one of his editors, Louis Paschal Setier, perhaps. I had probably ordered some such document and was waiting for it to arrive. In the Archives de la Seine, one tends to spend more time waiting than actually doing research. Waiting idly, I must have opened a drawer and leafed through other papers. By chance, at the letter D, I read: "Alexandre Dumas (père). Josephine's Debts, L.a.s., 2p."

I grabbed an order form, filled in my name, address, and the document number—8 AZ 282—and sent it off immediately. But I had to wait patiently before I could finally hold those two square blue sheets of paper in my own hands.

Cécile, for example) have chosen *Le Chevalier de Sainte-Hermine* as title, thus placing the emphasis on Hector's rank with the Sainte-Hermine family. Furthermore, we thus conform to the eight-syllable count of some of Dumas's other titles: *Le Comte de Monte-Cristo, Le Vicomte de Bragelonne.* . . .

3 Victor Hugo, *Les Contemplations,* Book V, XV.

Here I transcribe the document exactly as I read it then, without correcting any punctuation or spelling:

Josephine's Debts

Despite the additional note placed in yesterday's *Le Pays* and reproduced in *Le Moniteur,* not only does our collaborator and friend Alexandre Dumas maintain his assertions, but he adds for the edification of those interested some additional support for the proofs he has already provided.

Bourrienne is speaking, and he is the only person who can verify the accounts of the First Consul and those of Josephine:

"One can well imagine the First Consul's angry mood. Although I had only admitted half of the debt, he clearly suspected that his wife was hiding something. However, he said:

"'Well then, take six hundred thousand francs. Use the money to liquidate her debts and don't let me hear about this again. I give you authority to threaten her suppliers not to give them anything at all unless they relinquish some of their enormous profits. They need to learn not to be so free with selling on credit.'"

Here I could have shown the power of a man who, having set himself above the Constitution of the Year VIII by his actions on the 18th Brumaire, was not afraid of placing himself above the Tribunal de Commerce by not paying his wife's debts, or at least by agreeing to pay only half. But it appears that six hundred thousand francs in those days were enough to pay debts of twelve hundred thousand, since Bourrienne adds:

"I finally had the satisfaction, after lively disputes, of taking care of everything with the six hundred thousand francs."

It is true that he adds:

"But Madame Bonaparte soon returned to the same excesses. Her inconceivable mania for spending was the primary cause of all her problems. Her reckless use of money made for permanent disorder in her household, up until the second marriage with Bonaparte, when, so people have said, she settled down."

We cannot accuse Bourrienne of being spiteful to Josephine, for he remained her best friend up until the end. Never does he fail to seize an opportunity to praise Josephine, and never does he speak of her without expressing his gratitude for all the kindness she has bestowed upon him.

And now let us listen to the man who must have known the most about Josephine's debts, for he is the one who paid them.

"Josephine," said the Emperor, "had that excessive taste for luxury, for untidiness, for lack of restraint in her spending that is so typical of

Creoles. It was impossible to know how her accounts stood. She always owed something. And so there were always constant quarrels when it came time to pay her debts. Often she would send word to her suppliers that they should only ask for half of what she owed them. Even on the Isle of Elba, Josephine's bills would swoop down on me from all over Italy." (page 400) *Mémorial de Ste-Hélène*, vol. 3.

Let us conclude with the parallel Napoleon makes between his two wives:

"At no time in the life of the first were there attitudes or positions other than pleasing or seductive. It would have been impossible to catch her or to see any problem in what she was doing; she used all imaginable art to favor her attractiveness, but with such mystery that no one could have guessed. The second, on the other hand, never even suspected that there might be something to gain in innocent artifice.

"One was always slightly off the mark about what was true, and her first reaction was always negative. The other never tried to dissimulate, and beating around the bush was not in her nature. The first never asked her husband for anything, but she always owed something to everyone else. The second never hesitated asking when she needed anything, but that was quite rare. She would never have considered buying something without paying for it immediately. However, both were good, sweet, and strongly attached to their husband. But you have probably already guessed which woman is which. Whoever has seen them can recognize the two empresses." (page 407) *Mémorial de Ste-Hélène*, vol. 3.

My dear director, that is what I could have written to Monsieur Henry d'Escamps, but I thought that it would be useless to furnish copy gratis for *Le Pays*, if you yourself might place some value upon it.

I contented myself with writing the following letter:

"To Monsieur the editor of the newspaper *Le Pays*,

Monsieur,

Your answer is not an answer. I was speaking of the twelve hundred thousand francs of debts Josephine contracted from 1800 to 1801, that is, over a period of one year. I was not speaking of debts from 1804 to 1809. I leave the accounts for those five years to Monsieur Ballouhey, to Monsieur de Lavalette, and to you, not doubting that the three of you together will be able to give an account that is as exact as what Monsieur Magne accomplished for the lost four billion used over a seven or eight year period to balance the budget.

Please accept, Monsieur, my very best wishes.

Alexandre Dumas"

The handwriting and the signature were indeed those of Alexandre Dumas senior, not junior, and not those of General Matthieu Dumas or of any other Dumas, for the Dumases are legion.

I had found; I now had to search.

So Dumas had portrayed Josephine plagued by her creditors in a text published in *Le Moniteur universel* and had drawn the wrath of Monsieur Henry d'Escamps of *Le Pays*. Dumas was answering his contradictor, in a letter to be published, by citing the sources he had used; and that is all that I could affirm. The Dumas text itself was unknown to me. I verified that it had not been catalogued in any of the Alexandre Dumas bibliographies (neither in Reed nor in *Alexandre Dumas père: A Bibliography of Works Published in French, 1825-1900* by Douglas Munro). Of course, as is often the case with Dumas, the document was not dated.

Today I am incapable of remembering in detail all the various paths I took in trying to reach my goal. I must have looked in vain for a biographical sketch of Henry d'Escamps, and I probably remembered that Pierre Magne had been Minister of Finances between 1867 and 1870. I fruitlessly exhumed the brochure *Letter addressed May 16, 1827 to Monsieur le Comte de Lavalette, by Monsieur Ballouhey, former budget secretary of Her Majesty the Empress Josephine, in-octavo, 1843,* found in the second volume of Monsieur le Comte de Lavalette's *Mémoires* (p. 376); I must have deduced that because it was publishing a text sullying Josephine's reputation, *Le Moniteur universel* could only have ceased being the official newspaper of the Second Empire. And that change must have taken place on January 1, 1869, when the *Journal officiel* was founded.

Whatever my path may have been, I can imagine myself one day under the dome of the periodical room in the Bibliothèque Nationale, working in one of those little booths that look like confessionals, scrolling through a microfilm from the newspaper covering the first trimester of 1869, and discovering not the letter I had just uncovered (a letter that was never published, neither in *Le Moniteur universel* or in *Le Pays*), not an article by Dumas about Josephine's debts, but a serialized novel, a very long novel, unfortunately unfinished: one hundred eighteen chapters running, rather irregularly, from January 1 to October 30, 1869. Nearly a year of serials! I can imagine that I must have been as happy as if I had discovered El Dorado. It was Alexandre Dumas's final novel, a novel interrupted by illness and death, the novel on which his indefatigable pen finally had come to a stop.

Using all the funds at my disposal, a few months later I was able to obtain a photocopy of those chapters, and I eagerly attacked the thick bundle. At the time, though, no one was discussing whether Dumas should some day be in the Pantheon. But Guy Schoeller, director at the publishers

Bouquins, loved Dumas (in the ninth grade, bent over his desk, he would read *Le Comte de Monte-Cristo* during his Latin class), and he agreed to include *Hector de Sainte-Hermine* in the series "The Great Novels of Alexandre Dumas," of which I was the director. Because of changes in the editorial policies of the publisher, he was unable to carry out the project, however, and returned to me the manuscript.

"But when will you finally publish *Hector*?" my impatient friend Christophe Mercier kept asking each time I would meet him. I had told him about my secret child.

Today it has become a reality, thanks to Jean-Pierre Sicre, who has every bit as much panache as Guy Schoeller and who is his worthy successor.

"*Habent sua fata libelli*" ("Each book has its own destiny"), Dumas used to delight in saying, quoting Terentianus Maurus.

The novel is reconstructed

Approximately one hundred and twenty years before the rediscovery of the text you will be reading, Alexandre Dumas, at his house on the Boulevard Malesherbes, was seated at his worktable or lying in his low bed and writing on his sky-blue paper, on 21-by-27-centimeter sheets, the first sentence of his novel: "'Now that we are in the Tuileries,' the First Consul said to his secretary Bourrienne, as they entered the palace where Louis XVI had made his next-to-last stop between Versailles and the scaffold, 'we must try to stay.'"

The year before, on October 25, 1867, *La Petite Presse* had published in serial form *Les Blancs et les bleus,* which, in four autonomous sequences—"Les Prussiens sur le Rhin," "Le Treize Vendémiaire," "Le Dix-Huit Fructidor," and "La Huitième Crusade"—had painted a vast tableau of the history of France from December 1793 to August 1799, that is, from the Terror to Bonaparte's return from Egypt: "The book we are writing is far from being a novel, and perhaps it is not enough of a novel for some readers. We have already said that it has been written to accompany history step by step," Dumas had noted.[4] And he also said, "It should be obvious in the work we place before our readers that we are more a novelizing historian than a historical novelist. We believe we have displayed sufficient imagination to be allowed to demonstrate exactitude, trying to maintain, however, sufficient flights of poetry to facilitate reading and seduce the reader and avoid history stripped of all ornamentation."[5]

---

4 "Le Dix-Huit Fructidor," chapter XXVIII.
5 "Le Dix-Huit Fructidor," chapter XVI.

To the same end, in November 1866, writing as a historian, the novelist had sent the following letter to Napoleon III, Caesar's mediocre nephew:

Illustrious colleague,

When you undertook writing the life of the man who conquered the Gauls,[6] every library was eager to place its documents at your disposal.

The result was a work that is superior to others because it incorporates the greatest quantity of historical documents.

Occupied as I am just now with writing the history of another Caesar named Napoleon Bonaparte, I need documents relating to his appearance on the world's scene.

In short, I would like to have every brochure published about the 13th Vendémiaire.[7]

I asked for them all at the Library, and they refused to give them to me.

The only means left to me is to ask you, my illustrious colleague, to whom nothing is refused, to request those brochures in your name from the Library and to put them at my disposal once you have received them.

If you are willing to grant my request, you will have rendered me a service I shall never forget.

I have the honor to be, with respect,

Illustrious colleague of *La Vie de César*,

Your humble and very grateful colleague.

Alex. Dumas[8]

If one is to believe *Le Journal du Havre* of August 27, 1867, the letter bore fruit. Upon the intervention of Victor Duruy, Minister of Public Instruction, Dumas was likely given access to the sources he requested. And the writer had been able to describe the appearance on the world scene of Napoleon Bonaparte, "the man who illuminated the first part of the nineteenth century with his glorious torch."[9]

If we read *Les Blancs et les bleus* carefully, we note that Hector de Sainte-

6 Under the name of Napoleon III, the following book had been published: *Histoire de Jules César*, Imprimerie impériale, 1865–1866, 3 volumes in-folio; H. Plon, 1865–1866, 2 gr. in-octavo.

7 "Le Treize Vendémiaire," the second part of *Les Blancs et le bleus*, was published in *La Petite Presse* (July 18–August 21, 1867) after *Le Mousquetaire* ceased to appear.

8 Published in *Le Journal du Havre*, on August 27, 1867, and in *La Petite Presse*, on August 31, 1867. The letter seems to be contemporaneous with the transformation of *Les Nouvelles* into *Mousquetaire*, of which Dumas becomes the director (November 18, 1866). The new journal announces *Les Blancs et les bleus*, the continuation of *Les Compagnons de Jéhu*, only on December 20, and prints the preface the next day. The novel begins to appear in serial form on January 13, 1867.

9 "La Huitième Croisade," chapter XVII.

Hermine, the hero of the newly discovered novel, makes a furtive appearance when his brother Charles declares to Cadoudal that if he is guillotined, "just as my elder brother inherited vengeance from my father [guillotined], just as I have inherited vengeance from my elder brother [shot], my younger brother will inherit my own vengeance."[10]

He still does not have a given name and no particular characteristics except his rank among his brothers. He is simply the youngest son held in reserve. The mission precedes the individual.

He will need another year before he himself dons the cloak of a novel's hero.

In the meantime, A. Dumas attempted his final journalistic adventure with *Le D'Artagnan,* an adventure that he eventually found to be moribund and which he abandoned in order to spend the summer in Le Havre, at the exciting maritime exposition. Indeed, he seemed to appear everywhere: at the Hotel Frascati, at the Spanish bull corridas, at the Harfleur races, and at the theater, where he sponsored performances benefiting impoverished actors, all the while finding the time to continue working on *Création et rédemption,* a novel he had begun sixteen years earlier in Brussels, with his collaborator Alphonse Esquiros:[11] "Because he must work until four in the afternoon, you cannot be annoyed with him for not receiving visitors before then," his secretary Georges d'Orgeval writes.

As for what follows, how he conceived of and began writing *Hector,* I am forced to summarize what my ten years of research have allowed me to reconstitute.

It was probably in Le Havre, near the end of that summer, that Dumas dictated to his secretary of the moment, perhaps that same Orgeval, a letter for Paul Dalloz, director of *Le Moniteur universel.* Dalloz was printing, at that moment, his *Causeries sur la mer,*[12] as well as conversations on other topics, like insecticides, volcanoes, mustards, and something called "four-thief vinegar."

We ask that the timid reader skip the following letter,[13] to which we make no changes, and read it only after finishing the book. For it completes what is incomplete and finishes the outline of the novel's events (with many gaps, it is true). Alexandre Dumas's first movement always carries him toward the impossible. The canvas he proposes here is immense: nothing less

---

10 "Le Treize Vendémiaire," chapter VII.
11 Printed in *Le Siècle* between December 29, 1869, and May 22, 1870, and also published by Michel Lévy, in two parts: *Le Docteur mystérieux* and *La Fille du marquis.*
12 *Causeries sur la mer.* Preface and notes by Cl. Schopp. Marly-le-Roi, Editions Champflour, 1995, 144 pages.
13 We acquired this letter in 1991.

that the continuation of the history of that other Caesar, Napoleon I, from the moment he begins his rise toward the zenith to when he sinks beyond the horizon.

Here, my dear friend, is what I am proposing.

A novel of 4 or of 6 volumes entitled *Hector de Sainte-Hermine*.

Hector de Sainte-Hermine is the last member of a noble family in the Juras (Besançon). His father the Comte de Sainte-Hermine was guillotined, making his son, Léon de Sainte-Hermine, swear that he would die, as he himself did, for the Royalist cause. Léon de S[ain]te-Hermine died before the firing squad in the Harnem fortress.[14] He made his younger brother Charles de S[ain]te-Hermine swear to die for the Bourbon cause as he did. And Charles de S[ain]te-Hermine, head of the Companions of Jehu, was guillotined in Bourg-en-Bresse,[15] making the third brother, Hector de Sainte-Hermine, promise to follow the example his father and two older brothers had set for him.

Consequently, Hector joined the Companions of Jehu, swore a loyalty oath to the Bourbons and obedience to Cadoudal. And although he was deeply in love with a young Creole girl under Josephine's protection, and although she loved him too, he never dared declare his love, slave as he was to the ties binding him to the Bourbons and to the obedience he swore to Cadoudal.

But once peace is restored to La Vendée, Cadoudal comes back to Paris and has a meeting with Bonaparte, who offers him the rank of colonel or a pension of one hundred thousand francs if he will give up the struggle.

Cadoudal refuses, declares to Bonaparte that since he cannot stay in France he will go to England. As he is embarking, he sends his friend Coster de S[ain]t-Victor to free all his men from the oath of loyalty they had sworn to him.

And only then is Hector de S[ain]te-Hermine, freed from his oath, able to declare to Mademoiselle de La Clémencière his love for her and to ask for her hand in marriage.

His request is granted immediately. Everything is made ready for the wedding, and the day has been set. They are signing the contract, and just as Hector has picked up the pen, a masked man appears, comes over to him, and hands him a note.

Hector pauses, reads the note, lays down the pen, grows pale, gives a cry, and rushes out like a madman.

14 Auenheim, "two and a half leagues from Bischwiller, . . . the headquarters were in Auenheim," cf. *Les Blancs et le bleus*, ch. XV–XVI.
15 Cf. *Les Compagnons de Jéhu*.

The note is an order to go immediately to the Andelys Forest to rejoin his friends, the Companions of Jehu.

This is what has happened.

Cadoudal has faithfully kept his promise, but Fouché, trying to instill fear in Bonaparte, creates bands of arsonous brigades that in Cadoudal's name begin to ravage farms in Normandy and Brittany.

Cadoudal, whose name has been compromised, leaves England, comes back into France over the Biville cliffs, and requests hospitality at a farm.

By chance a band of arsons, led by a false Cadoudal, has planned to burn the farm that very night.

The arsons seize the farmer, his wife, and his children. They put their feet to the fire, and their cries alert Cadoudal, who comes in holding a pistol in each hand.

"Who among you is Cadoudal?" he asks.

"I am," a masked man replies.

"You are lying!" Cadoudal says to him, blowing his brains out. "I am Cadoudal!"

And since the oath made to him has been broken, he sends word to all his agents that he is continuing his campaign and that they should obey him as before.

This is the order Hector receives at the very moment he is signing the marriage contract, and that is why he rushes out of the reception room and takes the mail coach for Les Andelys.

The attack on a stagecoach takes place. Hector is wounded, taken prisoner. and imprisoned in Rouen. He is acquainted with the Prefect and asks him to come to the prison, telling him he absolutely must see Fouché, the Minister of Police. The Prefect assumes the responsibility of letting him out of prison, answering for him, and taking him by coach to Paris. They go to see Fouché.

The young man admits his guilt and asks for the favor of being shot without his name being made public. He was about to be allied with a family as noble as his own, about to marry a woman he adored, and he would like to disappear without casting either blood or shame on the woman who was to be his wife.

Fouché climbs into his carriage, goes to the Tuileries, and tells everything to Bonaparte. Bonaparte merely responds: "Grant him the favor he requests; have him shot."

Fouché insists that the prisoner be kept alive. Bonaparte turns his back and walks out.

Fouché contents himself with hiding the prisoner away, planning to speak about it later with Bonaparte.

The fiancée is in despair. Nobody can tell her what has happened to her lover. The conspiracy led by Pichegru, Cadoudal, and Moreau goes on. Cadoudal is arrested. Pichegru is arrested. Moreau is arrested. Trial. Situation in Paris during the trial. Inside the First Consul's mind. Cadoudal's execution. Pichegru manages to strangle himself. Moreau goes into exile.

Napoleon is crowned.

The evening of the coronation, Fouché goes to see him.

"Sire," he says, "I've come to ask what should be done with the Comte de S[ain]te-Hermine."

"What is all this about?" Bonaparte asks.

"He is that young man who requested the favor of being shot without his name being made public."

"Well, was he not shot?" the Emperor asks.

"Sire, I thought that the Emperor, on the day of his coronation, would not refuse me the first favor I would ask. I ask that the young man be pardoned, for I grew up with his father."

"Have him sent as a simple soldier to join the army, where he can get himself killed."

Hector de Sainte-Hermine goes off as a simple soldier, and during the Empire's long struggle with the rest of the world, he tries to get himself killed as the Emperor had ordered. But with every peril he encounters he performs some brilliant action, so that he rises through all the ranks for which the Emperor does not need to be involved, which is to say up to the rank of a captain.

From that time on, Napoleon, who has recognized the name, twice refuses further promotions. At Friedland, however, having witnessed a brilliant feat performed by the poor disgraced man, but not realizing who he is, Napoleon goes up to him and says:

"Captain, I promote you to major."

"I am unable to accept," Hector answers.

"And why not?"

"Because Your Majesty does not realize who I am."

"Who are you?"

"I am the Comte Hector de Sainte-Hermine."

Napoleon whirls around on his horse and gallops off.

Twice they try to promote Hector de Sainte-Hermine to major, but only at the battle of Eylau does the Emperor agree to sign his promotion order.

On the way back from Russia, Hector proposes leading the sled that will carry Napoleon back to France.

Napoleon has just removed his cross to give it to him when the mujik takes a step back and says: "Excuse me, Sire, I am the Comte de Sainte-Hermine."

Napoleon reattaches his cross.

The campaign of 1814 arrives. A major comes to Bonaparte carrying a letter from Marshall Victor at the moment when Napoleon has once again become an artillery gunner on Surville Mountain. A bomb falls at Napoleon's feet. The major shoves Napoleon aside and throws himself between him and the bomb.

The bomb explodes. Napoleon is safe and sound, and although he does recognize Hector de Sainte-Hermine, he pulls off his cross and hands it to him, saying:

"I believe there is nothing you would not do!"

Napoleon abdicates; the entire Sainte-Hermine family surrounds him. Hector is barely thirty-five years old, and his career will no doubt be magnificent if he wants to continue serving the Bourbons whom his ancestors, his father, and his two brothers served. They propose a commission as Capitaine des Mousquetaires, the equivalent of general, and he accepts.

However, during his first audience with Louis XVIII, he offends the king's susceptibilities by calling him Majesty. The king tells him that the word "majesty," having been profaned by the usurper, is no longer used. Now the word "king" is used, and people speak of him in the third person.

As he leaves his audience, Hector meets a beggar asking for alms.

He gives the man a coin.

"Ah," the beggar says, "that is not enough for an old comrade."

"Me, your comrade?"

"Or companion, if you prefer. Companion of Jehu. I was with you on that memorable evening when you allowed yourself to be captured. So you see that I cannot be satisfied with alms."

"You are right. You deserve better. Come to Rue de Tournon, number 11. That is where I live."

"When?"

"Immediately. I shall be waiting for you."

Hector gallops off, arriving ten minutes before the beggar.

He puts a pair of pistols in his pocket, sends his domestic off on an errand, and waits.

The beggar rings. Hector opens the door. He takes him to his study, opens a secretary, and says: "Take what you want."

As the beggar reaches out and grabs a handful of gold, Hector pulls a pistol and blows his brains out. Then he closes the doors, comes back to the Tuileries, asks to see the king, and tells him what has just happened.

He explains that he was a stagecoach robber, for the purpose of raising money for Cadoudal and serving the Royalty.

Louis XVIII, still disgruntled by the word "majesty," is willing to grant him pardon, but only on the condition that he resign his commission and leave France.

"Thank you, Sire," Hector answers.

He leaves for Italy, gets on a boat in Livorno and arrives at the Isle of Elba. There he finds Napoleon.

He has returned to join him and dedicate himself to Napoleon's fortune.

He comes back from the Isle of Elba with Napoleon, becomes a general at the battle of Ligny, participates in the battle of Waterloo, comes back to Paris with Ney. Labédoyère is sentenced to death along with them.

And then, Mademoiselle de La Clémencière, who has spent twelve years in a convent faithful to her first love, comes and throws herself at the feet of King Louis XVIII, begging him to pardon Hector.

Louis XVIII refuses, saying: "If I pardon the man you love, I shall also have to pardon Ney and Labédoyère, and that is impossible."

"Well then, Sire," answers Mademoiselle de La Clémencière, "grant me one last favor. As soon as Comte Hector is dead, allow me to carry off his body and bury him in our family vault. Not having been able to live with him in this world, at least I will sleep beside him throughout eternity."

King Louis XVIII writes on a sheet of paper:

"As soon as the Comte de Sainte-Hermine is dead, I authorize delivering his body to Mademoiselle de La Clémencière."

Mademoiselle de La Clémencière is Cabanis's cousin. She asks him if there is a narcotic that simulates death so well that the prison doctor, who must confirm that the prisoner is dead, could be fooled.

Cabanis himself prepares the narcotic. They are able to slip it to Hector, and the very night he is to be shot the doctor at the Conciergerie confirms his death.

At three in the morning, Mademoiselle de La Clémencière shows up with a post chaise at the prison gates and hands them Louis XVIII's order to give her the body.

The paper being in order, she is given the body, and they leave for Brittany. But on the way Mademoiselle de La Clémencière gives Hector an antidote, and once again he is in the arms of the woman he loved twelve years before, whom he still loves, but whom he has never expected to see again!

A. Dumas.[16]

It is also during one of the writer's short stays in Paris that Paul Dalloz visits Dumas at his last residence in the capital, 79 Boulevard Malesherbes. The director of the newspaper and his serial novelist agree on the conditions for publication, and the terms are confirmed the next day in a contract letter written by Dumas, undated, as is the case for most of his letters. He is to deliver the first of the six volumes of the novel he is writing especially for *Le Grand Moniteur universel* (the title at that moment is *Hector de Sainte-Hermine*), so that the publication can begin on January 1, 1869, and continue without interruption. According to normal practice, Dalloz can interrupt publication, but in his personal opinion, it would be better to continue publishing the episodes regularly. The price is established at 40 centimes a line. The work will become the author's property after it is published recto and verso in *Le Moniteur,* but his editor (Michel Lévy frères) cannot place any volume on sale until two months have elapsed after its appearance in *Le Moniteur.*

"I pray that God will keep you in his holy protection," he concludes.[17]

At the beginning of November 1868 the writer is back in Paris, in his studio, where, as it is described by Mathilde Shaw, "he had arranged his bedroom and assembled souvenirs of his family and friends: the portrait of his father, his mulatto face full of energy and loyalty; some watercolors given to him by his friend William III of Holland when he was heir to the throne; and finally a collection of quite handsome old weapons."

His age, though, has finally caught up with him. He is often ill and must remain in his large low bed, which faces the beautiful portrait of his son by Louis Boulanger.[18]

However, he does still have the strength to contemplate the future when, pen in hand or dictating if his hand is trembling too much, he delves into the past—the near past for him, since as a child he lived through the events he presents—as he throws himself into *Hector de Sainte-Hermine.* Although he does not realize it, it will be his final novel.

---

16 The handwritten document is torn and at the end there are a few gaps that we have attempted to fill. The signature is clearly in Dumas's handwriting.

17 Catalogue Roy David, 2001.

18 Cf. *Alexandre Dumas en bras de chemise.* Texts assembled and presented by Cl. Schopp, Paris, Maisonneuve & Larose, 2002, 256 p.

The following episode tomorrow or soon (or never)

When we consider the rhythm of the serial's publication, we notice that the first volume, comprising twenty-two chapters that were published between January 1 and February 9, appears regularly in *Le Moniteur*'s columns. It appears daily, except for Monday, which offers a serial play. The serialized novel is placed, as tradition demands, at the bottom of the first and second pages of the newspaper (except on January 9 and 17), and only on the front page from January 21 on (except for the last episode, which is found once again on both the first and second pages).

The second volume (or the second part of the first volume, as is indicated when it is delivered), with twenty-six chapters, meets with more upheaval. It begins on February 16, after the customary suspension of several days, and appears regularly until February 23, after which there is a series of interruptions ranging from several days (from February 24 until March 1; March 30; April 4 and 6; May 4, 5, 18, 22, 23, 26, and 28) to three weeks (April 8 to 28). It is completed on June 5.

What conclusions can we draw from these very specific observations? That Dumas gave the complete first volume (or the first part of the first volume) to Paul Dalloz before January 1, 1869, the date the first episode was published, and that then he had difficulty meeting the deadlines imposed by the daily publication?

Might events in his life help explain such difficulty? During the entire month of February, he was actively engaged in rehearsals for *Les Blancs et les bleus*, his play in five acts and eleven tableaux adapted from the first part ("Les Prussiens sur le Rhin") of the novel with same name. On March 4, he goes to Saint-Point, near Mâcon, to bury his old friend Lamartine. On Sunday, March 7, he attends a dinner dance beginning at 12:30 a.m., in honor of the one hundredth performance of the revival of *La Dame de Monsoreau*, in the Grand Hôtel du Louvre, where "for ladies, formal evening dress is forbidden," and "for men, formal dress in not required." But his health is failing, and the day after the ball his daughter Marie writes to a friend that she is taking care of her sick, tired father. "I have no time to myself with my beloved father whom you know. My own work, his work, and obligations of all kinds make my poor existence a perpetual pillage in which everyone takes things that belong to him or even things that do not," she adds. At the end of March, probably hoping to regain his health, he accepts the hospitality of Olympe Audouard ("a charming woman," he would say, with "only one flaw . . . she is always sick at the wrong time") at her little house in Maisons-Laffitte. He stays five or six weeks, and from there probably sends episodes one at a time to Dalloz by train. That perhaps explains the gaps in publication that we have pointed out. The good forest air in Saint-Germain does not appear to have had the beneficial effect he had counted on, since, around May 10, he admits to his son: "It is true, my hand does tremble, but don't worry about a situation that is only temporary. Too much rest makes my hand tremble. What do you expect? My hand is so used to working that when it has seen me do it the injustice of dictating instead of writing myself, it begins to tremble from anger. As soon as I start writing seriously myself, my hand will regain its majestic bearing."[19] And again, in June, just as he has finished the second volume: "I am better, and although I am not writing myself, it is only because writing is too fatiguing."[20]

The second part of the second volume (also designated as the second volume) in *Le Moniteur universel* comes immediately after the first part, on June 6. It is published regularly, although there are a few interruptions (June 10; July 3 and 6; August 5, 15, 17; and September 4, 8, and 26), which might be due to editorial necessities rather than to lack of copy. Its final episode appears on September 30. Clearly, the manuscript, in one or more bundles, was delivered in its entirety to Paul Dalloz before Dumas left for Brittany, probably on Tuesday, July 20, when he is feeling "worn out by slave labor. For the past fifteen years I have produced no fewer than three volumes a month. My imagination is edgy, my head is throbbing, and I am completely ruined. But I have no debts."

He spends that summer in Roscoff, where he continues working on his *Grand Dictionnaire de cuisine*. To Jules Janin, he writes:

> For the past year and a half, suffering from physical disabilities, supported only by moral will, I am obliged to draw the strength I need from momentary rest periods, from breaths of fresh sea air. . . . I have just come from Roscoff, where I expected to be able to finish the work from simple memories, but I needed to do a great deal of research and tiring work.
>
> Why did I choose Roscoff, the point that extends the furthest into the sea at Finistère?
>
> Because I hoped to find solitude, inexpensive living, and tranquility."[21]

19 Signed document: BnF, n.a.fr. 24641, fol. 150; only the signature is in Dumas's handwriting. The text of the letter was dictated.
20 Signed document: BnF, n.a.fr. 24641, fol. 151; only the signature is in Dumas's handwriting.
21 Published in the *Grand Dictionnaire de cuisine*, Paris, Alphonse Lemerre, 1872, p. 87–94, this preface-letter appears to date from September 1869.

Another undated letter to Pierre Margry, an assistant conservator in the Archives at the Ministry of the Marine, can obviously be closely linked with the writing of the second part; but it also raises some difficult questions.

Monsieur,
I arrived from St-Malo this morning and found your excellent letter. Needless to say, I accept your offer. I hope that you are young and nimble, because I suffer from a heart disease that keeps me from walking. Otherwise I would not dare tell you that I await you whenever you can come, for I am always at home. The sooner you come, the greater will be my pleasure to see you. I am acquainted with the work of Garnerey [*sic*] and I have seen nothing more picturesque about Surcouf. If you can give me some details about the coast of India, I would be much obliged to you.[22]

I place in your good graces my great uncle the bailiff Davy de La Pailleterie.
A thousand attentive compliments.
Alex Dumas[23]

Clearly, this letter answers an offer to write a biographical note on the Bailiff of the Order of Malte Charles Martial Davy de La Pailleterie (1649–1719?). It seems that Margry had read the first episodes of the second part of *Hector de Sainte-Hermine,* since he brought up Surcouf's name in the lost letter. Furthermore, thinking about the Burmese chapters, published beginning on July 13, Dumas asks him for "details about the coast of India." We could therefore appropriately suppose a trip by Dumas to Saint-Malo, unknown by biographers, between the beginning of June and the beginning of July. However, the chapters about Saint-Malo at the beginning of the second part seem to indicate that Dumas was familiar with the area before writing or revising them, and that would situate his stay there in May.

The publication of the third part begins immediately, on October 2, and ends October 30, without almost no interruption (only the 22nd and the 26th), and the episodes are now printed at the bottom of page two. Dumas did not leave Roscoff until about the middle of September. Had he worked

22 Louis Garneray, *Voyages, aventures et combats:* vol. I, *Corsaire de la République;* vol. II, *Le Négrier de Zanzibar,* Paris, Phébus, 1984 and 1985.
23 Handwritten document: Société des Amis d'A. Dumas, Glinel collection R 8/54; only the signature is in Dumas's handwriting. Mention: Alexandre Dumas before 1870.

on *Hector de Sainte-Hermine* while he was there? There is nothing to confirm that. We must therefore suppose that he wrote part three upon his return to Paris.

Dumas is perhaps alluding to his work on part three when he writes to his former collaborator Cherville:

> My good Cherville,
> I am both the most loving and the most forgetful of men. But I am forgetful only because of my immense workload and my boring distractions. I still love my friends.
> I never see you, and that is unfortunate.[24]

"End of part three (soon to be continued)," are the words written above the signature (Alexandre Dumas) of the last episode on October 30, although the last chapter, "La Chasse aux bandits" ("In Pursuit of Bandits"), has scarcely been sketched out and the resolution of the intrigue has been left hanging (how will René-Léo manage to reach Il Bizzarro?).

So the search begins as we scroll anxiously through spools of microfilm from *Le Moniteur universel*. For November-December 1869, nothing. January and February, nothing. And so on. Desperately, nothing. We have to give up: The continuation must never have been published.

And yet, we do have documents attesting that Dumas did not drop his pen in October 1869 and that he continued writing.

First, there is a letter to the same Pierre Margry, at the beginning of 1870:

> *L'Indipendente* Editor in Chief: Alexandre Dumas
> 10th year
> Offices: Paris, Boulevard Malesherbes, 107
> Naples, Strada di Chiaia, 54
> C.A. Goujon,[25] director.
>
>   Paris, January 15, 1870
> Dear Sir,
> Please do come dine with us this evening.
> If you are able and if you have them available, can you lend me:

---

24 Handwritten document: Société des Amis d'A. Dumas. The signature alone is in Dumas's handwriting. The rest was dictated.

25 "Administratore" of *L'Indipendente*, founded in 1860 in Naples by A. Dumas–in charge of writing the general news and reviews for the San Carlo Theater. Margry continued to direct the newspaper after Dumas left in 1864. Forced to leave Naples in 1868, he came back to Paris to see the old writer, accompanying him to Spain (1870), then to Puys.

1. *Le Manuscrit du Baron Fain*—1812.

2. Waren—*L'Inde.*

3. Ségur—*Campagne de Russie.*

You will be able to respond over some white turkey and a lobster that I have received from Roscof [*sic*].

All the best,

Alex Dumas.

[address:] Monsieur Margri [*sic*], Archivist in the Ministry of the Navy.[26]

Which book could the requested documentation have been used for? *Le Manuscrit de 1812, contenant le précis des événemens de cette année pour servir à l'histoire de l'empereur Napoléon* by Baron Fain (Paris: Delaunay, 2 vols. in-octavo); *L'Inde anglaise, avant et après l'insurrection de 1857, par le comte Edouard de Warren* (Paris: Louis Hachette, 1857–1858, 2 vols.), the third edition "revised and considerably expanded" of a work that appeared earlier with the title *L'Inde anglaise en 1843 et L'Inde anglaise en 1843-1844; L'Histoire de Napoléon et de la grande armée pendant l'année 1812, par le général comte Paul-Philippe de Ségur* (Paris: Baudoin frères, 1824, 2 vols.), which had gone through numerous editions. The three works all dealt with subjects relating more or less directly to the plot of *Hector de Sainte-Hermine.*

It would appear, then, that the writer was getting ready to recount the disasters of the Russian campaign of 1812. The reader had left Hector-René-Léo in Calabria at the end of the year 1806; might the author have intentionally made a leap of six years? The events of the first episode ran from February 19 until the beginning of April 1801; the events of the second, from April 1801 to June 1804; of the third, from July 9, 1804, until February 7, 1806; and of the fourth, from June to October 1806. No time gap appears between the various episodes. Why, then, suddenly, would Dumas have adopted a different narrative strategy? Or, on the other hand, should we believe that after his novel had ceased being published in the columns of *Le Moniteur universel,* he continued to write other chapters—which would have taken his hero up to the year 1812?

For me, doubt became certainty when I discovered at the beginning of the 1990s, in the book *Sur les Pas d'Alexandre Dumas père en Bohème* (in which Maria Ullrichovà indexes the Dumas manuscripts his daughter Marie had given to Prince Metternich), the following description (pages 190 and 191):

---

26 Handwritten document: Société des Amis d'A. Dumas, Glinel collection R 8/56; only the signature is in Dumas's handwriting. Mention: Alex. Dumas.

The manuscript number 25, having the title *Le vice-roi Eugène-Napoléon, fragment autographe,* is composed of twenty-seven sheets of light blue paper, with a format of 21.2 cm by 26.5 cm, numbered from 1 to 27 and written on only one side.

The first page carries the title of the first chapter, which runs through sheet nine: *"Son Altesse Impériale le Vice-Roi Eugène-Napoléon"* ("His Imperial Highness, Viceroy Eugene-Napoleon"), from *"On sait . . ."* ("We know") to *". . . le Vice-Roi"* ("the viceroy).

On page ten can be read the words: *"Le déjeuner"* ("At lunch"), designating a new chapter, from *"Les deux battans. . ."* ("The double doors") to *". . . monsieur, dit-il"* ("Please join us, monsieur") (sheet 18). [cf. p. 740, 745]

On page nineteen a new chapter begins, entitled *"Préparatifs"* ("Preparations"), from *"Une grande carte . . ."* ("A large map") to *". . . inclinée devant lui"* ("bowed respectfully"). [cf. p. 746, 752]

Summary: the follow-up of the Treaty of Campo Formio envisions the destiny of the Republic of Venice. Napoleon gave Eugène Beauharnais the title of Prince of Venice. His residence was in Udine, on the banks of the Roya. On April 8, 1809, a young officer named René appeared at his home, carrying dispatches from Napoleon announcing that in two or three days they would be attacked by Duke John. At lunch, René was asked to narrate his life's story, full of adventures. He was a prisoner, sailor, traveler, soldier, hunter, and bandit. He fought at Cadiz and Trafalgar, was sent to serve Joseph and Murat. Along with his military qualities, he was also a good musician and played for the princess one of his own compositions that was admired by everyone there."[27]

---

27 The collection is deposited in Prague, Stádni Ústrední Archiv. Among the numerous manuscripts preserved there are included:

Manuscript number 1, signed by Alex. Dumas and entitled *Hector de S. Hermine, fragments autographes,* is composed of twenty-five sheets of light blue paper, with a format of 21.5 cm x 27 cm, written on only one side. The sheets are numbered as follows: Sheet 1, then sheets 6 to 21, and finally 224, 224 bis, up to 230. The first page, carrying the title of the manuscript, shows us that it is the first volume and the first chapter of a work by Dumas, whose traditional autograph can be found on each of the pages. It is only when we reach page 21 that fourteen lines are added in a different hand. In the first chapter, with the title "Les dettes de Joséphine" ("Josephine's Debts"), four pages are missing from pages 1 to 9. Pages 10 to 19 are labeled "Comment ce fut la Hollande [*sic*, pour la ville de Hambourg] qui paya les dettes de Joséphine" ("How the Free City of Hamburg Paid Josephine's Debts"). Chapter III, which is not designated, pages 20 to 21, has the title "Georges Cadoudal." The text goes from: *"Nous voilà aux Tuileries . . ."* to *". . . dans cette ville."* [They are probably the first two pages of chapter one, which begins *"Nous voilà aux Tuileries"* ("Now that we are in the Tuileries . . .")].

Pages 224 to 230 constitute the chapter *"Le Prisonnier"* ("The Prisoner"). The text goes from *"Une heure après . . ."* to *". . . et sortit."* This chapter is designated "End of the first part,"

At the time of this discovery I was the only person alive who had read *Hector de Sainte-Hermine*. In spite of the disjointed nature of the summary, I could not but recognize a fragment opening a new episode of the unfinished novel I had read. Immediately I wrote to the Ústrední Archiv in Prague, from which several months later I would receive a photocopy of the manuscript pages I was so impatiently awaiting.

It was indeed the same hero setting out on a new perilous sequence, which would perhaps lead him to some glorious action on the battlefield at Wagram (1809). However, those pages, far from solving an enigma, proposed another nagging one. Did not the existence of this manuscript fragment suggest that additional fragments might have been destroyed or preserved by jealous or ignorant collectors, fragments that might have allowed me to fill in further gaps?

The publication we are undertaking today is also an appeal to search for the lost manuscripts.

POLEMIC

So the rediscovered letter to Henry d'Escamps that allowed me to rediscover the novel echoed the polemic triggered by the novel's first chapter, entitled "Les Dettes de Joséphine."

For on January 8, on the front page of *Le Pays,* which, since the coup d'état of December 2, 1851, had been the semiofficial newspaper of the prince-president who then became Emperor Napoleon III, Henry d'Escamps had viciously attacked Dumas without naming him. In his eyes, and in the eyes of the Bonapartists, Dumas was guilty of besmirching Empress Josephine's image:

> *Josephine's debts.* We ask the reader to believe that the title he has just read is not our own. It is the title of a serial that has just appeared in the first issues of *Le Moniteur universel.* The author puts the First Consul, his wife, and Monsieur de Bourrienne, his secretary, on stage and gives them language and sentiments that are both odious and ludicrous, against which history loudly protests. In order to show how unseemly such a publication is, a few of its features will suffice.

---

and signed "Alex. Dumas." [This is our chapter XLVIII, entitled "Après deux [*sic*] années de prison" ("After Three Years in Prison") and beginning in this manner: *"Une heure ne s'était pas écoulée . . ."* ("After the conversation . . . not an hour had yet gone by. . . .")].

One page, page 224, supplementary, does not belong to the ensemble of the above-mentioned pages. The text goes from *"Peu de personnes . . ."* to *". . . suit un ami."* [passage from chapter XXII.]

After refuting at length the impropriety of what he has done, the author concludes with a hymn to Josephine:

"Our memory of the Empress, moving out from under the clouds in which malevolence and foolishness have sometimes tried to envelop her, will remain as a halo of glory and clemency placed above Napoleon's victorious brow, and for the French people who loved her so, she will always be, as for posterity, 'good Josephine.'"

Alexandre Dumas is probably not displeased about the furor surrounding the initial publication of his novel.

But, in answer to the Bonapartists, with supporting documents, he seizes the opportunity in another letter to present at some length his conception of history, and incidentally, to chip away at the image of Napoleon III, liberator of Italy. The letter in question, written on January 9 or 10, is printed in *Le Moniteur universel* on January 11, 1869, preceded by the words: "We are sending the following letter to the director of the newspaper *Le Puy*, asking him to please publish it."

"To Monsieur the Director of *Le Puy*

Monsieur,

There are two ways of writing history.

One *ad narrandum,* to narrate, as does Monsieur Thiers.

The other *ad probandum,* to prove, as does Michelet.

The second method seems to us to be the better of the two, and this is why:

The first consults official documents, *Le Moniteur,* newspapers, letters and acts deposited in archives, that is, events written down by those who carried them out, and consequently, almost always modified them to their own advantage.

An example would be Napoleon on Saint Helena, looking back over his life and arranging it for posterity.

I saw in Monsieur de Montholon's hand the original of the letter announcing Napoleon's death to Hudson Lowe.

It had been modified in three places by Napoleon himself in his own handwriting.

Thus, even as he was dying, Napoleon was arranging a Napoleonic death for himself.

That method, in our opinion, is not the truth, but the paraphrase of the following maxim of Monsieur de Talleyrand: 'Speech was given to us to disguise our thoughts.'

The second method is totally different. It establishes a chronology of events, that is, of uncontestable facts. And then it seeks the causes and results of those events in contemporary memoirs.

And finally it draws a conclusion that those who write only to narrate

are unable to do. But those who write to prove are able to use such conclusions successfully.

Thus, for example, history *ad narrandum* would say:

The unity of Italy was accomplished under Napoleon III's lofty protection.

And history *ad probandum* would say:

The unity of Italy was accomplished in spite of Napoleon III's opposition. He adopted as a fait accompli the conquest of Sicily but did not
authorize Garibaldi to cross the Messina Straits, and the grand dukes of
Tuscany and others fell in spite of the support they received on Monsieur Walewski's orders from our consul in Livorno, who, because he
failed, was sent to America.

It is by following such a method, by entering into the smallest details,
that I have written four hundred volumes of historical novels that are
truer than history.

And I shall prove it to you, using as an example the novel *Hector de
Sainte-Hermine,* for which you do me the honor of troubling yourself
about.

First of all, allow me to cite, on the necessity of studying historical
figures carefully, a page from Madame d'Abrantès, who was not only a
witty woman but also an individual with imperial blood, since she descended from the Comnènes.

This is what she says about that excellent woman named Josephine,
whom people called Our Lady of Victories and who, they say, made off
with Napoleon's fortune.

'There are people,' says Madame d'Abrantès, 'who belong to history.
Josephine is among those people. Therefore, whether we consider her as
Mademoiselle de la Pagerie, as the wife of Monsieur de Beauharnais, or
as Madame Bonaparte, she is a person whom we must observe in great
detail. It will be with the help, the reconciliation, and the comparison of
such observations that posterity will possess a portrait of Josephine that
truly resembles her. Those objects that often seem the least important
sometimes furnish material for deep reflections. Josephine, as the wife of
the man who governed the world, and upon whom she herself exerted
some dominion, is clearly an important historical figure to study, although in and of herself she is of little interest in any area. However, she
needs to be examined carefully.

'There is one constant truth, and that is the unusual reputation, already at that time, that Madame Bonaparte established for herself. I shall
often have the opportunity to show her in her true light. Her true light
was somewhat doubtful whenever she was not guided by Monsieur de
Bourrienne. For he had gained control of her mind, or rather, of her fee-

ble character, and as soon as she was in Milan, she found herself, unsuspectingly, under his direct control.'[28]

So, Monsieur, as you see, there are two paragraphs. One of them tells us that Josephine is a historical figure who must be studied in all her facets, and the other that Monsieur de Bourrienne had completely taken control of her mind or, rather, of her feeble character.

Now we shall allow Bourrienne himself to tell you how he got along with the First Consul and with Madame Bonaparte:

'During the first months that Bonaparte lived in the Tuileries, he always slept with his wife. Every evening he would go down to Josephine's bedroom using a small staircase that led to a dressing room attached to a study that had once been the small chapel of Marie de Medicis. I never failed to use that small staircase when I went to Bonaparte's bedroom.

'And when he came up to our office, he always came through the same dressing room.'[29]

You might say, Monsieur, that Bourrienne could not possibly have gone into Bonaparte's bedroom in the morning while Josephine was still in bed.

You will see that many other things were permitted, and even required, of him:

'Among the particular instructions Bonaparte had given to me, there was one that was quite unusual.

'"During the night," he had said to me, "you will come into my bedroom as little as possible. Never awaken me when you have good news to tell me. With good news, there is no urgency. But if ever there is bad news, wake me up at immediately, for then, there is not a moment to lose."'

You see, Monsieur, that Bourrienne was authorized to enter Bonaparte's room during the night. So he must have had a key to the room, and if necessary, he could enter at any time. Or rather, in all probability, since the stairway communicated with Bonaparte's office, the key remained in the door.

Here is another passage indicating that he had orders to come in every morning at seven o'clock:

'Bonaparte was a sound sleeper. He slept so soundly that he wanted me to wake him up every morning at seven o'clock. So I was the first to enter his room, but often, when I tried to wake him up, he would say, still half asleep:

---

28 *Mémoires de la duchesse d'Abrantès* [Paris: L. Mame, 1835], page 279, volume 2.
29 *Mémoires de Bourrienne* [Paris: L'advocat], page 228, volume 3.

'"Ah, Bourrienne, please, just let me sleep a little longer."

'When there was nothing very urgent, I would not come back until eight.'[30]

After being in the Tuileries for a year, Bourrienne said positively that Bonaparte gave up his conjugal habit of sleeping every night with his wife and that sometimes, after being out at night with Duroc or for some other reason, he would sleep in bachelor's quarters he had set up on the second floor. On such days, Bourrienne, not aware of Bonaparte's nighttime escapade, would enter, as usual, the First Consul's bedroom and find Josephine there alone.

Besides, does it not seem to you, Monsieur, that there is something more indecent about seeing a man and a woman together in bed, even if they are husband and wife, than seeing a woman alone, in those days close to the era when women often received visitors while still in bed?

Now, we shall, if you allow, move on to Josephine's debts. Her debts had caused such a stir that nobody dared talking to the First Consul about them.

'One evening, at eleven thirty, Monsieur de Talleyrand brought up this delicate matter. As soon as he was gone, I went into the small office where Bonaparte was alone. He said to me:

'"Bourrienne, Talleyrand has just talked to me about my wife's debts. I have the money from Hamburg. Ask him exactly how much. Make sure she owns up to everything, because I want get to the end of all this once and for all. But do not pay without showing me the bills from all those rascals. They are a bunch of thieves."

'Up until then my fear of a nasty scene, the very thought of which made Josephine tremble, had always kept me from bringing up the subject with the First Consul. But I was pleased that Monsieur de Talleyrand had taken the initiative and so resolved to do everything in my power to bring the unpleasant business to an end.

'I saw Josephine the very next day. At first she was delighted with her husband's arrangements. But that was not to last. When I asked her the exact amount she owed, she begged me not to insist and to be satisfied with what she would admit to. I said to her:

'"Madame, I should not conceal the First Consul's mood. He believes you owe a considerable amount, and he is ready to settle everything. You will need to listen to sharp criticism and witness a violent scene, I have no doubt, but the scene will be the same for the amount you confess to as for an even greater amount. If you conceal a large part of your debts, when some time has passed, the rumors will begin again. They will again reach the First Consul's ears and his anger will explode even more violently. Believe me, you must own up to the entire amount. The results will be the same. You will have to listen but once to the horrible things he will say to you. If you hold back now, you will hear them over and over."

"'I shall never be able to own up to the whole amount; that is impossible. Do me the service of never repeating what I am going to confess to you. I owe, I believe, approximately twelve hundred thousand francs. But I am willing to admit to only six hundred thousand. I shall contract no further debts, and I shall pay off the rest little by little with what I can set aside."

"'Here, Madame, I must repeat my earlier observations. Since I do not believe he expects your debts to be as much as six hundred thousand francs, I can guarantee that you will experience no greater unpleasantness for twelve hundred thousand francs than for six hundred, and by asking for the maximum, you can ask once and for all."

"'I can never do that, Bourrienne. I know him, and I could never stand his violent reaction."

'After a quarter of an hour discussing the same topic, I was obliged to give in to her insistence and to promise to admit to only six hundred thousand francs when I spoke to the First Consul.

'You can imagine the First Consul's furious reaction. He suspected that his wife was concealing something, but he said to me:

"'Well, take six hundred thousand francs, but settle all of her debts with that amount, and I never want to hear about this matter again. I authorize you to threaten to give her suppliers nothing at all if they do not relinquish some of their exorbitant profits. They need to learn not to be so easy about selling on credit."

'Madame Bonaparte gave me all her bills. The exaggerated prices, due to her suppliers' fear of not being paid until much later and losing money, were hard to believe. It also seemed to me that actual deliveries were exaggerated. I noticed on the bill presented by the milliner thirty-six expensive hats for one month. There were heron-feathered hats costing 1,800 francs and other feathered hats costing 800. I asked Josephine if she wore two hats a day. She exclaimed that there surely had been some mistake. The saddler's exaggerations both in prices and in goods he had never delivered were ridiculous. I shall not go on about the other suppliers. It was the same kind of robbery.

'I made good use of the First Consul's authority, and I spared neither reproach nor threats. I am ashamed to say that the majority of her suppliers were satisfied with half of what they had been demanding. One of them accepted 35,000 francs instead of 80,000, and he had the gall to tell me that he was still making a profit.

'In the end I was pleased, after intense negotiations, to liquidate all her debts with the 600,000 francs. But Madame Bonaparte soon returned to the same excesses. Fortunately, money became less scarce. Her inconceivable mania for spending was the primary cause of all her problems. Her reckless profusion made for permanent disorder in her household, up until the second marriage with Bonaparte, when, so people have said, she settled down. I cannot say as much for her when she became Empress in 1804.'[31]

And furthermore, Monsieur, there is one thing you may not be aware of. Approximately two years ago, I won a lawsuit of great importance for those of us who are historical novelists.

In my study of the road to Varennes,[32] I had said that at the top the hill from which the whole town can be seen, the king was expecting to find an escort. But since the dragoons were not there, one of the bodyguards escorting the king got out and knocked at the door of a house where they could see light through the shutters.

The queen and Monsieur de Valory also started toward the house, but the door was pulled shut again as they approached. The bodyguard stepped up, pushed it open, and found himself facing a man about fifty years old, wearing a dressing gown, legs bare, with slippers on his feet.

It was a gentleman whose name I do not want to repeat. In his quality as major and as Chevalier de Saint-Louis, he had twice sworn loyalty to the king. But, on this occasion, his courage failed him. Recognizing the queen, he first refused to answer, then stammered something, and finally closed the door, leaving his august travelers in as much of a predicament as before. The grandson, pious guardian of his ancestors' honor, took me to court for libel against his grandfather. The court declared that, since it was possible, as I was doing, to base one's opinions on two contemporary witnesses, any man having played a role in historical events was accountable to history, and consequently threw out the grandson's suit and required that he pay court costs.

That, Monsieur, is what I wanted to tell you, thanking you for the opportunity you have provided for proving to the public that in my books I write only what is supportable by historical proof.

Alexandre Dumas"

31 *Mémoires de Bourrienne*, page 30 and following, volume 4.
32 As a "Causerie" printed in *Le Monte-Cristo* between January 28 and April 22, 1858, "La Route de Varennes" was included the same year in Brussels in "la collection Hetzel" before being picked up in 1860 by Michel Lévy.

Published the next day in the columns of *Le Pays,* the letter is accompanied by the following remarks by Henry d'Escamps:

The editors of *Le Moniteur universel* appeal to our feelings of collegiality, asking us to publish the preceding letter. We are delighted to do so because it confirms all of our claims.

Speaking about the novel, our contradictor invokes two methods of writing history, the method used by Monsieur Thiers and the one used by Monsieur Michelet. He modestly places himself in the company of such names, adding that in his opinion, the best way of writing history is to do research, not in serious public documents, but in the memoirs of the time.

We have no intention of arguing with such theories, but the reader will agree with us that we can only be surprised to see the author, when talking about the Empress who was idolized by the French people, when there is such an abundance of other documents, depend upon the memoirs of Monsieur de Bourrienne, the memoirs of the man who had to leave the First Consul's service under delicate circumstances. Such a collaborator can only bring misfortune to those who borrow his pen and his quotations.

Indeed, with the quotations he so rashly presents here, the author of the novel in question has chosen precisely the ones that prove the opposite of what he intended.

I cite as an example one of these passages. Monsieur Bourrienne says: "I asked Josephine if she wore two hats a day. She exclaimed that there surely had been some mistake." In spite of her denial, in spite of the testimony of Bourrienne himself, the novelist accepts and maintains the information as truth. We leave to sensible people the task of choosing between us and the author.

Such are the author's historical proofs. He needed to choose between Monsieur le Comte Lavalette, whom we evoked, and Monsieur Bourrienne. He chose the latter.

We could refute the preceding letter line by line, but we do not want to appear to be defending the memory of a person respected even by foreigners.

The reader will understand as we do that some things are indisputable. As for the novel's author, he obliges us to remind him that there is one faculty for the novelist, as for the historian, that can never replace imagination, talent, or wit, and that is a moral sense.

As we see, the letter I rediscovered in the Archives de la Seine was a response to that commentary. Alas, the stir raised about the first episode faded quickly away, and the rest of the novel seems to have been greeted with indifference. Such, at least, is what we are led to believe by the following short note by Pierre Margry. He evokes one of his visits to see the bedridden old writer, and it pains me every time I read it:

> One evening, when I went to his bedside after leaving my office, a priest, editor of a work to which Dumas had lent his pen, was there. He complimented Dumas on his *Comte de Ste-Hermine,* saying that he enjoyed following his story. (He was being paid 10 sous per line).
>
> "You are the only one, Monsieur l'Abbé, who has told me this. Nobody speaks to me about it. And I see that I am reaching my end."
>
> "Oh, don't talk like that. . . . You will continue to charm us for a long time. You [will recover] your health."
>
> "No, no. I can feel that death is near."
>
> "Let's not talk about that," said the abbé.
>
> "No, no. On the contrary, let's do talk about it. I need to prepare."[33]

Every time I read those words all these years later, I feel a rush of fraternal sympathy with the Abbé François Moret, for he understood that Alexandre Dumas the novelist, at the end of the 1860s, though he was no longer considered fashionable by the readers of the big newspapers, was still master of his art.

THE UNFINISHED CATHEDRAL

Historical novels, as we know, appear only late in Dumas's career, which at the beginning was essentially based in the theater. Before the historical novel, and like a number of essays with historical narration, he first composed chronicles of historical scenes, themselves introduced by general reflections about French history, in his work *Gaule et France,* which defines the general orientation of his thought.[34] In that book he divides national history into four epochs based on land ownership: feudalism, seigneury, aristocracy, and individual property. His materialist vision, dominated by the law of progress over which God (most often and for facility), Nature, or Providence is watching, was to be the thread connecting the different historical scenes, and indeed, it would also link his later historical novels.

Reading one of Dumas's historical novels means looking at things in the perspective of *Gaule et France.* Thus, *La Reine Margot, La Dame de Mon-*

---

33 Handwritten document: Société d'Amis d'A. Dumas, Glinel collection R 8/71.
34 *Gaule et France,* Canel and Guyot, 1833, in-octavo, 375 pages.

soreau, and *Les Quarante-Cinq* are novels showing the decadence of the seigneury; *Les Trois Mousquetaires, Vingt ans après,* and *Le Vicomte de Bragelonne* seal the fall of the seigneury and the advent of the absolute monarchy; *Les Mémoires d'un médecin* marks the death of the aristocracy; *Les Blancs et les bleus, Les Compagnons de Jéhu,* and *Le Chevalier de Sainte-Hermine* bring us into the modern age, of which the Comte de Monte-Cristo is the hero. The admirable narrative qualities and dramatic essence of certain scenes should not hide the general plan to which Dumas, as we shall see in this novel, remains faithful to the end.

Following the extraordinary success of his first novels (*Les Trois Mousquetaires, Vingt ans après*), the novelist reveals his grand project to Bérenger:

> The rest of my life is made up of compartments filled in advance, with future work already sketched out. If God grants me another five years to live, I shall have exhausted French History from Saint-Louis up to the present day. If God grants me ten more years, I shall have linked Caesar to Saint-Louis. . . . I ask your pardon for the vanity you may perhaps see in these lines, but there are certain men in whose eyes I would like to appear as I really am, and certainly, you are the foremost among those men.[35]

Dumas thus proposes translating the history of France into novels, but he sets as his principle not to write his novels *in* history, where the trappings of the past (décor, costumes, archaic speech) would only constitute a picturesque background as in those novels called troubadour novels, but rather novels *about* history, in which the heroes, even more than individuals, would be representatives of one of those social classes whose antagonisms make up the framework of individual and collective events and constitute the most solid material of all national history. The narrative has in truth only one heroine, that same France of which each named hero is only an incarnation in his particular place, time, and social position.

In *Les Compagnons de Jéhu,* of which *Le Chevalier de Sainte-Hermine* is the continuation, he returns to that same plan, defining and naming it:

> Perhaps those who read each of our books separately might be surprised to see that on certain details we spend time that seems inordinate for the novel in which they are found. That is because we are not writing an isolated book; but . . . we are filling or are trying to complete an immense framework. For us, the presence of our characters is not limited to their

---

35 Quoted in Benjamin Pifteau, in *Alexandre Dumas en bras de chemise,* op. cit., pages 64–69.

appearance in one book. The person you see as aide-de-camp in one novel [Murat], you will discover again as king in a second, then outlawed and shot in a third. Balzac composed a great and beautiful work entitled *La Comédie humaine*. Our own work, begun at the same time as his, but which of course we shall not attempt to describe, can be entitled *Le Drame de la France*."[36]

In *Le Drame de la France*, the forces at play, to keep the reader's interest (and Dumas has no other aesthetic credo than the Aristotelian to instruct while entertaining), must assume the different aspects of the human condition and find expression in all of the protagonist's emotions, his "loves, hates, shame, glory, joys and pains." In the poignant portrayal of a human being thrown into the very history he is constructing, most often as a blind instrument, the often-forgotten past is linked to the present, the ancient to the contemporary, as readers of novels meet historical characters. The writer restores to forgetful society a memory that can shed light on the obscurity of the present. The noise and furor of distant times find their echoes in the present furor, but no longer is it the Shakespearean idiot narrating. The narrator is a poet, a retrospective prophet who can distinguish order in chaos and uncover necessity where chance seems to reign. The book is, above all, the reading of another book whose author could be God. Beneath his unassuming legend, Dumas claims nothing less than to follow in the footsteps of prophets by finding in the past some signs for the future. His undertaking, whether or not he was fully conscious of it, deals particularly with the difficult birthing process of the modern world, from the beginnings of absolute monarchy to the advent of the Republic. A Dumas novel is never a novel turned only toward the past. Although the writer may long for bygone values, he never gives in to nostalgia for the good old days. He orients his historical narrative toward the present and the future, that is, toward the regeneration of humankind. The different epochs are like circles in which the writer places the reader to spiral up toward the social perfection he wishes to create. The past is not worth being restored unless it can help explain the present and foreshadow the future. Thus we should never be surprised that most of Dumas's novels are set in the seventeenth and eighteenth centuries, the prehistory of the present.

When, in the evening of his life (not five years, but twenty-five years later), the old writer considered the work he had accomplished, though he could rightly be proud of the monuments he erected, he could not fail, like it or not, to realize the gaps. He had not "exhausted French History from

36 *Les Compagnons de Jéhu*, chapter XLIV.

Saint-Louis up to the present day." In particular, there remained a gaping hole between 1799 (*Les Compagnons de Jéhu*) and 1815 (*Le Comte de Monte-Cristo*). Of course, Napoleon Bonaparte had indeed appeared in *Les Blancs et les bleus,* on the 13th Vendémiaire and during the Egyptian campaign, but he was still Bonaparte and not yet Napoleon.

Was Dumas's grand cathedral, like so many others, destined to remain incomplete? Porthos dies when he is crushed by the ceiling vault in the Locmaria grotto; Dumas dies while trying to construct an arched vault linking two bodies of his work. His final work as a builder is precisely this *Chevalier de Sainte-Hermine*, in which he projects Napoleon's problematic figure and sets up as a fictional counterweight the last representative of the Sainte-Hermine family, Hector, whose brother Léon was shot in *Les Blancs et les bleus* and whose second brother, Charles, was guillotined in *Les Compagnons de Jéhu*. Charged with the responsibility of pursuing the family's vengeance entrusted first to his brothers, the Comte and then the Vicomte, the "Chevalier," who in turn becomes the Comte, will escape the executioner but be sentenced by Fouché to live as a phantom. In that way he becomes the actor in and the witness to both the Emperor's glorious acts and his base actions, and he becomes one of the Emperor's admiring victims. He will meet Josephine, Fouché, Talleyrand, Cadoudal, Chateaubriand, the Duc d'Enghien, corsairs, police spies, society women, bandits such as Fra Diavolo and Il Bizzarro, and a thousand and one other brilliant walk-ons who play out their roles in this great fresco marked by fascinating excess.

This was, of course, not the first time Dumas was attempting to bring the Empire back to life through the novel form. In 1852, had he not already planned a story line including, along with fictional characters, Napoleon, Talleyrand, the twelve marshals, all the contemporary kings, Marie-Louise, and Hudson Lowe? His writing of that massive tale *Isaac Laquedem* was halted by time's censure and never got beyond the prologue.

NAPOLEON IN THE "DRAME DE LA FRANCE"

If in 1868, at the dusk of the writer's life, Napoleon already belongs to History, he is also linked to the writer's beginnings.

Young Dumas (he was thirteen years old) managed to see the modern Caesar twice. He evokes those meetings in a lecture given in 1865 at the Cercle national des Beaux-Arts in Paris:

Napoleon left the Isle of Elba on February 15 [1815]. On March 1, he landed in Golfe-Juan. On March 20, he entered Paris.

Villers-Cotterêts was on the route the army was taking to march on the enemy.

After a year of Bourbon reign, that is, after a year negating a quarter century of our history, it was great joy, I have to admit, for the wife and son of a revolutionary general to see those old uniforms, those cockades rediscovered on the Elba-Paris road hidden away with drums and those glorious tricolored flags riddled with bullet holes from Austerlitz, Wagram, and the Moskova River.

For us, seeing that old guard was a marvelous experience. They were soldiers whose likes we no longer see today, the living personification of the imperial period we had just traversed, France's glorious, living legend.

In three days, thirty thousand men, thirty thousand giants, marched by, purposeful, calm, almost somber. Not one who did not believe that the grand Napoleonic edifice, built by each man's blood, weighed heavily on them all, like those lovely caryatids at Le Puget that frightened the Chevalier de Bernin when he landed in Toulon. They all seemed proud to bear that weight, even though they could sense that they were beginning to bend beneath it.

Oh! Let us not forget! Let us never forget those men who were marching purposefully toward Waterloo, toward their tombs. They were devoted; they were courageous; they were honorable. It was France's purest blood, twenty years of struggle against the whole of Europe; it was the Revolution, our mother. It was the glory of the past and the freedom of the future. It was not French nobility, but the nobility of the French people.

I saw them all march by, all of them, including the last of those old men who had fought in Egypt. Two hundred Mamelukes, with their red trousers, their white turbans, and their curved swords.

There was something not only sublime but religious, holy, and sacred in those men who, sentenced as fatally and as irrevocably as ancient gladiators, could say as they did:

"Caesar, morituri te salutant." ("Caesar, those who are about to die salute you.")

However, these men were going to die not for pleasure but for a people's independence, not forced but of their own free will, of their own volition. . . .

They kept marching by!

One morning, the sound of their boots died away. The last notes of their music faded away.

The music they played was *"Veillons au salut de l'Empire."* ("Let's be sure the Empire is saved.")

And then the newspapers announced that Napoleon would leave Paris on June 12 to join the army.

Napoleon always took the same road that his guard had taken. So Napoleon too would be coming through Villers-Cotterêts.

I admit that I had a burning desire to see the man who, by leaning on France with the full weight of his genius, had also had a great effect on me, a poor atom lost among thirty-two million people. And he continued to weigh heavily on me, though he did not even know I existed.

On the 11th, the news was official. His horses had been reserved at the relay station.

He was to leave Paris at three in the morning. So he would be passing through Villers-Cotterêts at about seven or eight.

By six that morning, after a sleepless night, I was waiting at the edge of town with the most able part of the population, that is, those who could run as fast as the imperial carriages.

For it was not as he passed that one would be able have the best view of Napoleon, but rather at the relay station.

I realized that, and as soon as I saw the dust raised by the first horses a quarter of a league away, I started running toward the station.

As I got nearer, not taking the time to look back, I could hear the wheels thundering behind me, closer and closer.

I made it to the station. I turned around and saw three carriages flying in like a whirlwind, scorching the paving stones, drawn by sweaty horses and driven by postilions who were dressed in their finest, with powder and ribbons.

Everyone rushed toward the Emperor's carriage.

I was naturally among the first.

I saw him!

He was seated in the back on the right-hand side, dressed in a green uniform with white lapels, and wearing the badge of the Légion d'Honneur.

His face was pale and sickly, but it was as handsome as an antique medallion, seemingly hewn roughly from a block of ivory, for it had the yellowish tinge of ivory, and his head was bowed. On his left was Jerome, ex-king of Westphalia, the youngest and most faithful of his brothers. Facing Jerome on the front seat was Le Tort, the aide-de-camp.

The Emperor, as if being roused from sleep or coming out of deep thought, raised his head, looked around without really seeing and asked:

"Where are we?"

"In Villers-Cotterêts, Sire," a voice answered.

"Six leagues from Soissons, then?" he asked.

"Six leagues from Soissons. Yes, Sire."

"Hurry."

And he fell back into the somnolence that had been interrupted by the halt.

They had already changed horses, and there were new postilions in the saddles. Those who had just climbed down were waving their hats and shouting:

"Long live the Emperor!"

They cracked their whips. Napoleon nodded slightly in good-bye. The horses galloped off and disappeared around the corner on the road to Soissons.

The gigantic vision had faded.

Six days went by, and during those six days we heard about crossing the Sambre, taking Charleroi, the battle of Ligny, and the combat of Les Quatre-Bras.

So the first echoes were echoes of victory.

On the 18th, the day of the Battle of Waterloo, we learned about what had transpired on the 15th and 16th.

We impatiently awaited further news. The 19th went by without bringing anything new.

The Emperor, so said the newspapers, had visited the battlefield at Ligny and had brought help to the wounded.

General Le Tort, whom I had seen sitting opposite the Emperor in his carriage, had been killed when Charleroi was taken.

The Emperor's brother Jerome, who had been seated beside him, had had the pommel of his sword smashed by a bullet at Les Quatre-Bras.

The 20th inched by slowly and sadly. The sky was dark and stormy. Torrents of rain had been falling for three days, and people were saying that with such weather they probably had not been able to fight.

Suddenly the rumor begins to spread that some men, bearers of grim news, have been arrested and taken to the courtyard at the town hall.

Everyone rushes to the town hall, and of course I am among the first to get there.

And indeed, there are seven or eight men, some still in the saddle and others standing beside their horses, surrounded by crowds that are keeping them in custody.

They are bloodied, covered with mud, in tatters!

They claim to be Polish, and they can speak only a few words of French.

A retired officer who speaks German comes up. He questions them in German.

More at ease in that language, they begin to talk.

They say that Napoleon attacked the English on the 18th. The battle,

they say, began at noon. At five, the English were beaten. But at six o'-
clock, Blücher, who had marched rapidly to the battlefield, arrived with
forty thousand men and swung the battle in favor of the enemy. "Decisive battle. The French army is not simply retreating. It has been
routed."

The Poles are the vanguard of those who are fleeing.

It is now about three in the afternoon. In forty-eight hours, these men
have come all the way from Planchenois.

They averaged more than a league and a half per hour. Couriers of
misfortune sprout wings.

I run back home and tell my mother what I have just seen. She sends
me to the relay station. That is always where you can hear the freshest
news.

I sit down and wait.

At seven o'clock a courier arrives. He is wearing the Emperor's green
and gold livery.

He is covered with mud; his horse is trembling with fatigue and has to
brace its four legs to keep from collapsing.

The courier requests four horses for a carriage following him. They
bring him another horse that is already saddled. They help him up; he
digs his spurs into the horse's sides and disappears.

People questioned him in vain. He knew nothing or simply refused to
tell what he did know.

They lead the four horses he requested from the stable. The horses
are harnessed and stand awaiting the carriage.

A low rumbling announces that the carriage is almost there.

We can see it coming around the corner. It stops by the door.

The stationmaster starts toward it in astonishment.

I grab him by his clothing:

"It's him, it's the Emperor," I said.

"Yes!"

It was the Emperor, just where I had seen him a week before in a similar carriage, with one aide-de-camp sitting beside him and another opposite.

But now Jerome and Le Tort were no longer there. . . .

It was indeed the Emperor, the same man, the same pale face, sickly
and impassible.

Except that his head was bowed still further.

Was it simply fatigue?

Was it because he had gambled for the world and had lost?

Like the first time, sensing that the carriage had stopped, he raises his
head, looks around with his typical vacant stare that can quickly become

piercing when he concentrates on a man or on the horizon, those two mysterious things behind which a danger can always be lurking.

"Where are we?" he asks.

"In Villers-Cotterêts, Sire," the stationmaster answers.

"So we're eighteen leagues from Paris?"

"Yes, Sire."

"Hurry up!"

So, like the first time, after a similar question, using almost the same words, he gives the same order and leaves almost as quickly.

It was three months to the day that he had returned to the Tuileries after coming back from Elba.

However, between March 20 and June 20, God had dug an abyss in which his fortune was swallowed up.

And that abyss was Waterloo.[37]

"That man who, by leaning on France with the full weight of his genius, also had a great effect on me": Indeed, the child who watches Napoleon pass by is an heir not of material goods, since his father's death left his mother almost penniless, but of something much more important—a glorious inheritance, an inheritance diverted by that man, the Emperor, who has just passed.

Dumas will return time and time again to that recent, painful past, linked for him to his childhood. That episode will color his entire life.

It was General Dumas, the writer's father, whom the Convention had called to its defense when, on the 12th Vendémiaire of the year IV (October 4, 1795), the counterrevolutionary rebellion had reached the Paris sections.

The Convention sent General Alexandre Dumas, commander-in-chief of the Army of the Alps, on leave at the time, the following letter. Its very brevity demonstrates how urgent things were:

"General Alexandre Dumas will return to Paris immediately to take command of the army."

The Convention's order was taken to the Hôtel Mirabeau. But General Dumas had left three days earlier for Villers-Cotterêts, where he received the letter the morning of the 13th.

Meanwhile, the danger was growing by the hour. There was no way they could wait for the man they had sent for. Consequently, during the

37 The manuscript of this lecture is preserved in Prague, Stádni Ústřednř Archiv, Hore c. 2750 (Metternich collection, Ms. 44).

night, Barras, the representative of the people, was named commander-in-chief of the Army of the Interior. He needed a second in command. He chose Bonaparte.

Thus, the hour that rings once in the life of every man, opening up his future, had rung in vain for my father. He took a mail coach immediately, but he did not reach Paris until the 14th.

He found the sections vanquished and Bonaparte general-in-chief of the Army of the Interior.[38]

So the grand role had already been given to Bonaparte. General Dumas would be able to play only secondary roles, even though sometimes they would become nearly epic (the conquest of Mont-Cénis or the defense of the Klausen bridge, which earned him the nickname Horatius Coclès of the Tyrol on March 24, 1797).

Having embarked on the Egyptian adventure as a cavalry commander, General Dumas was nostalgic for revolutionary ideals and did not hide his mistrust for his fortunate rival. Everything made him suspicious of the general-in-chief's personal ambition. In his *Mémoires,* his son presents the famous meeting between General Dumas and Bonaparte that had "such a great influence on my father's future and on my own," when Bonaparte asks him to explain a meeting of disgruntled generals:

"Yes, the Damanhur meeting did take place. Yes, the generals, discouraged by the first march, wondered what the expedition's purpose was. Yes, they thought they perceived a motive of personal ambition rather than of public interest. Yes, I said that for the glory and honor of our homeland I would go to the ends of the world, but that if it were simply one of your personal whims, I would halt after the first step. And what I said that evening I am now repeating to you. If the miserable creature who brought you my words reported anything other than what I have just told you, not only is he a spy, but even worse, he is a slanderer."

Bonaparte looked for a moment at my father. And then, with some affection, he said:

"So, Dumas, you are able to separate your mind into two parts. You place France in one and me in the other. You believe that I can separate my own interests from those of France, my own fortune from France's fortune."

"I believe that the interests of France must come before those of any man, no matter how great he may be. . . . I believe that a nation's fortune should not be subject to the fortune of any individual."

38 Alexandre Dumas, *Mes mémoires,* chapters V and XII.

"So, you are ready to part ways with me?"

"Yes, if ever I believe that you are parting ways with France."

"You are making a mistake, Dumas," Bonaparte said coldly.

"That is possible," my father answered. "But I cannot accept dictatorships, not Sylla's any more than Caesar's."

"And what are you asking for?"

"To return to France at the first opportunity."

"Fine. I promise that I shall place no obstacle in your way."

"Thank you, General. That is the only favor I ask of you."

And with a bow, my father went to the door, pulled the latch, and walked out.

As he left, he could hear Bonaparte mumbling several words, among which he thought he could make out the following:

"Only a blind man would refuse to believe in my fortune."[39]

Leaving the coasts of Egypt after the Cairo revolt, "Dumas the black man," as Bonaparte called him, was also leaving behind a great destiny.

A storm forced his ship to take port in the Kingdom of Naples, where he was kept prisoner until March 1801. When he returned home sick and penniless, he wrote the following:

> But, General First Consul, you are aware of the misfortunes I have encountered. I hope that you will not permit the man who shared your efforts and perils to languish as a beggar. I have another concern: I have been listed among inactive generals. So, at my age and with my name, have I been discharged? At my rank, I am the most senior general. My feats of arms speak for me, for they had a powerful effect on events. I have always led to victory those who are defending our country. I appeal to your heart. (July 1802)

Although Dumas was allowed to receive his discharge pay (26 Fructidor, year X/September 13, 1802), he was no longer listed among the major-generals of the Republic. Bonaparte had sealed his military death.

> My health is gone and I am doomed to hardship and misfortune. Misery and sorrow are eating away at my life. The only thing that keeps me from despair is the thought that I have served under your orders and that often you showed me marks of your kindness and esteem. Sooner or later, I hope that you will deign to ease my fate. . . . I beg you to arrange

39 *Mes mémoires*, op. cit., chapters V and XII.

back payment for the time I spent in captivity in Sicily: 28,500 francs. (September 1803)

He was paid neither sooner nor later. He died in 1806, leaving his wife and children with no means of subsistence. A few hours before he died, he expressed the wish to be buried in the fields of Austerlitz.

Thus Dumas, faithful all his life to his father's memory, has mixed emotions regarding the Emperor, for they included both attraction and repulsion. On the one hand, the Emperor is the solar genius who for twenty years made France drunk with glory. On the other hand, he is the "Corsican ogre" who bled the country by taking her sons year after year and who, in Dumas's own "novel," is the true assassin of the writer's father.

However, during the Restoration and his captivity in Saint Helena, as well as after his death, as the Bourbons lost their popularity, the Emperor's image soon began to take on mythical proportions in the eyes of the very people who for a time held him in contempt: "Things got to the point where, without knowing why, and despite all the reasons we had to curse Napoleon, my mother and I had come to despise the Bourbons even more, though they had done nothing to us and may have even helped us more than harmed us."

That is why it is scarcely surprising to find that the young Dumas is employed as a ledger clerk in the service of the Duc d'Orléans (the future Louis-Philippe) and that he can be found in Bonapartist salons such as the one held by Antoine Vincent Arnault. Republicans, liberals, and Bonapartists are now making common cause against the Bourbons who are supported by the Company of the Holy Sacrament. Nor is it surprising to see, when he publishes his first verse, poems that glorify the imperial epic, poems such as "Leipsick" [*sic*] or the "Aigle blessé" dedicated to that same Antoine Vincent Arnault. We must note, however, that he sings more of defeats than of victories.

The Trois Glorieuses, the three days in July 1830 that effect the overthrow of old King Charles X, the last of the Bourbons to reign over France, give new life to the celebration of the imperial myth. No fewer than seven Napoleons face or will face the stage lights, far from battle fire and bivouacs: *Napoléon à Schoenbrünn* in the Théâtre de la Porte Saint-Martin, with fabulous box-office success, and others at Les Nouveautés, Le Vaudeville, Les Variétés, L'Ambigu-Comique, La Gaieté, and Le Cirque-Olympique. Alexandre Dumas, a young up-and-coming writer after *Henri III et sa cour*, is pursued by the director of the Odéon, Harel, who, promising him a fortune, also wants a Napoleon. Finally the young author agrees.

With the help of a collaborator (Cordellier Delanoue), he sketches out a basic structure: A spy, whom the Emperor saved from execution in Toulon, follows him throughout his prodigious career, all the way to Saint Helena. He includes twenty-three scenes taken from imperial history and hagiography, drawn from sources that we have been able to identify: Bourrienne's *Mémoires; Histoire de Napoléon* by the Baron Norvins; *Victoires, conquêtes, revers et guerres civiles des Français de 1792 à 1815; Mémorial de Sainte-Hélène* by Las Cases.

Dumas creates a Napoleon in conformity with his legend: a genius whose thought soars too high to be understood by his mediocre contemporaries; a man betrayed by politicians who change with the wind, politicians whose fortunes he has made and who, at the time the play is being written, are moving en masse to support Louis-Philippe. Only the people, represented by the illiterate soldier from Lorraine, remain faithful to the end. The people are those who have just fought in the barricades of 1830 to chase out the Bourbons.

Opening night, January 10, 1831, presents a strange spectacle, like a riot or setting off for battle. National guardsmen fill the theater. The rising curtain is greeted by exclamations. The decors are superb: In a redoubt near Toulon, through the doors and windows people can see the city under siege and the chain of rocks on which the forts were built. Then follow the Saint-Cloud fair, the apartment and then the gardens at the Tuileries, the interior of the King of Saxony's palace in Dresden, the Borodino heights, a room in the Kremlin, a small farmhouse on the near side of the Beresina, the heights of Montereau, a salon in the Faubourg Saint-Germain, a Paris street, a room in the Fontainebleau Palace, the courtyard of the Cheval-Blanc in the same palace, the port of Portoferraio, the Jamestown Valley on Saint Helena. . . . This succession of scenes indicates that the play, after a rapid presentation of Napoleon Bonaparte's ascension, concentrates on the Emperor's fall. It portrays primarily the beaten man.

During the intermissions, drummers and trumpeters of the National Guard play martial music. Frédérick Lemaître, who plays Napoleon, doesn't look at all like the Emperor. But he is wearing the little gray costume; he lies dying on Saint Helena. That is enough. At first people weep, and then they applaud frenetically. As people leave, they boo Delaître, the poor actor who has the misfortune of playing the role of Hudson Lowe.

Dumas has no illusions about the literary quality of the work. If he were to have any illusions, his royalist friend Alfred de Vigny would disabuse him: "Bad work, bad action!" he writes. "Out of anger against the king,

Dumas has put harsh words about the Bourbons into *Napoléon*. 'They were ungrateful to me,' he says. I've criticized him for heaping scorn on the vanquished."

Such is the criticism to which the young author is responding in the preface to the play, which he dedicates to "the French nation." He refutes all accusations about ingratitude:

I am the son of the Republican general Alexandre Dumas, who died in 1806, following eleven attempts to poison him in the prisons of Naples.

He died in the emperor's disgrace because he refused to adopt his system of colonization in Egypt (and he was wrong to refuse), and because he did not agree to sign the municipal registers at the time of the emperor's accession to the throne (and he was right not to sign).

My father was one of those men of iron who believe that one's soul is one's conscience, who do exactly what it prescribes, and who die poor.

For my father did die poor. He was owed twenty-eight thousand francs of back pay, and they were not given to his widow. They owed his widow a pension, but she never received it. The blood my father shed serving the Republic was paid neither by the Empire nor by the Restoration. I give thanks to the Restoration and to the Empire, because they liberated me.

More speculation than literary work, the play, entitled *Napoléon Bonaparte, ou Trente ans de l'histoire de France,* might, however, have led Dumas to reflect on Napoleon's role in French history. "How can the same man be so strong at the beginning of his career and so weak at the end? Why, at a given moment, when he is forty-six years old and in the prime of his life, does his genius abandon him, his fortune betray him?" he wonders. Two years later, in his book *Gaule et France* (1833), he arrives at an answer: Napoleon is only an instrument in God's hand; once God no longer needs him, he breaks him:

Three men, in our opinion, have been chosen by God throughout eternity to achieve the work of regeneration: Caesar, Charlemagne, and Napoleon.

Caesar prepares the way for Christianity.

Charlemagne prepares the way for Civilization.

And Napoleon Liberty.

. . . When Napoleon took France on the 18th Brumaire, it was still feverish from civil war. And in one of its excesses, it had leaped so far ahead of other peoples that other nations could not keep pace. The equilibrium of general progress was disturbed by an excess of individual progress. It was liberty gone mad, and according to the kings, it needed to be chained up to be healed.

Napoleon appeared with his double instinct of despotism and war; his double nature, both popular and aristocratic, lagged behind French ideas but was ahead of the ideas of the rest of Europe; he was a conservative man for domestic issues, but a man of progress in foreign affairs.

The foolish kings declared war on him!

And then Napoleon took what was the purest, the most intelligent and the most progressive in France. He formed armies and sent his armies all over Europe. Everywhere they carried death to kings and a breath of life to the people. Everywhere the spirit of France passed, Freedom followed with giant steps, throwing revolutions into the wind like a farmer sowing wheat.

[Then comes the disastrous Russian campaign.] By then, Napoleon's mission is complete, and the time of his fall has arrived. For now his fall will be as useful for freedom as his rise to power had once been. The Tsar, so careful before a victorious enemy, will perhaps be imprudent before a vanquished enemy. . . .

So God removes his protective hand from Napoleon, and so that divine intervention can this time be clearly seen in human affairs, it is no longer simply men fighting men. The order of the seasons is inverted, and snow and cold march in at double time. An army is killed by the elements. . . .

So thus, at intervals of nine hundred years, as living proof of what we have just said, the greater the genius, the blinder it seems to be:

Caesar, a pagan, paves the road to Christianity.

Charlemagne, a barbarian, paves the road to Civilization.

Napoleon, a despot, paves the road to Liberty.

Might not we be tempted to believe that they are one and the same man reappearing at fixed intervals under different names to carry out the same plan?

This providentialist view of Napoleon's destiny will rarely vary under the writer's pen. In particular, it forms the foundation for his *Napoléon,* a publishing agreement he reached in 1839, greeted less than enthusiastically by readers: "I expected in this episode [the Battle of Waterloo] to see him unfold the full power of his talent, the full energy of his thought and style, but no. It seemed nothing more than 10 well-written and well-chosen pages of *Victoires et conquêtes,*" writes Marco de Saint-Hilaire, who will provide one of the sources for the second volume of *Le Chevalier de Sainte-Hermine.*

Nothing will change, not even his relationship with Bonaparte. On September 13, 1832, in the course of his travels in Switzerland Dumas visited Queen Hortense in the Arenenberg castle. In Florence, beginning in June of 1840, he becomes such a good friend of the Bonaparte family that when he is back in France in 1844 he says the family "charges him with looking at the four manuscripts written by General Montholon [then in prison along with Louis-Napoleon Bonaparte, the future Napoleon III] devoted to the Emperor's captivity," and he asks the minister Tanneguy Duchatel to "grant him the greatest possible freedom in his power to see the prisoners of Ham five or six times."[40] The authorization is granted:

On the way to Belgium, we [Dujarier, manager of *La Presse,* and Dumas] stopped one day in Ham. I had been received in Arenenberg, twelve years earlier, by Queen Hortense, and I thought I should not pass through the city where her son was in prison without going to see him to thank him for his mother's hospitality. Besides, since that time, in Florence I had had the honor of meeting King Louis, King Jerome, and King Joseph. With apologies to the Congress of Vienna, I especially use the word "king" to refer to those who are king no longer, and for me the greatest monarchs are those who have fallen or are already dead. Prince Louis, though a prisoner, was for me still a French prince, and as such, he had the right to my homage.

I spent the first visit talking about the imperial family with His Highness Prince Louis, while you were in another apartment working out the details of your publication with Monsieur le Comte Montholon. The next day, when I went back to bid the prince good-bye, he and Comte Montholon asked me to review the proofs of the book you were going to edit, for Comte Montholon would be unable to do so since he was a prisoner thirty or forty leagues from Paris. I accepted, first of all for the prince, and then as well for the whole exiled family that was speaking to me through his voice and to which, by accepting, I could render the only service in my power."[41]

The *Récits de la captivité de l'empereur Napoléon à Saint-Hélène,* written by General Montholon and rewritten by Dumas (large fragments of the manuscript are preserved in Prague), would be published, in two volumes, by Paulin in 1847.

40 Austria, National Archives, AB XIX 3325 dr I.
41 Letter published in *La Presse,* December 24, 1844.

Dumas's view of Napoleon as an instrument of Providence is repeated in the lecture we have already cited, when, in beautiful dialogical style, Dumas addresses the Emperor himself:

No, Sire, your glory did not suffer, for you were struggling against destiny. Those victors we called Wellington, Bulow, and Blücher were only wearing men's masks, and they were genies sent by the Most High to combat you, for you had rebelled against him by choosing the cause of kings when he had charged you with the cause of the people.

Providence, Sire, Providence!

One entire night, Jacob wrestled with an angel he thought was a man. Three times he was brought down, he, Israël's best wrestler! And when morning came, thinking about his triple defeat, he thought he would go mad.

You, too, were brought down three times, Sire. Three times you felt the knee of the divine victor on your quivering breast!

At Moscow, at Leipzig, at Waterloo.

Such is the vision that overwhelms Dumas when, with one final deeply felt effort, he tries to fill the gap in his *Drame de la France*. He portrayed Bonaparte in *Les Blancs et les bleus,* and he will follow the course of Napoleon's star in *Le Chevalier de Sainte-Hermine.*

The novel begins one year before the author's birth in 1802, the same year his contemporary and good friend Victor Hugo had sung:

> *Ce siècle avait deux ans! Rome remplaçait Sparte,*
> *Déjà Napoléon perçait sous Bonaparte,*
> *Et du premier consul, déjà, par maint endroit,*
> *Le front de l'empereur brisait le masque étroit.*
> (This century was two years old! Rome was replacing Sparta,
> Napoleon was already emerging from beneath Bonaparte,
> And already, in many places, the emperor's brow
> Was breaking through the First Consul's tight mask.)

MONTE-CRISTO'S SON

In opposition to the historical Goliath, Dumas sets up a fictional David: the "chevalier" Hector, last remnant of the Comtes de Sainte-Hermine. His father guillotined after the Carnation Conspiracy; his eldest brother, Léon, an émigré with Condé's army, shot; the other brother, Charles, Companion of Jehu, guillotined. The young cavalier, along with the family's title, also inherits its vengeance.

Young Hector is therefore an avenger, as was Edmond Dantès, the Comte de Monte-Cristo, before him. One might think that Dumas-Hamlet is assigning to Hector, although he is only the hero of a novel, the task of avenging Dumas himself on Napoleon, his father's killer.

When Hector enters society, and the novel, although he is as handsome as Antinoüs, he is nothing but an ordinary young aristocrat dressed in a red velvet coat, tight suede pants, shoes with little diamond buckles, and in a supreme touch of elegance, a diamond buckle, larger than the diamonds on his shoes but with the same shape, on the braid of his hat.

But then Edmond Dantès, too, was hardly distinguishable from the other sailors around him.

Above all, Hector, like Dantès a young man in love, is relieved when the changing historical situation, the end of the Chouan uprising, removes his obligation to seek vengeance. After the leave Cadoudal granted his troops, Hector remarks:

> I would once again be in control of my own person, after my father and my two brothers had promised me to a monarchy that I knew only through my family's devotion and through the misfortunes our devotion had brought down upon our house. . . . I was twenty-three years old; I had an annual income of one hundred thousand francs. I was in love, and supposing that I was loved, the gates of paradise that had long been guarded by the destroying angel were now opening before me.

However, like Dantès, when in prison Hector undergoes an initiation as he descends into the abyss. Locked away three years in the Temple, when Hector gets out, he is a different man, or rather a superman. The obvious sign of his metamorphosis is his name change: Whereas the plebian Edmond Dantès assumed the title the Comte de Monte-Cristo, the aristocratic Hector de Sainte-Hermine borrows the plebeian name René. But, while Dantès benefited from the offices of the Abbé Faria even as he suffered more than fifteen years in the Château d'If, Hector had no such sublime initiator. He had to manage his transmutation from man into superman all by himself. In the novel, once Hector enters prison, he completely disappears from the story line, which continues with Bonaparte, until his "tight mask" finally breaks. Dumas does not pick up Hector again until he leaves prison. So the reader, though he can appreciate the effects of Hector's transformation, at first has no idea what caused it. In time, however, the narrator and Hector himself do reveal some of what occasioned the metamorphosis.

During those "three years of sadness and winter," during which "all the joys of [his] youth, all the flowers of his adolescence were broken," Hector changed physically, but not so much, as Dantès did, that he cannot recognize himself when he looks in the barber's mirror in Livorno:

During that long reclusion, his face had lost its youthful glow, and his rosy cheeks had given way to a dull complexion with thin, swarthy layers. His eyes seemed larger from straining to see in the dark. His beard had grown, giving a masculine frame to his face. Everything in his physiognomy was divided into three almost indistinct nuances that blended together: thought, reverie, and melancholy.

At the origin of his transformation seems to be the force of will alone. Hector hardened his body:

Most young people have the need to expend physical energy, and he met that need through gymnastic exercises. He had requested cannon balls of different sizes and with practice was finally able to lift and juggle even the heaviest.[42]

He had practiced, using a cord attached to the ceiling, climbing the cord using only his hands. He had invented all those gymnastic exercises, not to complete his education as is the case with young men in our day, but rather simply to pass the time.

He cultivated his mind by studies:

And finally, during his three years in prison, Sainte-Hermine had studied in great depth everything that one can study alone: geography, mathematics, and history. Passionate for travel in his youth, speaking German, English, and Spanish as well as he spoke his mother tongue, he had heavily used the privilege he had been granted of borrowing books, and he had traveled through his maps since he was unable to travel in the real world.

India . . . had especially attracted his interest and had been the object of particular study, although he never thought studying that particular

---

42 Reading this passage, one cannot help but recall General Dumas's renowned physical strength: The mulatto giant had the reputation of being able, with his two hands wrapped around a stable rafter and his legs around his horse, to lift the horse from the ground! Nor can one help thinking that Bonaparte, his young companion at arms, short of stature and weak as he then was, might have felt some jealousy toward the powerful "Dumas the black man" who was so proud of his Herculean strength.

area of the world would be useful. He assumed he was fated to perpetual imprisonment.

But especially, he spent many hours reflecting on the history and final purpose of mankind, and his quest led him to doubts like those of Hamlet and Faust:

I spent three years reflecting on these mysteries. I descended into the un-fathomable depths of one side of life, and I came out the other, not knowing how or why we are alive, how or why we die, telling myself that God is a word that is useful for naming what we seek. When I die I shall learn who God is, unless death is more silent than life. . . . Instead of making a God of the universe who established gravity and universal harmony among celestial bodies, we have tried to create God in our own image, a personal God. We ask him to explain, not the great atmospheric cataclysms, but our little individual misfortunes. We pray to a God whom our human minds cannot fathom and whom human tools cannot measure. And yet he is everywhere, if he does exist. We pray as did people in ancient times. They would pray to their household god, a small statue a cubit tall, always in sight and available. We pray as the Indian prays to his fetish, as the African prays to his gris-gris. Depending on whether an event is painful or happy, we ask: "Why did you do that? Why did you not do that?" Our God never answers, because he is too distant, and besides, he is not concerned with our petty passions. So then we are unjust toward him, for we blame him for our misfortunes. And that makes us not only unhappy, but also blasphemous and sacrilegious.
    . . . We are nothing but little atoms caught up in a nation's cataclysms, crushed between a world that is coming to an end and a world that is be-ginning, dragged along by collapsing royalty and a rising empire. Ask God why Louis XIV weakened France by losing so many men during his wars, why he ruined the treasury with his lavish marble and bronze caprices. Ask Louis XIV why he undertook disastrous policies in order to be able to say something that was no longer true when he said it: "The Pyrénées no longer exist." Ask him why, influenced by a woman's whims and bent under a priest's yoke, he made Holland wealthy and ru-ined France by revoking the Edit de Nantes. Ask God why Louis XV continued his grandfather's ruinous work. . . . Ask God why, against his-tory's advice, Louis XV followed the advice of a corrupt minister and why, failing to keep in mind that alliance with Austria always brought misfortune to the fleur-de-lys, he brought an Austrian princess to the French throne. Ask God why he gave to Louis XVI, instead of royal virtues, bourgeois instincts, which included neither respect for his word

nor the firmness required for the head of a family. Ask him why he allowed the king to take an oath he did not intend to keep, why he allowed him to seek outside help against his subjects, and why he brought such an august head down to the level of a scaffold designed for vulgar criminals.

. . . That is how you can understand why I did not remain with your family though I had found a father and two sisters. That is how you can see why my father died on the same scaffold, still red with the king's blood. Why my eldest brother was shot, why my second brother was guillotined, and why I myself, in order to keep my sacred promise, had to follow a path, without conviction or enthusiasm, which, just as I was about to reach happiness, ripped all hope from me. I was thrown into the Temple for three years and then delivered over to the false clemency of a man who, by granting me life, condemned me to a life of misfortune.

. . . I believe in a God who created the worlds, who drew their paths in the ether. But because of that, he has no time to be concerned with the misfortunes or happiness of two little atoms creeping over the surface of this terrestrial globe.

Through the mouth of the young, disabused man, we can hear the voice of the old writer nearing death. And that is why *Le Chevalier de Sainte-Hermine* rings true like a testament, like words spoken on a deathbed.

And that is when Hector begins to differ from his "elder," the Comte de Monte-Cristo. Whereas Dantès is motivated by a desire for personal vengeance, Hector, "without enthusiasm or conviction," is only obeying a promise of vengeance imposed upon him by honor and by History.

"Condemned to misfortune," Hector is an indomitable force, moving, it seems at first, at random. However, the young royalist avenger has discovered a value that is superior to class hatred or partisanship, a value for which he will fight:

He had needed to read voraciously and reflect at length in order to understand that devotion outside of the law can sometimes turn criminal and that the only devotion near to the heart of God is devotion to one's country.

The son of the Republican general, grandson of the aristocrat Davy de la Pailleterie and a black slave, grandson as well (on his mother's side) of Claude Labouret, first a domestic servant of the Duc d'Orléans and then an ordinary lower-middle-class citizen in Villers-Cotterêts, Dumas blends his disparate origins together in the melting pot of the nation. Therefore Hector is fighting neither for nor against Napoleon, himself only an avatar in the history of mankind. Since Hector has not been allowed to love, he offers his life without purpose in sacrifice to France. Initially a witness to Napoleonic history, he becomes an actor only to glorify his country.

> *Mourir pour la patrie,*
> *C'est le sort le plus beau, le plus digne d'envie,*
> (Dying for one's country
> Is the most glorious, the most enviable fate.)

Such were the words the Girondin chorus in the final scene of *Le Chevalier de Maison-Rouge* was singing already in 1847 in the Théâtre-Historique.

Death was propitious for Alexandre Dumas. In Dieppe, he did not have to hear the Prussian fanfares.

PART I

BONAPARTE

I

Josephine's Debts

~:~

"NOW THAT WE ARE in the Tuileries," Bonaparte, the First Consul, said to Bourrienne, his secretary, as they entered the palace where Louis XVI had made his next-to-last stop between Versailles and the scaffold, "we must try to stay."

Those fateful words were spoken at about four in the afternoon on the 30th Pluviose in the Revolutionary year VIII (February 19, 1800).

This narration begins exactly one year to the day after the First Consul's installation. It follows our book *The Whites and the Blues*, which ended, as we recall, with Pichegru fleeing from Sinnamary, and our novel *The Companions of Jehu*, which ended with the execution of Ribier, Jahiat, Valensolles, and Sainte-Hermine.

As for General Bonaparte, who was not yet general at that time, we left him just after he had returned from Egypt and landed back on French soil. Since the 24th Vendémiaire in the year VII he had accomplished a great deal.

First of all, he had managed and won the 18th Brumaire, though the case is still being appealed before posterity.

Then, like Hannibal and Charlemagne, he crossed the Alps.

Later, with the help of Desaix and Kellermann, he won the battle of Marengo, after first losing it.

Then, in Lunéville, he arranged peace.

Finally, on the same day that he had David's bust of Brutus placed in the Tuileries, he re-established the use of "madame" as a form of address. Stubborn people were still free to use the word "citizen" if they wanted, but only yokels and louts still said "citizeness."

And of course only the proper sort of people came to the Tuileries.

Now it's the 30th Pluviose in the year IX (February 19, 1801), and we are in the First Consul Bonaparte's palace in the Tuileries.

We shall now give the present generation, two thirds of a century later, some idea of his study where so many events were planned. With our pen we shall draw as best we can the portrait of that legendary figure who was considering not only how to change France but also how to turn the entire world upside down.

• • •

His study, a large room painted white with golden moldings, contains two tables. One, quite beautiful, is reserved for the First Consul; when seated at the table, he has his back to the fireplace and the window to his right. Also on the right is a small office where Duroc, his trusty aide-de-camp of four years, works. From that room they can communicate with Landoire, the dependable valet who enjoys the First Consul's total confidence, and with the large apartments that open up onto the courtyard.

The First Consul's chair is decorated with a lion's head, and the right armrest is damaged because he has often dug into it with his penknife. When he is sitting at his table, he can see in front of him a huge library packed with boxes from ceiling to floor.

Slightly to the right, beside the library, is the room's second large door. It opens up directly to the ceremonial bedroom, from which one can move into the grand reception room. There, on the ceiling, Le Brun painted Louis XIV in full regalia, and there a second painter, certainly not as gifted as Le Brun, had the audacity to add a Revolutionary cockade to the great king's wig. Bonaparte is in no rush to remove it because it allows him to say, when he points out the anomaly to visitors: "Those men from the Convention years were certainly idiots!"

Opposite the study's only window, which allows light into this quite sizable room and looks out over the garden, stands a large wardrobe that's attached to the consular office. It is none other than Marie de Médicis's oratory, and it leads to a small stairway that descends to Madame Bonaparte's bedroom below.

Just like Marie-Antoinette, whom she resembles in more ways than one, Josephine hates the state apartments. Consequently, she has arranged her own little safe haven in the Tuileries, as had Marie-Antoinette at Versailles.

Almost always, at least at the time we are speaking of, the First Consul would enter his office in the morning through that wardrobe. We say "almost always," because after they moved to the Tuileries the First Consul also had a bedroom separate from Josephine's. He slept there if he came home too late at night, so as not to disturb his wife, or if some subject of discord—and such moments, though not yet frequent, were beginning to occur from time to time—had precipitated an argument that left them for a time not on speaking terms.

The second table is nondescript. Placed near the window, it affords the secretary a view of thick chestnut tree foliage, but in order to see whoever may be walking in the garden he has to stand up. When he is seated, his back is turned just slightly to the First Consul, so the secretary has to turn his head only a bit to see him. As Duroc is rarely in his office, that is where the secretary often receives visitors.

Bourrienne is that secretary.

The most skillful artists competed with each other to paint or sculpt Bonaparte's, and later Napoleon's, features. But the men who lived most closely with him, although they could recognize in such statues or portraits the extraordinary man's essence, say that no single image of the First Consul or the Emperor exists that is a perfect likeness.

When he was First Consul, they managed to paint or sculpt his prominent cranium, his magnificent brow, the hair that he plastered down over his temples and let fall to his shoulders, his tanned face, long and thin, with its meditative physiognomy.

As Emperor, in their depictions, his head resembles an antique medallion and his pale, unhealthy skin marks a man who will die young. They could draw his hair as black as ebony, to show off his dark complexion to full effect, but neither the chisel nor the brush could render the dancing flames in his eyes or capture the somber cast of his features when he was in deep thought.

With the speed of lightning the expression in his eyes obeyed his will. In anger, nobody looked more fearsome; in kindness, no one's gaze was more caressing. Indeed, for each thought that traversed his soul he had a different expression.

He was short of stature, scarcely five feet three inches tall, and yet Kléber, who stood a head taller than he, once said to him as he placed his hand on his shoulder, "General, you are as big as the world!" And at that moment he did seem truly a head taller than Kléber.

He had lovely hands. He was proud of his hands and cared for them as a woman might have done. In conversation, he would frequently glance at them with admiration. Only on his left hand would he wear a glove; he kept his right hand bare, ostensibly so it would be ready should he want to reach out to someone he might choose to so honor, but in reality it was so he could admire his hand and shine his nails with a cambric handkerchief. Monsieur de Turenne, part of whose job it was to help the Emperor dress, came to the point where he would order gloves only for his left hand, thus saving six thousand francs a year.

He could not stand inactivity. Even in his private apartments he would constantly pace up and down, all the while leaning slightly forward, as if the weight of every thought in his head was forcing his neck to bend, and holding his hands clasped behind his back. His right shoulder would frequently jerk, and at the same time the muscles in his mouth would tighten. These ticks, these habits of mind and body, some people mistook for convulsive movements from which they deduced that Bonaparte must be subject to epileptic attacks.

He was passionate about bathing. Sometimes he would stay in his bath for two or three hours while the secretary or an aide read him the newspapers or a pamphlet the police had brought to his notice. Once he was in his bath, he would leave the hot faucet open, with no concern if the bath overflowed. Often, when Bourrienne, soaked with steam, could bear it no longer, he would ask if he could open the window or leave the room. In general, his request was granted.

Bonaparte truly loved to sleep. When his secretary woke him at seven, he would frequently complain, saying: "Oh, just let me sleep a little longer." "Don't come into my bedroom at night," he would say. "Never wake me up for good news, for there's no hurry to hear good news. But if ever there is bad news, wake me up immediately, for then there's not a moment to be lost."

As soon as Bonaparte was arisen, his valet Constant would shave him and brush his hair. Bourrienne, meanwhile, would read him the newspapers, first *Le Moniteur* and then the English or German papers. Bourrienne would barely have read the headlines from one of the dozen French newspapers being published at that time before Bonaparte would say: "That's enough; they say only what I let them say."

Once he was dressed and ready for the day, he would go up to his study along with Bourrienne. There he would find the letters he would need to read that day and the reports from the day before that he would need to sign.

At exactly ten o'clock the door would open and the butler would announce: "The general is served."

Breakfast was simple, only three dishes plus dessert. One of the dishes was almost always the chicken prepared with oil and onions that he had been served as well on the morning of the Battle of Marengo, and since that day the dish has been called chicken Marengo.

Bonaparte drank only a little wine, a Bordeaux or Burgundy, and then, after breakfast or dinner, he would have a cup of coffee. If he worked unusually late at night, at midnight he would have a cup of chocolate.

Early on, he began to use tobacco, but only three or four times a day, in very small amounts, and he always carried it in very elegant gold or enamel boxes.

On this particular day early in our Revolutionary year IX, as usual, Bourrienne had come down to the study at six thirty, opened the letters, and placed them on the large table, the most important ones on the bottom, so that Bonaparte would read them last and they would be fresh in his mind.

When the clock struck seven, he went to wake the general. Bourrienne had a key to Bonaparte's bedroom, so he could enter whenever necessary, at any time of day or night.

To his great surprise, he found Madame Bonaparte alone in bed. She was weeping.

Bourriene's first instinct was to turn and leave. But Madame Bonaparte, who admired Bourrienne and knew that she could count on him, stopped him. She asked him to sit down on the bed beside her.

Bourrienne was worried. "Oh, madame," he asked. "Has anything happened to the First Consul?"

"No, Bourrienne, no," Josephine had answered. "Something has happened to me."

"What, madame?"

"Oh, my dear Bourrienne. How unfortunate I am!"

Bourrienne began to laugh. "I bet I can guess what's wrong," he said.

"My suppliers," stammered Josephine.

"Are they refusing to supply you?"

"Oh, if that's all it was!"

"Could they be so impertinent as to ask to be paid?" asked Bourrienne with a laugh.

"They are threatening to sue me! Imagine how embarrassing it would be for me, my dear Bourrienne, if an official order landed in Bonaparte's hands!"

"Do you think they would dare?"

"There is no doubt in my mind."

"Impossible!"

"Look here."

And out from under her pillow Josephine pulled a sheet of paper imprinted with a symbol of the Republic. It was an official summons demanding of the First Consul the sum of forty thousand francs in payment for gloves delivered to Madame Bonaparte his wife. As chance would have it, the order had fallen into Madame Bonaparte's hands rather than her husband's. The proceedings were being carried out on behalf of Madame Giraud.

"Damn!" said Bourrienne. "This is serious! Did you authorize your entire household to buy gloves from that woman?"

"No, my dear Bourrienne; those forty thousand francs worth of gloves were for me alone."

"For you alone?"

"Yes."

"You must not have paid anything for ten years!"

"I settled accounts with all my suppliers and paid them last year on the first of January. I paid three hundred thousand francs. I remember how angry Bonaparte was then, which is why I'm quaking now."

"And you have worn forty thousand francs worth of gloves since the first of January last year?"

"Apparently so, Bourrienne, since that's what they're asking."

"Well, then, what you expect me to do about it?"

"If Bonaparte is in good humor this morning, perhaps you could bring up the subject with him."

"First of all, why is he not here with you? Have you quarreled?" Bourrienne asked.

"No, not at all. He was feeling fine last night when he left with Duroc to check out, as he says, what Parisians are thinking about. He probably came home late and, not wishing to disturb me, went to sleep in his bachelor's quarters."

"And if he is in good humor and I do speak to him of your debts, when he asks me how much you owe, how shall I answer?"

"Ah, Bourrienne!" Josephine hid her face behind her sheet.

"So, the figure is frightening?"

"Enormous."

"How much?"

"I don't dare tell you."

"Three hundred thousand francs?"

Josephine gave a sigh.

"Six hundred thousand?"

Another sigh, even heavier than the first.

"I must say that you are indeed beginning to frighten me," said Bourrienne.

"I spent the whole night adding sums up with my dear friend Madame Hulot, who is very good at such things. As you know, Bourrienne, I don't have a head for figures."

"So how much do you owe?"

"More than twelve hundred thousand francs."

Bourrienne gave a start. "You're right," he said, and he was no longer laughing. "The First Consul will indeed be furious."

"Let's just tell him it's half that amount."

"Not a good strategy," said Bourrienne shaking his head. "While you're at it, I advise you to admit everything."

"No, Bourrienne. Never!"

"But what will you do about the other six hundred thousand francs?"

"First of all, I shall contract no more debts, because they make me too unhappy."

"But how about the other six hundred thousand?" Bourrienne asked again.

"I shall pay them out of what I can save."

"That won't work. Since the First Consul is not expecting the figure of six hundred thousand francs, he will make no more of a fuss for twelve hundred thousand than for six. On the contrary, since the blow is more violent, he will be in even greater shock. He will give you the twelve hundred thousand francs, and you will be over and done with it."

"No, no," cried Josephine. "Don't make me do that, Bourrienne. I know him too well. He'll fly into one of his rages, and I can't stand seeing him get so violent."

At that moment Bonaparte's bell rang for his office boy, probably to find out where Bourrienne was.

"That's him," said Josephine. "He's already in his study. Hurry, and if he's in a good mood, you know. . . ."

"Twelve hundred thousand francs, right?"

"Heavens, no! Six hundred thousand, and not a penny more!"

"That's what you wish?"

"Please."

"Very well."

And Bourrienne hurried up the little staircase to the First Consul's study.

II

How the Free City of Hamburg Paid Josephine's Debts

WHEN BOURRIENNE RETURNED to the study, the First Consul was reading the morning mail that the secretary had laid out for him on his desk. He was wearing the uniform of a Republican division general, a frock coat without epaulettes with a simple gold laurel branch, buckskin pants, a red vest with wide lapels, and boots with their tops turned down. At the sound of his secretary's footsteps, Bonaparte turned his head.

"Oh, it's you, Bourrienne," he said. "I was just ringing Landoire to have him call you."

"I had gone down to Madame Bonaparte's room, thinking I would find you there, General."

"No, I slept in the large bedroom."

"Ah," said Bourrienne. "In the bed that belonged to the Bourbons!"

"Well, yes."

"And how did you sleep?"

"Poorly. And the proof is that I'm already here and you did not have to awaken me. It's all too comfortable for me."

"Have you read the three letters I set aside for you, General?"

"Yes, the wife of a sergeant-major in the consular guard who was killed at Marengo is asking me to be the godfather of her child."

"How should I answer her?"

"Tell her I accept. Duroc can stand in for me. The child's name will be Napoleon. The mother will receive an annuity of five hundred francs that will revert to her son. Answer her in those terms."

"And how about the woman who, believing in your good luck, asks you for three lottery numbers?"

"She's crazy. But since the woman believes in my star and is sure she'll win if I send her three numbers, though she has never won before, tell her that you can only win the lottery on those days you don't bet anything. As proof tell her that she has never won anything when she has bought tickets, but on the day that she has not bought a ticket she has won three hundred francs."

"So, I am to send her three hundred francs?"

"Yes."

"And the last letter, General?"

"I was just beginning to read it when you came in."

"Keep reading; you will find it interesting."

"Read it to me. The writing is scribbly and difficult to read."

With a smile, Bourrienne picked up the letter. "I know why you're smiling," said Bonaparte.

"Ah, I don't think you do, General," replied Bourrienne.

"You're no doubt thinking that someone with handwriting like mine should be able to read anyone's, even the scribbling of cats and public prosecutors."

"Well, you're right."

Bourrienne began to read:

"'Jersey, February 26, 1801

"'I believe, General, that since you are back from your extensive voyages, I can now, without being indiscreet, interrupt your daily occupations by reminding you who I am. However, you may be surprised that such a feeble excuse is the subject of the letter I have the honor of addressing you. You will remember, General, that when your father was forced to take your brothers out of the school in Autun and came to see you in Brienne, he found himself penniless. He asked me to lend him twenty-five louis, which I was pleased to do. Since his return, he has not had the opportunity to pay me back, and when I left Ajaccio, your good mother offered to give up some of her silver to reimburse me. I rejected her offer and told her that I would leave the promissory note signed by your father with Monsieur Souires and that she should pay it when she was able and it convenient. I judge that she had not yet found the appropriate time to do so when the Revolution took place.

"'You may find it strange, General, that for such a modest sum I am willing to trouble your occupations. But my situation is very difficult just now, and even such a small amount seems large to me. Exiled from my country, forced to find refuge on this island I abhor, where everything is so expensive that one has to be rich to live even simply, I would deem it a great kindness on your part if you would enable me to have that tiny sum which in earlier days would have been meaningless to me.'"

Bonaparte nodded. Bourrienne noticed his reaction.

"Do you remember this good man, General?" he asked.

"Perfectly well," said Bonaparte. "As if it were yesterday. The sum was counted out in Brienne before my very eyes. His name must be Durosel."

Bourrienne looked down at the signature. "That's right," he said. "But there's another name, one more illustrious than the first."

"What is his full name, then?"

"Durosel Beaumanoir."

"We must find out if he's from the Beaumanoir family in Brittany. That's a good name to have."

"Shall I keep reading?"

"Go ahead."

Bourrienne continued:

"'You will understand, General, that when a man is eighty-six years old and has served his country for more than sixty years without the slightest interruption, it is difficult to be sent away and forced to find refuge on Jersey, where I try to subsist on the government's feeble attempts to help French émigrés.

"'I use the word "émigrés" because that is what I was forced to become. Leaving France had never been in my plans, and I had committed no crime except for being the most senior general in the canton and being decorated with the great cross of Saint-Louis.

"'One evening they came to kill me. They broke down my door. I was alerted by my neighbors' shouts and barely had the time to escape with nothing but the clothes I had on my back. Seeing that I risked death in France, I abandoned all that I owned, real estate and furniture, and since I had no place to put my feet in my own country, I joined one of my older brothers here. He had been deported and was senile, and now I wouldn't leave him for anything in the world. My mother-in-law is eighty years old, and they have refused to give her a portion of my estate, on the pretext that everything I owned had been confiscated. Thus, if things don't change, I shall die bankrupt, and that saddens me greatly.

"'I admit, General, that I have not adapted to the new style, but according to former customs,

"'I am your humble servant.

"'Durosel Beaumanoir'"

"Well, General, what do you say?"

"I say," the First Consul replied with a slight catch in his voice, "that I am profoundly moved to hear such things. This is a sacred debt, Bourrienne. Write to General Durosel, and I shall sign the letter. Send him ten thousand francs and say that he can expect more, for I would like to do more for this man who helped my father. I shall take care of him. But, speaking of debts, Bourrienne, I have some serious business to talk about with you." Bonaparte sat down with a frown.

Bourrienne remained standing near his chair. Bonaparte said, "I want to talk to you about Josephine's debts."

Bourrienne gave a start. "Very well," he said. "And where do you get your information?"

"From what I hear in public."

Like a man who has not fully understood but who dares ask no questions, Bourrienne leaned forward.

"Just imagine, my friend"—Bonaparte sometimes forgot himself and dropped formal address—"that I went out with Duroc to find out for myself what people are saying."

"And are they saying many negative things about the First Consul?"

"Well," Bonaparte answered with a laugh, "I nearly got myself killed when I said something bad about him. Without Duroc, who used his club, I believe we might have been arrested and taken to the Château-d'Eau guardhouse."

"Still, that fails to explain how, in the midst of all the praise for the First Consul, the question of Madame Bonaparte's debts came up."

"In fact, in the midst of all that praise for the First Consul, people were saying horrible things about his wife. They're saying that Madame Bonaparte is ruining her husband with all the clothes she's buying; they're saying she has debts everywhere, that her cheapest dress cost one hundred louis and her least expensive hat two hundred francs. I don't believe a word of that, Bourrienne, you understand. But where there's smoke, there's fire. Last year I paid debts of three hundred thousand francs; she reminded me that I had not sent her any money from Egypt. All well and good. But now things are different; I'm giving Josephine six thousand francs a month for clothes. That should be enough. People used the same kinds of words against Marie-Antoinette. You must check with Josephine, Bourrienne, and set things straight."

"You'll never know," Bourrienne answered, "how happy I am that you yourself have brought up this subject. This morning, as you were impatiently waiting for me to appear, Madame Bonaparte asked me to talk to you about the difficult position in which she finds herself."

"Difficult position, Bourrienne! What do you mean by that, monsieur?" Bonaparte asked, suddenly reverting back to more formal speech.

"I mean that she is being harassed."

"By whom?"

"By her creditors."

"Her creditors! I thought I had got rid of her creditors."

"A year ago, yes."

"Well?"

"Well, in the past year, things have totally changed. One year ago she was the wife of General Bonaparte. Today she is the wife of the First Consul."

"Bourrienne, that's enough. My ears have heard enough of prattle."

"That's my opinion, General."

"It is up to you to take care of paying everything."

"I would be happy to. Give me the necessary sum, and I shall quickly take care of it, I guarantee."

"How much do you need?"

"How much do I need? Well, yes. . . ."

"Well?"

"Well, Madame Bonaparte doesn't dare tell you."

"What? She doesn't dare tell me? And how about you?"

"Nor do I, General."

"Nor do you! Then it must be a colossal amount!"

Bourrienne sighed.

"Let's see now," Bonaparte continued. "If I pay for this year like last year, and give you three hundred thousand francs. . . ."

Bourrienne didn't say a word. Bonaparte looked at him worriedly. "Say something, you imbecile!"

"Well, if you give me three hundred thousand francs, General, you would be giving me only half of the debt."

"Half!" shouted Bonaparte, getting to his feet. "Six hundred thousand francs! . . . She owes . . . six hundred thousand francs?"

Bourrienne nodded.

"She admitted she owed that amount?"

"Yes, General."

"And where does she expect me to get the money to pay these six hundred thousand francs? From my five-hundred-thousand-franc salary as consul?"

"Oh, she assumes you have several thousand franc bills hid somewhere in reserve."

"Six hundred thousand francs!" Bonaparte repeated. "And at the same time my wife is spending six hundred thousand francs on clothing, I'm giving one hundred francs as pension to the widow and children of brave soldiers killed at the Pyramids or Marengo! And I can't even give money to all of them! And they have to live the whole year on those one hundred francs, while Madame Bonaparte wears dresses worth one hundred louis and hats worth twenty-five. You must have heard incorrectly, Bourrienne, it surely cannot be six hundred thousand francs."

"I heard perfectly well, General, and Madame Bonaparte realized what her situation was only yesterday when she saw a bill for gloves that came to forty thousand francs."

"What are you saying?" shouted Bonaparte.

"I'm saying forty thousand francs for gloves, General. What do you expect? That is how things are. Yesterday she went over her accounts with Madame Hulot. She spent the night in tears, and she was still weeping this morning when I saw her."

"Well, let her cry! Let her cry with shame, or even out of remorse! Forty thousand francs for gloves! Over how many months?"

"Over one year," Bourrienne answered.

"One year! That's enough food for forty families! Bourrienne, I want to see all those bills."

"When?"

"Immediately. It's eight o'clock, and I don't see Cadoudal until nine, so I have the time. Immediately, Bourrienne. Immediately!"

"You're quite right, General. Now that we have started, let's get to the end of this business."

"Go get all the bills, all of them, you understand. We shall go through them together."

"I'm on my way, General." And Bourrienne ran down the stairway leading to Madame Bonaparte's apartment.

Left alone, the First Consul began to pace up and down, his hands clasped behind his back, his shoulder and mouth twitching. He started mumbling to himself: "I ought to have remembered what Junot told me at the fountains in Messoudia. I ought to have listened to my brothers Joseph and Lucien who told me not to see her when I got back. But how could I have resisted seeing my dear children Hortense and Eugene? The children brought me back to her! Divorce! I shall keep divorce legal in France, if only so I can leave that woman. That woman who gives me no children, and she's ruining me!"

"Well," said Bourrienne as he reentered the study, "six hundred thousand francs won't ruin you, and Madame Bonaparte is still young enough to give you a son who in another forty years will succeed you as consul for life!"

"You have always taken her side, Bourrienne!" said Bonaparte, pinching his ear so hard the secretary cried out.

"What do you expect, General? I'm for everything that is beautiful, good, and feeble."

In a rage, Bonaparte grabbed up the handful of papers from Bourrienne and twisted them back and forth in his hands. Then, randomly, he picked up a bill and read: "'Thirty-eight hats' . . . in one month! What's she doing, wearing two hats a day? And eighteen hundred francs worth of feathers! And eight hundred more for ribbons!" Angrily, he threw down the bill and picked up another. "Mademoiselle Martin's perfume shop. Three thousand three hundred and six francs for rouge. One thousand seven hundred forty-nine francs during the month of June alone. Rouge at one hundred francs a jar! Remember that name, Bourrienne. She's a hussy who should be sent to prison in Saint-Lazare. Mademoiselle Martin, do you hear?"

"Yes, General."

"Oh, now we come to the dresses. Monsieur Leroy. Back in the old days there were seamstresses, now we have tailors for women—it's more moral. One hundred fifty dresses in one year. Four hundred thousand francs worth of dresses! If things keep going like this, it won't be six hundred thousand francs, it'll be a million. Twelve hundred thousand francs at the least that we'll have to deal with."

"Oh, General," Bourrienne hastily said, "there have been some down payments made."

"Three dresses at five thousand francs apiece!"

"Yes," said Bourrienne. "But there are six at only five hundred each."

"Are you making fun of me?" said Bonaparte with a frown.

"No, General, I'm not making fun of you. All I'm saying is that it's beneath you to get so upset for nothing."

"How about Louis XVI? He was a king, and he got upset. And he had a guaranteed income of twenty-five million francs."

"You are—or at least when you want to be, you will be—more of a king than Louis XVI ever was, General. Furthermore, Louis XVI was an unfortunate man, you'll have to admit."

"A good man, monsieur."

"I wonder what the First Consul would say if people said he was a good man."

"For five thousand francs at least they could give us one of those beautiful gowns from Louis XVI's days, with hoops and swirls and panniers, gowns that needed fifty meters of cloth. That I could understand. But with these new, simple frocks—women look like umbrellas in a case."

"They have to follow the styles, General."

"Exactly, and that is what makes me so angry. We're not paying for cloth. At least if we were paying for the cloth, it would mean business for our factories. But no, it's the way Leroy cuts the dress. Five hundred francs for cloth and four thousand five hundred francs for Leroy. *Style!* . . . So now we have to find six hundred thousand francs to pay for style."

"Do we not have four million?"

"Four million? Where?"

"The money the Hamburg senate has just paid us for allowing the extradition of those two Irishmen whose lives you saved."

"Oh, yes. Napper-Tandy and Blackwell."

"I believe there may in fact be four and half million francs, not just four million, that the senate sent to you directly through Monsieur Chapeau-Rouge."

"Well," said Bonaparte with a laugh, delighted by the trick he had played on the free city of Hamburg, "I don't know if I really had the right to do what I did, but I had just come back from Egypt, and that was one of the little tricks I'd taught the pashas."

Just then the clock struck nine. The door opened, and Rapp, who was on duty, announced that Cadoudal and his two aides-de-camp were waiting in the official meeting room.

"Well, then, that's what we'll do," said Bonaparte to Bourrienne. "That's where you can get your six hundred thousand francs, and I don't want to hear another word about it." And Bonaparte went out to receive the Breton general.

Scarcely had the door closed than Bourrienne rang the bell. Landoire rushed in. "Go tell Madame Bonaparte that I have some good news for her, but since I don't dare leave my office, where I am alone—you understand, Landoire; *where I am alone*—I would like to ask her to come see me here."

When he realized it was good news, Landoire hurried to the staircase.

Everyone, from Bonaparte on down, adored Josephine.

III

The Companions of Jehu

⇗·⇖

IT WAS NOT THE FIRST TIME that Bonaparte tried to bring Cadoudal back to the side of the Republic in order to gain that formidable partisan's support.

An incident that had occurred on Bonaparte's return from Egypt was imprinted deeply in his memory.

On the 17th Vendémiaire of the year VIII (October 9, 1799), Bonaparte had, as everyone knows, disembarked in Fréjus without going through quarantine, although he was coming from Alexandria.

He had immediately gotten into a coach with his trusted aide-de-camp, Roland de Montrevel, and left for Paris.

The same day, around four in the afternoon, he reached Avignon. He stopped about fifty yards from the Oulle gate, in front of the Hôtel du Palais-Egalité, which was just beginning again to use the name Hôtel du Palais-Royal, a name it had held since the beginning of the eighteenth century and that it still holds today. Urged by the need all mortals experience between four and six in the afternoon to find a meal, any meal, whatever the quality, he got down from the coach.

Bonaparte was in no particular way distinguishable from his companion, save for his firm step and his few words, yet it was he who was asked by the hotel keeper if he wished to be served privately or if he would be willing to eat at the common table.

Bonaparte thought for a moment. News of his arrival had not yet spread through France, as everyone thought he was still in Egypt. His great desire to see his countrymen with his own eyes and hear them with his own ears won out over his fear of being recognized; besides, he and his companion were both wearing clothing typical for the time. Since the common table was already being served and he would be able to dine without delay, he answered that he would eat at the common table.

He turned to the postilion who had brought him. "Have the horses harnessed in one hour," he said.

The hotelier showed the newcomers the way to the common table. Bonaparte entered the dining room first, with Roland behind him. The two young men—Bonaparte was then about twenty-nine or thirty years old, and Roland twenty-six—sat down at the end of the table, where they were separated from the other diners by three or four place settings.

Whoever has traveled knows the effect created by newcomers at a common table. Everyone looks at them, and they immediately become the center of attention.

At the table were some regular customers, a few travelers en route by stagecoach from Marseille to Lyon, and a wine merchant from Bordeaux who was staying temporarily in Avignon.

The great show the newcomers had made of sitting off by themselves increased the curiosity of which they were the object. Although the man who'd entered second was dressed much the same as his companion—short leather pants and turned-down boots, a coat with long tails, a traveler's overcoat and a wide-brimmed hat—and although they appeared to be equals, he seemed to show a noticeable deference to his companion. The deference was obviously not due to any age difference, so no doubt it was owed by a difference in social position. Furthermore, he addressed the first man as "citizen," while his companion called him simply Roland.

What usually happens in such situations happened here. After a moment of interaction with the newcomers, everyone soon looked away, and the conversation, interrupted for a moment, resumed as before.

The subject of the conversation greatly interested the newly arrived travelers, as their fellow guests were talking about the Thermidorian Reaction and the hopes that lay in now reawakened Royalist feelings. They spoke openly of a coming restoration of the House of Bourbon, which surely, with Bonaparte being tied up as he was in Egypt, would take place within six months.

Lyon, one of the cities that had suffered hardest during the Revolution, naturally stood at the center of the conspiracy. There a veritable provisional government—with its royal committee and royal administration, a military headquarters and a royal army—had been set up.

But, in order to pay these armies and support the permanent war effort in the Vendée and Morbihan, they needed money; and lots of it. England had provided a little but was not overly generous, so the Republic was the only source of money available to its Royalist enemies. Instead of trying to open difficult negotiations with the Republic, which would have refused assistance in any case, the royal committee had organized roving bands of brigands who were charged with stealing tax revenues and with attacking the vehicles used for transporting public funds. The morality of civil wars, very loose in regard to money, did not consider stealing from Treasury stagecoaches as real theft, but rather as a military operation.

One of these bands had chosen the route between Lyon and Marseille, and as the two travelers were taking their place at the common table, the subject of conversation was the hold-up of a stagecoach carrying sixty thousand francs of government funds. The hold-up had taken place the day before on the road from Marseille to Avignon, between Lambesc and Port-Royal.

The thieves, if we can use that word for such nobly employed stage-coach robbers, had even given the coachman a receipt for what they took. They had made no attempt, either, to hide the fact that the money would be crossing France by more secure means than his stagecoach and that it would buy supplies for Cadoudal's army in Brittany.

Such actions were new, extraordinary, and almost impossible for Bonaparte and Roland to believe, for they had been absent from France for two years. They did not suspect what deep immorality had found its way into all classes of society under the Directory's bland government.

This particular incident had taken place on the very same road Bonaparte and his companion had just traveled, and the person telling the story was one of the principal actors in that highway drama: the wine merchant from Bordeaux.

Those who seemed to be most interested in all the details, aside from Bonaparte and his companion, who were happy simply to listen, were the people traveling in the stagecoach that had just arrived and was soon to leave. As for the other guests, the people who lived nearby, they had become so accustomed to these episodes that they could have been giving the details instead of listening to them.

Everyone was looking at the wine merchant, and, we must say, he was up to the task as he courteously answered all the questions put to him.

"So, Citizen," asked a heavyset man whose tall, skinny, shriveled-up wife was pressing up against him, pale and trembling in fear, so much so that you could almost hear her bones knocking together. "You say that the robbery took place on the road we've just taken?"

"Yes, Citizen. Between Lambesc and Pont-Royal, did you notice a place where the road climbs between two hills, a place where there are many rocks?"

"Oh, yes, my friend," the woman said, holding tight to her husband's arm. "I did see it, and I even said, as you must remember, 'This is a bad place. I'm glad we're coming through during the day and not at night.'"

"Oh, madame," said a young man whose voice exaggerated the guttural pronunciation of the time and who seemed to exercise a royal influence on the conversation of the common table, "you surely know that for the gentlemen called the *Companions of Jehu* there is no difference between day and night."

"Indeed," said the wine merchant, "it was in full daylight, at ten in the morning, that we were stopped."

"How many of them were there?" the heavyset man asked.

"Four of them, Citizen."

"Standing in the road?"

"No, they appeared on horseback, armed to the teeth and wearing masks."

"That is their custom, that is their custom," said the young man with the guttural voice. "And then they must have said, did they not?, 'Don't try to defend yourselves, and no harm will come to you. All we are after is the government's money.'"

"Word for word, Citizen."

"Yes," continued the man who seemed to have all the information. "Two of them got down, handed their bridles to their companions, and asked the coachman to give them the money."

"Citizen," the large man said in amazement, "you're telling the story as if you had witnessed it yourself!"

"Perhaps the gentleman was there," said Roland.

The young man turned sharply toward the officer. "I don't know, Citizen, if you intend to be impolite with me. We can speak about that after dinner. But, in any case, I am pleased to say that my political opinions are such that, unless you were intending to insult me, I would not consider your suspicion as an offense. However, yesterday morning at ten o'clock, when those gentlemen were stopping the stagecoach four leagues away, these gentlemen here can attest to the fact that I was having lunch at this very table, between the same two citizens who at this moment are doing me the honor of sitting at my right and my left."

"And," Roland continued, speaking this time to the wine merchant, "how many of you were in the stagecoach?"

"There were seven men and three women."

"Seven men, not counting the coachman?" Roland repeated.

"Of course," the man from Bordeaux answered.

"And with eight men you let yourself be robbed by four bandits? I congratulate you, monsieur."

"We knew whom we were dealing with," the wine merchant answered, "and we were not about to try to defend ourselves."

"What?" Roland replied. "But you were dealing with brigands, with bandits, with highway robbers."

"Not at all, since they had introduced themselves."

"They had introduced themselves?"

"They said, 'We are not brigands; we are the Companions of Jehu. It is useless to try to defend yourselves, gentlemen; ladies, don't be afraid.'"

"That's right," said the young man at the common table. "It is their custom to let people know, so there can be no mistake."

"Well," Roland continued, while Bonaparte kept silent, "who is this citizen Jehu who has such polite companions? Is he their captain?"

"Sir," said a man whose clothing looked very much like that of a secular priest, and who seemed to be a resident of the city as well as a regular at the common table, "if you were more acquainted than you seem to be in reading Holy Scripture, you would know that this citizen Jehu died some two thousand six hundred years ago, so that consequently, at the present time, he is unable to stop stagecoaches on the highway."

"Sir priest," Roland said, "since, in spite of the sour tone you are currently using with me, you seem to be well educated, allow a poor ignorant man to ask for some details about this Jehu who died twenty-six hundred years ago but is nevertheless honored by having companions who carry his name."

"Sir," the man of the church answered in the same clipped tone, "Jehu was a king of Israel, consecrated by Elisha on the condition that he punish the crimes of the house of Ahab and Jezebel and that he put to death all the priests of Baal."

"Sir priest," the young officer laughed, "thank you for the explanation. I have no doubt that it is accurate and certainly very scholarly. Except I have to admit that it has taught me very little."

"What do you mean, Citizen?" said the regular customer at the table. "Don't you understand that Jehu is His Majesty Louis XVIII, may God preserve him, consecrated on the condition that he punish the crimes of the Republic and that he put to death all the priests of Baal—that is, all the Girondins, the Cordeliers, the Jacobins, the Thermidorians; all those people who have played any part over the last seven years in this abominable state of affairs that we call the Revolution!"

"Well, sure enough!" said Roland. "Indeed, I am beginning to understand. But among those people the Companions of Jehu are supposed to be fighting, do you include the brave soldiers who pushed the foreigners back out of France and the illustrious generals who led the armies in the Tyrol, the Sambre-et-Meuse, and Italy?"

"Yes. Those men, and especially those men."

Roland's eyes grew hard, his nostrils dilated, he pinched his lips and started to stand up. But his companion grabbed his coat and pulled him back down, and the word "fool," which he was about to throw in the face of his interlocutor, stayed between his teeth.

Then, with a calm voice, the man who had just demonstrated his power over his companion spoke for the first time. "Citizen," he said, "please excuse two travelers who have just come from the ends of the earth, as far away as America or India, who have been out of France for two years, who don't know what's happening here, and who are eager to learn."

"Tell us what you would like to know," the young man asked, apparently having paid only the slightest attention to the insult Roland had been about to spit at him.

"I thought," Bonaparte continued, "that the Bourbons were completely reconciled to exile. I thought the police were sufficiently well organized to keep bandits and robbers off the highways. And finally, I thought that General Hoche had completely pacified the Vendée."

"But where have you been? Where have you been?" said the young man with a loud laugh.

"As I told you, Citizen, at the ends of the earth."

"Well, then. Let me help you understand. The Bourbons are not rich; the émigrés, whose property has been sold, are ruined. It is impossible to pay two armies in the West and to organize one in the Auvergne mountains without any money. So the Companions of Jehu, by stopping stagecoaches and pillaging the coffers of our tax officers, have set themselves up as tax collectors for the Royalist generals. Just ask Charette, Cadoudal, and Teyssonnet."

"But," ventured the Bordeaux wine merchant, "if the gentlemen calling themselves the Companions of Jehu are only after the government's money. . . ."

"Only the government's money, not anyone else's. Never have they robbed an ordinary citizen."

"So yesterday," the man from Bordeaux continued, "how did it happen, then, that along with the government's money they also carried off a bag containing two hundred louis that belonged to me?"

"My dear sir," the young man answered, "I've already told you that there must have been some mistake, and as sure as my name is Alfred de Barjols, that money will be returned to you some day."

The wine merchant sighed deeply and shook his head like a man who, in spite of the reassurances people are giving him, still is not totally convinced.

But at that moment, as if the guarantee given by the young man who had revealed his own name and social rank had awakened the sensibilities of those for whom he was giving his guarantee, a horse galloped up to the front door. They could hear footsteps in the corridor; the dining room door was flung open, and a masked man, armed to the teeth, appeared in the doorway.

All eyes turned to him.

"Gentlemen," he said, his voice breaking the deep silence that greeted his unexpected appearance, "is there among you a traveler named Jean Picot who was in the stagecoach that was stopped between Lambesc and Port-Royal by the Companions of Jehu?"

"Yes," said the wine merchant in astonishment.

"Might you be that man, monsieur?" the masked man asked.

"That's me."

"Was nothing taken from you?"

"Yes, there was. I had entrusted a sack of two hundred louis to the coachman, and it was taken."

"And I must say," added Alfred de Barjols, "that just now this gentleman was telling us about his misfortune, considering his money lost."

"The gentleman was mistaken," said the masked stranger. "We are at war with the government, not with ordinary citizens. We are partisans, not thieves. Here are your two hundred louis, monsieur, and if ever a similar error should take place in the future, just remember the name Morgan."

And with those words the masked man set down a bag of gold to the right of the wine merchant, politely said good-bye to those seated around the table, and walked out, leaving some of them in terror and the others in stupefaction at his daring.

At that moment word came to Bonaparte that the horses were harnessed and ready.

He stood and asked Roland to pay.

Roland dealt with the hotel keeper while Bonaparte got into the coach. Just as Roland was about to join his companion, he found Alfred de Barjols in his path.

"Excuse me, monsieur," the young man said to him. "You were beginning to say something to me, but the word never left your lips. Might I know what kept you from pronouncing it?"

"Oh, monsieur," said Roland, "the reason I held it back was simply that my companion pulled me back down by my coat pocket, and so as not to be disagreeable to him, I decided not to call you a fool."

"If you intended to insult me in that way, monsieur, might I therefore consider that you have now done so?"

"If that should please you, monsieur. . . ."

"That does please me, because it offers me the opportunity to demand satisfaction."

"Monsieur," said Roland, "we are in a great hurry, my companion and I, as you can see. But I will be happy to delay my departure for an hour if you think one hour will be enough to settle this question."

"One hour will be sufficient, monsieur."

Roland bowed and hurried to the coach.

"Well," said Bonaparte, "are you going to fight?"

"I could not do otherwise, General," Roland answered. "But my adversary appears to be very accommodating. It should not take more than an hour. I shall hire a horse as soon as this business is over and shall surely catch up with you before you reach Lyon."

Bonaparte shrugged.

"Hothead," he said. And then, reaching out his hand, he added, "Try at least not to get yourself killed. I need you in Paris."

"Oh, relax, General. Somewhere between Valence and Vienne I shall come tell you what happened."

Bonaparte left.

About one league beyond Valence he heard a horse galloping behind him and ordered the coachman to stop.

"Oh, it's you, Roland," he said. "Apparently everything went well?"

"Perfectly well," said Roland as he paid for his horse.

"Did you fight?"

"Yes, I did, General."

"How?"

"With pistols."

"And?"

"And I killed him, General."

Roland took his place beside Bonaparte and the coach set off again at a gallop.

IV

The Son of the Miller of La Guerche

BONAPARTE NEEDED ROLAND in Paris to help him organize the 18th Brumaire. Once the 18th Brumaire was over, what Bonaparte had heard and seen with his own eyes at the common table in Avignon came back to him. He resolved to do all he could to track down the Companions of Jehu and try to bring Cadoudal around to support the Republic.

It was Roland to whom Bonaparte entrusted that mission.

Roland left Paris, gathered some information in Nantes, and took the road toward La Roche-Bernard. There, he was able to get information that sent him to the village of Muzillac. For that is where Cadoudal could be found.

Let us enter the village with Roland. Let us walk up to the fourth thatched-roof house on the right and look in through an opening in one of the shutters. There we see a man dressed like a rich Morbihan peasant. His collar, his lapels, and the edges of his hat are trimmed with one gold stripe the width of a finger. His clothing is made of gray wool, with a green collar. His outfit is complete with Breton suspenders and leather gaiters coming up nearly to his knees. His saber is lying on a chair, and on the table a pair of pistols are within reach. The blaze in the fireplace reflects off two or three gun barrels.

The man is seated at the table. Light from a lamp shines on his face and on some papers he is attentively reading. His expression is open and joyous. Curly blond hair frames his face, his bright blue eyes give it life, and when he smiles, he displays two rows of white teeth that clearly have never needed to be touched by a dentist's brush or tools. He is nearly thirty years old.

Like his fellow countryman Du Guesclin, he has a large, round head. Consequently, he is as well known by the name General *Tête-Ronde* as he is by the name George Cadoudal.

George was the son of a farmer in the parish of Kerléano. He had just finished an excellent education in the secondary school in Vannes when the Royalist insurrection's first appeals were made. Cadoudal responded, gathered together his hunting and partying companions, led them across the Loire, and offered his services to Stofflet.

But Monsieur de Maulevrier's former game warden had his prejudices. He did not like nobility and liked the bourgeoisie even less. Before agreeing to take Cadoudal, he wanted first to see him at work, and Cadoudal asked for nothing more.

Already the next day there was combat. When Stofflet saw Cadoudal charge the Blues without concern for their bayonets or guns, he could only say to Monsieur de Bonchamps, who was standing beside him, "If some cannonball doesn't carry off that *tête ronde,* he will make a name for himself." The name stuck with him.

George fought in the Vendée until Savenay was routed, when half of the Vendée army died on the battlefield and the other half faded away like smoke.

After three years of prodigious feats of strength, skill, and courage, he crossed back over the Loire and returned to the Morbihan.

Once back on his native soil, Cadoudal fought on his own account. As general-in-chief, he was adored by his soldiers, who obeyed him at a simple signal. Thus Stofflet's prophecy came true. Replacing La Roche-Jacquelein, d'Elbee, Bonchamps, Lescure, Charette, and even Stofflet himself, Cadoudal became their chief rival in glory and their superior in force. He alone continues to fight against the government of Bonaparte, who has been consul for two months and is now about to leave for Marengo.

Three days ago, Cadoudal learned that General Brune, victor at Alkmaar and Castricum, savior of Holland, has been named general-in-chief of the Western armies. Now in Nantes, he is at all costs supposed to wipe out Cadoudal and his Chouans.

So, that being the case, Cadoudal has no choice but to take it upon himself to prove to the general-in-chief that he is not afraid and that intimidation is the last weapon that Brune should use against him.

At this particular moment he is dreaming up some brilliant maneuver with which to dazzle the Republicans. Suddenly he raises his head. He has heard a horse galloping. The horseman must surely be one of his own for to enter Muzillac without difficulty, he'd have had to pass through the Chouans spread out along the road from La Roche-Bernard.

The horseman stops at the front door of the thatched hut and comes face to face with George Cadoudal.

"Oh, it's you, Branche-d'Or," Cadoudal says. "Where have you come from?"

"From Nantes, General."

"Any news?"

"Bonaparte's aide-de-camp has come with General Brune on a special mission for you."

"For me?"

"Yes."

"Do you know his name?"

"Roland de Montrevel."

"Have you seen him?"

"As I see you now."

"What kind of man is he?"

"A handsome young man about twenty-six or twenty-eight years old."

"And when is he getting here?"

"An hour or two after me, probably."

"Have you alerted our men along the highway?"

"Yes. He will be able to pass freely."

"Where is the Republican vanguard?"

"In La Roche-Bernard."

"How many men are there?"

"Approximately one thousand."

At that moment they heard a second horse galloping up. "Oh!" said Branche-d'Or, "can that be him already? That's impossible!"

"No, because the man arriving now is coming from Vannes."

The second horseman stopped by the door and entered as had the first. Although he was wrapped in a large coat, Cadoudal recognized him immediately. "Is that you, Coeur-de-Roi?" he asked.

"Yes, General."

"Where are you coming from?"

"From Vannes, where you sent me to keep an eye on the Blues."

"Well, what are they doing?"

"They are starving, and to get some food, General Harty is planning to steal our stores in Grand-Champ. The general himself will lead the expedition, and so they can move rapidly, the column will be made up of only one hundred men."

"Are you tired, Coeur-de-Roi?"

"Never, General."

"And how about your horse?"

"He has run hard but can surely cover three or four leagues more without collapsing. With two hours of rest. . . ."

"Two hours of rest and a double ration of oats, and then your horse will need to cover six leagues!"

"He can do it, General."

"In two hours you will leave, and you must give the order in my name to evacuate the village of Grand-Champ at daybreak."

Cadoudal paused for a moment and turned to listen. "Ah," he said. "This time it must be him. I hear a horse galloping up on the La Roche-Bernard road."

"It's him," said Branche-d'Or.

"Who?" asked Coeur-de-Roi.

"Someone the general is expecting."

"Now, my friends, please leave me alone," said Cadoudal. "You, Coeur-de-Roi, get to Grand-Champ as quickly as possible. You, Branche-d'Or, wait in the courtyard with thirty men ready to carry a message to all parts of the country. I trust you can arrange to have the best possible supper for two brought here to me."

"Are you going out, General?"

"No, I'm simply going to meet the person who's arriving. Quickly, go to the courtyard and stay out of sight!"

Cadoudal appeared on the threshold of the front door just as a horseman, bringing his mount to a stop, was looking around uncertainly.

"He's right here, monsieur," said George.

"Who is right here?" the horseman asked.

"The man you are looking for."

"How did you guess that I'm looking for someone?"

"That is not difficult to see."

"And the man I'm looking for. . . ."

"Is George Cadoudal. That is not hard to guess."

"Huh," responded the young man in surprise.

He jumped down from his horse and began to tether it.

"Oh, just throw the bridle over his neck," said Cadoudal, "and don't worry about him. You will find him here when you need him. Nothing ever gets lost in Brittany. You are on loyal ground." And then, showing him the door, he said, "Please do me the honor of entering this humble hut, Monsieur Roland de Montrevel. I can offer you no other palace for tonight."

However much Roland was master of himself, he was unable to hide his astonishment from George. More from the light of the fire that some invisible hand had just stirred up than from the light of the lamp, George could study the young man who was trying in vain to figure out how the person he was looking for, and at, had been notified of his arrival ahead of time. Judging that it would be inappropriate to display his curiosity, Roland sat down on the chair Cadoudal offered and stretched his boots out toward the fire in the fireplace.

"Are these your headquarters?" he asked.

"Yes, Colonel."

"They are guarded in a strange way, it seems to me," said Roland, looking around.

"Do you say that," asked George, "because you didn't meet a soul on the highway between La Roche-Bernard and here?"

"Not a soul, I must say."

"That does not prove the highway was unguarded," said George with a laugh.

"Well, then it was guarded by owls, for they seemed to be accompanying me from tree to tree. And if that is the case, General, I withdraw my comment."

"Exactly," Cadoudal replied. "Those owls are my sentinels. They have good eyes, and they have the advantage over men of being able to see in the dark."

"Nonetheless, if I hadn't taken care to get directions in La Roche-Bernard, I never would have found a soul to show me the road."

"If at any place along the road you had called out, 'Where might I find George Cadoudal?' a voice would have answered, 'In the town of Muzillac, the fourth house on the right.' You saw no one, Colonel. However, there are now approximately fifteen hundred men who know that Monsieur Roland de Montrevel, the First Consul's aide-de-camp, is meeting with the miller of Kerléano."

"But if they know I'm the First Consul's aide-de-camp, why did your fifteen hundred men allow me to pass?"

"Because they had received orders not only to allow you free passage but also to help you if you should need them."

"So you knew I was coming?"

"I knew not only that you were coming but also why you were coming."

"Well, then, there's no reason for me to tell you."

"Yes, there is. For hearing what you have to say will be a pleasure."

"The First Consul wishes peace, but a general peace, not a partial one. He has signed a peace treaty with the Abbé Bernier, d'Autichamp, Châtillon, and Suzannet. He considers you a brave and loyal adversary and is saddened to see you alone continuing to stand up to him. So he has sent me here to talk to you directly. What are your conditions for peace?"

"Oh, my conditions are quite simple," said Cadoudal, laughing. "If the First Consul gives the throne back to His Majesty Louis XVIII, and if he in turn becomes the king's constable, his lieutenant-general, and head of his army and navy, at that very instant I shall convert our truce into a treaty of peace and, further, shall become the first soldier in his ranks."

Roland shrugged. "But you surely know that's impossible; the First Consul has already positively refused that request."

"Well, that is why I am inclined to continue hostilities."

"When?"

"Tonight. And you have arrived just in time to witness the spectacle."

"But you do know that the generals d'Autichamp, Châtillon, and Suzannet as well as the Abbé Bernier have laid down their arms?"

"They are from the Vendée, and as Vendeans, they can do as they wish. I am Breton and a Chouan, and in the name of Bretons and Chouans I can do as I wish."

"So you are condemning this unfortunate country to a war of extermination, General?"

"It is martyrdom, to which I convoke all Christians and Royalists."

"General Brune is in Nantes with the eight thousand French prisoners the English have just turned over to us."

"That is good fortune they would not enjoy with the Chouans, Colonel. The Blues have taught us not to take prisoners. As for the number of our enemies, it is not our custom to worry about that. Numbers are only a matter of details."

"But you know that if General Brune and his eight thousand prisoners, together with the twenty thousand soldiers he is inheriting from General Hédouville, are insufficient, the First Consul is determined to march against you himself, with one hundred thousand men if necessary."

"We shall be grateful for the honor he bestows upon us," said Cadoudal, "and we shall try to prove to him that we are worthy adversaries."

"He will burn down your cities."

"We shall then withdraw to our thatched-roof huts."

"He will burn down your huts."

"We shall live in the woods."

"You will give it some thought, General."

"Please do me the honor of staying with me for twenty-four hours and you will see that I have already thought about it."

"And if I agreed?"

"You would gratify me, Colonel. Only don't ask more than I can give you: a bed under a thatched roof, one of my horses so you can accompany me, and a safe-conduct for when you leave."

"I accept."

"Your word, monsieur, never to act counter to the orders I give you, never to try to thwart any surprises I might attempt."

"I am too curious about what you'll be doing for that. You have my word, General."

"Even when things happen before your very eyes?" asked Cadoudal insistently.

"Even if things take place before my very eyes, I renounce my role as an actor and will remain a spectator. I want to be able to say to the First Consul, 'I saw.'"

Cadoudal smiled. "Well, you will see," he said.

At that moment the door opened, and two peasants carried in a table already completely set. Steam was rising up from a crock of cabbage soup and a slab of bacon. An enormous jug of cider, newly drawn, foaming up and overflowing, stood between two glasses. There were two place settings: obviously an invitation to the colonel to sup with Cadoudal.

"You see, Monsieur de Montrevel," said Cadoudal, "my men hope you will do me the honor of supping with me."

"And it's good they do," answered Roland, "for I am starving, and if you didn't invite me, I would try to take what I could by force." The young colonel sat across from the Chouan general.

"Please excuse me for the meal I'm serving you," said Cadoudal. "I do not receive hardship bonuses like your generals, and you have somewhat cut off my food supply by sending my poor bankers to the scaffold. I could pick a quarrel with you on that score, but I know that you used neither trickery nor lies and that everything happened loyally among soldiers. So I have nothing to complain about. And what's more, I need to thank you for the money you managed to send to me."

"One of the conditions Mademoiselle de Fargas set when she identified her brother's murderers was that the sum she received was to be sent to you. We—that is, the First Consul and myself—have kept our promise, that is all."

Cadoudal bowed slightly; with his own insistence upon loyalty, he found all that perfectly natural. Then, speaking to one of the Bretons who had borne the table, he said, "What can you give us along with this, Brise-Bleu?"

"A chicken fricassee, General."

"That's the menu for your meal, Monsieur de Montrevel."

"It's a real feast. There's only one thing I fear."

"What is that?"

"As long as we're eating, things will be fine. But when we need to drink. . . ."

"Ah, you don't like cider," said Cadoudal. "Damn! This is embarrassing. Cider and water. I have to admit that my wine cellar has nothing else."

"That is not the problem. To whose health will we be drinking?"

"So that's what troubling you, Monsieur de Montrevel," said Cadoudal in a dignified tone. "We shall drink to the health of our common mother, to the health of France! We serve France with different minds, but, I hope, with the same love.

"To France, good sir!" said Cadoudal, filling his glass.

"To France, General!" replied Roland, clinking his glass against the general's.

Their consciences clear, they both sat down gaily, and with good appetites they dug into the cabbage soup. The elder of the two was not yet thirty years old.

V

The Mousetrap

A BELL WAS RINGING vibrantly, playing "Ave Maria." Cadoudal pulled out his watch. "Eleven o'clock," he announced.

"You know that I am at your orders," Roland answered.

"We have an expedition to complete six leagues away. Do you need some rest?"

"Me?"

"Yes. If so, you may sleep for an hour."

"Thanks, but that is unnecessary."

"In that case," said Cadoudal, "we shall leave when you are ready."

"And your men?"

"Oh, my men! My men are ready."

"Where?"

"Everywhere."

"I'll be damned. I'd like to see them!"

"You'll see them."

"But when?"

"Whenever you want. My men are quite discreet. They show themselves only when I give the signal."

"So that if I wanted to see them. . . ."

"You have only to tell me; I shall give the signal and they will appear."

Roland began to laugh. "Do you doubt it?" asked Cadoudal.

"Not in the slightest. Only . . . Let's go, General."

"Let's go."

The two young men wrapped themselves in their coats and stepped outside.

"Let's get on our horses," said Cadoudal.

"Which horse shall I take?" asked Roland.

"I thought you would be pleased to find your own horse well rested, so I chose two of my horses for our expedition. Take your pick. They are both equally good, and each has in its saddle holsters a pair of English-made pistols."

"Already loaded?" Roland asked.

"And loaded with great care, Colonel. That's a job I never entrust to anyone else."

"Well, then, let's mount," said Roland.

Cadoudal and his companion climbed up onto their saddles and started down the road toward Vannes. Cadoudal rode beside Roland, while Branche-d'Or, the major general of Cadoudal's army, rode twenty paces behind them.

As for the army itself, it remained invisible. The road, so straight it seemed to have been drawn by a tight rope, appeared to be totally deserted.

When they had ridden approximately a half league, Roland grew impatient: "Where in the devil are your men?"

"My men? . . . On our right, on our left, in front of us, behind us; everywhere."

"That's a good one," said Roland.

"I'm not joking, Colonel. Do you think me so imprudent as to venture out without scouts in the midst of men so experienced and vigilant as your Republicans?"

Roland kept silent for a moment; and then, with a doubtful gesture, he said, "You told me, General, that if I wished to see your men, all I needed to do was say so. Well, I'd like to see them now."

"All of them or just a part?"

"How many did you say would be with you?"

"Three hundred."

"Well, then, I'd like to see one hundred and fifty."

"Halt!" Cadoudal ordered.

Bringing his hands to his mouth, he imitated the call first of a screech owl, then of a barn owl. For the first call, he turned to the right, and for the second, to the left. The last plaintive notes had barely died away when suddenly on both sides of the road shadowy human shapes appeared. Crossing the ditch that separated them from the road, they began lining up on both sides of the horsemen.

"Who is in command on the right?" asked Cadoudal.

"I am, General," answered a peasant, stepping forward.

"Who are you?"

"Moustache."

"Who is in command on the left?" Cadoudal inquired.

"I am, Chante-en-Hiver," answered a second peasant as he stepped forward.

"How many men do you have with you, Moustache?"

"One hundred, General."

"How many men are with you, Chante-en-Hiver?"

"Fifty, General."

"So, are there one hundred fifty in all?" asked Cadoudal.

"Yes," the two Breton leaders answered together.

"Does that match your figure, Colonel?" asked George with a laugh.

"You are a magician, General."

"No, I am only a poor Chouan, just another unfortunate Breton. I command a troop in which each brain knows what it's doing and in which each heart beats for the two great principles of this world: religion and royalty." Then, turning toward his men: "Who is commanding the vanguard?" he asked.

"Fend-l'Air," the two Chouans answered.

"And the rear guard?"

"La Giberne."

"So we can safely continue on?" Cadoudal asked the two Chouans.

"As if you were going to mass in your village church," Fend-l'Air answered.

"Let's continue on, then," Cadoudal said to Roland. And turning back to his troops, he said: "Now scatter, my good men!"

In an instant, every man had leaped across the ditch and disappeared. For a few seconds, the horsemen could hear branches rustling and a trace of footsteps in the underbrush. Then nothing at all.

"Well," said Cadoudal. "Do you believe that with such men I have anything to fear from your Blues, however brave and skillful they might be?"

Roland sighed. He agreed totally with Cadoudal.

They continued riding.

About one league from La Trinité, they saw on the road a dark mass that kept getting larger. Suddenly it stopped.

"What's that?" asked Roland.

"A man," said Cadoudal.

"I can see that," Roland answered. "But who is it?"

"By his speed, you ought to have guessed that it's a messenger."

"Why has he stopped?"

"Why, because he saw three men on horseback, and he doesn't know if he should continue forward or start back."

"What will he do?"

"He's waiting before he decides."

"Waiting for what?"

"A signal, of course."

"And will he respond to the signal?"

"Not merely respond; he'll obey it. Would you like him to come forward or move backward? Or to jump to one side?"

"I would like him to come forward," said Roland. "That way we can find out what news he's bringing."

The Breton leader imitated a cuckoo's call with such perfection that Roland looked around for the bird. "It's me," said Cadoudal. "No need to look around."

"So the messenger will start toward us?"

"No, he is already on his way."

And indeed, the messenger had begun moving rapidly forward. In just a few seconds he was beside his general.

"Ah!" Cadoudal said. "Is that you, Monte-à-l'Assaut?"

The general leaned forward, and Monte-à-l'Assaut whispered a few words in his ear.

"I have already been warned by Bénédicité," said George.

After exchanging several words with Monte-à-l'Assaut, Cadoudal twice more imitated the call of a barn owl and then once again a screech owl. In an instant he was surrounded by his three hundred men.

"We're getting close," he said to Roland, "and we need to leave the highway."

Just above the village of Trédion they started out across the fields. Then, leaving Vannes on their left, they reached Trefféan. But instead of following the road into the village, the Breton leader went to the edge of a little woods that extends from Grand-Champ to Larré and ventured no farther. Cadoudal seemed to be waiting for some news.

A grayish glow appeared in the direction of Trefféan and Saint-Nolff. It was the first glimmer of dawn, but a thick layer of fog arising from the ground made it impossible to see more than fifty steps ahead.

Suddenly, about five hundred steps away, they heard a cock crow. George pricked up his ears. The Chouans looked at each other and laughed. The cock crowed once more, closer this time. "It's him," said Cadoudal. "Answer him."

Roland heard a howl three steps away; it imitated a dog with such perfection that the young man, although forewarned, looked around for the animal that was howling so lugubriously. At the same moment, out of the fog, the two horsemen saw a man coming rapidly toward them.

Cadoudal moved forward a few feet, then raised his finger to his mouth to warn the man to speak quietly. "Well, Fleur-d'Epine," George asked, "have we got them?"

"Like a mouse in a trap. Not a single one will return to Vannes if that is your wish, General."

"Oh, I could ask for nothing more. How many of them are there?"

"One hundred men, commanded by General Harty in person."

"How many carts?"

"Seventeen."

"Are they far from here?"

"Approximately three quarters of a league."

"What road are they following?"

"The road from Grand-Champ to Vannes."

"That's exactly what we need."

Cadoudal called together his four lieutenants: Branche-d'Or, Monte-à-l'Assaut, Fend-l'Air, and La Giberne. The general gave each his orders, and each in turn gave a screech-owl call to his fifty men.

The fog was getting thicker and thicker. In less than a hundred steps each band of fifty men disappeared into it like a host of shadows.

Cadoudal remained with a hundred men and Fleur-d'Epine.

"Well, General," asked Roland when Cadoudal returned, "is everything going as planned?"

"Pretty much," answered Cadoudal, "and in a half hour you will be able to judge for yourself."

"Not if the fog stays as thick as this."

Cadoudal looked around him. "In a half hour the fog will have completely dissipated. Shall we use this time to eat a bit and have a morning drink?"

"Well, General," said Roland, "I admit that the five or six hours of riding have given me quite an appetite."

"And I," said George, "I don't mind telling you that I always like to eat as well as I can before battle. When you leave for eternity, it's best to leave, whenever possible, on a full stomach."

"Ah!" said Roland. "You are going to fight?"

"That's why I'm here, and since we are dealing with your Republican friends and with General Harty in person, I doubt that they will surrender without a fight."

"Do the Republicans know that they will be fighting against you?"

"They suspect nothing."

"So you are planning a surprise for them?"

"Not completely. Given, as I have told you, that the fog will dissipate in about twenty minutes, they will be able to see us as well as we can see them. Brise-Bleu," Cadoudal continued, "do you have something to give us for breakfast?"

The Chouan who seemed to be in charge of food nodded and went into the woods. He came back out, behind him a donkey carrying two baskets.

A coat was spread out on a little mound, and there Brise-Bleu laid out a roast chicken, a piece of cold salt pork, some bread, and buckwheat crêpes. Since they were on a campaign, he thought it important also to provide the luxury of a bottle of wine and a glass. "There, do you see?" said Cadoudal to Roland.

Roland need no further invitation. He leaped down from his horse and handed the bridle to a Chouan. Cadoudal did the same.

"Now," said Cadoudal, turning toward his men. "You have twenty minutes to do the same as we. Those who have not finished eating in twenty minutes are forewarned that they will be fighting on an empty stomach."

As if awaiting this invitation, they all pulled from their pockets a piece of bread and a buckwheat crêpe and, minus the chicken and pork, followed the example of their general and his guest.

As there was only one glass, Cadoudal and Roland both drank from it. In the light of the dawning day, they ate side by side, just as two hunting friends might.

From one moment to the next, as Cadoudal had predicted, the fog was becoming less dense. Soon, a half league away on the road from Grand-Champ to Plescop, they could see the force of two hundred Chouans led by Monte-à-l'Assaut, Chante-en-Hiver, La Giberne, and Fend-l'Air.

Inferior in numbers—fewer than one hundred—the Republicans had stopped and were waiting for the fog to dissipate so they could estimate enemy numbers and determine what kind of force they would be facing.

At the sight of the Republicans confronting a force three times their strength, at the sight of their blue uniforms, the color that gave them their nickname, the Blues, Roland stood up suddenly. As for Cadoudal, he remained nonchalantly stretched out on the grass, finishing his meal.

Roland had only to glance at the Republicans to realize they were lost. Cadoudal watched the succession of emotions that crossed the young man's face. "Well," Cadoudal asked after a moment of silence that allowed Roland to evaluate the situation, "do you think I have taken the proper dispositions, Colonel?"

"You might even say your proper precautions, General," said Roland with a mocking smile.

"Is it not one of the First Consul's customs," asked Cadoudal, "to accept his advantages when the occasion permits?"

Roland bit his lips. "General," he said, "I have a favor to ask and I hope you will not refuse."

"What is it?"

"The permission to go die with my comrades."

Cadoudal got to his feet. "I was expecting such a request," he said.

"Then will you grant it?" said Roland, his eyes sparkling with joy.

"Yes, but first I would like to request a service from you," said the Royalist leader in his dignified tone.

"Speak, monsieur."

And Roland waited, no less serious and no less proud than the Royalist chief. Old France and New France found their epitomes in those two men.

VI

The Combat of the One Hundred

ROLAND LISTENED.

"The service I ask of you, monsieur, is to negotiate with General Harty for me."

"To what end?"

"I have several proposals to make before we begin battle."

"I presume," said Roland, "that among the proposals which you do me the honor of charging me with, you are not including one that asks him to lay down his arms?"

"On the contrary, Colonel. You must understand that such a proposal is at the top of my list."

"General Harty will refuse," said Roland, clenching his fists.

"Probably," Cadoudal answered calmly.

"And then?"

"And then I shall offer him the option of two other proposals that he will be perfectly free to accept without forfeiting his honor and without damaging his reputation."

"May I know what they are?" Roland asked.

"You will know them at the appropriate time. Please be so good as to begin with the first proposal."

"Spell it out for me."

"General Harty and his one hundred men are surrounded by a force three times stronger. You know it, and you can say as much to him. I offer them safe conduct, but they must lay down their arms and swear that for five years they will not serve against the Vendée or Brittany."

"A useless message," said Roland.

"That would be better than getting crushed, both him and his men."

"True, but he will prefer to have them crushed and himself crushed with them."

"Beforehand, it would be good, however, to make him the proposal."

"As for that, you are right," said Roland. "My horse?"

They brought his horse to him. He leaped into the saddle and rapidly crossed the space separating them from the waiting group.

General Harty's surprise was great when he saw an officer wearing the uniform of a Republican colonel coming toward him. He moved three paces toward the messenger, who introduced himself, explained how he happened to be with the Royalist Whites, and conveyed Cadoudal's proposal. As the young officer had predicted, the general refused.

Roland galloped back toward where Cadoudal was waiting. "He refuses!" he shouted as soon as he was within earshot.

"In that case," said Cadoudal, "take him my second proposal. I don't want to have anything to blame myself for afterwards, having to answer to an honorable judge such as you."

Roland bowed. "Let us move on the second proposal," he said.

"Here it is," answered Cadoudal. "General Harty is on horseback, as am I. He will leave the ranks of his soldiers and ride out to meet me in the space between the two armies. Like me, he will be carrying his saber and his pistols. And then we can decide the issue between ourselves. If I kill him, his men will accept the conditions I've dictated, not to serve for five years against us; for you surely understand that I cannot take any prisoners. If he kills me, his men will have free passage to Vannes with their supplies intact and with no fear of attack by my troops. Ah! I hope this is a proposal you would be able to accept, Colonel?"

"I do accept it," said Roland.

"Yes, but you are not General Harty. For the moment, just be content with your role as negotiator. And if this proposal—which, in his place, I would not pass up—is not enough to satisfy him, well, you will come back, and, good soul that I am, I shall make him a third one."

Roland galloped back to the Republicans and General Harty, who were waiting impatiently for him. He conveyed his message to the general.

"Colonel," the general answered, "I must give account to the First Consul for my actions. You are his aide-de-camp, and when you return to Paris, I charge you with being my witness when you speak to him. What would you do in my place? I will do what you would do."

Roland winced. An expression of deep gravity spread over his face. He paused to reflect. Then, a few moments later: "General," he said, "I would refuse."

"Give me your reasons," Harty answered, "so that I may see if they are in accordance with my own."

"The outcome of a duel is totally uncertain, and you cannot subject the destiny of one hundred brave men to such chances. In a business such as this, where each is engaged for himself, each man should defend his hide as best he can."

"Is that your opinion, Colonel?"

"Yes, on my honor."

"It is mine as well. So, take my answer back to the Royalist general."

Roland returned to Cadoudal as fast as he had ridden to meet Harty.

Cadoudal smiled when he heard the Republican general's answer. "I suspected as much," he said.

"How could you suspect such an answer, since I'm the one who gave it to him?"

"And yet you were of a different opinion a short while ago."

"Yes, but you accurately reminded me that I was not General Harty. Let us hear your third proposal," Roland continued a little impatiently, for he was beginning to realize that ever since the negotiations had gotten under way, Cadoudal had been coming off the better.

"The third proposal," said Cadoudal, "is an order, the order that two hundred of my own men withdraw. General Harty has one hundred men, I shall keep one hundred. Ever since the Combat of the Thirty, Bretons have had the custom of fighting face to face, chest to chest, man to man, and we prefer to battle one against one rather than three. If General Harty is the victor, he can walk over our bodies and return to Vannes without danger from the two hundred men who will not participate in the combat. If he is vanquished, he will not be able to say that he failed because he was greatly outnumbered. Go on, Monsieur de Montrevel, go back to your friends. I give them now the advantage of numbers, since you alone are worth ten men."

Roland raised his hat.

"What do you say, monsieur?" asked Cadoudal.

"It is my custom to salute those I see as great, and I salute you."

"Colonel," said Cadoudal, "one last glass of wine. Let each of us drink to what he loves most, to what he is most sorry to leave behind, to what he hopes to see again in heaven."

He took the only glass, filled it halfway, and handed it to Roland. "We have only one glass, Monsieur de Montrevel. You drink first."

"Why first?"

"Because you are my guest, and also because there's a proverb that says he who drinks after another shall know what the other person is thinking. I want to know what you are thinking, Monsieur de Montrevel."

Roland drained the glass and handed it back to Cadoudal. As he had done for Roland, he filled the glass halfway, and then emptied it in turn.

"So, do you know now what I was thinking?" asked Roland.

"Help me," laughed Cadoudal.

"Well, here are my thoughts," replied Roland without guile. "I'm thinking that you are a good man, General, and I would be honored if now that we are about to fight each other, you would agree to shake my hand."

More like two friends parting than like two enemies preparing to fight, the two young men shook hands. With simple grandeur, they each then executed a military salute.

"Good luck!" said Roland to Cadoudal. "But permit me to doubt that my wish will come true—though I say this from my lips, not my heart."

"May God protect you, Monsieur de Montrevel," said Cadoudal, "and may He grant that my own wish come true, for it expresses the sum of my best thoughts."

"By what signal will we know you are ready?" asked Roland.

"We shall shoot into the air."

"Very well, General."

Putting his horse to a gallop, for the third time Roland crossed the space between the Royalist and the Republican generals. Cadoudal pointed toward him. "Do you see that young man?" he asked his Chouans.

Everyone looked at Roland. "Yes, General," the Chouans answered.

"By the souls of your fathers, consider his life sacred! You may capture him, but take him alive and with no harm to a hair on his head."

"Very well, General," the Bretons replied.

"And now, my friends," he continued in a louder voice. "Remember that you are the sons of those thirty heroes who once fought thirty Englishmen, ten leagues from here, between Ploërmel and Josselin: the sons of victors! Our ancestors were made immortal by that combat of the Thirty. Now prove yourselves as illustrious in this combat of the One Hundred."

"Unfortunately," he added quietly, "this time we are fighting not the English, but our own brothers."

The fog had disappeared; with a golden tint the first rays of the springtime sun mottled the Plescop plain. It would be easy to see whatever maneuvers the two armies made.

As Roland returned to the Republican side, Branche-d'Or's men began to withdraw so that only Cadoudal and his force of one hundred men would be left to face General Harty and his Blues.

The men who had been dismissed from the combat separated into two groups: one marched toward Plumergat, the other toward Saint-Avé. The road was soon clear.

Branche-d'Or came back to Cadoudal. "Your orders, General," he said.

"One only," the general answered. "Pick eight men and follow me. When you see the young Republican I had breakfast with fall from his horse, you and your men shall throw yourselves upon him and take him prisoner before he can get away."

"Yes, General."

"You know I want to see him again safe and sound."

"I understand, General."

"Choose your men; and if he gives his word, you may act as you will."

"And if he won't give his word?"

"You will bind him so that he is unable to flee, and you will hold him until the battle is over."

Branche-d'Or sighed.

"It will be unhappy for us," he said, "to stand there twiddling our thumbs while our compatriots are spreading out to fight."

"God is good," said Cadoudal. "Go on, there will be enough for everyone to do."

Then, seeing the Republicans amassed for battle, Cadoudal called for a gun. He shot once into the air. At the same moment, within the Republican ranks two drummers began to beat out the charge.

Cadoudal stood up in his stirrups. "My sons," he said, his voice sonorous, "has everyone offered up his morning prayer?"

In unison they answered: "Yes, yes!"

"If anyone has forgotten to pray or has not found the opportunity to," Cadoudal pronounced, "now is the time!" Five or six peasants dropped to their knees.

The drums were moving rapidly closer. "General! General!" several voices called out impatiently, but the general pointed to the kneeling Chouans. And the impatient men waited while their fellows, each in his own time, finished their prayers.

When the last of them had risen to his feet, the Republicans had already covered about a third of the distance between the two camps. Their bayonets fixed, they were marching in three rows, thirty to a row. Behind them marched the officers in serried ranks, with Roland riding ahead of one row and General Harty between the other two. No one else rode on horseback. Among the Chouans, there was only one horseman: Cadoudal. Branche-d'Or had tied his mount to a tree so that he could fight on foot with the eight men charged with taking Roland prisoner.

"General," said Branche-d'Or, "the prayers are over, and everyone is ready."

Cadoudal assured himself that was so, and then with command in his voice he shouted: "All right, my men, everybody scatter!"

Scarcely had he given the order than the Chouans, waving their hats in one hand and brandishing their guns with the other, spread out over the plain to cries of "Long live the king!" Fanning farther outward, they took the shape of an immense crescent, with George and his horse at the center.

In an instant the Republicans, who held their ranks, were overrun, and the shooting began. As almost all of Cadoudal's men were poachers, they were good shots. And they were armed with English rifles, which could shoot twice as far as general-issue guns. Although the Chouans, who had fired first, appeared to be out of range, some of their death's messengers managed to reach the Republican ranks nonetheless.

"Forward!" General Harty shouted.

His soldiers continued to march with bayonets extended, but in a matter of seconds there was nobody facing them.

Cadoudal's one hundred men had disbanded; his army had become snipers, with fifty men splayed on each side of the Republican ranks. General Harty ordered an about-face to the right and to the left, and then his command rang out:

"Fire!"

But to no success. For the Republicans were firing at individual men, while the Chouans were shooting at a mass of soldiers in formation. Their shots almost always reached their mark.

Roland saw the disadvantages of the Republican position. He looked around, and in the middle of the smoke he descried Cadoudal standing immobile like an equestrian statue: The Royalist leader was waiting for him. With a cry, Roland rode straight for him.

As for Cadoudal, he galloped toward the brave Republican but stopped fifty paces away from him.

"Get ready," Cadoudal said to Branche-d'Or and his men.

"Rest easy, General. We're ready," Branche-d'Or replied.

Cadoudal drew a pistol from the saddle holster and loaded it. Roland, his saber in hand and his body leaning down over his horse's neck, was charging. He was only twenty paces away when Cadoudal slowly raised his hand and took aim at Roland. At ten paces, he fired.

Roland's horse had a white star in the middle of its forehead. Cadoudal's bullet struck the middle of the star. The horse, mortally wounded, rolled with its rider at Cadoudal's feet.

Cadoudal put his spurs to his horse's flanks, and it leaped over the fallen horse and rider. Branche-d'Or and his men were ready. Like a pack of jaguars they pounced on Roland, who lay trapped under his horse's body.

The young man dropped his saber and reached for his pistols. But before he could put hand to holster, two men had seized each of his arms, while the other six dragged the horse off his legs. They worked with such coordination that it was apparent a plan had been laid in advance.

Roland roared in anger. Branche-d'Or handed him his hat.

"I will not surrender," Roland shouted.

"There's no reason you need to surrender, Monsieur de Montrevel," Branche-d'Or answered politely.

"And why not?" asked Roland, wasting his efforts in a desperate, useless struggle.

"Because you have been captured, monsieur."

The obvious truth precluded any reasonable response Roland might make. "Then kill me," he shouted.

"We have no intention of killing you, monsieur."

"Then what do you want?"

"Your word that you will take no further part in this combat. At that price, we'll set you free."

"Never!" cried Roland.

"Excuse me, Monsieur de Montrevel. What you are doing is not very loyal," Branche-d'Or responded.

"Not loyal! Ah, you wretch! You are insulting me because you know that I can neither defend myself nor punish you."

"I am not a wretch, and I am not insulting you, Monsieur de Montrevel. All I'm saying is that by not giving your word and by forcing us to guard you, you are depriving the general of nine men who could be of use to him. That is not the way the great Tête-Ronde treated you. He had two hundred men more than you, and he sent them away. Now we are only ninety-one against your one hundred."

A flame flashed through Roland's eyes, then suddenly he went pale. "You are right, Branche-d'Or," he said. "Whether or not I can expect help, I surrender. You may go fight with your companions."

Shouting for joy, the Chouans released Roland. Then, waving their hats and guns and crying "Long live the king!" they rushed into the melee.

VII

Blues and Whites

ROLAND STOOD ALONE for a moment. He was now free, but he had been disarmed literally by his fall and figuratively by his word. He contemplated the little mound where he and Cadoudal had shared a breakfast; it was still covered with the cloak that had served as a tablecloth. From there he could survey the whole battlefield, and if his eyes had not been clouded by tears of shame, he would not have missed the slightest detail.

Like the demon of war, invulnerable and relentless, Cadoudal was standing upright on his horse in the midst of the fire and smoke.

As the heat of his anger dried his tears of shame, Roland noticed more. Out in the fields where green wheat was beginning to sprout, he counted the bodies of a dozen Chouans who lay scattered here and there on the ground. But the Republicans, in their compact formation on the road, had lost more than twice that number.

The wounded on both sides dragged themselves into the open field, where, like broken serpents, they tried to rise and continue fighting, the Republicans with their bayonets, the Chouans with their knives. Or they would reload their guns, then manage to get up on one knee, and fire, and fall back again onto the ground.

On both sides the combat was relentless, unceasing, pitiless. Civil war, a merciless and unforgiving civil war, was translating its hate into blood and death across the battlefield.

Cadoudal rode back and forth through the human redoubt. From twenty paces he'd fire, sometimes with his pistols, sometimes from a double-barreled gun that he'd then toss to a Chouan for reloading. Every time he shot, a man would fall. General Harty honored Cadoudal's maneuvers by ordering an entire platoon to fire at him.

In a wall of flame and smoke, he disappeared. They saw him fall, him and his horse, as if struck by lightning.

Ten or twelve men rushed out of the Republican ranks, but they were met by an equal number of Chouans. In the terrible hand-to-hand combat, the Chouans with their knives seemed to have the upper hand.

Then, suddenly, Cadoudal was again among them; standing in his stirrups, he wielded a pistol in each hand. Two men fell, two men died.

Thirty Chouans joined him to form a sort of wedge. Now wielding a regular-issue rifle, using it as a club, Cadoudal led his thirty men into their enemy's ranks. With each swing the giant felled a man. He broke through the Blues' battalion, and Roland saw him appear on the Republican side of the battle lines. Then, like a wild boar that turns back on a fallen hunter to rip out his entrails, Cadoudal reentered the fray and widened the breach.

General Harty rallied twenty men around him. Holding their bayonets in front of them, they bore down on the Chouans who had formed a circle around their general. Harty's horse had been disemboweled, so with his clothing full of bullet holes and blood flowing from two wounds, he marched on foot with his twenty men. Ten of them fell before they could break the Chouan circle, but Harty made it through to the other side.

Ready though the Chouans were to pursue him, Cadoudal in a thunderous voice called out: "You should not have let him pass, but since he's already through, let him withdraw freely." The Chouans obeyed their leader as if his words were sacred.

"And now," Cadoudal cried, "let the firing cease! No more killing! Only prisoners!"

And with that, everything was over.

In that horrible war both sides shot their prisoners: the Blues because they considered the Chouans and the Vendeans to be brigands; the Whites because they didn't know what to do with the Republicans they captured.

The Republicans tossed aside their guns to avoid handing them over to their enemy. When the Chouans approached them, they opened their cartridge pouches to show that they had spent their last ammunition.

Cadoudal started his march over to Roland.

During the final stages of the battle, the young man had remained seated; with his eyes fixed on the struggle, his hair wet with sweat, his breathing pained and heavy, he had waited. When he saw that fortune had turned against the Republicans and him, he had put his hands to his head and dropped facedown to the ground.

Roland seemed not to hear Cadoudal's footsteps when he walked up to him. Then slowly the young officer raised his head; tears were coursing down both cheeks.

"General," said Roland. "Dispose of me as you will. I am your prisoner."

"Well," laughed Cadoudal, "we cannot make a prisoner of the First Consul's ambassador, but we can ask him to do us a service."

"What service? Just give the order."

"I don't have enough ambulances for the wounded. I don't have enough prisons for the prisoners. Take it upon yourself to lead the Republican soldiers, both the prisoners and the wounded, back to Vannes."

"What are you saying, General?" Roland exclaimed.

"I put them in your care. I regret that your horse is dead. I am sorry too that my own horse was killed, but Branche-d'Or's horse is still available. Please accept it."

Cadoudal saw that the young man was reluctant. "In exchange, do I not still have the horse you left in Muzillac?" George said.

Roland understood that he had no choice but to match the noble character of the person he was dealing with.

"Will I see you again, General?" he asked, getting to his feet.

"I doubt it, monsieur. My operations call me to the Port-Louis coast, and your duty calls you back to the Luxemburg Palace." (At that time, Bonaparte was still living there.)

"What shall I tell the First Consul, General?"

"Tell him what you saw, and tell him especially that I consider myself greatly honored that he has promised to see me."

"And given what I have seen, monsieur, I doubt that you will ever need me," said Roland. "But in any case, remember that you have a friend close to General Bonaparte." He extended his hand to Cadoudal.

The Royalist leader took his hand with the same candor and confidence he had shown before the battle. "Good-bye, Monsieur de Montrevel," he said. "I'm sure there's no need for me to remind you to do justice to General Harty? A defeat of that kind is as glorious as a victory."

Branche-d'Or's horse had meanwhile been brought to the colonel. He leaped into the saddle. Taking one last look around the battlefield, Roland heaved a great sigh. With a final good-bye to Cadoudal he then started off at a gallop across the fields toward the Vannes highway, where he would await the cart with the prisoners and the wounded that he had been charged with taking back to General Harty.

Each man had received ten pounds on Cadoudal's orders. Roland could not help but think that Cadoudal was being generous with the Directory's money, sent to the West by Morgan and his unfortunate companions. And Morgan's companions had paid for that money with their heads.

The next day, Roland was in Vannes. In Nantes, he took the stagecoach to Paris and arrived two days later.

As soon as Bonaparte learned that he was back, he summoned Roland to his study.

"Well, then," Bonaparte asked when he appeared, "what about this Cadoudal? Was he worth the trouble you put yourself through?"

"General," Roland answered, "if Cadoudal is willing to come over to our side for one million, give him two, and don't sell him to anyone else even for four."

Colorful as the answer was, it was not sufficient for Bonaparte. So Roland had to recount in detail his meeting with Cadoudal in Muzillac, their night march under the singular protection of the Chouans, and finally the combat, in which, after prodigious feats of courage, General Harty had yielded to the Royalists.

Bonaparte was jealous of such men. Often he had spoken with Roland about Cadoudal, in the hope that some defeat would encourage the Breton leader to abandon the Royalist party. But soon Bonaparte was crossing the Alps and concentrating not on civil war but on foreign wars. He had crossed the Saint-Bernard pass on the 20th and 21st of May and the Tessino River at Turbigo on the 31st. On June 2nd he entered Milan. After conferring with General Desaix, who was just back from Egypt, he spent the night of the 11th in Montebello. On the 12th, Bonaparte had set his army in position on the Scrivia and finally, on June 14, 1800, he had waged the Battle of Marengo. There, tired of life, Bonaparte's aide-de-camp Roland had been killed in the explosion he himself had ignited when he set fire to a munitions wagon.

Bonaparte no longer had anyone to talk to about Cadoudal. Still, he thought often about the Breton brigand. Then, early in February 1801, the First Consul received a letter from Brune containing this letter from Cadoudal:

General,

If I had to fight only the 35,000 men you currently have in the Morbi-han, I would not hesitate to continue the campaign as I have done for more than a year, and by a series of lightning-quick movements, I would destroy them to the last man. But others would immediately replace them, and prolonging the war would only result in the greatest of disasters.

Please set the date for a meeting, giving your word of honor. I shall come to see you without fear, alone or with others. I shall negotiate for me and for my men, and I shall be tough for them alone.

George Cadoudal

Beneath Cadoudal's signature, Bonaparte wrote: "Set a meeting promptly. Agree to all his conditions, provided that George and his men lay down their arms. Insist that he come see me in Paris, and give him a safe-conduct. I want to see this man close-up and form my own judgment of him." And in his own hand he addressed the letter "To General Brune, Commander-in-Chief of the Western Army."

As it happened, General Brune was camped on the same road between Muzillac and Vannes where the Battle of the One Hundred had taken place two years before. There General Harty had been defeated, and there Cadoudal now appeared before General Brune. Brune extended his hand and led Cadoudal, along with his aides-de-camp Sol de Grisolles and Pierre Guillemot, across a trench where all four sat down.

Their discussion was just about to begin when Branche-d'Or arrived with a letter so important (so he'd been told) that he thought he should de-liver it immediately to the general, wherever he happened to be. The Blues had allowed him passage to his leader, who, with Brune's permission, took the letter and quickly perused it.

His face betraying no emotion, Cadoudal finished the letter, folded it back up, and tossed it into his hat. Then he turned toward Brune. "I'm all ears, General," he said.

Ten minutes later, everything was decided. The Chouans, officers and soldiers alike, would all return freely to their homes without harassment, not then or in the future, and they would not take up arms again except by direct orders from Cadoudal himself.

As for Cadoudal himself, he asked that he be granted the right to sell the few parcels of land, the mill, and the house that belonged to him and with the money from the sale be allowed to settle in England. He asked for no in-demnity whatever.

As for a meeting with the First Consul, Cadoudal declared that he would consider it a great honor. He said he'd be ready to go to Paris as soon as he had arranged with a notary in Vannes for the sale of his property and with Brune for a safe-conduct.

As for his two aides-de-camp, other than permission for them to accompany him to Paris so they could witness his meeting with Bonaparte, he asked only for the same conditions he had obtained for his men—pardon for the past, safety for the future.

Brune asked for pen and ink.

The treaty was written on a drum. It was shown to George, who then signed it, as did his aides-de-camp. Brune signed last and gave his personal guarantee that the document would be faithfully executed.

While a copy was being made, Cadoudal pulled the letter he had received out of his hat. Handing it to Brune, he said, "Read this, General. You will see that I did not sign the treaty because I needed money." For indeed, the letter from England announced that the sum of three hundred thousand francs had been deposited with a banker in Nantes, with the order that the funds be made available to George Cadoudal.

Taking the pen, Cadoudal wrote on the second page of the letter: "Sir, Send the money back to London. I have just signed a peace treaty with General Brune, and consequently I am unable to receive money destined for making war."

Three days after the treaty had been signed, Bonaparte had a copy in hand, along with Brune's notes detailing the meeting.

Two weeks later, George had sold his property for a total of sixty thousand francs. On February 13, he alerted Brune that he would be leaving for Paris, and on the 18th *Le Moniteur,* the official record, published this announcement:

> George will be going to Paris to meet with the government. He is a man thirty years of age. The son of a miller, fond of battle, having a good education, he told General Brune that his whole family had been guillotined but that he wished to be associated with the government. He said that he wanted his links with England to be forgotten, and that he had only sought out England in order to oppose the regime of 1793 and the anarchy that seemed then about to devour France.

Bonaparte was right to say, when Bourrienne offered to read him the French newspapers, "That's enough, Bourrienne. They say only what I let them say."

The newspaper report of course had come directly from Bonaparte's office, and with customary skill it combined both foresight and hate. In his foresight, the First Consul was improvising Cadoudal's rehabilitation by attributing to him the desire to serve the government. And in his hate, he was charging him with crimes against the regime of 1793.

On February 16, Cadoudal arrived in Paris. On the 18th, he read the brief piece about him in *Le Moniteur*. For a moment he was tempted to leave without seeing Bonaparte, hurt as he was by the newspaper's tone. But he decided it was better to accept the proposed audience and make his profession of faith to the First Consul. Accompanied by two witnesses, his officers Sol de Grisolles and Pierre Guillemot, he would go to the Tuileries as if he were going to a duel. Through the War Ministry, he sent word to the Tuileries that he had arrived in Paris. He received back a letter setting the audience for the next day, on February 19, at nine in the morning.

And that was the meeting to which the First Consul Bonaparte was hurrying so eagerly, once he had sorted out Josephine's debts.

VIII

The Meeting

THE THREE ROYALIST LEADERS were waiting in the large room that people continued to officially call the Louis Quatorze Room; unofficially, they called it the Cockade Room.

All three wore the typical Royalist uniform, for that was one of the conditions Cadoudal had set. The gray jacket with a green collar was simply adorned with a gold stripe for Cadoudal and a silver one for each of his officers. They also wore Breton suspenders, large gray gaiters, and white quilted vests. Sabers hung at their sides. And their soft felt hats sported a white cockade.

Duroc, when he saw them, placed his hand on Bonaparte's arm, and the First Consul stopped to look at his aide-de-camp. "What's the matter?" he asked.

"They have their sabers," said Duroc.

"So?" Bonaparte replied. "They aren't prisoners."

"No matter," said Duroc. "I'll leave the door open."

"Indeed, it's not necessary. They are enemies, but loyal enemies. Do you not recall what our poor comrade Roland said about them?"

Briskly Bonaparte walked into the room where the three Chouans were waiting. He signaled to Rapp and the two other officers who were present that they should station themselves outside.

"Here you are at last!" said Bonaparte, recognizing Cadoudal from the description his former aide-de-camp had given him. "A friend we have in common, whom we had the misfortune to lose at the Battle of Marengo, Colonel Roland de Montrevel, told me very good things about you."

"I am not surprised," Cadoudal answered. "During the short time I had the honor of knowing Monsieur Roland de Montrevel, I was able to recognize in him the most gentlemanly feelings. But, although you may know who I am, General, I must introduce to you the two men accompanying me, as they have also been admitted into the honor of your presence."

Bonaparte bowed slightly, as if to indicate that he was listening.

Cadoudal placed his hand on the older of the two officers. "Taken to the colonies as a young man, Monsieur Sol de Grisolles crossed the sea to return to France. During the crossing, he was shipwrecked and found floating alone on a plank in the middle of the ocean, barely conscious and about to be swallowed up by the waves. Later, a prisoner of the Revolution, he cut through his dungeon walls, escaped, and the next day he was fighting in our ranks. Your soldiers had sworn to take him at all costs, and during discussions about peace, they invaded the house where he had taken refuge. Alone, he defended himself against fifty soldiers. When he'd spent all his cartridges, he could only surrender or else throw himself out a window twenty feet from the ground. Without hesitation, he leaped and, landing among the Republicans, rolled over, got back to his feet, killed two of his enemy, wounded three others, took off running and escaped in spite of the bullets whistling uselessly around him.

"As for this man," Cadoudal said, pointing to Pierre Guillemot, "he too was surprised in a farmhouse where he was enjoying a few hours of rest. Your men entered his bedroom before he could grab his saber or rifle, so he picked up an axe and split open the head of the first soldier who approached him. The Republicans backed off. Guillemot, still brandishing his axe, reached the door, parried the thrust of a bayonet that barely touched his skin, and escaped across the fields. When he came to a barrier where a soldier stood guard, he killed the guard and leaped over the barrier. And when a Blue in pursuit of him was at his heels, Guillemot turned around and split open the man's chest with one swing of his axe. Finally he was free to come join my Chouans and me.

"As for me. . . ." Cadoudal added, bowing modestly.

"As for you," Bonaparte interrupted, "I know more about you than you yourself would tell me. You picked up where your fathers left off. Instead of the Combat of the Thirty, you were the victor at the Combat of the One Hundred, and some day people will call the war you have been waging the war of the giants." Then, stepping forward, he said, "Come, George. I'd like to speak to you alone."

George hesitated a moment, but followed him all the same. He would have preferred that his two officers also hear any words he and the head of the French republic would exchange.

Bonaparte, however, said nothing until they were out of earshot. Then he spoke: "Listen, George," he said, "I need energetic men to help me to finish the task I've undertaken. I used to have near me a heart of bronze on which I could depend as if he were me myself. You met him: Roland de Montrevel. A despondency I could never fully understand led him to suicide, for his death truly was a suicide. Are you willing to join me? I have proposed the rank of colonel for you, but you are worth more than that, I know, and I can offer you the rank of major general."

"I thank you from the depths of my heart, General," George responded, "but you would think less of me if I accepted."

"Why do you say that?" Bonaparte asked quickly.

"Because I swore allegiance to the Bourbons, and to the Bourbons I'd remain faithful even if I'd accept."

"Come now," said the First Consul, "is there no way I can get you to join me?"

Cadoudal shook his head.

"You have heard people slandering me," said Bonaparte.

"General," answered the Royalist officer, "might I be permitted to repeat the things people have told me?"

"Why not? Do you think I'm not strong enough to hear the bad as well as the good that people speak of me?"

"Please note that I affirm nothing. All I shall do is repeat what people say," said Cadoudal.

"Go ahead," said the First Consul, a slightly worried smile on his face.

"They say that you were able to come back to France so successfully, without hindrance by the English fleet, because you had made a treaty with Commodore Sidney Smith. They say the terms of the treaty allowed you to return without threat on the agreed-to condition that you would restore our former kings to the throne."

"George," said Bonaparte, "you are one of those men whose esteem I value and whom, consequently, I'd not want to give any cause for slander. Since returning from Egypt I have received two letters from the Comte de Provence. If such a treaty with Sir Sidney Smith had existed, do you think the count would have failed to make reference to it in one of the letters he did me the honor of sending? I shall show you these letters, and you can judge for yourself if the accusation brought against me has any basis."

In the course of their walking, they'd come to the Louis Quatorze Room's door. Bonaparte opened it. "Duroc," he said, "go ask Bourrienne to send me the two letters from the Comte de Provence as well as my response. They are in the middle drawer of my desk, in a leather portfolio."

While Duroc carried out the assigned task, Bonaparte continued: "How astonished I am to see how much your former kings constitute virtually a religion to you plebeians! Suppose I did restore the throne—something I'm not at all inclined to do, I tell you—what would be in it for you people who have shed your blood to see the throne restored? Not even the confirmation of the rank you have fought to obtain. A miller's son a colonel? Come now. In the royal armies, was there ever a colonel who was not a nobleman born? Among the ungrateful nobility has ever a man risen so high because of his own worth or even for services rendered? Whereas with me, George, you can rise to any rank or level. For the higher I rise, the higher shall I raise those surrounding me. . . . Ah, here are the letters. Give them to me, Duroc."

Duroc handed him three documents. The first one Bonaparte opened bore the date of February 20, 1800, and we have copied the Comte de Provence's letter from the archives without changing a single word.

Whatever their apparent conduct may be, men such as you, monsieur, never cause concern. You have accepted a high position, and I am grateful to you for that. Better than anyone else, you know what strength and power are necessary for a great country's happiness. Save France from its own fury, and you will have fulfilled my heart's deepest wish; give it back its king, and future generations will bless your memory. Your importance to the country will always be too great for me to pay the debt my ancestor and I owe you by some high appointment.

Louis

"Do you see any allusion to a treaty in that letter?" asked Bonaparte.

"General, I admit that I do not," George answered. "And you didn't answer the letter?"

"I must say that I thought there was no hurry, and I expected I would receive a second letter before deciding. It was not long in coming. A few months later, this undated letter arrived." He passed it to Cadoudal.

You have surely known for a long time, General, that my esteem for you is assured. If you were to doubt that I am capable of gratitude, propose your own position and set the destiny of your friends. As for my principles, I am French. Lenient by nature, reason makes me even more so.

No, the victor at Lodi, Castiglione, and Arcole, the conqueror of Italy and Egypt, cannot prefer vain celebrity to true glory. However, you are wasting precious time. We can guarantee France's glory. I say "we" because to accomplish that, I need Bonaparte, and because Bonaparte cannot do it without me.

General, Europe has its eyes on you, glory awaits you, and I am impatient to bring peace back to my people.

Louis

"As you see, monsieur," Bonaparte said, "there's no more reference to a treaty in the second letter than there was in the first."

"Dare I ask, General, if you answered this one?"

"I was about to have Bourrienne answer the letter and sign it when he pointed out to me that since the letters were penned by the Comte de Provence himself, it would be more appropriate for me to respond in my own handwriting, however bad it may be. Since it was an important matter, I did the best I could, and the letter I wrote was at least readable. Here's a copy," said Bonaparte, handing George a copy Bourrienne had made of the letter he himself had written to the Comte de Provence. It contained this refusal:

I received your letter, monsieur; I thank you for your kind words.

You ought not wish to return to France; you would need to tread over one hundred thousand cadavers.

Sacrifice your interests to France's peace and happiness. History will be grateful.

I am not unfeeling about your family's misfortunes, and I shall be pleased to learn that you have everything you need for a peaceful retirement.

Bonaparte

"So," asked George, "was that indeed your final word?"

"My final word."

"And yet history provided a precedent. . . ."

"The history of England, not our own history, monsieur," Bonaparte interrupted. "Me playing the role of Monck? Oh no! If I had to choose and if I wanted to imitate an Englishman, I would prefer Washington. Monck lived in a century when the prejudices that we fought against and overturned in 1789 were still strong. Even if Monck had tried to become king, he would not have been able to. A dictator perhaps, but nothing more. To do more, he would have needed Cromwell's genius. A quality lacking in Richard, Cromwell's son, who was not able to retain power—of course he was an idiot, the typical son of a great man. And then, some fine result, the restoration of Charles II! Replacing a puritan court with a libertine court! Following his father's example, he dissolved three or four parliaments and tried to govern alone, then set up a cabinet of lackeys that attended more to matters of royal debauchery than to the business of the court. He was greedy for pleasure and stopped at nothing when money was at stake. He sold Dunkirk to Louis XIV—Dunkirk, which was England's key possession in France. And he had Algernon Sidney executed, on the pretext that he was party to some nonexistent conspiracy, when, in fact, Sidney had refused not only to attend the commission that sentenced Charles I to death but also, adamantly, to sign the act ordering the royal execution.

"Cromwell died in 1658, when he was fifty-nine years old. During the ten years he was in power, he had the time to undertake many changes but to complete only a few. In fact, he was trying to accomplish complete reform: political reform by replacing a monarchy with a republican government, and religious reform by abolishing Catholicism in favor of Protestantism. Well, if you assume I shall live as long as Cromwell, to the age of fifty-nine—it's not very long, is it?—I have about thirty more years: three times as many as Cromwell had. And you see that I'm not trying to change things. I'm content to continue things the way they are. I'm not overthrowing things, but rather raising them back up."

Cadoudal laughed. "What about the Directory?"

"The Directory was not a government," replied Bonaparte. "Is it possible to establish power on a rotten foundation like the Directory's? If I had not returned from Egypt, the Directory would have collapsed under its own corrupt weight. All I had to do was nudge it a little. France wanted nothing to do with the Directory. And for proof of that, look at how France welcomed me back. What had the Directory done with the country in my absence? When I returned I found poor France threatened on every side by an enemy that already had a foothold inside three of its borders. I had left the country in peace; I found it now at war. I had left with victories behind me; I returned to defeats. I had left the country's coffers with millions from Italy; on my return I found misery and spoliatory laws everywhere. What has become of those one hundred thousand soldiers, my companions in glory, men whom I knew by name? They are dead. While I was taking Malta, Alexandria, Cairo; while I was engraving with the point of our bayonets the name of France on pylons in Thebes and on obelisks in Karnak; while I was avenging the defeat of the last king of Jerusalem at the base of Mount Thabor—what was the Directory doing with my best generals? They allowed Humbert to be taken in Ireland; they arrested and tried to dishonor Championnet in Naples. Schérer retreated, thus obliterating the victorious path I had laid out in Italy. They let the English invade the coast of Holland; they got Raimbault killed in Turin, David at Alkmaar, and Joubert at Novi. And when I asked for reinforcements to keep Egypt, munitions to defend it, wheat to plant for its future, they sent me congratulatory letters and decrees stating that the Army of the Orient was meritorious and the pride of France."

"They thought you could find all you needed in Acre, General."

"That is my only failure, George," said Bonaparte, "and if I had succeeded, I swear, I would have surprised all of Europe! If I had succeeded! I'll tell you what I would have done then. I would have found the pasha's treasures in Acre and enough weapons to arm three hundred thousand men. I would have roused and armed all of Syria, where everyone decried Djazzar's cruelty; I would have marched on Damascus and Aleppo. My army would have grown larger and larger as I advanced, and I would have announced to the people the abolition of all servitude and of the pasha's tyrannical government. I would have marched to Constantinople and overthrown the Turkish Empire. I would have founded a great new empire in the Orient that would have guaranteed my place in history. And then I would have come back to Paris through Adrianople or Vienna—after wiping out the house of Austria!"

"That's like Caesar's plan when he declared war on the Parthians," Cadoudal answered coldly.

"Ah, I was sure we would come back to Caesar," said Bonaparte with a laugh, his teeth clenched. "Well, as you see, I'm willing to accept discussion on whatever grounds you choose. Suppose that when he was twenty-nine years old, as I am now, Caesar, instead of leading a patrician life of debauchery in Rome and accumulating the greatest debts known in his time, suppose that he had been instead the Citizen First Consul. Suppose that at twenty-nine his campaign in Gaul had already been finished, his Egyptian campaign completed, and his Spanish campaign successfully ended. Suppose, I repeat, that he was twenty-nine instead of fifty years old—the age at which Victory, who loves only the young, begins to abandon bald brows—do you think he would not then have been both Caesar and Augustus?"

"Yes," Cadoudal replied brusquely, "unless he had happened first to find Brutus, Cassius, and Casca in his path with their daggers."

"So," said Bonaparte with sadness, "my enemies are counting on assassination! In that case, it'll be easy for them, and especially for you, since you are my enemy. What is preventing you at this very moment, if you have the same convictions as Brutus, from striking me down as he struck Caesar? We are alone, the doors are closed. You have your saber. You could surely be upon me before my guards could stop you."

"No," said George. "No, we are not counting on assassination. I believe it would require grave circumstances for one of us to decide to become an assassin. But the chances of war remain. One simple rebellion could cost you all your prestige, a cannonball could take off your head the way it did Marshal Berwick's, or a bullet could strike you like Joubert and Desaix. And then what will become of France? You have no children, and your brothers. . . ."

Bonaparte stared hard at Cadoudal, who completed his thoughts with a shrug. Bonaparte clenched his fists. George had found the chink in his armor.

"I admit," said Bonaparte, "that from that point of view you are right. I risk my life daily, and daily my life could be taken. But even if you do not believe in Providence, I do. I believe that nothing happens by chance. I believe that when Providence, on August 13, 1769, exactly one day after Louis XV had rendered the edict uniting Corsica to France, allowed a child to be born in Ajaccio, a child who would carry out the 13th Vendémiaire and the 18th Brumaire, it had great designs and supreme plans in store for him. I was that child, and Providence has always kept me safe in the midst of great dangers. Since I have a mission, I fear nothing. Because my mission is my armor. If I am mistaken; if, instead of living the twenty-five or thirty years I think are necessary to accomplish my goals, I am struck twenty-two times with a dagger like Caesar, or my head is blown off by a cannonball like Berwick's, or a bullet hits me in the chest like Joubert or Desaix—then that is because Providence has its own good reasons for allowing such things to happen, and Providence will then provide what France needs. Believe me, George, Providence never fails great nations.

"A moment ago we were talking about Caesar, and you evoked for me the image of him collapsing at the feet of Pompey's statue after he'd been stabbed by Brutus, Cassius, and Casca. When Rome in mourning attended the dictator's funeral ceremonies, when the people set fire to his assassins' homes, when the Eternal City trembled at the thought of a drunken Anthony or the hypocrite Lepidus and wondered where from the four corners of the earth would rise the genius who'd put an end to the civil wars, no one even thought to consider he'd be an Apollonian schoolboy, Caesar's nephew, young Octavius. A baker's son from Velletri, coated with the flour of his ancestors. A feeble child afraid of heat, cold, thunder, everything? Who could have seen in him the future master of the world when limping, pale, his eyes blinking like a bird's in a spotlight, he passed in review Caesar's old bands of soldiers? Not even Cicero, perspicacious Cicero: '*Ornandum et tollendum* (Cover him with flowers and raise him to the skies),' he said. Well, the child they should have celebrated and then gotten rid of at the first possible moment tricked all the graybeards in the Senate and reigned almost as long over Rome, the city that had assassinated Caesar because it did not want a king, as did Louis XIV over France.

"George, George, don't fight the Providence that has created me, for Providence will break you."

"Well," George answered with a bow, "at least I shall be broken as I follow the path and religion of my fathers, and God will forgive me my error, the error of a fervent Christian and a pious son."

Bonaparte placed his hand on the young leader's shoulder. "So be it," he said, "but at least remain neutral. Let events take their course, let thrones quake and crowns fall. Usually it's the spectator who has to pay to follow the game, but I'll pay you to watch me in action."

"And how much will you give me to do that, Citizen First Consul?" asked Cadoudal.

"One hundred thousand francs a year, monsieur," Bonaparte answered.

"If you can give one hundred thousand francs a year to a simple partisan leader, how much will you give the prince he has been fighting for?"

"Nothing, sir," said Bonaparte disdainfully. "In your case, what I'm paying for is your courage, not the principles that drive you. I would like to prove that for me, a self-made man, men exist by their works alone. Please accept, George. I beg you."

"And if I refuse?" asked George.

"You'll be making a mistake."

"Will I nonetheless be free to journey wherever I want?"

Bonaparte went to the door and opened it.

"Duroc!" he called.

Duroc appeared.

"Please make sure," he said, "that Monsieur Cadoudal and his two friends can move around Paris as freely as if they were in Muzillac. And if they would like passports for any country in the world, Fouché has been ordered to provide them."

"Your word is enough for me, Citizen First Consul," said Cadoudal, bowing once more. "I shall be leaving this evening."

"Might I ask where you'll be going?"

"To London, General."

"So much the better."

"Why so much the better?"

"Because there you'll see up close the men you've been fighting for, and once you've seen them. . . ."

"Yes?"

"Well, you will compare them to those you've been fighting against. However, once you're out of France, Colonel. . . ." Bonaparte paused.

"I'm waiting," said Cadoudal.

"Please don't come back without letting me know. If you do not let me know, you must not be surprised to be treated as an enemy."

"That will be an honor for me, General, since by treating me thus you prove that I am a man to be feared."

George said goodbye to the First Consul and withdrew.

The next day the newspapers read:

Following the meeting George Cadoudal had obtained with the First Consul, he asked permission to withdraw freely to England.

He was granted permission on the condition that he would not return to France without the government's authorization.

George Cadoudal promised to release his men from their oath. As long as he fought, they were committed to support him; by retreating, he has freed them from their obligations to him.

And indeed, on the very evening of his meeting with the First Consul, George was writing in his own hand a letter to his cohorts in every part of France.

Because a protracted war seems to be a misfortune for France and ruin for my region, I free you from your oath of loyalty to me. I shall never call you back unless the French government should fail to keep the promise it gave to me and that I accepted in your name.

If there should happen to be some treason hidden beneath a hypocritical peace, I would not hesitate to call once more on your fidelity, and your fidelity, I am sure, would respond.

George Cadoudal

IX

Two Companions at Arms

≈·≈

WHILE BONAPARTE WAS MEETING with Cadoudal in the Louis Quatorze salon, Josephine, certain that Bourrienne was alone, put on her dressing gown, wiped her reddened eyes, spread a layer of rice powder on her face, slipped her Creole feet into sky-blue Turkish slippers with gold embroidery, and quickly climbed the little stairway connecting her bedroom to Marie de Medicis's oratory.

When she arrived at the study door, she stopped and, bringing both hands up to her heart, peered guardedly into the room. Determining that Bourrienne was indeed alone—writing, with his back to her—she tiptoed across the room and laid her hand on his shoulder.

Smiling, for he recognized the light touch of her hand, Bourrienne turned around.

"Well," Josephine asked. "Was he very angry?"

"Yes," Bourrienne said. "I must admit that it was a major storm, if a storm with no rain. But there was thunder and lightning indeed."

"In short," Josephine added, moving directly to the only point that interested her, "will he pay?"

"Yes."

"Do you have the six hundred thousand francs?"

"Yes, I do," said Bourrienne.

Josephine clapped her hands like a child just relieved of its penitence.

"But," Bourrienne added, "for the love of God, don't run up any more debts, or at least be reasonable."

"What do you call reasonable debt, Bourrienne?" asked Josephine.

"How do you expect me to answer that? The best thing would be to run up no debt at all."

"You surely know that is impossible, Bourrienne," Josephine answered with conviction.

"Perhaps fifty thousand francs. Maybe one hundred thousand."

"But, Bourrienne, once these debts have been paid, and you are confident that you can pay them all with the six hundred thousand francs . . ."

"Yes?"

"Well, my suppliers will then no longer refuse me credit."

"But how about him?"

"Who?"

"The First Consul. He swore that these would be the last debts he would pay on your account."

"Just as he also swore last year," said Josephine with her charming smile.

Bourrienne looked at her in stupefaction. "Truly," he said, "you frighten me. Give us two or three years of peace and the few measly millions we brought back from Italy will be exhausted; yet you persist. . . . If I have any advice to give you, it is to allow him some time to get over this bad mood of his before you see him again."

"But I can't! Because I really must see him right away. I have set up a meeting this morning for a compatriot from the colonies, a family friend, the Comtesse de Sourdis and her daughter, and not for anything in the world would I have him fly into a fit of rage in the presence of these fine women, women whom I met in society, on their first visit to the Tuileries."

"What will you give me if I keep him up here, if I get him even to have his lunch here, so that he'd have no reason to come down to your rooms until dinnertime?"

"Anything you want, Bourrienne."

"Well, then, take a pen and paper, and write in your own lovely little handwriting. . . ."

"What?"

"Write!"

Josephine put pen to paper, as Bourrienne dictated to her: "I authorize Bourrienne to settle all my bills for the year 1800 and to reduce them by half or even by three quarters if he judges it appropriate."

"There."

"Date it."

"February 19, 1801."

"Now sign it."

"Josephine Bonaparte. . . . Is everything now in order?"

"Perfectly in order. You can return downstairs, get dressed, and welcome your friend without fear of being disturbed by the First Consul."

"Obviously, Bourrienne, you are a charming man." She held out the tips of her fingernails for him to kiss, which he did respectfully.

Bourrienne then rang for the office boy, who immediately appeared in the doorway. "Landoire," Bourrienne said, "inform the steward that the First Consul will be taking lunch in his office. Have him set up the pedestal table for two. We shall let him know when we wish to be served."

"And who will be having lunch with the First Consul, Bourrienne?"

"No business of yours, so long as it's someone who can put him in a good mood."

"And who would that be?"

"Would you like him to have lunch with you, madame?"

"No, no, Bourrienne," Josephine cried. "Let him have lunch with whomever he chooses, just so he does not come down to me until dinner." And in a cloud of gauze she fled the room.

Not two minutes later, the door to the study burst open and the First Consul strode straight to Bourrienne. Planting his two fists on the desktop, he said, "Well, Bourrienne, I have just seen the famous George Cadoudal."

"And what do you think of him?"

"He is one of those old Bretons from the most Breton part of Brittany," Bonaparte replied, "cut from the same granite as their menhirs and dolmens. And unless I'm sadly mistaken, I haven't seen the last of him. He's a man who fears nothing and desires nothing, and men like that . . . the fearless are to be feared, Bourrienne."

"Fortunately such men are rare," said Bourrienne with a laugh. "You know that better than anyone, having seen so many reeds painted to look like iron."

"But they still blow in the wind. And speaking of reeds, have you seen Josephine?"

"She has just left."

"Is she satisfied?"

"Well, she no longer carries all her Montmartre suppliers on her back."

"Why did she not wait for me?"

"She was afraid you would scold her."

"Surely she knows she cannot escape a scolding!"

"Yes, but gaining some time before facing you is like waiting for a change to good weather. Then, too, at eleven o'clock she is to receive one of her friends."

"Which one?"

"A Creole woman from Martinique."

"Whose name is?"

"The Comtesse de Sourdis."

"Who are the Sourdis family? Are they known?"

"Are you asking me?"

"Of course. Don't you know the peerage list in France backward and forward?"

"Well, it's a family that has belonged to both the church and the sword as far back as the fourteenth century. Among those participating in the French expedition to Naples, as best as I can recall, there was a Comte de Sourdis who accomplished marvelous feats at the Battle of Garigliano."

"The battle that the knight Bayard managed to lose so effectively."

"What do you think about Bayard, that 'irreproachable and fearless' knight?"

"That he deserved his good name, for he died as any true soldier must hope to die. Still, I don't think much of all those sword-swingers; they were poor generals—Francis I was an idiot at Pavia and indecisive at Marignan. But let's get back to your Sourdis family."

"Well, at the time of Henri IV there was an Abbesse de Sourdis in whose arms Gabrielle expired; she was allied with the d'Estrée family. In addition, a Comte de Sourdis, serving under Louis XV, bravely led the charge of a cavalry regiment at Fontenoy. After that, I lose track of them in France; they probably went off to America. In Paris, they live behind the old Hôtel Sourdis on the square Saint-Germain-l'Auxerrois. There is a tiny street named Sourdis that runs from the Rue d'Orleans to the Rue d'Anjou in the Marais district, and there's the cul-de-sac called Sourdis off the Rue des Fossés-Saint-Germain-l'Auxerrois. If I'm not mistaken, this particular Comtesse de Sourdis, who in passing I must say is very rich, has just bought a lovely residence on Quai Voltaire and is living there. Her house opens onto the Rue de Bourbon, and you can see it from the windows in the Marsan pavilion."

"Perfect! That's how I like to be answered. It seems to me that these de Sourdises are closely related to those living in Saint-Germain."

"Not really. They are close relatives of Dr. Cabanis, who shares, as you know, our political religion. He is even the girl's godfather."

"That improves things. All those dowagers who live in Saint-Germain are not good company for Josephine."

At that moment Bonaparte turned around and noticed the pedestal table. "Had I said that I would be having lunch here?" he asked.

"No," Bourrienne answered, "but I thought it would be better if today you had lunch in your study."

"And who will be doing me the honor of having lunch with me?"

"Someone I have invited."

"Given the way I was feeling, you had to be very sure that the person would please me."

"I was quite sure."

"And who is it?"

"Someone who came from far away and arrived at the Tuileries while you were with George in the reception room."

"I had no other meetings scheduled."

"This person came without a scheduled meeting."

"You know that I never receive anyone without a letter."

"This person you will receive."

Bourrienne got up, went to the officers' room, and simply said, "The First Consul is back."

At those words, a young man rushed into the First Consul's study. Although he was only about twenty-five or twenty-six years old, he was wearing the casual clothes of a general. "Junot!" Bonaparte exclaimed joyously.

"By God, you were quite right to say that this man did not need a letter! Come here, Junot!" The young general did not hesitate, but when he tried to take Bonaparte's hand and raise it to his lips, the First Consul opened his arms and pulled Junot tightly to his breast.

Among the many young officers who owed their careers to Bonaparte, Junot was one of those he loved the most. They had met during the siege of Toulon, when Bonaparte was commanding the battery of the sansculottes. He had asked for someone who could write beautifully, and Junot, stepping from the ranks, introduced himself. "Sit down there," Bonaparte said, pointing to the battery's breastwork, "and write what I dictate." Junot of course obeyed.

He was just finishing the letter when a bomb, tossed by the English, exploded ten steps away and covered him with dirt. "Good!" said Junot with a laugh. "How convenient! We didn't have any sand to blot the ink." Those words made his fortune.

"Would you like to stay with me?" Bonaparte asked. "I shall take care of you." And Junot answered, "With pleasure." From the outset the two men understood each other.

When Bonaparte was named general, Junot became his aide-de-camp. When Bonaparte was placed on reserve duty, the two young men shared their poverty, living off the two or three hundred francs that Junot received each month from his family. After the 13th Vendémiaire, Bonaparte had two other aides-de-camp, Muiron and Marmont, but Junot remained his favorite.

Junot participated in the Egyptian campaign as a general. So, to his great regret, he had to part with Bonaparte. He performed feats of courage at the battle of Fouli, where he shot dead the leader of the enemy army with his pistol. When Bonaparte left Egypt, he wrote to Junot:

I am leaving Egypt, my dear Junot. You are too far away from where we are embarking for me to take you along with me. But I am leaving orders with Kléber for you to leave in October. Finally, wherever I am, whatever my position, please know that I will always give you proof positive of our close friendship.

Good-bye and best wishes,

Bonaparte

On his way back to France on an old cargo ship, Junot fell into the hands of the English. Since then, Bonaparte had heard no news of his friend, so Junot's unexpected appearance created quite a stir in Bonaparte's quarters.

"Well, finally you're back!" exclaimed the First Consul. "I knew you idiotically let yourself be caught by the English by remaining so long in Egypt. What I don't know is why you waited five months when I had asked you to leave as soon as possible."

"Good heavens! Because Kléber would not let me leave. You have no idea how difficult he made things for me."

"He no doubt feared that I'd have too many of my friends in my ranks. I know no love was lost between us, but I never thought he'd demonstrate his enmity in such a petty way. Plus, he wrote a letter to the Directory—do you know about that? What's more," Bonaparte added, raising his eyes heavenward, "his tragic end closed all our accounts, and both France and I have undergone a major loss. But the irreparable loss, my friend, is the loss of Desaix. Ah, Desaix! Such a grave misfortune to have smote our country."

Totally absorbed in his pain, Bonaparte paced up and down a moment without saying a word. Then, suddenly, he stopped in front of Junot. "So, what do you want to do now? I have always said that I would furnish proof of my friendship when I could. What are your plans? Do you want to serve?"

Then, the look in his eyes difficult to read, Bonaparte asked jovially, "Would you like me to have you join the Rhine army?"

Junot cheeks grew flushed. "Are you trying to get rid of me?" he said. After a pause, he continued: "If such are your orders, I shall be happy to show General Moreau that the officers in the army of Italy have not forgotten their work in Egypt."

"Well," said the First Consul with a laugh, "my cart is getting before my horse! No, Monsieur Junot, no, you'll not leave me. I admire General Moreau a great deal, but not so much that I would give him one of my best friends." Then, his brow creased, he continued more seriously: "Junot, I'm going to give you command of Paris. It's a position of trust, especially just now, and I could not make a better choice. But"—he glanced around as if he feared someone might be listening—"you must give it some thought before you accept. You'll need to age ten years, because the position requires not only gravity and prudence to the extreme; it also demands the utmost attention to everything related to my safety."

"General," Junot exclaimed, "on that score. . . ."

"Silence, my friend, or at least speak more softly," Bonaparte said. "Yes, you must watch over my safety. For I am surrounded by danger. If I were still simply the General Bonaparte I was before and even after the 13th Vendémiaire, I would make no effort to avoid danger. In those days my life was my own; I knew its worth, which was not very much. But now my life is no longer my own. I can say this only to a friend, Junot: My destiny has been revealed to me. It is the destiny of a great nation, and that is why my life is threatened. The powers that hope to invade France and divide it up would like to have me out of their way."

Raising his hand to his brow as if he were trying to chase away a troublesome thought, he remained pensive for a moment. Then, his mind moving rapidly from one idea to another—he'd sometimes entertain twenty different ideas at once—Bonaparte resumed: "So, as I was saying, I shall name you commander of Paris. But you need to get married. That would be appropriate not only for the dignity of the position, but it is also in your own best interest. And by the way, be careful to marry only a rich woman."

"Yes, but I would like her to be attractive as well. There's the problem: All heiresses are as ugly as caterpillars."

"Well, set to work immediately, for I am appointing you commander of Paris as of today. Look for an appropriate house, one not too far from the Tuileries, so that I can send for you whenever I need you. And look around; perhaps you can choose a woman from the circle in which Josephine and Hortense move. I would suggest Hortense herself, but I believe she loves Duroc, and I would not want to go against her own inclinations."

"The First Consul is served!" said the steward, carrying in a tray.

"Let's sit down," said Bonaparte. "And in a week from now, you shall have rented a house and chosen a wife!"

"General," said Junot, "while I don't doubt I can find a house in a week, I would like to request two weeks for the wife."

"Agreed," said Bonaparte.

X

Two Young Women Put Their Heads Together

AS THE TWO COMPANIONS AT ARMS were sitting down at their table, Madame la Comtesse and Mademoiselle Claire de Sourdis were announced to Madame Bonaparte.

The women embraced and, gracefully grouping themselves, they inquired after each other's health and spoke of the weather, as was the mode of aristocratic society. Madame Bonaparte then had Madame de Sourdis sit beside her on a chaise longue, while Hortense took it upon herself to show Claire around the palace, as she was visiting for the first time.

The two girls, though about the same age, made a charming contrast. Hortense was blonde, fresh as a daisy, velvety as a peach. Her golden hair fell down to her knees, and her arms and hands were somewhat thin, for she still awaited Nature's last touch to turn her into a woman. In her graceful appearance she combined both French vivaciousness and Creole sweetness. And, to complete the charming picture, her blue eyes shone with infinite gentleness.

Her companion had no cause for jealousy in regard to grace and beauty. Both girls were Creoles, but Claire was taller than her friend, and she had the dark complexion that Nature reserves for the southern beauties she seems to favor. Claire had sapphire blue eyes, ebony hair, a waist so slender two hands could span it, and hands and feet as tiny as a child's.

Both had received excellent educations. Hortense's education, interrupted by her forced apprenticeship until her mother got out of prison, had been organized so intelligently and assiduously that you would not imagine it had ever been interrupted at all. She could draw very nicely, was an excellent musician, indeed composed music, and wrote romantic poetry, some of which has been passed down to us, not simply because of the author's elevated position but rather because of its intrinsic value. In fact, both girls were painters, both were musicians, and both spoke two or three foreign languages.

Hortense showed Claire her study, her sketches, her music room, and her aviary. Near the aviary, they sat down in a little boudoir that had been painted by Redouté. There they spoke about society parties, now beginning to reappear more brilliant than ever; about balls, which were vigorously starting up again; and about handsome, accomplished dancers. They talked about Monsieur de Trénis, Monsieur Laffitte, Monsieur d'Alvimar, and both Coulaincourts. They complained about the necessity, at every ball, to dance at least one gavotte and one minuet. And two questions arose quite naturally.

Hortense asked, "Do you know Citizen Duroc, my stepfather's aide-de-camp?"

And Claire wondered, "Have you had the opportunity to meet Citizen Hector de Sainte-Hermine?"

Claire did not know Duroc.

Hortense did not know Hector.

Hortense more than nearly dared admit that she loved Duroc, for her stepfather, who himself greatly admired Duroc, had given his blessing. Indeed, Duroc was one of those young generals for whom the Tuileries was such a proving ground in those days. He was not yet twenty-eight, his manners were quite distinguished, and he had large but not deeply set eyes. He was taller than average, slender and elegant.

A shadow hovered over their love, however. For while Bonaparte supported it, Josephine did not. She wanted Hortense to marry Louis, one of Napoleon's younger brothers.

Josephine had two declared enemies within Napoleon's family, Joseph and Lucien, who had very nearly obtained Bonaparte's agreement, on his return from Egypt, that he would never see Josephine again. Since his marriage to Josephine, Bonaparte's brothers were constantly pressing him to divorce, on the pretext that a male child was necessary to realize his ambitious plans. It was an easy argument for them to make, since it appeared they were working against their own interests.

Joseph and Lucien were both married, Joseph perfectly and appropriately. He had married the daughter of Monsieur Clary, a rich merchant from Marseille, and was thus Bernadotte's brother-in-law. Clary had a third daughter, perhaps more charming than her sisters, and Bonaparte asked for her hand in marriage. "Heavens, no," the father answered. "One Bonaparte in my family is enough." If he had agreed, the honorable merchant from Marseille would one day have found himself father-in-law to an emperor and two kings.

As for Lucien, he had made what society calls an unequal marriage. In 1794 or 1795, when Bonaparte was still known only for having taken Toulon, Lucien accepted the position of quartermaster in the little village of Saint-Maximin. A Republican who changed his name to Brutus, Lucien would not permit saints' names of any kind in his village. So he had rebaptized Saint-Maximin; the village became Marathon. Citizen Brutus, from Marathon. That had a nice ring to it, he thought.

Lucien-Brutus was living in the only hotel in Saint-Maximin-Marathon. The hotelkeeper was a man who had given no thought to changing his name, Constant Boyer, or that of his daughter, an adorable creature named Christine: Sometimes such flowers grow in manure, such pearls in mud.

Saint-Maximin-Marathon offered Lucien-Brutus no society life and no distractions, but he soon discovered he needed neither, because he had found Christine Boyer. Only Christine Boyer was as wise as she was beautiful, and Lucien realized there was no way he could make her his mistress. So, in a moment of love and boredom, Lucien made her his wife. Christine Boyer became not Christine Brutus, but Christine Bonaparte.

The general of the 13th Vendémiaire, who was beginning to see his fortune clearly, grew furious. He swore he would never forgive the husband, never receive the wife, and he sent both of them to a little job in Germany. Later he softened; he did see the woman, and he was not displeased to see his brother Lucien Brutus become Lucien Antoine before the 18th Brumaire.

Lucien and Joseph both became the terror of Madame Bonaparte. By marrying Bonaparte's nephew Louis to her daughter, Josephine hoped to interest him in her own fortune and to strengthen her protection against the two brothers.

Hortense resisted with all her might. At that time, Louis was quite a handsome young man, if barely twenty years old, with nice eyes and a kind smile—he looked rather like his sister Caroline, who had just married Murat. While he was not at all in love with Hortense, although he did not find her unattractive, he was too passive to resist the forces at play. Nor did Hortense hate Louis. But she was in love with Duroc.

Her little secret gave Claire de Sourdis confidence. She too ended up admitting something, precious little though it was to admit.

She too was in love, if we can call it love. It would be more appropriate to say that she was in thrall to an image, a mystery in the shape of a handsome young man.

He was twenty-three or twenty-four, with blond hair and dark eyes. His features seemed almost too regular for a man, and his hands were as elegant as a woman's. He was put together so precisely, each part of him so completely in harmony with the whole, that one could readily see that the outward form of the man, however fragile in appearance, hid Herculean strength. Even before the time of Chateaubriand and Byron, who created darkly romantic heroes like René and Manfred, he bore a troubled brow whose pallor bespoke a strange destiny. For terrible legends were attached to his family name—legends known only imperfectly, but they came stained with blood. Yet nobody had ever seen him parade an air of exaggerated mourning, like so many who had lost so much during the Republic, and never had he made show of his pain at dances and salons and social gatherings. In fact, when he did appear in society, he had no need of any such affectations to try to attract attention. People just naturally looked at him. Usually, though, he eschewed the pastimes of his hunting and travel companions, who had never yet managed to drag him to one of those youthful parties which even the most rigid agree to attend sooner or later. And nobody remembered ever having seen him laugh aloud and openly the way most young people do, or even having seen him smile.

There had long been alliances between the Sainte-Hermine and the Sourdis families, and, as is customary in such noble houses, the memory of those alliances remained important. So when by chance young Sainte-

Hermine had come to Paris, he had never failed, since Madame de Sourdis had come back from the colonies, to visit her, for he observed the demands of protocol, and never had his visits been other than formal.

The two young people had had occasion to meet, in society, over the past several months. Besides the polite greetings they exchanged, however, words had been spoken sparingly, especially by the young man. But their eyes had spoken eloquently. Hector apparently did not hold the same control over his eyes as he did over his words, and each time he encountered Claire, his gaze made known how lovely he found her and how perfectly she matched all his heart's desires.

At their first meetings Claire had been moved by his expressive eyes, and since Sainte-Hermine seemed to her an accomplished gentleman in every way, she had permitted herself to look at him too less guardedly. She had also hoped that he would invite her to dance so that a whispered word or the pressure of his hand might affirm the meaning she'd read in his gaze. But, strangely for the time, Sainte-Hermine, the gentleman who took fencing lessons with Saint-Georges and who could shoot a pistol as well as Junot or Fournier, did not dance.

During the balls he attended, Sainte-Hermine would stand coldly and impassibly at some bay window or in a corner of the room. In that, he became an object of bewilderment for all the gay young women who wondered what secret vow might be depriving them of such an elegant dance partner—for he always dressed with such taste in the latest style.

Claire had wondered, too, at Sainte-Hermine's reserve in her presence, especially since her mother seemed to admire the young man greatly. She spoke as highly about his family, decimated by the Revolution, as she did of him, and she knew that money could not be an obstacle to their union. The substantial fortunes of the two families were roughly equal.

One can understand the impression the mysterious young Sainte-Hermine might make on a young girl's heart, especially on a young Creole girl's heart, with the combination of his physical features and moral qualities, his elegance and strength. Claire's image of him occupied her mind while biding its time to take over her heart.

Hortense made her hopes and desires clear to Claire: She wanted to marry Duroc, whom she loved, rather than Louis Bonaparte, whom she did not—that essentially was the secret she whispered to her friend. But it was not the same, for Claire's storybook passion made it difficult for her to speak quite so plainly. At the same time that she described Hector's features in great detail to her friend, she tried also to understand as best she could the shadows surrounding him.

Finally, after Claire's mother had called twice, after she had stood up and embraced Hortense, as if the idea had just come to mind—as Madame de Sévigné observes, the most important part of a letter is in the postscript— she said: "By the way, dear Hortense, I am forgetting to ask you something."

"What is that?"

"I understand that Madame de Permon is giving a great ball."

"Yes. Loulou came to see my mother and me and invited us herself."

"Are you going?"

"Yes, of course."

"My dear Hortense," Claire said in her most endearing voice, "I would like to ask a favor."

"A favor?"

"Yes. Get an invitation for my mother and me. Is that possible?"

"Yes, I think so."

Claire leaped with a joy. "Oh, thank you!" she said. "How will you go about it?"

"Well, I could ask Loulou for an invitation. But I prefer having Eugene do it. Eugene is close to Madame de Permon's son, and Eugene will ask him for what you desire."

"And I shall go to Madame de Permon's ball?" cried Claire joyously.

"Yes," Hortense answered. Then, looking her young friend in the eye, she asked, "Will he be there?"

Claire turned as red as a beet and dropped her eyes. "I think so."

"You will point him out to me, won't you?"

"Oh! You'll recognize him without me doing that, my dear Hortense. Have I not told you that he can be picked out from among a thousand?"

"How sorry I am that he is not a dancer!" said Hortense.

"How do you think I feel?"

The two girls kissed each other and parted, Claire reminding Hortense not to forget the invitation.

Three days later Claire de Sourdis received her invitation by mail.

XI

Madame de Permon's Ball

THE BALL FOR WHICH Mademoiselle Hortense de Beauharnais's young friend had requested an invitation was the social event of the season for all of fashionable Paris. Madame de Permon would have needed a mansion four times the size of her own to welcome all those eager to attend, and she had refused to issue further invitations to more than one hundred men and more than fifty women despite their ardent requests. But, because she had been born in Corsica and linked from childhood to the Bonaparte family, she agreed immediately when Eugene Beauharnais made his request, and Mademoiselle de Sourdis and her mother both received their admission cards.

Madame de Permon, whose invitations were in such demand even though her name sounded a bit like the name of a commoner, was one of the grandest women of the times. Indeed, she was a descendant of the Comnène family, which had given six emperors to Constantinople, one to Heraclea, and ten to Trebizond. Her ancestor Constantin Comnène, fleeing the Muslims, had found refuge first in the Taygetus mountains and later on the island of Corsica. Along with three thousand of his compatriots who followed him as their chief, he settled there after buying from the Genoa senate the lands of Paomia, Salogna, and Revinda.

In spite of her imperial origins, Mademoiselle de Comnène fell in love with and married a handsome commoner whom people called Monsieur de Permon. Monsieur de Permon had died two years earlier, leaving his widow with a son of twenty-eight, a daughter of fourteen, and an annuity of twenty-five thousand pounds.

Madame de Permon's high birth and her common marriage were reflected in her salon, which she opened to prominent figures in both the old aristocracy and the young democracy. Among officers in the new military and notables in the arts and sciences were names that would soon rival the most illustrious of those in the old monarchy. So it was that in her salon you could meet Monsieur de Mouchy and Monsieur de Montcalm, the Prince de Chalais, the two De Laigle brothers, Charles and Just de Noailles, the Montaigus, the three Rastignacs, the Count of Coulaincourt and his two sons Armand and August, the Albert d'Orsay family, the Montbretons. Sainte-Aulaire and the Talleyrands mingled with the Hoches, the Rapps, the Durocs, the Trénis, the Laffittes, the Dupaty family, the Junots, the Anissons, and the Labordes.

With her twenty-five-thousand-pound annuity Madame de Permon maintained one of Paris's most elegant and best appointed mansions. She especially enjoyed the splendor of her flowers and plants, and her home had become a veritable greenhouse. The vestibule was so filled with potted trees and flowers that you could no longer see the walls, yet it was so skillfully illuminated with colored glass that you would have thought you were entering a fairy palace.

In those days, balls began early. By nine o'clock, Madame de Permon's rooms were open and brightly lit, and she, her daughter Laura, and her son Albert were awaiting their guests in the salon.

Madame de Permon, still a beautiful woman, was wearing a white crepe dress, decorated with bunches of double daffodils and cut in the Greek style, with cloth draped over her breasts and held at her shoulders with two diamond clips. She had commissioned Leroy on the Rue des Petits-Champs, who was all the rage for his dresses and hats, to make her a puffy hat with white crepe and large bunches of daffodils like the ones on her dress. She wore daffodils in her jet black hair as well as in the folds of the hat, and she was holding an enormous bouquet of daffodils and violets from Madame Roux, the best florist in Paris. In each ear sparkled a diamond worth fifteen thousand francs, her only jewelry.

Mademoiselle Laura de Permon's dress was quite simple. Her mother thought that since she was only sixteen, she should glow with her own natural beauty and not try to outshine anyone with her clothes. She was wearing a pink taffeta dress of a style similar to her mother's, with white narcissus in a crown on her head and at the hem of her dress, along with pearl clips and earrings.

But the woman whose beauty was supposed to reign over the ball, which was being given in honor of the Bonaparte family and which the First Consul had promised to attend, was Madame Leclerc, the favorite of Madame Laetitia and her brother Bonaparte as well, so people said. To ensure her triumph, she had asked that Madame Permon allow her to dress at the mansion. She had had Madame Germon make her dress and she had arranged for Charbonnier to do her hair (he had done Madame de Permon's as well). She woud make her entrance at the precise moment when the rooms were filling up but not yet full. That was the best moment if you wished to create a sensation and make sure you'd be seen by everyone there.

Some of the most beautiful women—Madame Méchin, Madame de Périgord, Madame Récamier—were already there when at nine thirty Madame Bonaparte, her daughter, and her son were announced. Madame de Permon rose and walked to the center of the dining room, a courtesy she had offered nobody else.

Josephine was wearing a crown of poppies and golden wheat, which also embellished her white crepe dress. Hortense too was dressed in white, her only accent being fresh violets.

At about the same time, the Comtesse de Sourdis arrived with her daughter. The countess was wearing a buttercup-yellow tunic adorned with pansies. Her daughter, whose hair was arranged in the Greek style, wore a white taffeta tunic embroidered with gold and purple. She was ravishing. Bands of gold and purple perfectly highlighted her dark hair, while a gold and purple cord accented her tiny waist.

At a signal from his sister, Eugene de Beauharnais hurried over to the new arrivals. Taking the countess's hand, he escorted her to Madame de Permon.

Madame de Permon rose to greet the countess, then had her sit to her left; Josephine was seated on the hostess's right. Hortense offered her arm to Claire, and they seated themselves nearby.

"Well?" Hortense asked, her curiosity getting the better of her.

"He is here," said Claire, all atremble.

"Where?" asked Hortense eagerly.

"Well," said Claire, "do you see where I am looking? In that group there, the man wearing the garnet-colored velvet suit, tight suede pants, and shoes with small diamond buckles. And there's a much larger diamond buckle around the braid on his hat."

Hortense's eyes followed Claire's. "Ah, you were right," she said. "He is as handsome as Antinous. But he doesn't look so melancholic at all. Your dark, mysterious hero is smiling at us very pleasantly."

And indeed, the face of the Comte de Sainte-Hermine, who had not taken his eyes off Mademoiselle de Sourdis since she had entered the room, radiated inner peace and joy. When he saw Claire and her friend looking at him, he walked timidly but gracefully over to them.

"Would you be so kind, mademoiselle," he said to Claire, "as to grant me the first quadrille or the first waltz you will be dancing?"

"The first quadrille, yes, monsieur," Claire stammered. She had turned deathly pale when she saw the count walking toward her, and now she could feel blood rushing to her cheeks.

"As for Mademoiselle de Beauharnais," the count, Hector, continued, bowing to Hortense, "I await the order from her lips to confirm my rank among her numerous admirers."

"The first gavotte, monsieur, if you please," Hortense answered, for she knew that Duroc did not dance the gavotte.

After a bow of thanks, Count Hector moved nonchalantly toward the crowd surrounding Madame de Contades, who had just arrived. Her beauty had attracted all eyes, but just then another murmur of admiration rippled through the crowd. Some new pretender to beauty's throne had arrived. The beauty competition was now open; the dancing itself would not begin until the First Consul appeared.

It was Pauline Bonaparte—Madame Leclerc—who now approached. Those who knew her called her Paulette. She had married General Leclerc on the 18th Brumaire, the day that had given her brother Bonaparte's career such a fortunate nudge forward.

Entering from the room where she had just dressed, with perfectly studied coquetry she was just beginning to pull on her gloves: a gesture that called attention to her lovely, plump white arms adorned with gold cameo bracelets. Her hair was done up in small bands of fine leather that looked like leopard skin, and attached to them were bunches of gold grapes; it faithfully copied the coif of a bacchante on a cameo that might have come from ancient Greece. Her dress was made of the finest Indian muslin, like woven air, as Juvenal said. Its hem was embroidered with a garland in gold leaf two or three inches wide. A tunic in pure Greek style hung down over her lovely waist and was attached at her shoulders by costly cameos. The very short sleeves, slightly pleated, ended in tiny cuffs, which were also held in place by cameos. Just below her breasts she wore a belt of burnished gold, its buckle a lovely engraved stone. The ensemble was so harmonious, and her beauty so delicious, that when she appeared, no other woman graced the room.

"*Incessu patuit dea,*" said Dupaty as she passed.

"Do you insult me in a language I do not understand, Citizen Poet?" asked Madame Leclerc with a smile.

"What?" answered Dupaty. "You are from Rome, madame, and you don't understand Latin?"

"I've forgotten all my Latin."

"That is one of Virgil's hemistiches, Madame, when Venus appeared to Aeneas. Abbé Delille translated it like this: 'She walks by, and her steps reveal a goddess.'"

"Give me your arm, flatterer, and dance the first quadrille with me. That will be your punishment."

Dupaty didn't need to be asked twice. He held out his arm, straightened his legs, and allowed himself to be led by Madame Leclerc into a boudoir, where she stopped on the pretext that it was cooler than the larger rooms. In reality, though, it was because the boudoir offered an immense sofa that enabled the divine coquette to display her couture and her beauty to best effect.

As she passed Madame de Contades, the most beautiful woman in the room only so long as Madame Leclerc had not been present, the grand coquette cast a defiant glance. And she had the satisfaction of seeing all her rival's admirers abandon Madame de Contades in her armchair and gather now around the sofa.

Madame de Contades bit her lips until they bled. But in the quiver of revenge that every woman wears at her side, she found one of those poisoned arrows that can mortally wound, and she called to Monsieur de Noailles. "Charles," she said, "lend me your arm so I can go see up close that marvel of beauty and clothing that has just attracted all of our butterflies."

"Ah," said the young man, "and you are going to make her realize that among these butterflies there is a bee. Sting, sting, Countess," Monsieur de Noailles added. "These low-born Bonapartes have been nobles for too short a time. They need to be reminded that they are making a mistake in trying to mix with the old aristocracy. If you look carefully at that parvenu, you will find, I am sure, the stigmata of her plebian origins."

With a laugh, the young man allowed himself to be led by Madame de Contades, who, nostrils flared, seemed to be blazing a trail. Once she'd reached the crowd of flatterers surrounding the lovely Madame Leclerc, she elbowed her way up to the front row.

Madame Leclerc afforded her rival a smile, for no doubt Madame de Contades felt obligated to pay her homage.

And indeed, Madame de Contades proceeded with a politesse that in no way disabused Madame Leclerc of her impression. Madame de Contades added her voice to the hymns of praise and admiration being offered up to the divinity on the sofa. Then, suddenly, as if she had just made a horrible discovery, she cried out, "Oh, my God! How terrible! Why does such a horrible deformity have to spoil one of nature's masterpieces!" she exclaimed. "Must it be said that nothing in this world is perfect? My God, how sad!"

At this strange lamentation, everybody looked first at Madame de Contades, then at Madame Leclerc, then at Madame de Contades again. They were obviously waiting for her to explain her outburst, but Madame de Contades continued only to lament this sad case of human imperfection.

"Come now," her escort finally said. "What do you see? Tell us what you see!"

"What do you mean? Tell you what I see? Can you not see those two enormous ears stuck on both sides of such a charming head? If I had ears like that, I would have them trimmed back a little. And since they have not been hemmed, that shouldn't be difficult."

Barely had Madame de Contades finished when all eyes turned toward Madame Leclerc's head—not to admire it, but rather to remark her ears. For until then no one had even noticed them.

And indeed, Paulette, as her friends called her, did have unusual ears. The white cartilage looked signally like an oyster shell, and, as Madame de Contades had pointed out, it was cartilage that nature had neglected to hem.

Madame Leclerc did not even try to defend herself against such an impertinent attack. Instead, she availed herself of that resource any woman wronged might use: She uttered a cry and collapsed.

At the same moment, her erstwhile admirers heard a carriage rolling up

to the Permon mansion, and a horse galloping, then a voice calling out
"The First Consul!"—all of which distracted everyone's attention from
the bizarre scene that had just transpired.

Except that, while Madame Leclerc was rushing from the boudoir in
tears and the First Consul was striding in through one of the ballroom
doors, Madame de Contades, her attack triumphant but too brutal perhaps,
was stealing out through another.

XII

The Queen's Minuet

MADAME DE PERMON WALKED up to the First Consul and bowed with
great ceremony. Bonaparte took her hand and kissed it most gallantly.

"What's this I hear, my dear friend?" he said. "Did you really refuse to
open the ball before I arrived? And what if I had not been able to come before one in the morning—would all these lovely children have had to wait
for me?"

Glancing around the room, he saw that some of the women from the
Faubourg Saint-Germain had failed to rise when he came in. He frowned,
but showed no other signs of displeasure.

"Come now, Madame de Permon," he said. "Let the ball begin. Young
people need to have fun, and dancing is their favorite pastime. They say
that Loulou can dance like Mademoiselle Chameroi. Who told me that? It
was Eugene, wasn't it?"

Eugene's ears turned red; he was the beautiful ballerina's lover.

Bonaparte continued: "If you wish, Madame de Permon, we shall dance
the monaco. That's the only dance I know."

"Surely you are joking," Madame de Permon answered. "I have not
danced in thirty years."

"Come now, you can't mean that," said Bonaparte. "This evening you
look like your daughter's sister."

Then, noticing Monsieur de Talleyrand, Bonaparte said, "Oh, it's you,
Talleyrand. I need to talk to you." And with his Foreign Affairs Minister he
went into the boudoir where Madame Leclerc had endured her embarrassment just moments before.

Immediately, the music began, the dancers chose partners, and the ball
was under way.

Mademoiselle de Beauharnais, who was dancing with Duroc, led him over to Claire and the Comte de Sainte-Hermine, for everything her friend had told her about the young man had piqued her interest.

Monsieur de Sainte-Hermine was proving to be no less talented on the ballroom floor than he was in other areas. He had studied with the second Vestris, the son of France's own god of dance, and he did his teacher great honor.

During the Consulate years, a young man of fashion considered it requisite to perfect the art of dancing. I can still remember having seen, when I was a child, in 1812 or 1813, the two Monbreton brothers—the very same who were dancing at Madame de Permon's ball this evening a dozen years earlier—in Villers-Cotterêts, where a grand ball brought together the entire beautiful new aristocracy. The Montbretons came from their castle in Corcy, three leagues away, and guess how they came. In their cabriolets. Yes, but their domestics rode inside the cabriolet, while they themselves, wearing their fine pump dancing shoes, held on to straps in the back, on the springboard where normally their valets stood, so that on the road they could continue to practice their intricate steps. Arriving at the ballroom door just in time to join the first quadrille, they had their domestics brush the dust off their clothes and threw themselves into the lively reel.

However brilliantly the Montbretons may have danced at Madame de Permon's, it was Sainte-Hermine who impressed Mademoiselle de Beauharnais , and Mademoiselle de Sourdis was proud to see that the count, who had never before deigned to dance, with skill and grace could hold his own with the best dancers at the ball. Although Mademoiselle de Beauharnais was reassured on that point, there was still another that worried the curious Hortense: Had the young man spoken to Claire? Had he told her the cause of his long sadness, of his past silence, of his present joy?

Hortense ran to her friend and, pulling her into a bay window, asked: "Well, what did he say?"

"Something very important concerning what I told you."

"Can you tell me?" Spurred by curiosity, Mademoiselle was using the informal *tu* form with her friend Claire, though normally in conversation they used formal address.

Claire lowered her voice. "He said he wanted to tell me a family secret."

"You?"

"Me alone. Consequently, he begged me to get my mother to agree that he might be able to speak to me for an hour, with my mother watching but far enough away that she'd not be able to hear what he'd say. His life's happiness, he said, depended on it."

"Will your mother permit it?"

"I hope so, for she loves me dearly. I have promised to ask my mother this evening and to give him my answer at the end of the ball."

"And now," said Mademoiselle de Beauharnais, "do you realize how handsome your Comte de Sainte-Hermine is, and that he dances as well as Gardel?"

The music, signaling the second quadrille, called the girls back to their places. The two young friends had been, as we have seen, quite satisfied with how well Monsieur de Sainte-Hermine had danced the quadrille. But then, it was only a quadrille. There were yet two tests to which every unproven dancer was put: the gavotte and the minuet.

The young count had promised the gavotte to Mademoiselle de Beauharnais. It's a dance we know today only by tradition, and though we may think it quite ridiculous, it was de rigeur during the Directory, the Consulate, and even the Empire. Like a snake that keeps twisting even after it has been cut into pieces, the gavotte could never quite die. It was, in fact, more a theatrical performance than a ballroom dance, for it had very complicated figures that were quite difficult to execute. The gavotte required a great deal of space, and even a large ballroom could accommodate no more than four couples at the same time.

Among the four couples dancing the gavotte in Madame de Permon's grand ballroom, the two dancers whom everyone loudly applauded were the Comte de Sainte-Hermine and Mademoiselle de Beauharnais. They were applauded so enthusiastically, in fact, that they drew Bonaparte both out of his conversation with Monsieur de Talleyrand and out of the boudoir to which they'd withdrawn. Bonaparte appeared in the doorway just as his stepdaughter and her partner were completing the final figures, so he was able to witness their triumph.

When the gavotte ended, Bonaparte beckoned the girl over. She leaned forward so he could kiss her forehead. "I congratulate you, mademoiselle," he said. "It is clear that you have had a graceful dancing master and that you have benefited from his lessons. But who is the handsome man with whom you were dancing?"

"I do not know him, General," said Hortense. "We met for the first time this evening, and he invited me to dance when I was speaking with Mademoiselle de Sourdis. Or rather, he didn't invite me; he put himself at my orders. I am the one who told him that I wanted to dance the gavotte and when I wanted to dance it."

"But you surely know his name!"

"He calls himself the Comte de Sainte-Hermine."

"Well," said Bonaparte with an expression of ill humor, "another person from the Faubourg Saint-Germain. This dear Madame de Permon insists on filling her house with my enemies. When I came in, I chased off Madame de Contades, a crazy woman who thinks I am worth no more than the last second lieutenant in my army. When she talks about my victories in Italy and Egypt, she says that 'I could do as much with my eyes as he can with his sword.' That is unfortunate," Bonaparte continued, looking at Hortense's partner, "for he would make a handsome hussar officer." Then, waving the girl back to her mother, he said: "Monsieur de Talleyrand, you who know so much, do you know anything about the Sainte-Hermine family?"

"Let me see," said Monsieur de Talleyrand, putting his hand on his chin and leaning his head back, his customary way of reflecting. "In the Juras, near Besançon, we do have a Sainte-Hermine family. Yes, I met the father, a distinguished man who was guillotined in 1793. He left three sons. As to what has become of them, I have no idea. This man perhaps is one of those sons, or a nephew, though I was not aware the man I met had a brother. Would you like me to find out?"

"Oh, don't bother."

"It will be easy. I have seen him talking to Mademoiselle de Sourdis— look, he is speaking to her at this very moment. Nothing easier than asking her mother. . . ."

"No, that is not necessary, thanks. And how about the Sourdis family? Who are they?"

"Of excellent nobility."

"That's not what I am asking. What are their political leanings?"

"I believe there are only the two women, and they have joined us, or at least they would like nothing more than to be so counted. Two or three days ago Cabanis was speaking about them; he knows them well. The girl is marriageable, and has, I believe, a dowry of a million. It would be a good match for one of your aides-de-camp."

"So it is your opinion that it would be appropriate for Madame Bonaparte to see them?"

"Perfectly appropriate."

"Thank you. That's what Bourrienne already told me." Then, turning to his hostess, Bonaparte asked, "But what is wrong with Loulou? It looks to me as if she is near tears. Dear Madame de Permon, how can you make your daughter so sad on a day like this?"

"I want her to dance the queen's minuet, and she won't."

At the mention of the queen's minuet, Bonaparte smiled.

"And why won't she?"

"How should I know? A caprice. Truly, Loulou, you aren't being good. Your refusal to dance is not worth the cost of having Gardel and Saint-Amand as your instructors."

"But, Mother," Mademoiselle Permon answered, "I would be happy to dance your minuet, much though I hate it, only I don't dare dance it with anyone but Monsieur de Trénis. I have promised the dance to him."

"Well, then," Madame de Permon asked. "Why isn't he here? It is already half past twelve."

"He said that he had two other balls to attend before ours and that he'd not get here until very late."

"Ah," said Bonaparte. "I am delighted to know there's at least one man in France busier than I am. But just because the much-celebrated Monsieur de Trénis has not kept his word is not reason enough, Mademoiselle Loulou, to deprive us of the pleasure of seeing you dance the queen's minuet. He is not here. That is not your fault, so choose another partner."

"How about Gardel?" said Madame de Permon.

"But he's my dance teacher," objected Loulou.

"Well, then, take Laffitte. After Trénis, he is the best dancer in Paris." She'd barely spoken his name when they espied Monsieur Laffitte walking close by in the ballroom. "Monsieur Laffitte! Monsieur Laffitte! Come over here," Madame de Permon called out to him.

Monsieur Laffitte could not have been more gallant or obliging; he was also quite elegant and handsome. "Monsieur Laffitte," said Madame de Permon, "please do me the pleasure of dancing the queen's minuet with my daughter."

"Of course, madame!" cried Monsieur Laffitte. "You fulfill my greatest desire, and I give my word of honor. Of course, it will mean a duel with Monseiur de Trénis," he added with a laugh. "But I am happy to take the risk. However, not knowing I would be granted this honor, I failed to bring a hat."

To understand Monsieur Laffitte's last comment, the reader must know that the final bow of the minuet, its high point, the capstone of that monument to formal dancing, had to be executed with a Louis XV-style hat. No other hat would do. So there was a search, there was a flurry, and soon a hat was found.

The minuet was danced with immense success, and Monsieur Laffitte was leading Mademoiselle de Permon back to her mother when Monsieur de Trénis—late, flustered, out of breath—appeared. Having failed to keep his promise to Mademoiselle Loulou, he was more astonished than furious in encountering the two dancers. The minuet he was supposed to dance—and everyone knew he was supposed to dance the minuet—not only had been danced without him but, as was clear from the bravos just beginning to fade away, had been danced without him triumphantly.

"Ah, monsieur," Mademoiselle de Permon said in great embarrassment, "I waited until after midnight for you, just look at the clock, and the minuet had been announced for eleven. Finally, at midnight, my mother insisted that I dance with Monsieur Laffitte," and with a laugh, she added, "and the First Consul gave the order."

"Mademoiselle," said Monsieur de Trénis, "Madame de Permon could indeed require such a sacrifice of you since she is the mistress of the house. She owed her guests the minuet and unfortunately, I was late, so she was within her rights. But, as for the First Consul," said Monsieur de Trénis, turning to Bonaparte and staring down at him, for he was five inches taller than the general, "to give the order to begin a dance which, in reality, cannot be danced consummately except by me, he mistakenly goes beyond his authority. I do not interfere with his doings on the battlefield, so he should leave affairs of the salon to me. I don't pluck the leaves from his laurels, so he should likewise let mine be."

Haughtily he walked over to Mademoiselle de Permon and, sitting beside her, said: "I am philosophical enough to be consoled at not having danced that dance with you, especially since it was my fault, late as I was. Neither can I be upset that you did not keep your word, yet there would have been a crown to be won had we danced the queen's minuet together. I would have danced it gravely, seriously; not sadly as Monsieur Laffitte did. Still, I was pleased to see it, and having seen it, I shall never forget it."

Around Monsieur de Trénis a large circle had gathered to listen to him expressing his disappointment. Among them was the First Consul, who was tempted to think he was dealing with a crazy man.

"But," said Mademoiselle de Permon to Monsieur de Trénis, "you worry me. What have I done?"

"What have you done? Why do you ask, mademoiselle, you who dance so well that I am delighted to promise to dance the minuet with you? You who have practiced the minuet with Gardel! Oh, there's no word to describe it. How you can dance the minuet with a man who is little more on the ballroom floor than a quadrille dancer. I repeat, a quadrille dancer. No, mademoiselle, no. Never in his life will Monsieur Laffitte be able to bow properly and execute the great hat step. No, I say it loud and clear, never, never has he been or will he be able to do that."

Noticing smiles on several faces, Trénis continued: "So, does that surprise you? Well, I shall tell you why he has never been able to properly perform the bow, the bow by which we all judge a minuet dancer. It's because he does not know how to put his hat on properly. Putting one's hat on properly is everything, gentlemen. Ask these ladies who have their hats made by Leroy but who have Charbonnier put them on for them. Ah, ask Monsieur Garel about putting on the hat; he will explain it to you. Anyone can put a hat on. I can even say that everyone can put a hat on, but some do it better than others. But how many can do it with the proper dignity, with the proper composure governing the movement of the arm and forearm? . . . May I?"

And taking in hand the enormous three-cornered hat, Monsieur de Trénis went to stand before a mirror. Then, singing the music that accompanies the minuet's bow, he executed the salute with perfect grace and supreme seriousness. After which, he placed the hat back on his head with all the pomp such an occasion requires.

Leaning on Monsieur de Talleyrand's arm, Bonaparte said to the diplomat, "Ask him how he gets along with Monsieur Laffitte. After that outburst he directed toward me, I dare not ask him myself."

Monsieur de Talleyrand asked the question with the same gravity he'd assume if he were asking how England and America were getting along since their last war.

"But of course we get along as well as two men of such equal talent can possibly manage," he answered. "However, I must admit that he is a magnanimous rival, a good sport, never jealous of my much-acknowledged success. It is true that his own successes may make him indulgent. His dances are strong and lively, and he is better than I in the first eight measures of the *Panurge* gavotte—of that there's no question. But in the *jetés*, for example, that is where I crush him. In general, he whips me in the calf muscles, but I stomp him in the marrow!"

"Well," said Monsieur de Talleyrand, "you can rest easy, Citizen First Consul. There will be no war between Monsieur de Trénis and Monsieur Laffitte. I would like to be able to say as much about France and England."

While the pause in the ball allowed Monsieur de Trénis the leisure to expand upon the niceties of putting on the hat, Claire undertook negotiations with her mother about a subject she considered far more important than the matter of concern to Monsieur de Talleyrand and the First Consul, whether or not there would be peace between Paris's two best dancers or between France and the world. The young count, who kept his eyes on her the entire time, saw by the smile on Claire's face that he had in all probability won his case with her mother.

He was not mistaken.

On the pretext of getting some air in one of the less crowded rooms, Mademoiselle de Sourdis took Mademoiselle de Beauharnais's arm, and as they passed the Comte de Sainte-Hermine, she whispered these words: "My mother agrees that tomorrow at three in the afternoon you may present yourself at our door."

XIII

The Three Sainte-Hermines

༚

The father

The next day, as three o'clock was striking on the pavilion clock, Hector de Sainte-Hermine knocked at the door of the Hôtel de Sourdis, whose lovely terrace, covered with orange trees and rose laurels, looked out over the Quai Voltaire. The door opened onto the Rue de Beaune. It was the great door, the door of honor. Another, smaller door, nearly invisible as it was painted the color of the wall, opened out onto the quay.

The great door opened. The Swiss guard asked for the visitor's name and allowed him to pass. A valet, alerted no doubt by Madame de Sourdis, was waiting in the antechamber. "Madame," he said, "is not receiving today. But Mademoiselle is in the garden, and she offers her mother's excuses to Monsieur le Comte."

The count followed the valet to the garden gate. "Follow this path," the valet told him. "Mademoiselle is at the other end, under the jasmine arbor."

And indeed, beneath the rays of a lovely March sun, Claire, wrapped in an ermine cloak, seemed to be a bloom, like one of those first spring flowers we call snowdrops because they return so early. Spread out under her feet lay a thick Smyrna carpet to protect her light blue velvet slippers from the cold ground. When she noticed Sainte-Hermine, although she had been expecting him and had heard the clock strike three, her cheeks turned pink and hid for an instant how marvelously lily-white they were. She rose with a smile illuminating her face.

Sainte-Hermine walked faster, and when he drew near, she pointed to where her mother was sitting at one of the drawing-room windows overlooking the garden. From there she could keep the two young people in sight, although she would not be able to hear a word they were saying. Sainte-Hermine bowed deeply to her, to show her both his thanks and his respect.

Claire offered him a chair, and once he was seated, he spoke: "I shall not, mademoiselle, try to make you understand how happy I am to be able to talk freely alone with you for a moment. For a year I've been awaiting this moment, granted to me now by Heaven's goodness, and upon it will depend the fortune or the misfortune of my entire life, although I've only been able truly to harbor such a hope for the last three days. You were kind enough to tell me at the ball that you noticed the anxiety I seemed to experience in your presence, as well as the pain and the joy you suspected were in my heart. I am going to tell you the cause of my anxieties, perhaps at greater length than necessary, but I cannot expect you to understand me unless I present you all the necessary details."

"Speak, monsieur," said Claire. "Anything coming from you, you may be sure, will be worthy of my interest."

"We are—or rather, since I'm the only member of my family left, I should say, I am—from a noble family in the Juras. My father, a high-ranking officer under Louis XVI, was among those defending him on August 10. Only, instead of fleeing like all the princes and courtiers, he stayed, and even when the king was dead, he hoped that all was not lost and that they would be able somehow to help the queen escape from the Temple. To that end, he gathered together a large sum of money. Among the municipal guards he found a young man from the South—his name was Toulan— who had fallen in love with the queen and had pledged her his heart. My father resolved to join forces with Toulan, or rather to use his position as a guard in the Temple, to save the prisoner.

"Then my oldest brother Léon de Sainte-Hermine, who was growing tired of being no use to the cause whose religion he had long espoused, solicited my father's permission to leave France and serve in Condé's army. Once he received that permission, he went directly to join the prince.

"Meanwhile, my father made arrangements with Toulan. At that time, a large number of people, including several of the queen's devoted servants, were still asking the municipal guards, on whom such favors depended, if they could see her. So, the guards would arrange for the queen's friends to be in the path their noble prisoner would follow when she went down into the garden to get some fresh air, as she did twice a day. Sometimes, if the guard looked the other way, it was possible for the queen's old devotées to exchange a word with her or even to slip her a note. It is true that they were risking their necks, but there are times when one's neck counts for little.

"Because Toulan had some obligation to my father and his gratitude to him thus coincided with his love for the queen, he agreed to allow my father and mother into the Temple. On the pretext of their wish to see the queen, my father and mother, dressed like rich Jura peasants, would come to the Temple, put on a Besançon accent, and ask for Monsieur Toulan. He, in turn, would place them somewhere on the queen's path.

"Among the prisoners in the Temple and the Royalists there was a whole system of signals that they employed to communicate as surely as did ships on the sea. On the day of my father and mother's visit, as the queen was leaving her room, she found a wisp of straw leaning up against the wall, which meant: 'Stay alert, someone is looking out for you.' The queen had not immediately seen the straw; it was Madame Elisabeth, less preoccupied than she, who called it to the attention of her sister-in-law.

"As soon as the two prisoners stepped into the garden, they noticed that Toulan was on duty. The queen counted on the poor young man's love for her. She had bound him to her destiny with six words. On the sure chance that she'd see him one day on duty, she had written on a piece of paper that she always carried next to her bosom: *Ama poco che teme la morte!* (He who fears death loves little!) And one day she did see him, and she had slipped him the note. Even before he had read it, Toulan's heart had leaped with joy. And after he'd read it, he had vowed that from that that day forward he was going to prove to the queen that he had no fear of death.

"He placed my father and mother in the tower staircase so that the queen would hardly be able to pass without touching them. My mother was holding a lovely bouquet of carnations, and when the queen saw them, she cried out, 'Oh, what lovely flowers, and how sweet they smell!' My mother pulled out the most beautiful carnation and held it out to the queen, who looked inquiringly at Toulan for permission to accept it. Toulan nodded almost imperceptibly.

"In ordinary circumstances, everything that was transpiring would have been quite unremarkable. But not in those extraordinary days when danger lay only a breath away. The queen suspected that a note might be hidden in the carnation's calyx, and she quickly slipped the flower into the bodice of her dress. My mother the Comtesse de Sainte-Hermine held up well under the pressure, although during the exchange, my father told us, her face went paler and more sallow than the tower walls.

"The queen had the courage not to cut short at all the time she usually spent walking in the garden and returned to her quarters at the usual hour. However, as soon as she was once again alone with the Madames Elisabeth and Royale, she pulled the flower from her bodice. And in fact, the calyx did contain a note written on silk paper in a tiny hand. It offered this consolation:

Day after tomorrow, on Wednesday, ask to go down to the garden. They will allow you to do so with no difficulty, since orders have been given to allow you this favor whenever you ask. After walking around the garden three or four times, pretend to be tired. Go over to the canteen in the middle of the garden and ask Madame Plumeau if you can sit down.

It is important for you to ask permission at exactly eleven o'clock in the morning so that your liberators can coordinate their movements with your own.

Then, after a moment, pretend to be even weaker, and faint. The doors will be closed while help is summoned, and you will be alone with Madame Elisabeth and Madame Royale. Immediately the trapdoor to the cellar will open. Hurry down through the opening with your sister and daughter, and all three of you will be saved.

"Three factors conjoined to instill confidence in the three prisoners: Toulan's presence, the wisp of straw standing against the wall in the corridor, and the note's precise details. Besides, what risk was there in trying? Their torture could not be greater than it was already. So they agreed. They would do exactly what the note instructed.

"Two days later, on Wednesday, at nine in the morning, the queen, behind the curtains of her bed, reread the note my mother had hidden in the carnation and assured herself that she'd not deviate from its instructions. Then, after tearing it up into tiny pieces, she went into Madame Royale's room.

"Returning almost immediately, she called to the guards on duty. She had to call twice before they answered, as they were having breakfast, but finally one of them appeared at the door. 'What do you want, Citizeness?' he asked her.

"Marie-Antoinette explained that Madame Royale was ill from lack of exercise, because she went out only at noon, when the sun was too hot for her to walk through the garden. So the queen was asking permission to change the time she and Madames Royale and Elisabeth walked from noon until two o'clock to ten until noon. Would the guard take her request to General Santerre, upon whom such permission depended, she asked, then added that she would be deeply grateful to him.

"The queen had spoken her gratitude with such grace and charm that the guard was smitten, and, lifting his red bonnet from his head, he said, 'Madame, the general will be here in a half hour; as soon as he's arrived, we shall pass along your request.'

"Then, as he was withdrawing—as if trying to convince himself that he was breaching no duty by yielding to the prisoner's request, that he was doing so out of his sense of equity, not out of weakness—he said: 'That's only right. When you look at it, it's only right!'

"'What's only right?' the other guard asked.

"'That the woman be allowed to take her sick daughter outside.'

"'Of course,' said the other. 'They can walk from the Temple to the Place de la Révolution. We can escort them there.'

"The guard's answer caused the queen a shiver, but she remained resolute: She would follow to the letter the instructions she had received.

"At nine thirty Santerre arrived. He was an excellent man, if a trifle brusque, a trifle brutal. He had been unjustly accused of ordering the terrible drumroll that interrupted the king's speech on the scaffold, and he'd never got over it. Unfortunately, he had made the mistake of getting on the wrong side of the Assembly and the Commune—and nearly lost his head.

"Santerre granted the permission requested, and one of the municipal guards returned to the queen's room with the general's favorable decision. 'Thank you, monsieur,' said the queen with the charming smile that had been the downfall of Barnave and Mirabeau.

"Then, turning toward the little dog that on its hind legs was jumping up and down behind her, she said, 'Ah, Black, you should be happy too. Yes, we're going to walk outside.' Turning back to the guard, she asked, 'So, we'll be going out. At what time?'

"'At ten o'clock. Is that not the time you yourself requested?' The queen bowed, and the guard left.

"Alone, the three women looked at one another with anxiety, an anxiety mixed with hope and joy. Madame Royale threw herself into the queen's arms. Madame Elisabeth walked over to her sister-in-law and reached out her hand. 'Let us pray,' said the queen. 'But let us pray in such a way that no one will suspect we are praying.'

"At ten o'clock they heard the sound of weapons. 'It's the changing of the guard,' said Madame Elisabeth.

"'Then they'll come get us,' said Madame Royale.

"'Courage,' said the queen, growing as pale as her two companions.

"'It is ten o'clock,' shouted someone down below, 'bring the prisoners down.'

"'Here we are, citizen,' the queen answered.

"The first door opened, and the three prisoners entered a dark corridor. In the semidarkness, they were able at least to hide their feelings.

"The little dog ran on before them, but when it got to the door of the room where its master had lived out his last days, it stopped abruptly and, whimpering, pushed its nose against the crack under the door. Its plaintive whimpers deepened into that painful moaning people call the death bark.

"The queen passed quickly by the door, but a few feet farther on she had to pause and lean against the wall. The two women drew in tightly behind her, and they waited, motionless, even after little Black caught up with them.

"'Well!' a voice cried out. 'Is she coming down or not?'

"'Here we are,' said the queen with great effort, as she proceeded the rest of the way down.

"When she reached the bottom of the spiral staircase, the drummer summoned the guard, not to honor her, but to demonstrate the armed force that made futile any attempt to escape. The heavy door opened slowly; its hinges squeaked.

"The three prisoners made their way quickly from the courtyard to the garden. Insulting graffiti and obscene figures drawn by soldiers in their spare time covered the courtyard walls, but the weather was magnificent, the sun not yet so hot as to be unbearable.

"The queen walked for about three quarters of an hour. Then, at ten minutes to eleven, she went to the canteen, where a woman named Mother Plumeau sold sausages, wine, and alcohol to the soldiers. The queen was already at the door, and just about to walk in and ask permission to sit down, when she noticed that Simon, the shoemaker and one of her most fervent enemies, was just finishing his breakfast at the table. So she decided to leave.

"But Black had already run in, and to no avail she called to the dog, who was sniffing at the trapdoor to the cellar where the widow Plumeau kept her food and drink. Insistently, the dog pushed its nose into the cracks around the trapdoor.

"Quaking, guessing what had attracted the dog's attention, the queen called out sharply for the little dog to come back. But Black appeared not even to hear her, or if he did, he refused to obey. Instead, the dog began to growl. Then he was barking ferociously.

"A light came on suddenly in the shoemaker's brain as to why the dog was so stubbornly refusing to obey its mistress. Up from the table in a flash, Simon ran to the door and called out: 'To arms! Treason! To arms!'

"'Black! Black!' the queen called in desperation, but the dog, unheeding, barked only more furiously still.

"'To arms!' Simon continued shouting. 'To arms! There are aristocrats in Citizen Plumeau's cellar, they've come to save the queen. Treason! Treason!'

"'To arms!' the municipal guards shouted in return as they grabbed their guns and rushed toward the queen and her two companions. They were soon surrounded and led by the guardsmen back to the tower.

"Even at that, Black refused to leave or cease. The poor animal's instinct had betrayed him. Still barking and scratching at the trapdoor, he was mistaking help for danger.

"A dozen national guardsmen entered the canteen. His eyes burning, Simon shouted, 'There, under the trapdoor! I saw the trapdoor move, I'm sure.'

"'Weapons ready!' the guards shouted out. You could hear the sound of guns being loaded, while Simon continued shouting 'There, right there!'

"The officer grabbed the ring on the trapdoor, but even with two of the strongest guards assisting him, the door wouldn't budge.

"'They're holding the trapdoor down,' shouted Simon. 'Shoot through it; fire!'

"'But what about my bottles?' the widow Plumeau cried. 'You're going to break my bottles!'

"'Stop your bawling, both of you!' said the officer. 'And you,' he addressed the guards, 'bring some axes and chop open the door.'

"His men obeyed, and the officer said, 'Now, get ready, and fire into the trapdoor as soon as we open it.'

"They began breaking the door open with the ax, and once the opening was large enough, twenty rifle barrels were lowered toward it. Only there was no one to be seen. The officer lit a torch and tossed it into the cellar. Still, no one.

"'Follow me!' the officer ordered as he hurried down the stairway into the empty cellar.

"'Forward!' shouted the municipal guards, rushing after their leader.

"'Ah, Widow Plumeau,' Simon cried, shaking his fist at her, 'so now you loan your cellar to aristocrats trying to free the queen!'

"But Simon unjustly accused the good woman. For someone had broken through the cellar wall from a tunnel three feet wide and five feet high that ran toward the Rue de la Corderie. On the tunnel floor many people had left their tracks.

"The officer set off quickly down the tunnel, but after only ten steps he encountered an iron grate and had to stop. 'Stop!' the officer called out to the soldiers hard on his heels. 'We can go no farther. I want four men to stay here and shoot anyone who shows up. I am going to make my report. The aristocrats have attempted to free the queen.'

"That was what came to be known as the Carnation Plot. The three principal actors were my father, the Chevalier de Maison-Rouge, and Toulan, and it led both my father and Toulan to the scaffold. The Chevalier de Maison-Rouge, who hid in a tannery in the Faubourg Saint-Victor, was able to escape unscathed.

"Before his execution, my father asked my elder brother to follow his example and to die as he did, for his sovereigns."

"And how about your brother?" Claire murmured, clearly shaken by his tale. "Did he obey your father's request?"

"You shall see," Hector answered, "if you allow me to continue."

"Oh, please, go on!" cried Claire. "I'm all ears and all heart!"

XIV

Léon de Sainte-Hermine

⁂

"A SHORT TIME AFTER my father was executed, my mother, who had fallen ill upon hearing of his death, also died.

"I was unable to send my brother Léon word about this new misfortune because we'd had no news of him since the Battle of Berchem. But I wrote to my brother Charles in Avignon, and immediately he rushed back to Besançon.

"All that we knew about the Battle of Berchem and my brother's fate came from the Prince de Condé himself. In her worry, my ailing mother had sent a messenger to him, but the messenger failed to return before my mother died. He arrived, in fact, on the same day as my brother did from Avignon.

"So we learned that on December 4, 1793, the Prince de Condé was headquartered in Berchem, where twice Pichegru launched an attack, but he was unable to hold the village after driving the prince out. When the émigrés retook the village, Léon performed extraordinary feats. Indeed, he was the first to enter the village, but then he disappeared and even the companions following close behind him had no idea where. They searched among the dead but did not find him. The general opinion was that, having advanced too rapidly in pursuit of the Republicans, he had been taken prisoner. Which was no better than death, since every prisoner who'd borne weapons was formally charged before the council of war and then shot.

"In the absence of news we had accepted that painful explanation when we were visited by a young man from Besançon who had been with the Rhine army. I say young man, but he was really just a child, scarcely fourteen years old, the son of one of my father's former friends. He was only a year younger than I; we had been raised together. His name was Charles N.

"I was the first to see him. As I knew that he had been with General Pichegru for three months, I ran up to him, shouting: 'Charles! Is that you? Have you any news of my brother?'

"'Alas, yes,' he replied. 'Is your brother Charles also here?'

"When I answered yes, he said, 'Well, then, send word to him. What I have to tell you requires his presence.'

"My brother soon appeared, and I told him Charles was bringing us news of Léon.

"'Bad news, right?'

"'I'm afraid so. Otherwise he would have already told us.'

"Then, without answering but smiling sadly, my young comrade pulled a garrison cap from under his vest and presented it to my brother. 'You are now the head of the family,' he said. 'This relic now belongs to you.'

"'What is this?' my brother asked.

"'The cap he was wearing when he was brought before the firing squad,' Charles answered.

"'So, it's all over?' my older brother asked, dry-eyed, though from my eyes, in spite of myself, tears were falling.

"'Yes.'

"'And he indeed did die?'

"'Like a hero!'

"'God be praised! Our honor is intact. . . . There must be something in this cap?'

"'A letter.'

"My brother ran his hands over the cap, felt the paper, cut the lining with his pocketknife, and pulled out a letter: "'To my brother Charles,'" he read. "'First of all, and above all, keep the news of my death from our mother as long as possible.'"

"'So he died without knowing that our poor mother preceded him to death?' my brother asked.

"'No,' said Charles. 'I told him myself.'

"My brother turned back to the letter and continued reading:

""'I was captured in Berchem. My horse was shot out from under me, and when it fell I was caught underneath. There was no way to defend myself. I threw my sword aside, and four Republicans pulled me loose. They led me to the fortress in Auenheim to shoot me. Short of a miracle, nothing could save me.

""'My father had given his word to the king that he would die for the Royalist cause, and so he did. I gave my word to my father to defend to death the same cause, and so I am. You gave me your word, and so you will. If you too die, Hector will avenge us.

""'A prayer on my mother's tomb. A fatherly kiss to Hector.

""'Adieu.

""'Léon de Sainte-Hermine

""'P.S. I don't know how I shall be able to get this letter to you, but God will provide a way."'"

"My brother raised the letter to his lips, gave it to me to kiss, and placed it against his heart. Then he said to Charles, 'You were there when he died, you said?'

"'Yes!' Charles answered.

"'In that case, tell me the whole story and don't leave out a single detail.'

"'It's quite simple,' said Charles. 'I was on my way from Strasbourg to Citizen Pichegru's headquarters in Auenheim, when, just beyond Sessenheim, a squadron of about twenty infantrymen, led by a captain on horseback, caught up with me. The twenty men were marching in two rows.

"'In the middle of the road, like me, a cavalry soldier was walking. It was easy to see that he was in the cavalry, because he was wearing riding boots with spurs. A large white coat covered him from the shoulders down, and all I could see of him was a young, intelligent face that seemed familiar to me. He was wearing a garrison cap, of a shape unusual in the French army.

"'The captain saw me walking near the young man in the white coat, and since I looked younger than I really am, he kindly asked, "Where are you going, my young citizen?"

"'"I'm going to General Pichegru's headquarters," I replied. "Do I still have far to go?"

"'"About another two hundred yards," the young man in the white coat answered. "Look, there, at the end of this avenue we've just started down, you can see the first houses in Auenheim." It seemed strange that he nodded toward the village instead of pointing to it.

"'"Thank you," I told him, and began walking faster, away from him, since he didn't seem to appreciate my presence. But he called me back.

"'"By my faith, young friend," he said, "if you are not in too much of a hurry, you should slow down and travel with us. That would give me time to ask you about our country."

"'"What country?"

"'"Come now!" he said. "Are you not from Besançon, or at least from the Franche-Comté?"

"'I stared at him in astonishment. His accent, his face, the way he held himself—everything about him brought back childhood memories. Clearly, I had known this handsome young man in the past.

"'"Of course," he said with a laugh, "perhaps you want to remain incognito."

"'"Not at all, Citizen," I answered. "I was just thinking of Theophrastus, to whom the Athenians had given the nickname Good Speaker, and after he had lived in Athens for fifty years, a fruit-seller identified him as a native of the Island of Lesbos."

"'"You are well-read, monsieur," my traveling companion said. "That is a luxury in such times as these."

"'"Not really," I answered. "I am going to join General Pichegru, who himself is well-read, and I'm hoping, thanks to a recommendation I am carrying for him, to get a job as his secretary. And how about you, citizen?" I added, goaded by curiosity. "Are you with the army?"

"'He began to laugh. "Not precisely," he said.

""'Well, then," I went on, "you must be attached to the administration."

""'"Attached," he repeated, and laughed again. "Yes, that's right, you have chosen the right word, monsieur. However, I am not attached to the administration; I am attached to myself."

""'"But," I said, lowering my voice, "you are using formal address with me, and you even called me monsieur out loud. Are you not afraid that you might lose your place?"

""'"Ah! Say, Captain," the young man in the white coat shouted, "this young citizen is afraid I might lose my place because I'm still using formal address and am calling him monsieur. Do you know anyone who would like to have my place? If so, I bow to such a man."

""'"Poor fellow!" the captain muttered with a shrug.

""'"Say, young man," my traveling companion said, "since you are from Besançon—and you are from there, are you not?"

"'I nodded that I was.

""'"Then you must know the Sainte-Hermine family."

""'"Yes," I answered. "A widow and three sons."

""'"Three sons. Yes, that's right," he added with a sigh. "There are still three of them. Thank you. How long has it been since you left Besançon?"

""'"Scarcely seven or eight days ago."

""'"So you can give me any recent news?"

""'"Yes, but it's sad news as well."

""'"Go on, tell me."

""'"The evening before I left, we went, my father and I, to the countess's funeral."

""'"Ah!" the young man said, raising his eyes to the heavens, "the countess has died!"

""'"Yes."

""'"It's for the best." He raised his eyes again, and two large tears rolled down his cheeks.

""'"What do you mean, it's for the best?" I objected. "She was a saintly woman."

""'"All the more reason," the young man replied. "Was it not better for her to die from illness rather than from the sadness of learning that her son went before the firing squad?"

""'"What?" I cried. "The Comte de Sainte-Hermine has been shot?"

""'"No, but he will be."

""'"When?"

""""When we get to the fortress at Auenheim."

""""So the Comte de Sainte-Hermine is in the fortress?"

""""No, but that is where they are taking him."

""""And he'll be shot?"

""""As soon as I get there."

""""Are you the one charged with the execution?"

""""No, but I shall give the order to fire. They never refuse that favor to a good soldier taken with arms in hand, even if he is an émigré."

""""Oh, my God!" I cried in horror. "Are. . . ?"

"'Again, the young man burst into laughter. "That is why I laughed when you were asking me to be careful. That is why I was proposing my place to anyone who might want it, for I had no fear of losing it. As you were saying, I am indeed *attached!*" And only then, with a shake of his shoulders to open his coat, did he show me his bound hands and two arms attached behind him.

""""But then," I cried in terror, "you are. . . ."

""""The Comte de Sainte-Hermine, young man. You see that I was correct in saying that it was better for my poor mother to die."

""""Oh, my God," I cried.

""""Fortunately," the Comte went on, his teeth clenched, "my brothers are still alive."

"In one voice, we both shouted yes, my brother and I, and vowed that we'd avenge him," said Hector.

"So," Mademoiselle de Sourdis asked, "that was your brother they were going to shoot?"

"Yes," Hector answered. "Is it enough for you to know the result, or would you like to know the details of his final moments? These details, each word of which made our own hearts beat doubly faster, may be of slight interest to you, since you never knew poor Léon."

"Oh, on the contrary, tell me everything," Mademoiselle de Sourdis cried out. "Don't leave out a single word. Was not Monsieur Léon de Sainte-Hermine a relative of mine, and do I not have the right to follow him all the way to his tomb?"

"That is exactly what we said to my young friend Charles."

"'You can imagine,' young Charles continued, 'how upset I was to learn that the man walking beside me, a man full of youth who could speak so lightly of events, was going to die. And that he was a compatriot, the head of one of our most important families, the Comte de Sainte-Hermine.

"""Is there no way to save you?" I whispered.

"""Frankly, I have to say that I don't see any," he answered. "If I did, I'd try it without wasting another second."

"""Although I'm unable to offer you any great service, I would like to be useful to you in some way, and while I can't save you from death, perhaps I can at least make your death less painful, to help you somehow in the face of it."

"""Since I first saw you I have been turning an idea over in my head."

"""Tell me what it is."

"""There may be some danger, and I don't want it to frighten you."

"""I'm ready to do anything to serve you."

"""I would like to send news to my brother."

"""I take it upon myself to do it for you."

"""It's a letter."

"""I shall take it to him."

"""I could give it to the captain. He's a good man; he would probably have it sent to its destination."

"""With the captain," I answered, "it's only probable. With me, it's certain."

"""Well, then, listen carefully." I stepped closer, and he said, "The letter has already been written; it's sewn into my cap."

"""Very well."

"""You must ask the captain for permission to be present at my execution."

"""Me!" I answered, and my forehead broke out in cold sweat.

"""Don't dismiss the idea out of hand. An execution is always interesting. Many people attend them simply for the enjoyment of it."

"""I haven't the courage. . . ."

"""Come now. Everything happens so quickly."

"""I couldn't! Never!"

"""Let's say nothing more about it then," said the count. "All you need to tell my brothers, if you happen to run into them, is that we met as they were about to send me to the firing squad." And he began to whistle the tune from *Vive Henry IV.*

"'I quickly moved still closer. "Excuse me," I said. "I'll do whatever you want me to do."

"""Well, now, you're a very kind boy. Thank you!"

"""But. . . ."

"""What?"

"""But you have to be the one who asks the captain if I can be present. I could not bear it if they thought that I wanted to watch for pleasure."

""""Very well. I shall tell him that we are from the same region, and I'll ask him to let me send something of mine to my brother, my cap, for instance. Such things happen all the time. Besides, you understand, there is nothing suspicious about a garrison cap."

""""No."

""""When I give the order to fire, I shall toss it aside. Don't act too much in a hurry to pick it up. Wait until I'm dead."

""""Oh!" I gasped, turning pale. My whole body began to tremble.

""""Who has a little alcohol for my young fellow countryman?" your brother asked. "He's cold."

""""Come here, my good boy," said the captain. He handed me his flask. I drank a swallow, then thanked him.

""""At your service. . . . A swallow, Citizen Sainte-Hermine?" he shouted to the prisoner.

""""Thank you very much, Captain," he answered. "I never drink alcohol."

"'I walked back to where he was, and he continued with his instructions to me. "So, when I'm dead, you'll pick up my cap, but treat it as if it were a thing of no importance. But you realize of course that my last wishes, the last wishes of a dying man, are sacred, and that the letter I've hidden in the cap must be delivered to my brother. If the cap is inconvenient, slip out the letter and toss the cap into a ditch somewhere. As for the letter, are you sure you won't lose it?"

""""No," I said, trying to hold back my tears. "I mean, I'm sure."

""""You won't misplace it?"

""""No, no! You can rest easy."

""""And you will give it to my brother yourself?"

""""Yes, I shall do so myself."

""""To my brother Charles, the elder. He has the same name as you, so it will be easy to remember."

""""To him and to no other."

""""Be sure of that! So, and then he'll ask you how I died, and you'll tell him. And he'll say, 'Good, I had a good brother,' and when his turn comes, he'll die like me."

"'We came to a fork in the road; one road led to General Pichegru's headquarters, the other to the fortress. I tried to speak, but no words came to my mouth. I looked at your brother beseechingly. He smiled.

""""Captain," he said. "A favor."

""""What favor? If it's in my power. . . ."

""""Perhaps it's a weakness, but you'll keep it between us, won't you? At the moment of my death, I would like to embrace a fellow countryman. This young man and I are both from the Juras, both our families live in Besançon and are friends. Someday he will go back home, and he will tell how we happened to meet and how he accompanied me until my final moments. Then he will tell how I died."

"'The captain looked at me; I was weeping. "Of course!" he said. "If that is what would please you both."

"""I don't believe," your brother said with a laugh, "that it will please the boy very much, but it will indeed please me."

"""Since it's you who are making the request."

"""So, you agree?" the prisoner asked.

"""I agree," the captain answered.

"""You see," he said as I walked beside him, "so far things are going perfectly well."

"'We marched up the hill, were recognized, and walked across the drawbridge. For a moment we waited in the courtyard while the captain went to announce to the colonel that we had arrived and to communicate to him the execution orders.

"'A few minutes later, he reappeared in the doorway. "Are you ready?" he asked the prisoner.

"""Whenever you are, Captain," the prisoner answered.

"""Do you have any comments to make?"

"""No, but several favors to request."

"""I shall grant whatever lies within my power."

"""Thank you, Captain."

"'The captain walked over to your brother. "We may serve under enemy flags, but we are still both French, and good men can spot each other at first sight. What do you wish?"

"""First, that you remove these ropes, which make me look like a thief."

"""That is only just. Untie the prisoner."

"'I rushed over and grabbed the count's hands; I had untied him before anyone else had time to draw near.

"""Oh!" said the count, flexing his arms under his coat. "It feels good to be free."

"""And now," asked the captain, "what else do you wish?"

"""I would like to be the one to give the order to fire."

"""You may give the order. Anything else?"

"""I would like to send some souvenir to my family."

"""You know it is forbidden for anyone to accept letters from political prisoners before they are shot. Anything else, yes."

"""I don't want to cause any problems. This is my young countryman, Charles. As you have authorized, he will be accompanying me to the place of execution. He can take responsibility for giving my family, not a letter, but something of mine. This old cap, for example."

"'"Is that all?" asked the captain.

"'"I think so," the count answered. "It is time. I'm beginning to get cold feet, and cold feet are what I hate most in the world. Let's go, Captain—I presume you are coming with us."

"'"It's my duty."

"'The count bowed, and with a laugh like a man who is pleased at having gotten what he wanted, he shook my hand.

"'"Which way?" he asked.

"'"This way," said the captain, starting out at the head of the column. Following him, we passed through a gate and entered a second courtyard where sentinels were walking back and forth on the ramparts above. The wall at the back of the courtyard was peppered with bullet holes at about a man's height.

"'"Ah, here we are!" said the prisoner, and without instruction or command he walked over to the wall.

"'The clerk read the sentence. Your brother nodded as if he accepted it. Then he said, "Excuse me, Captain. I would like a few words with myself."

"'The captain and the soldiers, realizing that he wanted to pray, stepped away. For a moment your brother remained immobile, his arms crossed, his head bowed down against his chest, his lips moving, though no sound came from them. When he raised his head, there was a smile on his face. He embraced me, and as he did, like Charles I of England, he whispered: "Remember."

"'Weeping, I bowed my head.

"'Then with a strong voice: "Attention!" said the condemned man.

"'The soldiers got ready. The count paused, and as if he did not want to give the order to fire with his head covered, he pulled off his cap, tossed it aside. It fell at my feet.

"'"Are you ready?" asked the count.

"'"Yes," replied the soldiers.

"'"Ready, aim, fire! Long live the K—" His "King" was lost in the detonations, and seven bullets tore through his chest.

"'He fell to the ground facedown. I had dropped to my knees; I was weeping as I'm weeping now.'"

"And indeed, the poor child was sobbing as he told us how our brother died. We too, Mademoiselle; I swear, we too were weeping hot tears," Hector said.

"My elder brother, now the head of the family, reread the letter and embraced Charles. Then, with his arms raised, on the holy relic that was all that remained of our brother, he promised to avenge his death.

"Oh, what a sad story, monsieur!" said Claire, wiping her tears.

"Should I continue?" asked Hector.

"Indeed, yes," said the girl. "For never have I heard a more heart-wrenching story."

XV

Charles de Sainte-Hermine [1]

HECTOR DE SAINTE-HERMINE PAUSED for a moment to let Mademoiselle de Sourdis pull herself together. Then he continued: "As you said, a sad story. And it gets worse. For soon after we received the painful news of Leon's death, my brother Charles disappeared. He did leave me a rather long letter, though, that said in pretty much these words:

"'You don't need to know, my dear child, where I am or what I'm doing. As you might suspect, I am striving to carry out what I swore I would do: seek vengeance.

"'You are now all alone. But you are sixteen years old, and with misfortune as your teacher you will quickly become a man.

"'You understand what I mean by becoming a man. A true man is like a solid oak tree with its roots in the past and its branches in the future. It can stand up to anything—to heat, cold, wind, rain, storms, weapons, and gold.

"'Keep both your mind and your body active; become skillful in all kinds of physical activities—there is no lack of money or teachers. While you are in the provinces, spend twelve thousand francs a year on horses, guns, weapons, and lessons in riding and fencing. If you go to Paris, spend double that amount, but always with the same purpose of becoming a man.

"'Do whatever is necessary always to have at hand ten thousand francs in gold. Be prepared to deliver it to any messenger who comes in Morgan's name—you will know his signature—and presents you with a letter marked with the sign of a dagger.

"'Whenever people speak of Morgan, you alone will know that they are really talking about me.

"'Follow to the letter these instructions, but consider them more as advice than orders. And once a month, at least, reread this letter.

"'Always be ready to take my place, to avenge me, and to die,' he charged me, and signed the letter 'Your brother, Charles.'"

"So, mademoiselle," Hector continued, "now that you know that Morgan and Charles de Sainte-Hermine are one and the same person, I no longer need to recount for you my brother's activities. For like all, you know that as the leader of the Companions of Jehu he soon became famous all over France and even in other countries. From Marseille to Nantua, France was his kingdom for more than two years.

"Twice more I received letters from him, marked with the seal and signature to which he had alerted me. Each time he asked for the same amount, and each time I sent it to him.

"The man named Morgan meanwhile became both the terror and the darling of the South of France. The Royalist party deemed the Companions of Jehu to be like knights and avowed their legitimacy. The authorities, on the other hand, tried to sully them by calling them bandits, brigands, and stagecoach robbers, but they were unable to tarnish Jehu's prestige. All over the South one could openly say he stood with the Companions of Jehu without having anything to fear from the local authorities.

"As long as the Directory lasted, everything went well. The government was already too weak for foreign wars, so domestic war was unthinkable. But then Bonaparte came back from Egypt.

"By chance, in Avignon he witnessed one of the many courageous operations typical of the Companions of Jehu, and he witnessed their code of ethics too. For along with money belonging to the government, they had mistakenly carried off a bag containing two hundred louis that belonged to a wine merchant from Bordeaux. While taking a meal at the common table in an inn, the merchant was complaining about the wrong done to him when in broad daylight my brother strode into the dining room, masked and armed to the teeth. He walked over to the table, offered his excuses, and put down in front of the merchant his two hundred louis.

"Chance had it that General Bonaparte and his aide-de-camp Roland de Montrevel were eating at the same table, so he saw firsthand the kind of men he was dealing with. And he realized that it was not the English but the Companions of Jehu who were providing support to the Chouans. He made the decision to exterminate them and sent Roland south with full authority to do whatever was needed.

"But Roland could not find a single traitor willing to identify the people Roland had sworn to exterminate. Nor did the caves, forests, or mountains betray the lair of the men who themselves refused to betray their king. It was an unexpected event, produced by a woman's hand, that brought about the downfall of those whom the weapons of entire regiments had been unable to reach.

"You know about the terrible political turmoil that, like an earthquake, is now rocking the city of Avignon. Well, imagine one of those riots in which people pitilessly cut each other's throats, in which they battle an enemy as long as they have one ounce of breath and even after the enemy has breathed his last. And imagine then how a certain Monsieur de Fargas had been not only killed but burned and eaten by cannibals whose actions far outstripped any primitives in the Pacific isles. His assassins were liberals.

"His two children, though, escaped the carnage and fled. Nature had made a mistake with de Fargas's son and daughter, for it had given the young man the heart of a girl and the sister the heart that should have been her brother's. Both of them, Lucien and Diana, with Diana giving her full support to her brother, swore to avenge their father.

"Lucien joined the Companions of Jehu, but during a raid he was captured. Unable to stand up to the torture of sleep deprivation, he revealed the names of his accomplices. To protect him from the vengeance of the Companions of Jehu, his captors moved him from Avignon to a prison in Nantua, but one night a week later, a band of armed men stormed the prison and carried him off to a monastery in Seillon.

"Two nights after that, the corpse of Lucien de Fargas was placed in the town square in front of the Préfecture, just across from the hotel Les Grottes de Ceyzériat, where his sister Diana was living. The body was naked, and the well-known dagger of the Companions of Jehu was planted in his heart. Hanging from the dagger was a piece of paper on which Lucien, in his own hand, had written: 'I shall die because I failed to keep my sacred oath. The dagger found planted in my chest will prove that I die the victim not of a cowardly assassin but of avenging justice.'

"At daybreak Diana was awakened by a loud noise under her windows. She somehow knew that the noise had something to do with her, and that a new misfortune awaited her. She put on a dressing gown, and without even tying up her hair, which had come loose in her sleep, she opened the window and leaned out over the balcony.

"Scarcely had she glanced down at the street than she let out a scream, jumped back, and, like a madwoman, pale as a ghost, her hair flowing, hurried down to the square and threw herself on the corpse in the middle of the crowd, crying 'My brother! My brother!'

"Now a stranger had been witness to Lucien's death. He had been sent by Cadoudal, so he knew all sorts of passwords that would open any door.

This is the letter that served as his passport; I copied it because it has something to do with me.

"'My dear Morgan,' he read, 'I'm sure you have not forgotten that at our meeting on Rue des Postes you offered to be my treasurer in case I should pursue war alone without any foreign or domestic help. Our defenders have all been killed, either as they fought or by a firing squad. D'Autichamp went over to the Republic. Only I still stand unswerving in my beliefs, invincible here in my Morbihan.

"'My army of two or three thousand men is sufficient for my campaign. Although they are not asking for any salary, they must still have food, weapons, and ammunition. Ever since what happened in Quiberon, the English have sent us nothing.

"'If you provide the money, we shall furnish the blood. That is not to say, God forbid, that if necessary, you too would not be willing to give blood of your own. No, your devotion is far greater than anyone's, and it makes ours pale in comparison. If we are captured, we shall be shot, whereas if you are taken, you will die on the scaffold. You write that you have large amounts of money. If I can be sure of receiving thirty-five to forty thousand francs a month, that will be sufficient..

"'I am sending you a mutual friend, Coster de Saint-Victor. His name alone should be enough to make you realize you can trust him completely. I am giving him the little catechism to study so he can find his way to where you now are hiding. Give him the first forty thousand francs if you have them and keep safe the rest, for it is much less to me than it is to you. If you are unable to stay where you are because persecution is too great, come to this part of France to be with me.

"'Whether near or far, I love you and thank you.

"'George Caudoudal

"'General of the Army of Brittany

"'PS: You apparently have, my dear Morgan, a young brother about nineteen or twenty years old. If you don't think me unworthy of leading him into his first battles, send him to me. He will be my aide-de-camp.'

"After consulting all the Companions, my brother responded:

"'My dear general,

"'We received your good, courageous letter, thanks to your brave messenger. We have approximately one hundred fifty thousand francs in our coffers, and so we are able to do what you request. Our new associate, to whom I am giving the name Alcibiade on my own authority, will leave this evening with the first forty thousand francs. Each month you will receive from the same bank the forty thousand francs you need. In case of death or dispersion, the money will be buried in as many different places as we have multiples of forty thousand francs. Herewith is the list of those who will know where the money is hidden.

"'Our brother Alcibiade arrived just in time to witness an execution, by the way. He has seen how we punish traitors.

"'I thank you, my dear general, for your generous offer concerning my younger brother. But my intention is to keep him out of danger until the time comes for him to replace me. My father died on the guillotine, bequeathing his vengeance to my older brother. My older brother died before the firing squad, bequeathing his vengeance to me. I shall likely die, as you say, on the scaffold. But I shall die bequeathing my vengeance to my younger brother. And then it will be his turn to follow the same path we have taken, and he will contribute, as we have, to the triumph of our noble cause. Or he will die as we have died. That is the reason I am required to take it on myself to deprive him of your patronage, though I do ask you to keep him as a friend.

"'As soon as possible, send us back our dear brother Alcibiade. For us it is a double pleasure to be able to send you our message with a messenger like him.

"'Morgan'

"As my brother said, Coster de Saint-Victor did indeed witness the punishment. Lucien de Fargas was judged and executed before his eyes. Afterward, at midnight, two horsemen left the Seillon monastery by the same gate. One, Coster de Saint-Victor, was leaving for Brittany to meet Cadoudal, carrying forty thousand francs from Morgan. The other, the Comte de Ribier, with Lucien de Fargas's body lying across his horse, was on his way to place the traitor's corpse in the square by the Préfecture."

Hector paused a moment, then said, "Pardon me, my story seemed so simple at first, only now it seems to have gotten so complicated it's taking on the shape of a novel. I'm obliged to follow events as they progress, of course, but for fear of describing too many catastrophes I shall try to be as brief as possible."

"Oh, on the contrary, don't leave anything out, I beg you," said Mademoiselle de Sourdis. "I find all the people you are talking about quite fascinating, especially Mademoiselle de Fargas."

"Well, I was just about to get back to her. For three days after she had religiously attended to the burial of the body, identified as her brother, on the square in Bourg-en-Bresse, a young woman appeared at the Palais de Luxembourg and requested an audience with Citizen Director Barras. He was in a meeting. The valet, noticing that she was young and attractive, showed her into the pink boudoir, where Citizen Barras conducted his more amorous meetings. A quarter of an hour later, the same valet announced Citizen Director Barras.

"Barras entered triumphantly, placed his hat on a table, and walked toward the visitor, saying: 'You wanted to see me, madame? Here I am!'

"The young woman, lifting her veil to reveal her astounding beauty, stood up as he approached. Barras stopped in amazement. Then he moved quickly forward and tried to take her hand as he gestured that she should sit back down.

"But she, keeping her hands in the folds of her long veil, said, 'Please excuse me, but I must remain standing as befits a supplicant.'

"'A supplicant!' said Barras. 'Oh, a woman like you does not beg; she gives orders, or at the very least she makes demands.'

"'Well, that is what I'm also doing. In the name of the earth that gave us both life, in the name of my father, your father's friend, in the name of outraged humanity, in the name of failed justice, I come to you to demand vengeance.'

"'Vengeance?'

"'Vengeance,' Diana repeated.

"'Vengeance is a harsh word,' Barras said, 'for one so lovely and young.'

"'Monsieur, I am the daughter of the Comte de Fargas, assassinated by the Republicans in Avignon, and the sister of the Vicomte de Fargas, who has just been killed in Bourg-en-Bresse by the Companions of Jehu.'

"'Are you sure, madame?'

"She showed him a dagger and a sheet of paper. 'The dagger is well known in its design,' she said, 'even if the dagger explained nothing at all, and the paper will remove any doubts as to the murder and its cause.'

"Barras studied the weapon. 'And this dagger. . . .' he began.

"'Was planted in my brother's chest.'

"'The dagger by itself proves nothing,' said Barras. 'It could have been stolen or counterfeited purposely simply to complicate the investigation.'

"'Yes, but read this paper, written and signed in my brother's hand.'

"Barras read Lucien's last words, avouching his failure to keep his oath to the Companions of Jehu. 'And this is truly your brother's writing?' Barras asked.

"'Yes, it is.'

"'What do these words mean: "I die the victim not of a cowardly assassin but of avenging justice?"'

"'That means that when he fell into your agents' hands and was tortured, my brother broke his oath by naming his accomplices. I'm the one,' Diana added with a strange laugh, 'who should have joined the Companions, not my brother.'

"'How is it possible that a murder like that took place without my knowing anything about it?'

"'It does not speak well for your police,' Diana said with a smile.

"'Well, since you seem to be so well informed, tell us the names of the people who killed your brother. Once we have caught them, their punishment will be swift.'

"'If I knew their names,' answered Diana, 'I would not have to come see you. I'd have planted a knife in them myself.'

"'Well,' said Barras, 'as you look for them, so shall we.'

"'But should it be I who looks for them?' Diana asked. 'Is that my job? Am I the government or the police? Is it my responsibility to keep watch over people? My brother was arrested and put into prison, a prison belonging to the government, which now has to answer to me for my brother. The prison has betrayed its prisoner. So the government owes me an answer. Since you are the head of government, I ask you, I demand, "Give me back my brother!"'

"'You loved your brother?'

"'I adored him.'

"'And you want to avenge him?'

"'I would trade my life for the lives of his assassins.'

"'What if I offered you a way, whatever it might be, to discover the murderer? Would you accept?'

"Diana hesitated a moment, then said boldly, 'Whatever it is, I shall do what's necessary.'

"'Well, then,' said Barras, 'if you are willing to help us, we shall help you.'

"'What must I do?'

"'You are attractive; very attractive, indeed.'

"'My beauty has nothing to do with it,' said Diana without lowering her eyes.

"'On the contrary,' said Barras, 'beauty has everything to do with it. In this grand struggle we call life, beauty comes to women not as some heaven-sent gift merely to please the eyes of a lover or husband, but as a potent weapon, a means of attack and defense.'

"'Tell me more,' Diana replied.

"'The Companions of Jehu keep no secrets from Cadoudal. He is their true leader, for essentially they work for him. He knows their every name from top to bottom.'

"'And so?' Diana wondered.

"'So? Nothing could be simpler. Go to Brittany, join Cadoudal, introduce yourself as a victim of your devotion to the Royalist cause, gain his confidence. It will be easy for you, because Cadoudal will not be able to look at you without falling in love. And sooner or later you'll have all the names of these men, these bandits, whom we have had so much trouble finding. Provide us those names, that is all I ask, and you shall have your revenge, I guarantee. In addition, if through your influence you're able to get that stubborn rebel to give up his struggle, I don't need to tell you that the government would set no limits. . . .'

"Diana raised her hand. 'Careful, Citizen Director, one more word and you'd be insulting me.' Then, after a moment's silence: 'I'd like to request twenty-four hours to consider,' she said.

"'Take your time, madame,' said Barras. 'I am always at your orders and shall be waiting.'

"'Tomorrow at nine p.m., right here,' said Diana. She then took the dagger from Barras's hands and picked up her brother's letter from the table. She slipped them inside her bodice. She said good-bye and left.

"The next evening at the appointed hour Mademoiselle Diana de Fargas was again announced at the palace, and the director hurried back to the pink boudoir.

"'I've come to a decision, monsieur. However, you will understand that I shall need a safe-conduct so that the Republican authorities will know who I am. In the life I shall be leading, it is possible I could be caught bearing arms against the Republic. I know that you send even women and children to the firing squad, for you wage a war of extermination—well, that is between you and God. So while I may be captured, I have no wish, you can be sure, to be shot before enjoying my revenge.'

"'I had anticipated your request, and so as not to delay your departure, the papers you need I have already had prepared. Here are clear orders from General Hédouville; they transform those whom you fear into your protectors. With this safe-conduct, you can go anywhere in Brittany or the Vendée.'

"'Very well, monsieur!' said Diana. 'Thank you.'

"'If it's not too indiscreet, may I ask when you plan to leave?'

"'This evening. My horses and coach await me outside the palace gates.'

"'Allow me to ask one somewhat delicate question. It is my duty to ask.'

"'Go ahead, monsieur.'

"'Do you have money?'

"'I have six thousand gold francs in this box, and that's better than sixty thousand francs' worth of assignats. As you see, I have my own resources to fund my battles.'

"Barras reached out to shake the lovely traveler's hand, but she took no notice of his polite gesture. She merely curtsied and withdrew.

"'What a charming viper,' said Barras. 'I would not want to be the one to provide it warmth.'"

XVI

Mademoiselle de Fargas

"MADEMOISELLE DE FARGAS and Coster Saint-Victor happened to meet by chance just below the village of La Guerche, about three leagues from where Cadoudal was camped.

"Coster Saint-Victor, one of the most elegant men of the time, a rival of the First Consul Bonaparte for the favors of one of the most beautiful actresses of the day, spotted the lovely woman in the open carriage. When the carriage was forced move more slowly on an upgrade, he was able to draw near easily since he was on horseback.

"At first Diana tried to remain coldly distant with the stranger, but he greeted her so politely, and his speech and compliments were so gentlemanly, that she remained aloof no longer than was appropriate for people who meet while traveling. Then, too, the region was completely new to her, and danger could be waiting anywhere. This traveler apparently knew the country very well, so he could prove to be useful to her, perhaps even telling her where Cadoudal could be found.

"Both of them had assumed a false identity. Coster Saint-Victor had told her that his name was d'Argentan and that he was a government tax officer in Dinan. Diana had introduced herself as Mademoiselle de Rotrou, the postmistress in Vitré. From statement to statement they shared false information, but eventually they both spoke something true. To each other both divulged that they were looking for Cadoudal.

"'Are you acquainted with him?' Saint-Victor, or d'Argentan, had asked.

"'I've never set eyes on him,' Diana answered.

"'Well, then, mademoiselle, I shall be pleased to offer my services,' said d'Argentan. 'Cadoudal is a close friend of mine, and we are getting so near the place where we shall meet him that I can with no risk, I believe, admit that I am not really a government tax agent but rather an officer in Cadoudal's ranks. If you need a reference to be able to see him, mademoiselle, I shall be doubly pleased that chance—in this case I will say Providence—has placed you on my path.'

"'Since we are making admissions, I am no more postmistress in Vitré than you are a tax officer in Dinan. I am the last of a well-known Royalist family and I've a vow of vengeance to fulfill. I am seeking to serve with him.'

"'In what capacity?' d'Argentan asked.

"'As a volunteer,' said Diana.

"Coster looked at her in surprise, and then said, 'Well, yes, in the end that should be possible. Dumouriez after all had as aides-de-camp the two Fernig girls. We live in such strange times that we have to get used to everything, even to those things that seem unbelievable.' At that, they let the matter drop.

"In La Guerche they had met and passed a detachment of Republican soldiers on its way to Vitré. At the bottom of the hill below La Guerche they came upon some logs barricading the road. 'By Jove!' said Coster, 'I would not be at all surprised if Cadoudal were behind this barricade.'

"He came to a halt and motioned to Diana's carriage to stop. He imitated the hoot first of a screech owl, then of a barn owl, and was answered by the cry of a crow. 'We've identified each other as friends,' he told Diana. 'Even so, it's best if you wait here. I'll come back to get you.'

"Two men appeared and opened up a path through the barricade. Diana watched as her traveling companion threw himself into the arms of a man whom she assumed to be the elusive Cadoudal himself.

"Soon the man crossed the barricade and walked toward Diana. As he neared the carriage, he took off his felt hat. 'Mademoiselle,' he said, 'either you continue on your way or you do me the honor of asking for hospitality. I can only ask you to decide quickly. In less than an hour the Republicans will be here, and as you can see'—he motioned to the barricades—'we are ready to welcome them. Not to mention,' he went on, 'the fifteen hundred men hidden in the Scotch broom who will soon begin to make music the likes of which you have never heard.'

"'Monsieur,' said Diana, 'I have come to request your hospitality, and I am thankful that chance allows me the opportunity to witness a spectacle I have always wanted to see: a battle.'

"Cadoudal bowed and motioned to his men, who made a passageway just large enough for the carriage. Once Diana found herself on the other side of the barricade, she discovered, in addition to the fifteen hundred Cadoudal had said were in the broom, a thousand more lying prone with their rifles ready. And hidden back in the underbrush were about fifty horsemen, their horses' bridles in hand.

"'Mademoiselle,' Cadoudal said to Diana, 'please don't think ill of me for attending to my military duties. As soon as I've taken care of them, I shall return.'

"'Please, gentlemen, don't worry about me,' said Diana. 'If only there were a horse. . . .'

"'But I've got two,' said d'Argentan. 'I shall put the smaller at your disposal. Unfortunately it is saddled for battle and for a man.'

"'Which is exactly what I need,' said Diana. And when she saw the young man taking his saddlebag off the horse, she said with a laugh, 'Thank you, Sir Government Tax Officer from Dinan!' And then she closed the carriage door.

"Ten minutes later, the first shots rang out on the hilltop about a quarter of a mile from the barricade, and the battle was under way. At the same time, the carriage door opened and a young man in an elegant Chouan costume stepped down. He was wearing a velvet vest. Two double-barreled pistols protruded from his white belt, a white feather waved from his felt hat, and at his side hung a light saber. On the horse that Coster Saint-Victor's servant gave to him, he galloped off with an ease that betrayed an excellent horseman. He took his place among the ranks of the cavalry serving under the Breton leader.

"I shall not recount the battle," Hector went on, "except to tell you that the Blues were totally defeated; after displaying prodigious courage, they retreated and rallied around their leader, Colonel Hulot, in the village of La Guerche.

"Although the day had not brought great material gains to Cadoudal and his men, the moral effect was immense. For Cadoudal, his twenty-five hundred men not only had stood up to four or five thousand veteran soldiers hardened by five years of fighting, but had also pushed them back into the town from which they had tried to sally, and he'd cost the Blues four or five hundred men. Thus the insurrection in Brittany, following on the heels of the insurrection in the Vendée, got under way with a victory.

"Diana had fought in the front ranks, had often shot with her rifle, and three or four times, in close battle, had had occasion to use her pistols. As for Coster Saint-Victor, he came back, his Chouan jacket over his shoulder, with a bayonet wound in his arm.

"'Monsieur,' the girl said to Cadoudal, who had been hidden in the smoke while fighting in the front rows throughout the whole battle, 'before the battle, you said that once it was over, you would attend to my purposes in coming to join you. Now that the combat is indeed over, I would hope you'd allow me a place among your troops.'

"'In what capacity?' Cadoudal asked.

"'As a volunteer. For have I not just proven to you that noise and smoke do not frighten me?'

"Cadoudal scowled; his face became stern. 'Madame,' he said, 'your proposal is more serious than it first appears. I am going to tell you something strange. I was first called to become a churchman, and I willingly took all the vows one normally takes when entering orders, nor did I ever break any of them. Now, I have no doubt that you would be a charming aide-de-camp, brave in the face of all. And I believe that women are as good as men. For centuries—from the time of Epicharis, who, while being tortured at Nero's orders, bit off her tongue so she would not be able to betray her accomplices, up until the time of Charlotte Corday, who rid the earth of a monster before whom men trembled—we have seen constant proof of women's courage. But in our regions where religion is important, especially in our old Brittany, there are prejudices that can harm a military reputation just as they can force a military leader to operate contrary to his beliefs. Still, in their camps, some of my colleagues have welcomed sisters and daughters of Royalists who had been killed. Did we not owe them the help and protection they requested?'

"'And who says, monsieur,' cried Diana, 'that I myself am not the daughter or sister of a murdered Royalist, perhaps both, and that I do not have the same claim to the protection you speak of?'

"'In that case,' said the supposed d'Argentan with a smile, 'how is it that you are carrying a passport signed by Barras and made out to the postmistress of Vitré?'

"'Would you be so kind as to show me your own passport?' Diana riposted.

"'Ah! What a good answer,' said Cadoudal, intrigued by Diana's strong will and cool demeanor.

"'And then you will explain how, since you are General Cadoudal's friend, almost his right arm, you have the right to circulate, as the tax officer in Dinan, throughout the territory of the Republic?'

"'Go ahead, speak,' said Cadoudal. 'Explain to the lady how you are a tax officer in Dinan.'

"'And then she can explain how she is postmistress in Vitré?' d'Argentan responded.

"'Oh, that is a secret that I would never dare reveal to our modest friend Cadoudal. However, if you push me, I can tell you, at the risk of making him blush, that in Paris, hidden on Rue des Colonnes near the Feydeau Theatre, there is a young woman named Aurélie de Saint-Amour to whom Citizen Barras can refuse nothing. Nor can she refuse anything to me.'

"'Well, then,' said Cadoudal, 'the name d'Argentan on my friend's passport hides a name he uses as a pass among all those bands of Chouans, Vendeans, and Royalists wearing the white cockade in France and abroad. Your traveling companion, mademoiselle, who no longer has anything to hide now that he has nothing more to fear, is not a tax collector for the Republican government in Dinan, but rather the intermediary between General Tête-Ronde and the Companions of Jehu.' Diana winced almost imperceptibly when she heard that word.

"'And I must say,' offered the counterfeit d'Argentan, 'that I was witness to a horrible execution when I was last among the Companions. The Vicomte de Fargas, who had betrayed the association, was stabbed in my presence.'

"Diana could feel her blood draining from her face. If she had told them her real name, or if she now revealed it, she would not be able to meet the objectives of her journey. To the sister of the Vicomte de Fargas, who had been judged and sentenced by the Companions of Jehu, never would Cadoudal or d'Argentan reveal the executioners' names or their whereabouts. So she said nothing, as if she were waiting for d'Argentan to finish his thought.

"Cadoudal continued: 'His name is not d'Argentan, but rather Coster Saint-Victor, and even he had given no other guarantee of his loyalty to our holy cause than the wound he has just suffered.'

"'Unless it's a wound merely to prove his devotion,' said Diana coldly. 'That would be easy.'

"'What do you mean?'

"'Watch!'

"Diana pulled from her belt the sharp dagger that had killed her brother and struck her arm at the same place where Coster had been wounded. She struck with such force that the blade went into one side of her arm and out the other. Then, holding her wounded arm, with the dagger still in it, out toward Cadoudal, she said, 'Would you like to see if I am of noble birth? Look! My blood is no less blue, I trust, than Monsieur Coster Saint-Victor's. Would you like to know how I can claim your trust? This dagger proves that I am affiliated with the Companions of Jehu. Would you like to know my name? I am the goddaughter of that Roman woman who, to give her husband courage, pierced her own arm with a knife. My name is Portia!'

"Coster Saint-Victor gave a start, and while Cadoudal was looking admiringly at the avenging heroine, he said, 'I can attest that the blade with which this girl has just struck herself is indeed a dagger belonging to the Companions of Jehu. The proof is that I have here one just like it that the company's leader gave to me on the day of my initiation.' And he pulled from his cloak a dagger in every way identical to the one in her arm.

"Cadoudal extended his hand to Diana. 'From this moment on, mademoiselle,' he said, 'if you no longer have a father, I am your father. If you no longer have a brother, you are now my sister. Since we are living at a time when everyone is forced to hide his true name under another, your name, like the worthy Roman you are, shall be Portia. From now on, you are part of our army, mademoiselle, and as your first action has earned you a rank of leader, once our surgeon has bandaged your wound, you will attend the council I shall be holding.'

"'Thank you, General,' said Diana. 'As for the surgeon, he's not needed for me any more than he's needed for Monsieur Coster Saint-Victor. My wound is no more serious than his.' Pulling the dagger from the wound in which it had until then remained, she rolled up her sleeve and displayed her lovely arm. Then, turning to Coster Saint-Victor, she said, 'Comrade,' she said, 'please be so good as to lend me your tie.'

"For two years Diana remained with the army of Brittany without anyone ever learning her real name. For two years she participated in every battle Cadoudal waged and shared with the general all the dangers and his fatigue, her devotion to him apparently complete. For two years she swallowed her hatred for the Companions of Jehu and vaunted their exploits, glorified their names: Morgan, d'Assas, Adler, and Montbar. For two years, the handsome Coster de Saint-Victor, who had never met a woman insensible to his charms, besieged the woman named Portia with his love, but in vain. Finally, after two years, her long perseverance was rewarded.

"The 18th Brumaire burst on the scene in France. Immediately the new dictator's thoughts turned to the Vendée and Brittany. Cadoudal realized that serious war was about to break out in France. He realized, too, that to wage war he needed money. And that only the Companions of Jehu would be able to furnish it.

"Coster Saint-Victor had just taken a bullet in the thigh, so this time he could not be expected to assume his tax collector's role. Cadoudal thought of Portia. Again and again she had proved her devotion and courage, and with Coster Saint-Victor unavailable, Cadoudal could think of no one better to complete the delicate mission: Dressed like a woman, she could travel anywhere in France undisturbed, and if she traveled by carriage, she could carry considerable sums of money. He consulted the wounded man, who agreed with him completely. Diana was summoned to the general's bedside, where he laid out his plan. He wanted her to establish contact, by using letters from Cadoudal and Coster Saint-Victor, with the Companions of Jehu, then return to him with the money that was now more necessary than ever, what with hostilities about to break out even more fiercely than before.

"Diana's heart leaped with joy as he spoke, but not a flicker of emotion on her face betrayed what was happening in her heart. 'Although the task will be difficult,' she said, 'I ask for nothing more than the opportunity to complete it. In addition to letters from the general and Monsieur Coster Saint-Victor, however, I shall need all the topographical information, as well as all the watchwords and passwords, necessary for reaching the secret site of their meetings.'

"Coster Saint-Victor gave her everything she needed. She left with a smile on her face and vengeance in her heart."

XVII
The Ceyzériat Caves

"BARRAS NOW BEING totally powerless, Diana did not even think of going to him when she arrived in Paris. Instead, she asked for an audience with First Consul Bonaparte.

"It was two or three days after Roland had returned from his mission to Cadoudal. We know how little attention Roland paid to women, and he walked right past Diana without even wondering who she was.

"She said in her request for an audience that she had a means to catch the Companions of Jehu and that she would share it once certain conditions, which she wanted to discuss with the First Consul himself, were met.

"Bonaparte hated women who were involved in politics. Fearing that he was dealing with some adventuress, he sent her letter to Fouché and asked him to see what Mademoiselle de Fargas was like."

Hector paused for a moment to ask, "Do you know Fouché, mademoiselle?"

"No, monsieur," Claire answered.

"He represents supreme ugliness. Porcelain eyes that cross, thin yellow hair, ashen skin, a snub nose, a crooked mouth filled with ugly teeth, a receding chin, and a beard of the reddish sort that makes his face look dirty—that's Fouché for you.

"Beauty has a natural abhorrence for ugliness. So, when Fouché came to see Mademoiselle de Fargas—his air both servile and insolent, beneath which one could spot the former seminarian's false humility—the lovely Diana's every moral and physical sense revolted.

"The Minister of the Police had been announced, and that title, which opens all doors, also opened Diana's, until she saw the hideous creature. She pulled back on her sofa and did not even ask Fouché to sit down.

"He chose an armchair nonetheless, and with Diana staring at him, making no attempt to hide her revulsion, he said, 'Well, my little woman, we have revelations to make to the police and a deal to propose?'

"Diana looked around with such great surprise that the skillful magistrate assumed immediately that he was right. 'What are you looking for?' he asked.

"'I'm trying to determine to whom you might be speaking, monsieur.'

"'To you, mademoiselle,' said Fouché insolently.

"'Then you are quite mistaken, monsieur,' she said. 'I am not a little woman. I am an important woman, daughter of the Comte de Fargas, murdered in Avignon, and the sister of the Vicomte de Fargas, murdered in Bourg. I did not come to make a revelation to the police or to arrange any kind of deal with them. I leave that to those who have the misfortune of being its employees or at its head. I have come to demand justice, and as I doubt,' she said, getting to her feet, 'that you have any relationship with that chaste goddess, I would be much obliged to you if you would kindly realize that you came to the wrong door when you came here.'

"When Fouché failed to move from his armchair, either out of stupefaction or insolence, she left him sitting there and returned to her bedroom. She locked the door.

"Two hours later, Roland de Montrevel, sent by the First Consul, arrived and escorted her to Bonaparte's quarters. Having led her to the meeting room with every consideration due a woman, as his distinguished education, supervised by his mother, had taught him, he withdrew to tell Bonaparte she had arrived.

"A few minutes later Bonaparte entered. 'Well,' he said, as he responded to Diana's bow with a benevolent nod, 'apparently that oaf Fouché thinks he is still dealing with his typical low-class women. That he treated you quite inappropriately, please forgive him. What else can you expect from someone who was a homework supervisor for Oratorians?'

"'From him, Citizen First Consul, I could not have expected anything better, but I would have expected a different messenger from you.'

"'You are quite right,' said Bonaparte. 'And you have taught us two good lessons in the process. But now here I am. Apparently you have something interesting to tell me. Speak.'

"'As you are apparently unable to listen without pacing about, and since I do need you to listen to me, shall we walk together?'

"'As you please,' said Bonaparte. 'One thing I dislike when I give audience to women is that they never walk.'

"'Perhaps. But when a woman serves as Cadoudal's aide-de-camp for two years, she gets used to walking.'

"'You have been Cadoudal's aide-de-camp for two years?'

"'Yes.'

"'How is it possible, then, that Roland, my own aide-de-camp, knows you neither by sight or by name?'

"'For the reason that in Brittany I was known only by the name of Portia; and because when he was with Cadoudal, I was always careful to keep my distance.'

"'Ah, you're the one who stabbed herself in the arm to gain acceptance among the ranks of the Chouans?'

"'Here's the scar,' said Diana, pulling up her sleeve.

"Glancing at her lovely arm, Bonaparte seemed to notice only the scar. 'A strange wound,' he said.

"'The dagger that caused it is stranger still,' said Diana. 'As you see.' And she showed the First Consul the dagger, made entirely of metal, that was borne by the Companions of Jehu.

"Bonaparte carefully examined the unique design as he considered the damage, surely dreadful, its blade might inflict. 'And how did you come by this dagger?' he asked.

"'I pulled it from my brother's chest. It had been planted in his heart.'

"'Tell me about it, but quickly, because my time is precious.'

"'No more precious than the time of a woman who's been waiting two years for her vengeance.'

"'Are you Corsican?'

"'No, but I am speaking to a Corsican, and he will surely understand me.'

"'What do you want?"

"'I seek the lives of those who took my brother's life.'

"'Who are they?'

"'I told you in my letter. The Companions of Jehu.'

"'And you even added that you knew a way to capture them.'

"'I have their passwords and two letters, one from Cadoudal and one from Coster Saint-Victor, for Morgan, the Companions' leader.'

"'You are sure you can arrange their capture?'

"'I am sure, provided that I can work with a brave, intelligent man such as Monsieur Roland de Montrevel and that we have a sufficient number of soldiers.'

"'And you said that you would set some conditions. What are they?'

"'First of all, that they not be granted pardon.'

"'I never pardon thieves and assassins.'

"'And also, that I be allowed to complete the mission entrusted to me.'

"'What mission?'

"'I am on my way to collect the money for Cadoudal. It's a mission for which he had to reveal his secrets to me.'

"'You are asking for the freedom to do with the money as you wish?'

"'Ah, Citizen First Consul,' Mademoiselle de Fargas said, 'such words could ruin forever the good impression that I would otherwise have of our conversation.'

"'Then what in the devil do you want to do with the money?'

"'I want to be sure it reaches its destination.'

"'You are asking me to allow you to deliver money to the very men who are making war on me? Never!'

"'Well, then, General, please allow me to leave. There is nothing to keep us any longer.'

"'Oh, what a hard head!' said Bonaparte.

"'You should say "what a hard heart," General.'

"'What does that mean?'

"'That it is not the head that refuses shameful proposals, but rather the heart.'

"'But I cannot furnish weapons to my enemies.'

"'Do you have complete confidence in Monsieur Roland de Montrevel?'

"'Yes.'

"'Do you know that he will do nothing contrary to your honor and to the interests of France?'

"'I am sure.'

"'Well, then. Entrust this undertaking to him. I shall arrange with him the means to ensure its success and the conditions on which I shall lend a hand.'

"'So be it,' said Bonaparte.

"Then, as rapid as usual when making decisions, he immediately called to Roland, who had remained just outside the door. 'Roland,' he said as soon as the aide-de-camp had entered, 'I'm giving you full authority. You will work together with Mademoiselle de Fargas, and whatever the cost, you will get rid of these highway gentlemen who, all the while that they are stopping and robbing stagecoaches, put on such grand aristocratic airs.'

"Then, with a slight bow to Diana de Fargas, he said, 'Don't forget. If you succeed, it will be a great pleasure to see you again.'

"'And if I fail?'

"'I never recognize those who fail.' With those words he strode out and left Diana alone with Roland.

"Despite Roland's distaste for any operation involving a woman, he found Diana de Fargas to be so far from the typical that he treated her as a good, loyal companion. She was as pleased by his familiarity as she had been put off by Fouché's insolence. Everything was fixed in less than an hour, and they agreed to set out that very evening, on separate roads, for Bourg-en-Bresse, their headquarters.

"You can be sure, with all the information she had, including the watchwords and passwords, along with letters from Cadoudal and Coster Saint-Victor, Diana de Fargas easily gained entry to the Seillon monastery, where the four leaders were meeting. She was dressed once again like a Chouan and was using the name Portia.

"Nobody had the slightest suspicion, not that the messenger was a woman, because even the clothes of a man could not conceal that Diana was a woman, but that she was Mademoiselle de Fargas, the sister of the man they had killed in punishment for his betrayal.

"Since the total amount Cadoudal was asking for, one hundred thousand francs, was not readily available in the abbey, they arranged to meet Diana at midnight in the Ceyzériat caves, where they would give her the forty thousand still wanting.

"The first thing Roland did when Diana had told him about the arrangements was to summon the captain of the gendarmerie and the colonel of the dragoons garrisoned in the town. When they arrived, he showed them the papers giving him full authority.

"He found the colonel to be a passive instrument ready to put himself, with the number of men required, at Roland's disposal. On the other hand, the captain of the gendarmerie was an old soldier full of rancor toward the Companions of Jehu, who, as he himself said, for the past three years could not stop causing trouble for him. Ten different times he had seen them, talked to them, and pursued them. Every time, either because of their better horses, tricks, skills, or strategy, the old soldier had ruefully to admit, they had escaped.

"Once, at a moment when they expected it least, the captain had happened upon them in the Seillon forest. The brigands had bravely engaged in combat, killed three of the gendarmerie men and then withdrawn, carrying off with them two of their own wounded. So he had come to despair of ever getting the better of Morgan and his men. Now he wanted one thing only: not to be forced by government orders to have to deal with them. And here was Roland, come to drag him out of his pleasant rest, to disturb him in his tranquility, or rather in the apathy into which he had settled.

"But as soon as Roland had pronounced the Ceyzériat caves as the place the leaders of the Companions said they would meet Diana, the old officer sat thoughtfully for a moment, then removed the three-cornered hat from his head as if it were impeding his thought process, laid it on the table, and said, blinking as he spoke, 'Wait a moment . . . wait a moment! The Ceyzériat caves, the Ceyzériat caves . . . we've got them.' And he placed his hat back on his head.

"The colonel broke into a smile. 'He's got them!' he said.

"Roland and Diana looked doubtfully at each other. They had less confidence in the old captain than did the colonel.

"'Let's hear what you have to say,' said Roland.

"'When the demagogues tried to demolish the church in Brou,' said the old captain, 'I came up with an idea.'

"'I'm not at all surprised,' said Roland.

"'It was a way to save not only our church but also the magnificent tombs inside.'

"'By doing what?'

"'By turning the church into a storeroom for fodder for the cavalry.'

"'I understand,' said Roland. 'Hay saved the marble. You are quite right, my friend, that was a great idea.'

"'So they turned the church over to me. And then I decided to visit it inside and out.'

"'We're listening religiously, Captain.'

"'Well, at one end of the crypt I discovered a small door opening onto a tunnel. After I walked about a quarter of a league, I found the tunnel was blocked by a gate, but on the other side were the Ceyzériat caves.'

"'I'll be damned,' said Roland. 'I'm beginning to see what you mean.'

"'Well, not me,' said the colonel of dragoons.

"'And yet it's quite obvious,' said Mademoiselle de Fargas.

"'Explain things to the colonel, Diana,' said Roland, 'and show him you did not waste your time while you were Cadoudal's aide-de-camp for two years.'

"'Yes, please explain,' said the colonel, spreading his legs apart, leaning on his sword, opening wide his eyes, and blinking, as he looked up.

"'Well,' said Mademoiselle de Fargas, 'with ten or fifteen men the captain will enter through the church in Brou and guard that entrance to the tunnel, whereas we will attack the outside entrance with twenty men or so. The Companions of Jehu will then attempt to escape by the other entrance which, they believe, is known only to them. There they will find the captain and his men. That's it, they're caught in the crossfire.'

"'Exactly,' said the captain, astonished that a mere woman could have come up with such a plan.

"'How stupid of me!' said the colonel in disgust. Roland nodded his agreement.

"Then he turned toward the captain. 'However, Captain, it is important for you to be at the church entrance ahead of time. The Companions don't go to the caves before nightfall, and they use only the outside entrance, of course. I shall go in with Mademoiselle de Fargas, and we shall be disguised as Chouans. I shall get the forty thousand francs. As we're leaving, thanks to the password that will let me approach the two sentinels, I shall silence them with my knife. We shall hide the forty thousand francs or entrust them to a gendarme. Then we shall turn around, go back into the caves, and attack the Companions. When they realize there's a surprise attack, they will try to escape, but at the gate they will find their way blocked by the captain and his gendarmes. They will either have to surrender or be killed, from the first to the last man.'

"'I'll be at my post this morning before daybreak,' said the captain. 'I'll take along enough food for the entire day. And battle tonight!' He drew his sword and struck the wall several times. Then he returned the sword to its sheath.

"Roland allowed the old soldier some time for his heroic gestures, and when the soldier had calmed down, he slapped him on the shoulder. 'There will be no changes to our plans. At midnight, Mademoiselle de Fargas and I shall enter the caves to get our money, and a quarter of an hour later, with the first gunshot you hear, there will be battle, as you say, my good captain.'

"'Battle!' the colonel of dragoons echoed.

"Once more Roland went over what they had agreed upon so that everyone knew exactly what to do. Then he took leave of the two officers, the captain of the gendarmerie, whom he would see only in the caves, and the colonel of dragoons, whom he would not see until two thirty.

"Everything happened the way it had been arranged. Diana de Fargas and Roland, using the identities and costumes of Bruyère and Branche-d'Or, entered the Ceyzériat caves after exchanging the watchwords with the two sentinels, one at the base of the mountain and the other at the cave entrance.

"Inside, they learned something disappointing: Morgan had had to leave. Montbar and the two other leaders, d'Assas and Adler, were governing in his absence. They suspected nothing and handed the forty thousand francs over to Diana and Roland.

"It was clear that the Companions were planning to bivouac that night in the caves. But without their chief leader. So no matter how successfully Roland and Diana accomplished their mission, their victory would be incomplete if they were unable to take Morgan along with the others.

"Might Morgan come back during the night? If he were to, when? With their plans already set in motion, Roland and Diana decided to proceed, as it would be better to capture three leaders than to let four of them escape. Further, unless Morgan left the country, it would be easier to take him alone rather than with three other leaders and their band. Once Morgan realized how isolated he was, perhaps he would surrender.

"Thanks to the watchwords, Roland was able to again approach the sentinel at the cave's entrance without arousing suspicion. After a brief exchange, the sentinel collapsed and fell facedown on the ground. Roland had knifed him. The second fell like the first, without a cry.

"Then, on hearing the agreed-upon signal, the colonel appeared with his twenty dragoons. Though not an intelligent man, the colonel was a veteran soldier as brave as his sword, which he had drawn as he advanced at the head of his men. Roland joined him on his right, Diana on his left.

"They had not taken more than ten steps into the cave when two gunshots rang out. The fire came from one of the stagecoach thieves who, sent by Montbar to Ceyzériat village, had just then happened upon Roland's dragoons. One of the shots went wild; the other broke a man's arm.

"'To arms!' someone shouted; and a man rushed into one of the twenty or thirty rooms on either side of the main tunnel where torches flickered on the walls; his rifle was still smoking. 'To arms!' he shouted. 'To arms! It's the dragoons!'

"'I'll take command,' cried Montbar. 'Put out all the lights! Retreat toward the church!'

"They all promptly obeyed; they understood the danger. Hard on the heels of Montbar, who knew the tunnel's every twist and turn, they followed him deeper and deeper into the caves.

"Suddenly, Montbar thought he heard, some forty yards ahead, someone whisper an order—and then the sound of guns being cocked. 'Halt!' he said, his voice tense, his hand raised.

"'Fire!' ordered a voice up ahead.

"'Facedown!' shouted Montbar.

"Scarcely had they dropped to the floor than the tunnel was lit by a terrible explosion. All those who'd had the time to obey Montbar's order heard the bullets whistle over their heads. Among those who had not, two or three collapsed. In the light of the explosion, brief though it was, Montbar and his companions recognized the uniform of the gendarmes.

"'Fire!' Montbar shouted in turn.

"Twelve or fifteen shots rang out, and once again the dark vault grew bright. Three of the Companions of Jehu lay stretched out on the ground.

"'Our escape has been cut off,' said Montbar. 'We must go back. Our only chance, if we have one, is through the forest.'

"As Montbar and his companions, at a run, started back, a second volley from the gendarmes shook the tunnel. A couple of sighs and the sound of a body hitting the ground evidenced that it had not been without effect.

"'Forward, my friends!' Montbar cried. 'Let's sell our lives for what they're worth, as dearly as possible.'

"'Forward!' his companions repeated.

"But as they moved forward, Montbar was worried by the smell of smoke. 'I think those scoundrels are trying to smoke us out,' he said.

"'I'm afraid so,' Adler agreed.

"'They must think they're dealing with foxes.'

"'When they see our claws, they'll know we are lions.'

"The more they advanced, the thicker the smoke rose, and the brighter grew the glow. They made the final turn. About fifty paces from the opening to the cave, a large fire, set more for its light than for smoke, was burning. In the light of the fire, they could see the dragoons' guns and swords gleaming.

"'And now we shall die,' cried Montbar. 'But first let us kill!'

"He was the first to leap into the circle of light, shooting from both barrels of his shotgun into the dragoons. Then, the emptied shotgun tossed aside, he pulled his pistols from his belt and, lowering his head, rushed toward the dragoons."

"I won't even try," said the young count to Claire, "to tell you everything that happened then. It was a horrible battle, the swearing and cursing and shouting like the skies rumbling, the pistol shots like bolts of lightning. And when the pistols had been all discharged, they turned to the daggers.

"The gendarmes joined the battle, wielding their weapons in the dense, smoky red air, stumbling, falling, getting back up, falling once more. You could hear roars of rage and cries of agony. And sometimes a man's last gasp.

"The killing lasted about a quarter of an hour, maybe twenty minutes. At the end, twenty-two bodies lay dead in the Ceyzériat caves. Thirteen of them were dragoons or gendarmes; nine were Companions of Jehu.

"Overwhelmed by numbers, only five Companions had survived. They had been taken alive, and Mademoiselle de Fargas regarded them as might the ancients' Nemesis, while the gendarmes and dragoons, swords in hand, surrounded them.

"The old captain's arm was broken, and the colonel had been shot in the thigh. Roland, covered with the blood of his opponents, had not sustained even a scratch.

"Torches were lit, and they all started back toward town. Two of the prisoners had to be carried on stretchers because they were unable to walk.

"As the weary procession was reaching the highway, a horse came galloping toward them. Roland stopped. 'Keep moving,' he said. 'I'll stay to see who this is.'

"When the horseman was about twenty paces away, Roland called out, 'Who's there?'

"'One more prisoner, monsieur,' the horseman answered. 'I was not able to be present for the battle, so I insist on being present at the scaffold! Where are my friends?'

"'Here, monsieur,' said Roland.

"'Please excuse me, monsieur,' Morgan said. 'I would like to claim my rightful place with my three friends, the Vicomte de Jahiat, the Comte de Valensolles, and the Marquis de Ribier. . . . I am the Comte Charles de Sainte-Hermine.'

"The three prisoners cried out in admiration. Diana cried out in joy. She now had all her prey; not one of the four leaders had escaped.

"The same night, according to the promise Roland had made to Diana and she to Cadoudal, the one hundred thousand francs from the Companions of Jehu left for Brittany.

"Now that the Companions of Jehu were in the hands of justice, Roland's mission was completed. He came back to his post with the First Consul, then left for Brittany, where in vain he tried to persuade Cadoudal to join the Republican cause, returned to Paris, and accompanied the First Consul on his Italian campaign, in which he was killed at Marengo.

"As for Diana de Fargas, she was too caught up in her hatred and too thirsty for vengeance not to savor it until the bitter end. The trial would soon get under way, come to its conclusion, and end with a quadruple execution that she would most assuredly not miss.

"In Besançon I was alerted that my brother had been arrested, and I hurried to Bourg-en-Bresse where the jury would be meeting. The investigation began. There were six prisoners in all, the five who had been taken in the caves and the one who had joined them voluntarily. Two were so seriously wounded that within a week of their arrest they died from their injuries.

"At first the four remaining Companions were to be judged by a military tribunal and condemned to the firing squad, but the law intervened, declaring that political crimes would now be tried by civil courts. Thus the sentence would be the scaffold. The guillotine is ignominious; the firing squad is not. In a military court, the prisoners would have admitted everything; in the civil court, they denied all.

"Arrested under the names d'Assas, Adler, Montbar, and Morgan, they declared that they did not recognize those names. They said they were:

Louis-André de Jahiat, born in Bâgé-le-Châtel in the Ain, twenty-seven years of age; Raoul-Frédéric-Auguste de Valensolles, born in Sainte-Colombe in the Rhône, twenty-nine years of age; Pierre-Auguste de Ribier, born in Bollène in the Vaucluse, twenty-six years of age; and Charles de Sainte-Hermine, born in Besançon in the Doubs, twenty-four years of age."

XVIII
Charles de Sainte-Hermine [2]

"THE PRISONERS ADMITTED they belonged to a group that had joined Monsieur de Teyssonnet, who was gathering an army in the Auvergne mountains. But they categorically denied that they had ever had the slightest connection with the stagecoach thieves named d'Assas, Adler, Montbar, and Morgan. They could make such brazen declarations because the stagecoaches had always been robbed by masked men. In only one case had the face of one of the leaders ever been seen, and that was my brother's face.

"When they attacked the stagecoach running between Lyon and Vienne, a boy of about ten or twelve, who was in the cabriolet with the coachman, picked up the coachman's pistol and shot at the Companions of Jehu. But the coachman, having foreseen just such a situation, had been careful not to load any bullets in his pistols. The boy's mother, unaware of the coachman's precaution, was so afraid for her son that she had fainted. My brother immediately tried to help her—he gave her some salts to breathe and tried to calm her shaken nerves—but as she thrashed about, she inadvertently knocked off Morgan's mask and had been able to see Sainte-Hermine's face.

"Throughout the trial, the public had great sympathy for the accused men. Each man's alibi was proven by letters and witnesses, and the woman who had seen the bandit Morgan's face declared that he was not among the four accused men. Furthermore, nobody had been harmed by their attacks, and nothing was taken but the treasure, and no one cared much about the treasure since there was no way of knowing who it belonged to really.

"The four men were about to be acquitted, when the president, turning unexpectedly to the woman who had fainted, asked, 'Madame, would you be so good as to tell the court which of these gentlemen was gallant enough to provide the help you needed when you felt faint?' The woman, caught unawares by the question, perhaps thought that while she was absent the four accused had admitted who they were. Or maybe she thought it a ploy to attract more sympathy for the accused men. Whatever she thought, she pointed to my brother and said, 'Monsieur le Président, it was Monsieur le Comte de Sainte-Hermine.'

"Thus, the four accused men, all of them protected by the same indivisible alibi, were all of them brought down together and delivered to the hand of the executioner. 'By Jove, *Capitaine,*' said de Jahiat, stressing the word 'captain,' 'that will teach you what being gallant is all about.'

"One cry of joy arose in the courtroom. Diana de Fargas was triumphant.

"'Madame'—my brother bowed to the woman who had identified him—'you have just caused four heads to fall with one single blow.' Realizing what she had done, the woman fell to her knees and begged for forgiveness. But it was too late!

"I was in the audience that day, and felt about to faint myself. I also felt undying love for my brother.

"On that very day, the four condemned men were sentenced to death.

"Three of them refused to appeal. The fourth, Jahiat, resolutely did not. He told his companions he had a plan; and so they'd not attribute the delay he'd requested to any fear of dying, he explained that he was in the process of seducing the jailer's daughter and that he hoped, with her, to find a way of escaping during the six or eight weeks the appeal would take. The three others, no longer objecting, joined with Jahiat and signed the papers requesting an appeal.

"Once they had latched on to the idea of escape, the four young souls clung to the possibility of life. It was not that they feared death, but death on the scaffold held no appeal as it lacked honor and conferred no prestige. So they encouraged Jahiat on their behalf to pursue his work of seduction, and in the meantime they tried to enjoy what was left of life as much as they could.

"The appeal did not offer much hope. For the First Consul had declared clearly his intention to crush all those bands of Royalist sympathizers until he had wiped them out completely.

"I myself exhausted all possible steps and every prayer to reach my brother. It was impossible.

"The accused men were ideal, I must say, as objects for everyone's sympathies. They were young and handsome; they dressed in the latest fashion. They were confident without being haughty: all smiles with the public and polite with their judges, although they did sometimes make fun about what was happening. Not to mention that they belonged to some of the most important families of the province.

"The four accused men, the oldest of them not yet thirty, who had defended themselves against the guillotine but not against the firing squad, who had admitted they might deserve death but who asked to die as soldiers, composed an attractive tableau of youth, courage, and magnanimity.

"As everyone expected, their appeal was denied.

"Jahiat had managed to win the love of Charlotte, the jailer's daughter, but the lovely girl's influence over her father was not so great that she could arrange a means for the prisoners to escape. Not that Comptois, the chief jailer, didn't pity the young men. He was a good man, a Royalist at heart, but, above all, an honest man. He would have given his right arm to prevent the misfortune befalling his four prisoners, but he refused sixty thousand francs to help them escape.

"Three gunshots fired outside the prison conveyed the news to the condemned men that their sentence had been upheld. That night, Charlotte brought each of the prisoners a pair of loaded pistols and a dagger; it was all the poor girl was able to do.

"The three gunshots and the imminent execution of the four condemned but admired young men alarmed the commissioner, and he requested the largest group of armed men that could be mustered. At six in the morning, as the scaffold was being constructed in the Place du Bastion, sixty horsemen stood ready for battle just outside the gate to the prison courtyard. Behind them, more than a thousand people were amassing in the square.

"The execution was set for seven o'clock. At six, the jailers entered the condemned men's cells. The evening before, they had left their prisoners in shackles and without weapons. Only now they stood free of their shackles, and they were armed to the teeth. Their suspenders were crossed over their bared chests, their wide belts bristled with weapons.

"When it was least expected, the crowd heard what sounded like fighting. Then they saw the four condemned men burst forth from the prison. The crowd cried out as one—in awe, in fear—for surely something terrible was about to happen, these four prisoners looking like gladiators entering the ring.

"I managed to push my way to the front row. I saw them cross the courtyard. They saw that the enormous gate was closed and that on the other side of it, in an unbreakable line, gendarmes were standing motionless with their rifles at their knees.

"The four men stopped, put their heads together; seemed to confer for a moment.

"Then Valensolles, the oldest, strode up to the gate, and with a gracious smile and noble bow, he greeted the horsemen: 'Very well, gentlemen of the Gendarmerie.' Then, turning toward his three companions, he said:

'Adieu, my friends.' And then he blew his brains out. His body did three pirouettes, and he fell facedown to the ground.

"Next, Jahiat left his companions and walked over to the gate, where he cocked his own two pistols and pointed them toward the gendarmes. He did not shoot, but five or six gendarmes, thinking they were in danger, lowered their rifles and fired. Two bullets pierced Jahiat's body. 'Thank you, gentlemen,' he said. 'Thanks to you I can die like a soldier.' And he collapsed onto Valensolles's body.

"In the meantime, Ribier had seemed to be trying to determine how he in his turn would die. Finally, he appeared to have come to a decision.

"He eyed a column in the courtyard. Ribier walked straight over to it, pulled the dagger from his belt, placed the point against the left side of his chest and set the handle against the column. Then he took the column in his arms, and after he'd saluted the spectators and his friends one last time, with his arms he squeezed the column until the dagger's blade had completely disappeared into his breast. For a moment he remained standing. Soon, though, his face turned ghastly pale, and his arms loosened their hold on the pillar. His knees buckled. He fell, dead.

"The crowd stood mute, frozen in terror at the same time it was rapt in admiration. Everyone understood that these heroic men were willing to die, but that like ancient Roman gladiators, they wanted to die honorably.

"My brother was the last of them. As he surveyed the crowd he caught sight of me. He put his finger to his mouth, and I realized that he was asking me to stay strong and keep quiet. I nodded, but in spite of myself tears coursed down my cheeks. He motioned that he wished to speak. Everyone grew silent.

"When you witness a spectacle of that kind, you are as eager to hear words as to see action, for words help to explain actions. Still, what more could the crowd ask for? They had been promised four heads, all four falling uniformly and monotonously in the same manner. Instead, they were now being given four different deaths, each one more inventive, dramatic, and unexpected than the one before. The crowd knew that this last hero planned to die in a way at least as original as the other three.

"Charles held neither pistol nor dagger in his hands, though his belt held both. He walked around Valensolles's body, then stood between the bodies of the other two, Jahiat and Ribier. Like an actor in a theater, he bowed grandly and smiled at the spectators.

"The crowd erupted in applause. Eager as everyone was to see what was coming, not a single person among them, I dare say, would not have given a portion of his own life to save the life of the last Companion of Jehu.

"'Gentlemen,' said Charles, and God only knows the anguish I felt as I listened to him, 'you have come to see us die, and you have already seen three of us fall. Now it is my turn. I ask nothing better than to satisfy your curiosity, but I've come to propose a deal.'

"'Speak! Speak!' people shouted from all sides. 'Whatever you ask will be granted.'

"'All but your life!' cried a woman's voice—the same voice that had expressed triumph and joy at the sentencing.

"'All but my life, of course,' my brother repeated. 'You saw my friend Valensolles blow out his brains, you saw my friend Jahiat get shot, you saw my friend Ribier stab himself, and you would like to see me die on the guillotine. I can understand that.' His calm demeanor and sardonic words, spoken with no emotion, sent a shiver through the crowd.

"'Well,' Charles went on, 'like a good sport I would like to die at your pleasure as much as at my own. I am prepared to have my head fall, but I wish to walk to the scaffold on my own, as if I were going to a meal or a ball, and, as an absolute condition, without anyone touching me. If anyone comes near'—he pointed to the two pistols in his belt—'I shall kill him. Except for this man,' Charles continued, looking over to the executioner. 'This business is between him and me, and proper procedures need to be followed.'

"The crowd seemed to accept the condition, for on all sides people shouted: 'Yes! Yes! Yes!'

"'Do you hear?' Charles addressed the officer of the gendarmerie. 'Indulge me, Captain, and things will be fine.'

"The officer wanted nothing better than to make some concessions. 'If I leave your hands and feet free,' he said, 'do you promise to attempt no escape?'

"'I give you my word of honor,' said Charles.

"'Well, then,' said the officer. 'Move aside and let us carry off the bodies of your companions.'

"'Yes, that's only right,' said Charles. Then, turning toward the crowd, he noted: "You see, it's not my fault. I am not the cause of the delay; rather, these gentlemen are.' He gestured toward the executioner and his two helpers loading the bodies on a cart.

"Ribier was not yet dead. He opened his eyes, as if he were looking for someone. Charles took his hand. 'Here I am, good friend,' he said. 'Rest assured, I am joining you!' Ribier's eyes closed again; and his lips moved, but no sound came from them, only a reddish foam.

"'Monsieur de Sainte-Hermine,' said the brigadier when the three bodies had been removed. 'Are you ready?'

"'I await you, monsieur,' Charles answered, bowing with exquisite politeness.

"'In that case, please step forward.' Charles moved to the middle of the gendarmes.

"'Would you prefer to go by carriage?' said the officer.

"'By foot, monsieur. By foot. I want these people to know that I myself am allowing this extravaganza at the guillotine. Were I in a vehicle, people might think that fear kept me from walking.'

"The guillotine had been set up on the Place du Bastion. They crossed the Place des Lices, which takes its name from the carousel that stood there in older times, and then walked along the walls beside the gardens of the Hôtel Monbazon. The cart came first, then a detachment of ten dragoons. Then the condemned man, who now and then glanced over at me. Then, about ten paces behind, the gendarmes, led by their captain.

"At the end of the garden wall, the cortege turned to the left. And suddenly, through the opening between the garden and the grand hall, my brother caught a glimpse of the scaffold—and I could feel my own knees buckle. 'Bah!' he said. 'I had never seen a guillotine. I did not realize they were so ugly.'

"Then, as quickly as a passing thought, he pulled the dagger from his belt and plunged it to the hilt into his chest.

"The captain spurred his horse and reached out to stop him, while the Comte pulled one of the double-barreled pistols from his belt and cocked it, saying: 'Stop! We agreed that nobody would touch me. I will die alone, or three of us will die together. The choice is yours.'

"The captain stopped his horse and pulled it back.

"'Let's keep walking,' said my brother.

"With my eyes fixed on my beloved brother and my ears straining to hear his every word as my mind recorded every gesture, I remembered again what Charles had written to Cadoudal: how he had refused to allow me to learn my military career at Cadoudal's side; hoe he'd said that he was keeping me in reserve so that I could avenge his death and continue his work. I kept swearing under my breath that I would do what he expected of me, and from time to time a glance from him strengthened my resolve.

"In the meantime, he kept walking, blood dripping from his wound.

"When he reached the foot of the scaffold, Charles pulled the dagger from the wound and stabbed himself a second time. Still he remained standing. 'Truly,' he raged, 'my soul must be firmly set in my body.'

"The helpers waiting on the scaffold removed the bodies of Valensolles, Jahiat, and Ribier from the cart. At the guillotine the heads of the first two, already corpses, fell without a single drop of blood. Ribier, though, let out a groan, and when his head was cut off, blood gushed out. The crowd shivered.

"Then it was my brother's turn. As he waited he had kept his eyes on me almost constantly, even when the executioner's assistants tried to pull him up onto the scaffold, and he said: 'Don't touch me. That was our agreement.'

"He climbed the six steps without stumbling. When he reached the platform, he pulled the dagger from his chest and stabbed himself a third time. He let out a horrible laugh that came accompanied by spurts of blood from all three wounds. 'Well, that's it,' he said to the executioner. 'That should be enough. Manage as best you can.'

"Then, turning to me, he cried, 'Do you remember, Hector?'

"'Yes, my brother,' I answered.

"With no help, he lay down on the deadly plank. 'There,' he said to the executioner. 'Is this acceptable?'

"The falling blade was the answer. But, filled with that implacable vitality that had kept my brother from dying at his own hand, his head, instead of falling into the basket with the others, bounced over its rim, rolled along the platform, and dropped to the ground.

"I burst through the row of soldiers restraining the crowd from the open space between them and the scaffold. As quickly as I could, before anyone could stop me, I picked up that dearly beloved head in my two hands and kissed it.

"His eyes opened and his lips moved beneath my own—Oh! I swear to God, his head recognized me. 'Yes, yes, yes!' I said. 'You can be sure that I will obey you.'

"The soldiers had made a movement to stop me, but several voices had shouted out: 'It's his brother!' And all the soldiers stayed where they were."

XIX

The End of Hector's Story

❧

HECTOR HAD NOW BEEN speaking for two hours. Claire was weeping so profusely that he wasn't sure he should continue. He paused. The tears pearling in his eyes showed what he was thinking.

"Oh, please go on! Go on!" she said.

"It would be according me a great favor," he said, "for I have not yet said anything about myself."

Claire reached out her hand to him. "How you have suffered," she murmured.

"Wait," he said, "and you will see that you are just the person to make me forget it all."

"I didn't know Valensolles, Jahiat, and Ribier very well, only by sight. But through their association with my brother, who had joined them in death, they were my friends. I gave them all a proper burial. Then I returned to Besançon. I put our family affairs in order and began to wait. What was I waiting for? I didn't know what, only that it was something on which my fate would depend. I didn't think it necessary that I go looking for it, but I felt compelled to be ready whenever it should come.

"One morning, the Chevalier de Mahalin was announced. I did not recognize the name, and yet in my heart a painful chord began to vibrate as if it bore for me a strange familiarity. The man behind the name was young, twenty-five or twenty-six, perfectly attired, and irreproachably polite.

"'Monsieur le Comte,' he said, 'you know that the Company of Jehu, so painfully smitten by the loss of its four leaders, and especially your brother, is beginning to reform. Its leader is the famous Laurent, though beneath that ordinary name hides one of the most aristocratic family names of the South. Our captain is reserving an important place in his army for you, and he has sent me to ask if you would like, by joining us, to keep the promise given by your brother.'

"'Monsieur le Chevalier,' I answered, 'I would be lying if I told you that I have much enthusiasm for the life of a wandering cavalier, but as I did promise my brother, and as my brother promised me to your cause, I am ready.'

"'Shall I tell you, then, where we are meeting?' asked the Chevalier de Mahalin. 'Or are you coming now with me?'

"'I am coming now with you, monsieur.'

"I had a trusty servant named Saint-Bris. He had served my brother too, and I installed him in our house and left him master of it all, making him really more my steward than my servant. That done, I gathered up my weapons, climbed on my horse, and rode off.

"We were to meet Laurent somewhere between Vizille and Grenoble. In two days' time, we were there.

"Laurent, our chief, was truly worthy of his reputation. He was like one of those men to whose baptism fairies are invited, and each one blesses him with a virtuous quality, but there's always one fairy who's been overlooked and he arrives to burthen the infant with the one defect that counterbalances all of his virtues. Laurent had been endowed with that beauty typical of the South and typically masculine: brilliant eyes, lustrous dark hair, and a thick dark beard, his fiercely handsome face tempered by a charming blend of kindness, strength, and affability. Left on his own when he was scarcely beyond his tumultuous youth, he lacked a solid formal education, but he was worldly-wise, and he possessed a nobleman's grace and politesse, as well as a charismatic quality that naturally attracted people to his fold. But he was also unusually violent and quick-tempered. As much as his gentleman's education normally kept him within acceptable boundaries, he would still frequently, suddenly, explode; and an angry Laurent, the imperfect Laurent, appeared to be no longer of humankind. And the rumor would spread, wherever he happened to be: 'Laurent is angry; men will die.'

"Justice was as concerned about Laurent's band as it had been about Saint-Hermine's group. Large forces were deployed. Laurent and seventy-one of his men were captured and sent to Yssingeaux in the Haute-Loire to answer for their actions before a special court convened expressly for their trial.

"But Bonaparte was still in Egypt then. Power resided in weak hands, and the little town of Yssingeaux treated Laurent and his band more like a garrison than like prisoners. The prosecution was timid, the witnesses were ineffectual, the defense was bold. It was led by Laurent himself, who took responsibility for everything. His seventy-one companions were acquitted; he was sentenced to death.

"Laurent returned to the prison as nonchalantly as he had left. By then, the supreme beauty with which Nature had endowed him, the *corporal recommendation*, as Montaigne has called it, had already produced its effect. Every woman in Yssingeaux felt sorry for him, and for more than a few of them, pity had transferred itself into a much more tender feeling. Such was the case of the jailer's daughter, although Laurent was not aware of it.

"Two hours after midnight, Laurent's cell door opened as it had for Pierre de Médicis, and the girl from Yssingeaux, like the girl in Ferrare, spoke these sweet words: 'Non temo nulla, bentivoglio!' ('Have no fear, I love you!') His angel savior had seen him only through the prison bars, but his magnetic seductive powers had touched her heart and ruled her senses. A few words were exchanged; so were rings. And Laurent walked free.

"A horse was waiting in a neighboring village, she'd told him, and there she would meet him. Dawn broke. As he fled through the shadows, Laurent caught a glimpse of the executioner and his helpers setting up the deadly machine. For he was supposed to be executed at ten that morning, the execution having been rushed to take place only one day after the sentencing so as to coincide with market day, when everyone from the neighboring villages would be in Yssingeaux. Of course, when the sun's first rays struck the guillotine in the square, and when the identity of the illustrious prisoner who'd climb the steps to the platform became known, no one was giving any more thought to the market.

"Waiting in the nearby village, Laurent worried not for himself but for the woman who had saved him. Laurent became impatient. Several times he rode out toward Yssingeaux, each time riding closer to the town, to try to get information, but without success. Finally, caught up in the heat of the moment, he lost his head: He assumed that his savior had herself been captured and that she, as his accomplice, would in his place be climbing the scaffold to the guillotine. So he rides into town, his horse spurred to a gallop, and as he passes by, people shout in astonishment when they realize that the man they were expecting to see guillotined is riding free on horseback. He rides past the gendarmes who'd been posted to escort him from his cell; he reaches the square where the scaffold awaits him, and espying the woman he's looking for, he pushes his way to her, reaches down, pulls her up behind him, and gallops off to the cheers of the whole town. All those who had come to applaud his head as it fell were now applauding his flight, his escape, his salvation.

"That is what our leader was like, the leader who followed my brother. Such was the man under whose tutelage I learned to fight.

"For three months I lived daily under the strain of our battles and at night I slept wrapped up in my coat, my hand on my gun, pistols in my belt. Then the rumor of a truce began to spread. I came to Paris, promising to return to my companions at the first call. I came because I had seen you once—please excuse my frankness—and I needed, I yearned, to see you again.

"I did of course see you again, but if by chance your eyes happened to fall on me, you surely remember my face betrayed my deep sadness, my unconcern, and I might even say my apparent distaste for all of life's pleasures. For how indeed, given the precarious position in which I found myself—obeying not my own conscience but another fatal, absolute, imperious power that exposed me to the possibility of being wounded if not killed in a stagecoach attack, or, even worse, being captured—how could I dare say to a lovely, sweet girl, the flower of the world in which she blossoms and the laws of which she accepts, how could I dare say to her: 'I love you. Are you willing to accept a husband who has placed himself outside the law, for whom the greatest happiness possible is to be shot dead in cold blood?'

"No, I could not declare my love. I had to be content just to be able to see you, to be intoxicated by the sight of you, to be where you were likely to be, and all the while pray that God would accomplish a miracle, that the rumored truce would become real peace, though I hardly dared to hope.

"Finally, about four or five days ago, the newspapers announced that

Cadoudal had come to Paris, that he had met with the First Consul. The same evening the same newspapers reported that the Breton general had given his word to no longer attempt any action against France, if the First Consul, for his part, would take no further action against Brittany or against him.

"The next day"—Hector pulled a sheet of paper from his pocket—"the next day I received this circular letter written in Cadoudal's own hand:

"'Because a protracted war seems to be a misfortune for France and ruin for my region, I free you from your oath of loyalty to me. I shall never call you back unless the French government should fail to keep the promise it gave to me and that I accepted in your name.

"'If there should happen to be some treason hidden beneath a hypocritical peace, I would not hesitate to call once more on your fidelity, and your fidelity, I am sure, would respond.'

"You can imagine my joy when I received this leave. Once again I would be in control of my own person; no longer was I promised by the word of my father and my two brothers to a monarchy that I knew only through my family's devotion and through the misfortunes that devotion had brought down upon our house. I was twenty-three years old; I had an annual income of one hundred thousand francs. I was in love, and supposing that I was also loved, the gates of paradise that had long been guarded by the angel of death were now opening up before me. Oh, Claire! Claire! That is why I was so happy when you saw me at Madame de Permon's ball. I could finally ask you to meet me like this. Finally I could tell you that I loved you."

Claire lowered her eyes and made no answer, which in itself was almost an answer.

"Now," Hector went on, "everything I have just told you, all these histories hidden away out in the provinces, is completely unknown in Paris. I could have kept it hidden from you, but I chose not to. I wanted to tell you my whole life's story, to explain by what destiny I was led finally to make my confession to you—knowing that you might suppose my actions to be a mistake or even a crime—so that I might receive absolution from your own lips."

"Oh, Hector dear!" cried Claire, carried away by the quiet passion that had been governing her for nearly a year. "Oh, yes, I forgive you! I absolve you," and forgetting that she was under her mother's watchful eyes, she added, "I love you!" And threw her arms around his neck.

"Claire!" cried Madame de Sourdis, her voice showing more surprise than anger.

"Mother!" answered Claire, blushing and about to faint.

"Claire!" said Hector, taking her hand. "Don't forget that everything I have told you is for you alone. It must be a secret between us, and since I love only you, I have no need for forgiveness from anyone but you. Do not forget. And especially, remember that I shall be truly alive only when I receive your mother's answer to the request I have made. Claire, you have told me that you love me. I am placing our happiness in your love's hands."

Without another word Hector left. But his heart, athrill with the freedom and joy of a prisoner whose death sentence has just been commuted, was not silent.

Madame de Sourdis was waiting impatiently for her daughter. Claire's spontaneity, when she threw herself into the arms of the young Comte de Sainte-Hermine, had seemed out of character. She wanted an explanation.

The explanation was clear and rapid. When the girl reached her mother, she simply dropped to her knees and pronounced these three words: "I love him!"

Our characters are molded by nature to prepare us for the times we need them to survive. It was thanks to such natural strength that Charlotte Corday and Madame Roland were able to say, one to Marat and the other to Robespierre: "I hate you." Likewise, Claire could say to Hector: "I love you."

Madame de Sourdis helped Claire up from her knees, had her sit down next to her, and then questioned her, but these are the only words the mother got out of her daughter: "My dear mother, Hector told me a family secret that he believes he must hide from everyone except the girl he wants to make his wife. I am that girl. He solicits the favor of coming to ask your permission for a marriage we desire more than anything. He is free, he has an annual income of one hundred thousand francs, and we love each other. Think about it, Mother dear. But a refusal on your part would be a calamity for both of us!"

Having spoken firmly but respectfully, Claire then bowed to her mother and started to walk away.

"And if I say yes?" said Madame de Sourdis.

"Oh, Mother," cried Claire, throwing herself into her arms, "how good you are and how I love you!"

"And now that I have reassured your heart," Madame de Soudis said, "sit down and let us speak reasonably."

Madame de Sourdis seated herself on a sofa. Claire sat in front of her, on a cushion, and took her mother's hands. "I'm all ears, Mother," said Claire with a smile.

"In times like ours," said Madame de Sourdis, "it is absolutely necessary to belong to some party. I believe that Hector de Sainte-Hermine numbers himself among the Royalists. Yesterday, when I was chatting with your godfather Dr. Cabanis, a great man of science who also has good sense, he congratulated me on the friendship Madame Bonaparte has for me. He believes strongly that you should likewise become as close as possible to her daughter Hortense. In his opinion, that is where your future lies.

"As you know, Cabanis is the First Consul's personal doctor, and he is convinced the First Consul, in his genius, will not be content to stay where he is situated now. A man does not risk something like the 18th Brumaire just to sit in a consul's armchair; he does it rather to rule from a throne. So those who attach themselves to Bonaparte's star before the veil of the future is rent will be carried along with him in the whirlwind of his destiny; along with him they will rise.

"The First Consul, we know, loves to bring great families, rich families, over to his side. In that regard, Sainte-Hermine leaves nothing to be desired. He has an income of one hundred thousand francs; his family goes back to the Crusades. His entire family, too, has died for the Royalist cause, so truly, he owes nothing more to their campaign. He is of an age that has allowed him to remain thus far outside of political events. Whereas his father and two brothers all gave their lives for old France, he has not yet pledged anything to any party. It is up to him, then, by accepting a position with the First Consul, to live for new France.

"Please note that I am not making this step on his part a condition for your marriage. I would be more than pleased to see Hector join the side of the First Consul. If he refuses, however, it is because his conscience tells him that he must, and only God can judge the human conscience. Whichever path he chooses, he will be my daughter's husband nonetheless, and no less will he be my beloved son-in-law."

"When might I write to him, Mother?" Claire asked.

"Whenever you like, my child," answered her mother.

That very evening, Claire sent him a message, and the next day before noon, as soon as he could appropriately appear, Hector was knocking again at the front door.

This time he was taken directly to see Madame de Sourdis, who welcomed him with open arms, like a mother. They were still holding each other tightly when Claire opened the door, and seeing them, she cried, "Oh, Mother. How happy I am!" Madame de Sourdis again opened her arms, so that she could embrace both of her children.

The marriage was agreed upon. All that was left to discuss with the young Comte was the matter of his joining the First Consul's administration.

Hector, with Madame de Sourdis on his left and Claire on his right, was

seated on the sofa with his future mother-in-law's hand in his on one side
and his fiancée's on the other. Claire took it upon herself to explain to Hector the high opinion that Dr. Cabanis held of Bonaparte and to present
Madame de Sourdis's hope regarding Hector's future. Hector kept his eyes
fixed attentively on Claire as she tried to repeat word for word her mother's
reasoning on the matter.

When she had finished, Hector bowed to Madame de Sourdis, and looking even more intently at Claire than he had while she was speaking, he
said, "Claire, based on what I told you yesterday, and I am not sorry to
have gone on at such length, put yourself in my place and answer your
mother. Your answer will be my answer."

The girl thought for a moment and then threw herself into her mother's
arms. "Oh, Mother!" she cried, shaking her head. "He cannot. His
brother's blood flows between them."

Madame de Sourdis bowed her head. It was clear that she felt great disappointment. She had dreamed of a high rank in the army for her son-in-
law; and for her daughter, a high position at the court.

"Madame," said Hector, "please don't think that I am among those people who praise the old regime to the detriment of the current one, or that I
am blind to the First Consul's great qualities. I saw him the other day for
the first time at Madame de Permon's ball, and rather than feeling repulsed,
I was attracted to him. I admire his campaign of '96 and '97 as a masterpiece of modern strategy and an exemplar of his military genius. I am less
enthusiastic, I'll admit, about his Egyptian campaign, which could have no
happy outcome and was no more than a mask to cover his immense thirst
for fame: Bonaparte fought and won where Marius and Pompey had also
fought and won. By that, he hoped to awaken and amend ancient echoes that
for centuries had repeated no names but those of Alexander and Caesar.
How tempting. But it was an expensive fantasy that cost our country so much
money and so many men! As for the most recent campaign, at Marengo, that
was a campaign only for personal glory, undertaken to give a firm footing
to the legitimacy of the 18th Brumaire and to force foreign governments to
recognize the new French government. But, as everyone knows, Bonaparte
was not a military genius. He was lucky, like a gambler who is about to lose
and then draws two trump cards. And what trump cards they were! Kellermann and Desaix! The 18th Brumaire was no more than a conspiracy
whose lucky success in the end barely justifies its author's means. What if it
had failed? What if his attempt to overthrow the established government
had been ruled a rebellion, a crime of treason? Then in the Bonaparte family at least three heads would have rolled. Chance served him well when he
returned from Alexandria, fortune was on his side at Marengo, and his

boldness saved him in Saint-Cloud. But a temperate man, a man not blinded by passion, would never mistake three lightning flashes, however bright they might be, for the dawn of a great day. If I were completely free of my background, if my family had not stood firmly in the Royalist camp, I would have no objection to linking my own fortune to Bonaparte's, although I consider him an illustrious adventurer who once fought a war for France and two other times for himself. Now, to prove to you that I am not prejudiced against him, I promise that the first time he does something great for France I shall come over to his side. For to my great astonishment, and although I owe my most recent loss to him, I do admire him in spite of his faults and in spite of myself. That is the kind of influence that those of a superior nature exert upon those lesser beings around them, and I feel that influence."

"I understand," said Madame de Sourdis. "But will you at least permit one thing?"

"It is not for me to permit," said Hector, "but rather for you to order."

"Will you allow me to ask the First Consul and Madame Bonaparte for their assent to Claire's marriage? Connected as I am to Madame Bonaparte, I can hardly do otherwise. It is simply a step that etiquette demands."

"Yes, but on the condition that if they refuse, we will proceed anyway."

"If they refuse, you will carry off my darling Claire and I shall come to forgive you wherever you have taken her. But rest assured, they will not refuse me."

And with that assurance, permission was granted to Madame de Sourdis to seek the blessing of the First Consul and Madame Bonaparte on the marriage of Claire de Sourdis to Monsieur le Comte Hector de Sainte-Hermine.

XX

Fouché

THERE WAS ONE MAN whom Bonaparte hated, feared, and tolerated all at the same time. He is the man who appeared for a moment to talk to Mademoiselle de Fargas when she was setting her conditions for delivering up the Companions of Jehu.

Bonaparte, when he began pulling away from the influence of Fouché, was obeying that admirable instinct more typical of animals than of humans: to remove oneself from beasts that may prove to be harmful.

Joseph Fouché, Minister of the Police, was a creature both ugly and harmful. It is rare that what is ugly is good, and in Fouché's case, his morality, or rather his immorality, was equal to his ugliness.

Bonaparte saw men as nothing but means or obstacles to him. For Bonaparte the general, Fouché, on the 18th Brumaire, had been a means. For Bonaparte the First Consul, Fouché could indeed become an obstacle. He who had conspired against the Directory in favor of the Consulate might as easily conspire now against the Consulate in favor of some other government. Fouché had become a man whom Bonaparte needed to bring down after having raised him up, and given the current political situation, bringing him down would be difficult. For Fouché was one of those men who, as they climb, cling to every rough edge, hold on to every farrow, make every mark and scar their own so they never want any point of support at any level once they have arrived.

Indeed, Fouché was attached to the Republic by his vote to have the king killed; to the Terror, by his bloody incursions into Lyon and Nevers; to the Thermidorians, by his role in bringing down Robespierre; to Bonaparte, by his participation in the 18th Brumaire; and to Josephine, through the terror that had been inspired by Joseph and Lucien, Fouché's avowed enemies. He was attached to the Royalists by services he had rendered to individuals as Minister of the Police, after having attacked the class as a whole when he was proconsul. As director of public opinion, he had turned the office to his own uses, and his police, instead of serving the general populace, had become simply Fouché's police, a force in service to the minister's schemes. All over Paris, all over France, Fouché's agents sang in praise of his abilities. Stories of his extraordinary skill abounded, the best indicator of that skill being his ability to make everyone believe the stories to be true.

Fouché had been Minister of the Police since the 18th Brumaire. No one, not even Bonaparte himself, could understand how the First Consul could have allowed Fouché to have such powerful influence over him. The situation bothered Bonaparte increasingly. Outside Fouché's presence, when the minister's magnetism no longer had any effect, in his every cell Bonaparte rebelled against Fouché's sway. When the First Consul spoke of him, his words, cutting and spiteful, betrayed his anger. Yet when Fouché next appeared, the lion again lay down, calmed if not tamed.

One thing in particular bothered Bonaparte: Fouché never entered wholeheartedly into his grandiose plans, unlike his brothers Joseph and Lucien, who not only entered into them but helped to move them forward. One day, though, Bonaparte did have it out with Fouché.

"Be careful," the Minister of the Police had said, "if you restore the royalty, you will have worked for the Bourbons, for sooner or later they will get back on the throne that you have reestablished. Nobody would dare to prophesy what combination of lucky events and of cataclysms we might have to live through before that happened, but we need nothing more than our own intelligence to judge how long you and your descendants would need to fear such a possibility. You are moving rapidly in the direction of the old regime, in form if not in content, so that occupation of the throne will soon be just a question not of government but of which family sits in it. If France must give up its hard-fought-for freedom and return to the good pleasure of the monarchy, why should it not prefer the former race of kings that gave us Henri IV and Louis XIV? You have given France nothing but the despotism of the sword!"

Bonaparte bit his lip as he listened, but he did listen. And in that moment decided to abolish the Ministry of Police. On that very Monday, at his brother's insistence—he had gone to spend the day with his brother at Mortefontaine—he signed an abolition order and put it in his pocket.

The next day, on his return to Paris, though pleased with his decision, he knew what a blow it would be for Josephine. So he tried to be charming with her when he got back, which gave some hope to the poor woman, for whenever she looked beyond her husband's gaiety or sadness, beyond his ill humor or cheerfulness, she saw nothing but divorce.

Seated in her boudoir, he was giving orders to Bourrienne when she slipped over to him and, sitting in his lap, stroked his hair and then put her fingers near his mouth for him to kiss them. When his kiss met her burning hand, she asked, "Why did you not take me with you yesterday?"

"Where?" he asked.

"Wherever you went."

"I went to Mortefontaine, and since I know there's some hostility between you and Joseph. . . ."

"Oh, and you could also add between me and Lucien. I say Lucien as well as Joseph because both of them are hostile to me. I am not hostile to anyone. I could ask for nothing better than to get along with your two brothers, but they hate me. So you should realize how worried I am whenever you are with them."

"Relax. All we discussed yesterday was politics."

"Yes, politics. Like Caesar with Anthony. Did they try the wrappings of royalty on you?"

"What? You know Roman history?"

"My friend, all I know about Roman history concerns Caesar, and every time I read it I quake."

She was silent a moment. Bonaparte frowned, but there was no holding her back now that she had started: "Please, Bonaparte, I beg you, do not make yourself king. I know that evil Lucien is pressing you to do so, but you must not listen to him. It would be the end of all of us."

Bourrienne, who had often given the same advice to his schoolmate, was afraid that Bonaparte would fly into a rage. But instead, he began to laugh. "You're crazy, my poor Josephine," he said. "All those dowagers from the Faubourg Saint-German must be telling you such tales, as well as your La Rochefoucauld. Stop bothering me."

At that moment the Minister of Police was announced. "Do you have anything to say to him?" asked Bonaparte.

"No," said Josephine. "It's you he must be on his way to see; he no doubt wants merely to greet me in passing."

"When you've finished, send him to me," said Bonaparte, standing up. "Come, Bourrienne."

"If you have no secrets to tell him, why do you not see him right here? I'd have you longer here with me."

"Indeed, I was forgetting that Fouché is a friend of yours," said Bonaparte.

"A friend of mine?" remarked Josephine. "I do not allow myself friends among your ministers."

"Well," said Bonaparte, "he will not be a minister for long. But no, I have no secrets to impart." Then, turning toward Constant, who had announced Fouché, he said affectedly, "Show the Minister of Police in."

On entering, Fouché seemed surprised to find Bonaparte there with his wife. "Madame," Fouché said, "this morning my business is with you, not the First Consul."

"With me?" said Josephine in astonishment and with some worry.

"Oh," said Bonaparte. "Then let's see what this is all about." And to show that he had regained his earlier good humor, he pinched his wife's ear.

Tears welled in Josephine's eyes—why did Bonaparte have always to make his little love gesture so painful? But she kept her smile.

"Yesterday," said Fouché, "Dr. Cabanis came to see me."

"Good God!" said Bonaparte. "What made that benign philosopher venture into your den?"

"He came to ask if I believed, madame, before any official visit would be arranged, that a certain marriage in his family would have your blessing, and if it did, whether you would take it upon yourself to obtain the First Consul's consent."

"Well, now! You see, Josephine," said Bonaparte with a laugh, "people are already treating you like a queen."

"But," said Josephine, "thirty million French people can get married without the slightest objection from me. Who could be giving so much thought to etiquette as to check with me?"

"Madame la Comtesse de Sourdis, whom you honor sometimes by receiving her here. She is marrying her daughter Claire."

"To whom?"

"To the young Comte de Sainte-Hermine."

"Tell Cabanis," Josephine answered, "that I enthusiastically support their union, and unless Bonaparte has some reason not to approve it. . . ."

Bonaparte thought for a moment. Then, turning to Fouché: "Come up to my office," he said, "when you leave Madame. Come, Bourrienne."

Scarcely had Bonaparte and Bourrienne disappeared than Josephine, placing her hand on Fouché's arm, confided, "He went to Mortefontaine yesterday."

"Yes, I know," said Fouché.

"Do you know what he and his brothers talked about?"

"Yes."

"Was it about me? Did they talk about divorce?"

"No: Be reassured on that point. They were talking about something else entirely."

"Was it about the monarchy?"

"No."

Josephine sighed. "Well, in that case, little does it matter what they talked about!"

Fouché smiled that dark sardonic smile so characteristic of him. "However," he said, "since you will probably be losing one of your friends. . . ."

"Me?"

"Yes."

"I will?"

"Yes."

"Why?"

"Because he has protected your interests."

"Who are you talking about?"

"I cannot divulge his name. His disgrace is still a secret. I've come to warn you so you can choose someone else."

"Where do you expect me to find this other person?"

"In the First Consul's family. Two of his brothers are against you. Align yourself with the third."

"Louis?"

"Exactly."

"But Bonaparte insists on giving my daughter in marriage to Duroc."

"Yes, but Duroc does not seem quite so eager to enter into marriage, and his indifference is offensive to the First Consul."

"Hortense bursts into tears every time we talk about it. I don't want it to look like I am sacrificing my daughter; she says that she has given her heart."

"Well," said Fouché, "does anyone really have a heart?"

"Oh, I do!" said Josephine. "And I am proud of it."

"You?" said Fouché with his sarcastic laugh. "You don't have only one heart, you have. . . ."

"Careful!" said Josephine. "You are about to say something disrespectful."

"I'll not say a word. As Minister of Police, I must remain silent. Otherwise people might say I am revealing secrets from the confessional. So, as I've nothing further to tell you, allow me to go and announce to the First Consul some news he is not expecting to hear from my lips."

"What news?"

"Yesterday he signed an order for my resignation."

"So you are the person I shall be losing?" Josephine asked.

"Yes, that's correct," said Fouché.

The realization elicited a sigh from Josephine as she placed her hand over her eyes. "Oh, don't worry!" said Fouché, walking over to her. "It won't be for long."

In order not to display too great a familiarity, rather than taking the little stairway up to Bonaparte's office, Fouché left through Josephine's outside door, then came back in through the clock pavilion and went up to the First Consul's study.

The First Consul was working with Bourrienne. "Ah!" he said to Fouché as he came in, "you can explain something to me."

"What, sire?"

"Who this Sainte-Hermine is who's asking for my approval of his marriage with Mademoiselle de Sourdis."

"Let us understand one another, Citizen First Consul. It is not the Comte de Sainte-Hermine who is asking for your approval to marry Mademoiselle de Sourdis, but rather Mademoiselle de Sourdis who is asking for your approval to marry Monsieur de Sainte-Hermine."

"Is that not the same thing?"

"Not entirely. The Sourdis family is a noble family that has joined our side, whereas the Sainte-Hermine family is a noble family that we would like to have join us."

"So they have been holding out?"

"Worse than that. They have been combatting you."

"Republicans or Royalists?"

"Royalists. The father was guillotined in '93. The oldest son was shot. The second son, whom you met, was guillotined in Bourg-en-Bresse."

"I met him?"

"Do you remember a masked man who appeared when you were dining at the common table in a hotel in Avignon? He carried a bag containing two hundred louis, which he'd stolen by mistake from a Bordeaux wine merchant in a stagecoach?"

"Yes, I remember him well. Ah, Monsieur Fouché, that is the kind of man I need."

"It is not devotion to an earlier regime, Citizen First Consul, that drives men like him; it's really just a matter of self-interest."

"How right you are, Fouché. Well, how about the third one?"

"The third son will be your friend if you want."

"How's that?"

"Obviously, it is with his agreement that Madame de Sourdis, skilled in flattery, is asking for your blessing of her daughter's marriage as if you were a king. Give your blessing, sire, and instead of being your enemy, Monsieur Hector de Sainte-Hermine will have no choice but to become your friend."

"Fine," said Bonaparte. "I shall give it some thought." Rubbing his hands in satisfaction at the thought that someone had just fulfilled a formality that used to be associated with French kings, he then proceeded: "Well, Fouché. Any news?"

"Just one piece of news, but it's quite important, especially for me."

"What's that?"

"Yesterday, in the green room at Mortefontaine, with Lucien, the Minister of the Interior, holding the pen, you dictated and signed my dismissal and my admission to the Senate."

In a gesture familiar to Corsicans, Bonaparte ran his thumb twice over his chest in the sign of the cross, and said: "Who told you such a story, Fouché?"

"One of my agents, of course."

"He was mistaken."

"He was so far from mistaken that my dismissal is right there, on that chair, in the side pocket of your gray frock coat."

"Fouché," said Bonaparte, "if you limped like Talleyrand, I would say that you were the devil himself."

"You no longer deny it, am I right?"

"Of course not. Besides, your dismissal has been arranged with the most honorable terms."

"I understand. It is surely to my credit, during all the time I have been in your service, that you have never noticed any of your silver missing."

"Now that France is at peace and the Ministry of Police is unnecessary, I can send its minister to the Senate so that I know where to find him if ever the ministry needs to be reestablished. I am aware that in the Senate, my dear Fouché, you will have to give up your administration of gambling, which provides you a source to streams of gold, but you already have so much money you cannot possibly enjoy it all. And your domain in Pont-carré, which I knew you would like to keep expanding, is really already quite large enough for you."

"Do I have your word," said Fouché, "that if the Ministry of Police is reestablished it will be for no one other than for me?"

"You have my word," said Bonaparte.

"Thank you. And now, may I announce to Cabanis that Mademoiselle de Sourdis, his goddaughter, has your blessing to marry the Comte de Sainte-Hermine?"

"You may."

Bonaparte nodded slightly, Fouché answered with a deep bow, and departed.

The First Consul, his hands behind his back, paced up and down silently for a few moments. Then, stopping behind his secretary's chair, he said, "Did you hear that, Bourrienne?"

"What, General?"

"What that devil Fouché just said to me."

"I never hear anything unless you order me to listen."

"He knew that I had retired his ministry, that I had done so at Morte-fontaine, and that the dismissal order was in the pocket of my gray frock coat."

"Ah," said Bourrienne. "That is not so surprising. All he needed to do was to give your brother's personal valet a pension."

Bonaparte shook his head. "All the same, that man Fouché is dangerous."

"Yes," said Bourrienne, "but you have to admit that a man whose subtlety can surprise you can be a useful man in times like these."

Silent for a moment, the First Consul then said, "I've promised him that at the first signs of trouble I will call him back. I shall probably keep my word."

He rang for the office boy. "Landoire," Bonaparte said, "look out the window and see if a carriage is ready."

Landoire leaned out the window. "Yes, General," he said.

The First Consul pulled on his frock coat and picked up his hat. "I'm going to the Conseil d'Etat."

He started toward the door, then stopped. "Bourrienne," he said, "go down to Josephine and tell her that not only does Mademoiselle de Sourdis's marriage have my blessing but also that Madame Bonaparte and I shall sign her marriage contract."

XXI

In Which Fouché Works to Return to the Ministry of Police, Which He Has Not Yet Left

FOUCHÉ WENT BACK to his office furious. He still had a role to play, but the role was limited. Outside of the police, Fouché had only secondary power, which to him was of no real value. For nature had endowed him with crossed eyes so that he could look in two directions at once and with big ears that could hear things from all directions. Add to that his subtle intelligence and his temperament—nervous, irritable, worrying—all of which went wanting without his ministry.

And Bonaparte had hit upon the truly sensitive point. In losing the police, he was losing his control over gambling, so he was also losing more than two hundred thousand francs a year. Although Fouché was already extremely rich, he was always trying to increase his wealth even if he could never really enjoy it. His ambition to extend the boundaries of his domain in Pontcarré was no less great than Bonaparte's to move back the borders of France.

Fouché threw himself into his armchair without a word to anyone. His facial muscles were quivering like the surface of the ocean in a storm. After a few minutes, however, they stopped twitching, because Fouché had found what he was looking for. The pale smile that lit up his face indicated, if not the return of good weather, at least a temporary calm. He grabbed the bell cord that hung above his desk and pulled it vigorously.

The office boy hurried in. "Monsieur Dubois!" Fouché shouted.

A moment later the door opened and Monsieur Dubois entered. Dubois had a calm, gentle face, with a kindly, unaffected smile, and he was scrupulously neat. Wearing a white tie and a shirt with cuffs, he pranced more than he walked lightly in, and the soles of his shoes slid over the carpet as if they were a dancing master's.

"Monsieur Dubois," said Fouché, throwing himself back in his armchair, "today I need all your intelligence and discretion."

"I can vouch only for my discretion, Monsieur le Ministre," he answered. "As for my intelligence, it has value only when guided by you."

"Fine, fine, Monsieur Dubois," said Fouché a little impatiently. "Enough compliments. In your service, is there a man whom we can trust?"

"First I need to know what we will be using him for."

"Of course. He will travel to Brittany, where he will organize three bands of fire-setters. One fire, the largest, must be set on the road between Vannes and Muzillac; the other two, wherever he likes."

"I'm listening," said Dubois, noting that Fouché had paused.

"One of the bands will call itself Cadoudal's band, and it will pretend to have Cadoudal himself at its head."

"According to what Your Excellency is saying. . . ."

"I shall let you use those words for now," said Fouché with a laugh, "especially since you've not much time left appropriately to use them."

Dubois bowed, and, encouraged by Fouché, he went on: "According to what Your Excellency is saying, you need a man who can shoot if necessary."

"That, and whatever else is necessary."

Monsieur Dubois thought for a moment and shook his head. "I have no one like that among my men," he said.

But, when Fouché gestured impatiently, Dubois recalled: "Wait a moment. Yesterday a man came to my office, a certain Chevalier de Mahalin, a fellow who was a member of the Companions of Jehu and who asks for nothing better, he says, than well-paid dangers. He is a gambler in every sense of the word, ready to risk his life as well as his money on a throw of the dice. He's our man."

"Do you have his address?"

"No. But he is coming back to my office today sometime between one and two o'clock. It is now one o'clock, so he must be there already or else he will be soon."

"Go, then, and bring him back here."

When Monsieur Dubois had left, Fouché pulled a file from its box and carried it over to his desk. It was the Pichegru file, and he studied it with the greatest attention until Monsieur Dubois returned with the man he'd talked about.

It was the same man who had visited Hector de Sainte-Hermine regarding the promises he'd made to his brother and who then had led him to Laurent's band. Now disbanded, with nothing more to be done in Cadoudal's cause, the good man was looking elsewhere for work.

He was probably between twenty-five and thirty years old, well built, and quite handsome. He had a pleasant smile, and you could have said he was likeable in every respect, except for a troubled and disturbing look in his eyes that often caused people he dealt with worry and concern.

Fouché examined him with a penetrating look that enabled him to take any man's moral measure. In this man he could sense the love of money, great courage, though he seemed more ready to defend himself than to attack another, and the absolute will to succeed in any undertaking. That was exactly what Fouché was looking for.

"Monsieur," said Fouché, "I have been assured that you would like to enter government service. Is that correct?"

"That is my greatest wish."

"In what role?"

"Wherever there are blows to receive and money to be earned."

"Do you know Brittany and the Vendée?"

"Perfectly well. Three times I have been sent to meet General Cadoudal."

"Have you been in contact with those serving just beneath him?"

"With some of them, and particularly with one of Cadoudal's lieutenants—he's called George II because he looks like the general."

"Damn!" said Fouché. "That might be useful. Do you believe you could raise three bands of about twenty men each?"

"It is always possible, in a region still warm from civil war, to raise three bands of twenty men. If the purpose is honorable, honest men will easily make up your sixty, and for them all you will need are grand words and elegant speech. If the purpose is less principled and demands secrecy, you will still be able to enlist mercenaries, but to buy their questionable consciences will cost you more."

Fouché gave Dubois a look that seemed to be saying, "My good man, you have indeed come up with a real find." Then, to the chevalier, he said, "Monsieur, within ten days we need three bands of incendiaries, two in the Morbihan and one in the Vendée, all three of them acting in Cadoudal's name. In one of the bands a masked man must assume the name of the Breton general and do all that he can to convince the populace that he really is Cadoudal."

"Easy, but expensive, as I have said."

"Are fifty thousand francs enough?"

"Yes. Unquestionably."

"So then, we are agreed on that point. Once your three bands have been organized, will you be able to go to England?"

"There is nothing simpler, given that my background is English and that I speak the language as well as I do my mother tongue."

"Do you know Pichegru?"

"By name."

"Do you have a means of getting introduced to him?"

"Yes."

"And if I asked you how?"

"I would not tell you. After all, I need to keep some secrets; otherwise, I would lose all my value."

"So you would. And so you will go to England, where you will check out Pichegru and try to discover under what circumstances he would be willing to come back to Paris. Were he to wish to return to Paris but finds money to be lacking, you will propose funds in the name of Fauche-Borel. Don't forget that name."

"The Swiss bookseller who has already made proposals to him in the name of the Prince de Condé; yes, I know him. And were he to wish to return to Paris and needs money, to whom should I turn?"

"To Monsieur Fouché, at his domain in Pontcarré. Not to the Minister of Police, the difference is important."

"And then?"

"And then you will return to Paris for new orders. Monsieur Dubois, please count out fifty thousand francs for the chevalier. By the way, chevalier. . . ."

Mahalin turned around.

"If you should happen to meet Coster Saint-Victor, encourage him to come back to Paris."

"Does he not risk arrest?"

"No, all will be forgiven, that I can affirm."

"What shall I say to convince him?"

"That all the women in Paris miss him, and especially Mademoiselle Aurélie de Saint-Amour. You may add that after being a rival to Barras for her charms, it would be a shame for him not also to be a rival to the First Consul. That should be enough to help him make up his mind to return, unless he has even more extraordinary liaisons in London."

Once the door had shut on Dubois and Mahalin, Fouché quickly had an orderly carry the following letter to Doctor Cabanis:

My dear doctor,

The First Consul, whom I have just seen in Madame Bonaparte's apartments, could not have more graciously received Madame de Sourdis's request concerning her daughter's marriage, and he is pleased to see such a marriage take place.

Our dear sister can therefore plan her visit to Madame Bonaparte, and the sooner the better.

Please believe me your sincere friend,

J. Fouché

The next day, Madame la Comtesse de Sourdis presented herself in the Tuileries. She found Josephine radiant and Hortense in tears, for Hortense's marriage with Louis Bonaparte was almost certain.

Josephine had realized the day before that, whatever mysterious reason lay behind it, her husband was in good humor, so she had asked to have him come see her on his return from the Conseil d'Etat.

But, when he got back, the First Consul had found Cambacérès waiting for him—he'd come to explain two or three articles of the code that Bonaparte had found to be not sufficiently clear—and the two of them had worked until quite late. Then Junot had shown up to announce his marriage with Mademoiselle de Permon.

News of this marriage pleased the First Consul far less than the one arranged for Mademoiselle de Sourdis. First of all, Bonaparte had himself been in love with Madame de Permon; in fact, before marrying Josephine, he had tried to marry her. But Madame de Permon had refused, and he still held a grudge. Furthermore, he had advised Junot to marry someone rich, and now Junot, on the contrary, was choosing a wife from a ruined family. His future wife, on her mother's side, was descended from former emperors in the Orient and the girl, whom Junot had familiarly called Loulou, came from the Comnène family as well, but she had a dowry of only twenty-five thousand francs. Bonaparte promised Junot he would add one hundred thousand francs to the basket. Also, as governor of Paris, Junot could be guaranteed a salary of five hundred thousand francs. He would simply have to manage with that.

Josephine had meanwhile waited impatiently for her husband all evening. But he had dined with Junot, and then they had gone out together. Finally, at midnight, he had appeared in his dressing gown and with a scarf over his head, which meant he would not retire to his own rooms until the next morning. Josephine's face had beamed with joy: Her long wait had been worth it. For it was during such visits that Josephine was able to solidify her power over Bonaparte. Never before had Josephine so insistently pressed her case for the marriage of Hortense to Louis. When he'd gone back up to his own rooms, the First Consul had very nearly agreed to the betrothal of his stepdaughter to his brother.

So, when Madame de Sourdis arrived, Josephine was eager to tell her of her good fortune. Claire was dispatched to console Hortense.

But Claire didn't even try. She knew only too well how difficult it would have been for her herself to give up Hector. Instead, she wept with Hortense, and encouraged her to bring up the question with the First Consul as he surely loved her too much to consent to her unhappiness.

Suddenly a strange idea came to Hortense: She and Claire, with their mothers' permission, should consult Mademoiselle Lenormand and have their fortunes told.

It was Mademoiselle de Sourdis who acted as ambassador, presenting to their mothers their wish and asking their permission to put it into execution. The negotiation was long, with Hortense listening at the door and trying to hold back her sobs.

Claire came joyously back. Permission was granted, on the condition that Mademoiselle Louise not leave the presence of the two girls even for a moment. Mademoiselle Louise, as we believe we have pointed out, was Madame Bonaparte's principal maid, and Madame Bonaparte had complete confidence in her.

Mademoiselle Louise was given strict orders, and she swore on everything that was holy to do her duty. Heavily veiled, the two girls climbed into Madame de Sourdis's carriage, which was a morning carriage without a coat of arms. The coachman was told to stop at number six, Rue de Tournon; he was not told whom they were going to see.

Mademoiselle Louise was the first to climb down from the carriage. She had her instructions, so she knew that Mademoiselle Lenormand lived in the back of the courtyard and to the left. She would then lead the girls up three steps and knock on the door to the right.

She knocked, and when she asked to come in, she and the two girls were led into a study off to one side, not generally open to the public.

They were informed that each girl would be received separately, because Mademoiselle Lenormand never worked with more than one person at the same time. The order in which they would be received would be determined by the first letter of their family name. Thus Hortense Bonaparte would be first. Still, she had to wait a half hour.

The arrangement greatly upset Mademoiselle Louise, for she had been ordered never to let the girls out of her sight. If she remained with Claire, she'd lose sight of Hortense. If she accompanied Hortense, she'd lose sight of Claire.

They took the question to Mademoiselle Lenormand, who found a way to reconcile the situation. Mademoiselle Louise would remain with Claire, but Mademoiselle Lenormand would leave the door of the study open so that the maid would be able to keep her eyes on Hortense. At the same time, she would be far enough away from Mademoiselle Lenormand that she would not be able to hear what the prophetess was saying.

Naturally, both girls had requested the grand set of cards. What Mademoiselle Lenormand saw in the cards for Hortense seemed to impress her greatly. Her gestures and facial expressions indicated growing astonishment. Finally, after she had again shuffled the cards well and carefully studied the girl's palm, she stood up and spoke like one inspired. She pronounced just one sentence, which brought an incredulous expression to her subject's face. In the face of Hortense's pressing questions, she remained mute and refused to add a single word to her declaration, except to say: "The oracle has spoken; believe the oracle!"

The oracle signaled to Hortense that her time was up and summoned her friend.

Although it was Mademoiselle de Beauharnais who had proposed coming to consult Mademoiselle Lenormand, Claire, after what she had seen, was equally eager to learn her future. She hurried into the prophetess's study. She had no idea that her future would astonish Mademoiselle Lenormand as much as had her friend's.

With the confidence of a woman who believed in herself and hesitated to offer improbable utterances, Mademoiselle Lenormand read Claire's cards three times. She studied Claire's right hand, then the left, and in both palms she found a broken heart, the luck line cutting through the heart line and forking toward Saturn. In the same solemn tone she had assumed in her pronouncement for Mademoiselle de Beauharnais, she spoke her oracle for Mademoiselle de Sourdis. When Claire rejoined Mademoiselle Louise and Hortense, she was as pale as a corpse, and her eyes were filled with tears.

The two girls did not say one word further, did not ask a single question, so long as they were under Mademoiselle Lenormand's roof. It was as if they feared that any utterance on their part might bring the house down around their heads. But, as soon as they were settled in the carriage and the coachman had started the horses off at a gallop, they both asked at the same time: "What did she tell you?"

Hortense, the first to be received, was the first to answer. "She said: 'Wife of a king and mother of an emperor, you will die in exile.'"

"And what did she tell you?" Mademoiselle de Beauharnais asked eagerly.

"She said: 'For fourteen years you will be the widow of a man who is still alive, and the rest of your life the wife of a dead man!'"

XXII

In Which Mademoiselle de Beauharnais Becomes the Wife of a King without a Throne and Mademoiselle de Sourdis the Widow of a Living Husband

SIX WEEKS HAD PASSED since the two girls had visited the prophetess living on Rue de Tournon. Mademoiselle de Beauharnais had, in spite of her tears, married Louis Bonaparte, and that very same evening Mademoiselle de Sourdis had been going to sign her marriage contract with the Comte de Sainte-Hermine.

Mademoiselle de Beauharnais's repugnance for her marriage might lead one to believe that she was repulsed by the First Consul's brother. That was not the case at all. It was simply that she loved Duroc. Love is blind.

Louis Bonaparte was then about twenty-three or twenty-four years old. He was a handsome young man—in fact, he resembled his sister Caroline— though he appeared to be a little cold. He was well educated and had true literary instincts. Upright, kind, and very honest, he never for a minute presumed that the title of king in any way changed the rules and duties of the human conscience. He is perhaps the only prince who, reigning over a foreign people, elicited at least a bit of gratitude and love in his subjects, just as Desaix had done in upper Egypt. He was a just sultan.

Before we leave that loyal-hearted man and the charming creature he was marrying, let us say that the marriage happened suddenly, for no other reason than for Josephine's incessant hounding.

"Duroc," Josephine told Bourrienne, repeatedly, "would give me no support. Duroc owes everything to his friendship with Bonaparte, and he would never dare stand up to his protector's brothers. On the other hand, Bonaparte has great fondness for Louis, who has not the slightest ambition and never will. For me, Louis will be a counterbalance to Joseph and Lucien."

As for Bonaparte, he took this position with Bourrienne: "Duroc and Hortense love each other. Whatever my wife might do, they are a good fit and shall marry. As for me, I am fond of Duroc; he comes from a good family. After all, I gave Caroline to Murat and Pauline to Leclerc. So I can surely give Hortense to Duroc, for he's a fine man, as good as they come. As he is now a major general, there is no reason to oppose this marriage. Besides, I have something else in mind for Louis."

However, the same day the girls went to consult Mademoiselle Lenormand, Hortense, urged on by her friend, tried to enlist, and ensure, the support of her stepfather one more time. After dinner, finding herself alone with Bonaparte, she knelt down gracefully at his feet, and using all her feminine charms on the First Consul, she told him that the proposed union between her and Louis would mean her eternal unhappiness, and while giving full justice to Louis's virtues, she repeated that she loved only Duroc and that Duroc alone could make her happy.

Bonaparte made a decision.

"Fine," he said. "Since you insist on marrying him, marry him you will, but I warn you that I must set some conditions. If Duroc accepts them, then all is well. But if he refuses, then this is the last time I shall go against Josephine's wishes on this subject, and you will become Louis's wife."

Walking briskly, as he did when he had made a decision, in spite of any unpleasantness his decision might provoke, Bonaparte went to Duroc's office but failed to find him, the eternal idler, at his post. "Where is Duroc?" he asked, visibly upset.

"He has gone out," Bourrienne answered.

"Where do you think he might be?"

"At the Opera."

"Tell him, as soon as he returns, that I have promised him to Hortense, that he will marry her. But I want the wedding to take place in two days at the latest. I shall give him five hundred thousand francs. I shall name him commander of the eighth military division. He will leave for Toulon the day after his wedding, and we shall live separately as I do not want a son-in-law in my house. I do want to have this matter settled once and for all, so tell me this evening if he is in agreement."

"I don't believe he will be," said Bourrienne.

"Then she shall marry Louis."

"Is she willing?"

"She has no choice but to be willing."

At ten, on Duroc's return, Bourrienne communicated the First Consul's intentions. But Duroc shook his head. "The First Consul does me a great honor," he said, "but I shall never marry a woman under such conditions. I prefer now to take a stroll near Palais-Royal."

With that, Duroc picked up his hat, and with no apparent concern he left. His attitude, to Bourrienne's eye, only served to prove that Hortense was mistaken about the intensity of the feelings the First Consul's aide-de-camp had, or pretended to have, for her.

The wedding of Mademoiselle de Beauharnais and Louis Bonaparte took place in the little house on Rue Chantereine. A priest came to bless their union. At the same time Bonaparte had him bless Madame Murat's marriage.

Far from occasioning the sad atmosphere that had hung over poor Hortense's wedding, Mademoiselle de Sourdis's wedding held every promise of light and joy. The two lovebirds, who were apart only between eleven at night and two in the afternoon, spent all the rest of their time together. The most elegant merchants, the most popular jewelers in Paris, had been ransacked by Hector to produce a collection of wedding presents worthy of his fiancée. The opulent offerings were the talk of Parisian high society; Madame de Sourdis had even received letters from people who wanted to view them in person.

Madame de Sourdis had been expecting no more than a simple agreement from the First Consul and Madame Bonaparte, so she was in a tizzy about the favor he had bestowed upon her by proposing to come and sign the marriage contract himself. It was a favor he granted only to his closest friends, for it was of necessity followed by a gift of money or a present, and the First Consul, not a stingy man but by nature more thrifty than generous, did not spend money like water.

The only person less than pleased with the honor was Hector de Sainte-Hermine. Bonaparte's show of honoring his fiancée's family worried him. Younger than his brothers, he had never embraced the Royalist cause as actively as they had, but in spite of his admiration for the First Consul's genius, Hector had not reached the point where he truly liked him. He could not put out of his mind his brother's brave but painful death and all the bloody details that accompanied it, or the fact that it was the First Consul who had ordered it and who, in spite of strong pleading, had refused to grant a reprieve or pardon. So every time he met Bonaparte, he felt his face begin to sweat and his knees weaken, and against his own will he would avert his eyes. He feared one thing only, and that was to be forced some day, by his high rank or his great fortune, either to serve in the army or to go into exile. He had warned Claire that he would rather leave France than accept any position in the army or civil service. Claire had said it was totally up to him, that in such an event he should do what he needed to do. All she had demanded of her fiancé was that he would allow her to accompany him wherever he might go. That promise was all her tender, loving heart needed.

Claude-Antoine Régnier, who since then became Duke of Massa, had been named chief judge and prefect of the police. He worked in concert with Junot, now governor of Paris, as well as with Bonaparte himself and his aide-de-camp, Duroc. On the day that Bonaparte was to sign Mademoiselle de Sourdis's marriage contract, he spent an hour with Régnier, for the news recently had been disturbing. Once again the Vendée and Brittany were in upheaval. It did not appear this time to be civil war; rather, shadowy bands of incendiaries were traveling from farm to farm and from chateau to chateau, where they were forcing farmers and proprietors to give them their money and then torturing them most atrociously. The newspapers were reporting instances of poor souls whose hands and feet had been burned to the bone.

In an order written to Régnier, Bonaparte had asked the prefect to gather all the files relating to this business of burnings. Five such events had been confirmed within the past week: The first, in Berric, where the Sulé River takes its source; the second, in Plescop; the third, in Muzillac; the fourth, in Saint-Nolff; the fifth, at Saint-Jean-de-Brévelay. There appeared to be three leaders at the head of the roving bands, but some superior officer no doubt was in control of them all. And that officer, if one were to believe the police agents, was Cadoudal himself. One could only conclude that he had not kept his word to Bonaparte; that instead of withdrawing to England as he had promised, he was fomenting a new uprising in Brittany.

Bonaparte, who normally was correct in his assumption that he could read a man's character well, shook his head when the chief judge tried to lay on Cadoudal the despicable crimes they were trying now to solve. How could that be possible? That sharp mind that had discussed with Bonaparte, without giving an inch, the interests of peoples and their kings; that pure conscience content to live in England on his own family's wealth; that heart without ambition who turned down the position of aide-de-camp to the most important general in Europe; that unselfish soul who refused one hundred thousand francs per year to stand by and watch while lesser men tore each other apart—how could a man like that have lowered himself to such a vile activity as burning, the most cowardly act of banditry of all?

Totally impossible!

And Bonaparte had forcefully said as much to his new prefect of police. He had then given orders for the most skillful agents with broad powers to leave Paris and pursue relentlessly the conscienceless murderers. Régnier promised to send the best of his men to Brittany that very day.

By then, it was already almost ten in the evening, and Bonaparte sent word to Josephine that they would be leaving shortly to visit Madame de Sourdis and the young couple.

The countess's magnificent hotel was gleaming with light. The day had been warm and sunny, and the first flowers and leaves were beginning to break out of their cottony prisons. The warm spring breezes danced in the flowering lilacs that seemed to forest the garden from the castle windows to the terrace along the quay. Beneath those intriguingly scented canopies, colored lamps were burning, and whiffs of perfume and snatches of song wafted from the open windows, while on the drawn curtains the guests cast moving shadows.

Among the guests were the most elegant people in Paris. There were the government officials, that marvelous staff of generals, the oldest of whom was no more thirty-five: Murat, Marmont, Junot, Duroc, Lannes, Moncey, Davout—already heroes at an age when one is normally only a captain. There were poets: Lemercier, still proud of the recent success of his *Agamemnon;*Chénier, who had written *Timoléon,* then given up theater and thrown himself into politics; Chateaubriand, who had just discovered God at Niagara Falls and in the depths of America's virgin forests. There were famous dancers without whom grand balls could not be held: Trénis, Laffitte, Dupaty, Garat, Vestris. And there were the new century's splendid stars who had appeared in the East: Madame Récamier, Madame Méchin, Madame de Contades, Madame Regnault de Saint-Jean-d'Angély. Finally, there was the brilliant young crowd, made up of men like Caulaincourt, Narbonne, Longchamp, Matthieu de Montmorency, Eugène de Beauharnais, and Philippe de Ségur.

From the moment the word got out that the First Consul and Madame Bonaparte not only were attending the wedding celebration but also would be signing the marriage contract, all society sought an invitation. Guests filled the ground floor and the first story of Madame de Sourdis's spacious hotel, and they spread out onto the terraces, there to seek relief from the hot, stuffy rooms in the cool evening air.

At quarter to eleven, a mounted escort was seen leaving the Tuileries gates, with each man carrying a torch. Once they had crossed the bridge, the First Consul's carriage, rolling at a triple gallop, surrounded by torches, swept by in the thunder of hoofbeats and a whirlwind of sparks before it disappeared into the hotel courtyard.

In the midst of a crowd so dense that it seemed impossible for anyone to penetrate, a passage magically opened and, inside the ballroom, widened into a circle that allowed Madame de Sourdis and Claire to approach the First Consul and Josephine. Hector de Sainte-Hermine walked behind Claire and her mother, and though he paled visibly on seeing Bonaparte, he nonetheless stood nobly before him.

Madame Bonaparte embraced Mademoiselle de Sourdis and placed on her arm a pearl necklace worth fifty thousand francs. Bonaparte greeted the two women, then moved toward Hector. Not suspecting that Bonaparte indeed meant to address him, Hector began to step aside. But Bonaparte stopped to face him.

"Monsieur," said Bonaparte, "if I had not been afraid you would refuse it, I would have brought a gift for you as well, an appointment to the consular guard. But I understand that some wounds need time to heal."

"For such cures, General, no one has a more skillful hand than you. However. . . ." Hector sighed and raised his handkerchief to his eyes. "Excuse me, General," said the young man, after a pause. "I would like to be more worthy of your kindness."

"That is what comes from having too much heart, young man," said Bonaparte. "It is always the heart that suffers."

Turning again to Madame de Sourdis, the First Consul exchanged a few words with her, and complimented Claire. Then he noticed Vestris.

"Oh, there's young Vestris," he said. "He lately did me a kindness for which I shall be eternally grateful. He was coming back to perform at the Opera after a short illness, and the performance happened to fall on a day that I was having a reception at the Tuileries. He changed his performance date so as not to conflict with my reception. . . . Come, Monsieur Vestris, please demonstrate your inimitable courteousness by asking two of these ladies to dance a gavotte for us."

"Citizen First Consul," answered this son to the god of dance in an Italian accent that the family had never been able to eradicate, "we are pleased to have just the dance for you, a gavotte I composed for Mademoiselle de Coigny. Madame Récamier and Mademoiselle de Sourdis dance it like angels. All we need is a harp and a horn," he said, rolling his "r"s, "if Mademoiselle de Sourdis is willing to play the tambourine as she dances. As for Madame Récamier, you know that she is unbeatable in the shawl dance."

"Come, my ladies," said the First Consul. "You surely cannot refuse the request that Monsieur Vestris has made and which I support with all my power."

Mademoiselle de Sourdis would have been happy to escape the ovation given to her, but once her dancing master Vestris had chosen her, and after the First Consul had added his bidding, she did not wait to be asked again.

She was dressed perfectly for this dance. Her white dress, accented by her dark skin, had two clusters of grapes on the shoulders, while grape leaves in reddish autumn colors ran the length of her gown. She also wore grape leaves in her hair.

Madame Récamier was wearing her customary white dress and her red Indian cashmere shawl. The creator of the shawl dance, which had so successfully been taken from the ballroom to the theater, Madame Récamier performed her invention with no want of modesty yet without a hint of constraint as no theater bayadère or professional actress has demonstrated since. Beneath the undulations of the supple cashmere cloth, she was able to reveal her charms at the same time she was pretending to hide them.

The dance lasted nearly a quarter of an hour and ended in a crescendo of applause, to which the First Consul added his own. At his signal, the entire room exploded in bravos. Amidst the boisterous praise, Vestris seemed to be walking on air as he took full credit for all that poetry of form and movement, of expression and attitude.

Once the gavotte had finished, a servant in livery whispered a few words to the Comtesse de Sourdis, to which she responded, "Open the drawing room."

Two doors slid open, and in the marvelously elegant drawing room, brightly lit, two men of the law were seated at a table lit by two candelabras, between which the marriage contract was awaiting the signatures with which it would soon be honored. The only people authorized to enter the drawing room were the twenty or so who would be signing the contract, which would first be read aloud for the benefit of the other wedding guests.

As the contract was being read, a second lackey in livery entered. As unobtrusively as he could, he slipped over to the Comte de Sainte-Hermine and in a whisper said, "Monsieur le Chevalier de Mahalin asks to speak to you at this very moment."

"Have him wait," said Sainte-Hermine, who was standing attendant in the small study at one side of the drawing room.

"Monsieur le Comte, he says that he must see you at this very instant. Even if you were to have the pen in your hand, he would request that you lay it down on the table and come to see him before you sign . . . oh, there he is at the door."

With what looked like a gesture of despair, the count joined the Chevalier outside the drawing room. Few people noticed the discreet exit, and those who did were unaware of its unfortunate significance.

After the contract had been read, Bonaparte, always in a hurry to finish what was under way, as eager to leave the Tuileries when he was there as he was to return when he was out, picked up the pen that was lying on the table. Without wondering whether he should be the first to sign, he hastily placed his signature on the contract, and then, just as four years later he would take the crown from the pope's hands and place it himself on Josephine's head, he handed his wife the pen.

Josephine signed, then passed the pen to Mademoiselle de Sourdis, who instinctively looked around worriedly, but in vain, for the Comte de Sainte-Hermine. Filled with anxiety, she signed her name and tried to hide her concern. But it was the Comte's turn next to sign.

A murmur disturbed the drawing room as heads turned in search of the bridegroom. Soon there was no choice but to call out for him. Only there was no answer.

For a long moment, in surprised silence, the guests looked at each other, all of them, wondering what could have happened to the count at the very moment his presence was indispensable and his absence a complete lapse of etiquette.

Finally someone mentioned that during the reading of the contract, a young well-dressed stranger had appeared in the dorway to the drawing room and had exchanged a few whispered words with the count before leading him off, more like his executioner than his friend.

Still, the count might not have left the house. Madame de Sourdis rang for a servant and ordered him to organize a search for the absent bridegroom. For several minutes, amidst the buzz of six hundred stunned wedding guess, servants could be heard calling out to each other from one floor to the next.

Then one of the servants thought to ask the coachmen out in the courtyard if they had seen two young men. Several of them had, as it happened. They'd noticed that one of the young men had been hatless in spite of the rain. They reported that the two men had rushed down the steps and leaped into a carriage, shouting, "To the stagecoach house!" and the carriage had galloped off. One of the coachmen was certain he had recognized the young man without a hat: It was the Comte de Sainte-Hermine.

The guests looked at each other in stupefaction. Then, out of the silence, they heard a voice shout: "The carriage and escort for the First Consul!" They all respectfully allowed Monsieur and Madame Bonaparte, along with Madame Louis Bonaparte, to pass. And as soon as they had left, pandemonium struck.

Everyone rushed from the elegant rooms of Madame de Sourdis's grand house as if there were a fire.

Neither Madame de Sourdis nor Claire, however, had any inclination to stop them. Fifteen minutes later they found themselves alone.

Madame de Sourdis, with a painful cry, rushed to her daughter's side. Claire was trembling, about to faint. "Oh, Mother, Mother!" she cried, bursting into sobs as she collapsed into the countess's arms, "it is just what the prophetess predicted! My widowhood has begun."

XXIII

The Burning Brigades

WE SHOULD EXPLAIN why Mademoiselle de Sourdis's fiancé disappeared so incomprehensibly just as the marriage contract was to be signed. For the guests, his disappearance was the cause for surprise; for the countess, it prompted all sorts of speculations, each new one more improbable than the last. For her daughter, it elicited incessant tears.

We have seen that Fouché summoned the Chevalier de Mahalin to his office the day before news of his dismissal was to be publicly announced. Hoping to get back his ministry, Fouché then planned with Mahalin the organization of burning brigades in the West.

The bands of incendiaries had soon begun to appear, and already they had left their mark. Scarcely two weeks after the Chevalier had left Paris, it was learned that two landowners had been burned, one in Buré and the other in Saulnaye. Again, terror was spreading throughout the Morbihan.

For five years civil war had raged in that unfortunate region, but even in the midst of its most horrible outrages against humanity, never had such banditry as this been practiced. To find robbery and torture of the kind that accompanied these burnings, one had to go back to the worst days of Louis XV and to the horrors of religious discrimination under Louis XIV.

Terror came in bands of ten, fifteen, or twenty men who seemed to rise out of the earth and move like shadows over the land, following ravines, leaping across stiles; and any peasants who had ventured out late in the night had to hide behind trees or throw themselves facedown behind hedges, or else fall prey to the brigands. Then, suddenly, through a half-open window or a poorly closed door, they would burst into some farmhouse or chateau and, taking the servants by surprise, bind them up. Next, they would light a fire in the middle of the kitchen; they'd drag the master or mistress of the house over to it and lay their victim down on the floor with his feet to the flames until pain forced him to reveal where his money was hidden. Sometimes they would then free their prisoner. Other times, once they'd got the money, if they feared they might be identified, they would stab, hang, or bludgeon to death the unfortunate they had robbed.

After the third or fourth episode of that kind, after the authorities had indeed confirmed the fires and murders, the rumor began to spread, at first secretly, then quite openly, that Cadoudal himself strode at the head of those gangs. The brigands and their leader always wore masks, but some who had seen the largest of the bands stalk through the night were sure they had recognized the leader as George Cadoudal—by his size, by his bearing, and especially by his large round head.

This was difficult to believe. How could George Cadoudal, who acted so honorably in all things, have suddenly become the contemptible chief of a shameless, pitiless burning brigade?

Yet the rumor kept growing. More and more people claimed they had recognized George, and soon *Le Journal de Paris* officially announced that Cadoudal, in spite of his promise not to be the first to open hostilities— Cadoudal who had disbanded his Royalist forces—had now scraped together fifty or so bandits with whom he was terrorizing the countryside.

In London, Cadoudal himself might not have happened upon the article in *Le Journal de Paris,* but a friend showed it to him. He took the official announcement as an accusation against him, and he saw the accusation as a flagrant attack on his honor and loyalty.

"Very well," he said, "by attacking me the French authorities have broken the pact we swore between us. They were unable to kill me with gun and sword, so now they are trying to kill me with calumny. They want war, and war they shall have."

That very evening George embarked on a fishing boat. Five days later it landed him on the French coast, between Port-Louis and the Quiberon peninsula.

At the same time, two other men, Saint-Régeant and Limoëlan, were also leaving London to go to Paris. As they would be traveling through Normandy, they'd enter the country by the cliffs near Biville. They had spent one hour with George the day they left, to receive their instructions. Limoëlan had considerable experience in the intrigues of civil war, and Saint-Régeant was a former naval officer, skilled and resourceful, a sea pirate who had become a land pirate.

It was on such lost men—rather than the likes of Guillemot and Sol de Grisolles—that Cadoudal was now forced to depend to execute his plans. In any case, it was clear that his goals and theirs were one and the same.

This is what transpired.

Near the end of April 1804, at about five in the afternoon, a man wrapped in a greatcoat galloped into the courtyard of the Plescop farm owned by Jacques Doley. A wealthy farmer, Doley lived there with his sixty-year-old mother-in-law and his thirty-year-old wife, with whom he had two children: one a boy of ten, the other a girl of seven. He had ten servants, both men and women, who helped him run the farm.

The man in the greatcoat asked to speak to the master of the house and closed himself up in the milk room with him for a half hour, but then failed to reappear. Jacques Doley came back out of the room alone.

During dinner, everyone noticed how quiet and preoccupied Jacques seemed to be. Several times his wife spoke to him, but he did not answer. After the meal, when the children tried to play with him as they usually did, he gently pushed them away.

In Brittany, as you know, the servants eat at the master's table. On that day, they too noticed how sad Doley was, and found it surprising because by nature he was quite jovial. Just a few days before, the Château de Buré had been burned, and that is what the servants were talking quietly about during the meal. As Doley listened to them, he raised his head a few times as if he were about to ask something, but each time without interrupting them. From time to time, though, the old mother made the sign of the cross, and near the end of the servants' tale, Madame Doley, no longer able to control her fear, moved closer to her husband.

By eight in the evening, it was completely dark. That was when all of the servants usually retired, some to the barn, some to the stables, but Doley seemed to be trying to delay them, as he gave them a series of orders that kept them from leaving. Also, now and then he would glance at the two or three double-barreled shotguns hanging on nails above the fireplace, like a man who would rather have them in hand.

Soon, however, each servant had left in turn, and the old woman went to put the children in their cribs, which stood between their parents' bed and the outside wall. She returned from the bedroom to kiss her daughter and son-in-law good-night, then went to her own bed in a little cabinet attached to the kitchen.

Doley and his wife retired to the bedroom, which was separated from the kitchen by a glass door. Its two windows, protected by tightly closed oak shutters, opened out onto the garden. Near the top of the shutters, two small diamond-shaped openings admitted daylight even when the shutters were closed.

Although it was the time that Madame Doley, like all farm people, normally got undressed and went to bed, that evening, some vague worry troubled her out of her routine. She did finally get into her nightclothes, but before she'd actually get into bed she insisted that her husband check all the doors to be sure they were securely locked.

The farmer agreed, shrugging his shoulders like a man who thinks it is an unnecessary precaution. The first door he checked was the one that led from the kitchen to the milk room, but since it had only a few openings for light and no outside entrance, she did not disagree when her husband said, "To get in there, anyone would have to come in through the kitchen, and we have been in the kitchen all afternoon."

He checked the courtyard gate; it was firmly locked with an iron bar and two bolts. The window too was secure. The door of the bake house had only one lock, but it was an oak door and a prison lock. Finally, there was the garden door, but to get to it, you would have to scale a ten-foot-high wall or break down the courtyard door, itself impregnable.

Somewhat reassured, Madame Doley went back into the bedroom but she still couldn't keep from trembling. Doley sat down at his desk and pretended to be looking over his papers. Yet, whatever power he had over himself, he was unable to hide his worry, and the slightest sound would give him a start.

If he had begun to worry because of what he had learned during the day, he indeed had valid reasons. Roughly one hour from Plescop, a band of about twenty men was leaving the woods near Meucon and starting across open fields. Four were on horseback, riding in front like a vanguard and wearing uniforms of the Gendarmerie Nationale. The fifteen or sixteen others following on foot were not in uniform, and they were armed with guns and pitchforks. They were trying their best not to be seen. They stuck to the hedgerow, walked along ravines, crawled up hillsides, and got closer and closer to Plescop. Soon they were only a hundred paces away. They stopped to hold council.

One of the men moved out from the band and circled his way around to the farm. The others waited. They could hear a dog barking, but they could not tell if it came from inside the farm or a neighboring house.

The scout came back. He had walked around the farmhouse but had found no way in. Again they held council. They decided that they would have to force their way in.

They advanced. They stopped only when they reached the wall. That's when they realized that the barking dog was on the wall's other side, in the garden.

They started toward the gate. On its side, so did the dog, barking even more ferociously. They had been discovered; their element of surprise was lost.

The four horsemen in gendarme uniforms went to the gate, while the bandits on foot pressed themselves back against the wall. Now sticking its nose under the gate, the dog was barking desperately.

A voice called out, a man's voice: "What's the matter, Blaireau? What's wrong, old boy?"

The dog turned toward the voice and howled plaintively.

Another voice called out from a little farther away, a woman's voice: "You are not going to open the gate, I hope!"

"And why not?" the man's voice asked.

"Because it could be brigands, you imbecile!"

Both voices went quiet.

"In the name of the law," someone shouted on the other side of the gate: "Open up!"

"Who are you, to speak in the name of the law?" the man's voice asked.

"The gendarmerie from Vannes. We have come to search Monsieur Doley's farm. He has been accused of giving refuge to Chouans."

"Don't listen to them, Jean," said the woman. "It's a trick. They're just saying that to get you to open the gate."

Jean, the gardener, was of the same opinion as his wife, for he had quietly carried a ladder over to the courtyard wall and climbed up to its top. Looking over, he could see not only the four men on horseback but also roughly fifteen men crowded up against the wall.

Meanwhile, the men dressed like gendarmes kept shouting: "Open up in the name of the law." And three of them began pounding at the gate with the butt end of their guns while threatening to break it down if it was not opened.

The noise of their pounding reached all the way to the farmer's bedroom. Madame Doley's terror increased. Shaken by his wife's alarm, Doley was still trying to bring himself to leave the house and open the gate when the stranger emerged from the milk room, grabbed the farmer's arm, and said: "What are you waiting for? Did I not tell you I'd take care of everything?"

"Who are you speaking to?" cried Madame Doley.

"Nobody at all," Doley answered, hurrying out from the kitchen.

As soon as he opened the door, he could hear the gardener and his wife talking to the bandits, and although he was not duped by the bandits' trickery, he called out: "Well, Jean, why are you so stubbornly refusing to open up to the police? You know that it is wrong to try to resist them. Please excuse this man, gentlemen," Doley continued, walking toward the gate. "He is not acting on my orders."

Jean had recognized Monsieur Doley. He ran up to him. "Oh, Master Doley," he said. "I'm not mistaken. You are. They aren't real gendarmes. In the name of heaven, don't open up."

"I know what's happening and what I have to do," said Jacques Doley. "Go back to your rooms and lock yourself in. Or if you are afraid, take your wife and go hide in the willows. They will never look there for you."

"But you! What about you?"

"There's someone here who has promised to defend me."

"Come on, are you going to open up?" roared the leader of the supposed gendarmes, "or must I break the gate down?" And once again they pounded three or four times on the gate with the butts of their guns, which threatened to knock the gate off its hinges.

"I said I was going to open up," shouted Jacques Doley.

And he did.

The brigands swarmed over Jacques Doley, grabbing him by the collar. "Gentlemen," he said. "Don't forget that I willingly opened the gate for you. You realize that I have ten or eleven men working here. I could have given them weapons. We could have defended ourselves from behind these walls and done severe damage before surrendering."

"But you didn't. Because you thought you were dealing with gendarmes and not with us."

Jacques showed them the ladder placed against the wall. "Yes, except that Jean saw you all from up on that ladder."

"Since you did open the gate, what do you expect?"

"That you will be less demanding. If I had not opened the gate, you might have burned my farm in a moment of rage!"

"And who's to say that we won't burn your farm in a moment of joy?"

"That would be unnecessary cruelty. You want my money, fine. But you do not wish my ruin."

"Well, now," said the chief, "finally someone who's reasonable. And do you have a lot of money?"

"No, because a week ago I paid all my bills."

"The devil take you! Those are not the kind of words I want to hear."

"They may not be what you want to hear, but they are the truth."

"Well, then, we were given bad information. For we were told that you'd have a large sum of money here."

"Someone lied to you."

"No one ever lies to George Cadoudal."

By now, they had gotten closer to the farmhouse and were pushing Jacques Doley into the kitchen. The brigands, unused to such coolness from one of their prey, were looking in astonishment at the farmer.

"Oh, gentlemen, gentlemen," said Madame Doley, who had once again gotten up and left the bedroom, "we'll give you everything you want, but please you won't hurt us, will you?"

"Say," said one of the brigands, "you're like an Auray eel, crying before you're skinned alive."

"Enough words," said the chief. "The money!"

"Woman," said Doley, "give them the keys. These gentlemen will look themselves. That way they cannot accuse us of trying to fool them."

The woman looked at her husband with surprise, and made no move to obey. "Give them the keys!" he said again. "When I say give them, you give them."

Agape, the poor woman could not understand why her husband was so readily acquiescing to the brigands' demands. But she gave the leader the keys, then watched in fear as he walked over to the huge walnut wardrobe, the kind in which farmers usually lock up their most valuable possessions, beginning with their linens.

In one drawer they found silverware. The chief grabbed it up and tossed it onto the middle of the tiled kitchen floor. To Madame Doley's great surprise, she counted only six place settings when there should have been eight. In another drawer they'd had a sack of silver and a sack of gold, about fifteen thousand francs in all. But however much the chief dug through the drawer, to the woman's great astonishment, all he came up with was the sack of silver.

The wife tried to exchange a look with her husband, but he did not look back. One of the brigands, however, caught the flash of her glance. "Well, now, Mother," he said, "is your august husband trying to trick us?"

"Oh, no, gentlemen!" she cried. "I swear."

"Perhaps you know more than he does. Very well, we'll start with you then."

The brigands emptied the wardrobe but found nothing else of value to them. They emptied a second wardrobe as well and found only four louis, five or six six-pound crowns, and a few coins hidden in a bowl. "I think you might be right," said the chief to the brigand who had accused the woman of trying to trick them.

"Someone warned him we were coming," said one of the bandits, "and he has buried his money."

"Thunderation!" said the chief. "We have ways of getting money to come out of the ground. Come, bring me a bundle of wood and some straw."

"Why?" cried the woman in terror.

"Have you ever seen a pig roast?" the chief asked her.

"Jacques! Jacques!" the woman cried. "Do you hear what they're saying?"

"Of course I can hear," said the farmer. "But what do you expect? They are the masters, and we have no choice but to let them do whatever they want."

"Oh, Jesus!" cried the woman in desperation, as two brigands came from the bake house, one carrying a bundle of straw, the other some sticks. "How can you be so compliant?"

"I trust that God will not permit such an abominable crime as the destruction of two creatures whom I cannot call innocent of any sin, but certainly they're innocent of any crime."

"What do you mean?" asked the chief. "Is God going to send an angel to protect you?"

"It would not be the first time," said Jacques, "that God would show himself through a miracle."

"Well, we'll see about that," said the chief, "and to give him the opportunity to kill two birds with one stone, we'll burn the sow along with the boar." Shouts of laughter greeted his joke, all the more so because it was crude.

The brigands grabbed Jacques Doley, tore off his shoes, pants, and stockings. They ripped off the woman's skirt. They tied them up separately but similarly, with their hands behind their backs and made them sit on the floor with their legs stretched out. When the fire had caught, they pushed the farmer and his wife by the shoulders until their feet were just a few inches away from the flames. Both cried in pain at the same time.

"Wait!" said one of the brigands, "I've just found the piglets. We need to roast them along with the father and mother." Into the room he dragged a child in each hand; he'd found them quaking and weeping on the floor behind their mother's bed.

Jacques Doley could stand no more. "If you are a man," he shouted, "it is time to keep the promise you made!"

Scarcely had he pronounced those words than the milk house door was thrown open. A man came out, his arms extended, and in each hand he held a double-barrelled pistol.

"Who is the man they call George Cadoudal?" the man asked.

"I am," said the tallest and heaviest of the masked men, getting to his feet.

"You're lying," said the stranger. And he shot the bandit point-blank in the chest.

"I myself am Cadoudal," he said. The impostor fell, dead.

The bandits took a step backward. They had indeed recognized the real Cadoudal, who, they'd assumed, was still in England.

XXIV

Counterorders

IT WAS CADOUDAL, and not a man among the band of indenciaries—or in all of the Morbihan—who would dare to raise a hand against him or hesitate to obey a single one of his orders. So the second in command, who was still holding the children, released them and walked over to Cadoudal. "General," he said. "What are your orders?"

"First of all, untie those two poor people."

The bandits quickly did Cadoudal's bidding. Madame Doley collapsed in an armchair, then drew her two children into her arms and pulled them to her breast. Her husband rose to his feet, walked over to Cadoudal, and shook his hand.

"And now?" asked the second in command.

"Now," said Cadoudal, "I've been told that there are three brigades like yours."

"Yes, General."

"Who had the audacity to gather you together to do this odious work?"

"A man came from Paris; he told us that you would be back to join us within a month; he said that we should gather in your name."

"Fighting against the government as Chouans I could understand. But burning, never! Am I an arsonist?"

"We were even told to choose the man among us who most resembled you, so that people would believe you were already here. We called him George II. What must we do now to atone for our mistake?"

"Your mistake was to believe that I could ever become the leader of a band of brigands like you, and there is no way to atone for that. Carry my orders to the other groups: They must disband and cease their odious activities immediately. Then send word to all the former leaders, and especially to Sol de Grisolles and Guillemot, asking them to take up arms and prepare once again to embark on a campaign under my command. However, they must not make a move or raise their white flag until I say so."

The bandits withdrew without a word.

The farmer and his wife restored order to their wardrobes. The linen once more took its place on the shelves and the silverware in the drawers. A half hour later, the room looked as if nothing out of the ordinary had happened there at all.

Madame Doley had not been mistaken. Her husband had indeed taken precautions. He had hidden some of the silverware as well as the sack of gold, which contained probably twelve thousand francs. The Breton peasant, among all peasants, is the most defiant and perhaps the most provident. In spite of Cadoudal's promise, Doley had worried that things might turn out badly, and in that case, he wanted to protect at least some of his fortune. And so he had done.

After seeing to Jean and his wife and then carrying out George II's body, Monsieur and Madame Doley relocked their doors. Cadoudal, who had eaten nothing since morning, now sat at a simple supper, as if his day had passed without event. Refusing the bed the farmer offered, he stretched out on fresh straw in the barn.

The next day, scarcely had he arisen when Sol de Grisolles arrived. Living in Auray, about two and a half leagues from Plescop, he had been roused by one of the brigands who'd hoped to please Cadoudal by telling Grisolles without delay that Cadoudal was nearby. The news greatly astonished Grisolles, for he believed, like everyone else, that Cadoudal was in London.

Cadoudal told him the whole story and showed him the traces of fire and blood on the kitchen's tile floor. These burning brigades had surely been a police plot, devised to nullify the treaty that Cadoudal had signed with Bonaparte by accusing the Breton general of breaking it. So Cadoudal concluded; and in light of that, he said, he was once more free to act as he wished: which was what he wanted to talk to Sol de Grisolles about.

His first intention was to inform Bonaparte that by virtue of what had recently happened in Brittany, he was withdrawing his word. Still, with proof incontrovertible that he had nothing to do with the new wave of banditry in the west—for indeed he had stopped it at his own life's peril—he would not declare a war between sovereign powers, since that would be impossible for him to carry out; rather, he would undertake vengeance Corsican style. He wished to charge Sol de Grisolles with communicating the vendetta. It was a charge that Grisolles accepted immediately, for he was a man who never backed away from what he believed to be his duty.

Grisolles would then join Laurent, wherever Laurent happened to be, and have him put his Companions of Jehu back into operation at once, with the understanding that Cadoudal himself would lose no time in going first to London and then returning to Paris to set his own plans into execution.

Once he had given his instructions to Sol de Grisolles, Cadoudal said good-bye to his hosts, begged their forgiveness for having used their home as the theater for the horrors the day before, and mounted his horse. While Grisolles was heading to Vannes, Cadoudal was galloping to the beaches at Erdeven and Carnac, where his boat, only apparently a fishing boat, was plying along the coast.

Three days later, Sol de Grisolles was in Paris, requesting from the First Consul a safe-conduct and a meeting for a matter of the greatest importance. The First Consul sent Duroc to his hotel, but Grisolles, apologizing politely like a true gentleman, declared that he could repeat only to General Bonaparte the message he carried from General Cadoudal. Duroc reported back to the First Consul and then returned to escort Grisolles to the Tuileries.

Bonaparte, it turned out, was quite upset about the Cadoudal matter.

"So," he said without allowing Sol de Grisolles time to speak, "that is how your general keeps his word. He agrees to leave for London, and instead he stays in the Morbihan where he raises bands of burning brigades who rampage all over, as if he were Mandrin or Poulailler. But I have given orders. All the authorities have been alerted. If he is taken, he will be shot like a bandit without a trial. Don't tell me it's not true. *Le Journal de Paris* has published an article, and my police reports agree. Besides, people have recognized him."

"Will the First Consul permit me to answer," said Sol de Grisolles, "and to prove my friend's innocence with a few words?" Bonaparte shrugged.

"And if in five minutes you admit that your newspapers and your police reports are wrong and I am in the right, what will you say?"

"I will say . . . I will say that Régnier is an idiot, that is all."

"Well, General. A copy of *Le Journal de Paris* reporting that Cadoudal had never left France and was raising burning brigades in the Morbihan ended up in his hands in London. He immediately boarded a fishing boat and came back to France, landing on the Quiberon peninsula. He hid at a farm that was to be burned that very night, and he burst from his hiding place just as the leader of the brigade, who claimed himself to be Cadoudal, was about to torture the farmer. The farmer's name is Jacques Doley; the farm is called Plescop. Cadoudal walked straight up to the man who had usurped his name and blew out his brains, saying: 'You are lying. I am Cadoudal.'

"And then he asked me to tell you, General, that in fact it was you, or at least your police, who had tried to sully his name by placing at the head of the burning brigades a man of his size and stature, a man who looked enough like him to be mistaken for him. He took vengeance on the man by killing him right there on the spot. That done, he ran the others off the farm they had presumed to seize, although there were twenty of them and he was but one."

"What you are telling me is impossible."

"I saw the body, and here is a letter from two farmers attesting to it all." Grisolles placed under the First Consul's eyes the written account of the night's events. It was signed by Jacques Doley and his wife.

"So," Grisolles continued, "Cadoudal now frees you from your promise and takes back his own. He is unable to declare war since you have stripped him of all his means of defense, but he declares upon you a Corsican vendetta. For you he adopts the code of your own country: *Defend yourself! He will defend himself!*"

"Citizen," Duroc cried, "do you know whom you are speaking to?"

"I am speaking to a man who gave us his word as we gave him ours, who was bound as we were, and who had no more right to violate that word than did we."

"He is right, Duroc," said Bonaparte. "Still, we need to know if he's telling the truth."

"General, when a Breton gives his word. . . ." Sol de Grisolles cried.

"A Breton can be mistaken or tricked. Duroc, go get Fouché."

Ten minutes later, Fouché was in the First Consul's office. The former Minister of Police had scarcely cleared the doorway when Bonaparte called out, "Monsieur Fouché, where is Cadoudal?"

Fouché began to laugh. "I could answer that I have no idea."

"Why do you say that?"

"Because I am no longer Minister of Police."

"You still hold the office. . . ."

". . . but am on the way out."

"No more joking, Fouché. But, yes, you are on the way out. I am still paying you, however, and you still have the same agents, so you can still tell me what I need to know as you still are, technically, officially minister. I asked you where Cadoudal was."

"As of now, he must be back in London."

"So he had left England?"

"Yes."

"For what reason?"

"To blow out the brains of a fellow who had assumed his identity."

"And did he kill him?"

"Right in the presence of the fellow's twenty men at the Plescop farm. But this man," he said, pointing to Sol de Grisolles, "can tell you more than I can about the matter. He was close by when it happened. Plescop, I believe, is only two and a half leagues from Auray."

"What?! You knew all that and you did not alert me?"

"Monsieur Régnier is prefect of police. It was his job to let you know. I am just an ordinary citizen, a senator."

"So it's clear, the prefecture is a job honest men will never know properly how to do," said Bonaparte.

"Thank you, General," said Fouché.

"Indeed. All you need is for people to think that you're an honest man. In your place, Fouché, I would aim for something higher.

"Monsieur de Grisolles, you are free to go. As a man and as a Corsican, I accept the vendetta that Cadoudal announces. Let him defend himself, and I will defend myself. But, if he is captured, there shall be no mercy."

"That is exactly how he expects it to be," said the Breton with a bow, and took his leave.

"Did you hear, Monsieur Fouché?" said Bonaparte when the door had closed on the two of them. "He has declared a vendetta. It's your job to protect me."

"Make me Minister of Police once again, and I'll be happy to protect you."

"You're a fool, Monsieur Fouché. As bright as you think you are, you're a fool. For the less you are Minister of Police, visibly at least, the easier it will be for you to protect me, since no one will mistrust you. Besides, it has been only two months since I abolished the Ministry of Police, so I cannot very well restore it without good reason. Save me from some great danger; then I shall restore it. Meanwhile, I shall open for you a credit line of five hundred thousand francs from secret funds. Use it as you need, and when it runs out, let me know. Above all, I want you to see to it that no misfortune befalls Cadoudal. I want him taken alive!"

"We shall try. But to do that, he first needs to come back to France."

"Oh, he'll be back!—you can be sure of that. I'll be expecting to hear from you."

Fouché bowed to the First Consul, and, returning to his carriage as quickly as possible, he leaped up onto it rather than climbing inside, and called out, "Back to my office!" Once there, as he climbed down, he said to his coachman, "Go get Monsieur Dubois. And if possible, make sure he brings Victor along."

A half hour later, the two men Fouché had summoned were in his office. Although Monsieur Dubois reported to the new prefect of police, he had remained faithful to Fouché, not on principle but for reasons of self-interest. He realized that Fouché's disfavor would not last forever, so he was careful not to betray Fouché: not Fouché the man, but rather Fouché the minister who might make him his fortune. He, along with three or four of his best agents, like the especially skillful Victor, had remained completely at Fouché's service.

There were two piles of gold stacked on the fireplace mantel when Dubois and his agent entered the office of the real Minister of Police. Victor, a man of the people, had not had the time even to change his clothes.

"We did not want to waste a single moment," said Dubois. "I bring you one of my most reliable men, dressed just as he was when I received your message."

Without answering, Fouché walked over to the agent, and, attending Victor with his cross-eyed gaze, he said, "Damn it, Dubois. This may not be the man we need after all."

"What kind of man do you need, Citizen Fouché?"

"I've got a Breton leader we have to follow, perhaps to Germany, certainly to England. I need a respectable man, someone who can shadow him with ease, inconspicuously, in cafés, in clubs, and even in parlors. I need a gentleman, and you have brought me a bumpkin from the Limousin."

"Oh, how true!" said the agent. "I'm not one for cafés, clubs, and parlors very much, but drop me into taverns, popular dances, and cabarets and you'll find me in my element sure." He winked at Dubois, who had been regarding his agent with surprise but was quick to understand.

"So," said Fouché, "you must immediately send me a man who could comfortably attend an evening party at the regent's. To him I shall give my instructions." Taking two louis from a third stack of gold, he said to Victor, "Here, my friend. This is for the trouble you've taken. If I ever need you for more ordinary observations, I shall ask for you. But not a word to anyone about coming to see me here today."

"Not a word," said the agent, speaking in the accent of his region, "and I accept with pleasure. You ask for me, you say nothing to me, and you give me two louis to keep silent. Nothing simpler."

"Fine, fine, my man," said Fouché. "Now you may go."

Both men returned to Fouché's carriage. Fouché himself was a little annoyed to have wasted time, but since he had not told Dubois the sort of surveillance he required, he realized the fault was mostly his own fault.

Still, he did not have to wait long for the second man. Within a quarter of an hour, he was announced. "I said to let him come in!" he shouted impatiently. "Send him in!"

"Here I am, here I am, Citizen," said a young man, about twenty-five or twenty-six years old, with dark hair and bright, intelligent eyes; he was impeccably dressed and looked to be quite familiar with high society. "I lost no time getting here, and here I am!"

"It's about time!" said Fouché, as he studied him through his lorgnette. "You are just the man I need."

After a moment's silence. during which he continued his examination, Fouché asked, "Do you know what this is all about?"

"Yes! It's about following a suspicious citizen, maybe go to Germany and surely to England. Nothing easier. I speak German like a German and English like an Englishman. Be assured, too, I shall never let him out of my sight. So all I need is for someone to point him out to me, or to see him once, or to know where he is and who he is."

"His name is Sol de Grisolles, and he is Cadoudal's aide-de-camp. He lives on Rue de la Loi, and his hotel is called L'Unité. He has perhaps already left the city. In that case it will be necessary to pick up his trail. I need to know everything he does." Taking the two stacks of gold from the fireplace mantel, Fouché added, "Here. This will help you gather information."

The young man held out his perfectly gloved hand and put the money in his pocket without counting it. "And now," said the young dandy, "should I give back the Limousin's two louis?"

"What do you mean? The Limousin's two louis?" asked Fouché.

"The two louis you gave me a few minutes ago."

"I gave them to you?"

"Yes, and to prove it, here they are."

"Well," said Fouché, "in that case this third stack is also yours—consider it a bonus. Now, go on, waste no more time. I want information this evening."

"You will have what you need." The agent walked out as pleased with Fouché as Fouché was pleased with him.

Later that evening, Fouché received the first dispatch:

I've taken a room in the Hotel L'Unité, Rue de la Loi, and my neighbor is Sol de Grisolles. From the balcony that connects our four windows, I was able to see how his room is arranged. A sofa, ideal for conversation, is set right against my wall. I've made a hole, almost invisible, allowing me to see and hear everything. The citizen Sol de Grisolles, who did not find the person he was looking for at the Mont-Blanc Hotel, will wait for him until two in the morning. He has alerted the Hotel L'Unité that one of his friends would be coming to see him late.

I will be the unsuspected third party to their conversation.

The Limousin

PS: Tomorrow, first thing, I'll send a second dispatch.

The next morning as day was breaking, Fouché was greeted with a second message with the following information:

The friend the citizen Sol de Grisolles was expecting is the famous Laurent, called handsome Laurent, head of the Companions of Jehu. The order that Cadoudal's aide-de-camp delivered to Laurent was that all the affiliates of the famous company should be reminded of the oaths they have taken. Next Saturday they will be resuming their attacks, first by stopping the stagecoach from Rouen to Paris in the Vernon forest. Whoever is not at his post will be punished by death.

The citizen Sol de Grisolles is leaving at ten in the morning for Germany. I'll be leaving with him. We will pass through Strasbourg, and as best I can understand, we are going to the residence of Monsieur le Duc d'Enghien.

The Limousin

The two messages fell like two rays of sunshine on Fouché's chessboard, and they allowed the Minister of Police who was "on the way out" a clear picture of Cadoudal's own chess game. Cadoudal had not made an empty threat to Bonaparte by declaring a vendetta. For at the same time he was re-activating the Companions of Jehu, to whom he had given conditional leave, and he was now sending his aide-de-camp all the way to see the Duc d'Enghien. He was tired, no doubt, of the way the Comte d'Artois and his son kept hesitating. They were the only princes with whom Cadoudal had been in contact, and though they were always promising to send him money and men and to grant him their royal protection, they had never come through. Now he was going directly to the last member of the Condé family, that warrior race, to find out if he would be willing to provide more effective aid than simply his encouragement and best wishes.

Once his devices were set, Fouché would wait patiently, like a spider at the edge of its web.

That day, in both Vernon and Les Andelys, near the highway from Paris to Rouen, the gendarmerie received the order to keep their horses saddled day and night.

XXV

The Duc d'Enghien [1]

MONSIEUR LE DUC D'ENGHIEN LIVED in the little Ettenheim chateau, on the right bank of the Rhine about twenty kilometers from Strasbourg in the Grand-Duchy of Baden. He was the grandson of the Prince de Condé, who was himself the son of the one-eyed Prince de Condé who cost France so dearly during the regency of Monsieur le Duc d'Orléans. Just one Condé, and he died young, separated the one-eyed duke from the Condé whose victories at Thionville and in the Battle of Nördlingen won him the name The Great Condé. His great greed, rotten morals, and cold cruelty proved him indeed to be the son of his father, Henri II de Bourbon. Condé's strong desire to occupy the French throne prompted him to dis-close that Anne d'Autriche's two sons, Louis XIV and the Duc d'Orléans, were not in fact the sons of Louis XIII, which could easily have been true.

It was with Henri II de Bourbon that the celebrated Condé family changed character. No longer generous, it became greedy; no longer gay, it became melancholic. Although history states that he was the son of Henri I de Bourbon, Prince de Condé, chronicles from that time protest against the filiation and assign him a quite different father. Apparently Henri I's wife, the duchess Charlotte de la Trémouille, had been living in adultery with a Gascon page when suddenly, after a four-month absence, her husband returned home with no warning. The duchess quickly made a grim decision; after all, an adulterous woman is already halfway down the road to a murder. She afforded her husband a royal welcome. Although it was wintertime, she managed to find some lovely fruits, and with him she shared the most beautiful pear in the basket. The knife she used to cut the pear had a golden blade, and one side of it had been bathed with poison. The prince died that very night.

Charles de Bourbon reported the news of the death to Henri IV, and attributed the cause to papal decree: "His death was caused by Pope Sixtus V's excommunication," he said. "Yes," Henri IV replied, never one to pass up an opportunity to be witty, "the excommunication didn't hurt, *but something else lent a hand.*"

An investigation was opened, and serious charges were leveled against Charlotte de Trémouille. Henri IV asked that all the trial documents be delivered to him, and then threw every bit of them into the fire. When he was asked the reasons for his unusual action, he replied simply, "It is better for a bastard to inherit the Condé name than for such a great name to disappear forever."

So a bastard did inherit the Condé name, and he brought into that parasitic branch of the once noble family vices that had rather go unnamed. Rebellion, certainly, was the least of them.

Our position is different from that of other novelists. If we fail to report such details, we are accused of not knowing history any better than some historians. And if we do reveal them, then we are accused of trying to sully the reputation of the royal families.

But let us hasten to add that the young prince Louis-Antoine Henri de Bourbon had none of the failings of his father, Henri II de Bourbon, who, had he not been imprisoned for three years, would never have come back to his wife, though she was the most beautiful creature of the time. And none of the failings of the Great Condé, whose amorous relationship with Madame de Longueville, his sister, were the talk of Paris during the Fronde; or of Louis de Condé, who, while he was regent of France, simply emptied the state's coffers into his own and those of Madame de Prie.

No, the young prince Louis-Antoine was a fine-looking young man of thirty-three years. He had emigrated with his father and the Comte d'Artois, and in '92 he had joined the corps of émigrés that had gathered along the Rhine. For eight years he had been at war against France, it is true, but he fought in order to combat principles that his princely education and royal bias forbade him to support. When Condé's army was disbanded, as it was after the Lunéville peace treaty, the Duc d'Enghien could have moved to England, as had his father, his grandfather, other princes, and most of the émigrés. But because of a love affair no one knew about then, although it has become common knowledge since, he chose to set up residence, as we have said, in Ettenheim.

There he lived like an ordinary citizen. The immense Condé fortune, which had been built with gifts from Henri IV, the possessions of the Duc de Montmorency (who was decapitated), and the plunders of Louis le Borgne, had all been confiscated by the Revolution. The émigrés living around Offenburg often came to pay their respects. Sometimes the young men would organize large hunting parties in the Black Forest. At other times the prince would disappear for six or eight days, then reappear suddenly, without anyone knowing where he had been. His absences elicited all sorts of conjectures, and with neither confirmation nor denial, he simply let people think and say whatever they wanted to, no matter how strange their speculations and no matter the cost to his reputation.

One morning, a stranger came to Ettenheim. He had crossed the Rhine at Kehl, then followed the Offenburg road, and finally presented himself at the prince's door. The prince had been gone for three days.

The stranger waited. On the fifth day, the prince returned home. The stranger told the prince his name and the name of the man who had sent him. He asked that he be received at such time that the prince found it to be convenient. The prince invited the stranger in straightaway.

Sol de Grisolles was the stranger's name.

"You have been sent by the good Cadoudal?" the prince asked. "I just read in an English newspaper that he had left London and returned to France to avenge an insult made to his honor, and that once the insult had been avenged, he had gone back to London."

Cadoudal's aide-de-camp recounted the adventure as it had happened, without omitting a single detail. He told the prince, too, that he'd been sent to the First Consul to declare the vendetta. Then he spoke of his mission to Laurent, whom he had ordered, in Cadoudal's name, to call the Companions of Jehu back to the work they had been doing before Cadoudal had relieved them of their duties.

"Have you nothing more to tell me?" the young prince asked.

"Yes, I do, Prince," said the messenger. "I need to tell you that in spite of the Lunéville peace agreement, war will break out with renewed ferocity against the First Consul. Pichegru has finally come to an understanding with your father, and he will join in the cause with all the hate that's been kindled by his exile in Sinnary. Moreau is furious at how little recognition his victory at Hohenlinden has received, and he is tired of seeing the Rhine army and its generals sacrificed for the troops in Italy. So he too is ready to place his forces and his immense popularity behind a rebellion. And there is more. There is something almost nobody knows anything about, and I am to reveal it to you, Prince."

"What is that?"

"Within the army a secret society is being established."

"The Philadelphian Society."

"Are you familiar with it?"

"I have heard about it."

"Does Your Highness know who its leader is?"

"Colonel Oudet."

"Have you ever seen him?"

"Once in Strasbourg, but he did not realize who I was."

"What does Your Highness think of him?

"He seemed to me to be a bit young and a little frivolous for the huge undertaking he has dreamed up."

"Yes, Your Highness is not mistaken," said Sol de Grisolles. "Still, Oudet was born in the Jura mountains, and he has all the physical and moral strength of mountain people."

"He's barely twenty-five years old."

"Bonaparte was only twenty-six when he undertook his Italian campaign."

"He started out as one of ours."

"Yes, and we first met him in the Vendée."

"And then he went over to the Republicans."

"Which is to say he grew tired of fighting against Frenchmen."

The prince gave a sigh. "Ah! I too," he said, "am tired of fighting Frenchmen."

"Never—and may Your Highness accept the opinion of a man who is not quick to praise—never have such natural and such contrasting qualities been united in one man as they are in this Oudet. He is as naïve as a child, brave as a lion, giddy as a girl, and as tough as an old Roman. He is active and relaxed, lazy and relentless, changeable in mood and unchanging in his resolutions, sweet and strict, tender and terrible. I can add only one more thing in his honor, Prince: Men such as Moreau and Malet have accepted him as their leader and have promised to obey him."

"So, at the present time the three leaders of the society are. . . ."

"Oudet, Malet, and Moreau. Philopœmen, Marius, and Fabius. A fourth will join them, Pichegru, and he will take the name Themistocles."

"I see there are quite diverse elements in this association," said the prince.

"But very powerful ones. Let us first get rid of Bonaparte, and once his place is empty, then we can worry about the man or the principle that we need to fill it."

"And how do you intend to get rid of Bonaparte? Not by assassination, I hope?"

"No, but rather in combat."

"Do you think that Bonaparte will accept a Combat of Thirty?" the prince asked with a smile.

"No, Prince. But we shall force him to accept it. At least three times a week he goes to his country house, La Malmaison, with an escort of forty or fifty men. Cadoudal will attack him with a like number, and God will decide between them."

"Indeed, that is combat and not assassination," said the prince thoughtfully.

"But in order for the plan to be completely successful, Your Highness, we need the assistance of a French prince, a brave, popular French prince such as you. The Dukes of Berry and Angoulême, as well as your father and the Comte d'Artois, have made and broken so many promises that we can no longer count on them. So I've come to tell you, Milord, that all we are asking for is your presence in Paris, so that when Bonaparte is dead the people will be drawn back to royalty by a true prince from the House of Bourbon, one who is able and eligible to occupy the throne immediately."

The prince took Sol de Grisolles's hand. "Monsieur," he said, "I thank you from the depths of my heart for both your and your friends' esteem. I shall give you, to you personally, some warrant for that esteem, perhaps, by divulging to you a secret that nobody knows, not even my father.

"But to the brave Cadoudal, to Oudet, Moreau, Pichegru, and Malet, this is my response: 'For nine years I have continued the campaign. For nine years, I swear by my life, which I risk daily and which is unimportant, I have been filled with disgust and contempt for those powers who call themselves our allies and use us only as instruments. Those powers have made peace, yet they did not deign to include us in their treaty. All the better. Alone now, I will not perpetuate a parricidal war, like the war in which my ancestor the Great Condé drowned part of his glory. You will tell me that the Great Condé was waging war against his king, and I against France. From the point of view of these new Republican principles that I am fighting against, and on which I can personally make no pronouncement, my ancestor's excuse could rightly have been that he was fighting against nothing more than a king. I have fought against France, yes, but as a minor figure. I never declared war, nor did I bring it to an end. I left everything to destiny. To fate I answered: "You have summoned me; here

I am." But now that peace has been made, I will do nothing to change what has been done.' That's what you will tell my friends.

"And now," he added, "this is for you, but for you alone, monsieur. And please assure me that the secret I'm about to confide in you will never leave your breast."

"I so swear, my lord."

"Well, and please forgive my weakness, monsieur: I am in love." The messenger drew back.

"Weakness, yes," the duke repeated, "but happiness at the same time. A weakness for which I risk my neck three or four times a month by crossing the Rhine to see an adorable woman, a woman whom I love. People think an estrangement from my cousins and father is keeping me in Germany. No, monsieur. What is keeping me here in Germany is my love, my burning, superlative, invincible love, which is more important to me than my duty. People wonder where I go, they wonder where I am, they think I'm conspiring. Alas! Alas! I am in love, and that is all!"

"Love is a grand and sacred thing when it can make a Bourbon forget even his duty," Grisolles murmured with a smile. "Do not forsake your love, my prince. And may you be happy! That, you may be sure, is man's true destiny." Grisolles rose to his feet to take leave of the prince.

"Oh," said the duke, "you cannot leave just like that."

"Why should I stay?"

"Hear me out a little longer, monsieur. Never before have I spoken to anyone about my love, and my love overwhelms me. I have confided in you, but that is not enough. I want to tell you about it in full. You have stepped into the happy, joyous side of my existence, for she has made it so, and I must describe for you how beautiful she is, how intelligent, how devoted. Please have dinner with me, monsieur, and after dinner, well, then you may leave me, but at least I shall have had the luxury of talking to you about her for two hours. I have been in love with her for three years. Just think of that, and I have never spoken one word to anyone about her."

So Grisolles stayed for dinner. And for two hours the duke spoke only about her. He laughed, he wept; he savored and shared his love in every detail. Finally, squeezing his new friend's hands, the duke embraced Grisolles as he left.

Strange, the effects of friendship! In one day, a stranger had entered the young prince's heart more deeply than any of the friends who had never left his side.

The very same evening, Cadoudal's messenger was on his way to England, and the police agent whom Fouché had enlisted to report the messenger's every action sent the following message:

Left one hour later than the citizen S. de G.

Followed him stage by stage. First across the Kehl bridge; then had supper with him in Offenburg, in the same room, and he suspected nothing.

Spent the night in Offenburg.

Left at eight in the morning, by mail coach, a half hour after him.

Spent the night in the hotel La Croix, and the citizen S. de. G. in the hotel Rhin et Moselle.

Since my presence in Ettenheim might have been suspect, I said that I had come because of a letter from the last bishop prince of Strasbourg, Monsieur de Rohan-Guéménée, so famous for the role he played in the necklace affair. As for the bishop prince in Ettenheim, I introduced myself to him as an émigré, saying I did not want to pass through the region without paying my respects. He is full of vanity, so I praised him a great deal and thus gained his confidence enough that he invited me to have dinner with him. I took advantage of our brief friendship to ask him about the Duc d'Enghien. He and the prince rarely see each other, but, in a tiny city like Ettenheim with only three thousand five hundred souls, each man always knows what the other is doing.

The prince is a handsome young man of thirty-two or thirty-three years of age, with thinning blond hair. He is tall and strong, courteous and courageous. His life is surrounded by mystery, inasmuch as he disappears on occasion without anyone knowing where he has gone. However, His Grandeur has no doubt that the prince goes to France, or at least to Strasbourg, for twice he has met him on the Strasbourg road, once coming through Offenburg and once through Benfeld.

Citizen S. d. G. was graciously welcomed by the Duc d'Enghien, who invited him for dinner and who no doubt accepted his proposals, for he walked back with his guest to his carriage and shook his hand affectionately when they separated.

The citizen S. de G. is on his way to London. He left at eleven tonight. At midnight I too will leave.

In case I should need to stay in London, please open a line of credit of one hundred louis for me at the French embassy, so that no one else knows about it.

The Limousin

PS: Don't forget, milord, that the Companions of Jehu are to return to battle this afternoon, and that as their first action they are to rob the Rouen stagecoach in the Vernon Forest.

We trust that our readers now understand why the Comte de Sainte-Hermine disappeared so suddenly.

Once he had received his leave from Cadoudal, Sainte-Hermine was so eager to believe that he was truly free that he had finally asked for the hand of Mademoiselle de Sourdis, and her hand had been granted.

We have seen with what pomp the marriage contract was prepared and how Hector had so nearly signed it. We have seen how the Chevalier de Mahalin had rushed into the house of Madame de Sourdis and stopped Sainte-Hermine just as he was about to go into the drawing room and enter his signature. Then Mahalin, pulling the count into the light from a chandelier, had shown him Cadoudal's order that Laurent should take up arms again, and Laurent's order to the Companions of Jehu to ready themselves for battle anew.

Hector had cried out in pain. The foundation of all his happiness was collapsing beneath him. His fondest dreams, nurtured for the past two months, had evaporated. He could not, by signing the contract, risk some-day making Mademoiselle de Sourdis the widow of a highway robber whose head had fallen on the scaffold. Chivalry vanished before his eyes; he could no longer view his situation in the mirror of his dreams, he had to place it under reality's magnifying glass. All that was left for him was flight.

He hesitated not one second. Shattering his destiny with three words, he said, "We must flee!" And he rushed from the house with the Chevalier de Mahalin.

XXVI

In the Vernon Forest

THE FOLLOWING SATURDAY, around eleven in the morning, two men rode out of the village of Port-Mort. Following the road that links Les Andelys and Vernon, they passed through L'Isle and Pressagny until they reached Vernonnet. There they crossed the old bridge with its five mills to reach the Paris-Rouen highway. At the end of the bridge, when one turns to the left, the Bizy Forest offers a shady arcade, and the two horsemen rode in the trees just off the highway, though not so deep in the forest that they were unable see any carriages passing by on the highway.

When they had been riding through Pressagny, two other horsemen leaving Rolleboise started down the left bank of the Seine. Once they'd left Port-Villez and Vernon behind them, they arrived at the spot where the other two riders had headed into the forest. They stopped to confer with each other; then, after a moment's hesitation, they too resolutely disappeared into the forest.

Scarcely had they covered ten paces when someone cried out: "Who's there?"

"Vernon!" the newcomers answered.

"Versailles!" said the two men who had arrived earlier.

At the same time, on the forest road running diagonally from Thilliers-en-Vexin to Bizy, two more horsemen appeared, and, using the same watchwords, they joined the other four. Having identified themselves to each other, the six horsemen waited in silence.

A bell struck midnight. They counted the twelve strokes one by one. Almost immediately after the last, they heard a rumbling off in the distance.

Each horseman placed his hand on his fellow's arm, saying, "Listen!"

As one, they answered, "Yes."

They all understood, and all their hearts beat faster, as if echoing the hoofbeats and wheels of the approaching carriage. The forest echoed the sound of their pistols being cocked.

Suddenly, the stagecoach's two lanterns appeared. Not one of the six men breathed, their pounding now in their ears.

The stagecoach advanced. It was maybe ten paces away when two of the men surged forward to grab the horses and the four others rushed toward the doors, shouting, "Companions of Jehu! Do not resist!"

The stagecoach stopped, but in one moment from the doors came a shocking volley of shots, and in the next, a voice cried out, "Let's be off!" And the four strong Percherons galloped away with the carriage.

Two of the Companions of Jehu lay stretched out on the ground. A bullet had gone through one man's temple; he was lost, and his horse had fled. The second man, trapped under his horse, was struggling in vain to reach the pistol he'd lost when he fell. The other four horsemen had dashed into the forest or toward the river, crying: "We've been betrayed! Run for your life!"

Four gendarmes galloped up. They leaped down from their horses and, grabbing the man who had just managed to recover his pistol, prevented him from blowing out his brains. That hope gone, all the man's energy seemed to drain from his body. He heaved a deep sigh and fainted. Blood was gushing from a large cut on his scalp. The gendarmes took the wounded man to the Vernon prison.

When he regained his senses, he thought he was awaking from a dream. A lamp was burning—more so that his captors could see him, when they bothered to look through the peephole in the door to his cell, than for him to be able to see—but it did allow him to contemplate where he might be.

Then everything came back to him. He put his head in his hands and began to sob.

The cell door opened, and the prison director, summoned by the sound of his sobbing, asked the man if there was anything he wanted. The prisoner stood up, and, shaking his head, he dispensed with his tears and said, "Monsieur, can you give me a pistol so I can blow out my brains?"

"Citizen," replied the director, "you are asking me for the only thing that, along with your freedom, I am forbidden to grant you."

"In that case," said the prisoner, sitting back down, "I need nothing at all." And nothing could bring him to say another word.

The next morning at nine, another man—the public prosecutor—entered his cell. He was still sitting on the stool onto which he had collapsed the night before. The blood from his scalp wound had coagulated, and his head was stuck to the wall; evidently he had not moved even an inch during the night.

The public prosecutor had come to interrogate him, but the prisoner refused to answer any of his questions, saying, "I will answer only to Monsieur Fouché."

"Do you have revelations to make to him?"

"Yes."

"On your word of honor?"

"On my word of honor."

The news had spread about the stagecoach holdup, and everyone knew how important their prisoner was. So the public prosecutor did not hesitate a moment. He called for a four-person carriage and had the prisoner carried to it, tightly bound. He sat beside the prisoner, stationed two gendarmes on the seat across from them, and placed a third one up on the seat with the driver. The carriage got under way. Six hours later, they had arrived at the home of Citizen Fouché.

The prisoner was led up to the antechamber on the second floor. The public prosecutor left the prisoner in there with the gendarmes while he himself stepped into Fouché's office. Five minutes later, he returned for the prisoner, whom he ushered into the office of the Senator Citizen Fouché de Nantes. (Fouché had just begun to add "de Nantes" to his family name; he liked its aristocratic ring.)

The prisoner had suffered his tight restraints throughout the long trip, and the ropes that bound him still were causing him considerable pain. Fouché noticed. "Citizen," he said, "if you give me your word not to try to escape while you are at my house, I shall have those ropes removed. They seem to be hurting you."

"They are indeed," said the prisoner.

Fouché rang for his office boy. "Toutain," he said, "cut loose or untie that man's ropes."

"What are you doing?" asked the public prosecutor.

"You see what I'm doing," said Fouché. "I'm having his ropes removed."

"But what if he takes advantage of his freedom?"

"I have his word."

"And if he doesn't keep his word?"

"He will not fail to keep it."

The prisoner sighed with relief and flexed his bloody hands; the rope had indeed cut into his flesh. "There now," said Fouché. "Are you ready to answer?"

"I said that I wanted to speak to you alone. Once we are alone, I shall speak."

"But first, citizen, please sit down. Monsieur the Prosecutor, you've heard what he said. You will not need to wait long to know what he has to say further. As the trial will be in your hands, your curiosity will no doubt be fully satisfied." He shook the public prosecutor's hand, and the man, contrary to his wishes surely, left immediately.

"And now, Monsieur Fouché. . . ."

But Fouché stopped the prisoner. "There is no reason for you to trouble yourself, monsieur," he said. "I already know everything."

"You do?"

"Your name is Hector de Sainte-Hermine; you come from an important family in the Juras. Your father died on the scaffold; your elder brother was shot at the Auenheim fortress. Your younger brother was guillotined in Bourg-en-Bresse. After his death, you in turn joined the Companions of Jehu. Cadoudal, after his meeting with the First Consul, freed you from your commitment, and you seized the opportunity to ask for the hand of Mademoiselle de Sourdis, for you are in love with her. As you were about to sign the marriage contract, to which the First Consul and Madame Bonaparte had already lent their signatures, one of your companions arrived and transmitted to you Cadoudal's order. You disappeared. They looked for you everywhere in vain. Yesterday, when the Rouen-Paris stagecoach had passed, after you and five companions had attacked it, you were found lying on the road under your dead horse; you were only partially conscious. You wanted to speak to me in the hope that I would let you blow your brains out and you would thus die incognito. Unfortunately I am unable to effect that hope. If I were able, word of honor, I would render you that service."

Hector stared at Fouché with astonishment. Then, quickly surveying the room, on the minister's desk he eyed a stylus as sharp as a dagger. He leaped for it, but Fouché stopped him. "Careful, monsieur," he said. "You are going to fail to keep your word, and that would be unworthy of a gentleman."

"How so, pray tell?" shouted the young count, trying to pull his chafed wrists from Fouché's grasp.

"Killing oneself is like running away."

Sainte-Hermine let the stylus fall and himself collapsed onto the carpet, where he began shaking convulsively.

Fouché observed him, and when he saw that Hector's pain had passed its peak, he said: "Listen, there is someone who might be able to grant what you wish."

Sainte-Hermine quickly pulled himself to one knee. "Who is that?"

"The First Consul."

"Oh!" cried the young man. "Please ask him to grant my request. Let me be shot behind a wall before an investigation can take place, and let it be done without my name being pronounced, so that even those who shoot me do not know who I am."

"Will you give me your word to wait here, that you will not try to flee?"

"You have my word! You have my word, monsieur! But in heaven's name, bring me back my death."

"I shall do the best I can," said Fouché with a laugh. "Your word. . . ."

"On my honor!" cried Sainte-Hermine, reaching out his hand.

The public prosecutor was still waiting in the antechamber. "Well?" he said when Fouché appeared.

"You may return to Vernon," said Fouché. "We no longer need you."

"But what about my prisoner?"

"I am keeping him here."

With no further explanation to the magistrate, Fouché hurried down the stairs and jumped into his carriage, shouting: "To the First Consul's!"

XXVII

The Bomb

⟡

THE HORSES HAD BEEN CHAMPING at the bit while they waited, and they galloped off when they received the order. At the Tuileries, they stopped of their own accord; they stopped there regularly.

Bonaparte was with Josephine. Fouché did not wish to be received in her apartment as he did not want to have a woman involved in his quivering political web. He asked Bourrienne to announce him.

The First Consul came up to the study immediately. "Well, Citizen Fouché, what is the matter?"

"Since I have many things to tell you, Citizen First Consul, I had no fear of disturbing you."

"So you should have done. So now, what do you have to tell me?"

"With Monsieur Bourrienne present?" Fouché whispered.

"Monsieur Bourrienne is deaf; Monsieur Bourrienne is dumb; Monsieur Bourrienne is blind," the First Consul answered. "Speak."

"I set one of my most skillful agents to follow Cadoudal's man," said Monsieur Fouché. "That very same evening he, Sol de Grisolles, had a meeting with Laurent, the leader of the Companions of Jehu, who immediately called his men back into action."

"And then?"

"Grisolles left for Strasbourg, crossed the Kehl bridge, and went to Ettenheim to pay a visit to the Duc d'Enghien."

"Fouché, you have not been paying enough attention to that young man. He is the only member of his family who has enough energy to fight and enough heart to fight bravely. It has been reported that he has even come to Strasbourg two or three times. You need to keep your eyes on him."

"Relax, Citizen First Consul. We are watching him."

"Do we know what they did while they were together, what they talked about?"

"What they did? They dined. What they said is more difficult to discern, since they were alone."

"And when did they part?"

"That evening at eleven o'clock Citizen Sol de Grisolles left for London. At midnight, my agent left as well."

"Is that all?"

"No. I still have the most important thing to tell you."

"I'm listening."

"The Companions of Jehu have resumed their campaign."

"When?"

"Yesterday. Last night they stopped a stagecoach."

"And they robbed it?"

"No. I had been forewarned and had placed some gendarmes in the stagecoach, and when they heard the order to stop and not to resist, instead of obeying, they began firing. One of the Companions of Jehu was shot dead; another was taken prisoner."

"Some miserable creature?"

"No." Fouché shook his head. "On the contrary."

"A nobleman?"

"One of the best."

"Has he made any important revelations?"

"No."

"Will he?"

"I don't believe so."

"We must find out who he is."

"I already know."

"His name is?"

"Hector de Sainte-Hermine."

"What? That young man whose marriage contract I signed? Who disappeared at the moment he himself was summoned to sign?"

Fouché nodded.

"Get his trial under way at once," Bonaparte shouted.

"That may compromise some of the finest names in France."

"Well, then, have him shot behind a wall somewhere, or behind a hedge, in a ditch."

"That is what I've come to request on his part."

"Well, his wish is granted."

"Allow me to take the good news to him."

"Where is he now?"

"At my house."

"What do you mean, at your house?"

"Yes, I have his word that he will not flee."

"So he's a man with a heart?"

"Yes."

"Should I see him?"

"As you wish, Citizen First Consul."

"No, I think not. I might myself get soft and pardon him."

"And at the moment, that would set a very bad example."

"You are right. Go, and make sure everything is over by tomorrow."

"Is that your final word?"

"Yes. Adieu."

Fouché bowed and exited. Five minutes later, he was back home.

"Well?" asked Hector, his hands joined as if in supplication.

"Granted," Fouché answered.

"Without a trial? And the news will not get out?"

"Your name will not be pronounced. From this moment on, you no longer exist for anyone."

"And when will I be shot? For I will be shot, won't I?"

"Yes."

"When will that be?"

"Tomorrow."

Sainte-Hermine grabbed Fouché's hands and squeezed them in gratitude. "Ah! Thank you! Thank you!"

"And now come with me."

Sainte-Hermine followed him like a child. Again the carriage was still
waiting at the door. Fouché motioned for him to climb into the carriage,
then climbed in after him. "To Vincennes," he ordered.

If the young count still had any doubts, the mention of Vincennes reassured him, for military executions took place at Vincennes. On their arrival, they both climbed down from the carriage and were introduced into the
fortress. Monsieur Harel, the governor, came to meet Fouché. Fouché whispered a few words to him, and the governor bowed obediently. Fouché
prepared for his departure.

"Farewell, Monsieur Fouché," said Sainte-Hermine, "and many
thanks."

"We may see each other again," Fouché answered.

"What?" cried Sainte-Hermine. "What do you mean?"

"Well, by God, who knows?"

Meanwhile, Saint-Régeant and Limoëlan had arrived in Paris. So had the
Limousin, as Fouché called him, and he had already alerted the Minister of
Police that Saint-Régeant and Limoëlan had arrived from London. Both
men were hotheads, though they complied with their orders from Cadoudal,
for whom they were acting as scouts, as it were. Cadoudal's presence in
Paris would depend on whether their mission was a success or not.

Nobody knew exactly how they were planning to attack the First Consul. By "nobody," we are referring to those four people who actually knew
the two men were in Paris. Perhaps even they themselves did not know
how they were going to do it.

The First Consul made no effort to stay out of sight. He would go out
walking on Rue Duroc in the evening, and he would often travel by himself
in his carriage during the day. Three or four times a week he would go to
La Malmaison, but with only a few men to escort him. He would frequently
attend the Comédie-Française or the Opera.

Bonaparte was not a man of letters. He judged the whole of a work by
its details. He loved Corneille, not for his poetry, but for the thoughts his
poetry expressed. When on occasion he quoted French verse, rarely were
the quotations accurate, and yet he loved literature.

Music he found to be a way of relaxing; for him, as for every Italian, it was a sensual pleasure. He was nonetheless unable to carry a tune even two measures long. Still, he admired such masters as Gluck, Beethoven, Mozart, and Spontini. And Haydn, whose oratorio *The Creation* was the most popular work of the day.

The story of the Hungarian maëstro Haydn had become legendary. He was the son of a poor wheelwright, who, in addition to making wheels, played the harp as a strolling musician. His wife liked to sing, and little Joseph, only five or six years old, scraping at a board, would pretend to accompany her. As performers, the family traveled from village to village. It was the schoolmaster in Hainburg who spotted in Joseph what he thought was an extraordinary talent for music. He took the boy in, taught him the rudiments of composition, and found him a job as choir boy in Saint Stephen's, the cathedral in Vienna. For seven or eight years people flocked to the city to hear his magnificent countertenor, which he lost when his voice changed. With his voice he also lost his means of livelihood, and the young man was about to go back to his village when a poor wigmaker, himself a musician, took him in. The wigmaker was happy to offer shelter to the man whose lovely voice he had so admired in the cathedral for all those years, while Haydn, now assured that he would not starve to death, was industrious. Working sixteen hours a day, he composed his first work, the opera *The Crippled Devil*, which was presented in the theater at the Carinthian Gate. From that moment on, he was secure.

When Haydn was thirty, he entered the household of Prince Esterhazy, who supported him for his next thirty years. Of course, he was already famous when the prince afforded him his patronage. Princes often appear in the lives of great artists, but they often arrive late. How would the poor survive without the other poor?

Once honors began showering down on Haydn, he, out of gratitude, married the wigmaker's daughter, and, we should add in passing, she in turn gave him as much happiness as Xanthippe did to Socrates.

In 1804 the French Opera had scheduled for performance Haydn's celebrated oratorio, and the First Consul had announced early on that he would attend opening night. At three in the afternoon of that day, Bonaparte turned to his secretary to say: "By the way, Bourrienne, you will not be dining with me this evening. I am going to the Opera, and I shall be taking along Lannes, Berthier, and Lauriston. If you would like to go on your own, you may, but you are otherwise free this evening."

However, when it was time to leave, Bonaparte, worn out from the day's work, wasn't sure that he really wanted to go out. He hesitated from eight o'clock until about a quarter after.

During those fifteen minutes, this is what was happening outside the Tuileries:

Two men appeard in Rue Saint-Nicaise, a narrow street (it no longer exists) through which the First Consul had to pass. Their horse was pulling a wagon on which they had loaded a barrel of powder. When they got halfway down the street, one of the two pulled a coin from his pocket and gave it to a little girl who, in exchange, agreed to watch his horse. Then one of the men ran to a spot where he could see the Tuileries clearly enough to send a signal, while the other man stayed nearby, so that on signal he could light the fuse of their infernal bomb.

As the bells were tolling eight fifteen, the man watching the Tuileries called out, "Here he comes!" The second man, at the cart, lit the fuse and ran off immediately. At the same time, through the gates of the Louvre, the First Consul's carriage, drawn by four horses and followed by a contingent of grenadiers on horseback, burst like a whirlwind. They had just turned into the little street when the driver—his name was Germain, though the First Consul called him César—saw a horse and cart blocking the road. Without trying to stop or hold back his horses, he shouted, "Cart! To the right!"

He meanwhile pulled to the left, and the little girl, afraid that she'd be run over along with the cart she was guarding, heeded his order and pulled to the right. The First Consul's carriage passed; so did its escort. Scarcely had they all disappeared around the first corner than they heard a terrible explosion, as if ten artillery guns had fired at one and the same time.

The First Consul exclaimed, "Somebody has just shot at us! Stop, César!" César obeyed.

Bonaparte leaped down. "Where is my wife's carriage?" he asked. (Madame Bonaparte, by some miracle—or by an argument with Rapp over the color of a cashmere shawl—had been delayed.)

The First Consul looked around him. Ruins everywhere. Two or three houses had been torn open by the explosion; one was totally leveled. Groans of the wounded hung in the air. Two or three bodies lay lifeless on the ground.

Every glass window in the Tuileries had been shattered, as had all the windows in the carriages of both the First Consul and Madame Bonaparte. Madame Murat had been too shaken to continue on to the Opera, so she was conveyed back to the palace.

Bonaparte assured himself that no one in his entourage had been wounded. He was relieved not to have discovered Josephine's carriage anywhere near. He dispatched two grenadiers to inform her that he had escaped safe and unharmed and to entreat her to join him at the Opera.

Then, climbing back in his carriage, he cried, "To the Opera, at top speed! People must not think me dead."

News of the catastrophe had already reached the Opera. People were saying that assassins had blown up an entire section of Paris. They were saying that the First Consul had been very seriously injured. Or that he was dead. Only then the door to his box opened and there he was, seating himself as usual near the front and looking as calm and impassible as ever.

A universal shout arose from every heart. For everyone there, excepting his personal enemies, Bonaparte was the bronze pillar of France. On him everything depended: military victories, national happiness, public fortune, France's tranquility, world peace.

The cheering intensified when Josephine too appeared. Pale and trembling, she made no attempt to hide her fright. Then she looked bravely, lovingly, at the First Consul, her concern shadowing her eyes.

Bonaparte stayed at the Opera only a quarter of an hour. He was eager to return to the Tuileries, so that he could relieve his heart of the anger engulfing him. It seemed that all the hatred he had harbored for the Jacobins had been revived, and whether it was entirely real or in fact political posturing, he needed to allow its expression.

What is strange about these attempts to create a dynasty, as they were undertaken first by Napoleon, then by the elder and the younger branches of the Bourbons, and even now by the government under which we are currently living, is the fatal and destructive instinct that compels them unwittingly to wed their ambition to delusions so like those in Louis XVI's ill-fated throne and Marie-Antoinette's anti-national royalty. It seems that the enemies of those two unfortunate people, who at the guillotine expiated the faults of Louis XIV and Louis XV, should also be the enemies of any new throne, no matter what isolated branch of the monarchy it might belong to. If that was not one of Bonaparte's faults, it was certainly one of his errors.

As the explosion of the two carters' bomb had been heard all over Paris, the large reception room on the ground floor that opened up onto the terrace of the Tuileries had been instantly crowded with people. They had come to read in the master Bonaparte's eyes, for Bonaparte was already the master, their destiny. They had come to learn to whom they should attribute this new crime; they had come to hear who should stand accused. The First Consul's opinion wasn't long in coming.

Although that very day Bonaparte had had a long conversation with Fouché during which the minister had talked about Royalist plots, he seemed to have forgotten all that completely. As nervous and upset at the palace as he had been calm and collected at the Opera, he said as he entered, "This time, gentlemen, there are no nobles involved, nor are there priests, Chouans, or Vendeans. It's the work of the Jacobins; the Jacobins alone tried to assassinate me. I know exactly who I'm dealing with, and nobody can tell me otherwise. It's those filthy scoundrels, the Septembrists, who are always conspiring even when they're not engaging in open rebellion; like a *bataillon carré*, they confront society and every succeeding government. Not a month goes by without people like Ceracchi, Aréna, Topino-Lebrun, and Demerville trying to kill me. Always the same cadre. The bloodthirsty Septembrists, those Versailles assassins, those brigands of May 31st, those Prairial conspirators, they are the authors of every crime against every different government. If we cannot restrain them, we must wipe them out. We must purge France of her vermin. No pity for the blackguards. Where is Fouché?"

He stomped his feet impatiently. "Where is Fouché?" he repeated.

Fouché appeared; his clothing was covered with plaster and dust. "Where have you come from?" Bonaparte asked.

"From where it's my duty to have been," Fouché answered. "From the ruins."

"Well? Do you still insist it's the Royalists?"

"Citizen First Consul," said Fouché, "I will not speak until I am certain of what I'm saying. And when I accuse, you may be sure that I will be accusing the real perpetrators."

"The real perpetrators, in your opinion, are not the Jacobins?"

"The real perpetrators are those who committed the crime, and they are the ones I am looking for."

"Well, by God, they should not be hard to find."

"Very hard, on the contrary."

"But I know who they are. I need not depend on your police, I can do my own policing. I know who the authors of this crime are, and when I find them, as I will, I shall inflict on them exemplary punishment. Until tomorrow, Monsieur Fouché; I shall be waiting for what you uncover. Until tomorrow, gentlemen."

With that, Bonaparte went up to his apartments. In his office, he found Bourrienne, whom he asked, "Do you know what happened?"

"Of course," Bourrienne answered. "By this time all of Paris knows."

"Yes, and so Paris also must know who the guilty people are."

"Be careful. Those whom you name Paris will accuse."

"Those whom I name, by God! I shall name the Jacobins."

"That is not Fouché's opinion. He claims it was a conspiracy involving two people, three at the very most. He says that any conspiracy must be handled by the police."

"Fouché has his reasons for not agreeing with me. Fouché is protecting his own—was he not one of their leaders? Am I not aware of what he did in Lyon and in the Loire? So, Lyon and the Loire help me understand Fouché. Good night, Bourrienne."

He went to his room in a calmer frame of mind. His anger had been spent.

Meanwhile, Fouché had returned, as he had said, to the ruins. All around the Rue de Saint-Nicaise he had set up a police cordon to protect as much as possible the scene of the explosion. There he had turned the Limousin loose. In police circles, the Limousin was called Victor Quatre-Faces, because he could so skillfully play four completely different roles—as a man of the people or a cultured gentleman, as an Englishman or a German— but on this occasion he had no need to change his language or wear a disguise. He had only to put into play the invaluable faculties nature had given him, his intelligence and instinct in solving the most baffling and mysterious of plots.

Fouché found him sitting on the rubble of a broken-down wall; he was lost in thought. "Well, Limousin?" Fouché asked.

"Well, citizen. I thought I should question the coachman, for he alone, sitting high up on the driver's seat, would have been able to see what was in the street when they entered it. What César told me I'm sure is true."

"You don't think that he might have been blinded by fear, or perhaps even drunk?"

The Limousin shook his head. "César is a good man," he said. "His real name is Germain, but Bonaparte gave him the name César in Egypt the day he saw him first attack three Arabs, then kill two of them, and finally take the third one prisoner. The First Consul, who hates to owe anything to anyone, might say he was drunk, but he was not."

"Well, what did he see?" asked Fouché.

"He saw a man run toward the Rue Saint-Honoré after dropping something behind him. And he saw a girl holding the bridle of a horse that was harnessed to a cart on which there was a barrel. The girl certainly didn't know what was on the cart, which was a barrel of powder, and what the man had dropped was a lighted fuse."

"We must find and question the girl," said Fouché.

"This girl?" the Limousin answered. "Take a look; here's her leg." He showed Fouché a foot; it still wore a blue cotton stocking and a shoe, but it was no longer attached to a body.

"How about the horse? Is anything left of it?"

"The head and one thigh. In the middle of the forehead there's a white star. Plus, I have a few pieces of its hide, enough to get a description."

"And the cart?"

"For that, we must wait. I'm having all the pieces of metal set aside. To-morrow I'll take a look."

"Limousin, my friend, I'm putting you in charge of this business."

"Then I must be completely in charge."

"I cannot speak for the First Consul's own police."

"No matter, as long as yours don't get in my way."

"Mine will keep their distance, as if nothing at all happened."

"Then things will turn out fine."

"Can you guarantee it?"

"When I get hold of something at one end, I always reach the other."

"So you must. There will be a thousand crowns for you the day you do."

More certain than ever that the Jacobins had not been involved, Fouché returned home.

The next day around two hundred people, all of them known for their revolutionary opinions, were arrested. After debating several alternatives, Bonaparte decided to deport them on the basis of a consular decree for which he'd need—and would get—Senate approval.

The day before the decree was to be approved, all the detainees were forced to parade one by one before a jury of four men: One was a horse dealer, another sold seeds, the third rented carts, and the fourth was a cooper. None of them recognized among the parade of detainees either of the two men who'd set off the explosion, and thus far, nobody assumed that more than two men were involved, although a third might possibly have played a smaller role.

The little jury had been chosen with the help of the unfortunate horse's remains and the Limousin's ingenuity. The day after the event, in all the newspapers and on street-corner posters, everyone could read the following notice, drafted by the Limousin:

The prefect of police alerts all citizens that the little cart which carried the barrel of powder with iron hoops that exploded yesterday at 8:15 PM in the Rue Saint-Nicaise, just opposite the Rue de Malte, as the First Consul was passing, was harnessed to a mare. It was a bay draft horse with a ragged mane, a cropped tail, a nose like a fox, pale flanks and rump, a mark on its head, white spots on both sides of its back and roan-colored under its main on the right side, of indeterminate age, about a meter fifty tall, which is about four feet six inches, fat and in good health, without any marks on thigh or neck to indicate that it belonged to any depot.

Anyone knowing who might own this mare or who might have seen it pulling the little cart is invited to give any information they have to the

prefect of police, either verbally or in writing. The prefect offers a reward to the person who can lead us to the owner. People are also invited
to come identify the mare's remains, and to come as soon as possible because of rapid putrefaction.

All of the horse dealers in Paris heeded the call, and on the very first day
the mare was identified by the one who had sold it. When he asked to speak
to the prefect, the officers sent him to the Limousin. The horse dealer then
gave the Limousin the name and address of the seed dealer to whom he had
sold the mare.

The Limousin sent for the seed dealer, who identified the horse's remains and said that he had sold the mare to two men claiming to be traveling merchants. Having talked to them on two or three occasions, the seed
dealer remembered them well. He was able to provide some description:
One was dark-haired, he said, and the other man's hair was light brown.
The taller of the two was about five feet six or seven inches; the other was
perhaps three inches shorter. One carried himself like a military man; the
other seemed to be an ordinary middle-class citizen.

The following day, a man who rented carts appeared at the prefecture. He
also was able to identify the mare, which had been kept in one of his barns
for a few days, and his description of the two men who owned the horse and
rented its cart matched that of the seed dealer. The fourth of the jurors, the
cooper, had sold the two men the barrel and had himself put the hoops on it,
he told the Limousin.

No doubt the Limousin's job was made easier by the public's enthusiasm
for the First Consul. Witnesses, like the four men chosen to be jurors, simply appeared of their own accord, without waiting to be called. Anyone
with information that might shed light on the mysterious business was
eager to share it with the authorities, to help them add to the facts of the
case, rather than keep it to himself.

For all that, the upshot so far had been only one mediocre result. And
that was to confirm Fouché's opinion that none of the Jacobins who'd been
arrested was guilty, since not one of them had been identified as the supposed traveling merchants by the four men on the Limousin's little jury.

There was, however, another result. The prison doors were opened to two
hundred twenty-three people. Still, Bonaparte had one hundred and thirty
other political prisoners that he was now even more determined to punish.

Bonaparte's determination, as it turned out, did not sit well with the
Conseil d'Etat, particularly with Monsieur Réal. A member of the Conseil
d'Etat and a historiographer of the Republic—the founder of the *Journal
de l'opposition* and of the *Journal de patriotes de 1789,* he had been a prose-

cuting attorney at the Châtelet, the former prosecutor having been relieved of his duties by Robespierre for being too moderate—Réal took Bonaparte to task: He claimed that Bonaparte had in fact set out to persecute his personal enemies rather than to prosecute the true perpetrators of the crime.

"But," cried Bonaparte, "I am after the Septembrists."

"The Septembrists!" Réal answered. "If there are any, may they perish to the last man. But what is a Septembrist? Perhaps Monsieur Roederer, who might be considered a Septembrist by the Faubourg Saint-Germain; perhaps Monsieur de Saint-Jean-d'Angély, who might be considered a Septembrist by émigrés in power."

"Is there not a list of such people?"

"Yes, of course, there are lists," Monsieur Réal answered. "On the first list I see the name of Baudrais, who has been a judge in Guadeloupe for five years. I also see the name of Pâris, clerk of the revolutionary court, but he's been dead for six months."

Bonaparte turned toward Monsieur Réal. "Who drew up these lists?" he asked. "There are surely plenty of those incorrigible Babeuf anarchists left."

"And I too would be on that list," said Réal, "if I were not a member of the council. For I defended Babeuf and those accused with him in Vendôme."

Bonaparte, a man who always demonstrated great mastery over his emotions, then said, "I see that emotions have deeply colored a state question. We must look at the question again, but with equity and sincerity."

Another man would never have forgiven Réal for the embarrassment of proving him wrong during an official meeting of the Conseil d'Etat. Bonaparte would continue to pursue the political enemies he had sworn to bring down, but he also took note of the honest man he had met on his path, and he would reward him too. Six months later, Réal had become a deputy to the Minister of Police.

The Conseil d'Etat deemed it necessary to Bonaparte's plans to deport one hundred and thirty Jacobins. What did it matter to him whether they were guilty or not?

XXVIII
The Real Perpetrators

BONAPARTE DREW ALL THE ADVANTAGE he could from the plot organized by his still unknown assassins. Once he had succeeded in deporting the one hundred and thirty Jacobins in the aftermath of the assassination attempt, he turned his attention to an earlier conspiracy, one that had landed its strategists—Aréna, Topino-Lebrun, Ceracchi, and Demerville—in jail. Their case had not yet come to court, and the explosion in the Rue Saint-Nicaise gave Bonaparte the opportunity to set the trial date speedily. Their cases were tried, and the four conspirators were found guilty and executed while the more recent plot against Bonaparte was still the major topic of public conversation.

Fouché, already certain from his agent's report that he would soon have in hand the true authors of the bomb, came to see Bonaparte before their arrest, in order to discover what specific actions he might want to take. Flushed with the success of his deportation decrees, and having seen the last of the Jacobin revolutionaries leave France cursed by an ignorant population, Bonaparte scarcely paid any attention at all to Fouché's question. This was his answer: "Get rid of all those low-class courtesans, all those immoral women, infesting the area around the Tuileries."

Bonaparte had noticed that the prostitutes in those wretched little rooms so close to the palace often were involved not only in conspiracies but also in every variety of crime. His concern that day, however, as Fouché soon realized, was the beautification of Paris, not his own personal safety. "But for the love of God!" cried Fouché, employing a phrase typical of supplications. "Give a little thought to your own safety!"

"Citizen Fouché," Bonaparte laughed. "Might you by chance believe in God? I would find that amazing."

"Though I do not believe in God," Fouché answered impatiently, "you will agree that I do believe in the devil, won't you? Well, then, in the name of the devil, to whom we shall soon be sending your conspirators' souls, I trust, give some thought to your safety!"

"Bah!" the First Consul said with his customary lack of concern. "Do you think it would be so easy to take my life? I have no set habits, I keep no regular hours. I never exercise at the same time, and my goings are as unpredictable as my comings. It's the same for the table. I've no special preferences for food. Sometimes I eat one thing, sometimes another, and I'm as likely to choose a serving from a dish set out of easy reach as from one that's right in front of me. Nor is this mode of behavior based on some system, you can be sure. It is just the way I am, and that is why I act as I do. But, my dear man, since you are so capable, since once again you will find the guilty parties, though it's already two weeks since they tried to kill me, I shall let you take all the appropriate measures and watch assiduously over me. That is now your responsibility."

So that Fouché would not think that he was mouthing a crowd-pleasing sort of bluster, Bonaparte went on: "Don't think that my peace of mind is lodged in blind fanaticism," he said, "any more than it is based on my faith in the diligence of your police officers. Another assassination plan will surely be put into play. But we don't know the details, and while there's an unlikely chance of its success, there's no sure way to guard against it. All of that is much too vague for a mind as positive and a character as absolute as mine. Facing real obstacles, I can rely on my intelligence to be effective and on my resources to meet the challenge. But how can we prevent ambush by some malcontent, or a knife thrust in the corridor at the Opera, a gunshot from a window, a bomb exploding on a street corner? I would need to be afraid of everything at every moment. Vain weakness! Protect myself at all times from everything? Impossible. It is no help to keep telling me about the danger I face at any moment. I am aware of that danger, but I put it out of my mind. And by putting it out of my mind I am free not to waste time thinking about it."

He continued: "I live by the power of my reason, or at least by my ability to keep my feelings and actions subservient to its authority. When I have decided that something is not within my means, or that it is unsuitable, I cease to waste time thinking about it. All that I'm asking you to do is not to take away my peace of mind. My peace of mind is my strength."

And when Fouché insisted that the First Consul at least agree to take some precautions, Bonaparte said, "Come now. Why don't you go on home? Go ahead and have those men arrested since you think you know who they are. Arrange for their trial; have them hanged, shot, or guillotined. Not because they tried to kill me, but because they are clumsy men. They missed me, and in missing me they killed twelve citizens and wounded sixty others instead."

Realizing that there was nothing more to be gained in arguing with the First Consul, Fouché took his advice and went home. There he found the Limousin waiting.

With his skills, the Limousin had gained Fouché's complete confidence. The police had been keeping watch on three men they believed might be Chouans who'd come to Paris to kill the First Consul; all three men had disappeared on the day of the bombing. Nor did they ever reappear, a fact that had led the Limousin to believe that they were the actual perpetrators of the crime. He knew the names of those three men. They were Limoëlan, a former Vendean, Saint-Régeant, and Carbon.

He could find no trace of Limoëlan or of Saint-Régeant. But he discovered that Carbon's sister was living in the Faubourg Saint-Marcel with her two daughters. He rented an adjacent room in the same building and made a show of holing up there for two days. On the third day, or rather the third night, after moaning and groaning loudly enough so that his neighbors could hear him through the thin walls, he dragged himself to their door, rang, and dropped to his knees.

One of the daughters opened the door. She found a man with little strength and almost no voice leaning against the wall. "Oh, Mother!" she cried. "It's our poor neighbor who's been moaning all day long."

The mother hurried out, helped him stand up, and led him to a chair inside. She asked how, in spite of their poverty, she and her daughters could help. "I'm starving," the Limousin answered. "I have not eaten a thing for three days. I don't dare go out into the streets because they are full of policemen. They're looking for me, I'm sure."

Carbon's sister first had him drink a glass of wine; then she gave him a chunk of bread, which he devoured as if indeed he had not eaten for three days. Since she and her daughters also feared the police, as they were Carbon's sister and nieces, they asked the man what he had done.

Seeming to yield reluctantly to their request, he admitted, or pretended to admit, that he had been sent to Paris by Cadoudal, so that he could join Saint-Régeant and Limoëlan. Since he had arrived in Paris the day after the assassination attempt in the Rue Saint-Nicaise, however, he had not been able to gather any information as to the whereabouts of either of the two. And that was unfortunate, because he had a guaranteed way of getting them to England.

The old woman and her two girls didn't open up to him that first day, but they did give him more bread and a bottle of wine. They also promised to provide him with food as long as he was living beside them, although he would have to pay for it, they said, since they were living, if not in misery, at least in poverty.

On the second day he learned that Carbon was the old woman's brother and that he had been living with his sister until the 7th Nivôse, when a young woman, Mademoiselle de Cicé, sent by Limoëlan's confessor, had come to get Carbon. She had taken him to a small congregation of the Sisters of Sacré-Coeur, where he was introduced as a priest who had not yet received authorization to return to France but had come back to Paris anyway, supposedly in the expectation of hearing in a few days that his name had been removed from the list of émigrés. Ensconced with the holy sisters, he was surely safe, for they, to show their gratitude to the First Consul for reopening the churches for public worship, had been holding a public mass daily to protect his precious life. Carbon never failed to attend.

Furthermore, the old woman knew all about the bomb conspiracy, for it had been planned under her very nose. She showed the Limousin the last of the twelve kegs of powder that had been used to fill the barrel. The keg still contained fourteen pounds of powder—an English mixture, of a very good quality, the Limousin noted. The other kegs had been broken up for firewood, which the three women had burned in the fireplace. One day Limoëlan had said to them, "Go easy with it, ladies, that's expensive wood." She also showed the Limousin the smocks two of the conspirators, Limoëlan and Carbon, had worn; she wasn't sure what had become of the smock Saint-Régeant had been wearing.

The Limousin still needed to find out which religious congregation was unwittingly sheltering Carbon. The three women themselves didn't know, but the false Chouan was so insistent about organizing with Carbon the conspirators' escape to England that the woman promised to bring him her brother's address the next day. She did know Mademoiselle de Cicé's address, and a visit there produced all the information the old woman—and the Limousin—wanted.

Since the masses said for the First Consul's safety were public, the Limousin and two other agents were able to enter the church without suspicion. In one corner of the choir the Limousin spotted a man praying so ardently that it could only be Carbon. He waited until the church emptied, then walked over to Carbon and arrested him. Carbon offered not the slightest resistance, because he had no idea that anyone knew who he was. Soon, however, Carbon was admitting everything. It was the only hope he had.

Carbon revealed that Saint-Régeant was hiding in a house on Rue du Bac, where he too was arrested. Once he realized that his accomplice had confessed to everything, he made no effort to defend himself or to protect Limoëlan. Here is the confession, copied from the record he himself signed:

Everything Victor has said about the purchase of the horse, boarding it with the seed merchant, buying a barrel with iron hoops, all that is true.

The day still had to be chosen, and we chose the evening when the First Consul would be going to the Opera to hear the oratorio *The Creation*.

We knew that he would have to take Rue Saint-Nicaise, one of the narrowest streets around the Tuileries, and that is where we resolved to place our bomb. The carriage was to come by at eight fifteen. At exactly eight o'clock, I was there with the cart, while Limoëlan and Carbon were each standing at one of the Louvre gates to give me the signal. Limoëlan and Carbon were dressed as carters, just as I was, and we had taken the cart to a spot just opposite Rue de Malte. And then, as I have said, they each went to their stations. Five minutes went by. Seeing that there was no signal, I left the cart, taking care to hand the horse's bridle to a young peasant girl. I gave her a coin for her help, and then I started up the street toward the Tuileries.

Suddenly I heard Limoëlan shouting: "Here he comes!" And at the same time I could hear a carriage and men on horseback coming toward me. I ran toward the cart, saying to myself, "My God, if Bonaparte is necessary for France's tranquility, shield him from the explosion and turn it on me." And all the while I was shouting to the girl "Run, run, get out of here!" I set fire to the tinder on the cart; it was supposed to act as a fuse.

The carriage and escort were almost upon me. The horse of one of the grenadiers threw me back against a house. I fell, got up again, and ran toward the Louvre. But I was able to take only a few steps. My last memory as I turned is seeing the tinder glowing like a spark and then the girl's silhouette against the cart. Then everything went black. I saw nothing more, heard nothing more, felt nothing more!

I found myself, not knowing how I got there, under one of the Louvre gates. How long had I been unconscious? I could not say. A chilly breeze brought me back to my senses. I remembered who I was and everything that had happened. But two things surprised me: one, that I was still alive; the second, that since I was still alive I had not been arrested. Blood was oozing from my nose and mouth. I had probably been taken for just another innocent passerby who had been wounded by the terrible blast. I ran to the bridge. I balled up my smock and threw it into the river. I did not know where to go, for I had assumed I would be blown to bits in the explosion and had not given any thought to seeking refuge in case I should survive. I found Limoëlan at home; we were living together. When he saw how badly I was wounded, he ran quickly to get a confessor and a doctor. The confessor was his uncle, Monsieur Picot de Closrivière, and the doctor was a young doctor who was a friend of his. That is when we learned that our attempt had failed.

"I did not want to use tinder," said Limoëlan. "If you had let me take your place as I was asking, I would have used a torch to set the fire. I would have been blown to bits, I know, but at least I would have killed Bonaparte."

That was all they learned from Saint-Régeant, and indeed that was all they needed to know from him.

Limoëlan was ashamed at having failed. Since he knew that the condition imposed on a political assassin was either to succeed or to die, not only did he not go back to see George Cadoudal, but he did not even set foot again in England. As devout as he was proud, seeing only the will of God in his actions and not wanting to subject himself to the judgment of mere mortals, he hired himself out as an ordinary sailor in Saint-Malo.

There was news eventually that he had retired to some foreign country and withdrawn from society, but even his party did not know what exactly had become of him. Fouché, though, never lost sight of him, and for a long time he kept his eye on the distant monastery where Limoëlan had become a monk. He corresponded only with his sister, and at the top of one of his letters, which he no doubt feared might be intercepted by English ships, Desmarets, the chief of the high police, read this remarkable invocation: "Oh, Englishmen! Please permit this letter to get through. It is from a man who has accomplished much and suffered greatly for your cause."

Two other Royalists were also linked to the assassination plot, but they played scarcely even a shadowy role in the final plan. They were Joyaut and Lahaye Saint-Hilaire, and like Limoëlan they were able to flee in all the uproar raised by Bonaparte's action against the Jacobins. They took the news to George Cadoudal and England that the latest plot in the battle for France had failed.

Saint-Régeant and Carbon were both sentenced to death. In spite of his revelations to the police, which had led to the arrest of his accomplice, Carbon could not get his sentence commuted. When the matter was brought up with Bonaparte, he appeared to have completely forgotten the trial of the would-be assassins and answered simply: "Since the sentence has been rendered, it must be carried out. It is none of my business." On April 21, Carbon and Saint-Régeant died without notice on the scaffold. It was still red from the blood of Aréna and his three fellow conspirators.

The day after their execution, the Limousin was on his way back to London with secret instructions.

XXIX
King Louis of Parma

~:~

WHEN A MAN'S EXISTENCE weighs supreme in a great nation's interests, honor, and destiny, when minds are led to foresee the success or collapse of a great fortune and begin to consider the possibilities that success or failure could mean, then friends and enemies stand facing each other, calculating the possible consequences of their hate for or their devotion to a man whose star is rising but who might be brought down at any moment. It is a time for augurs, for portents, for prognostication. Even dreams wield a secret influence, and everyone is ready to be guided into the unknown country of the future by one of those bright, vaporous phantasms that escape from night's kingdom through the gates of horn or the gates of ivory. Some diviners, out of their natural timidity or a mania for seeing the bad side of any circumstance or occasion, are easily alarmed and cannot refrain from giving absurd warnings about all sorts of imaginary dangers. Others, on the contrary, view the world from but a single perspective that sees only easy means and happy ends. They would press a Caesar or a Bonaparte in whatever direction he might blindly choose to go, without giving a thought to dangers unforeseen. Still others—those who have fallen; those on whom the man of genius or darling of chance or Providence has trampled—vent their impotent rage in sinister vows and threatening signs filled with bloody promises. These become the preoccupations of troubled minds in troubled times, and often of them criminal ideas are born. Feeble, brooding imaginations wallow in the murk of deadly plots and fatal devices: terror, assassination, revenge.

In troubled times—as when Caesar wanted Rome to name him king, or when Henri IV resolved to carry out the trial of Marie de Medicis and Concino Concini, or when Bonaparte, after the 18th Brumaire, wavered between becoming France's Augustus or George Washington—it seems that a price is always put on the head of any great man dedicated to his vision of public tranquility. And there are always ravenous hands eager to pick up Brutus's dagger or Ravaillac's knife in the hope of bringing down the obstacle that stands in the path of their ambitions, dreams, or principles.

Indeed, the entire first year of the Consulate saw an unending series of plots against the First Consul. Enemies from the 13th Vendémiaire, enemies from the 18th Fructidor, enemies from the 18th Brumaire; Royalists, Republicans, Companions of Jehu, Vendeans and Chouans—they all conspired at night in the forests, on the highways, in cafés, at the theater. Angered by the events in Saint-Cloud that Brumaire day, alarmed by the power Bonaparte then assumed as First Consul, indignant that he would not answer Louis XVIII's letters, both the Royalists and the Republicans, the Whites and the Blues, the only two true political parties left in France, began to call for vengeance and death.

"How do you expect me not to conspire?" Aréna would ask his judges. "Everyone is conspiring these days. There is plotting in the streets, plotting at social gatherings, plotting at every crossroads, plotting in public squares."

And Fouché himself would say, to prod Bonaparte out of his apathy regarding conspirators, "The air is full of daggers."

The air indeed was full of daggers when we saw Bonaparte solidly installed in the Tuileries and in protocol, which though it was not yet imperial protocol was still something more than princely protocol; when we saw that Josephine was now attended by four ladies in waiting and four palace officers at all times; when we saw her organizing receptions in her apartments, and when we saw her, in the formal apartments on the ground floor that opened onto the gardens, receiving ministers, the diplomatic corps, and foreigners of distinction; when we saw her, preceded by the Minister of Foreign Affairs, greet the ambassadors of all the European powers drawn to Paris by the universal peace, and when we then saw the door of the First Consul's living quarters flung open so that the First Consul could salute, with his hat still on, the dignitaries bowing before him; when we saw the second anniversary of the 18th Brumaire celebrated as a Day of Peace; when we saw the man whom the two legislative chambers had once declared an outlaw now negotiating with the pope, God's ambassador, just as he had negotiated with the ambassadors of earthly kings; when we saw him reopen the churches and have the Te Deum sung in Notre Dame by Cardinal Caprara; when we saw Chateaubriand, who had been banished from France and had found God in the virgin forests of America and at Niagara Falls, publish the *Génie du christianisme* in the same capital that, five years earlier, had celebrated along with Robespierre the Supreme Being and mandated worship of the Goddess Reason, whose deistic temple had been Philippe Auguste's basilica; when we saw Rome reconciled with the Revolution and the pope reaching out his hand to the signatory of the very treaty that had despoiled him of his provinces; and finally, when we saw the victor at Montebello, at Rivoli, at the Pyramids, and at Marengo bring to the two legislative assemblies peace on land with the Treaty of Lunéville, peace on the seas with the Treaty of Amiens, and peace in heaven with the Concordat; when we saw him become, in recompense for all his services, consul for life, a title that did not come, quite, with a throne; and when we saw England, our archenemy, fail to outmaneuver him in war or peace; when, for a moment, we could hope for a ruler who would be as wise in the future as he had been great in the past, for he possessed two qualities rarely given by God to one man, the vigor of great leaders' genius and the patience that ensures the fortune and glory of empires and their founders; when we could hope that after making France so great, after showering her with glory, after placing her at the head of nations, he would now prepare her for liberty; when we saw England begin to grow horrified and take it upon herself to stop in his tracks this new Washington, who, as powerful as the first as a legislator, was much more illustrious as a general.

Then we saw the First Consul, seizing an unexpected opportunity, astound Europe once again and raise doubts even more. To the king of Spain, who had aided Bonaparte in his war against Portugal, he promised that he would give the kingdom of Etruria to the infante of Parma, who had married the Spanish king's daughter. The peace treaty signed in Lunéville had ratified that promise.

The infante, Louis Bourbon-Parma, and his wife, destined by Bonaparte to reign over Tuscany, had just arrived at the border in the Pyrenees and had inquired as to the First Consul's orders. Bonaparte wanted very much to vaunt the royal couple in France and have them visit Paris before traveling on to Tuscany to take possession of the Florentine throne. The First Consul, who had begun to feel that in his office he could do whatever he wanted, delighted in all the ambiguities of the situation. It struck him as being worthy of the glory days of Rome, and he relished the idea of a king being established by a republic. He especially enjoyed the fact that the occasion would allow him to demonstrate that he had little to fear from a Bourbon's presence in France, for he was convinced that his own reputation put him beyond any comparison with that old race of rulers whose place, if not their throne, he now occupied. The visit would also provide him an enormous opportunity to show the world that Paris had at last been healed of all its revolutionary wounds, and to celebrate her recovery, in his position as a simple consul, if in a style more sumptuous than most European kings at the time would have been able to display, ruined as they all had been by the war that had enriched France.

Bonaparte met with his two colleagues, the provisional consuls Emmanuel Joseph Sieyès and Roger Ducos. All three deliberated for a long time about the protocol to be observed in regard to the king and queen of Etruria. They agreed first of all that the honored couple should remain incognito. They would thus be introduced under the names of the Count and Countess of Livorno, and they would be accorded the same protocol as that given the Tsarevitch Paul of Russia and Joseph II when they visited during

Louis XVI's day. Orders were issued to the appropriate civil and military departmental authorities all along the titled couple's route.

While France, proud of creating kings but pleased not to have one, cheered as the two young royals passed, Europe looked on with astonishment.

At a theater in Bordeaux, the Royalists decided to take advantage of the couple's presence and test public feeling. "Long live the king!" they cried out, and from every corner of the arose a ringing, loud response: "Down with kings!"

The royal couple arrived in Paris during the month of June. Although Bonaparte as First Consul was supposedly simply a temporary magistrate of a republic, he clearly represented France, and all the privileges of royal blood paled before his eminence; thus the two young people went first to see him. On the following day he returned the visit, but, to mark his distinction from his two colleagues, he had the provisional consuls visit the couple first.

It was at the Opera that the First Consul planned to present his guests to the Paris public. On the set day of the performance, however, either out of calculated self-interest or because he was really ill, an indisposed Bonaparte was unable to appear. Cambacérès replaced the First Consul, and once he had escorted the couple to the consuls' box, he took the Count of Livorno by the hand and introduced him to Paris. The audience responded with unanimous applause, perhaps not untinged by malicious intent.

The First Consul's indisposition prompted much conjecture as various parties read into Bonaparte's absence at the Opera intentions he had perhaps never had at all. His partisans said that he simply did not wish to present any Bourbon, whatever his nationality, to France. The Royalists asserted that it was his way of preparing France for a return of the deposed monarchy, whereas the few Republicans still remaining after the latest political blood-letting claimed that with royal ceremonies celebrated in his absence but by his authority, he was trying to accustom France to the idea of restoring monarchy.

The ministers followed the First Consul's demand for protocol, especially Monsieur de Talleyrand, whose aristocratic tastes had long disposed him toward the complete restoration of the old régime, of which, in terms of elegance of style and language, he was a perfect specimen. At his chateau in Neuilly, Monsieur de Talleyrand hosted for the traveling prince a magnificent party, and all of Parisian high society attended. In fact, many guests who would not have deigned to mingle at the Tuileries did appear at the home of the Minister of Foreign Affairs.

At Neuilly a surprise awaited the young couple, who were not yet acquainted with their future capital. During a brilliant light show the city of Florence suddenly appeared, and there, at its most Florentine, was the

Palazzo Vecchio. Then a company of men and women, all of them dressed in traditional Italian costumes, entertained them with dancing and singing, while a retinue of young girls presented flowers to the future sovereigns and victory wreaths to the First Consul.

The celebration, people said, had cost Monsieur de Talleyrand a million. But he had done what no one else could have accomplished: he'd brought over to the new government in one evening alone more partisans of the old regime than the Consulate had been able to attract in two years. Nostalgic for the old regime because of what they had lost, they were now beginning to believe that they might be able to regain good fortune under the new one.

Finally, the Count and Countess of Livorno were taken to La Malmaison by the Spanish ambassador, the Count of Azara. There the First Consul welcomed the appointed king as the head of a military house. But the king, totally unfamiliar witih military protocol and, to him, its bewildering display of stripes, swords, salutes, and ceremony, completely lost all countenance and threw himself into the First Consul's arms.

We are forced to admit that the poor young prince was an idiot, or nearly so. Although Nature had given him an excellent heart, it had refused him like qualities of the mind. It is true to say, too, that the monastic education he had received had served only to extinguish what little light might have arisen from his heart to illuminate his mind with a glimmer of intelligence.

Louis of Parma stayed at La Malmaison almost the entire six weeks he spent in France. Madame Bonaparte would take the young queen to her apartments, but as the First Consul never left his office until dinnertime, the aides-de-camp were obliged to try to entertain the young king, who was apparently incapable not only of engaging himself in any activity but also of enjoying himself.

"And," said the Duc de Rovigo, who was one of the First Consul's aides-de-camp at that time, "we really had to be patient with all the childish things that filled his head. When we knew him better, though, we had people send us games, the kinds of games parents usually give to children. And from then on he was never bored.

"We were pained by his uselessness. It was hard for us to watch a tall, handsome young man, one ordained to become a leader of men, quake at the sight of a horse he didn't dare or even know how to mount. He would spend his time playing hide-and-seek or leapfrog, and his entire knowledge seemed to comprise no more than his evening prayers or the grace he'd offer God before eating his soup and after drinking his coffee. It was in such hands that the destinies of a nation were going to be placed.

"When the young king left to go to his new states, the First Consul said to us: 'Rome can rest easy; that man will never cross the Rubicon.'"

God was kind enough to Etruria to take the young king to him after he had reigned for one year.

But Europe had not noted how ineffective the young prince was. All it had observed was that a new kingdom had been established. And it marveled at how strange were these French who cut off the heads of their own kings and then set up kings to rule other people.

XXX

Jupiter on Mount Olympus

OUR READERS MUST HAVE NOTICED our efforts to introduce the historical characters who play a role in our story without taking any side, just as they might introduce themselves impartially to history. We have never allowed ourselves to be influenced by personal memories of misfortunes within our own family, which date from the divisions between Bonaparte and Kléber in Egypt when my father took Kléber's side. Nor have we been influenced by the hosannas of Napoleon's eternal admirers, whose rule is to admire everything, no matter what, or by the new vogue, brought to pass by the opposition to Napoleon III, which is to criticize everything that has happened in the Napoleonic past in order to undermine the foundations on which Napoleon III's dynasty rests. No, I cannot say I have always been just, because no one can guarantee that, but at least I have been sincere, and I am sure that by now people have already confirmed my sincerity. In any case, our conviction is that by the time we are talking about, the First Consul realized that he had as much to gain from peace as from war, and he seriously desired peace. Though he was a man on whom fortune smiled when he gambled at the bloody game of battles which he knew so well, and which he trusted, we will not affirm that his sleep was not sometimes haunted by shades of Arcole and Rivoli. Nor can we affirm that from time to time his periods of wakefulness were not troubled by the sight of waving palm trees along the Nile or by the unyielding pyramids of Giza; nor that he was never drawn from his evening reveries by the dazzling snows of Saint-Bernard or by Marengo's blinding smoke. But we can affirm indeed that he could envision the golden fruits and oak-leaf wreaths that peace offers to those special people for whom destiny closes the door of Janus's temple.

In that regard, Bonaparte had accomplished at the age of thirty-one what Marius, Sylla, and Caesar had been unable to do during their entire lives.

But would he be able to maintain that peace that had been bought so dearly? And what about England? Had he not just clipped the claws and pulled the teeth of her three leopards? Would England allow Caesar enough time to become Augustus?

Yet peace was indeed necessary if Bonaparte expected to gain the French throne, just as war had been necessary for him to solidify its foundation at the expense of other European thrones. Bonaparte had no illusions about his eternal enemy's intentions. He knew that England had signed the peace treaty at Amiens only because, cut off from her allies, she could no longer continue the war, just as he knew that she would not allow France the time to reorganize its navy. Such reorganization would take four or five years. If you talked to Bonaparte about the French people's needs, about the advantages of peace, about the power he wielded over domestic order, over the arts, commerce, and industry—and, indeed, over all those areas that combine to make up public prosperity—he would not contradict you, but he would say that the future success of any of his accomplishments was possible only with England's help. Within two years, he was sure, England would try to weigh her navy on the world's scales and use her gold to influence the cabinet of every country in Europe. As sure as if he himself had participated in cabinet meetings in England, he was convinced that the peace he'd established in France was slipping through his fingers.

"Peace will be broken for sure," he would shout, his true thoughts pouring out like a river flooding its banks. "Surely England will break it. In that case, would it not be wise to act first? Would it not be better not to allow England the time to gain all the advantages and strike a terrible blow ourselves, unexpectedly, and surprise everyone?"

England's actions clearly justified Bonaparte's suspicions. Or rather, operating on the premise that Bonaparte desired war, England was priming that desire. What Bonaparte could in truth reproach his enemy for was that England was pushing him faster toward the goal of war than he himself would have wished.

The king of England had addressed a message to his parliament. In it he complained about the weapons being built, he said, in French ports, and he asked parliament to take the necessary precautions to counteract any aggression that was being prepared. Such bad faith angered the First Consul. With the long-hoped-for peace he had just brought to France, his popularity had doubled; now that peace was about to be broken.

There were other aggravations, too. According to the Treaty of Amiens, England was supposed to give up Malta but had failed to do so. She was also supposed to give up Egypt, but had not done so. She was supposed to give up the Cape of Good Hope, but was still holding on to it.

The First Consul decided that it was time to get out of an intolerably difficult situation that was in fact worse than war. He would speak to the English ambassador with total frankness; he would make it clear that he was adamant on two points negotiated at Amiens: the English evacuation of both Malta and Egypt. He would try something new: he would tell his enemies what is usually never said in such situations, the candid truth as to his own position.

On the evening of February 18, 1803, he invited Lord Whitworth to come to the Tuileries. He received him in his study, and after seating him at the end of a long table, he himself sat down at the other end. He was alone with the ambassador, as is appropriate in a meeting of this kind.

"Milord," he said, "I wanted to see you alone so as to be able to tell you plainly what my true intentions are: something no minister can do as well as I myself."

He then reviewed all his diplomatic relations with England since he had become consul. He reminded the ambassador that he had been careful to communicate immediately to the English government that he had been named consul. He reminded the ambassador that despite the insolence he had suffered from Pitt, he had with eagerness reopened negotiations with England as soon as he could honorably do so, and he had then made successive concessions in order to reach an agreement on the Treaty of Amiens. With more pain than anger, he expressed the sadness he felt on seeing that his efforts to live harmoniously with Great Britain had borne such little fruit. He reminded the ambassador that Britain's bad behavior, which should have ceased along with the hostilities, seemed on the contrary to have grown worse since the peace had been signed. He complained about the virulent attacks leveled against him by English papers and the horrible insults they were allowing émigré gazettes to publish about him; he complained about the welcome England everywhere afforded the French nobility exactly as the deposed monarchy wished. Finally, he demonstrated how Great Britain had its hand in every conspiracy laid against him.

"Every gust of wind rising in England," he said, "carries some new outrage along with an expression of ancient hate. And now look, milord. Now we are in an untenable situation. Do you or do you not plan to carry out the terms of the Treaty of Amiens?

"I myself have carried them out scrupulously. The treaty required me to evacuate Naples, Taranto, and the Roman states in three months, and within two, French troops had left each area. Yet it is now ten months ago that we both ratified the agreement, and English troops are still stationed in Malta and Alexandria.

"Do you want peace? Do you want war? Well, by God, if you want war, all you need to do is say so. If that is what you want, we will wage it ferociously until we have exterminated both our peoples. Do you want peace? If so, you must leave Malta and Alexandria.

"Malta, the rock on which so many fortifications have been built, has great naval importance, but of even greater importance, to my mind, is its link to French honor. What would people say if we allowed a solemnly signed treaty to remain thus violated? They would doubt our commitment. As for me, I have come to a decision. I would prefer seeing you in Montmartre and Chaumont than in Malta."

Lord Whitworth had not been expecting such an outburst. He remained silent and motionless, as he had not received instructions from his government in regard to such recriminations. He answered the First Consul's prolixity with only a few words.

"How do you expect," he asked the First Consul, "that in only a few months we can soothe animosities that have grown between our two nations in the course of a war that has lasted between two hundred fifteen and two hundred eighteen years? You know that English law is powerless against the press. Our law gives us no means of curbing writers, even those who daily insult our own government. And the pensions that have been granted the Chouans are for past services, not payments for future services. As for the welcome given to émigré princes, that is no more than the noble expression of hospitality on the part of the British nation."

"But that," Bonaparte cut in, "cannot justify the tolerance shown to French pamphleteers, nor the pensions given to assassins, nor the trappings of royalty accorded the Bourbon princes."

Bonaparte began to laugh. "To a man of your quality," he said, "I shall not attempt to point out the weakness of such arguments. Let us get back to Malta."

"Well, I can promise you," Lord Whitworth responded, "that at the present time our soldiers have no doubt left Alexandria. As for Malta, it would already have been evacuated were it not for the changes your politics have wrought in Europe."

"What changes are you referring to?" cried Bonaparte.

"Have you not arranged to have yourself named president of the Italian republic?"

"Have you such a poor memory for dates, milord?" Bonaparte replied. "Have you forgotten that the presidency was conferred upon me before the Treaty of Amiens?"

"And what of the kingdom of Etruria that you have created?" continued the ambassador. "Never did you consult England regarding that matter."

"You are mistaken, milord. England was indeed consulted, although that was an unnecessary formality. Furthermore, we were made to understand that England too would soon recognize the kingdom."

"England," said Lord Whitworth, "had asked you to accept the restoration of the king of Sardinia in his states."

"And I answered Austria, Russia, and you that not only would I not restore him but also that I refused to grant him any indemnity. You have always been aware, so it is not news to you, that I was planning to reunite the Piedmont to France. Such reunification is necessary as a complement to my power over Italy, an absolute power that will remain absolute. Now, look at this map of Europe spread out between us. Look, search. Is there in some tiny corner a single regiment of my army that should not be where it is? Is there any state that I am threatening or that I would like to invade? None, as you know. At least as long as peace is kept."

"If you were frank, Citizen First Consul, you would admit that you are still eyeing Egypt."

"It is true that I have given thought to Egypt, that I still give some thought to it, and that I shall give a lot more thought to it if you force me to go back to war. But may God keep me from compromising the peace we have enjoyed so briefly over the sequence and contents of my thought. The Turkish Empire is breaking up on every side and threatening to fall into ruin. Its place is not in Europe but in Asia; yet I shall work to enable it to endure as long as possible. If their empire collapses, however, I want France to have its share. You will agree that, if I had so desired, with the many ships I am sending to Saint-Domingue, nothing would have been easier for me than to divert one of them to Alexandria, where you still have four thousand men—four thousand men who should have left Egypt ten months ago. Far from being an obstacle to me, your four thousand troops could have provided me with a ready pretext. I could have invaded Egypt in twenty-four hours, justifiably, and this time you would not have taken it back. You believe that my power blinds me to the influence I may wield over public opinion in France and all over Europe today. Well, let me tell you, my power is not so great that I can simply decide to undertake aggression without motivation. If I were foolish enough to attack England without some serious cause, my political influence, which is really more a moral than a material influence, would immediately be lost in the eyes of Europe. As for France, I will need to prove that I am being attacked without provocation in order to raise national sentiment against you if you force me into war. For France, you will have to be totally in the wrong, and me not at all! And now, if you doubt my desire to preserve peace, listen and judge for yourself how sincere I am.

"I am thirty-two years old. At the age of thirty-two I have attained power and fame to which it would be difficult to add. Do you believe that I would blithely risk my power and fame in a desperate struggle? No, I would not, so I shall not decide to do so until the last possible moment. But then, just listen to what I shall do. I shall wage no war of skirmishes and blockades; I shall not burn a ship here or there, wherever, by chance, on the ocean, where the ocean can put out the fire. No, I shall be gathering together two hundred thousand men. No, I shall cross the Channel with an immense fleet of warships. Perhaps, like Xerxes, I shall leave my glory and fortune at the bottom of the sea! For with such expeditions one never turns back; you either succeed or die!"

Lord Whitworth looked at Bonaparte in surprise; he continued: "It seems strangely foolhardy to attack England, does it not, milord? But what do you expect? Where Caesar was successful, I too have been. Why should I not be successful, then, where William the Conqueror so famously succeeded? If you force me to do so, believe me, I have resolved to undertake such an endeavor, however foolhardy it may seem. I am willing to commit my army and myself to its accomplishment. I crossed the Alps in winter; I am able to make possible things that seem impossible to ordinary men. And, if I succeed, your last nephews will shed tears of blood because of the decisions that you force me to make. I can give you no other proof of my sincerity than to tell you unqualifiedly that I want peace. It is best for you and for me to honor the conditions set forth in the treaty. Leave Malta, leave Egypt, silence your newspapers, banish those who would assassinate me from your country, and act in accord with me. I promise total accord in return. Let us bring our two nations closer together, let us link them together, for together we can exert a sovereignty over the world that neither France nor England could ever exert alone. You have a navy that, even with all my resources, I could not match with ten years of effort. And I have five hundred thousand men ready to march under my orders wherever I decide to lead them. If you are masters of the sea, I am the master on land. So, rather than fighting, let us consider joining forces, for if we do, we shall be able to settle as we wish the destiny not just of Europe but of the world!"

Lord Whitworth communicated to the British government his conversation with the First Consul. Unfortunately, though he was an honest man, a man of the world, he was mediocre of intellect and had been unable to follow the First Consul's line of reasoning fully to its conclusion.

So, in response to Bonaparte's long, eloquent improvisation on power in the interest of peace as it was reported to King George, the British monarch sent the following message to parliament:

George the King,

His Majesty believes it necessary to inform the House of Commons that, given current military preparations under way in French and Dutch ports, he has deemed it appropriate to adopt new precautionary measures to ensure his country's security. Although the apparent purpose of those preparations is to send expeditions to the colonies, since there are currently highly important discussions under way between His Majesty and the French government whose outcome is uncertain, His Majesty has decided to send this communication to his faithful House of Commons, certain that although it shares his urgent and unwavering desire for the continuation of peace, His Majesty can nonetheless count with full confidence on its public spirit and generosity, knowing that it will make it possible for His Majesty to deploy any measures the circumstances seem to require for the honor of his crown and the essential interests of his people.

When the First Consul learned the contents of the English king's message from Monsieur de Talleyrand, he flew into a rage like those of Alexander. Monsieur de Talleyrand nonetheless managed to cajole him into promising that he would restrain himself and that he would leave any provocation up to the English. Unfortunately, Sunday came two days later, and with it the diplomatic visits at the Tuileries. Drawn by their curiosity, all the ambassadors were eager to see how Bonaparte might have taken King George's insult and what words he would choose in greeting the British ambassador.

The First Consul and Madame Bonaparte were playing with King Louis and Queen Hortense's first child, when Monsieur de Rémusat, palace prefect, announced that all the ambassadors had arrived.

"Has Lord Whitworth arrived?" Bonaparte asked brusquely.

"Yes, Citizen First Consul," Monsieur de Rémusat answered.

Bonaparte had been lying on the carpet. Relinquishing his grandchild, he stood up quickly and, taking Madame Bonaparte's hand, went through the doorway that opened out onto the reception room. He walked past the foreign ministers without responding to their greetings, without even looking at them, and strode directly over to the ambassador from Great Britain.

"Milord," he said, "have you any news from England?" But without giving him time to speak, he added: "So you really want war?"

"No, General," the ambassador answered with a bow, "we are too aware of the advantages of peace."

"So you want war," the First Consul continued loudly, as if he had not heard but so that everyone would be sure to hear him. "We fought for ten years, and now you want to fight for ten years more? How dare anyone say that France was rearming? How dare anyone lie so plainly to Europe! For there is not a single warship in our ports. Every capable vessel has been sent to Saint-Domingue. Only one French warship sits in port, and it is in Dutch waters, and everyone knows that it is destined for Louisiana. It was reported, too, that there is a disagreement between France and England. Yet I do not know of a single one. All I know is that the island of Malta has not been evacuated within the time limits imposed at Amiens, but I cannot imagine that your ministers would fail to honor England's commitment by refusing to carry out a solemn treaty. Nor would I suppose that with your warships you intend to intimidate the French people! You might kill them, milord; but intimidate them—never!"

"General," the ambassador answered, totally taken aback by this outburst, "there is only one thing we ask for, and that is to live peacefully with France."

"Well, then," cried the First Consul, "first of all you must respect our treaties! Woe to those who do not respect their treaties! Woe to those nations whose treaties must be covered with a black veil!"

Then, quickly changing his expression and tone so that Lord Whitworth could see that the insult had not been meant for him personally but for his government, he went on: "Milord, allow me to ask for news of the Duchess Dorset, your wife. After spending the bad season in France, she will be able to remain for the good season, I hope. Of course, that is not for me to say but for England to decide. And if we need to reopen hostilities, in the eyes of God and of men all responsibility will reside with those traitors who refuse to honor their obligations."

Then, taking his leave of Lord Whitworth and the other ambassadors, without another word to anyone, he left the entire diplomatic corps in the greatest stupefaction that it had experienced in quite a long while.

XXXI

War

THE DAM HAD BROKEN. Bonaparte's outburst at Lord Whitworth was the equivalent of declaring war. Indeed, from that moment on, despite her commitment to give up Malta, England felt honor-bound to keep it.

Unfortunately, at that time England was suffering the effects of the famously weak Addington and Hawkesbury ministry, one of those transition ministries that base their most important decisions on public opinion rather than on benefit to the government they are representing. When King George III of England found himself uncomfortably between Mr. Pitt the Tory and Mr. Fox the Whig, the king shared the opinions of Mr. Pitt but could not stand the man, and while he greatly admired Mr. Fox's character, he deemed the man's political opinions odious—in order not to choose either of the two famous rivals, he chose to make the interim Addington ministry permanent.

On May 11, the English ambassador asked for his passports. Never had an ambassador's departure had such an impact on the French public as did Lord Whitworth's. Every day since he'd made his request, two or three hundred people would gather and stand from morning to evening in front of the ambassador's residence. Finally, the carriages were ready for his homeward journey, and as all Paris knew that Lord Whitworth had done everything within his power to maintain the peace, the crowd that had gathered applauded as he left.

As for Bonaparte, like all men of genius, once he had decided to support peace, he had begun to appreciate its benefits and give free rein to his dreams and hopes for the betterment of a peacetime France. Now, suddenly thrown back into a warrior's camp, he resolved that if he could not as benefactor amaze France and the world, then he would astound them in another way. The deep antipathy Bonaparte had always felt toward England turned to violent rage and grandiose plans. He measured the distance between Calais and Dover. It was no greater than the distance he had covered when he crossed the Saint Bernard pass, and, he reminded himself, that had been done in midwinter, around precipices and over unmarked trails on a snow-covered mountain reputed to be uncrossable. By comparison, crossing the Channel was a simple transportation problem. If he had enough boats to land an army of one hundred fifty thousand men on the other side, conquering England would be no more difficult than conquering Italy had been.

But, in such an endeavor, whom could he count on? Whom should he fear? The Philadelphians? They remained a secret society. The Concordat? They had reawakened old animosities among Republican generals and had even created some new ones. And all those apostles of reason, men like Dupuis, Monge, and Berthollet, who scarcely acknowledged God's divinity, were hardly inclined to recognize in a general godlike qualities. As an Italian, Bonaparte had always been, if not religious, at least superstitious. He believed premonitions, prognostications, and omens. On occasion, when he freely aired his religious beliefs among the habitués in Josephine's circle, his listeners found his more fanciful ideas and theories worrisome.

One evening Monge said to him: "One must hope, Citizen First Consul, that we will never return to certificates of confession."

"One should never say never," Bonaparte answered sharply.

While the Concordat had patched things up between Bonaparte and the church, it had also put him at odds with part of the army, which in turn had brought a glimmer of hope to the Philadelphians. They felt the time had come to act, and a conspiracy evolved against the First Consul.

Accordingly, on a day when Bonaparte, accompanied by perhaps sixty generals and aides-de-camp, was reviewing his troops, the conspirators planned to knock him from his mount in the hope that he would then be trampled by the other horses' hooves. The two most prominent leaders of the conspiracy were Bernadotte, the commander of the Western Army who was then in Paris, and Moreau, who, poorly rewarded for the magnificent battle of Hohenlinden that had brought an end to war with Austria, was back on his lands in Grosbois, sulking.

At that same time, three lampoons appeared in Paris, all of them addressed to the French armies and all of them from army headquarters in Rennes, where Bernadotte was based. The lampoons spared no insults to "the Corsican tyrant," "the usurper," "the deserter who killed Kléber." For the news of Kléber's death had reached Paris, and in spite of the truth of the matter, and even in spite of appearances, Kléber's murder was being attached to the man to whom one half of France credited everything good in the country and to whom the other half attributed all the bad. The sarcasm in the lampoons extended from Bonaparte's bloody deeds to his banal moral pronouncements. Then came a call for insurrection and for the extermination of the entire Corsican clan.

The lampoons had been mailed to every officer—to four-star generals, commanders, major generals—but all of the packets had been intercepted by Fouché's police, except for the first one, which had been sent in a butter basket by stagecoach from Rennes to Citizen Rapatel, General Moreau's aide-de-camp in Paris. Fouché was preparing to go to the Tuileries with this proof of the military conspiracy when Bonaparte in fact sent for him so that they could peruse the list of the First Consul's friends and enemies.

Bonaparte had spoken only a few words before Fouché realized that the occasion could not be more opportune for his own business. With him he had a copy of each of the three lampoons.

Fouché knew, too, that Rapatel had received a bundle of the pamphlets. So there was no doubt that even if Moreau was not part of the conspiracy, he was certainly aware that these scabrous, dangerous lampoons were circulating through all the ranks of the army. Moreau himself, under pressure from his wife and mother-in-law, who had quarreled with Josephine and hated her, had engaged in the mockery of Bonaparte by making fun of his proposed Order of the Légion d'Honneur. Fouché told Bonaparte that following a fine dinner at Moreau's home, everyone had voted an honorary saucepan for the cook, and after a wild boar hunt, one of his dogs, who had been the best attacker and received three wounds to show for it, was decorated with an honorary collar.

Bonaparte was particularly sensitive to such attacks. Their frequency made them only more painful. He ordered Fouché to extract an explanation from Moreau immediately. Moreau responded to Fouché with a laugh and made light of the conspiracy. A "butter-pot conspiracy," he called it. As for his tomfoolery, he reasoned that since Bonaparte, as head of the government, was bestowing honorary sabers and guns, he surely could, in his own house, as its master, confer honorary pans and collars.

Though he rarely got indignant, an indignant Fouché reported back to Bonaparte, who flew into a blinding rage. "Moreau is the only person, aside from me, who's of any worth," he ranted. "It is not right that France should suffer, torn between us two. Were I in his place, and he in mine, I would offer to be his first aide-de-camp. And he thinks he's ready to govern! Poor France! Well, so be it! Have him come to the Bois de Boulogne tomorrow morning at four o'clock. His saber or mine will decide; I shall be waiting for him there. Do not fail to carry out my orders, Fouché. Add nothing, but, for sure, do not leave anything out."

Bonaparte waited. At midnight, Fouché came back. This time he had found Moreau more amenable, and Moreau had promised to present himself early the next morning at the Tuileries, where he had not appeared for a long time.

Bonaparte welcomed Moreau graciously and served him breakfast. As Moreau was leaving, Bonaparte presented him with a magnificent pair of diamond-studded pistols, saying: "I had intended to have your victories engraved on the pistols, but there was not enough room."

They shook hands as they parted, but there was no union in their hearts.

Matters with Moreau now calmed if not completely pacified, Bonaparte threw himself into his grander ventures. He wanted every port in Flanders and Holland to be surveyed; he wanted to know the layout, the size, how many people lived there, what supplies were held there. He put Colonel Lacuée in charge of the evaluation. He wanted to know the conditions of every boat and fishing vessel that sailed up and down the coast between Le Havre and Texel. He sent officers to Saint-Malo, Granville, and Brest to discover how many vessels were docked or harbored there. He had navy engineers build models of flatbed boats that could transport heavy cannons. He had all the forests along the Channel inspected to see how much wood they might be able to supply for building a fleet of warships. Knowing that the English were buying wood in the Roman States, he sent agents there too and had them buy wood that would prove to be indispensable for France.

The resumption of hostilities was supposed to be signaled by the immediate occupation of Portugal and the Gulf of Taranto.

England's bad faith had been so obvious that even among Bonaparte's worst enemies not a single man blamed him for the rupture between the two countries. Still, all of France was in great turmoil. We felt that our navy was inferior, but at the same time we were convinced that with enough time and money to build a large number of flatbed boats, we would be able to fight the English on land with cannon, in which case they would be vanquished.

As soon as the cost of the boats had been determined, the First Consul was inundated with construction proposals. The first came from the Loiret department, which imposed taxes in order to raise the three hundred thousand francs with which to build and arm a thirty-cannon frigate. Immediately, others fought to follow their example. Little towns like Coutances, Bernay, Louviers, Valognes, Foix, Verdun, and Moissac proposed that they build flatbed boats costing somewhere between eight thousand and twenty thousand francs. Paris, whose city symbol includes a ship, voted to provide a one-hundred-twenty-gun vessel; Lyon, a vessel of one hundred guns; Bordeaux, of eighty; Marseille, of seventy-four. The Gironde department contributed one million six hundred thousand francs. And finally, the Italian Republic allotted the First Consul four million francs to build two frigates, one to be called the *Président,* the other the *République Italienne.*

During this time, when Bonaparte was concentrating totally on military preparations and on foreign rather than domestic affairs, Savary received a letter from a former Vendean leader for whom he had done some service. Although the man had taken up arms against the Revolution, he was now hoping for nothing more than to live out his days peacefully on his own land. He told Savary that he had just had a visit from a band of armed men who were talking about foolish activities that, frankly, he himself had given up after the 18th Brumaire. He added that in order to keep the promise he had made to the government at that time and in order to protect himself against repercussions as a result of such visits, he was eager to report more fully on the event. He promised he'd come to Paris to provide more details as soon as the grapes had been harvested.

Savary knew how much importance the First Consul attached to being aware of every hint of conspiracy, for his sharp, analytic mind could see in the tiniest details the most secret intentions. The letter preoccupied him for several moments, but scarcely a quarter of an hour later he said to Savary, "Go spend several days with your Vendean leader. Study the Vendée and try to figure out what events are being prepared."

Savary left that very day, incognito.

When he reached his friend's house, he judged the situation to be so serious that he disguised himself as a peasant and forced his host to do the same. They then set out to find the band of men his Vendean friend had spoken about in his letter. Three days later, they happened upon a few men who had gotten separated from the band the day before. From them, Savary and his friend were able to glean all the details they needed. Convinced that one spark would be enough to set the Vendée and the Morbihan ablaze, Savary returned to Paris.

Bonaparte was greatly surprised by what Savary had to say. Indeed, the First Consul had assumed that the Vendée had ceased to be worrisome, particularly as George, according to police minister Régnier, was in London.

At the time, many prisoners who had been charged with spying or political intrigues were still being held in various Paris castles. No attempt had been made to bring them to trial, however. For Bonaparte himself had said that time would soon usher in a new era in which no one would need to worry again about such intrigues, and all those poor souls in prison could be set free.

But not now. Without consulting Fouché, the First Consul had Savary draw up a list of every person who had been arrested in the preceding year, along with the date of the arrest and a commentary on the prisoner's background.

Among those prisoners were two men, their names Picot and Lebourgeois, who had been arrested more than a year before, about the time of the bomb, in Normandy at Pont-Audemer, just as they were arriving from England. Their arrest papers carried a note in the margin: "Here to make an attempt on the First Consul's life." Why Bonaparte's eyes landed on those two names rather than on any number of others, nobody knows, but the First Consul indeed selected them and three men more to be tried before a commission.

Picot and Lebourgeois, despite the evidence against them, remained admirably calm as they stood up to the accusation. The commission found their complicity with Saint-Régeant and Carbon so evident that they were sentenced to death, but they went to the firing squad without in fact admitting anything. To the end they even seemed to be intent on defying authority; they died declaiming that the government would soon thrust France into war and that Bonaparte should be eliminated.

As for the three other accused men, two were acquitted. The third, a man named Querelle, was found guilty. A native of lower Brittany, he had served in La Vendée under the orders of George Cadoudal. Denounced by a creditor to whom he had had the misfortune of making only a partial payment of his debt, at his creditor's bidding he had been arrested as a conspirator.

Several hours after Picot and Lebourgeois had received their death sentences, Querelle too was sentenced, but by then his recent companions had been executed. As the two condemned men were leaving for their execution, they said to Querelle: "You must follow our example. We have pious hearts and honest minds, and we are fighting for throne and altar. We are dying for a cause that will open heaven's gates for us. You must die as we shall die, without a word, if you are condemned. God will count you among the martyrs, and you will enjoy every heavenly beatitude!"

As Querelle's two companions had foreseen, he was indeed condemned to die. At about nine in the evening the reporting judge sent to the chief of staff the order that Querelle be executed early the next morning according to the custom.

The chief of staff was at a ball. He returned home at about three in the morning, opened the letter, slipped it under his pillow, and fell asleep.

If the order had been given early enough for Querelle to have gone to his death along with his companions, he would no doubt have died bravely, supported by their courage and his own pride. But the delay, nearly a whole day spent in total isolation facing the possibility of death and then a long night awaiting its reality, filled him with terror. Late in the evening he began to convulse so violently that one would have thought his jailers had slipped him some poison. The prison doctor was called. He questioned the condemned man about his symptoms; certain Querelle had taken poison, the doctor insisted he tell him what kind of poison it was. In response, Querelle threw his arms around the doctor, put his mouth close to the doctor's ear, and whispered, "I was not poisoned. I am simply afraid!"

Taking advantage of an opportunity to get the poor man to speak, the doctor said, "You are bearing a secret that the police would like very much to know. Set your conditions. Perhaps you might be pardoned."

"Oh, never! Never!" crie the condemned man. "It is too late for that."

Finally, though, with the doctor's encouragement, Querelle asked for pen and paper, and he wrote to the governor of Paris saying that he had information to reveal.

Junot was no longer governor of Paris. Finding him too soft-hearted, Bonaparte had replaced Junot with Murat. So it was Murat who appeared at the Tuileries at about eleven that evening. The First Consul, preoccupied and worried, was talking with Réal in his office when suddenly the door opened and Savary announced the governor of Paris.

"Ah, it's you, Murat," said Bonaparte, taking a step toward his brother-in-law. "You must have some news, to have come at such an hour."

"Yes, General. I've just received a letter from a poor devil who is about to be executed tomorrow morning. He is requesting a chance to make revelations."

"Well," Bonaparte said lightly, "send the letter to the secretary of the commission that judged him. He can do whatever is necessary."

"That was my first thought," said Murat. "But in the letter there is a tone of such frankness and conviction that my interest was piqued. Here, read for yourself."

Bonaparte read the letter that Murat handed to him, but it didn't change his mind. "The poor devil. He's trying to gain one more hour of life, that's all. Do as I have told you." He handed back the letter.

"But, General," Murat insisted, "did you not notice that the man says clearly that he has important revelations to make?"

"Yes, of course. I read everything, and I've read many such overtures before, which is why I repeat that it is not worth our trouble to discover what the man might have to say."

"Who knows?" said Murat. "Leave the whole business to Monsieur Réal and me."

"Since you insist," said Bonaparte, "I won't stand in your way. Using your position, Réal, you go question him. Murat, you may accompany the judge if you like, but no reprieve, do you hear? I want no reprieve."

XXXII

Citizen Régnier's Police and Citizen Fouché's Police

IT WAS AFTER MIDNIGHT when Réal and Murat left the First Consul. Murat had been obliged to leave a large formal gathering that by chance he was hosting that evening, and he needed to return there. In any case, his own task had been completed: He had alerted the First Consul, and the First Consul had deferred to the appropriate authorities, in this case the judge, to whom Murat left the responsibility of visiting the prisoner.

Réal thought it would be best to see the prisoner about two hours before the execution, which was scheduled for seven that morning. If the man's revelations warranted it, Réal would have plenty of time to grant a reprieve. If they were unimportant, the execution could proceed.

As a man accustomed to manipulating human feelings, Réal was certain that military preparations taking place at daybreak around the prison would add to the pressure on the condemned man and prompt him all the more to tell everything.

As bad as Querelle's state was when, at the doctor's urging, he sent word to Murat about revelations he wanted to make, we must understand that when no response was forthcoming, his condition had gotten only worse while he'd been waiting for some word from the governor. But none had come. The poor man was in a sorry state. Reduced to sheer inertia, he surrendered to the waves of anguish and anxiety that overwhelmed him while he waited for death. Quaking, dreading the day's first light, he stared at the window opening onto the street.

At about five in the morning he gave a start when he heard the sound of a carriage stopping at the prison door. Alerted, he heard the sound of the massive door opening, and then closing, heavily. He heard the sound of footsteps in the corridor: three, maybe four people walking; they stopped at his door. The key screeched in the lock. The door opened. With one final ray of hope, he turned his head to see who was entering. He did not see the governor's splendid uniform, decorated with braid and embroidery, under the folds of his cloak. He saw a man dressed in black. Despite his friendly, open face, he seemed sinister.

Candles were lit in sconces on the wall. Réal considered the surroundings. Apparently the prisoner had been thought to be so close to death that they had placed him in the clerk's room. There was a bed, on which the prisoner had thrown himself fully dressed. The poor man was stretching out his hands to him. Réal could smell his fear.

Réal gestured to the guards. They left him alone with the man he had come to interrogate.

"I am the Conseiller d'Etat Réal," he said. "You announced your intention to make some revelations, and I have come to hear them."

The poor man began to tremble so violently that he was unable to respond. His teeth were chattering, his face was contorted. "Pull yourself together," said the state counselor, who had witnessed many a man facing imminent death, but never one with such naked terror. "I have come with the intention of being as benevolent as my difficult responsibilities permit. Do you think you can answer me now?"

"I shall try," said the poor fellow. "But what's the use? In two hours, will not everything be over?"

"I have no authority to make any promises," Réal answered. "However, if what you have to tell me is as important as you claim. . . ."

"Ah, you may judge for yourself," cried the prisoner. "But . . . what would you like to know? What do you want me to tell you? Guide me, I cannot think clearly."

"First relax, then answer my questions. What is your name?"

"Querelle."

"What was your occupation?"

"I was a health officer."

"Where did you live?"

"In Biville."

"Now you need to tell me what is on your mind."

"In the name of God in whose presence I shall soon appear, I will tell you the truth, but you will not believe me."

"I already believe you," said Réal. "You are innocent, are you not?"

"Yes, I swear." Réal's face registered disbelief.

"At least I am of what they accuse me," the prisoner added. "And I could have proven my innocence."

"Why didn't you?"

"Because I would have had to have used an alibi, and the alibi, by saving me from all this, would have ensured my downfall in another way."

"But you were indeed part of a conspiracy?"

"Yes, but not with Picot and Lebourgeois. I was never involved in that bomb business, I swear. At that time I was in England with George Cadoudal."

"How long have you been back in France?"

"For two months."

"So, you left George two months ago?"

"I did not leave him."

"What? You did not leave him? Since you are in Paris and he is in England, it seems to me that you must have left him!"

"George is not in England."

"Then where is he?"

"In Paris."

Réal leaned forward. "In Paris?" he cried. "Impossible!"

"Yet he is here, because we came together. I spoke to him the day before I was arrested."

So George had been in Paris for two months! Obviously this man's revelations were even more important than they had imagined. "And how did you enter France?" Réal asked.

"By the Biville cliffs. It was on a Sunday. We had been put to shore by a small English sloop. We nearly drowned because the sea was so high."

"Let me see now," said Réal. "This information may be of more moment than I thought, my friend. I cannot make any promises, however. . . . Go on. How many of you were there?"

"Nine at the first landing."

"And how many landings have there been since then?"

"Three."

"Who met you when you came ashore?"

"The son of a man who is a clockmaker by profession. He led us to a farm whose name I don't know. We stayed there three days, and then, moving from farm to farm, we came to Paris. Once here, some of George's friends came to meet us."

"Do you know their names?"

"I know only two of them, his former aide-de-camp Sol de Grisolles and a man named Charles d'Hozier."

"Had you ever seen them before?"

"Yes, in London, one year earlier."

"And then what happened?"

"The two gentlemen had George climb into a cabriolet. As for us, we entered Paris on foot through different barriers. In two months, I have seen George only three times, and then only when he sent for me. Furthermore, I have never seen him twice in the same place."

"And where was the last place you saw him?"

"At a wine merchant's, whose shop is on the corner of the Rue du Bac and the Rue de Varenne. When I was back in the street, I had scarcely taken thirty steps before I was arrested."

"Have you had any news about him since then?"

"Yes, he sent me one hundred francs through the Temple concierge."

"Do you believe he is still in Paris?"

"I am sure of it. He was expecting additional landings. But in any case, nothing was to happen until a prince from the house of France was present in Paris."

"A prince from the house of France!" cried Réal. "Did you ever hear his name?"

"No, monsieur."

"Very well, then," said Réal, getting to his feet.

"Monsieur," cried the prisoner, taking Réal's hands, "I have told you everything I know, at the risk of being called a traitor, a coward, and a wretch by my companions."

"Relax," said the state counselor. "You will not die, not today at least. I shall try to interest the First Consul in your favor, but you must not breathe a word of what you have told me to anyone. Otherwise I can do nothing for you. Take this money and get whatever you need to restore your strength. Tomorrow, no doubt, I shall be back."

"Oh, monsieur," said Querelle, throwing himself at Réal's feet, "are you quite sure I will not die?"

"I cannot guarantee it, but keep your mouth closed and remain hopeful."

However, because the First Consul's order—"No reprieve!"—had been so forceful, Réal dared only to say to the governor of the abbey: "Make arrangements with the warrant officer so that nothing happens before ten o'clock this morning."

It was then six o'clock, and Réal knew Bonaparte's instructions: "Never wake me for good news, only for bad." It seemed to Réal that the news was more bad than good.

Réal went straight to the Tuileries. He woke up Constant, and Constant aroused Rustan, the Mameluke who slept at Bonaparte's door. Rustan woke up the First Consul, as by then Bourrienne had begun to fall from his old schoolmate's favor and no longer enjoyed many of his former privileges. (By then, too, Bonaparte was no longer sharing the same room with Josephine.) To be sure no mistake had been made, Bonaparte had the Mameluke tell him twice that the state counselor was waiting to see him.

"Light the candles," Bonaparte said, "and have him come in." A candelabrum was placed beside the fireplace, near the First Consul's bed.

"Well! It's you, Réal," Bonaparte said as the counselor came in. "So, things are more serious than we first thought?"

"Very serious, General."

"What do you mean?"

"I have just learned something interesting."

"Tell me," said Bonaparte, resting his head in his hands, ready to listen.

"Citizen General," said the state counselor, "George is in Paris with his whole band."

"What?" said the First Consul, thinking he surely had misunderstood. Réal told him again.

"Come now!" cried Bonaparte with the characteristic pull of his shoulders that indicated he doubted something. "That cannot be possible."

"Nothing could be truer, General."

"So," cried the general, "that's what that scoundrel Fouché meant when he wrote to me yesterday evening: 'Take care, the air is full of daggers,' he said. I put his note on my night table and paid it no further attention."

He rang for Constant, who appeared immediately. "Call Bourrienne," Bonaparte ordered him.

Quickly awakened, Bourrienne was soon placing himself at the First Consul's disposal. "Write to Fouché and Régnier," Bonaparte said, "and tell them to come at once to the Tuileries to discuss the Cadoudal affair. Tell them to bring any information they have in its regard. Have two orderlies deliver the letters directly to them. Meanwhile, Réal will explain the whole business to me."

Réal repeated to Bonaparte word for word what Querelle had told him: how Cadoudal and his band had come by sloop from England and entered France via the Biville cliffs; how they had been welcomed by a clockmaker, whose name Querelle did not know, and taken to a farm; how they had traveled from farm to farm all the way to Paris; how, in Paris, Querelle had seen Cadoudal for the last time in a house on the corner of the Rue du Bac and the Rue de Varenne.

Once Réal had related all the information to the First Consul, he asked permission to return to the poor fellow he had left agonizing in the Abbey. He asked, too, if he could promise the man a temporary reprieve, given the importance of his revelations. This time Bonaparte agreed; he authorized Réal to promise Querelle, if not a total pardon, at least his life.

Réal then left the First Consul in the hands of his valet. By the time Régnier arrived, Bonaparte was already dressed. His head bowed, hands behind his back, forehead creased, he was pacing up and down.

"Ah, here you are, Régnier," said the First Consul. "What did you tell me yesterday about Cadoudal?"

"I said, Citizen First Consul, that I had received a letter to the effect that he was still in London and that he had dined three days ago in Kingston at the home of Mr. Addington's secretary."

At that moment in Régnier's account, Fouché was announced. "Have him come in," said Bonaparte, not at all displeased by the prospect of a confrontation between his two Ministers of Police: Régnier, the official minister, and Fouché, who was operating in secret.

"Fouché," said the First Consul, "I had you summoned to help us reach an agreement, Régnier and me. Régnier here claims that Cadoudal is in London, whereas I contend that he is in Paris. Which of us is right?"

"The man to whom I sent word yesterday, saying, 'Take care, the air is full of daggers.'"

"Do you hear that, Régnier? As I am the man who received Fouché's letter, I am the one who is right."

Régnier shrugged. "Would you care to show Monsieur Fouché the letter that I received from London yesterday?"

Still holding the letter Régnier had presented, the First Consul passed it to Fouché, who read the letter with middling interest, then asked, "Will the First Consul allow me to bring in a man who in fact returned from London with Cadoudal and accompanied him to Paris?"

"Yes, by God!" said Bonaparte. "That would be a pleasure."

Fouché opened the antechamber door to his agent Victor. Elegantly dressed, Victor looked for all the world like one of those young Royalists who, out of either true conviction or political fashion, were conspiring against the First Consul. Remaining near the door, he bowed respectfully.

"What is all this?" asked Bonaparte. "If this man truly entered France with Cadoudal, why is he still alive?"

"Because," Fouché replied, "he is the agent who I have had keeping an eye on Cadoudal. So as not to lose sight of him, he followed him on his return to France all the way to Paris."

"How long ago?" Bonaparte asked.

"Two months ago," Fouché replied. "If Monsieur Régnier cares to interrogate my agent himself, he would do him the greatest honor."

Régnier motioned the agent over. Bonaparte meanwhile studied the young man with great interest. His clothes were of the latest fashion, perfectly stylish, neither too little so nor too much; he might have just paid a morning visit to Madame Récamier or Madame Tallien. He bore himself well, and one suspected that he wore his radiant smile much the way he did his cloak.

"What were you doing in London, monsieur?" Régnier asked.

"Well, Citizen Minister," the agent replied, "I was doing what everyone else was doing, plotting against the Citizen First Consul."

"To what purpose?"

"For the purpose of gaining the recommendation of Their Highnesses the royal princes to Monsieur Cadoudal."

"Which princes are you speaking about?"

"The princes of the House of Bourbon, of course."

"And did you manage to get a recommendation to George?"

"Through Monsignor le Duc de Berry, yes, Monsieur le Ministre. I was indeed so fortunate. So much so that General George judged me worthy of joining the first expedition sent to France, which is to say the band of nine men who came with him."

"And who were those nine men?"

"Monsieur Coster Saint-Victor, Monsieur Burban, Monsieur de Rivière, General Lajolais, a man named Picot, Louis Picot, George's servant, not the same man who was just shot. There was also Monsieur Bouvet de Lozier, Monsieur Damonville, and the man named Querelle, the same who yesterday was sentenced to death. Also, of course, your servant, and finally George Cadoudal."

"And how did you arrive in France?"

"On a kind of cutter, with Captain Wright."

"Ah!," cried Bonaparte. "I know him. He is Sidney Smith's former secretary."

"Exactly, General," said Fouché.

"The weather was horrible," the agent went on. "We had trouble reaching the base of the Biville cliffs at high tide."

"Where is Biville?" asked Bonaparte.

"Near Dieppe, General," Fouché answered.

Bonaparte noticed that, due no doubt to a feeling of restraint unusual in a man of such apparent accomplishment, the agent never answered him directly; he was instead content to bow and allow Fouché to answer for him. His humility was touching. "When I question you," said Bonaparte, "you may answer me directly."

Once again, the agent bowed, then continued: "We were deposited at the foot of the Biville cliffs, which are about two hundred thirty feet high at that point."

"And how did you scale such a height?" Bonaparte asked.

"With the help of a rope the size of a ship's cable! We climbed up by the strength of our arms, with our feet against the cliff face, at a place where the rock forms a kind of chimney. From time to time, to help the climbers, there are knots in the cord, and there are even some wooden crosspieces on which you can rest for a moment, like parrots on their perches. I was the first to go; then came Monsieur le Marquis de Rivière, General Lajolais, Picot, Burban, Querelle, Bouvet, Damonville, Coster Saint-Victor, and finally George Cadoudal.

"When we got halfway up, several of us said we were tired. 'I warn you,' said George, 'I've just cut the cable behind me.' And indeed, we could hear the cable falling onto the rocks at the bottom of the cliff. Which left us hanging there between earth and sky. With no way back down, we had no choice but to keep climbing until we reached the top.

"We all finally made it safely. I admit, though, that by the time I reached the top I'd been so terrorized by the climb that I had to lie down flat on my stomach, for fear that if I got to my feet, vertigo would pull me back down over the cliff. Monsieur de Rivière, the weakest of us all, was almost unconscious at the end of it. Coster Saint-Victor was whistling a hunting song when he reached the top. As for Cadoudal, he was panting noisily but managed to say, 'For a man weighing two hundred sixty pounds, that is a tough climb.'

"Cadoudal then loosened the cable from the post to which it was tied and sent the second half of the cable down after the first. We asked him why. He answered that since the cable was normally used by smugglers, some poor devil, not realizing that it reached only halfway, might start down, and at the rope's end plunge a hundred feet to the rocks below.

"Once he'd dispatched the cable, Cadoudal imitated a crow call. A screech owl answered, and two men appeared. They were our guides."

"Monsieur Fouché said that George traveled from Biville to Paris, stopping at pre-arranged stations along the way. Did you notice where, specifically, you stopped?"

"Perfectly, General. I have given the list of stations to Monsieur Fouché, but my memory is good enough that if someone were willing to copy as I dictate, I can give you the names here and now."

Bonaparte rang for Savary, who responded promptly.

"Sit there"—Bonaparte pointed him toward a table—"and write what this man dictates." Savary sat down and picked up a pen.

"First of all," the agent began, "about a hundred paces from the cliff, there's a sailor house, which is used only to shelter from bad weather those who are about to embark or those who are waiting for people coming ashore. From there we moved to the first station, in Guilmécourt, the house of a young man named Pageot de Pauly; the second is a farm called La Potterie, in the commune of Saint-Rémy, where the Détrimont couple live; the third is in Preuseville, at the house of a man named Loizel. Allow me, Colonel," the agent continued with his customary politeness, "to point out that here our common path separated into three different routes, all three of which end up in Paris.

"On the easternmost route, the fourth station is Aumale, where a man named Monnier lives; the fifth, in Feuquières, at Colliaux's house; the sixth, in Monceau, at Leclerc's; the seventh, at Saint-Lubin, at Massignon's; the last, in Saint-Leu-Taverny, at Lamotte's.

"If we take the middle route from the fork, though, the fourth station is in Gaillefontaine, at the home of the Widow Le Seur; the fifth is at Saint-Clair, where Sachez lives; and the sixth is in Gournay, at the home of the Widow Cacqueray. But, if from the fork we follow the route to the west, the fourth station is in Roncherolles at the home of the Gambu couple; the fifth, in Saint-Crespin at the home of Bertengles; the sixth, in Etrépagny, where the Damonvilles live; the seventh, in Vauréal, at Bouvet de Lozier's; and the eighth, in Eaubonne, where a man named Hyvonnet lives. That is all."

"Savary, guard this list carefully. It will be useful," said the First Consul. "Well, what do you say to that, Régnier?" he asked.

"I say either my agents are imbeciles or that man is one clever scoundrel."

"Coming from you, Monsieur le Ministre," said the agent with another bow, "what you have just said can be considered high praise. But I am not a scoundrel. I am simply a man more perspicacious than most, and I have an unusual ability with disguise."

"And so," said Bonaparte, "what have you done with Cadoudal now that he's in Paris?"

"I have followed him to the three or four houses where he has stayed: first, from the Rue de la Ferme, then to the Rue du Bac, where he received Querelle just before he was arrested, and finally, today, to the Rue de Chaillot, where he is living under the name of Larive."

"But if you have known all that, monsieur, for so long—" Régnier began to Fouché.

"Yes, for two months," said Fouché, interrupting him.

"—why have you not arrested him?"

Fouché laughed. "Ah, excuse me, Monsieur le Ministre de la Justice," he said, "but until I myself am accused, I won't give up my secrets. Besides, this is a secret I have been keeping for General Bonaparte."

"My dear Régnier," remarked the First Consul, laughing, "I believe, after what we've just heard, that you can safely recall your agent from London. Now, as Minister of Justice, please see to it that the poor devil who, under his death sentence, told us what I have to accept as the truth since it fits in with what this man has just told us"—Bonaparte gestured toward Fouché's agent—"is not executed. I do not wish to pardon him completely, because I want to see how he behaves in prison. Keep your eyes on him; in six months you will bring me a report on his conduct. It remains, my dear Régnier, for me to express my regrets for having gotten you up so early, when your presence was not really required. Fouché, you stay here with me."

The agent moved to the far side of the room so that the First Consul and the true prefect of police could speak privately. Bonaparte moved closer to Fouché. "You said that you would tell me why you kept Cadoudal's presence in Paris a secret."

"I kept the information from you, Citizen First Consul, primarily so that you would not know anything about it."

"Stop joking," said Bonaparte with a frown.

"I'm not joking at all, Citizen General, and I'm sorry that today you have forced me to tell you. The honor you have bestowed upon me by admitting me into your presence has allowed me to study you. Don't frown, damn it—that's my job. You see, you are a man who lets secrets slip out easily when you become angry. As long as you remain calm and collected, there's no problem, for you keep your confidences closed up as tightly as champagne is corked in a bottle. But once you give sway to your anger, the bottle of champagne explodes, and everything erupts in foam."

"Monsieur Fouché," said Bonaparte, "I could do without such comparisons."

"And I, General, can do without divulging my secrets. Allow me to withdraw."

"Come now, don't get angry," said Bonaparte. "I want to know why you have not arrested George."

"You really want to know?"

"Absolutely."

"And if, because of you, I lose my battle of Rivoli, you will not hold it against me?"

"No."

"All right! I want to arrest all these men together in the same net, and I want you to be the first to proclaim such an incredible catch. I did not have Cadoudal arrested, because Pichegru arrived in Paris only yesterday."

"What? Pichegru arrived in Paris yesterday?"

"In the Rue de l'Arcade, if you please, because he has not yet had time to come to an agreement with Moreau."

"With Moreau!" cried Bonaparte. "You must be crazy! Have you forgotten that they are mortal enemies?"

"Ah! Because Moreau denounced Pichegru out of jealousy! You know better than anyone, Citizen First Consul, that Pichegru, whose brother the priest, to pay a debt of six hundred francs when he left unwillingly for Cayenne, had to call upon the general to sell his sword and epaulettes bearing this inscription: 'The sword and epaulettes belonging to the victor over Holland.' You know full well that Pichegru received no million from Monsieur Le Prince de Condé. Furthermore, you know that Pichegru, who never married and who, consequently, has neither wife nor children, was not able, in his treaty with the Prince de Condé, to command a pension of two hundred thousand francs for a nonexistent widow and one hundred thousand for unborn children. So it is that governments apply such slights and omissions against a man they would like to be rid of: a man whose great service is repaid only by ingratitude. Well, Moreau has admitted his error, and Pichegru arrived yesterday, ready to forgive him."

Hearing the news about the meeting of the two men he regarded as his greatest enemies, the Corsican in Bonaparte could not refrain from making a rapid sign of the cross. "But," he said, "once they have met, once they have come to an agreement, once those daggers filling the air are turned against me, will you get rid of them for me? Will you have them arrested?"

"Not yet."

"Then what in damnation are you waiting for?"

"I am waiting for the prince they themselves are waiting for to reach Paris."

"They are expecting a prince?"

"A prince from the House of Bourbon."

"They need a prince to assassinate me?"

"Who says they intend to assassinate you? Cadoudal has made it clear that he would never assassinate you."

"What were they trying to do with the bomb?"

"He swears to high heaven that he had nothing to do with the bomb."

"What does he want then?"

"He wants to fight you."

"Fight me?"

"Why not? The other day you yourself were ready to fight Moreau."

"But Moreau is Moreau. That is, he is a great general, a winner. I did call him the retreat general, it's true, but that was before Hohenlinden. And how do they expect to fight me?"

"One evening when you are making your way back to La Malmaison or Saint-Cloud with an escort of twenty-five or thirty men, a like number of Chouans, led by Cadoudal, armed as your men are armed and equal in numbers to them, will block your path, attack your escort, and kill you."

"And once I am dead, then what will they do?"

"The prince, who will be present during the combat but will not participate in it, will proclaim the monarchy. Without having moved so much as his little finger during the whole affair, he will take the name Louis XVIII, sit on his ancestors' throne, and the Consulate will have ended. You will simply be a glowing point of light in history, much like the sun, or Saturn, with golden satellites by the names of Toulon, Montebello, Arcole, Rivoli, Lodi, the Pyramids, and Marengo."

"Enough joking, Monsieur Fouché. Who is this prince who would now claim France and my heritage?"

"As for that, I must say that I am in the deepest ignorance. People have been expecting a prince to return for the past ten years, and still he has not done so. He was expected in the Vendée, and he never came. He was expected at Quiberon, and he didn't come. He is expected in Paris, and he will no more likely come to Paris than he did to the Vendée or Quiberon."

"Well, then, so be it!" said Bonaparte. "We shall wait for him. Can you answer for everything, Fouché?"

"I can answer for everything in Paris, provided that your police do not get in the way of mine."

"Agreed. You know that I am careless with precaution, so it will be your job to watch over me. By the way, don't forget to make a gift of six thousand francs to your agent. And make sure he does all that is possible to not lose sight of Cadoudal."

"Relax. If my agent loses sight of him, we have two reference points that will allow us to find him again."

"And they are what, those reference points?"

"Moreau and Pichegru."

Scarcely had Fouché taken his leave than Bonaparte called Savary. "Savary," Bonaparte said to his aide-de-camp, "bring me the description of any individuals who, in the department of the Seine-Inférieure, have been identified as stagecoach robbers or anything similar."

Since domestic peace had been restored, the police had prepared a list of all those who had participated in civil unrest or who had been arrested in those areas where stagecoach robberies had taken place. These suspect individuals fell into one of four categories: manipulators, participants, accomplices, and aiders and abettors.

They needed to find the clockmaker about whom both Querelle and Fouché's agent had spoken. While Bonaparte might have learned his name through Fouché's agent, he did not want to seem to attach too much importance to it, for fear of revealing his plan to Fouché. For he found Fouché's clairvoyance almost as painful as Régnier's blindness.

To find himself in the midst of an undefined danger, to be dependent upon an inefficient police force for protection, was for a man of Bonaparte's genius and character in itself a kind of humiliation. He wanted to see the situation through his own eyes, even if he could not see clearly! That is why he had Savary bring him the status of all the suspects in the department of the Seine-Inférieure.

Their first glance at the list from Eu and Le Tréport produced the name of a clockmaker: Troche. The father had once been arrested in Dieppe, and as he was evidently so heavily implicated in the affair, they knew they could not count on reliable information from him. But there was still the nineteen-year-old son, who surely knew as much as anyone about the past and any future landings at Biville. Using the semaphore network, Bonaparte telegraphed an order for the son to be arrested and brought straightaway to Paris. If he came by postal coach, he could be there the following morning.

Réal had meanwhile gone back to the prison, where he had found the poor condemned man in a pitiful state. In the clerk's room, from the barred window that looked out over the square, he had watched the preparations for his date with the firing squad. At daybreak, sometime between six and seven o'clock, the armed guards who would accompany him to the Grenelle plain, and there shoot him, had arrived. They stood in order in the square, while the carriage that would transport him waited by the gate with its door open and the step lowered.

He had watched as the orderly left to get the execution order from the governor of Paris, and the warrant officer, already on his horse, was waiting only for the orderly's return before proceeding with the execution. The mounted dragoons who would serve as the escort were also now waiting in formation, except for their officer, who had tied his horse's bridle to the bars of Querelle's window. For nearly three hours, Querelle had been suspended in that terrible, increasingly expectant state when finally, as the clock struck nine o'clock, he marked the arrival of the same carriage he had heard at five that morning. Then he watched the door to the clerk's room anxiously. He strained to hear any sounds in the corridor, and his heart began pounding with expectation.

At last the door burst open. Réal came in, a smile brightening his stern face.

"Oh, you would not be smiling," said the poor prisoner, throwing himself at the state counselor's feet and wrapping his arms around him, "if I were condemned to die!"

"I did not promise you a pardon," said Réal. "I promised you a reprieve, and that's all I am bringing, but I promise I will do all I can to save you."

"Please, then," cried the prisoner, "if you don't want me to die from anxiety, dismiss the dragoons, the carriage, the soldiers. They are here for me, I know, and as long as they remain I will never be able to believe what you are telling me."

Réal summoned the director: "The execution has been postponed," he said, "by the First Consul's order. Instead, you will put the prisoner in solitary confinement, and this evening you will take him to the Temple."

Querelle could finally breathe freely. The fact that the Temple was a prison for long detentions but not for dangerous criminals confirmed what

Réal had just told him. His eyes still trained on the window, he saw the steps of the carriage rise, the door close, and the carriage drive off. He saw the officer untie his horse, climb into the saddle, and take the lead of his men. Then he saw nothing more: His joy so excessive, he had fainted dead away.

The doctor was called and proceeded to let some blood. When the man came back to his senses, Réal promised once again to intercede on his behalf with the First Consul. That night, Querelle was taken to the Temple.

XXXIII
Empty-Handed

A SINGULAR CIRCUMSTANCE HAD put the police on Troche's trail. Two or three years before the time of our story, a skirmish had broken out between customs officials and a band of smugglers who had just reached shore. A few shots were exchanged, and on one of the charred pieces of wadding that remained on the ground afterward was the following address: "To Citizen Troche, clockmaker at. . . ." Everyone in Dieppe knew the clockmaker Citizen Troche, so there was no doubt on the part of the police that he had used a letter bearing his address as wadding when he loaded his gun. That letter that led to his arrest.

Citizen Troche had been brought to Paris from Dieppe five or six days previously. He was a crafty Norman between forty-five and fifty years old, and when he'd been brought face to face with Querelle and Querelle had appeared not to recognize him, he had chosen not to recognize Querelle either. Nonetheless, despite his denials, they were keeping the elder Citizen Troche locked up.

Then there was Troche the son, a big, naïve fellow about nineteen or twenty years old, who, however innocent-looking his face, was a better smuggler than he was a clockmaker. Nicolas Troche, too, had now been brought to Paris for questioning. Savary, dissembling, told him that his father had divulged everything, and the son proceeded unwittingly to do the same.

His confession did not compromise him greatly. Nicolas said that when he'd receive word smugglers wanted to come ashore, he would guide them with an agreed-upon signal. If the sea was calm, he would have them advance; if rough, he'd have them wait for a more opportune moment. After they'd land, he'd give them his hand when they reached the top of the cliff;

for then he'd pass them on to one of his friends and never deal with them again, except for the three francs per person they would give him when they were ready to leave again. For generations the Troche household had been engaging in such activity, with the eldest son always inheriting the trade. They'd earn a good thousand francs a year this way, but, Nicolas insisted, the only men they ever helped were smugglers.

Through an open door, Bonaparte was listening to the whole interrogation. Thus far all was as they had assumed.

Savary asked Troche if he was expecting another arrival. He answered that at the very time Savary had done him the honor of summoning him for this conversation, an English cutter was sailing back and forth down below the Biville cliffs, waiting for good weather before trying to land.

Savary knew what the First Consul's plans were. If young Nicolas confessed to another arrival—which he just had—Savary was to get back into the carriage with him and leave immediately for Dieppe in order to be ready for the next landing.

Young Troche was kept in custody all day long, for in spite of the aide-de-camp's diligence, he was not able to leave until seven that evening. He and Bonaparte had briefly considered having Nicolas join his father Jérôme Troche in prison. No matter to them that the young man preferred the sea breeze of the cliffs to stale prison air, but, as Nicolas pointed out, if he were not present with them on the cliffs to give the customary signals, the landing would not take place.

Troche was a true poacher. As long as he was hunting, it didn't matter for whom. Furthermore, the thought that his past path might lead him to the scaffold spurred him to collaborate in setting a trap for the new arrivals as zealously as he had aided those who had landed earlier.

Accompanied by a wagon carrying twelve elite gendarmes, Savary arrived in Dieppe twenty-four hours after leaving Paris at nightfall with authority from the Ministry of War to deal with any situation that might arise. Troche immediately got information about the landing signals.

The sea was still high, and the two-masted brig was still tacking back and forth, bad weather having made landing impossible. Savary took Troche to the coast at daybreak. The ship was in sight. From its present position, if the wind were right, it could make it to the base of the cliff with one tack.

Savary decided not to stay in Dieppe. Instead, disguised as respectable middle-class citizens, he and his twelve gendarmes, chosen from among the bravest in the regiment, left for Biville. Savary had sent the horses on ahead, and, guided by Troche, he and his men came to a house normally used to accommodate the people whom English ships brought to the coast.

The house was completely isolated, well outside the circle of police surveillance. It sat at the edge of the village and looked out over the sea. It offered seclusion and provided protection, for one could come or go without being seen.

Leaving his men outside the garden, Savary stepped over the hedge and walked toward the little house. Through a partially opened shutter, he could see a table set with wine, slices of bread, and chunks of butter. Savary called for Troche; he showed Troche the meal that had been prepared. "That's the meal that always awaits those arriving by sea," Troche explained. "It means that the landing will take place tonight, or tomorrow at the latest. The tide is beginning to ebb, and if they are not here in a quarter of an hour, they will come ashore tomorrow."

Savary waited in vain. Then he waited impatiently for the morrow. Rumor had it that the prince, without whom nothing could happen, or at least without whom George would do nothing, was himself aboard the ship.

At daybreak, Savary was standing on the cliff. The ground was covered with snow, and as he had walked toward the cliff, he had thought for a moment he would see what he was looking for. The wind was blowing violently from the sea, and the air was filled with white flakes, so he was unable to see more than ten paces. But he could hear quite well, and he heard voices rising from a path along the cliff.

Troche put his hand on Savary's arm. "Here come our men," he said. "I can hear Pageot de Pauly's voice." Pageot de Pauly, a young man about Troche's age, served as guide to the new arrivals in Troche's absence.

Savary sent his gendarmes to block the end of the path, while he, along with Troche and two other men, headed toward the place he had heard the voices. The early travelers, frightened by the sudden appearance of four men on the crest of the ravine, shouted "Stop!" But then Pageot, recognizing Troche, said, "Don't worry. Troche is with them!"

The two groups met. Pageot's men were just ordinary villagers who were coming to the cliff in expectation of a landing. A landing had in fact been attempted, but the skiff had been unable to make it to shore because the breakers were too heavy. The wind carried three words from the boat up to the villagers: "See you tomorrow!"

It was the third time the cutter had tried to put in the skiff without success. It was the third day that the cutter had had to sail again out to sea and, sailing back and forth, wait for the tides and weather to change. In the evening it would attempt to make the landing once more.

Savary spent the following night watching. Not only did nothing happen, but the next day they could barely see the cutter. It seemed to have set full sail for England.

Savary waited again the day after that to see if the ship would return. He also carefully examined the cable that the men who'd come ashore were using to scale the cliff. Though he himself was a man not easily discouraged, he would for sure rather participate in ten bloody battles than climb to the top of a cliff, this length of rope his only support, with the tempest meanwhile raging around him as he hung there suspended between the darkness above and the sea beneath.

He sent messengers daily to Bonaparte, and after the twenty-eighth day, he received a telegraph message from the First Consul ordering him to return to Paris. For Bonaparte had now become convinced that the cutter, whose presence had been reported for ten or twelve days by Savary, had not been carrying that famous French prince—the prince without whom George had declared he would not act—after all. And by himself, George was just an ordinary conspirator; only if he was acting in accordance with the Duc de Berry or the Comte de Provence was he the ally of a prince.

For Bonaparte had recently summoned Carnot and Fouché. Let us now see what Bonaparte himself said about that meeting in a manuscript the ship the *Héron* brought back from Sainte-Hélène:

However, the more things continued, the more dangerous the Jacobins were becoming, for they could not forgive how their friends had been punished. Given the dire situation, I summoned Carnot and Fouché.

"Gentlemen," I said, "after so many storms, I would like to believe that you are as convinced as I am that France's interests have never been in harmony with the different governments it has given itself since the years of the Revolution. No government has been established on the basis of France's geographical position, on the number and genius of its inhabitants. However peaceful the country may seem to you now, it is still sitting on a volcano. Lava is bubbling, and we must prevent an eruption at all costs. I, as do many right-thinking people, think that there is only one way to save France and guarantee forever the advantages of the liberty it has won. And that is to put France in the safekeeping of a constitutional monarchy in which the throne would be hereditary."

Carnot and Fouché were not surprised by my proposal. They had been expecting it. Carnot answered, in no roundabout way, that he could see I had my own eyes set on the throne.

"And what if I did," I replied. "How would that be a mistake, if it resulted in France's glory and peace of mind?"

"Because in a single day you would be destroying the work of an entire population, and you might have cause to repent."

I could see that there was nothing to be done with Carnot. So I broke off the conversation, planning to bring it up again with Fouché. And indeed, I summoned him a few days later.

Carnot had already divulged my secret, which, if truth be told, was no longer much of a secret. Not having requested discretion, I could hardly hold his indiscretion against him. After all, it was necessary for my plans to be made known so that I could find out how people were reacting.

Had the acts I promulgated since being at the head of things prepared the French people for seeing me take the scepter? And did they believe that my doing so would be likely to give them happiness and peace of mind? I have no idea. However, it is likely that the whole affair would have been settled amicably if some infernal genius, Fouché, had not gotten involved. If he truly believed the rumor he began to spread, then he is not so guilty. But if he spread the rumor to cause me problems, then he's a monster.

As soon as he was aware of my designs on the throne, Fouché, with the help of his agents, for he indeed made sure that the reports did not seem to be coming from him, circulated the news among the Jacobins that I wanted to restore the monarchy, and that my intention was to return the crown to its rightful heir. They added that, according to secret treaties, I would be supported in such an enterprise by every foreign power.

It was a diabolical invention, and it turned against me all those people for whom restoration of the Bourbons might jeopardize fortune or existence.

Since at that time I did not know Fouché very well, naturally I did not believe him capable of such an evil deed. As proof of what I'm saying, I had asked him to sound out public opinion. He had no trouble reporting the rumors being circulated because he had invented them himself.

"The Jacobins," he said, "will shed their last drop of blood before allowing the Bourbons to regain the throne. They are not afraid of a sovereign, and I believe they could even be persuaded that would be the best way to go. But what the Jacobins really object to is the Bourbons, because they are afraid they have everything to fear from them."

His comments, although they helped me foresee some obstacles, were not of the nature to discourage me, for I was not thinking at all about the Bourbons. I said as much to Fouché, asking what we might to do to refute such false rumors and convince the Jacobins that I was working for myself alone.

He asked for two days before responding.

Two days later, as he had promised, Fouché came back.

"The ship Colonel Savary was talking about in his correspondence disappeared on the eleventh day," he said. "That's because it was transporting only secondary agents, and it took them to Brittany, from where they could take different roads to Paris. You know them only too well—the princes of the House of Bourbon, the Comte d'Artois and the Duc de Berry—to believe that they would risk coming to fight you in Paris itself. For in spite of the appeals made to them, never did they risk coming to fight the Republicans in the Vendée. Monsieur le Comte d'Artois, an empty-headed dandy, is too busy proposing his degenerate love to the lovely English girls and ladies. And the Duc de Berry, as you know full well, has never seized any opportunity, in combat or in a duel, to prove his personal courage. But there does happen to be, near the Rhine, only six or eight leagues away from France, a noble, brave man who has proven his courage numerous times in fighting Republican troops. He's the son of the Prince de Condé, the Duc d'Enghien."

Bonaparte shuddered. "Be careful, Fouché. Although I have not told you frankly what my plans are for you in the future, I believe that sometimes you fear that I might patch things up with the Bourbons and that then, Monsieur le Régicide, you would find yourself in an awkward position. But know that if a Bourbon plots against me, and if such a plot is clearly proven, neither royal blood nor social standing would stop me from doing what I must. I want to achieve my fortune as it is written, as I think it is, on the book of destiny. Any obstacle I meet on my path will be overcome. However, I need to have right and my conscience on my side."

"Citizen," said Fouché, "it is not by chance nor is it out of personal interest that I speak to you of the Duc d'Enghien. After the interview you gave Cadoudal the honor of granting, when Sol de Grisolles, instead of going back to London with his general, left for Germany, I was eager to know what he was going to do on the other side of the Rhine. On my orders, the agent who had the honor of appearing before you the other day followed him. He is a very resourceful man, as you were able to see. He followed Sol de Grisolles to Strasbourg, he crossed the Rhine with him, he struck up a friendship with him on the way, and he arrived in Ettenheim with him. There the very first thing that Cadoudal's aide-de-camp did was present his respects to Monsieur le Duc d'Enghien, who invited him to dinner, keeping him there all evening until eleven."

"So," said Bonaparte sharply, seeing where Fouché was going, "your agent did not dine with him, did he? There is no way he can know what they said or what plans they made."

"What they said is not hard to guess, and whatever plans they made would be easy to surmise. But, without spending time on vain conjectures, let us stay with what we know. My man, as you may suspect, did not spend his eight hours of free time without gathering information. He learned that the Duc d'Enghien is often away from Ettenheim for seven or eight days at a time. He learned, in addition, that from time to time he spends a night, sometimes two, in Strasbourg."

"Nothing surprising about that," said Bonaparte. "I too have information about what he does in Strasbourg."

"And why does he go to Strasbourg?" asked Fouché.

"To see his mistress, Princesse Charlotte de Rohan."

"Now," said Fouché, "we still need to know if Madame Charlotte de Rohan, who is not the mistress but the wife of the Duc d'Enghien, since he married her secretly, though not apparently so that she could live with him in Ettenheim—so we still need to know if she remains in Strasbourg merely to provide a pretext for the prince. He comes to Strasbourg to see his wife, of course, but he might also be coming to Strasbourg to meet with his accomplices, and when he is in Strasbourg he is only twenty hours away from Paris."

Bonaparte frowned. "So that's it," he said. "People have been sure that they've spotted him here at the theater! I simply shrugged my shoulders and said it couldn't be true."

"Whether or not he ever came to the theater," said Fouché, "I invite the First Consul not to lose sight of the Duc d'Enghien."

"I can do better than that," said Bonaparte. "Tomorrow I shall send a trustworthy man across the Rhine. He will report to me directly, and as soon as he's back, we shall talk about this business once again."

He turned away from Fouché then, to show that he wanted to be alone. Fouché withdrew.

An hour later, the First Consul summoned the inspector of the Gendarmerie to his office. He wondered if the inspector might have an intelligent and discreet man who could go to Germany on a secret mission to verify the information Fouché's agent had gathered. The inspector said that he had exactly the man and asked how the First Consul wanted his instructions to be conveyed to the agent. Bonaparte replied that such serious business demanded the instructions be crystal-clear, so he would write them out that evening, then send them to the inspector, who would in turn give them to the officer. The officer was to leave immediately upon receiving them.

The instructions were:

Find out if the Duc d'Enghien really does leave Ettenheim mysteriously;
    Find out who among the émigré community is most often seen in his circles and who among them have the honor of seeing him most frequently;

Find out as well if he has any political connections with English agents at the small German courts.

At eight in the morning the officer was on the way to Strasbourg.

XXXIV

The Revelations of a Man Who Hanged Himself

WHILE THE FIRST CONSUL was writing out his instructions for the officer of the Gendarmerie, a tragic scene was being played out in the Temple prison.

Among the first prisoners taken when fears of conspiracy against the Consulate grew had been George's loyal servant Louis Picot. After his arrest at the wine shop in the Rue du Bac—on the same day the Limousin had seen George himself leaving the same establishment—the police had found a map in Picot's room. The map had led them to an address on Rue Saintonge, where they had surprised two other conspirators, Roger and Damonville, and barely missed a third, Coster de Saint-Victor.

The very evening he'd entered the Temple, Damonville had hanged himself. As a result, orders were given for the guards to check the prisoners' room twice during the night.

Another of Cadoudal's men, Bouvet de Lozier, had been arrested on February 12 at the house of a woman named Saint-Léger, on Rue Saint-Sauveur. Once inside the Temple, he had been secreted in a chamber near the common heated room, where he was immediately and brutally interrogated.

A Royalist officer about thirty-six years old, Bouvet de Lozier was George's chief warrant officer and one of his closest confidants. It was he who, under an assumed name, had organized all the various relay stations between Biville and Paris for Cadoudal's bands of men. He had also arranged to have Madame de Saint-Leger, in whose home he was lodging, rent a house in Chaillot, on the Grande Rue, number 6, which had become George's address, using the name Larive, when he reached Paris. Bouvet de Lozier was indeed one of George's most active agents.

Disheartened after his first interrogation, during which he had revealed more than he'd intended to, and fearful that he'd divulge still more in the second, he decided that he'd kill himself as his compatriot Damonville had done. And on February 14, at about midnight, using a black silk tie wrapped around the highest door hinge, he hanged himself. He was just losing consciousness when Savard, one of his jailers, came by on his nightly round.

The door to the interrogation room offered Savard some resistance, so with some force he pushed it open. Hearing a moan as he entered, he turned quickly around. He saw the prisoner hanging from a tie. He called for help.

The second jailer, suspecting a struggle, came running with a knife. "Cut it, Elie, cut it!" shouted Savard, pointing to the tie holding up the prisoner. Elie didn't lose a second. He cut the knot, and Bouvet dropped motionless to the floor.

They thought he was dead, but Fauconnier, the chief jailer, wanted to be sure. He had the jailers carry the body to the clerk's room, where the Temple doctor, Monsieur Suppé, could attend to him. The doctor found that the prisoner was still breathing, and he let some blood. A few minutes later, Bouvet de Lozier opened his eyes.

Soon after than, when he was strong enough to be moved, Bouvet was taken to see Citizen Desmarets, chief of the high police. There he also found Monsieur Réal, to whom the prisoner made a full confession. He then signed a written declaration as well.

The next morning at seven, just as the specially dispatched gendarme was leaving for Germany, Réal appeared at the First Consul's rooms, where the valet, Constant, was doing Bonaparte's hair.

"Ah, Monsieur le Conseiller d'Etat, do you have something new to report? I see you are here early."

"Yes, General. I have news of the utmost importance to communicate, but I would prefer to speak to you in private."

"Oh, don't worry about Constant. Constant is nobody."

"Since such are your wishes, General. You must know that Pichegru is in Paris."

"I know," Bonaparte replied. "Fouché has already told me."

"Yes! But what he did not tell you, what even Fouché does not know, is that Pichegru and Moreau are meeting and plotting together."

"Not one more word!" said Bonaparte, putting his finger to his mouth.

Bonaparte dressed hurriedly, then guided Réal to his office. "Now let us take a look at the matter!" he said. "You are right: if what you have just told me is true, the news is indeed of utmost importance." Bonaparte moved his thumb quickly over his chest in the sign of the cross.

When Réal had told him what had happened, Bonaparte asked, "And you say that in addition, you have a written declaration from him?"

"Here it is," said Réal. In his eagerness, Bonaparte nearly ripped it from Réal's hands, for it was indeed important that he know Moreau was participating in some plot against his life.

Moreau and Pichegru were the only two men equal to Bonaparte in military tactics. Pichegru, either unjustly or falsely accused of treason against France, had been sent to Sinnamary on the 18th Fructidor, and in spite of the miraculous way he had engineered his escape—aided, it seemed, by the hand of God—he no longer inspired fear in Bonaparte. Moreau, on the other hand, caused the First Consul concern. Still glowing from his battle at Hohenlinden, but poorly rewarded by Bonaparte for his beautiful, skillful victory, and now living as an ordinary man in Paris, Moreau continued to have a great following. Between the 18th Fructidor and the 13th Vendémiaire, Bonaparte had proscribed only the Jacobins, the party of extreme Republicans, and excluded them from all government activities. But now even the moderate Republicans, seeing the First Consul gain control of more and more power as he moved France toward monarchy, had become increasingly alarmed and had gathered together, if not in fact, at least in spirit, around Moreau. Further, he had the support of three or four other generals who had remained faithful to the principles of '89 and even of '93. Confronted by the unceasing conspiracy within the army, the open conspiracy of Augereau and Bernadotte, and the invisible conspiracy bred by Malet, Oudet, and the Philadelphians, Bonaparte found in Moreau an adversary clearly to be feared. An irreproachable Republican, like Fabius himself, whose name he was sometimes given— Fabius the temporizer who made a maxim of the need to allow men and principles the time to wear themselves down—Moreau was suddenly, without such allowance, throwing himself headlong into a Royalist plot that included on the one hand Pichegru the Condean and on the other George the Chouan.

Bonaparte smiled, looked up to the heavens, and uttered these words: "Decidedly, I must be living under a star!"

Then he turned to Réal. "Is this letter in his own handwriting?"

"Yes, General."

"Is it signed?"

"Yes, it is signed."

"Let's take a look."

He read avidly:

Pichegru is a man who has come back out through the gates of the tomb; he comes back still covered with the shadow of death, and he demands vengeance on those who by their perfidy cast him and his party into the abyss. Sent back to France to support the Bourbon cause, he finds himself now obliged to fight for Moreau or to give up the undertaking that has long been the only object of his mission. . . .

Bonaparte stopped reading. "What does he mean, 'fight for Moreau'?" he asked.

"Read on," said Réal.

A prince from the House of Bourbon was to come to France to place himself at the head of the Royalist party. Moreau had promised to join the Bourbon cause. But once the Royalists are back in France, Moreau retracts. He proposes that they work for him and name him dictator. Those are the facts; it is up to you to determine their full value.

A general who served under Moreau, Lajolais, is sent by him to meet with the prince in London. Lojolais adheres, in Moreau's name, to the principal points of the proposed plan. The prince makes ready to leave, but in meetings that take place in Paris between Moreau, Pichegru, and George, Moreau reveals his intentions and declares that he can act only for a dictator and never for a king. From that point on there is dissension and disbandment within the Royalist party.

I saw the same man, Lajolais, on January 25 in Paris, when he came to pick up George and Pichegru from the carriage I shared with them on the Boulevard de la Madeleine to take them to Moreau, who was waiting not far away. They had a meeting on the Champs-Elysées during which Moreau claimed that it was impossible to restore the king, and he proposed to put himself at the head of the government with the title of dictator, leaving the Royalists only the possibility of being his collaborators or his soldiers.

The prince was to come back to France only after hearing the result of the meeting between the three generals, after total unity, total agreement among them concerning the execution of their plan.

George rejected any idea of assassination or of bombs; he had explained things clearly back in London; he wanted nothing but a forceful attack in which he and his officers risked paying with their own lives. The object of the attack would be to seize the First Consul and consequently the government.

I do not know how much weight you will accord to the assertions of a man who only an hour ago was pulled back from a death he himself had sought and who can see before him the death an offended government has in store for him. But I cannot hold back my cry of despair or refrain from attacking the man who brought me down. Furthermore, you will be able to find facts confirming everything I have said as the grand trial in which I am implicated plays out.

Bouvet de Lozier

Bonaparte remained silent a moment after reading. It was clear from his intense concentration that he was trying to solve a problem. Speaking more to himself than Réal, he said, "The only man who could cause me worry, the only man who would have any chance against me, damning himself in such a clumsy way! It's impossible!"

"Would you like me to arrest Moreau immediately?" Réal asked.

The First Consul shook his head. "Moreau is too important," he said. "He is too directly opposed to me. Since I would be so well served by getting rid of him, I cannot expose myself to conjectures."

"But what if Moreau is indeed conspiring with Pichegru?" Réal objected.

"Do I need to tell you," Bonaparte went on, "that my only sources for knowing that Pichegru is in Paris are Fouché and this man of yours who tried to hang himself last night? All the English newspapers speak of Pichegru as if he were still in or near London. I am aware, of course, that all those newspapers are conspiring against me and plotting against the French government."

"In any case," said Réal, "I have ordered the barriers to be closed. Anyone trying to enter Paris will be carefully searched."

"And equally so those who are trying to leave," said Bonaparte.

"Are you not planning a grand military review the day after tomorrow, Citizen First Consul?"

"Yes."

"Well, you must cancel it."

"Why?"

"Because there may still be as many as sixty conspirators walking around freely in Paris. Once they see that all means of leaving the capital have been blocked, they may risk some desperate action."

"What does that have to do with me? Is it not your job to watch over me?"

"General," Réal replied, "we can take responsibility for your safety only if you cancel your military review."

"Monsieur le Conseiller, I shall say this once again," said Bonaparte. "We each have our own responsibilities. Yours is to watch over me so that no one assassinates me while I review my troops, and mine is to review my troops at the risk of being assassinated."

"General, that is imprudent."

"Monsieur Réal," Bonaparte replied, "you are speaking like a state counselor. In France, what is most prudent to have is courage!"

Dismissing Réal, Bonaparte said to Savary, "Have an orderly ride over to ask Fouché to come see me immediately."

Within ten minutes, Fouché's carriage had arrived from his house on the Rue du Bac at the gate of the Tuileries. By then Bonaparte was pacing nervously up and down.

"Come quickly!" he said at his first glimpse of Fouché. "Do you know that Bouvet de Lozier has just tried to hang himself in prison?"

"Yes, and I know as well," answered Fouché calmly, "that they got there in time to save him and that they took him to see Monsieur Desmarets, and that he also saw Monsieur Réal, was interrogated, and signed a declaration."

"In that declaration he said that Pichegru is in Paris."

"I told you as much, well before he did."

"Yes, but you did not tell me that he was here to plot with Moreau."

"Because I did not yet know that, or at least I was not absolutely certain. All I had then were suspicions, and I told you my suspicions."

"And today you are certain?" Bonaparte asked.

"You're a hard man," said Fouché. "We have to tell you everything that will happen before it happens, and then when it does happen we are credited with telling you nothing. Would you like to know exactly how we stand—on the condition that you allow me to carry things out to their conclusion as I wish?"

"I grant you no conditions, and I demand to know how things stand."

"Very well, as we each have our own role to play. Réal has Bouvet de Lozier, who hanged himself yesterday, and I have Lajolais, who perhaps will hang himself tomorrow. I've had Lajolais arrested, and I have interrogated him. If you would like to know about the interrogation, I have it here, in substance, minus the questions."

It read thusly:

I had known for a long time, through a common friend, a priest named David, that Pichegru and Moreau, formerly at odds with each other, had finally reconciled. I saw Moreau several times last summer. He expressed the desire to meet with Pichegru. In order to arrange a meeting, I went to London. There I saw Pichegru and spoke to him about Moreau's wishes. Pichegru told me that he had a similar wish and that he would be pleased to seize on such an opportunity to leave England.

Scarcely two weeks later an opportunity presented itself, and we took advantage of it. Pichegru then was living on the Rue de l'Arcade. The meeting was planned for the Boulevard de la Madeleine, near the Rue Basse-du-Rempart. Moreau came from where he lived, on the Rue d'Anjou-Saint-Honoré, by hackney cab. He got out at the Madeleine. I stayed in the cab, and it continued moving. The two generals met at the prescribed place. They walked together for about a quarter of an hour. I know nothing about what they said during that first meeting.

The two other meetings took place in Moreau's house, at the Rue d'Anjou-Saint-Honoré. The last time, I was waiting for Pichegru on the Rue de Chaillot, for he had changed lodgings. He came back quite displeased with Moreau. When I asked him why he was so displeased, he said: "Do you know what Moreau proposed? A man normally so unselfish, so like a Spartan at heart? He asked us to make him dictator. He would deign to accept a dictatorship! It seems that he is ambitious after all, and that he would like to reign. Well, I wish him success, but in my opinion, he does not have what it takes to govern France even for three months."

"Do you think we should arrest Moreau?" asked Bonaparte.

"I see no problem with that," said Fouché. "With his character as we know it, he will be no further along in three months than he is today. Of course we'll need to arrest Pichegru at the same time, so that their names can be pronounced in the same breath and displayed together on walls all over Paris."

"Do you know where Pichegru is living now?"

"As I am the one who found his lodging for him, with Leblanc, one of his former valets—yes. It cost me dearly, but I know everything he does."

"Will you then take responsibility for arresting Pichegru?"

"Of course. And you can have Réal arrest Moreau. That will not be difficult, and showing your confidence in the good counselor will cheer him up. Have him tell me the moment Moreau arrives at the Temple, and Pichegru will be there a half hour later."

"And now," Bonaparte moved on, "you know that I have a military review scheduled for Sunday. Réal advises me to cancel it."

"On the contrary, have your review," said Fouché. "It will have the greatest effect."

"How strange," said Bonaparte, looking at Fouché. "I do not think of you as being brave, yet you constantly give me the most courageous advice."

"By giving you courageous advice," said Fouché with his customary cynicism, "I myself am not required to take it."

The orders to arrest the two generals were signed at the same time, on the same table, with the same pen. Fouché took Pichegru's arrest order with him; Savary delivered the order for the arrest of Moreau to Réal.

Moncey, one of Moreau's best friends and the general commander of the Gendarmerie, was charged by Réal with the duty of arresting Moreau. Attached to the order, when it was shown to the grand judge and acting minister of police Monsieur Régnier, was a recommendation from Bonaparte:

> Monsieur Régnier,
> Before taking Moreau to the Temple prison, ask him if he would like to speak to me. In that case, bring him to me in your carriage. Everything might be settled between us.

There was no similar recommendation to Fouché for Pichegru. Yet the First Consul had known Pichegru for a long time, since he had been Bonaparte's teacher at the school in Brienne.

Bonaparte was not fond of his school memories. He had too often suffered ridicule because his family was not very noble in rank. Nor could they afford to send him more than very little money.

XXXV

The Arrests

BONAPARTE WAS NOT at all sanguine about the effect Moreau's arrest might have on people in Paris. So he preferred, if it were possible, to have Moreau arrested at Grosbois, his estate in the country.

It was around ten in the morning, on the day after the arrest orders had been issued, and Bonaparte still had not received any news. Eager to learn what was happening, he summoned Constant and sent him out to the Faubourg Saint-Honoré, where Moreau's house was situated in the Rue d'Anjou, to find out what he could about the progress of the arrests.

But all Constant saw were a few policemen. Actually, only he would have recognized that they were policemen, as he had often seen them around the Tuileries. He happened upon a policeman he was acquainted with, and when he inquiured about Moreau, the man answered that he was probably out in the country as they had not found him in his Paris house.

Constant was already leaving when the policeman, who'd recognized him as the First Consul's valet, came running after him; Moreau had just been arrested on the Charenton bridge, he said, and they had taken him to the Temple prison. He had shown no resistance; he'd merely climbed from his carriage into the policeman's cabriolet. At the Temple, when the grand judge Régnier asked if he might be willing to see Bonaparte, he'd answered that he had no reason to speak to the First Consul.

If, in Bonaparte's hate for Moreau, there was some injustice, in Moreau's hate for Bonaparte there was clearly abundant pettiness. Moreau's hate, however, came not from within himself but rather from two women, his wife and his mother-in-law. Madame Bonaparte had married Moreau to her friend Mademoiselle Hulot, like her a Creole from the island of Martinique. Sweet and kind, a girl with all the qualities that make for a good wife and mother, she loved her husband passionately and proudly bore his glorious name. Unfortunately, among her virtues was her deference in everything—opinions, wishes, desires—to her mother. And Madame Hulot was ambitious. She placed her son-in-law's reputation on a par with Bonaparte's, and she wanted her daughter to have a position equal to Josephine's. Her motherly love translated her dissatisfaction into ceaseless lamentation and endless recriminations, which were borne daily to Moreau by his wife. The old Roman's serenity soon passed; he became bitter, and his house became a center for all sorts of political and social malcontents. In the eyes of this opposition, the First Consul's every act became the object of mockery, scorn, or bitter criticism. Moreau had been a melancholic dreamer, but now he grew somber. He had been bitter, but now he grew hateful. The malcontent now became a conspirator.

In the hope that Moreau, once he was arrested and alone, beyond the reaches of his wife and mother-in-law, might reconcile with him, Bonaparte asked Régnier expectantly, after the arrest, "Well, are you bringing him to see me?"

"No, General. He said he had no reason to meet with you."

Bonaparte looked askance at the grand judge and shrugged. "That's what comes of dealing with an imbecile," he said: The question was, who was the imbecile? The grand judge of course assumed that Bonaparte was alluding to Moreau, but we believe that Bonaparte was speaking of his ineffectual minister of justice, Régnier.

Pichegru, too, had been arrested. But things had not gone so well with him as they had with Moreau.

Thanks to the Limousin's vigilance, Fouché had not lost track of Pichegru since he had arrived in Paris: from the Rue de l'Arcade to the Rue de Chaillot; from the Rue de Chaillot to the Rue des Colonnes, where Coster de Saint-Victor had hidden him, perhaps more safely than anywhere, in the maisonette of his old friend and lovely courtesan, the beautiful Aurélie de Saint-Amour. This last refuge, suitable as it would have been for Alcibiades, did not appeal to Pichegru's more austere tastes, and at the invitation of a former valet he took up residence in the Rue Chabanais.

Pichegru had stayed but two days with the courtesan, and it was in these two days that Fouché lost the general's trail. For two weeks Pichegru had been secure, until Fouché had found him again. Fouché had been keeping an eye on him for twelve days when, the day before the arrests were to be made, a man named Leblanc called at the offices of the governor of Paris and asked insistently to speak to General Murat himself. Murat, weighted down with his many responsibilities, at first refused to see him, but the name Pichegru could open any door. On being admitted, the fifty-year-old man said, "Monsieur le Gouverneur, I have come with an offer to deliver up Pichegru to you."

"To deliver him up or to sell him to me?"

The man remained silent for a moment, head bowed, before he said, "To sell him."

"How much?"

"One hundred thousand francs."

"Damn! That's expensive, my friend!"

"General," said the man, raising his eyes, "when someone commits such infamy, it must at least be well paid."

"Will I have his address this evening, and will I be able to arrest him tomorrow?"

"Once I receive payment, you will be free to do whatever you wish, and even to send my soul to the devil, if that be your good pleasure."

"We shall give you the money," said Murat. "Where is Pichegru?"

"Living with me, at number five Rue Chabanais."

"I would like to write down the description of the room."

"On the fifth floor, a room and a small closet, two windows looking out over the street, a door that opens onto the landing, and a door to the kitchen. I will give you the key to the kitchen door. I have made a copy, and my servant will let your men in there. I warn you that Pichegru always sleeps with a pair of double pistols at his reach and a dagger under his pillow."

Murat read the declaration and showed it to the traitor. "And now you have to sign it."

The man took the pen and signed: "Leblanc."

"I could cause you some trouble for your one hundred thousand francs," said Murat. "You know about the law against hiding criminals. Why did you wait two weeks before turning him in?"

"I did not know you were looking for him. He came to me as an émigré who had returned to Paris in order to have his name removed from the list of exiles. It was only yesterday that I became convinced he was in Paris for some other purpose, and I thought I would be rendering a good service to the government by having him arrested. And besides," said the traitor, lowering his eyes, "as I've told you, I'm not rich."

"You'll be rich now," said Murat, pushing the bills and the gold coins toward him. "May this money bring you happiness, but I doubt if it will."

Leblanc had not been gone an hour when Fouché was announced. Murat, being in Bonaparte's confidence, knew that Fouché was the true prefect of police.

"General," said Fouché, "you have just tossed one hundred thousand francs into the Seine for no reason at all."

"How's that?"

"By giving that amount to a rascal named Leblanc, who told you that Pichegru was staying with him."

"Well, I don't think the price was too high for a secret like that."

"But it was, since I've known for two weeks where he is and would have arrested him at the first order."

"But were you acquainted with the interior of the room so as to avoid any mistake?"

Fouché shrugged. "On the fifth floor, two windows looking out into the street, two doors, one to the kitchen, the other to the landing, two pistols, and a dagger under his pillow. Pichegru can be in the Temple whenever you wish."

"It must be done tomorrow. Tomorrow we are arresting Moreau."

"Fine," said Fouché. "Tomorrow at four in the morning he will be arrested. However, since I have been charged with the whole affair by the First Consul, I would like to carry it out myself."

"Go ahead," said Murat.

The next day, between three and four in the morning, using the information they had been given, Police Commissioner Comminges along with two lieutenants and four gendarmes went to number 5 Rue Chabanais. Comminges had selected strong, brave men, for everyone knew that Pichegru, a fierce soldier of prodigious strength, would not be taken without a struggle.

They woke the doorman as quietly as possible, in a few hushed words told him their purpose, and asked for Leblanc's cook.

Alerted the evening before, she was already dressed. She appeared quickly and led the police up the stairs. With the key her master had made, she opened the door of the kitchen, then let the six policemen and the commissioner into Pichegru's bedroom.

Pichegru was sleeping.

The six policemen threw themselves on the bed. Pichegru sat up, tossed two of them aside, and went for his pistols and dagger, only to discover they had been removed.

The four gendarmes together attacked him. In his nightshirt, almost naked, Pichegru was defending himself against three of them while the fourth was chopping at his legs with a saber. He fell like a dead weight. One gendarme put his boot on Pichegru's face, and almost immediately let out a scream. Pichegru had bitten through the heel, into his flesh, right to the bone. The three others bound him with heavy ropes, which they tightened into a tourniquet.

"You've won!" cried Pichegru. "That's enough!"

They wrapped him in a blanket, threw him into a cab, and with the police commissioner and two lieutenants he was driven to the Barrière des Sergents. By the time they arrived, Pichegru, it seemed, was no longer breathing. They loosened the ropes—in the nick of time, indeed, for he was about to expire.

One of the gendarmes, meanwhile, was taking the papers they had seized in Pichegru's room to the First Consul. Pichegru himself was delivered to Monsieur Réal's office, where he was interrogated by the state counselor. Marco Saint-Hilaire has preserved for us that first interrogation; it clearly indicates Pichegru's still-recalcitrant state.

"What is your name?" asked the state counselor.

"If you do not know my name," Pichegru answered, "you will surely understand that I am not the person who should tell you."

"Do you know George?"

"No."

"Where have you come from?"

"From England."

"Where did you land?"

"Where I managed to."

"How did you get to Paris?"

"In a carriage."

"With whom?"

"With myself."

"Do you know Moreau?"

"Yes, he is the man who denounced me to the Directory."

"Have you seen each other here in Paris?"

"If we had, it would have been with swords in hand."

"Do you know who I am?"

"Of course."

"I've often heard about you and admired your military talents."

"That is flattering for me," said Pichegru.

"We shall bandage your wounds."

"That is not necessary. Just go ahead and shoot me."

"Do you have a given name?"

"I was baptized so long ago that I have forgotten."

"Did not people used to call you Charles?"

"That is the name you gave me in the false correspondence attributed to me. However, that's enough. I will no longer answer your impertinent questions."

And indeed, Pichegru would say no more.

He was given some underwear and clothing that had been found in his room. One of the bailiffs served as his valet. When Pichegru entered the Temple, he was dressed in a brown coat with tails, a black silk tie, and boots with turned-down tops. A tight pair of pants held in place the bandages on his wounded legs and thighs. A white handkerchief wrapped around one of his hands was soaked with blood.

Once he'd finished the interrogation, Monsieur Réal had rushed to the Tuileries. Although by then all of Pichegru's papers had been delivered to Bonaparte, what absorbed the First Consul most was a report Pichegru had written about how to make French Guyana a healthier place. Evidently, while he had been in Sinnamary, Pichegru had taken notes on the climate, out of which, like a true engineer, he had composed his report during his stay in England. The report concluded that in his opinion only twelve to fourteen million francs were required to achieve satisfactory results.

Bonaparte was far more greatly impressed by Pichegru's report than he was by Réal's account of Pichegru's arrest and interrogation. He listened vaguely, and when Réal had finished, he said, "I'd like you to read this too." Bonaparte held out the report.

"What is it?"

"The work of an innocent man who happens to be mixed up with guilty men, as it sometimes happens. While he was away from France, instead of plotting against it, he kept trying to increase his nation's wealth and fame."

"Ah," said Réal, glancing at the report, "this is a report on Guyana and on ways to make our possessions on the continent healthier places."

"Do you know who wrote it?" asked Bonaparte.

"I see no name," said Réal.

"Well, it was Pichegru. Be kind to him, speak to him as one speaks to a man of worth, try to gain his confidence, bring the conversation around to Cayenne and Sinnamary. I am more than tempted to send him there as governor with a credit of ten or twelve million francs to carry out his plans."

Going back into his office, Bonaparte left Réal open-mouthed at the

First Consul's intentions regarding a man who had been sentenced to death.

Even though Pichegru, of the two rivals, was perhaps the man of more worth, Bonaparte hated him less, because he had already lost much of his popularity, whereas Moreau was still immensely admired. If Bonaparte had wanted to make a singularly favorable impression on the people of France, he could have forgiven Moreau and rewarded Pichegru. With such magnanimous actions, he would have cut off the conspiracy's head without fear of any protest.

XXXVI
George

George Cadoudal was still at large.

Whether Fouché had saved him for last, so that the other conspirators would have already incriminated themselves, or whether Cadoudal was simply more skillful, more capable, better informed, and richer with more means at his disposal than his fellows—once Moreau and Pichegru had been arrested, Fouché no longer had any reason to delay. He threw himself into tracking down Cadoudal. In a dozen or more houses, some skillful architect had provided for hiding places that were almost impossible to discover without the plans; they hid Cadoudal well. And no matter how often Fouché was sure he had picked up Cadoudal's trail, for all his formidable policing skills, George would manage somehow to slip through his fingers. He was always armed to the teeth, he slept fully clothed, he had unlimited funds. Pursued, he would always simply slip inside the door of the first house he'd come to and with persuasion, money, or threats secure new refuge. His artful disappearances had become the stuff of legends.

Like that night near the end of February, when he'd been flushed out of a house in which he'd found refuge: With a pack of policemen fast on his heels, George was running down the boulevard in the Faubourg Saint-Denis when he pulled himself up short, at bay like a stag coming upon a pond. Then he noticed the doorway, and the illuminated sign: "Guilbart, dental surgery." He rang the bell. The door opened, then closed behind him. The concierge asked where he was going, and he replied, "Monsieur Guilbart." Halfway up the stairs, he met the dentist's maid coming down, and faced with a man wrapped in a heavy coat who was trying to push by her, she concluded he was a thief.

To reassure her, George pulled a handkerchief from his pocket and held it to his cheek. "Is the dentist available, madame?" he asked, with a moan of pain.

"No, monsieur!" the maid answered.

"Where is he?" George asked.

"He's in bed. After all, it's midnight!"

"He will get up for me if he is a friend of humanity."

"Friends of humanity have to sleep like everyone else."

"Yes, but they get up when someone calls upon their generosity."

"Do you have a toothache?"

"You can see that I have a horrible toothache."

"Do you expect him to pull some teeth?"

"All of them, if necessary."

"Very well, then. However, you must know that he never pulls teeth for less than one louis per tooth."

"I shall give him two, if necessary."

The servant went back up the stairs, let George into the office, lit two candles beside the dentist's chair, and went into the bedroom. Five minutes later she came back to say that the dentist would be right out, and a moment later he appeared.

"Well, doctor," cried George, "I have been waiting impatiently."

"Well, now I'm here," said the doctor. "Sit down in the chair, please. There, that's good. Show me which tooth is hurting you."

"The tooth that's hurting me?"

"Yes."

"Look." George opened his mouth and displayed a straight row of pearls to the dentist.

"Oh!" said the doctor. "I've rarely seen such a lovely set of teeth. But which one is hurting?"

"It's like neuralgia, Doctor. Try to find which one."

"Which side?"

"On the right."

"You must be joking. Nowhere can I see a single damaged tooth."

"Do you think I've come here for fun, Doctor, asking you to pull a tooth? Strange fun!"

"Which tooth would you like me to pull?"

"This one," said George, pointing to his first molar. "How about this one?"

"Are you quite sure?"

"Quite sure. Hurry up."

"But, monsieur, I believe. . . ."

"It seems to me," said George with a frown, "that I have every right to ask you to pull out a tooth if it is bothering me." Moving, as if to rise from his seat, he displayed, perhaps intentionally, the handles of his two pistols and elegant dagger.

Unable to refuse anything to a man so well armed, the surgeon placed his forceps over the tooth, twisted, and pulled it out. George had not uttered a single sound. From the dentist he took a glass of water with a few drops of elixir in it, and very politely said, "Monsieur, it is impossible to have a more dexterous hand and a more powerful wrist than you do. But please allow me to say that I prefer English to French methods." He rinsed out his mouth and spat into the basin.

"And how does it happen that you have such a preference, monsieur?"

"Because the English pull teeth with pliers, and they pull straight up, allowing the tooth to stay in the same line. You French, on the other hand, you twist the tooth, forcing it to make a half turn. That's what causes all the pain."

"It did not appear that the pain was very great."

"That is because I have great control over myself."

"Are you French, monsieur?"

"No, I'm Breton."

George placed a double louis on the fireplace mantel. But he still had not heard the signal that would let him know the coast was clear, so he needed to buy more time. Monsieur Guilbart, however, was of no mind to displease such a well-armed client, who, in any case, appeared to find considerable enjoyment even in the most ordinary circumstances. Finally George heard a whistle.

It was the signal he'd been waiting for. He stood up, shook the doctor's hand affectionately, and hurried back down the stairs.

The doctor was not at all certain what had just happened, though it crossed his mind that he might have been dealing with a thief or a madman. Only the next day a policeman came to see him and presented him with a written description of George Cadoudal. Then the dentist was able to identify his strange client.

He did note one detail that made him pause: "He has an attractive mouth and all thirty-two of his teeth," he read, and to the policeman he reported, "That's a mistake! He no longer has all thirty-two teeth."

"Since when?" asked the policeman.

"Since last night, when I pulled one of them," answered Monsieur Guilbart.

Two days after George's midnight visit to the dentist, which, as I mentioned, became legend in police annals, two very important conspirators were arrested. This is how it happened. The story that you're about to read, however, is not merely a police legend or clerk's anecdote.

On the first steamboat I ever took from Genoa to Marseille, I met the Monsieur le Marquis de Rivière, and I was captivated by his conversation. But just as he was about to tell me how he'd gotten arrested, I got seasick. What is strange, though, is that even in the midst of my unbearable suffering his vibrant voice nonetheless reached me and seemed indeed to penetrate my mind; for he continued with his story until he realized how desperately hard I was trying to hide my suffering and at the same time listen to him. As a result, what he told me remains as clear in my mind today, forty years later, as if his narration and my mal de mer had happened only yesterday.

Monsieur de Rivière and Monsieur Jules de Polignac were bound by one of those friendships that only death can sever. They plotted together; they had come to Paris together; they expected to die together.

Once Moreau and Pichegru had been arrested, they too were being sought by the police. Not knowing where to hide, they decided to ask Comte Alexandre de Laborde for refuge. A young man about their age with family connections to the banking nobility, he had easily positioned himself in the First Consul's government.

On their way to Monsieur de Laborde's home, situated on the Rue d'Artois, just off the Chaussée d'Antin, the two friends paused when they reached the Boulevard des Italiens. Close by, at the Hanover pavilion, the Marquis de Rivière was taken aback to see on one of the pilasters the decree from the prefect of police announcing the death sentence for anyone caught hiding conspirators.

He took the disheartening news to Jules de Polignac, who was waiting on the boulevard. "My friend," he said, "we are about to do something extremely harmful, for if we ask the Comte de Laborde for refuge, we will be incriminating both him and his family. Surely with money, we'll be able to find another refuge just as safe as his. So let us keep looking."

Jules de Polignac, an upright man, accepted his friend's reasoning. They decided to part ways for a time and look separately for an appropriate place to hide.

That same evening the Marquis de Rivière met one of his former valets, a man named Labruyère, with whom the marquis had already refused to hide for fear of putting him in danger. This time, at his good servant's entreaties, he accepted.

He stayed with Labruyère for eighteen days with no problems, and he probably would have continued indefinitely to be safe there if his comrade Jules had not acted so unwisely. Jules was entering his own lodgings when

he learned that Armand, his brother, had just been arrested. Without thinking, he immediately rushed to report his misfortune to his friend Rivière,
who insisted that to be safely hidden, Jules now needed to stay with him.

"Did anyone see you come in here?" asked Rivière.

"Nobody, not even the doorman."

"In that case, you will be safe."

For six days they'd been been hiding together in Rivière's room when
one evening Jules, despite his friend's appeals, left for a rendezvous that, he
claimed, he had no choice but to keep. He did not go unrecognized. A policeman followed him back to the room, then spent the night watching the
house. The next day, Jules was arrested along with the Marquis de Rivière
in Labruyère's lodgings.

The police commissioner was that same Comminges who six days earlier
had arrested Pichegru. He took care to tell poor Labruyère that the law forbade citizens to house strangers, to which Labruyère answered that Monsieur de Rivière was not a stranger but a friend, and to a friend he would
always give refuge, even if the guillotine were waiting outside his door.

All three were taken for interrogation to Réal, the state counselor, and
the Marquis de Rivière spoke at once on behalf of his faithful valet. "Monsieur le Conseiller d'Etat," he began, "I warn you that neither my friend
nor I will answer any of your questions unless you give us your word that
no harm will come to the man who took us in. He did not even know why
we were in Paris."

The counselor gave his word. Monsieur de Rivière wished his former
valet well; shaking his hand, he said, "Adieu, my friend. I have arranged for
you to be spared, and I am happy at least for that."

On Friday, March 9, at six in the evening, at the police prefecture, a public safety agent named Caniolle received an order to go to the foot of the
Montagne Sainte-Geneviève and follow a cabriolet with the number 53 if
by chance it came by. Supposedly, the cabriolet was going to pick up
George, who was believed to be changing lodging and moving to rooms a
friend had rented for him at eight thousand francs a month.

The cabriolet came by empty, but Caniolle followed it anyway. He
guessed that it was on its way to pick up someone suspicious. Noticing that
the street was lined with policemen, Caniolle spoke with them and learned
that they had received instructions similar to his. They followed him.

The cabriolet was moving slowly. At the Place Saint-Etienne-du-Mont,
it turned into the Rue Sainte-Geneviève and stopped near an alley beside a
fruit-seller's shop.

There was no one in the alley, and the top of the cabriolet was down.
The driver went into the shop and began to light the lanterns. As he was

lighting the final one, George, his two friends Le Ridant and Burban, plus a fourth man, walked quickly out. George climbed into the cabriolet, and his three friends were about to follow when Caniolle pushed his way through them.

"What's this?" said Burban, pushing back. "Is there not enough room for you to pass on the other side of the carriage?"

"It seems to me," said the policeman, "that if one is doing no harm it is perfectly permissible to pass by."

George became wary; he suspected that the police had been watching his movements. He pulled Le Ridant into the cabriolet, and, without waiting for the others, he sent the horse off at a gallop.

The policemen had not wanted to arrest George in the streets, as they were sure he'd fight back and blood would be spilled on the pavement; so they had ordered the agent simply to follow the cabriolet. Caught by surprise, Caniolle had let it go off. Anxious now to catch up with it before it got out of sight, he cried, "Follow me!" With two policemen behind him, he set off in pursuit.

The cabriolet continued to put distance between George and the police in the Rue Saint-Hyacinthe, even though it was going uphill. Crossing the Place Saint-Michel, it stayed just as far ahead. It coursed down the Rue des Fossés-Monsieur-le-Prince, then the Rue de la Liberté. George had pulled the top up on the cabriolet, and when he looked back through the opening, he saw three men running after them. He handed Le Ridant the reins: "Use your whip! Someone's following us. Use the whip, faster, faster!" he shouted.

The cabriolet had sped through the streets like a whirlwind and was now coming out on the Carrefour de l'Odéon. But Caniolle had managed to catch up with it, and seizing his single change to grab the horse's bridle, he shouted, with effort, "Stop! Stop in the name of the law!"

In the mad rush of the cabriolet, the noise of its wheels, the hooves, had attracted a crowd. The horse, slowed by the bit, advanced a few more steps with Caniolle hanging from its bridle, and finally stopped.

Buffet, one of the other policemen, leaped up on the running board. He looked under the top of the cabriolet to see who was inside, and immediately two pistol shots rang out. Buffet fell back, shot twice through the forehead. At the same moment Caniolle's arm, the one holding the bridle, dropped to his side, broken.

George and Le Ridant jumped out from the cabriolet, one to the right, one to the left. Le Ridant had not gone ten paces before he was stopped. He made no effort to defend himself, but George, dagger in hand, was fighting two policemen. His dagger raised, he was about to strike one of his opponents when a hat-maker's helper named Thomas leaped on his back and wrapped his arms around George's shoulders. Two other spectators—one named Lamotte, a clerk in the lottery office on Rue du Théâtre-Français, the other a soldier named Vignal—also threw themselves on George and managed to wrench the dagger from his grasp.

Restrained at last, George was loaded into a cab and taken to the police prefecture, where Division Chief Dubois, along with Desmarets, interrogated him. He made a lasting impression on the two policemen. Remarked Desmarets: "I had always assumed that George, whom I was seeing for the first time, was like the old man living on a mountain and sending his assassins off to strike their targets. On the contrary, I found a man with a open expression, a frank gaze, good color, his eyes self-assured yet gentle, just like his voice. Although he was heavyset, his movements and way of carrying himself were sprightly. With a perfectly round head, curly hair worn short, no sideburns, he looked nothing like the leader of a murder conspiracy, the longtime ruler of the Breton countryside."

"Ah, how unfortunate!" Dubois shouted as he entered the interrogation room. "Do you know what you've just done? You have just killed one father and wounded another."

George began to laugh. "It's all your fault," he said.

"What do you mean, it's my fault?"

"You should have sent unmarried men to arrest me."

XXXVII
The Duc d'Enghien [2]

WE HAVE ALREADY SEEN how Fouché was plotting to bring about the death of the Duc d'Enghien, in which event Bonaparte would stand forever on bad terms not just with the House of Bourbon but with every other throne in Europe.

And now, one after the other, Moreau, Pichegru, and George, under interrogation, had each confirmed Fouché's assertions in regard to the duke as each had repeated the vague rumor that a prince in the House of Bourbon was supposedly coming to Paris so as to take leadership of the conspiracy.

We recall that Bonaparte, fearing that Fouché's hate might be leading his judgment astray, had dispatched a gendarme to Strasbourg to verify the facts of the case laid out by the interim unofficial minister of police, who had become the true minister once again. (Though they themselves did not realize it, Régnier the grand judge and Réal the state counselor served only as Fouché's pawns.)

The gendarme had set out on his mission.

When destiny decrees that a fateful or fortunate event shall occur, all things come together to serve its invincible force. It sweeps up all men and directs them toward the accomplishment of one grand purpose. What has characterized such grand events in modern times, without exception, is the limited influence that individual men have been able to exert over them. Even those reputed to be the strongest, the most gifted and skillful among men have proved to be unable to dominate, control, or alter the course of great events. Rather, they prove themselves to be powerful when by their will they ride in the sway of the event, and to be useless when they try to stand in its way. That was truly Bonaparte's fortune: to shine like a star so long as he himself represented the wishes and will of the people, then to be obliterated by a comet in 1811. Senselessly comparing himself to Roman emperors, he strove to link the cause of the Revolution to the cause of old monarchies, and in that he attempted the impossible. Philosophers are able to see with humble surprise the power of destiny at work above and within our societies; it acts in and by its own right. Not in superior genius or caste, then, should one seek the means or right to govern. And while it is possible to turn to one's profit the products of a political movement, one cannot take the credit for being able to do so.

Now, by chance, that gendarme, who in any other circumstance would have only been reflecting what others thought, in this matter had his own opinions. He'd left Paris already convinced that the Duc d'Enghien was the prince George was expecting. Furthermore, he believed himself to be the man chosen to shed light on the conspirators' plot; so from that moment on, he could see things only from his own point of view. He reported, first of all, that nothing was more true than the fact of the conspiratorial life the Duc d'Enghien was leading in Ettenheim and, secondly, that nothing was more true than that his week-long absences, for which hunting was the pretext, were indeed devoted to conspiracy.

Still, his absences, though the prince himself denied them later, can't have been a well-kept secret. Knowledge of them was public enough that his father, the Prince de Condé, wrote to him from England: "People are telling us here, my dear son, that you have been to Paris; others say that you have gone only to Strasbourg. You must agree that such trips have been an unnecessary risk to your life and liberty. As for your principles, I can rest easy on that score, for they are as deeply engraved in your heart as they are in ours." To which the prince responded: "Assuredly, my dear father, only someone who does not know me very well would have said or tried to make others believe that I could have set foot on Republican soil other than with the rank and position in which chance allowed me to be born. I am too proud to bow my head. The First Consul may perhaps be able to destroy me, but I shall never humble myself before him."

More serious than all that, though, was one of destiny's strange, terrible blows. When the gendarme inquired as to who normally associated with the prince, he was told that the prince's most frequent visitors were two British ministers, Sir Francis Drake of Munich and Sir Spencer Smith of Stuttgart, who, in spite of the distance, often traveled to Ettenheim. In addition, among his better acquaintances were an English commissioner, Colonel Schmidt, and General Thumery. Now, when pronounced by a German-speaker, the name Thumery sounds more like *Thumeriez*, and from there it's a small phonetic step to get to *Dumouriez*, which was what the gendarme evidently heard, for in his dispatch, he wrote "General Dumouriez" instead of "General Thumery." The Duc d'Enghien's presence along the Rhine thus assumed more serious proportions, in that it appeared France was bound by conspiracy: the followers of Moreau in Paris, at its center; of George and Pichegru in the West; and Dumouriez in the East. In a civil war, France would be gravely threatened by hostile forces.

And there was one more unfortunate circumstance. At that time, and I don't know if things are the same today, never did officers of the Gendarmerie report on any mission, whoever might have ordered it, without also sending a copy of their findings to their inspector general. So the gendarme's two reports came to Paris by the same mail. One was addressed to General Moncey, the other to Monsieur Réal. Both men worked with Bonaparte every day, and that day General Moncey appeared as usual. Immediately he took the dispatch from his pocket and showed it to Bonaparte. The report's effect on the First Consul was powerful. He could see an armed Bourbon standing at the gates of Strasbourg, ready to return to France, waiting only for the news that Bonaparte had been assassinated. He could envision a complete staff of celebrated émigrés attendant to the only prince who had been courageous enough to take the sword and defend the interests of the throne. He could imagine in alliance with this Royalist hope British ministers, British commissioners, and finally, more English than the English themselves, Dumouriez himself. He sent Moncey away, but he kept the report and ordered that he be left alone.

Moncey had been instructed to send orderlies to inform Fouché, the two other consuls, and Réal that they should be at the Tuileries at seven o'clock. But Bonaparte had already promised Chateaubriand an audience at seven, so he had his secretary Monsieur Méneval write to the author of the *Génie du christianisme* and ask him to delay their meeting until nine.

The fortunes of these two great men had been equally remarkable. Strangely, or simply coincidentally, they had both been born in 1769, and both were now thirty-two years old. They had been born three hundred leagues apart, yet their paths seemed bound to cross. They would meet, connect, separate, meet again and reconnect. They grew up without knowing each other, one sad in his studies behind tall school walls, where he was subject to those strict rules that make generals and statesmen; the other wandering along rocky beaches, the companion of winds and tides, with no book other than nature's own and no teacher other than God. Nature and God can make dreamers and poets of men. The one man always had a goal, and he reached his goal even though it was lofty, whereas the other had only desires, desires he never satisfied. One wanted to take the measure of space; the other wanted to conquer the infinite.

In 1791, the year that Bonaparte rejoined his family to wait out events for a semester, Chateaubriand sailed out of Saint-Malo for America, to look for the Northwest Passage to India. Let us follow the poet.

Chateaubriand leaves Saint-Malo on May 6 at six in the morning. He sails first to the Azores, where later he will send Chactas. The wind then carries him to the banks of Newfoundland; he goes through the straits and stops for two weeks in Saint-Pierre, where, lost in the fog that always covers the island, he wanders beneath the clouds and through the gusty wind, listens to the moaning of the invisible sea, and ventures out over the dead wooly heath, his only guide the sounds of a reddish torrent cascading over the rocks.

Traveling south from Saint-Pierre, eventually he reaches the latitudes of the coast of Maryland, and there he is becalmed. But what matters that to a poet? The nights are admirable, dawns splendid, dusks magnificent. Seated on deck, he watches the sun's fiery ball prepare to plunge into the waters behind the ship's rigging, out in the middle of the limitless ocean.

Finally, one day treetops appear above the waves. They might at first be mistaken for an expanse of darker green ocean water, except that they are motionless. Chateaubriand had reached America!

What a vast subject for this twenty-two-year-old poet to reflect upon! A world with an untrammeled destiny, an unmapped future, a world foreseen by Seneca, discovered by Columbus, named by Vespucci, its history waiting yet to be written by some latter-day Thucydides.

What a fortunate time to visit America! America, who from across the ocean had sent back to France the spirit of the revolution it had completed and the freedom it had won with the help of French swords.

It was strange now to witness a flourishing city being built at the very spot where William Penn had purchased a parcel of land from some wandering Indians one hundred years before. What a stirring sight to see a new nation being born of a bloody battlefield, as if some present-day Cadmus had sown men in the bullet-plowed land.

Chateaubriand stopped in Philadelphia not only to see the city but also to meet with Washington. Washington showed him a key to the Bastille that the victors in Paris had sent to him. Chateaubriand had nothing to show Washington, though had he seen the famous American on his way home, he could have shown him the *Génie du christianisme.*

All his life the poet would remember his visit with Washington the legislator, albeit by the evening after the visit Washington had probably already totally forgotten Chateaubriand. The president of the American people, who had served them as the general of their army and a founding father of their nation, Washington then was at the peak of his glory, whereas Chateaubriand still lingered in the obscurity of his youth, with barely a few rays of his brilliant future evident. Washington died without ever seeing any extraordinary accomplishment in the man who would say later of him and Napoleon: "Those who, like me, have seen both the conqueror of Europe and the American legislator will turn their eyes away from today's political scene: only buffoons, making us laugh or cry, who are not worth looking at."

Washington represented all that was worthy of interest in men among all the men Chateaubriand would see in American cities. But then, the young traveler hadn't crossed the Atlantic to the New World in order to observe men; for they are the same everywhere, after all. Rather, he was seeking, deep in America's virgin forests and out on its prairies as infinite as deserts, the voice that speaks in solitude.

Let us listen as the traveler himself speaks about his feelings. In those days, we must remember, the land, so admirably described and poeticized by James Fenimore Cooper, was still unknown. Gabriel Ferry, following in Cooper's path into the wilderness, had not yet written *Les Chercheurs d'or* or *Costal l'Indien.* Gustave Aimard had not yet drawn a world of legends out of the deep forests and given them literary life. No, every creature, every leaf, in the forest and out on the prairies existed still in a virgin state, as did the forest and prairies themselves. The man who'd first lift their veil would find them in that moment as pure and as chaste as they'd been on creation day.

When, after crossing the Mohawk, I found myself in a woods where no trees had ever been cut, much less visited, I fell into a state of inebriation. I went from tree to tree, wandering here and there, saying to myself: "Here, there are no paths, no cities, no narrow houses, no presidents, no republics, no kings. . . ." And in order to determine if I were truly able to enjoy my original rights, I gave free rein to all sorts of capricious acts, angering the big Dutchman who was my guide. Deep down he was sure I was crazy.

Once the traveler said his last good-bye to civilization, he had only the Indian longhouse for shelter, the ground for a mattress, a saddle for a pillow, his coat for a blanket, and the sky for a canopy over his bed. His horse, like his guide's, roamed freely, with a bell around its neck. Using their admirable instinct for survival, the horses never wandered far from the fires their masters lit to keep insects away and serpents at bay.

Chateaubriand had set out on a trip like Sterne's, except, instead of studying civilization, he was traveling a solitary path, journeying through solitude even as he quested for solitude. From time to time he'd come upon an Indian village, or unexpectedly encounter a wandering tribe. Then the man from civilization would give to the man of the wilderness a sign of universal brotherhood understood around the globe, and the native hosts would sing the song of the foreigner: "Here is the stranger, sent by the Great Spirit."

A child would then lead him by the hand to the longhouse and say, "Here is the stranger." The sachem would answer, "Child, take the man into my house."

Led by the child, the traveler would enter, and, like a guest among the ancient Greeks, he would sit down on the ashes beside the fire. The native men would offer him the peace pipe. He would smoke three times, and the women would sing the song of consolation: "The stranger has found a mother and a wife. The sun will continue to rise and set for him, as before." They would fill a maple wood cup with water. From this holy cup the traveler would drink half the water, then pass it to his host to drink the rest.

Instead of that scene from native life in the wilderness, does the reader prefer night, silence, meditation, and melancholy? The traveler paints the following scene. Just look:

Caught up in my thoughts, I got up and went some distance over to where a root was hanging out over a brook, and I sat down. It was one of those American nights that the human brush can never truly paint and which I remember with delight.

The moon was high in the sky. Here and there, in the uncluttered heavens, thousands of stars were twinkling. At times the moon seemed to rest on a cluster of clouds that looked like high mountain peaks capped with snow. And then the clouds would flatten, spreading out in diaphanous waves of white satin, or turn to light flakes of foam or to countless sheep wandering across the firmament's azure plains. At another moment, the celestial vault seemed to become a pebbly seashore with horizontal layers, parallel folds traced, as it were, by the regular ebb and flow of the sea. And then a gust of wind would rend the veil, and everywhere in the heavens huge banks of brilliantly white cotton would gather, looking so inviting that one could almost feel how soft and pliant they were. On the ground the scene was no less ravishing. The velvety, cerulean moonlight floated silently over the forest, reaching down between the trees, throwing sprays of light even into the deepest shadows. The tiny brook babbling at my feet disappeared beneath thickets of oaks, willows, and sugar maples, then reappeared farther downstream in clearings, bespangled now with the night's constellations. It resembled a shimmering blue ribbon, sewn with bits of diamonds and cut transversely by dark bands. On the other side of the brook, in a broad wild meadow, the moonlight slept motionlessly on the grass that lay spread out like a canvas. Depending on the wind, stands of birch trees, scattered here and there in the meadow, were sometimes at one with the ground, wrapped in pale gauze, and sometimes stood out darkly against the chalky background, like floating shadow islands on a motionless sea of light. Everything nearby was silent and peaceful, except for a few leaves falling, a sudden gust of wind, an occasional call of an owl. But off in the distance, one could hear the solemn roaring of Niagara Falls in the night's calm, extending out through the wilderness and dying away in far-off forests.

The grandeur, the melancholic surprise of that tableau, can never be expressed in human language. The loveliest European nights cannot give so grand a panorama. In our cultivated fields the imagination seeks in vain to expand. Everywhere it looks it can see human dwellings. But in this wilderness, the soul enjoys losing itself deep in an ocean of eternal forests. It loves wandering by starlight along immense lakes, looking out over awesome gorges carved by roaring waterfalls, plunging with masses of water, and thus becoming one with nature so wild and sublime.

In the night's silence the falls at Niagara thundered loudly as if to guide and draw the traveler to them. And each morning their roar was hidden in the thousand sounds of awakening nature. Finally one day he did reach them, and the splendid falls Chateaubriand had journeyed so far to find very nearly caused his death. On two occasions. We shall not attempt to tell the story ourselves. Here is what Chateaubriand says:

When I got there, I went to the falls, my horse's bridle wrapped around my arm. As I was leaning over to look, a rattlesnake moved in the bushes nearby. The horse was startled and it jerked backward, rearing up. As we neared the abyss, I could not pull the reins from my arm, and the horse, still frightened, was dragging me along. Its forelegs were already over the edge and its hind legs were all that was keeping it from falling. It appeared that I was done for, but then the horse made a supreme effort, whirled around, and ended up ten feet from the edge.

And that's not all. Saved from that accident, the traveler put himself in danger deliberately: Some men believe that they can tempt God with impunity. But let us allow the traveler himself to continue:

The ladder which had been there now was broken. In spite of my guide's warning, I decided to climb down to the bottom of the falls over a two-hundred-foot-high cliff. I started down. Although the falls were roaring down into the abyss below me, I kept my wits about me and managed to reach a point about forty feet from the bottom. But from then on, the vertical rock wall was too smooth to allow any foothold, for there were no roots or cracks. I was left hanging by my hands, unable to move down or climb back up. I could feel my fingers weakening from my body's weight, and I thought death was inevitable. There are not many men who have spent two minutes of their life as I did at Niagara Falls, hanging out over the abyss. My grip loosened and I dropped. By unexpected good fortune, I landed on the rocks alive. I could have been smashed to bits, but I was not seriously hurt. I landed a half inch from the edge, but I had not fallen in. When the cold spray began to penetrate, however, I realized that I had not gotten off as lightly as I had thought. I felt unbearable pain in my left arm; it was broken below the elbow. My guide was looking down and I showed him my problem. He went to get some savages who, with a great deal of difficulty, managed to pull me back up with birch ropes and take me to their village.

About the same time Chateaubriand was braving the wild in Niagara, a young lieutenant named Napoleon Bonaparte almost drowned while swimming in the Saône.

The traveler continues along the Great Lakes. From the shore of Lake Erie he could see Indians venturing out onto those perilous waters where such frightful storms frequently arise, and the journey is soon to prove to be frightening for him. First of all, the Indians hang their weapons from the stern of their birch-bark canoes as in ancient days the Phoenicians would

hang their gods, then they paddle off through snow flurries into waves that
rise higher than the canoes and seem constantly to be about to swallow
them up. The hunters' dogs, with their front paws up on the sides, howl
sadly, while their masters, stone silent, their only movements those necessary to forward the canoe, keep time with their paddles. The canoes move
in single file. In the prow of the first canoe stands a chief who, for encouragement and as an invocation, constantly repeats one word: *"Oha."*

> In the last canoe, in the stern, at the end of the line of men and boats,
> stands another chief, holding a long oar as a tiller. Through the fog,
> snow, and waves, one can see only the feathers that decorate the Indians'
> heads, the long necks of the howling dogs, and the torsos of the two
> sachems.
> Pilot and daemon.
> One might say they were the gods of those unknown far-off waters.

And now let us move from the perils of the lake to those of the shore:

> An area about twenty miles long is covered with water lilies. In the
> summertime, the leaves are crowded with entwined snakes. When the
> reptiles move in the sunlight, you can see their rings, golden, purple,
> and black. And then in those horrible double and triple knots, all you
> can see are shining eyes, triply-forked tongues, fiery mouths, tails armed
> with stingers and rattles that whip around in the air. There is a con-
> stant hissing, a sound similar to rustling dry leaves, arising from this foul
> Cocytos.

So the traveler wandered for a year: climbing down waterfalls; crossing
lakes; riding through forests; stopping in the midst of ruins in Ohio, there
to cast a questioning eye on the past's dark abyss; following the meander-
ing course of rivers, wedding his own voice morning and evening with the
universal voice of nature in proclaiming creation and God; crafting his
poem *Les Natchez;* forgetting Europe; subsisting on freedom, solitude, and
poetry.
    Wandering from forest to forest, lake to lake, prairie to prairie, he had
sometimes happened upon a frontier settlement, as he did one evening
when he noticed a log cabin on a farm near a stream. He stopped, and there
benefited by the settlers' hospitality. Night fell, and the only light in the
cabin came from the fireplace. Seated near the hearth, while his hostess was
preparing supper, he passed the time by reading an English newspaper by

the light of the fire. Scarcely had he picked the paper up than he was struck by four words: *"Flight of the king."*

It was the story of Louis XVI's flight and arrest in Varenne. The same newspaper reported that nobles were emigrating and gathering under the princes' flag. Their voice reached even the depths of the American wilderness with the call "To arms!" It seemed to him to be a fateful cry.

He returned to Philadelphia and from there crossed the sea. Propelled by a storm, the ship carried him to the French coast in eighteen days. In July 1792 he arrived in Le Havre, shouting, "The king is calling; here I am!"

As Chateaubriand was climbing on board the ship that would now take him to the king's aid, a young artillery captain, wearing a red cap and leaning against a tree on the terrace near the river, was watching Louis XVI at one of the windows in the Tuileries. The young officer murmured, "That man is lost."

"Thus," says the poet, "what seemed at the time to be my duty overturned my original plans and brought about the first of those events that marked my career.

"The Bourbons probably did not really need for a young Breton just back from deepest America to demonstrate his obscure devotion. If, continuing my travels, I had lit my hostess's lantern with the newspaper that changed my life, no one would ever have noticed my absence, for no one even knew I existed. It was a simple debate between my conscience and me that brought me back onto the world's stage. I could have done what I liked, since I was the only witness to that debate, but that witness was the one I most feared shaming."

Chateaubriand brought back with him *Atala* and *Les Natchez*.

XXXVIII

Chateaubriand

꿈ㆍ꿈

FRANCE HAS CHANGED a great deal in the traveler's absence. New men have come to the political fore: Barnave, Danton, Robespierre. Murat is still around, but he is more wild beast than man. And Mirabeau is already dead.

Our gentleman gets reacquainted with France. He meets, one after the other, important men in all the different political parties—important but doomed ultimately to the scaffold, many of them.

He visits the Jacobins; he mingles with the club's liberal aristocrats, its litterateurs, its artists. The club has attracted a host of outstanding people, including even some great lords, like La Fayette, the two Lameths, Laharpe, Chamfort, Andrieux, Sedaine. Chénier is there, his poetry representing a standard for the time to which it so completely belongs; still, in the final analysis, one cannot ask of a time more than it can give. There too are David, who revolutionized French painting, and Talma, who did the same for French theater; neither often misses a meeting. At the door invitations are checked by Laïs, the singer, and the son of the Duc d'Orléans. In the office is the author of the *Liaisons dangereuses*, the Chevalier de Laclos, his manners always elegant, his mien only somber.

A man is at the speaker's stand. His voice is weak and shrill, his face thin and sad. His hair is powdered. He is wearing a somewhat worn, faded olive-green suit with a white vest and a spotlessly clean shirt. It is Robespierre, the oracle of Jacobin society and republican France: a man who moves with the times and who, one day, will imprudently atempt to move ahead of the times only to slip and fall on Danton's blood.

Chateaubriand visits the Cordeliers. If the Jacobins are the aristocrats of the revolutionary movement, the Cordeliers are the people: hard to manage, active, violent; like their favorite writers, like Marat, who has his printing press in the chapel basement, like Desmoulins, Fréron, Fabre d'Eglantine, Anacharsis Cloots, and like the orators Danton and Legendre, those two butchers, one of whom changed Paris prisons into slaughterhouses. Like bees, around their hive, they all live close by: Marat, just opposite the Cordeliers; Desmoulins and Fréron, on Rue de la Vieille-Comédie; Danton, fifty yards away, in the Passage du Commerce; Cloots, on Rue Jacob; Legendre, on Rue des Boucheries-Saint-Germain.

Chateaubriand listens to all these noisy men: Desmoulins rasping, Marat stammering, Danton thundering, Legendre swearing, Cloots blaspheming. And they all frighten him.

He decides therefore to go abroad, where he plans to join those gentlemen gathering under the princes' banner. Alas, his plan encounters an impediment: in a word, money.

Unfortunately, Madame de Chateaubriand (the former Céleste Buisson de la Vigne) had brought with her as a dowry only assignats, and assignats were beginning to be worth less than ordinary white paper on which one at least can write a promissory note or a bill of exchange. Eventually, though, Chateaubriand found a notary who was able to loan him twelve thousand francs. He put the treasure in his wallet and the wallet in his pocket. On those twelve thousand francs depended his life, and his brother's.

But man proposes and Satan disposes. As it happened, the would-be future émigré met a friend, to whom he admitted that he had twelve thousand francs. The friend was a gambler, and gambling is contagious. And Monsieur de Chateaubriand soon found himself in a gambling house near the Palais-Royal, where he lost ten thousand five hundred of his twelve thousand francs.

What might have made him lose all sense and all his francs, however, actually helped him to regain them. For he was not a true gambler. Ready though his last one thousand five hundred francs might have been to follow the others, he put them in his pocket, rushed out of the accursed house, climbed into a cab, returned to the Impasse Férou, got back into his house, and discovered he had no wallet.

Concluding he had left the wallet in the cab, he ran back into the street; but the cab had gone. He set off after it, to no avail, although some children had seen the cab go by with a client. Fortunately, a commissioner knew the driver and where he lived, and he gave Chateaubriand the address.

Monsieur de Chateaubriand was waiting at his door at two in the morning when the coachman returned home. They checked the cab. Apparently the wallet had disappeared.

Having dropped off Monsieur de Chateaubriand near the Impasse Férou, the coachman had picked up three sansculottes and a priest; and he recalled the priest's address. By now, though, it was three in the morning, and you cannot wake up an honest man at such an hour. So the exhausted Monsieur de Chateaubriand returned home and went to sleep.

Not many hours later he was awakened by a visit from the priest, who restored to him his wallet and his fifteen hundred francs.

The very next day Monsieur de Chateaubriand left Brussels with his elder brother and a servant. Dressed like the brothers, the servant passed for a friend, if a friend with three faults: the first, being too respectful; the second, being too familiar; the third, being prone to dreaming and talking in his sleep. He commonly dreamt that officers were coming to arrest him, and the first night, when he tried to jump out of the stagecoach, evidently to escape, the two brothers managed to hold on to him. The second night they simply opened the stagecoach door, and still dreaming, he leaped out and fled into the countryside without his hat. The two travelers thought they were thus well rid of him, but one year later his deposition would cost Monsieur de Chateaubriand's elder brother his life.

Brussels was the Royalist meeting place, as Paris was only a five-day march away. (Pessimists said eight.) So there was some surprise that the brothers had come to Brussels instead of waiting in Paris, since the Royalists were planning soon to begin their would march on the capital. Furthermore, not even the Navarre regiment, in which Chateaubriand had once been a lieutenant, welcomed him.

Not as proud as their counterparts in the Navarre regiment, one of the Breton companies, similar to expeditionary forces, which were being dispatched to besiege Thionville, took the compatriot into their ranks. As we can see, Monsieur de Chateaubriand was not destined for a great army career. Formerly a cavalry captain who rode in royal carriages, he'd been demoted to second lieutenant, and now he was marching to Thionville as a simple infantryman.

On the march out of Brussels, Monsieur de Chateaubriand met Monsieur de Montrond, with whom he might have had another path in common. "Where are you from, monsieur?" the citizen asked the soldier.

"From Niagara, monsieur."

"Where are you going?"

"Wherever there is fighting."

Ten leagues farther along, Monsieur de Chateaubriand met a man on horseback. "Where are you going?" asked the horseman.

"I'm going to fight," said the man on foot.

"What do they call you?"

"Monsieur de Chateaubriand; and you?"

"Monsieur Frédéric-Guillaume." The man on horseback, it turned out, was the King of Prussia.

The year before his march to Thionville, Monsieur de Chateaubriand had started out on his quest for the Northwest Passage; he did not find it. Nor did he take Thionville. During the first expedition he had broken his arm; however, on the second, he injured his leg. It was struck by a burning beam, at about the same time that a young battalion leader named Napoleon Bonaparte received a bayonet wound in the thigh during the siege of Toulon.

A bullet also did its best to kill the Royalist volunteer, but stuffed between his clothing and his chest was the manuscript of *Atala*, which absorbed the shock. Unfortunately, he did not also escape smallpox, and along with his wound and the disease came a third calamity, one that for a Frenchman was even worse: a rout.

By the time the young émigré had gotten himself to Namur, he was near dying. Walking through the streets of Namur, trembling with fever, he found some pity from a poor woman who threw a blanket over his shoulders. It was filled with holes, but it was the only blanket she owned. Saint Martin gave only half of his cloak to a poor man, and he was later canonized.

Just outside Namur, Monsieur de Chateaubriand collapsed in a ditch. He was surely dying when the Prince de Line's company passed by, although he managed to stretch out an arm. Eying with pity the frail, trembling body, they put him in a wagon and took him to the gates of Brussels.

Belgians know how to benefit from the past, but they have not yet acquired the diviner's gift of reading the future; they did not guess that counterfeit editions of this young man's work would one day make Belgian publishers wealthy. What they did do was close their doors to the poor wounded man.

Exhausted, he lay down on the ground in front of an inn and waited. The Prince de Line's company had happened by to aid him in Namur; perhaps Providence would send someone to help him here. It's good to hope, even when you are dying.

Providence did not fail him. It sent his brother. Recognizing each other immediately, the two young men fell into each others' arms. While the younger brother's fortune had been ill, the elder Chateaubriand was rich. He had twelve hundred francs with him and gave his brother six. He wanted to take his younger brother with him back to Paris, but fortunately our poet was too sick to travel. He found shelter with a barber and came gradually back to life, while his brother returned to France, where the scaffold was waiting.

Healthy again after a long convalescence, Monsieur de Chateaubriand left for Jersey. Tired of being an émigré, he intended to go from there to Brittany and join the Vendeans. About twenty passengers had shared the cost of hiring a small boat. When a storm blew up, to escape the heavy sea, they had to go below deck, where it was stifling. The convalescent proved not to be very strong. Without fresh air and crushed by the mass of bodies, he had lost consciousness and, when they finally made port in Guernsey, he was about to expire.

They carried him off the boat and propped him against a wall. He turned his face toward the sun so as to ease his death. But again Providence appeared, this time in the shape of a bargeman's wife who happened to be walking by. She called to her husband, and with the help of three or four sailors, they lay the ailing man in a good bed. The next day they put him on a boat coming from Oostende. He was delirious when he arrived in Jersey.

It was not until the spring of 1793 that Monsieur de Chateaubriand had regained enough strength to travel. He left for England, where he hoped to join forces under a white Royalist flag. Once there, though, his health failed to continue to improve. Indeed, his lungs became congested, and the doctors he consulted ordered complete rest. They said that even with the best care and benefit of precautions, the poor man had no more than two or three years to live. Of course, the same death sentence had been delivered to Voltaire, the author of *La Pucelle*. Owing us at least a little compensation, God once again proved the doctors wrong.

To our benefit, the doctors' decree did force Monsieur de Chateaubriand to give up the gun. Instead, he again took up the pen. He wrote his *Essais;* he prepared an outline for the *Génie du christianisme*. Since those two distinguished works, so different in spirit, and no matter how great, were not going to keep him from starving to death, in his spare moments he practiced the art of translation, for which he was paid by the page. Such was his battle during the years 1794 and 1795.

Another man was also fighting against hunger then, and that was the young battalion leader who had taken Toulon. The director of the War Committee, Aubry, had nonetheless removed him from his artillery command, and he had come to Paris, where he had been offered command over a brigade in the Vendée. He had refused, and finding himself without a job, while Chateaubriand was translating, he was making notes about how to strengthen Turkey against invasions by the European monarchies.

By the beginning of September, at wit's end, the battalion leader had decided to throw himself into the Seine. He might have done it, too, had he not run into one of his friends: "Where are you going?" his friend asked.

"I'm going to drown myself."

"Why?"

"Because I'm penniless."

"I've got twenty thousand francs to share." And share he did. He gave ten thousand francs to the young officer, who decided not to drown himself.

On October 4, he went to the Feydeau theater. There he learned that the Lepelletier section of the National Guard had backed down Convention troops being led by General Menou and that the Convention was now looking for a general to turn things around.

The next morning at five o'clock, General Alexandre Dumas was receiving orders from the Convention to take command of the armed forces. But General Alexandre Dumas was not in Paris, so Barras was named general in his place, and he asked for and received the authorization to have Bonaparte, former battalion leader, named as his assistant.

October 5 is the 13th Vendémiaire. On that day Napoleon would rise from obscurity, thanks to his victory; Chateaubriand would arise from his own obscurity too, thanks to a literary masterpiece.

The events of the 13th Vendémiaire surely brought the general to the writer's attention, and when it appeared, the *Génie du christianisme* brought the poet to the general's attention.

At first, Bonaparte had reservations about Chateaubriand. When Bourrienne one day expressed surprise that the celebrated Chateaubriand's name had not yet appeared on the lists of personages worthy of appointment to important positions, Bonaparte replied, "You are not the first person who has mentioned that, Bourrienne. But I have already given a definitive answer. That man's ideas about liberty and independence could never be reconciled with mine. I prefer having him as a respected enemy rather than as an imposed friend. At best, I shall see about it later on. I might try him out at first in some secondary position, and if he does well, then help him move up." It was clear from his comments that Bonaparte greatly underestimated Chateaubriand's true importance.

Soon, however, the publication of *Atala* brought its author instant glory, and from that moment on the First Consul kept his eyes nervously on Chateaubriand, not least because he was jealous of anyone who drew the public's attention away from him. After *Atala* came the *Génie du christianisme,* which won Chateaubriand tremendous acclaim as it brought people's minds back to serious contemplation on the subject of religion.

One day Madame Baciocchi came to see her brother with a small book in her hand. "Read this, Napoleon," she said. "I'm sure you'll be pleased."

Bonaparte looked at the small volume absentmindedly. "Another novel ending in 'a,'" he said. "Do you really think I have the time for such silliness?" Still, he took the book from his sister's hands and laid it on his desk.

Madame Baciocchi then asked him to remove Monsieur de Chateaubriand's name from the list of émigrés. "Ah!" he said. "So it's Monsieur de Chateaubriand who wrote your Atala?"

"Yes, Brother."

"Fine. I shall read it when I find the time." Then, turning toward his secretary, he said, "Bourrienne, write to Fouché and tell him to remove Monsieur de Chateaubriand's name from the list of émigrés."

Since Bonaparte was not very well read and paid little attention to literature, as I've already said, it is not surprising that he did not know that Chateaubriand had written *Atala*. But he did read it, and with some pleasure. A short time afterward, Monsieur de Chateaubriand published the *Génie du christianisme,* and Bonaparte completely changed his initial opinions about the writer.

The first time Bonaparte and Monsieur de Chateaubriand met, but only in passing, was the evening Bonaparte signed the contract of the marriage between Mademoiselle de Sourdis and Hector de Sainte-Hermine. Bonaparte had intended to speak to the poet later that evening, but the evening had ended so abruptly and in such a strange manner that Bonaparte had gone back to the Tuileries without having given another thought to Chateaubriand.

The second time they met was at that magnificent party Monsieur de Talleyrand gave to honor the King of Parma just before he took possession of the Etrurian throne. Let us allow Chateaubriand himself to describe his impressions of that first scintillating encounter:

> I was in the grand gallery when Napoleon came in. He made a good first impression. I had only seen him once before and had never spoken to him. He had a warm, endearing smile, and his eyes were striking, framed as they were beneath his forehead by dark eyebrows. There was no trickery in those eyes, nothing theatrical or affected. The *Génie du Christianisme*, so much in the news at that time, had had an effect on Napoleon. Prodigious imagination lent fire to his cold political side. He would never have become what he was if the Muse had not been there. Reason carries out the poet's ideas. All men of great stature are composed of two natures, for they must be capable both of inspiration and of action. One develops the plan; the other carries it out.
>
> Bonaparte saw me and recognized who I was, I am not sure how. When he walked over to me, no one knew what he was looking for. People stepped aside one after the other. They each were hoping that the First Consul would stop and talk to them. He seemed a little impatient with them all. I stepped behind those guests closest to me. Suddenly Bonaparte called out:
>
> "Monsieur de Chateaubriand!"
>
> I was there by myself, as the others pulled back. But soon a circle formed around us. Bonaparte greeted me very simply. There were no compliments, no tedious questions, no preamble. He began speaking of Egypt and the Arabs, as if I had been a close friend and as if he were continuing a conversation we had started some time before.
>
> "I was always struck," he said, "when I saw the sheiks fall on their knees in the middle of the desert, turn toward the East, and touch the sand with their foreheads. What was that unknown thing they were worshiping in the East?"
>
> Bonaparte paused, and with no transition, moved to a different idea.
>
> "Christianity! Have not the ideologues tried to turn it into a system of astronomy? And even if it were, do they think they can convince me that Christianity is small? Even if Christianity is an allegory for the movement of the spheres, the geometry of the stars, whatever rational minds might claim, they have nonetheless plenty of grandeur left beyond what is loathsome."
>
> And forthwith Bonaparte walked away. As had been the case for Job, in my night, "a spirit passed before me; the hairs of my skin stood up; he

remained in front of me: I could not recognize his face and I heard his voice like a small breath."

My days have been a succession of visions. Hell and heaven have continually opened beneath my feet or above my head without me being able to probe their shadows or lights. On the shores of two different worlds I have met the man of the last century and the man of the new one, Washington and Napoleon. I was able to speak for a moment with one and the other. Both sent me back to my solitude, the first by a benevolent wish and the second by a crime.

I noticed that as Bonaparte circulated through the crowd he would look at me more deeply than he did when he was speaking to me. I kept my eyes on him, and like Dante, I was thinking:

"Chi è quel grande, che non per che curi
L'incendio?"

"Who is this great man who doesn't fear the flames?"

So they met, these two extraordinary men of equal and peerless stature: Chateaubriand as poet; Bonaparte as statesman. They stood unmatched in France at that time.

By that time, the French people had witnessed so much destruction that they were eager to take a moment's respite. But of all the destruction, what had been most ruined and abused, most abased and abraded, was religion. Revolutionaries had melted down church bells, overturned altars, smashed the statues of saints. They had slit priests' throats, they had invented false gods; like whirlwinds of heresy, they had swept through Paris to wither all life and eradicate all public discourse. They had turned Saint-Sulpice into the Temple of Victory, Notre-Dame into the Temple of Reason. The only true altar left was the scaffold, and there was no true temple except the Grève. Even the most rational men shook their heads in denial. Only a few noble souls maintained hope.

The *Génie du christianisme*, then, arrived like the first whiff of fresh air after the contagion, like a breath of life over the miasma of death. At the time when an entire nation had been screaming before bloody prison doors and dancing around the scaffold on the Place de la Révolution and shouting, "There is no more religion. God is no more!" was it not consoling to know that a man, far away on a peaceful night in the middle of virgin forests in America, had been lying on moss, his back against a century-old tree, his arms crossed, his eyes fixed on the moon whose shimmering rays seemed to be drawing his soul into heaven, while he'd been murmuring these words:

There is indeed a God! The grass in the valley and the cedars of Lebanon bless his name. The insect sings his praises, the elephant greets him at daybreak, the birds sing to him from their foliage, the wind murmurs to him in the forest, lightning proclaims his presence, and the Ocean roars his grandeur!

Only man says: "God is no more!"

Has man never, in his misfortune, lifted his eyes to heaven? Has he never looked up at those starry realms where worlds have been sown like sand? As for me, I have looked, and that suffices. I have seen the sun suspended over Western gates, draped in purple and gold. I have seen the sun, on the opposite horizon, rising like a silver lantern in the azure East.

At the zenith, those two celestial balls blended their ceruse and crimson tints, the sea turned the Orient into girandoles of diamonds and washed the Occident in pink. There on the bank, peaceful waves expired weakly one by one at my feet. The night's first silences and the day's final murmurs echoed softly on the hillsides, along the riverbanks, and in the valleys.

O God, whom I have never met, O God, whose name and dwelling place I do not know, invisible architect of this universe, you have given me an instinct so that I might sense everything. Absent a reason to understand everything, might you be only an imaginary being? Only a gilded vision of misfortune? Will my soul be separated from the rest of my mortal dust? Is the tomb an abyss with no exit or a portal opening up to another world? With cruel pity, has nature not placed hope of a better life in the heart of man, something better than human misery?

Forgive my weakness, Father of mercy. No, I do not doubt your existence, and whether you have destined an immortal career for me or whether I must simply move on and die, I adore your decrees in silence, and your insect confesses your truth!

We can understand the effect of such prose after Diderot's imprecations, after La Revellière's theophilanthropic speeches, after Murat's slobbering, bloody pages.

So Bonaparte, unable to turn his eyes away from the Revolution's abyss into which he was sliding, managed to halt this saving angel as he passed, this poet who had limned the first traces of light in that night of nothingness. And since he was about to send Cardinal Fesch to the embassy in Rome, the First Consul decided to make the great poet the ambassador's assistant. The eagle would summon the dove, and like the dove, he would be responsible for carrying an olive branch to the Holy Father.

Of course it was not enough to name Chateaubriand as secretary to the ambassador. The poet still had to accept the appointment.

XXXIX
The Embassy in Rome

BONAPARTE HAD ENJOYED his conversation with Monsieur de Chateaubriand. Monsieur de Chateaubriand, on the other hand, points out in his *Mémoires* that Bonaparte's questions flew so thick and fast that he never had time to answer. But those were the kinds of conversation that Bonaparte liked, the ones he could control. Little did it matter to Bonaparte whether Chateaubriand was involved or not. He had judged at one glance where and how the poet could be useful; he believed that some minds already know what others need to learn.

Assured in his inherent knowing, Bonaparte was a great discoverer of men. He wanted those men's talents to be devoted to him alone, however; he demanded that his mind always be the driving force in any alliance. A gnat flying off to mate without his permission was a rebel gnat.

Tormented by the desire to become not just someone but someone great, Chateaubriand could not tolerate for a minute the notion that he might be seen merely as an object, or a gnat. He flatly refused Bonaparte's offer.

When Abbot Emery, the father superior at the Saint-Sulpice seminary, a man of whom Bonaparte thought highly, heard about the refusal, he begged Chateaubriand to accept, for the good of religion, the position of first secretary to the ambassador to Rome. At first the abbot's appeals to Chateaubriand failed, but his persistence finally proved to be persuasive. Chateaubriand accepted.

As soon as his preparations were complete, Chateaubriand set out for Rome, for the ambassador's secretary needed to arrive before the ambassador. His trip through the plains of Lombardy offers a sample of Chateaubriand's inimitable prose style with its perfect blend of simplicity and grandeur. Here he describes our soldiers on foreign soil, and how wherever we go people either love us or hate us.

The French army was settled in Lombardy like a military colony. With some of their comrades posted here and there as sentinels, these foreigners from Gaul with their garrison caps and swords hanging at their sides like sickles over their thick jackets looked like busy, joyous reapers. They moved stones and situated cannons, drove carts, built hangars and shelters with branches. Horses were jumping, rearing up, prancing through the crowds like dogs trying to please their masters. Italian women were selling fruits from trays in the marketplace to this unruly army. Our soldiers would give them their pipes and lighters, saying, as the old Barbarians, their fathers, said to their beloved: "I, Fotrad, son of Eupert, of the race of Franks, I give you, Helgine, my beloved wife, in honor of your beauty, my house in Les Pins."

We are strange enemies. At first people think we are a little insolent, a little too gay, too rowdy. But no sooner have we left than they begin to miss us. Lively, witty, intelligent, the French soldier participates in the activities of the family that provides him lodging. He draws water from the well, like Moses for the daughters of Midian; he follows the shepherds, takes the lambs to be washed, splits wood, builds fires, stirs the cooking pot, holds the baby in his arms or rocks it to sleep in its cradle. His good humor and activity in everything speak of life. They begin to see him as a family conscript. But when the drum beats? Then their lodger runs for his musket, leaving his host's daughter in tears at the door, and leaves the hut, never thinking about the family again until he enters the Invalides.

As I was passing through Milan, a great people was beginning to open its eyes. For a moment Italy awoke from its slumber, remembering its genius as in a divine dream. It was useful to the rebirth of our own country. Compared to the pettiness of our own poverty, we were able to see the grandeur of what lay beyond the Alps, nourished as it was in the artistic masterpieces and grand reminiscences from the country's celebrated past when it was called Ausonia.. Then Austria arrived, placing its heavy mantel on the Italians. Austria forced them back into their coffins. Rome returned to its ruins, Venice to the sea. Venice sank, gracing the sky with its last smile; charmingly, it lay down in its waves, like a star which will never rise again.

Chateaubriand arrived in Rome on the evening of June 27, just two days before the much-celebrated feast of Saint Peter. He spent the 28th as a tourist, and for the first time he visited the Coliseum, the Pantheon, the Trajan column, and Sant Angelo castle. That evening, Monsieur Artaud, whom he was replacing, took the new arrival to a house near Saint Peter's Square, where they were able to watch the pyrotechnic display on Michelangelo's dome as well as dancers whirling in waltzes down below their open windows. Rockets from fireworks on Hadrian's piers lit up the night sky at Sant Onufro, high above Tasso's tomb.

The next day, he went to mass in Saint Peter's, with Pope Pius VII presiding. Two days later he was introduced to His Holiness. Pope Pius had him sit down beside him, a rare honor, because normally visitors remain standing in the presence of the pope. The *Génie du christianisme* lay open on a table.

When we consider that great mind we call Monsieur de Chateaubriand, we enjoy recalling, too, among his splendid sentences that appeal so much to the imagination, incidental details that speak to more common experience. For instance, Cardinal Fesch had rented the Lancelotti Palace, near the Tiber, and the new embassy secretary had been given the top floor, but no sooner had he entered his rooms than a swarm of fleas leaped onto his legs and in seconds his white pants were black with them. He had his office rooms thoroughly cleaned, then organized the space and began preparing passports attending to other equally momentous tasks.

In penmanship, he was just the opposite of me. My elegant hand has always provided me an unfailing advantage in my long career, but Chateaubriand's was a real obstacle to the performance of his duties. Cardinal Fesch would inevitably shrug at the sight of his signature, and since he had never read *Atala* or the *Génie du christianisme*, he was apt to wonder how a man whose signature scrawled over an entire page could possibly write anything worth reading.

In fact, he had little to do in his lofty position as first secretary at the embassy, a position that his enemies had nonetheless predicted to be beyond the reach of his particular intelligence. So he would look out over the mansard roofs and watch the neighbors. There were washerwomen who would wave to him. There was a yet-to-be-discovered singer who practiced daily and whose ceaseless melodies haunted him. He considered himself fortunate when a funeral procession passed by, for it not only relieved his boredom but also reminded him of death and turned his thoughts to the eternal poetry of the earth and heavens. Or he might be aggrieved to see a young mother, her face uncovered, being borne solemnly between two rows of penitents in white, her newborn, dead, with a wreath of flowers, lying at her feet.

During his first days there he made a regrettable mistake. The former king of Sardinia, who had been dethroned by Bonaparte, was stopping in Rome, and Chateaubriand went to pay him homage; for noble hearts are naturally attracted to what has fallen. That visit created a diplomatic storm that blew through the embassy palace. The first secretary drew the scorn of the entire diplomatic corps, and any whom he should happen to pass would turn away, button up their collars, and murmur, "He is done for!" There was, said Chateaubriand:

> . . . not one diplomatic idiot who did not look down on me from his stupidity. Everyone hoped I would fall, although I wasn't anyone really and did not count for much. No matter, it would mean that somebody was falling from favor, and people always enjoy that. In my simplicity, I

failed to realize the extent of my crime, and as has been the case since then, I did not give a fig for any particular position. Kings, to whom people thought I attached so great an importance, in my eyes were linked only to great misfortune. People wrote back to Paris about my stupid actions. Fortunately, I was dealing with Bonaparte. What should have sunk me ended up saving me.

Yes, Chateaubriand was bored, utterly. The secretaryship that his ill-wishers deemed to be above his worth and intelligence consisted mostly of trimming quills and sending letters. Given the problems in the political offing, his talents could have been put to good diplomatic use, but no one bothered to initiate him into the embassy's mysteries. Perfect though he would have been for working with chancery disputes, the greatest genius of the time was instead assigned duties any ordinary clerk could execute.

For who could attach import to a mission like delivering shoes! Albeit the Princess Borghese was delighted to receive the latest fashion in footwear from Paris, so delighted that she suffered the secretary to attend her while she tried on five or six pairs. Only very briefly, though, would she walk in her elegant new shoes through the old city streets that had once belonged to the She-Wolf's sons.

Chateaubriand had already decided to abandon a diplomatic career that afforded him little else than tedious tasks and political red tape when a personal misfortune saddened his heart as much as the work bored his mind. When he had returned from exile, he had been welcomed by a certain Madame de Beaumont. She was the daughter of the Comte de Montmorin: French ambassador to Madrid, a commander in Brittany, he had held the Foreign Affairs portfolio under Louis XVI, who greatly admired him. He had ended up on the scaffold, as had others in his family.

Because Chateaubriand draws his literary portraits with such poetry, rather than merely refer to them, we are always tempted to reproduce them directly, in that we assume the reader will admire them as much we have. So here is the portrait of his friend Madame de Beaumont, whom you do not know even by name, yet she will appear before you as if with her magic wand the pythonness Eudora herself had lifted the shroud from her face.

Madame de Beaumont, her face more homely than attractive, looked very much like her portrait painted by Madame Lebrun. Her face was thin and pale. Her almond-shaped eyes might have been considered too sparkling if an extraordinary sweetness had not softened them and made them more languorous, the way a ray of light traverses water. Her character was somewhat stiff and impatient due to the strength of her feelings and her inner suffering. With an exalted soul and a noble spirit, she had been born to a world from which her thoughts had withdrawn by choice and by misfortune. But when the voice of a friend called her from her thoughtful solitude, she always responded, and she would speak celestial words.

Doctors had recommended Mediterranean air for the ailing Madame de Beaumont, and Chateaubriand's presence in Rome helped her decide to follow their advice. Within her first few days in Italy, she noted a distinct improvement in her health. Indeed, any signs of an imminent demise seemed to have disappeared almost immediately. Monsieur de Chateaubriand escorted her around the ancient city in a carriage. They visited all the marvels of Rome. But one needs life to see, to love, to admire. Increasingly the woman was taking little pleasure in anything.

It was one of those beautiful October days found only in Rome, the day they went to the Coliseum. She sat down on a stone facing one of the altars that had been erected around the outside of the edifice. Looking up, she let her eyes rest a long moment on the portico, then on the walls that had witnessed the death of so many men and centuries. The ruins were decorated with thorns and columbines, yellowed by autumn and bathed in its light. Then the dying woman looked away from the sun, down across the steps to the arena. She saw the cross and said, "We must leave. I'm cold."

Monsieur de Chateaubriand took her home. She went to bed, and she never got up again. This is how her friend describes the story of her death:

She asked me to open the window, because the air felt oppressive. A ray of sunlight struck her bed and seemed to cheer her up. She reminded me of plans we had made to go to the country, and she began to cry.

Between two and three in the afternoon, Madame de Beaumont asked Madame Saint-Germain, the old Spanish maid who served with the affection her good mistress deserved, to move her to a different bed. The doctor objected, fearing that Madame de Beaumont might die as they were moving her. And then she told me she felt death was upon her. Suddenly, she threw off her blanket, reached out to me, and squeezed my hand. Her eyes lost focus. With her free hand, she began gesturing to someone she saw at the foot of the bed. And then, placing her hand on her breast, she said:

"There it is! There it is!"

In consternation, I asked her if she knew me. A half smile appeared in the midst of her distraction. She nodded slightly. Her thoughts were already otherworldly. Convulsions lasted several minutes. We held her in our arms, me, the doctor, and the servant. One of my hands rested on her heart, and it was beating rapidly close to her thin bones like a clock winding down.

Suddenly I could feel it stop. We laid her back on her pillow, a woman who had reached her final rest. Her head drooped over. Some of her curls slipped down over her forehead. Her eyes were closed; eternal night had fallen. The doctor held up a mirror and candle to the stranger's mouth. The mirror did not fog up, and the flame was motionless. All was over.

"I shall love you forever," says a Greek epitaph. "But, in the kingdom of the dead, do not drink the water of Lethe that will make you forget those whom you loved."

It was sometime afterward that Monsieur de Chateaubriand got the news that the First Consul had named him minister in Le Valais. Bonaparte, at least, perceived that the author of the *Génie du christianisme* was the kind of man whose true value would be realized on the front lines rather than in the offices of bureaucracy.

Chateaubriand returned to Paris. Grateful to Bonaparte for recognizing his worth, he dedicated the second edition of the *Génie du christianisme* to the general:

To the First Consul, General Bonaparte.

General,

You have kindly taken under your protection this second edition of the *Génie du christianisme*. That is one more witness to the favor you have shown for the august cause that is triumphant under your protection. We cannot fail to recognize in your destiny the hand of Providence. It has marked you from afar to carry out its prodigious plans. The people keep their eyes on you, and France, aggrandized by your victories, has placed its hope in you ever since you have made religion the foundation of the State and of its prosperity.

Continue reaching out to the thirty million Christians who are praying for you at altars you have given back to them.

I am, with deepest respect, General,

Your humble and obedient servant,

Chateaubriand.

Such was the relationship between the First Consul and Monsieur de Chateaubriand that evening when Bonaparte, in order to determine what action to take regarding the Duc d'Enghien, postponed for two hours the audience he had granted to the man he had named to be his minister in Le Valais.

XL
Resolve

BEFORE ENTERING our long parenthesis on the author of the *Génie du christianisme*, we mentioned that Bonaparte had asked to be left alone. Why he had done so was to allow his anger the opportunity to rise to the highest degree on the passion thermometer. Contrary to most men, whom solitude calms and reflection tempers, Bonaparte in that state let his imagination go wild and feed the tempest within him. And when the tempest raged, someone would inevitably be struck by lightning.

He dined alone, and when Monsieur Réal arrived that evening with the same report on the Duc d'Enghien that the First Consul had received that morning, but with different comments, he found the First Consul bent over a table on which large maps were spread out. Bonaparte was studying the area between the Rhine and Ettenheim, measuring distances and calculating marching times.

When Monsieur Réal came in, Bonaparte paused, and, placing one of his fists on the table, he said to the state counselor, "Well, Monsieur Réal. You are in charge of my police and see me daily. Yet you neglect to tell me that the Duc d'Enghien is only four leagues away from my border, organizing military plots."

"That is precisely what I have come to talk to you about," Monsieur Réal answered calmly. "The Duc d'Enghien is not four leagues from your border. Rather he is in Ettenheim, twelve leagues away."

"What are twelve leagues?" asked Bonaparte. "Was not George sixty leagues away? And Pichegru eighty? And how about Moreau, where was he? He was not even four leagues away, was he? He was living in Rue d'Anjou-Saint-Honoré, just four hundred paces from the Tuileries. All he had to do was give the signal and the next thing you knew, his two accomplices had joined him in Paris. Suppose they had succeeded: A Bourbon would be here in the capital and he would have been heir to everything that belongs to me. So, I am just a dog to be killed in the streets, whereas my assassins are sacred!"

At that moment Monsieur de Talleyrand arrived with the second and third consuls. Immediately Bonaparte confronted the Minister of Foreign Affairs: "What can your Minister Massias be doing in Karlsruhe while my enemies are busy forming armed groups in Ettenheim?"

"I know nothing of all that," said Monsieur de Talleyrand. "And Massias has sent me nothing on that subject," he added with his customary calm.

His manner of answering and defending himself never failed to exasperate Bonaparte.

"Fortunately," Bonaparte said, "the information I have received is sufficient. I shall be able to punish their conspiracies. The guilty man will pay with his head."

The First Consul was pacing up and down the room, as was his custom, and the Second Consul, Cambacérès, was doing the best he could to keep in step with him, but when he heard the words "The guilty man will pay with his head," he abruptly stopped. "I dare think," Cambacérès said, "that if such a man were in your power, such severity would not be necessary."

"What are you telling me, monsieur?" responded Bonaparte, looking him up and down. "You can be sure that I would never spare any man who sent assassins after me. In this affair I will follow my own counsel and will not listen to anyone's advice, especially not to yours, monsieur, for you seem to have become a protector of Bourbon blood since the day you voted death for Louis XVI. Even if all the laws of our country were not on my side, I would still be within my rights in that I'd be acting in accord with natural law. I am warranted by my rights of self-defense.

"The likes of Moreau and his friends are plotting daily to take my life. I am assailed on all sides, sometimes with daggers, sometimes with fire. People invent air guns, they build bombs. They surround me with conspiracy, set traps of all kinds. Daily, from far and near, there are attempts to kill me! If no power, no tribunal, on earth is able to protect me, should I not embrace my natural right to fight fire with fire? Who could blame me? Who would call that an odious crime? Blood calls for blood. To answer that call is a natural, infallible, inevitable reaction. Woe to the man who provokes it!

"Those who persist in fomenting civil unrest and political troubles may themselves end up being the victims. You need to be stupid or crazy to imagine that you as a family are granted the strange privilege of being allowed to constantly threaten my life without my having the right to give back as I receive. No one can reasonably claim to be above the law; no one can reasonably expect to destroy others and then depend on the law for their own protection.

"Personally, I have never done any harm to any Bourbon. A great nation has placed me at its head. Almost all of Europe has acceded to that choice. My blood, after all, is not mud, and it is time that we establish that my blood is the equal of theirs.

"What would have happened if I had insisted on additional reprisals? Which would have been within my power! More than once the Bourbons' fate was in my hands. Ten times, their heads were offered; ten times I refused the proposal with horror. And not because I thought it would be unjust, given the position I was in. But I found myself so powerful, and I believed the danger from them to be so slight, that I could only consider such actions to be base and gratuitous cowardliness. My grand maxim has always been that in politics as in war, any evil, even when it falls within the rules, is excusable only if it is absolutely necessary. Anything that goes beyond what is necessary is a crime."

Fouché still had not spoken. Bonaparte turned toward him, feeling that in him he would find an ally. Fouché's only response to the First Consul's silent plea, however, was to address Monsieur Réal: "Could not Monsieur le Conseiller d'Etat," he said, "help us understand the situation by showing us the statement made by the man Le Ridant, who was arrested at the same time as George? It is true that Monsieur might not yet know about his statement, for he received it from the hands of Monsieur Dubois only at two o'clock, and since he has been so busy over the past few hours, perhaps he has not yet had the time to read it."

Réal could feel his ears turning red. He had indeed received the paper and he had been told that it was important; nonetheless, without reading it, he had placed it in George's file, having promised himself to give it a glance at his first free moment. That free moment had never come; so although he knew about the statement, he had no idea what it contained.

Without a word, Réal opened his portfolio and began to search among the papers it contained. Fouché looked over his shoulder and pointed: "There it is," he said.

Bonaparte regarded Fouché with some surprise, as the man seemed to know better than Réal himself what was in the state counselor's portfolios.

The statement was quite serious. Le Ridant was confessing the existence of a plot and claiming that a prince was at its head—a prince who had already come once to Paris and who probably would be coming again. He added that with George he had seen a young man of about thirty-two, well mannered and elegantly dressed, who was clearly shown respect by everyone there; indeed, in his presence Pichegru had removed his hat.

Bonaparte stopped Réal from reading further: "Enough, gentlemen," he said. "Enough! It's clear that the young man for whom the conspirators showed such respect could not have been a prince who'd come from London, because for a whole month Savary was guarding the Biville cliffs. It can only have been the Duc d'Enghien. He can leave Ettenheim and be in Paris in forty-eight hours, then be back again in Ettenheim in the same number of hours after spending some time with his accomplices. So it is obvious how they'd organized the plan," he continued. "The Comte d'Artois was to come through Normandy with Pichegru, and the Duc d'Enghien through Alsace with Dumouriez. The two Bourbons, in order to return to

France, arranged to be escorted by the two most famous generals of the Republic.

"Call Colonel Ordener and Colonel Caulaincourt."

You will understand that once they had heard the First Consul present his opinion so emphatically, not one of othem dared to oppose his plans directly or indirectly. Consul Lebrun made a few vague comments; he feared the effect such events might produce in Europe. Cambacérès, in spite of the cruel words that had reduced him to silence, breached the subject of clemency once again, but Bonaparte simply answered, "Fine, I know why you are speaking as you do. It is out of devotion to me, and I thank you. But I will not let them attempt to kill me without defending myself. I shall make every conspirator quake and teach them never to dare any treachery again."

In fact, the dominant sentiment in Bonaparte's mind at that moment was neither fear nor vengeance, but rather the desire for all of France to realize that Bourbon blood, so sacred to Royalist partisans, was no more sacred to him than the blood of any other citizen in the Republic.

"Well, then," asked Cambacérès, "what have you decided?"

"It's simple," said Bonaparte. "We shall kidnap the Duc d'Enghien and be done with it."

They voted. Only Cambacérès dared maintain his opposition to the end. Now that the decision had been made in council, Bonaparte no longer bore the responsibility alone.

Outside the office, Ordener and Caulaincourt were waiting. Bonaparte called them in. Already he had determined that Colonel Ordener would go to the Rhine with three hundred dragoons, several brigades of gendarmes, and some pontoniers. His men would be given enough food for four days. In addition, the colonel would be given the sum of thirty thousand francs so that he would not need to depend upon the local population. They would cross the river at Rheinau, march directly to Ettenheim, surround the town, and take into custody the Duc d'Enghien and all the émigrés in his camp, especially Dumouriez. Meanwhile, another detachment, supported by several artillery pieces, would move through Kehl to Offenburg, where they would remain in observation until the Duc d'Enghien was once more back in French territory. As soon as he received absolute confirmation that the Duc d'Enghien was in France, Colonel Caulaincourt would call upon the Grand Duke of Baden to present him a diplomatic note explaining the action that had just been taken.

It was eight o'clock. Bonaparte dismissed the council, and, as if he were afraid he might change his mind, he ordered the two colonels, whose mission conferred upon them the rank of general, to set out that very evening.

Alone again, Bonaparte's face broke into an expression of triumph. Once accomplished, the action would be a source of eternal regret for him, but for the moment it inspired in him profound feelings of pride and satisfaction. His blood, he had now established, was equal to that of princes and kings, and no one, not even a crowned prince, had the right to spill it.

He looked at the clock. It showed a quarter past eight. His new secretary Monsieur de Méneval had witnessed the strange scene that had just taken place, and he had remained in case the First Consul needed him further. Bonaparte went over to the table where he was sitting, placed one finger on the table, and said, "Start writing!"

The First Consul to the Minister of War,
Paris, the 19th Ventôse, year XII (March 10, 1804)

You will give orders, Citizen General, to General Ordener, whom I am placing under your command, to take the mail coach to Strasbourg this very evening. He is to find lodging under an assumed name, and he is to see the major general.

The purpose of his mission will be to go to Ettenheim, to surround the town, and to capture the Duc d'Enghien, Dumouriez, an English colonel, and any other people who are associated with them. The major general, the sergeant from the Gendarmerie who scouted out Ettenheim, and the police commissioner will provide him all the necessary information.

You will order General Ordener to request three hundred men from the 26th Dragoons in Schelestadt. They will go to Rheinau, and they must be there by eight in the evening.

The division commander will send eleven pontoniers who must arrive in Rheinau by eight o'clock as well. They must also leave by mail coach or by borrowing horses from the light brigade, and they are not to take the ferry. They must ensure that four or five large boats are waiting so that in one trip they can transport three hundred horses.

The troops are to carry enough bread for four days as well as a good supply of cartridges. The major general will send a captain or another officer and a lieutenant from the Gendarmerie along with three or four brigades. Once General Ordener has crossed the Rhine, he will go to Ettenheim and march directly to where the Duke and Dumouriez live. Once he has completed his assignment, he is to return to Strasbourg.

On his way through Lunéville, General Ordener will request that the carabineer officer commanding the depot in Ettenheim take the mail coach to Strasbourg, where he is to await orders.

In Strasbourg, General Ordener will secretly send on ahead two agents, either military or civilian, and make arrangements for them to meet him.

You will give orders that on the same day, at the same time, two hundred men from the 26th Dragoons, under the orders of General Caulaincourt, will go to Offenburg, surround the town, and arrest the Baronne de Reich, if she has not already been captured in Strasbourg, as well as other agents of the English government, based on information provided by the prefect, Citizen Méhée, who is currently in Strasbourg.

From Offenburg, General Caulaincourt will send out patrols toward Ettenheim until he is sure that General Ordener has arrived. They are to provide support for each other. At the same time, the major general will have his three hundred cavalrymen cross at Kehl, with four light artillery pieces, sending a squadron of light cavalry to Wilstadt, between the two highways.

The two generals will take care that the greatest discipline reigns and that their troops take nothing from the local inhabitants. For that purpose you will give them each twelve thousand francs.

If it should happen that they are unable to carry out their missions but are hopeful that by staying three or four days and sending out patrols they might be able to do so, they are so authorized.

They will communicate to the bailiffs of the two towns that if they continue to give asylum to France's enemies, they will bring great misfortune down upon themselves.

You will order the commanding officer at Neufbrissac to send one hundred men across to the right bank with two cannons.

The positions at Kehl and on the right bank are to be evacuated as soon as the two detachments have returned.

General Caulaincourt will have approximately thirty gendarmes with him.

General Caulaincourt, General Ordener, and the major general will discuss the situation and make any appropriate changes to this plan.

If it should happen that neither Dumouriez nor the Duc d'Enghien are still in Ettenheim, they will send a special courier to keep us informed.

You will order the arrest of the postmaster in Kehl and any other individuals who might be able to give out information.

Bonaparte

Just as he was signing that crucial document, Citizen Chateaubriand was announced.

Both Monsieur de Chateaubriand and Bonaparte were now thirty-five years old. Both men were short, and appeared to be about the same height. But, whereas Bonaparte held his head high and looked straight ahead, Monsieur de Chateaubriand's head was sunk between his shoulders, and were it not, he would have been taller. In his *Mémoires* Chateaubriand claimed that his posture was typical of scions in warrior families, because their ancestors wore helmets.

All those who have had the honor of meeting Monsieur de Chateaubriand will agree with me, I am sure, that they have never known a man whose pride was greater than his, except for Bonaparte's. Chateaubriand's pride would soundly survive everything—the loss of his fortune as well as the loss of his political appointments and all the literary honors bestowed upon him—so at this moment of personal triumph, it had to have been immense. As for Bonaparte, he had but one more step to take to attain the highest political and social position a man could ever hope to reach, and his pride permitted no comparisons between him and other men, either in the past or the present. So Leviathan and Behemoth stood facing each other.

"You see, Monsieur de Chateaubriand," Bonaparte said, walking over to greet him, "I have not forgotten you."

"Thank you, Citizen First Consul. You have understood that there are men who are useful only in the appropriate place."

"Rather," said Bonaparte, "I have understood Caesar's words: 'Better to be first in one's own village than second in Rome.' The fact is," he continued, "you surely cannot have enjoyed working with my dear uncle, what with the cardinal's stingy tedium, the Bishop of Châlons and his small-town boasting, and the future Bishop of Morocco's continual lying."

"Monsignor Guillon," said Chateaubriand.

"You know his story," Bonaparte continued. "Taking advantage of a name that to the ear sounded very much like his own, he claims, after miraculously escaping from the massacre at Les Carmes, to have given absolution to Madame de Lamballe in La Force. Not a word of all that is true. What did you do to avoid boredom?"

"I lived as much as I could with the dead. I did what all foreigners do in Rome: I dreamed. Rome itself is a dream, one that must be seen by moonlight. From up on the Trinita del Monte, the buildings in the distance look like a painter's sketches or like the outlines of misty coasts seen from a vessel at sea. The great night star, a globe we can assume is itself a wondrous world, would cast its pale rays over Rome's deserted streets. It lit up lifeless avenues, Rome's courtyards and squares, those gardens where no one walks, the monasteries, the cloisters as quiet and deserted as the portico of the Coliseum. I wondered what had happened there eighteen centuries earlier, in that very place, at the same time of day. What men stepped through the shadows cast by those obelisks, after the obelisks had ceased to cast their shadows on Egypt's sands? Not only is ancient Italy dead, but medieval Italy, too, has disappeared. Yet there are still traces of both Italies in the

Eternal City. Modern Rome can flaunt its Saint Peter and masterpieces of art, and ancient Rome can boast its Pantheon, even among its ruins. One Italy recalls its consuls coming down from the Capitol; the other parades its pontiffs from the Vatican. The Tiber separates these two glorious cities set in the same dust, as pagan Rome sinks gradually into its tombs and Christian Rome slowly descends into its catacombs."

Bonaparte remained thoughtful during the poet's description of Rome. His ears were listening to what the poet was saying, but his eyes were set on some point off in the distance. "Monsieur," he said, "if I were going to Rome, especially as an attaché to the French embassy, I would see something different than the Rome of Caesar, Diocletian, and Gregory VII. I would see not only the heiress to the mother of the Roman world, the greatest empire that has ever existed. I would see the queen of the Mediterranean, that marvelous mirror in which the cities crowning civilizations from every era in turn have been reflected and to each other wed: Marseille, Venice, Corinth, Athens, Constantinople, Smyrna, Alexandria, Cyrene, Carthage, and Cadiz. Around its waters are grouped, just a few days apart, all three parts of the ancient world: Europe, Africa, and Asia.

"Thanks to the Mediterranean, the man who would become master of Rome and of Italy could go anywhere and everywhere: by the Rhone, into the heart of France; up the Eridano, into the heart of Italy; through the Straits of Gibraltar, to Senegal, the Cape of Good Hope, and the two Americas; through the Dardanelles, to the Marmara Sea, to the Bosporus, to the Black Sea, all the way to Tartary; through the Red Sea, to India, to Tibet, to Africa, to the immense Pacific Ocean; up the Nile, to Egypt, to Thebes, to Memphis, to Elephantine, to Ethiopia, to the desert and the great unknown. As if to prepare some future grandeur, greater perhaps than what Caesar imagined or Charlemagne accomplished, the pagan world developed around the Mediterranean. Christianity gathered it for a moment in its arms. Alexander, Hannibal, and Caesar were born on its shores. Perhaps people will one day be saying, 'Bonaparte was born in its bosom!' There is an echo in Milan that sings 'Charlemagne'; in Tunis the echo honors 'Saint Louis.' The Arab invasions spread out over one of its shores; the Crusades moved east on the other. Civilization has graced the Mediterranean for three thousand years. For eighteen centuries, Calvary has dominated it!

"So, if by chance you returned to Rome, I would dare to say to you: 'Monsieur de Chateaubriand, enough poets, enough dreamers, and enough philosophers have seen Rome as you have. It is time now for a practical man, instead of losing himself in dreaming about the city itself, to immerse himself in the horizon's depth. There is nothing more to be done with a city that has twice been the capital of the world. But there is everything to be done with that great plain we call the sea, a field always so easy to plow.' If some day I am master of Spain as I am now master of Italy, I will close the Straits of Gibraltar to England, even if it means building a citadel in the ocean's depths. And then, Monsieur de Chateaubriand, the Mediterranean will no longer be a sea. It will be a French lake.

"If ever a man of your intelligence should return to Rome, which is certainly possible, and if I should be in power, you would go, not as the embassy's first secretary, but as ambassador. And I would say to you: 'Do not encumber yourself with a library. Leave Ovid, Tacitus, and Suetonius in Paris. Take along only one map, the map of the Mediterranean, and never take your eyes off of it. Wherever I should happen to be in the world, I can promise you that I would look at it daily.'

"Good-bye for now, Monsieur de Chateaubriand."

XLI
Via Dolorosa

As BONAPARTE AND CHATEAUBRIAND were taking leave of each other, each having measured the other like two athletes planning to meet again for further combat and not at all like a subordinate bowing to a superior, General Ordener was leaving by mail coach for Strasbourg.

As soon as he reached Strasbourg, he went to see the division commander, who had been ordered to meet all his requests, even if their purpose was not clear. The commander immediately consigned to him General Fririon, the three hundred men from the 26th Dragoons, the pontoniers, and all the material General Ordener asked to be made available to him.

At the same time General Ordener was going to Schelestadt, under his orders a Gendarmerie sergeant in disguise was heading to Ettenheim, in order to ascertain that the prince and General Dumouriez were in fact there.

On the sergeant's return, with a report that both men were in Ettenheim, General Ordener left immediately for Rheinau. He arrived at eight in the evening, and, commandeering the ferry and five large boats that were tied together, he and his men crossed the Rhine.

By five in the morning, the prince's castle was completely surrounded.

Awakened by the sound of horses and the order to open his doors, the prince leaped out of bed, grabbed his double-barreled shotgun, opened the window, and took aim at Citizen Charlot, commander of the 38th squadron of the Gendarmerie Nationale, who was shouting at the servants and anyone else at the castle windows: "Open, in the name of the Republic!"

The prince was about to shoot—and if he had, it would have been all over for Citizen Charlot—when Colonel Grunstein, who had been sleeping in the room next to the prince's, rushed to the window and laid his hand on the barrel of the gun, and said, "Monsignor, have you already compromised yourself?"

"Not at all, my dear Grunstein," the prince answered.

"Well, then," said Grunstein. "It is useless to resist. We are surrounded, as you can see; bayonets are gleaming everywhere. As for the man you're aiming at, he is the commander. You must realize that if you kill him you will be bringing about your own ruin as well as ours."

"Fine," said the prince, throwing aside his gun. "Let them come in, but only if they break down the doors. I do not recognize the French Republic and will not open for it."

The prince meanwhile hurriedly got dressed. He heard a few shouts that fires should be set, but they were soon silenced. One man, running to the church to sound the tocsin, was arrested, and the alleged General Dumouriez (you remember that his name was not Dumouriez, but Thumery) was captured without resistance. The prince was led from his bedroom, and while gendarmes were gathering his papers, he was taken to a mill near the Tuilerie.

In fact, the soldiers had not had to break down the doors, for Sergeant Pferdsdorff, who had been sent to Ettenheim the day before and who had pointed out to Commander Charlot where the prince's various guests were sleeping, had led some gendarmes and a dozen dragoons from the 22nd Regiment into the house by way of the commons, after they'd climbed over the courtyard wall.

Once they had gathered all the prisoners together, no one could identify Dumouriez. Certainly the prince could not, for, as he said, General Dumouriez had never been in Ettenheim and he did not even know what the general looked like.

The people arrested were: the prince; the Marquis de Thumery; the Baron de Grunstein; Lieutenant Schmidt; the Abbé Weinborn, ecclesiastical judge for the bishopric of Strasbourg; the Abbé Michel, secretary of the bishopric of Strasbourg; Jacques, the Duc d'Enghien's private secretary; Simon Ferrand, his valet; and two servants, one named Pierre Poulain and the other Joseph Canone.

Straightaway the Duc d'Enghien expressed his fear of being taken to Paris. "Now that the First Consul has me, he will have me locked up," he said. "I am sorry," he added, "not to have shot at you, Commander. I would have killed you, your men would then have shot me, and everything would now be over."

Hay was spread in the bed of a cart for padding, and after the prisoners had climbed in, they were taken to the Rhine, with a row of gunmen on either side. At the Rhine, the prince was put on a boat that took him across to Rheinau. He walked to Plobsheim, where they stopped for breakfast as day had long since broken. After breakfast, the prince rode in a carriage with Commander Charlot and the sergeant; a gendarme climbed up on the seat with Colonel Grunstein. They reached Strasbourg at about five in the evening.

A half hour later, the prince was taken from Commander Charlot's house by cab to the citadel. There he rejoined his companions, who had come by cart or on horseback. The fortress commander had put them all in his reception room. They would spend the night on thin mattresses, on the floor, while three sentinels, two inside the room and one at the door, kept watch over them until dawn.

The prince slept poorly. He could not help worrying about how things might turn out. He thought back over information he had been given, and he was sorry not to have paid more attention to it.

On Friday, March 16, it was announced that he would be moved to different lodgings. General Leval, Commander of Strasbourg, and General Fririon, who had captured him, came to speak with him. The generals' bearing was stiff, the meeting more than chilly. The prince was then transferred to the pavilion on the right-hand side of the square as one leaves the city. He was able to communicate with Thumery, Schmidt, and Jacques, but neither he nor his servants were allowed to leave the pavilion, though he hoped to be granted permission to walk in the garden behind it. A contingent of twelve men and an officer guarded his door.

Nor was the prince permitted any contact with his friend the Comte de Grunstein, who was lodged on the other side of the courtyard; their separation saddened the prince. His sadness turned into despondency when he asked General Leval to send on a letter he had written to the princess his wife, and the general did not even offer him the courtesy of an answer. He could communicate with no one outside the pavilion.

At four-thirty they began to go through his papers. Colonel Charlot and a security officer read them in his presence, but hastily, apparently only superficially, before bundling them up in small packets to be sent to Paris.

The prince went to bed at eleven. Although he was completely worn out, he was unable to sleep. The major in charge, Monsieur Machine, looked in on him as he lay sleepless in bed and tried, to little avail, to console the distraught prince.

If the letter he had written to the Princesse de Rohan had been sent, the Duc d'Enghien still had received no answer on Saturday the 17th. He was near despair. That day they had him sign an official statement regarding his witnessing of their opening his papers, and that evening they told him he would likely be permitted to walk in the garden with the officer on guard and his prison companions. He ate supper and went to bed in a calmer frame of mind.

On Sunday the 18th, they roused him at one-thirty in the morning. He'd scarcely had time to dress and say good-bye to his friends before he was being marched out of the pavilion. Flanked by two officers and two gendarmes, he was led to a carriage with six post horses that was waiting in the square near the church. They pushed him into the carriage, where he was joined by Lieutenant Peterman and one of the gendarmes, while Sergeant Blitersdorff and the other gendarme climbed up on the seat.

The carriage arrived at the gates of Paris on the 20th, at eleven in the morning. It stood there for five hours, during which all the details of the terrible tragedy to ensue were probably being worked out. At four in the afternoon, by way of the outer boulevards, the carriage started for Vincennes. It arrived there after nightfall.

The consuls of the Republic had needed the time to prepare the following decree:

Paris, 29 Ventôse, year VII of the One Indivisible Republic
The government of the Republic decrees the following:

The ci-devant Duc d'Enghien, accused of bearing arms against the Republic, of having been and still being in the pay of England, of participating in plots organized by that power against the Republic's domestic and foreign security, will be brought before a military commission composed of seven members to be named by the Governor General of Paris, meeting in Vincennes.

The grand judge, the Minister of War, and the General Governor of Paris are charged with carrying out the present decree.

Bonaparte.
Hugues Maret.
The Governor General of Paris, Murat.

In the execution of such a decree, military law required that the division commandant—in this case, Murat, who was also governor general of

Paris—form the commission, bring its members together, and order the implementation of any sentence to be carried out.

When Murat unsealed the decree to enter his signature upon it, he let the document fall from his hands, so saddened he was by the sight of the official instrument bearing his name. Murat was courageous and rash, but a good man at heart. He had already learned of the consuls' resolve to arrest the Duc d'Enghien, and because he was tired of seeing his brother-in-law continually compromised in new conspiracies, he had applauded their action. But now that the Duc d'Enghien had been arrested and by the decree before him he himself was charged with carrying out the terrible consequences of that arrest, his courage failed him.

"Ah," he said in despair, tossing his hat away. "Ah! So the First Consul wants to dip my uniform in blood!"

He ran to the window, opened it, and shouted, "Harness the horses!"

Scarcely was the carriage ready than he was rushing into it with the cry "To Saint-Cloud!" For he did not want to execute unquestioningly an order that he considered a stain on Bonaparte and on himself.

He managed to get in to see his brother-in-law, to whom he expressed the fear and pain that were racking him. But Bonaparte, his face like a mask of bronze, concealed his own distress and doubts, and, taking refuge in what appeared to be utter impassivity, he treated Murat's misgivings as a weak man's cowardliness. To bring the discussion to a close, he said, "Well, since you are afraid, I shall be the one to give and sign the orders to be executed during this entire day."

We remember that the First Consul had ordered Savary to come back from the Biville cliffs, where he had been sent to await and arrest the princes as they came to shore. Savary was one of those rare men who, when they give of themselves in service to another, give their all, both body and soul. He had no opinions, he was without political sentiments, he hid no personal ambitions; he merely loved Bonaparte and served only the First Consul. And so when Bonaparte had had the orders drawn up and had signed them himself, it was Savary he entrusted to deliver them to Murat.

The orders were totally unambiguous. Having been violently rebuffed and ill treated by the First Consul, Murat, all the while cursing himself and virtually pulling out his hair, issued the order written in his name:

> To the government of Paris,
> the 29 Ventôse, year XII of the Republic
> The general in chief, governor of Paris,
> In execution of the government decree dated on this day, ordering that the ci-devant Duc d'Enghien shall be brought before a military

commission composed of seven members, chosen by the governor general of Paris, has named and is naming, to make up the aforementioned commission, the seven military officers whose names follow:

General Hulin, commander of foot grenadiers belonging to the Consuls' guard, president;

Colonel Guiton, commandant of the 1st regiment of cuirassiers;

Colonel Bazancourt, commandant of the 4th regiment of light infantry;

Colonel Ravier, commandant of the 18th regiment of heavy infantry;

Colonel Barrois, commandant of the 96th regiment of heavy infantry;

Colonel Rabbe, commandant of the 2nd regiment of the Paris municipal guard;

Citizen d'Autancourt, major in the gendarmerie d'élite, who will fulfill the function of captain rapporteur.

This commission will meet immediately in the Château de Vincennes to judge the accused without delay on the charges laid forth in the governmental decree, of which a copy will be given to the president.

J. Murat

We left our prisoner as he was entering Vincennes. The governor of that fortified castle, a man named Harel, had received its command as recompense for his help in the Ceracchi/Arena affair. By a strange coincidence, his wife was the foster sister of the Duc d'Enghien.

At first Harel had received no formal orders. Asked if he could house a prisoner, he'd said that he was unable to do so because there was only his own lodging and the council chamber. Then an official order did come: for him to prepare a room where a prisoner could sleep while awaiting his sentence. The order was followed by a request that he begin digging a grave in the courtyard. Harel answered that the request would be difficult to fulfill since the courtyard was paved. Where a grave could be dug, it was decided, was in the moat, and there it was dug before the prince's arrival.

The prince arrived at seven in the evening. Though hungry and cold, he did not look sad, and seemed otherwise not to bear any cause for worry. Since his room had not yet been warmed, the governor received him in his own apartment and found something for him to eat. When the prince sat down at the table, he invited the governor to share his meal, but Harel declined.

The prisoner asked Harel many questions about the castle keep and about events that had taken place there. The prince noted that he himself had been raised around Vincennes as he chatted amiably and seemingly completely at ease. Then he came back to his present situation: "Well," he said. "Do you know, my dear Governor, what they intend to do with me?"

The governor replied that he did not know and could not answer on that point. His wife, who could hear his conversation with the Duc d'Enghien from her bed in an alcove hidden by curtains, had earlier heard the order that her husband dig a grave; so she knew what the not-too-distant future held for the duke, and she could hardly hold back her sobs for her foster brother.

Tired as he was from the trip, the prince was eager to get to bed. Before he had fallen asleep, however, he was intruded upon by Lieutenant Noirot, Lieutenant Jacquin, Captain D'Autancourt, and two gendarmes, Nerva and Tharsis. With the assistance of the captain of the 18th regiment, Citizen Molin, a clerk chosen by the rapporteur, they began the interrogation.

"Your names, your age, and your position?" Captain d'Autancourt asked.

"I am Louis-Antoine-Henri de Bourbon, Duc d'Enghien, born on August 2, 1772, in Chantilly," the prince answered.

"When did you leave France?"

"I am unable to say precisely when, but I think it was on July 16, 1789. I left with the Prince de Condé, my grandfather; my father, the Duc de Bourbon; and the Comte d'Artois and his children."

"Where have you lived since you left France?"

"When I left France, I traveled with my parents first from Mons to Brussels, then on to Turin, where we stayed with the king of Sardinia approximately sixteen months. From there, again with my parents, I went to Worms, near the Rhine. At that time the Condé Corps was formed, and I joined the army. Before that, I had participated in the Brabant campaign with the corps led by the Duc de Bourbon, in the army of Duc Albert."

"Where did you retire to after the peace between the French Republic and the emperor of Austria was signed?"

"We finished the final campaign near Gratz. That is where the Condé Corps, which had been subsidized by England, was dissolved. I stayed on my own in or near Gratz for the next eight or nine months, waiting for news from my grandfather, who had gone to England and was negotiating how much money I would receive. During that time, I asked permission of the Cardinal de Rohan to visit his home, at Ettenheim in Brisgau. For the past two years that is where I have stayed. At the cardinal's death, I made an official request of the Elector of Baden to be allowed to remain there; he granted me that permission."

"Have you not gone to England? And is not that power paying you a salary?"

"I have never been in England. That power is granting me a salary, which is all I have to live on."

"Are you maintaining relationships with French princes in London, and have you been seeing them for a long time?

"Naturally I correspond with my father and my grandfather, whom I have not seen, if I remember correctly, since 1794 or 1795."

"What was your rank in Conde's army?"

"Vanguard commandant. Before 1796, I served as a volunteer in my grandfather's headquarters."

"Do you know General Pichegru?"

"I believe I have never seen him. I certainly have never had dealings with him. I know that at some point he wanted to meet with me, and I am glad that no such meeting ever occurred, given the vile means he has been accused of trying to use."

"Do you know General Dumouriez, and have you had dealings with him?"

"Not with him, either. I have never seen him."

"Have you not, since the peace, corresponded with individuals inside the Republic?"

"I have written to friends, but the letters have not been of a nature to cause concern for the government."

At that point Captain d'Autancourt ended the interrogation. After signing the transcription himself, he had Jacquin the squadron chief, Lieutenant Noirot, and the two gendarmes add their signatures, and finally the Duc d'Enghien as well. Before signing, the duke inserted the following lines:

> Before signing this transcription, I make an earnest request for a private audience with the First Consul. My name, my rank, my way of thinking, and the horror of my situation allow me to hope that he will not refuse my request.
>
> Louis-A.-H. de Bourbon

Meanwhile, Bonaparte had gone to La Malmaison, where he had ordered that he not be disturbed, for he wanted to be absolutely alone with his thoughts.

Madame Bonaparte, the young Queen Hortense, and all the women at court were in great despair, because they all had Royalist sentiments. Several times, Josephine, braving his bad moods, had gone so far as to raise questions regarding the recent nature of his justice. But Bonaparte had always answered with affected brusqueness: "Be quiet and leave me alone. You are only women and you know nothing about politics."

In the matter of the Duc d'Enghien Bonaparte had seemed to be especially distracted. On one occasion, trying to appear relaxed, he had walked up and down as was his custom with his hands behind his back and his head bowed, then finally he'd sat down at a table set for a game of chess and asked: "Well, now, which of you ladies will play chess with me?" In response, Madame de Rémusat had stood up and come over to the table, but scarcely had she sat down across from him than abruptly he'd knocked over the chess pieces and, without explanation, stormed out of the room.

In order to wash his hands of the whole business, Bonaparte, as we have seen, laid it all on Murat, to his brother-in-law's great despair. And it all was being played out in Vincennes.

Once the interrogation by Captain d'Autancourt had been finished, the prince, totally exhausted, had fallen asleep immediately. But not an hour had passed before the six men came back. They awakened the prince, had him get dressed, and escorted him down to the council chamber.

General Hulin, the commission president, had had an unusual military career. Born in Geneva in 1758, like everyone in Geneva he had become a clockmaker. He might have been making clocks still, if the Marquis de Conflans, impressed by the size and figure Hulin cut, had not made him his hunter and dressed him in a fancy embroidered uniform. When the first shots in the Revolution had been fired, Hulin had hurried to the Bastille, where, in his grand uniform, he was mistaken for a general and placed at the head of one of the first brave squads to enter the courtyard of the royal prison. He had subsequently borne the title of colonel, and nobody had contested it, until six weeks earlier, when he had received his promotion to general.

The courage Hulin had shown in 1789 was all the more remarkable because once the fighting was over, he had set himself in front of Governor de Launay and defended him as long as he could. Finally, yielding only in the face of overwhelming numbers, he had been unable to prevent the poor officer, as we know, from being cut to pieces. Perhaps it was the memory of his humanity that prompted Bonaparte to name him president of the commission that was to judge the Duc d'Enghien.

The prince was interrogated a second time with all possible consideration. It being a council of war, in the end, the options were clear-cut: If the prince was innocent, he would have to be released from Vincennes; if guilty, the sentence carried by his offense would have to be executed.

The verdict of the commission was unanimous. It read:

1) Unanimously, the commission declares Louis-Antoine-Henri de Bourbon, Duc d'Enghien, guilty of bearing arms against the French Republic;

2) Unanimously, guilty of offering his services to the English government, an enemy of the French people;

3) Unanimously, guilty of receiving and accrediting agents of the aforesaid English government, of procuring them means of spying inside France and of conspiring with them against the State's security, both domestic and foreign;

4) Unanimously, guilty of leading a gathering of French émigrés and others, in the pay of England; said corps having been formed on the borders of France in the area around Fribourg and Baden;

5) Unanimously, guilty of spying in Strasbourg, his aim to incite the surrounding departments to rebellion, thus creating a diversion favorable to England;

6) Unanimously, guilty of being one of the troublemakers and conspirators in the plot organized by the English against the First Consul's life; of being ready, in the event that the plot were successful, to return to France.

Only one question remained: that of punishment. It was resolved, like the others, unanimously. For the crimes of espionage, correspondence with enemies of the Republic, and conspiracy against the security of the State, both domestic and foreign, Louis-Antoine-Henri de Bourbon, Duc d'Enghien, was to pay with his life.

So, the commission had acted, although when its various members had arrived at Vincennes, not one of them had yet been told why he was being convoked. One of the colonels had been forced to wait by the entrance gate for an hour because the guards did not know who he was. Another, having received the order to report immediately to Vincennes, had concluded that he was being arrested and asked where he should present himself to be locked up.

As for the request the Duc d'Enghien had made for an audience with Bonaparte, one of the commission members had offered to convey the prince's wishes to the government, and the commission had agreed. But then a general seated behind the president had declared that the request was inappropriate. As he appeared to represent the First Consul, the commission had carried on, in disregard of the request, but no doubt on the assumption that after their discussion they would have ample time to satisfy the accused man's wishes. In fact, once the sentence had been rendered, General Hulin had picked up a pen to transmit the Duc d'Enghien's wishes to Bonaparte, only to be halted by the man who had raised the objection earlier: "What are you doing?" the man asked.

"I am writing to the First Consul," Hulin answered, "to communicate the wishes of the council and those of the condemned man."

"Your business is completed," said the man, taking away the pen. "Now it is up to me."

Savary had been present at the sentencing and had then gone to join the gendarmes d'élite on the castle esplanade. He was standing among them when the officer leading the legion's infantry approached him with tears in his eyes. A firing squad had been requested, he told Savary, to carry out the military commission's sentence.

"Give it to them," said Savary.

"Where shall I place it?"

"Where it cannot hurt anyone." For indeed, farmers in the Paris region were already traveling the roads with their carts to the various markets. After examining the possibilities, the officer determined the moat to be the safest place for the execution.

When the council had completed its interrogation of d'Enghien, he had gone back up to his room and promptly gone back to sleep. He was sleeping soundly when his escorts again awakened him and again had him get up and get dressed.

As yet unaware of his sentence, he was far from suspecting that he was being led to his death when they began descending the stairs that led to the moat of the fortress. "Where are we going?" he asked, and then, feeling the cool air below, he squeezed the hand of the governor, who was carrying the lantern, and whispered, "Are they going to throw me in the dungeon?"

Soon enough everything was explained to him. By the light of Governor Harel's lantern, the commission's sentence was read to him.

He listened impassively. Then from his pocket he pulled a letter he had no doubt written in the event of such an outcome. The letter contained a curl of his hair and a golden ring. He gave it to Lieutenant Norot, the officer with whom he had had the most contact since he had come to Vincennes and for whom he had the warmest feelings.

The commandant of the firing squad then asked: "Would you kneel down?"

"Why?" inquired the prince.

"To receive death."

"A Bourbon," the Duc d'Enghien replied, "kneels down before God alone."

The soldiers took a few steps backward and revealed the open grave. At the same moment, a little dog appeared. It had accompanied the duke all the way from Ettenheim and, escapting his room, had come to join him in the moat. Running back and forth between his legs, it was barking joyously.

The prince bent down to pat the dog. The soldiers began to prepare their weapons.

"Be careful about my little Fidèle," said the prince, "that's all I ask."

Then, straightening up, he added: "I'm all yours, gentlemen. Do what you need to do!"

In rapid sequence, the customary orders followed: "Ready! Aim! Fire!" There was a loud detonation. The prince fell.

He was laid fully dressed in the grave that had been readied for him, and, within minutes, his body was covered with dirt. The soldiers stomped on the ground, trying to wipe out any trace of the untimely grave.

Scarcely had the judgment been pronounced than all the commission members had tried to leave Vincennes. Each had asked for his carriage, but there was such confusion at the castle gates that not one of the men who had participated in sentencing the prince to death had yet left when by their judgment the fatal shots rang out. Only after the execution did the gates, which had been ordered shut, again open. With haste each man climbed into his carriage, and with haste each coachman, as ordered, distanced his passenger from the accursed castle. So it was that all those brave soldiers, who had so often faced death on the battlefield without a single thought of retreat, now fled from a ghost.

Savary, perhaps more affected than even the military commissioners, started back toward Paris as well. When he reached the barrier, he was surprised to meet the state counselor Monsieur Réal, who was heading out of the city. "Where are you going," Savary asked.

"To Vincennes," Monsieur Réal answered.

"And what are you going to do there?"

"I am going to interrogate the Duc d'Enghien as the First Consul has asked me to do."

"The Duc d'Enghien has been dead for a quarter hour now," said Savary.

Monsieur Réal cried out in astonishment, almost in fright, and turned pale. "Oh! Who was in such a hurry to bring about the poor prince's death?" he asked.

"At that moment," says Savary in his *Mémoires*, "I began to doubt that the death of the Duc d'Enghien had been orchestrated by the First Consul."

Monsieur Réal returned to Paris, while Savary went on to La Malmaison to report to Bonaparte. He arrived at eleven o'clock.

The First Consul seemed to be no less surprised than Monsieur Réal by Savary's announcement of the prince's death. Why had they not respected the prince's request to see him, Bonaparte wondered. "From what I know about his character," he said, "we could have worked something out between us."

Walking nervously up and down, Bonaparte cried, "There's one thing I fail to understand! It is clear that the commission made its decision based on what the Duc d'Enghien admitted. But what he admitted was only the beginning of his interrogation, not the occasion for immediate execution. The sentence was not supposed to be carried out at least until Monsieur Réal could interrogate him on one important point."

And he repeated: "It's beyond me! This is a crime that gets us nowhere. And it makes me appear odious!"

Shortly after eleven, Admiral Truguet, knowing nothing about the fatal turn of events, also arrived at La Malmaison, he to report to the First Consul on the proposed reorganization of the fleet in Brest. Because the First Consul was in close conversation with Savary, the admiral went into the drawing room and there found Madame Bonaparte weeping hot tears in great despair. She had just learned of the prince's execution, and she could not conceal her fears as to the consequences of this terrible catastrophe.

The admiral himself, upon hearing such unexpected news, began to tremble; he trembled more when he was told the First Consul was ready for him. As he passed through the dining room on his way to Bonaparte's study, the aides-de-camp invited him to share their lunch, but even if he'd had the time, he now had no appetite. He showed the aides his portfolio, he indicated that he was in a hurry, but he seemed unable to speak a word.

On finally reaching Bonaparte's study, he managed to say, with great effort, "Citizen First Consul, I have come to give you my report on the fleet in Brest."

"Thank you," said Bonaparte, still pacing up and down. Then, stopping, he said, "Well, Truguet. There is one less Bourbon."

"Bah!" said Truguet. "By chance has Louis XVIII died?"

"No. Nothing like that at all!" said Bonaparte heatedly. "I had the Duc d'Enghien arrested in Ettenheim. I had him brought to Paris, and at six o'clock this morning he was shot at Vincennes."

"What could the purpose of such a harsh act be?" Truguet asked.

"Well," said Bonaparte, "it was time to put an end to all the attempts being made on my life. Now nobody can say that I am trying to play the role of a Monck."

Shortly thereafter, Bourrienne, out of concern regarding Madame Bonaparte's condition, sent her a note asking if she could receive him. The return message being affirmative, Bourrienne hastened to La Malmaison, and as soon as he arrived he was introduced into the boudoir where Josephine sat in company with Madame Louis Bonaparte and Madame de Rémusat. All three were inconsolable in their grief.

"Ah! Bourrienne," Madame Bonaparte cried out when he appeared, "what a dreadful misfortune! If only you knew the state the First Consul has recently been in! He avoids us all; he seems to fear the presence of anyone. Who could have inspired him to such a deed?"

Bourrienne shared with the three women all the details he'd learned about the execution through Harel. "How cruel!" cried Josephine when he'd finished. "At least nobody can lay any blame with me, for I tried to dissuade him from such a sinister plan. Not that he had told me anything about it, but you know how I can always sense things. He admitted to everything, but if only you knew how harshly he treated me and how cruelly he refused to consider a single one of my supplications! I clung to him, I threw myself at his feet. 'Mind your own business,' he shouted angrily. 'This is not a woman's business. Leave me alone!' And he pushed me away with violence I had not seen since he returned from Egypt.

"What must Paris be thinking? I am sure that everywhere the people are cursing him, for here even his flatterers are in consternation. You know how he is when he is displeased with himself, how he tries to display the opposite. Nobody dares speak to him, the mood surrounding him is so somber.

"Here is a shock of hair and a gold ring that the poor prince begs me to send to someone who was dear to him. The lieutenant he gave them to passed them on to Savary, who gave them to me. Savary had tears in his eyes when he related to me the duke's last moments. He was so upset as to be embarrassed as he said, wiping his eyes: 'Ah, madame. It is unfortunate, but you cannot see a man like that die without feeling strong emotion.'"

Monsieur de Chateaubriand, who had not yet left for his embassy post in Le Valais, was strolling through the Tuileries gardens when he heard a man and woman shouting out the official news. The words stopped passersby in their tracks, as if they'd been petrified: "Judgment by the special military commission gathered in Vincennes, ordering the death sentence for Louis-Antoine-Henri de Bourbon, Duc d'Enghien, born in Chantilly on August 2, 1772."

Chateaubriand felt like he'd been struck by lightning, and for a moment he was as petrified as everyone else. When he got back home, he sat down immediately at his table and wrote out his resignation, which he sent to Bonaparte that very same day.

Bonaparte recognized Monsieur de Chateaubriand's handwriting. He turned the letter over several times in his hands without opening it. Finally he broke the seal, and after reading the letter, he angrily tossed it down on the table. "All the better!" he spat. "That man and I would never have been able to get along. He represents the past; I am the future."

Madame Bonaparte had been right to worry about the effect produced by the news of the Duc d'Enghien's death.

When the criers spread the news, Paris answered with a din of disapproval. Rumor spread. No one talked about the Duc d'Enghien's "sentence"; instead, the city talked about his "murder." Nor did anyone believe the prince was guilty in the least.

People began to make pilgrimages to the prince's grave. The authorities had been careful to cover the grave with sod, and no one would have been able to determine exactly where the unfortunate prince was buried if it had not been for the dog that was always lying at the spot. The pilgrims would stand looking at the grave until tears clouded their vision; then they would call out quietly: "Fidèle! Fidèle! Fidèle!" And the sad animal would answer them with long, mournful howls.

One morning the pilgrims searched in vain for Fidèle. The dog had become worrisome to the police. And had disappeared.

XLII

Suicide

WE RETURN TO PICHEGRU, who had at first denied everything. But once he had been identified by Moreau's personal valet as the man who always under mysterious circumstances would visit his master and be greeted respectfully—in his presence people doffed their hats—he stopped denying and linked his fortune to that of George Cadoudal.

At the Temple, Pichegru was placed in a room on the ground floor. The head of his bed stood against the window, which allowed him enough light to read by. Just outside the window a sentinel was stationed to watch whatever transpired in the room.

Only a small antechamber separated George and Pichegru. At night a gendarme remained in the antechamber, the key to which was held by the concierge, so even the gendarme was locked in, although he could give alarm or ask for help through the window. Standing by the door was another sentinel, whose post enabled him, if necessary, to alert the sentry box, which in turn was equipped to alert the concierge.

Pichegru was separated, too, by a partition from the room where Monsieur Bouvet de Lozier, the man who had tried to hang himself, was being held. Finally, three or four steps away to the right, on the vestibule, was the door to George's room, which was kept open day and night so that he was never out of the sight of two gendarmes and a brigadier.

For a time Pichegru also had in his room two gendarmes who observed his every move. After his conversation with Monsieur Réal, he asked if the two gendarmes could be removed, because their presence made him uncomfortable. The request was passed along to Bonaparte, who said with a shrug, "Why bother him for nothing? The gendarmes are there not to keep him from escaping but to keep him from killing himself, and a man who seriously wants to kill himself can always find a way."

They allowed Pichegru a pen and some ink, and he went about his work. The overtures made to him about draining Guyana had pleased him enormously. With his double-barreled imagination, that of a strategist and of a numbers man, along with the memories of his travels and hunting in the Guyana interior, he probably could readily picture himself at work there, and happily so.

Bonaparte's presentiment that Pichegru might be contemplating another, more fatal plan in regard to himself was not without basis. The Marquis de Rivière would later recall for Monsieur Réal and Monsieur Desmarets that one evening when he was walking through Paris with Pichegru, both of them fearing going home as much as being surprised in the streets, the general had stopped suddenly, and placing his pistol to his forehead, he had said, "Well, there is no reason to go any farther, let's stop right here."

Grabbing Pichegru by the arm, Monsieur de Rivière had pulled the pistol away from him and begged him to agree that for the time being at least he would not try to kill himself. Monsieur de Rivière had then taken the general to the home of a lady who was giving him shelter at her place in the Rue des Noyers. There Pichegru had laid his dagger on a table and said, "Another evening like that and it would be the end."

Charles Nodier, as he remembers the Revolution, tells a curious anecdote that would seem to foreshadow what was to take place eleven years later in the Temple prison. Pichegru often wore, as did all his staff, a black silk necktie with a small knot close to his neck. To distinguish himself from the *merveilleux* of the day, who wore voluminous ties like Saint-Just, the young man had made a point of tying his tie with one knot on the right-hand side. Under orders to sleep fully dressed, Pichegru and his two secretaries shared the same room, each with his own mattress on the floor, although Pichegru himself slept little and rarely went to bed before three or four in the morning.

One night Nodier was having trouble sleeping—he was dreaming that some Indian thugs were strangling him—and in his nightmare he felt a hand slip around his neck and begin untying his tie. He awakened with a start and opened his eyes. The general was kneeling beside him. "What? Is that you, General?" he asked. "Do you need me?"

"No," the general answered. "You are the one who needed me. You were struggling in your sleep, moaning. It was not hard to find out why. Your tie is tied too tightly; you need to loosen it a bit before you go to sleep, because otherwise you could cause yourself apoplexy or sudden death. It is a way to commit suicide."

During Monsieur Réal's visit with Pichegru, after they had talked about the colonization of Guyana, Monsieur Réal asked him if he wanted anything.

"Yes, books!" Pichegru had responded.

"History books?" Réal asked.

"My goodness no! I'm fed up with history. Send me Seneca. I am like the gambler."

"General," laughed Monsieur Réal, "the gambler asks for Seneca only when he's lost his last game. You are not yet at that point."

Pichegru also asked if they might have a portrait that was particularly dear to him. Monsieur Desmarets proved to be agreeable until someone pointed out that the portrait had been inventoried along with other items in evidence for the trial. So Pichegru received only the book. Finding the reasons for retaining the portrait to be poor, Pichegru said to the concierge, "Well, I have to believe, then, that Monsieur Réal was just playing games with me when he talked about Cayenne." Still, he impatiently awaited Monsieur Réal's next visit.

In the meantime, all the business about the Duc d'Enghien had been occupying Monsieur Réal. Loaded down with work, he never found the time to pay the general a second visit. That is when Pichegru must have decided to commit suicide.

He complained about the cold. Since there was a fireplace in his room, the concierge had the guards build a fire. They brought in an extra bundle of kindling so that it would be easier to restart the fire when it died down. Two days later, when they came into his room in the morning, they found Pichegru lying motionless on his bed. They called out to him. He was dead!

An hour after that, at about eight in the morning, Savary, who was on duty in the Tuileries, received a note from the officer in command of the guard post at the Temple that day. He was alerting Savary that a few minutes earlier General Pichegru had been discovered dead in his bed and that they were waiting for someone from the police department to certify the death and determine what had happened. Savary immediately sent the note to the First Consul, who summoned him, thinking that he might have additional information. As that was not the case, he said, "Quick, go get some more details! Damn! A lovely death for the man who conquered Holland!"

Savary did not waste a minute. He arrived at the Temple at the same time as Monsieur Réal, who had been sent by the grand judge to learn the details of the event. No one had yet entered the room except the guard who had discovered the accident. Escorted to the bed on which the general lay, Monsieur Réal and Savary identified him easily, although his face had turned deeply red as a result of the apoplexy.

The general was lying on his right side. Around his neck his tie was twisted like a small cable. Apparently he had knotted the tie around his neck, and after tightening it as much as possible, he had evidently taken a piece of kindling, maybe fifteen centimeters long, from the bundle by the fireplace, then forced the stick through the knot and twisted it until the silk tie was so tight that he began to lose consciousness. When his head fell to his pillow, with his weight pressing down on the stick, it would have been impossible for the knot to loosen. Apoplexy would not long have been long in coming. His hand was still on the little tourniquet beneath his neck.

Nearby, on the nightstand, a book lay open, as if someone's reading had been momentarily interrupted. It was the Seneca Monsieur Réal had sent him, and on the last page Pichegru would in all probability have read, Seneca says: "The man who wants to conspire must first of all not fear to die." The general must have believed, especially once the rumor of the Duc d'Enghien's death had reached him, that his only options were to appeal to the First Consul's clemency or to die. He'd made the choice.

Réal and Savary immediately questioned anyone who might be able to provide them details about Pichegru's strange and unexpected death; for Savary's first thought was that Bonaparte might be accused of killing the general. Savary started with the gendarme who had spent the night in the antechamber that separated George and Pichegru. The man had heard nothing at all during the night, he said, except that at about one in the morning Pichegru had been coughing incessantly. Because he could not get into the room to check on the beneral, he himself having been locked in the antechamber, he deemed it unnecessary to wake up the entire tower for only a cough. The gendarme posted by Pichegru's window offered Savary and Réal even less. He should have been able to see everything that happened in the prisoner's room, but in fact he had seen nothing.

Monsieur Réal was beginning to get desperate. "Even though we can absolutely prove that this was a suicide," he said, "whatever we do, people will still say that since we could not sway the prisoner, we had him strangled." And that's what people did indeed say, although they were mistaken.

And there was nothing that could have made the case against Moreau more difficult. The First Consul had really no reason to destroy Pichegru; he had plans for the general that would not only preserve his life but also increase Bonaparte's own popularity. By granting a pardon to Pichegru, his teacher at Brienne, and in addition, by sending him on an honorable mission to Cayenne, Bonaparte would have neutralized the ill effects of whatever punishment he should mete out to Moreau. Bonaparte hardly held the same grievances against Pichegru that he bore, rightly or wrongly, against Moreau. Furthermore, just when he was bearing the full weight of the Duc d'Enghien's sentence on his shoulders was not the time to be so recklessly augmenting the negative sentiments of the public. Bonaparte would have been horrified even by the suggestion of murdering Pichegru so odiously during the night.

"Ah," said the First Consul the next time he saw Réal as he pounded the table with his fist, "when I think that to colonize Guyana all he was asking for was six million negroes and six million francs!"

XLIII
The Trial

THAT POLICE MEASURES in regard to George Cadoudal had so carefully placed the peace officer Caniolle at the foot of the Montagne Sainte-Geneviève to wait for a cabriolet with the number 53 due to come by between seven and eight; that, at seven, he was able to spot the cabriolet and follow it to a door in an alley near a fruit-seller's shop; that, at seven-thirty, four people, including George and Le Ridant, emerged in the alley; and finally, that George was arrested on the basis of such exact information—all that was because, from London to Paris, and every day from the day he had arrived in Paris until Friday, March 9, George had never been out of sight of the most intelligent among Citizen Fouché's agents, the man known as the Limousin.

Fouché knew that George was not the kind of man to surrender without resorting to pistols or knife, and he had not wanted to expose his precious

Limousin to any danger from the fiery Breton chief's anger. Yet, not fully anticipating Cadoudal's reaction, he'd had him apprehended by married men rather than bachelors.

Fouché received the news of George's arrest at about nine-thirty in the evening. He shared it with the Limousin, who had been waiting in the next room. "You have heard the news," Fouché said when he'd finished, and before he added, "Now the only ones we still must capture are Villeneuve and Burban."

"Whenever you wish, we can take them. I know where they live."

"For them, we have plenty of time. However, do not lose sight of them."

"Did I ever let George out of my sight?"

"No."

"Will you allow me to mention one thing you yourself have lost sight of?"

"Me?"

"Yes."

"What is that?"

"George's money. When we left London, he was carrying one hundred thousand francs."

"Can you take responsibility for finding that money?"

"I shall do what I can. However, nothing disappears faster than money."

"Begin looking for it this evening then."

"Am I free until tomorrow at the same time?"

"Tomorrow I have a meeting with the First Consul at this time. I would not be sorry to be able to answer all of his questions."

The next evening, at nine-thirty, Fouché was on his way to the Tuileries, where he found the First Consul calm and in great spirits.

(This was before the decision had been made to arrest the Duc d'Enghien, let us not forget. In going back to George's arrest, we have taken a step backward in time.)

"Why were you not the one who came to tell me about George's arrest?" Bonaparte asked.

"Because," Fouché answered, "we need to allow other people to do a few things."

"Do you know the circumstances of the arrest?"

"He killed an agent named Buffet and wounded another named Caniolle."

"Apparently both were married."

"Yes."

"We must do something for the wives of those poor devils."

"I have thought of that. A pension for the widow and a bonus for the wounded man's wife."

"In all good conscience England should be paying."

"England will be paying."

"What do you mean?"

"England or Cadoudal. But, since Cadoudal's money is England's money, in fact, it will be England paying the pension."

"But I was told that he had only a thousand or twelve hundred francs on him, and that when they searched his house, they found nothing."

"He left London with one hundred thousand francs, and he spent thirty thousand since reaching Paris. So he still had seventy thousand, and that is more than enough for a widow's pension and a bonus for the wounded man."

"But where are those seventy thousand francs?" Bonaparte asked.

"Right here," said Fouché. On the table he placed a small sack of gold and bank notes.

Bonaparte emptied the sack of its contents and, with great interest, counted forty thousand francs in Dutch sovereigns; the rest was in paper money. "Well, how about that!" said Bonaparte. "Now Holland is paying my assassins."

"Not really; they are afraid that English gold might raise suspicions."

"And how did you get your hands on such a sum?"

"You know the old police maxim: *'Cherchez la femme!'*"

"Well?"

"I looked for the woman and found her."

"Tell me about that. Today I'm very curious."

"Well, I knew that a certain Izaï, a low-class courtesan, had attached herself to the conspirators and had rented a room from the fruit-seller where they would be meeting. She was following them into the alley when George climbed into the cabriolet. He seems to have suspected they were being watched, and he had just enough time to toss to her the sack he was carrying. She put it in her apron; he'd already shouted: 'To Caron the perfume seller!' Caniolle heard George's command, and as he prepared to pursue George he shouted to another agent, 'Follow that girl.'"

"Meaning what?" Bonaparte asked.

"Meaning follow that prostitute and don't lose sight of her. The girl wandered around through the streets and eventually came to the Carrefour de l'Odéon, at the very moment George was being arrested. A huge crowd had gathered, with everyone talking about the incident, and she dared not try to get through. Things got worse for her when she learned that it was

George who had been arrested, for she didn't dare return home. She took refuge with a friend, whom she asked to keep the package. I sent my men to that friend's house and found the package, and that was it. By God, it was no more difficult than that."

"And did you not arrest the girl?"

"Yes, we did. We had no further use for her. But what a saintly girl," Fouché added. "Heaven should have granted her better protection."

"Why do you say that, monsieur?" said Bonaparte with a frown. "You know that I don't appreciate ungodliness."

"But you don't know what the woman was wearing around her neck," Fouché answered the First Consul.

"How could you expect me to know something like that?" asked Bonaparte, who, in spite of himself, allowed his curiosity to draw him down the inconsequential path of Fouché's conversation, for Bonaparte lacked any ability to listen to almost anyone with even short patience.

"Well, she was wearing a medallion with this inscription: 'Piece of the true cross venerated in the Sainte-Chapelle de Paris and in the church of Saint-Pierre de Lille.'"

"That's good," said Bonaparte. "Send the girl to Saint-Lazare. And let the children of poor Buffet and Caniolle meanwhile be raised at government expense. You will give fifty thousand francs of the money you found at the home of the girl's friend to Buffet's widow and the rest to Caniolle. I shall add an annuity of one thousand francs from my own pocket for the Widow Buffet."

"Do you want her to die of joy?"

"Why do you say that?"

"Because she would have been satisfied enough with her husband's death."

"I don't understand," said Bonaparte impatiently.

"What? You don't understand that her husband was a scoundrel? That he would get drunk every night and beat his wife every morning. Our George, damn it, has killed two birds with one stone."

"Now that the business of George's arrest is finished," said Bonaparte, "send me the records of his interrogation as soon as you get them. I wish to keep a close watch on this whole affair."

"Here is the first report," said Fouché. "It is not like the Virgils and Horaces we give to students of the Oratorians in Paimboeuf, *ad usum Delphini*. No, it is pure, and the words come straight from George and Monsieur Réal themselves."

"Are the reports of these interrogations sometimes changed?"

"Have you not noticed that orators' speeches never read the same in *Le*

Moniteur as they sounded from the platform? Well, that is also true of these reports. We do not change them, but we do improve them."

XLIV

In the Temple

꠶꠶

FOUCHÉ HANDED A SHEET of paper to the First Consul. Bonaparte took it eagerly and, skipping the first questions, mere formalities required by the law, he started reading at the fourth.

"How long have you been in Paris?"

"Five or six months. I couldn't say exactly."

"Where have you been lodging?"

"Nowhere."

"What was your reason for coming to Paris?"

"To attack the First Consul."

"With a dagger?"

"No, with weapons similar to those carried by his own escort."

"Explain yourself."

"My officers and I counted Bonaparte's guards one by one. There are thirty of them. I and twenty-nine of my men were going to engage them in hand-to-hand combat after stretching two ropes across the Champs-Elysées to stop the escort and swooping down on them with pistols drawn. And then, sure of our right and fortified by our courage, we would have let God accomplish the rest."

"Who asked you to come back to France?"

"The princes. One of them was to join us as soon as I wrote that I had sufficient means to attain my goal."

"Whom did you meet with in Paris?"

"Allow me not to answer. I do not want to increase the number of your victims."

"Was Pichegru involved in your plans to attack the First Consul?"

"No. He refused to have anything to do with it."

"But, supposing that your plans had succeeded, might Pichegru have done something to benefit from the First Consul's death?"

"That is his secret, not mine."

"Supposing that your attack had succeeded, what plans did you and your fellow conspirators have?"

"To replace the First Consul with a Bourbon."

"And who was the Bourbon so designated?"

"Louis-Xavier-Stanislas, ci-devant Monsieur, whom we recognize as Louis XVIII."

"So the ci-devant French princes were in agreement with your plan and the manner in which you were to carry it out?"

"Yes, Citizen Counselor."

"Who was supposed to furnish the money and weapons?"

"The money had been in my possession for a long time. But I had no weapons."

Bonaparte turned the page over. There was nothing on the other side: at that point the interrogation ended.

"These plans are absurd," he said. "Trying to attack me with numbers equal to those of my escort."

"Can you complain about that?" asked Fouché with a smirk. "They had no desire to assassinate you. They wanted only to kill you. It would have been like another Combat of Thirty, a kind of medieval duel with seconds."

"A duel with George?"

"You were willing to fight Moreau without any witnesses."

"Moreau was Moreau, Monsieur Fouché, a great general, a taker of cities, a conqueror. If his retreat, returning to the French border from the heart of Germany, made him the equal of Xenophon, his battle at Hohenlinden made him the equal of Hoche and Pichegru, whereas George is no more than a bandit chief, a kind of Royalist Spartacus, a man whom one protects himself from but not whom one fights. Do not forget that, Monsieur Fouché."

At that, Bonaparte stood up. The work session with Fouché was over.

News of both the Duc d'Enghien's execution and Pichegru's suicide hit Paris in the space of a few days, and we must say that the cruel execution of the one made it difficult to believe the suicide of the other.

It was in the Temple, among the prisoners, that the news produced especially disastrous effects, and Réal's prediction to Savary, as they stood before Pichegru's dead body, came to pass: "Even though we can absolutely prove that this was a suicide," he'd said, "whatever we do, people will still say that since we could not sway the prisoner, we had him strangled."

One man, the Swiss bookseller Fauche-Borel, who had brought to Pichegru the Prince de Condé's first offers, had been arrested and brought to the Temple on July 1, 1803.

In turn, Moreau, Pichegru, and George had followed in the winter months of 1804, along with all the others involved in that grand conspiracy: Joyaut, who went by the name of Villeneuve; Roger, who used the name L'Oiseau; and finally even Coster Saint-Victor, who had escaped the police by changing his place of residence nightly, thanks to the help of all his lovely courtesans. When consulted about the elusive Saint-Victor, Fouché had recommended, "Place a man who can recognize him at Frascati's door, and you won't have to wait three days before you'll get him going in or coming out." On the second day, they got Coster Saint-Victor on his way out.

At the time of the Duc d'Enghien's arrest, one hundred and seven prisoners were being held in the Temple; the prison was so full, in fact, that there was no room for the prince. That is why he had to wait five hours at the barriers at the entrance to the city, until a temporary room was found for him at Vincennes, where he could be held while waiting for that room, as the gravedigger in *Hamlet* says, he could keep until the last judgment.

There was not a single prisoner in the Temple who was not absolutely convinced that Pichegru had been killed. Fauche-Borel not only asserts that Pichegru was strangled, he even names his stranglers. He writes (in 1807): "I was convinced that the killing was done by a man named Spon, brigadier in the elite company, along with two guards, one of whom, though he was in excellent health, died two days later, and the other, named Savard, was found to be one of the 1792 Septembrists."

Weighed upon by their conviction that someone in the Temple guard had strangled Pichegru under orders, the prisoners became suspicious when General Savary arrived there in full dress uniform and in the company of his entire, large staff, as well as Louis Bonaparte. They had come to see George Cadoudal, who, at that moment, had just been shaved. He was lying on his bed, his hands, in manacles, resting on his stomach. He and the two gendarmes guarding him virtually filled up the tiny tower room where he'd been placed after Pichegru's death; yet Savary and his staff crowded in. If they were gratififed by the Royalist general's present sad situation, he himself was mostly impatient to see them leave. And when they did, finally, after observing him and whispering among themselves for ten minutes, George asked the two gendarmes, "Why all those fancy uniforms?"

"That was the First Consul's brother," one of them answered, "along with General Savary and his whole staff."

"It's a good thing you had me in handcuffs," said George.

As preparations for the trial neared their completion, discipline in the Temple seemed to relax. The prisoners were allowed to leave their rooms and gather in the garden, although that did little to alter their antipathy, and often unconcealed hostility, toward Savary. He'd had free rein at the Temple since it had become a military prison, so naturally he was hated by all the prisoners. Still, loathing did not prevent him from appearing perhaps more often than he should have. One day, as Moreau was leaving his room, he came face to face with Savary, and with no acknowledgment, whirling around, he turned his back on Savary and shut the door.

As for General Moreau, there was nothing stranger or more touching than the deep respect he seemed to command from all the military men who were currently serving inside the prison. They would touch their hats and acknowledge him with a military salute. If he sat down, they would gather around him, and if he proved to be willing speak to them, they would humbly ask him to recount some of the glorious feats of arms that had set him above all the other generals and made him Bonaparte's rival. The prisoners were convinced that if he had called these soldiers of the Consulate to his aid, they would have rushed to open up the Temple doors for him and marched out behind him. No longer treated so strictly as the other prisoners, Moreau was allowed to see his young wife and child daily. From time to time he was presented with some excellent Clos-Vougeot wine, which he would always share with the sick, and with the not-so-sick too. Anyone who got sweaty playing royal tennis or prisoner's base was counted among the sick and got his glass of Clos-Vougeot.

What distinguished George and his companions from the other prisoners was their happy, carefree nature. They would play like schoolboys during recess, especially Coster de Saint-Victor and Roger, called L'Oiseau, who were two of the most handsome and elegant men in all of Paris. One day, during a game of prisoner's base, Roger had gotten exceptionally sweaty and pulled off his tie. "Did you know," Saint-Victor said to him, "that you have a neck like Antinous?"

"Well," Roger rejoined, "it's hardly worth complimenting me for it. In a week it will be chopped off."

Everything was soon ready for the defendants to appear before the criminal court and for the public debate to begin. The accused in these proceedings numbered fifty-seven. They received the order to be prepared for transfer to the Conciergerie.

The Temple took on a completely new aspect. The fifty-seven named defendants were heady with the prospect of ending their captivity, which for some would also be ending their life. They sang at the top of their lungs as they closed their trunks and tied up parcels. Some were singing; others were whistling. All of them were vying with each other in making loud, joyful noise. Sad, pensive thoughts oppressed only those who would be left behind in the Temple prison.

XLV

In the Courtroom

GEORGE HAD BEEN not only the most joyous but, we might say, also the craziest of all the prisoners. He had participated in every game, and when their repertory had been exhausted, he'd invented new ones. He had told the most fantastic stories, as with mordant wit and boundless verve he'd mocked the new empire now rising from the rubble of Louis XVI's throne. He had joyously sung farewell to the sinking ship that was the republic. But then came the hour when, he realized, he and his companions would have to pay personally for their Royalist loyalties, and he ceased playing, laughing, and singing. He sat down in a corner of the garden, gathered his aides-de-camp and officers around him, and spoke to them in a firm but affectionate tone:

"My good friends, my dear children, I have set the example for cheerfulness and unconcern up to this point. But now allow me to urge you, when you are in the courtroom, to maintain all the poise, sangfroid, and dignity you can muster. You will be appearing before men who believe they have the right to determine what is your freedom, your honor, and your life. I urge you especially never to answer with haste, anger, or arrogance any questions your judges put to you. Answer fearlessly, calmly, directly. Consider yourselves to be the judges of your judges. And should you feel that you're somehow not strong enough, remember that I am with you and that my fate will be no different from yours. If you live, I shall live; if you die, I too shall die.

"Be gentle, be indulgent, be brotherly one with another. Especially be affectionate and considerate. Do not blame each other for having been drawn into danger. For each man must answer for himself when the time for death approaches. May each man die well!

"Here in this prison, as in the years before, you have all undergone different experiences. Some have been good and some have been bad for you; for some men have called you friends while others have named you brigands. Give thanks both to those who have treated you well and to those who have treated you ill. Walk out of this prison with gratitude toward the first and without hatred for the second. Remember that our good king Louis XVI, who lived as you have lived in this same tower, was condemned as a traitor and a tyrant. Our Lord Jesus Christ himself "—and at the name of Christ they all raised their hats with one hand and made the sign of the cross with the other—"even our Lord Jesus Christ was reviled as an agitator and an impostor, was mocked and slapped and whipped. For especially when men are acting badly, they mistake the value of words and try to insult those whom truly they should exalt."

Rising to his feet, Cadoudal said "Amen" and crossed himself. The others did likewise. Then, pointing to the tower and calling them each by name, he had them file past him one by one, before he himself fell in behind them.

That same day, after the fifty-seven prisoners linked to the Moreau, Cadoudal, and Pichegru conspiracy had been transferred, only the secondary accomplices, those who had given the conspirators shelter or guided them in their nighttime activities, were left in the Temple. Not only were they now granted permission to walk in the courtyard and gardens, but they were also allowed to visit all the rooms and cells in the Temple; so for several days the prison was a noisy, tumultuous place. Moreover, on Palm Sunday, they were encouraged to organize a ball in the reception room, from which all the beds had been removed to provide them space to dance and sing.

The ball took place the same day the defendants appeared in court, though the dancers were not aware of that coincidence. One of them, a man named Leclère, was enjoying himself as much as the others, until he learned from a guard that the arguments, which would lead twelve of the defendants to their deaths, had begun. He rushed into the midst of his comrades and, stamping his feet loudly, called for silence. The room fell quiet.

"You miserable brutes!" Leclère admonished them. "Is it this kind of life you would pursue in this damnable prison when the very men who were living here among us and who have only recently left are soon to die? Now is the time for praying and chanting the *De profundis*, not for dancing and singing profane songs. Here is a man with a holy book in his hands. Let him read to us something edifying, something that speaks to our souls about death."

The man was Fauche-Borel's nephew, by name Vitel, and the book he bore was by Bourdaloue. It did not contain the *De profundis*, but it did have a sermon on death. To read it, Vitel climbed up on a table, and, forgoing frolic, all those good men listened to the whole sermon on their knees.

Elsewhere, the city was restive. Never before, not even during Vendémiaire or on the 18th Brumaire, had Bonaparte found himself in such a precarious position. To be sure, he had lost none of his reputation as a genius on the battlefield, but the death of the Duc d'Enghien had struck his prestige as a statesman a terrible blow. Added to that was Pichegru's problematic suicide, for the more that General Savary and the government laid out their proofs, one after the other, to demonstrate suicide, the more people doubted them, especially when forensic pathologists were claiming such a suicide to be impossible. And then came the Consulate's very unpopular accusations against Moreau, which the people quickly linked with the execution of the Duc d'Enghien that the government admitted and the killing of Pichegru that it denied.

What everyone saw clearly in the charges against Moreau was the First Consul's hateful envy of a rival. So certain was Bonaparte that Moreau would maintain his power with the populace even in the dock that there were long discussions to determine the number of guards to assign to him in the event of an uprising. Indeed, Bonaparte was worried enough that he forgave the grievances he held against Bourrienne and recalled him from exile to attend the court debates and report on them each evening to the First Consul.

What Bonaparte wanted above all, now that the Duc d'Enghien had been shot and Pichegru strangled, was for Moreau be found guilty and given a sentence that he, in turn, could pardon. So he sent out feelers to several judges intimating that he only wanted Moreau to be convicted so that he could then be pardoned by the First Consul. The feelers went no further than Judge Clavier, who replied: "And who then will grant us pardon?"

On the first day of the trial crowds flooded the streets around the Palais de Justice. Anyone of any importance in the capital strove to attend. The fact that there was no jury for the trial indicated how vital was the outcome for the government. At ten in the morning, the crowd parted to allow the twelve judges of the criminal court to pass. Dressed in their long red robes, they proceeded to the designated courtroom in the Palais and solemnly assumed their seats.

The twelve judges were Hémard, president; Martineau, vice-president; Thuriot, whom the Royalists called Tueroi (king killer); Lecourbe, the brother of the general with the same name; Clavier, who wittily addressed the issue of convictions and pardons; Bourguignon, Dameu, Laguillaumie, Rigault, Selves, and Grangeret-Desmaisons. The public prosecutor was Gérard; Frémyn was the clerk. Eight bailiffs had been assigned to the court, and the Temple doctor, Souppé, as well as the surgeon at the Conciergerie, had been ordered not to leave the courtroom.

The president called the defendants in. One by one they entered, each between two gendarmes. Among them was Bouvet de Lozier, his eyes downcast, not daring to look at those whom his failed suicide had betrayed. All the others wore countenances serious and confident.

Seated in the dock, Moreau appeared to be calm, distant, as if lost in daydreams. He was dressed in a long blue frock coat cut military style, but he was wearing nothing to indicate his rank. Seated nearby, separated from him only by the gendarmes, were Lajolais, his former aide-de-camp, and the handsome, young Charles d'Hozier, so elegantly dressed that he might have been going to a royal ball. George, whom everyone considered the most noteworthy of the defendants, was easily recognized by his huge head and powerful shoulders; with a steady, proud gaze he stared at each of the judges in turn as if he were challenging them to the death. At his side was Burban, who in battle used the names Malabry and Barco; and next to him, Pierre Cadoudal, known all over the Morbihan only as Bras-de-Fer, for he could fell an ox with his fist. The two Polignacs and the Marquis de Rivière, seated in the second row, attracted considerable attention because of their good looks, youth, and elegance, but all of them were outstripped by the handsome Coster Saint-Victor, who was seated next to Roger called L'Oiseau, the same man who prized his own handsome neck so lightly.

Legend had it that Coster Saint-Victor had earned Bonaparte's hatred not out of rivalry on the battlefield, as was the case with Moreau, but out of rivalry in love. Supposedly, they had run into each other in the bedroom of one of France's loveliest and most famous actresses at the time, and Coster Saint-Victor, pretending not to recognize the First Consul, had refused to yield his ground and thus remained master not on the field of battle but on the field of love.

The third bench seated those brave Chouans who had become involved in the whole affair because of their devotion to Cadoudal and the cause. They knew they had been risking their lives if they failed; had they succeeded, they would have returned to their simplicity of life in forest and field.

Among the forty-six defendants, to which the original fifty-seven had been reduced, were five women: the Denaud woman, the Dubuisson woman, the Gallois woman, the Monier woman, and the prostitute Izaï, to whom Cadoudal had entrusted the seventy thousand francs that Fouché used to pay a pension to the Widow Buffet and a bonus to Caniolle's wife.

The president began the interrogation by questioning the five witnesses—policemen and private citizens—who had helped arrest George. After they had made their depositions, the president addressed George.

"George," he asked, "do you have anything to say?"

"No," George answered, without looking up from the paper he was reading.

"Do you agree with the charges against you?"

"I agree," George answered, with no concern.

"The defendant George is requested not to read while he is being spoken to," said Thuriot, the examining magistrate.

"But what I am reading is quite interesting," George answered. "It is the official record of the session on January 17, 1793, during which you voted for the king's death."

Thuriot bit his lips. A murmur ran through the courtroom. The president quickly cut things short by continuing his interrogation: "You agree," he said to George, "that you were arrested at the place the witnesses have identified?"

"I do not know the name of the place."

"With your pistols, did you shoot twice?"

"I do not remember."

"Did you kill a man?"

"Really, I have no idea."

"You were carrying a dagger."

"That is possible."

"And two pistols?"

"Perhaps."

"Who was with you in the cabriolet?"

"I do not remember."

"Where were you living in Paris?"

"Nowhere."

"At the time of your arrest, did you not have lodgings in Rue de la Montagne-Sainte-Geneviève, with a fruit-seller?"

"At the time of my arrest I had lodgings in my cabriolet."

"Where did you sleep the night before your arrest?"

"The night before my arrest I did not go to bed."

"What were you doing in Paris?"

"I was strolling around."

"Did you see anyone else?"

"A multitude of tattletales who were following me."

"You can see that the defendant is refusing to answer," said the examining magistrate. "Move on to someone else."

"Thank you, Monsieur Thuriot. . . . Gendarmes, would you please have someone bring me a glass of water?" George asked. "After pronouncing the name Thuriot, I always like to rinse my mouth out."

One can understand how such interrogation might have aroused in the audience responses of both hatred and hilarity toward the government, and of sympathy toward George. In a sense, he had already sacrificed his life, and he was accorded the respect customarily extended to those who have been sentenced to death.

For four days everyone waited impatiently for interrogation of Moreau. Finally, on Thursday, May 31, Judge Thuriot began by introducing several witnesses for the prosecution, none of whom could identify Moreau. Thus, with a smile, the accused said disdainfully, "Gentlemen, not only can no prosecution witness identify me, but none of the defendants had ever seen me before I was incarcerated in the Temple."

They then read him the deposition made by Roland, one of Pichegru's men, who had declared during his interrogation that it had been painful for him when Pichegru had charged him with a mission to Moreau and that it had been even more painful when he had carried it out. The deposition brought Moreau to his feet; he addressed the president: "Either Roland is attached to the police," he said, "or he made that statement out of fear. I shall tell you how things went between the examining magistrate and him.

"He was not interrogated. No, they got nothing out of him. They said to him, 'You are in a horrible situation. You are going to be an accomplice in the conspiracy or a confidant. If you say nothing, you are an accomplice. If you confess, you'll be saved.' And so, to save his skin, this man concocted the fable you've just read. I ask every man of good faith and good sense, to what purpose would I have conspired?"

"Well," said Hémard, "so that you would be named dictator."

"Me, a dictator?" cried Moreau. "Then produce my supporters. Unless you count all French soldiers, since I have commanded nine-tenths of them and saved the lives of more than fifty thousand: They are my only supporters, my partisans. All of my aides-de-camp have been arrested, and all of my officers; however, no one has discovered even the shadow of a suspicion against them. People have spoken of my fortune. I began with nothing, and maybe I could have fifty million francs, but I own nothing more than a house in Paris and my land in Grosbois. As for my salary as general-in-chief, I earn forty thousand francs, though I trust no one will try to compare that amount to the services I have rendered."

At that moment a strange incident occurred. It seemed to have been pre-arranged between the general and Lecourbe, his aide-de-camp, so that people might see just how powerful the conqueror of Holland still was. Lecourbe walked into the courtroom with a child in his arms, Moreau's son, but the line of soldiers surrounding the courtroom did not recognize the child and refused to let him pass. So, lifting up the child, Lecourbe cried out, "Soldiers! Let your general's son pass." Scarcely had those words been pronounced than every military man in the courtroom presented arms, and the room exploded in applause. Voices cried out, "Long live Moreau!"

If at that moment Moreau had spoken, enthusiasm would have been such that the courtroom would have been overwhelmed and the prisoners would have been carried off in triumph. But Moreau said not a word. Not in any way did he participate in the episode.

"General," said Cadoudal, leaning over to whisper in his ear, "another session like this one and that same evening you will be able to sleep in the Tuileries."

XLVI

The Sentencing

∗∴∗

DURING THE COURT SESSION of June 2, one witness aroused great interest at a moment when it was least expected. The witness was Captain Wright, commander of the little brig that had landed the defendants at the foot of the Biville cliffs. Becalmed within sight of Saint-Malo, he had been attacked by five or six French longboats, and after a fight during which he took a bullet in the arm, he had been taken prisoner. His entrance produced a stir in the audience, with everyone standing on tiptoe so they could see the skinny little man.

He was wearing the uniform of the Royal English Navy, called the blue squadron, and his arm was in a sling. On inquiry, he answered that he was a lieutenant commander, thirty-five years of age, and that he lived in London at the home of his friend Commodore Sidney Smith.

As the witness had trouble standing, they brought him a chair. The captain thanked his judges, but after he was seated, he went so pale that it looked as if he was going to faint. Coster Saint-Victor hastened to offer him a bottle of cologne. Recovering, the captain stood back up and courteously bowed his thanks to Saint-Victor; then, mustering remarkable composure, he turned once more toward the judges.

The president attempted to continue the interrogation, but the captain shook his head: "I was taken following a combat," he said, "and made a prisoner of war. I demand all the rights I am due in my situation."

They read to him the text of his interrogation of May 21, to which the witness listened with undivided attention. Then he said, "Excuse me, Monsieur le Président, but I hear no reference to the threat of making me appear before a military commission and of being shot if I refused to give up my country's secrets."

"George, do you know this witness?" the president asked.

George looked at him and shrugged. "I have never seen him," he said.

"And you, Wright, will you now answer my questions?"

"No," the captain replied. "I am a prisoner of war, and I claim the rights and customs of war."

"Claim anything you want," the president answered. "The trial will continue tomorrow."

It was scarcely noon. Cursing President Hémard's lack of patience, everyone left.

The following day, crowds were already swarming around the Palais de

Justice at seven in the morning. Rumor had it that Moreau would be making a speech when the session opened.

Rumor had it wrong. Instead, though, the spectators were witness to a very touching scene.

The brothers Armand and Jules de Polignac, who'd been seated next to each other, without even a gendarme between them, would frequently squeeze each other's hands as if in their union they could defy the court as well as the death that might soon be separating them. That day, the court had been questioning Jules, and as his responses seemed to be incriminating him, Armand rose to his feet and pled, "Gentlemen, I beg you to look at this child. He is scarcely nineteen years old. Save his life. When he returned to France with me, he was simply accompanying me, nothing more. I alone am guilty, for I alone was conscious of what I was doing. I know you need heads. So take mine, I give it to you. But do not take the head of this young man. Rather than wrench him violently from life, grant him the time to find what he will be missing."

In protest, Jules then stood up and, throwing his arms around Armand's neck, he cried, "Oh, gentlemen! Do not listen to him. It is precisely because I am only nineteen, because I am alone in the world, and because I have neither wife nor children, that the sentence should fall on me. Armand, on the other hand, is a father. When I was very young, almost before I even knew my own country, I was forced to eat the bread of exile. My life outside of France is useless to France and to me. Take my head. I give it to you, but spare the head of my brother."

From that point on, everyone's interest, which until then had been focused on George and Moreau, widened to include all those fine, handsome young men, the last of France to remain loyal to the fallen throne. In them resided the best that the Royalist party, and even all of Paris, could offer in terms of nobility, refinement, and grace. With sympathetic ear the spectators attended their every word.

There was one moment that brought tears to every eye. President Hémard showed Monsieur Rivière the portrait of the Comte d'Artois, asking, "Defendant Rivière, can you identify this miniature?"

"I cannot see it well from here, Monsieur le Président," the marquis answered, "but please be so kind as to have it passed to me."

The president gave the miniature to a bailiff, who handed it to the defendant. No sooner was the portrait in his hands than he brought it to his lips. Then, clutching it to his heart, with a tear-filled voice he cried, "Can you really believe that I could not identify him? My last wish was to kiss him before I die. Now, gentlemen, you may pronounce my sentence, and I will walk to the scaffold blessing you."

Coster Saint-Victor, too, was the cause of some sensation. When the president asked him if had nothing else to say in his defense, he replied, "Yes, indeed. I would like to add that the defense witnesses I requested have not appeared. I also add that I am surprised to see that you are willing to mislead public opinion and pour abuse and shame not only on us defendants, but also on those who would defend us. This morning, when I read today's newspapers, I noticed with great sadness that the words attributed to me were completely false."

"Defendant," said the president, "these details have nothing to do with the case."

"On the contrary," objected Coster. "The protest I am making to the court is closely related to my case and to the case of my poor friends. The newspaper articles have painfully distorted the speeches of the lawyers defending us. As for me, I would be according my defense lawyer ingratitude if I, even when interrupted by the public prosecutor, did not recognize, by the homage I give him now, the zeal and talent he has displayed in my defense. Therefore I protest against the abuse and nonsense that paid tattlers and government scribblers have put in the mouths of these brave citizens for the press. I beg my lawyer, Monsieur Gautier, to receive the homage and gratitude that I owe him, and I ask him to continue to provide his noble, generous help up until the final moment." At that, with immense sympathy, the audience burst into unreserved applause.

Behind Coster Saint-Victor, on the third bench, sat seven Bretons from the Morbihan, distinguishable by their stocky builds and rugged faces that did nothing to conceal the brute forece that was wedded to their keen intelligence. Among them was George's domestic servant, Picot, whose personal vengeance on our soldiers had earned him the epithet Executioner of the Blues. He was a small man with short legs, powerful shoulders, and a pock-marked face. His hair was black, cut short and squared off in front. What gave distinction to his face was the sparkle in his little gray eyes, which were set deep beneath thick red eyebrows.

Scarcely had Coster Saint-Victor finished than Picot stood up, and speaking plainly, employing none of the polite locutions characteristic of his predecessor's social class, he said, "I have nothing to protest, but I do have something to denounce."

"To denounce?" asked the president.

"Yes," Picot went on. "I would like it noted by the court that when I arrived at the prefecture on the day I was arrested, they began by offering me two hundred gold louis, counting them right before my eyes, as well as my freedom, if I would tell them where my master, General George, lived. I said that I did not know, and that was the truth, because the general is always on the move. So Citizen Bertrand told the guard officer to fetch a gun hammer, along with a screwdriver, and then they tied me up and broke my fingers."

"That was a good lesson they gave you," President Hémard said, "and now you choose to tell us all that instead of the truth."

"It is the truth, God's own truth, pure," Picot replied. "The soldiers who were there can confirm it. Was them put my feet to the fire and crushed my fingers."

"You will note, gentlemen," said Thuriot, "that this is the first time the defendant has mentioned these incidents."

"Ah, so you say now," said Picot. "You yourself are well acquainted with the incident. For when I spoke to you in the Temple, was it not you that told me, 'Don't say a word about all that, and we'll take care of everything.'"

"You never mentioned a word to me in your depositions about any of what you are saying today."

"Why I did not was I was afraid you would start in again to mutilate and burn me."

"Defendant," cried the public prosecutor, "you can lie if you want, but at least don't be indecent in the presence of justice."

"Justice be a fine one. Justice wants me to be polite with it, when it won't be just with me."

"Quiet! That's enough!" said Hémard. Then, turning toward George, he said, "Have you anything to add to the words of your defense lawyer?"

"I do have something to add," George replied. "The First Consul did me the honor of granting me an audience, at which we agreed on several points. As carefully as these conditions were observed on my part, they were as baldly violated on the part of the government. Its agents organized burning brigades in the Vendée and the Morbihan. Under my name, they were committing such atrocities that I had no choice but to leave London and come back to Brittany, where I was forced finally to blow out the brains of one of the bands' leaders and identify myself as the real Cadoudal. I then sent my lieutenant Sol de Grisolles to Paris to inform Napoleon Bonaparte that from that day on a vendetta stood in effect between the two of us. He is Corsican, so he surely understood the meaning in that and acted accordingly. That is when I decided to return to France. I do not know if what I have done and what my friends have done constitutes a conspiracy; you know the law better than I do, gentlemen, and I rely on your consciences to judge us."

Another among the defendants was the Abbé David, a friend of Pichegru's, and it was because of that friendship that he now found himself in the prisoner's dock. Poised, placid in his demeanor, he evidenced no fear in the face of death. He rose to his feet; his voice firm, he said, "Pélisson never abandoned superintendent Fouquet when he was banned, and posterity has set him up as model of devotion. I hope that my loyalty to Pichegru during his exile will not prove to be any more harmful for me than was Pélisson's for Fouquet during his detention. The First Consul must have friends. Surely he has many friends, because, except maybe for Sylla, no one has treated his compeers better. Yet, if on the 18th Brumaire he had failed like many before him, he would, I suppose, have been sentenced to death. Or banished perhaps."

"What you are saying lacks common sense!" the president shouted.

"Perhaps banished," David repeated.

"Quiet!" Thuriot shouted.

"I'm sorry, but I must go on," the priest insisted, "and I ask you, in that case, would you blame his friends if they, in spite of his being banished, continued to correspond with him and did whatever was in their power to bring him back to France?"

Thuriot could not stop fidgeting in his seat. "Gentlemen," he shouted angrily, looking over at his colleagues and assessors, "the words we have just heard are totally out of place—"

But the Abbé David interrupted him: "Magistrates," he said with great calm, "my life is in your hands. I do not fear death. I know that during a revolution, when one is trying to remain an honest man, it is necessary to expect, and accept, anything."

As the court session came to an end, the two Polignac brothers again entered poignant pleas. "Gentlemen," said Jules, holding his hands together in supplication and leaning toward the judges, "because I was so emotional on hearing my brother's speech, I was able to give only cursory attention to my own defense. Now that I am calmer, I dare to hope, gentlemen, that what Armand said to you will not persuade you to pay any attention to the wish he formulated in my favor. I repeat, to the contrary, that if a scapegoat is needed, if one of us must succumb, then please save Armand; return him to dry his wife's tears. For I have no wife, and I am prepared to brave death. I am too young to have tasted so much of life that I shall miss it."

"No! No!," Armand shouted, pulling his brother back down to him and pressing him against his breast. "No, you shall not die! It is I who should die. I beg of you, my dear Jules, let the place be mine."

Even as the tender scene between the brothers pained the judges' consciences, the president shouted, "Court is adjourned!"

It was eleven o'clock when the judges left the courtroom for their chambers. The spectators, though, were loath to depart. Their number had increased each day, their curiosity piqued in their understanding that there were in fact two trials going on at the same time, Moreau's and Bonaparte's, for the destinies of the two generals were interlinked. No matter how long the decision would take, the crowd was willing to wait.

The deliberations were further delayed when Réal arrived to inform the judges that Moreau had to be administered some sentence, no matter how light, because if he were acquitted, there would be a coup d'état. Of course, a long deliberation was especially necessary to condemn a defendant everyone knew was innocent.

Five hours later, at four o'clock on the morning of June 10, the sounding of a bell sent a shiver through the crowd still waiting in the courtroom, for it was announcing that the judges were coming back into session. Dawn's first pale light was beginning to filter in through the windows and mingle with the last glow of the candles; it was that melancholy hour when the night struggles with the day for the glory of the morning. The air seemed to be fraught with uncertainty and expectancy, and a hint of terror, when a band of army men invaded the courtroom. They had taken their stations when a second bell rang out. The door to the chambers opened, and a bailiff in full voice announced: "The high court!"

President Hémard and the eleven other judges marched solemnly in and took their places. Then the defendants were ushered in.

The first category of prisoners was brought before the president. With one hand on his heart and the other holding the court's decree, he somberly read the sentence condemning the following men to death: George Cadoudal, Bouvet de Lozier, Rugulion, Rochelle, Armand de Polignac, Charles d'Hozier, Monsieur de Rivière, Louis Ducorps, Picot, Lajolais, Roger, Coster Saint-Victor, Deville, Armand Gaillard, Léhan, Pierre Cadoudal, Joyaut, Lemercier, Burban, and Mérille. President Hémard read the names slowly, and in the long pause after each name, the spectators collectively held their breath, their hearts scarcely beating, as they prayed the next name not be that of a family member or friend.

Twenty-one men stood condemned to death. Large though the number was, relief flooded the courtroom once the first list had been read. The president then proceeded to announce the rest of the decisions: "Given that Jean-Victor Moreau, Jules de Polignac, Le Ridant, Roland, and Izaï the prostitute are guilty of participating in the conspiracy, but attenuating circumstances having come to light during the inquest and the debates, the court reduces their sentences to two years of prison.

"The other defendants are acquitted."

The condemned men listened to their sentences calmly, without arro-

gance, fear, or disdain. George, however, did lean over to Monsieur de Rivière to say, "Now that we have finished with our earthly king, we need to
prepare to meet our heavenly one."

XLVII

The Execution

IN OTHER PLACES, worry over the defendants was perhaps even more intense than it was in the courtroom where their fate was being decided.
Josephine, Madame Murat, and Madame Louis, all three of them already
shaken by the death of the Duc d'Enghien and Pichegru's questionable suicide, were horrified at the thought now of executing twenty-one people;
such public butchery recalled the darkest days of the Terror.

It was not unreasonable, Josephine being horrified, for had not Fouché
once written that "the air is full of daggers"? The thread etched in those
words was never far from Josephine's mind, and she could not think of the
fresh hatred that twenty-one new deaths were sure to sire without imagin-
ing twenty-one more vengeful daggers hanging over her husband's breast.

The aggrieved sought out Josephine, Madame de Polignac's tears being
the first to fall on her imperial mantle. She hastened to Bonaparte's study to
plead the case of the noble young man who, to save his brother's head, had
offered his own. But Bonaparte refused to be moved by either his wife's
prayers or her tears: "You are always concerned about my enemies,
madame!" he said harshly. "Royalists or Republicans, they are all equally
incorrigible. If I pardon them, they will simply begin their intrigues over
again, and you will have to plead for them anew."

Alas! As she aged, her age every day reducing Bonaparte's hope for posterity, Josephine was losing her influence. She sent for Madame de Polignac
and suggested that she herself petition Bonaparte. Throwing herself at his
feet, Madame de Polignac begged a pardon for her husband Armand. "Armand de Polignac!" cried Bonaparte. "My childhood friend at military school!
Did he really need to plot against me? Ah, madame," he added, "those
princes who put their faithful servants at risk without sharing the danger
are indeed the ones who are truly guilty."

Madame de Polignac had barely left the Tuileries when Murat and his
wife arrived to ask pardon for Monsieur de Rivière. Murat, a good man at

heart, continued to despair over the role he had played, in spite of himself, in the Duc d'Enghien affair; he wanted, as he said, to erase the stain that Bonaparte had placed upon his uniform. In any case, Bonaparte heeded Murat's plea, and Monsieur de Rivière's pardon followed on the heels of Monsieur de Polignac's. It was granted with hardly a struggle.

Monsieur Réal brought the news of the pardon to Monsieur de Rivière, but he brought it with ulterior motives, as he hoped to gain something by it. "The Emperor appreciates courage and loyalty," said Réal, "and he might be willing to pardon you. Indeed, he would be pleased to see you enter his service, for he knows that you would keep your word if you gave it. Would you like a regiment?"

"I would be pleased and proud to lead French soldiers," Monsieur de Rivière answered, "but I cannot accept, having always served until now under a different flag."

"You have been in diplomatic service. Would it please you to be the French ambassador in Germany?"

"It was not by chance that I was sent to several German courts in the name of Monsieur and of the King. I was your enemy, Monsieur Réal, when I was carrying out those missions. So what would those German kings think of me if I were to begin negotiating for interests different from those I have been defending up until now? I would lose their esteem as well my own; therefore, I cannot accept."

"Then join the administration! Would you like a prefecture?"

"I am only a soldier; I would make a very poor prefect."

"Well then, what do you want?"

"Something quite simple: I have been sentenced; I want to undergo my punishment."

"You are a loyal man," Réal said as he withdrew. "If I can be of help, please let me know."

Réal then summoned Cadoudal. "George," he said, "I am prepared to request your pardon from the Emperor. He will be certain to grant it if you promise one thing—not to plot against the government. Will you instead accept a commission in the army?"

George shook his head. "My friends and comrades followed me back to France," he said. "In turn, I will follow them to the scaffold."

All noble hearts beat in sympathy for George. Thus Murat, having obtained pardon for Monsieur de Rivière, argued in favor of the same for the brave Breton.

"If Your Majesty has pardoned the Polignacs and others, why," he said, "would he not show the same clemency toward Cadoudal? George is a man of great character, and if Your Majesty is willing to grant him life, I would like him to be my aide-de-camp."

"By Jove," Napoleon answered, "I can see clearly why you might choose him, for so would I; but that devil of a man would then expect me to pardon all of his companions. And that is impossible, when some of his men killed openly in the streets of Paris. However, do as you like, as I am sure that whatever you do will be done well."

Murat visited the cell where George was locked up with his companions. The execution was scheduled to take place the following morning, so he was not surprised to find everyone in prayer. Not one man looked up when he came in. Murat waited until the condemned prisoners had finished their prayers, then pulled George aside to speak to him. "Monsieur," he said, "I have come in the name of the Emperor to offer you a position in the army."

"Monsieur," George replied, "I received the same offer this morning and I refused it."

"I will add to the offer that Monsieur Réal made you this morning. The same pardon will be granted to any of those men who should accompany you if they too would be willing to devote themselves to the Emperor's service and renounce without reserve their former loyalties."

"In that case," said George, "you will surely understand that the decision is no longer mine alone and that I must communicate your proposal to my comrades so as to find out what they think."

Cadoudal repeated aloud the offer that Murat had just whispered to him. Then, making no attempt to influence his comrades either for or against the proposal, he waited quietly.

Burban was the first to stand. Lifting his hat, he shouted, "Long live the king!"

And with the same words ten other voices drowned out his own.

Turning toward Murat, George said, "As you see, monsieur, we share one common thought and have only one cry: 'Long live the king!' Please be so kind as to communicate our words to those who have sent you."

The next day, June 25, 1804, a cart carried the condemned men to the foot of the scaffold.

It was almost unheard of in the whole bloody history of public executions for an exception to be made to the ordinary custom; but made it was. The leader of the conspiracy was to be executed first, at George's own request. As there had already been several attempts to obtain his pardon, he feared that if he mounted the scaffold last, his friends might die thinking that he might have been pardoned the moment before he took his final breath.

George was followed to the scaffold by four of his compatriots when an unusual incident interrupted and prolonged the bloody spectacle. Louis Ducorps, the sixth in line to die, and Lemercier, the seventh, surprised their executioners and the throng of onlookers by suddenly announcing they had revelations to make. They were taken to see the governor of Paris, and for an hour and a half the proceedings were delayed while they served up a number of unimportant revelations. In that hour and a half they hoped that the pardon promised to Coster Saint-Victor, the eighth in line, would arrive. The elegant CosterSaint-Victor meanwhile asked if they might not take advantage of the delay by summoning a barber to trim his hair. "For," he said to the executioner, "you see the crowd of women that's gathered here, most of them for me; indeed, I may know all of them. So for them if not for me you might grant my request for a barber that for the past four days in the prison has been refused, for by now I must look horrible." Again the request was refused, and as the minutes sped past Saint-Victor appeared to grow more agitated. When Ducorps and Lemercier were brought back, Saint-Victor's pardon had still not arrived. Down to the last man, the scaffold accommodated them all.

The clock on the Hôtel de Ville struck two. The conspirators against Bonaparte had met their destiny at the guillotine, and from that hour on Napoleon's power had been truly established. In 1799 he had overcome political resistance by breaking up the Directory; in 1802 he had overcome civil resistance by annulling the Tribunate; in 1804 he had vanquished all military resistance by foiling the conspiracy of the émigrés linked with Republican generals. Pichegru, his only rival, had strangled himself; Moreau, his only equal, was going into exile. After twelve years of struggles, terrors, and riots, of rivaling factions biting at each other's political heels, the Revolution was finally coming to an end. Over twelve years, gradually, it had been incarnated in Bonaparte; the republic had become a man, France had become Napoleon. No wonder, then, that the coins being minted in 1804 carried this epigraph: *"République française, Napoléon empereur."*

A month after the executions, on the evening of July 25, 1804, Fouché came to pay his customary visit to the new emperor. Bonaparte, in recompense for the good services that Fouché had rendered in exposing and thwarting conspiracy, had just restored him to his former position as Minister of Police. It was on that evening that Fouché, in tête-à-tête with Napoleon near the window and thinking it a favorable moment, said to him, "Well, sire, what shall we do with the poor fellow who has been in a cell in the Abbaye for the past three years awaiting your decision?"

"What poor fellow?"

"The Comte de Sainte-Hermine."

"The Comte de Sainte-Hermine? Who is he?"

"The man who was going to marry Mademoiselle de Sourdis and who disappeared the evening the contract was to be signed."

"That stagecoach robber?"

"Yes."

"He was never shot?"

"No."

"And yet I had so ordered."

"To invert Monsieur de Talleyrand's axiom, your first reaction is often the wrong one."

"And so . . . ?"

"I kept waiting for the second. In truth, spending three years in prison for the crime he committed seems to me punishment enough."

"Fine. Send him to the army as an ordinary soldier."

"Is he free to choose the branch?" asked Fouché.

"Let him choose," Bonaparte replied, "but he should never expect to become an officer."

"Fine, sire. It is up to him to force Your Majesty's hand."

PART II

NAPOLEON

XLVIII

After Three Years in Prison

꙳⫶꙳

NOT AN HOUR HAD GONE BY since the conversation between the Minister of Police and the Emperor when Fouché's doorman announced, "The prisoner is here."

Fouché turned around, and just outside the door he saw the Comte de Sainte-Hermine standing between two gendarmes. On a signal from the Minister of Police, the Comte de Sainte-Hermine entered the room.

Since the day he had been arrested, when Fouché had extended to him the hope of being shot without a trial, the minister and he had not spoken. For a week, two weeks, even a month, whenever a key had turned in his prison door, Sainte-Hermine would rush to the door, with the expectancy that he was at last being summoned to his execution. Eventually he had realized that, at least for the moment, he had to resign himself to life.

Then fear had seized him, the fear that they were keeping him alive so he could serve as a witness in the coming trials. He'd spent a month or two fostering this fear he himself had created, until one day it too evaporated, like his hope.

So tortured had his soul been first by hope, then by fear, that time had not weighed upon him. But then he'd grown bored. He'd asked for books; they'd granted his request. He'd asked for pencils, drawing paper, and mathematical instruments; they'd been brought. He'd asked for ink, writing paper, pens; they'd appeared. And when the long winter nights had arrived to darken his cell by four in the afternoon, he had asked for a lamp. They were reluctant at first, but the lamp too had appeared. Allowed though he was to walk in the garden for two hours of every day, he had never taken advantage of the opportunity for fear of being recognized. Thus had he existed for three years.

There is an age at which, in select individuals, misfortune seems only to enhance physical beauty and moral character. Hector was scarcely more than twenty-five years old, and his character was exceptional. During his long reclusion his face had lost its youthful glow, and his rosy cheeks had hollowed and given way to a darker, swarthy complexion. His eyes seemed to have grown larger, their gaze more penetrating, from his having to strain to see in the dark. His beard formed a strong, strikingly masculine face. In the play of any light, his physiognomy cast shadows of thought, reverie, and melancholy.

Young men have a need to expend physical energy, and Hector met that need through gymnastic exercises. He had requested cannonballs of different sizes, and with practice he was finally able to lift and juggle even the heaviest of them. To the ceiling he had attached a rope, which he could now climb by using only his hands. Whatever the benefits he bore from his strenuous physical education, Hector had invented his gymnastic exercises primarily to help him pass the time.

During his three years in prison, too, Sainte-Hermine had studied in great depth subjects he could study alone: geography, mathematics, history. Hector had been passionate for travel in his youth, and indeed he spoke German, English, and Spanish as well as he did his mother tongue. Now, employing heavily the privilege he'd been granted to borrow books, he had traveled in words and on maps where he could not journey in the world beyond his prison walls. India, for which Haider-Ali, his son Tippo Sahib, the Bailiff de Suffren, Bussy, and Dupleix had been ferociously fighting the English, had especially captured his interest. It hardly mattered that he thought such study would be of no particular use since he assumed that he was doomed to perpetual imprisonment in any case.

He had grown used to prison life, and the order to appear before the Minister of Police was a momentous event for him. We confess that he approached it with more than a little apprehension in his heart.

Hector recognized Fouché immediately. Fouché had not changed a bit, except that now he was wearing an embroidered jacket and people called him "monsignor." On the other hand, Fouché had to look twice at Sainte-Hermine and even then was barely able to recognize him.

As he stood before the Minister of Police, Sainte-Hermine's mind was flooded by painful memories. "Ah, monsieur," he said, breaking into their silence, "so this is how you have kept your promise?"

"Do you really hold it against me for having forced you to live?" asked Fouché.

Sainte-Hermine smiled sadly. "Is it really living," he asked, "being confined in a room twelve feet by twelve feet with bars on the windows and two bolts on each door?"

"One is surely more comfortable in a twelve-by-twelve room than in a coffin that measures only six feet long and two feet wide."

"However narrow the coffin may be, in death one is always comfortable."

"Would you insist as strongly on death today," asked Fouché, "as you did the last time I saw you?"

Sainte-Hermine shrugged. "No," he said. "I hated life then; today I am completely indifferent. Besides, since you have sent for me, doesn't that mean my turn has come?"

"Why might your turn have come?"

"Well, because now that you have finished with the Duc d'Enghien, Pichegru, Moreau, and Cadoudal, it seems to me that you might be ready to finish with the last Sainte-Hermine."

"My dear sir," Fouché replied, "when Tarquin wanted Sextus to know what his orders were, he did not cut down all the poppies in his garden, only those that stood the tallest."

"What should I understand from your answer, monsieur?" asked Hector, blushing. "That my head is not important enough to be cut off?"

"I do not mean to offend, monsieur, but you must admit that you are neither a prince with royal blood like the Duc d'Enghien, nor a conqueror like Pichegru, nor a great warrior like Moreau, nor a famous partisan like George."

"You are quite right," Hector replied with bowed head. "I am nothing compared to those you have named."

"However," Fouché went on, "you could become everything those men were, except for being a prince as you were not, alas, born with royal blood."

"Me?"

"Of course. In prison, have you been treated like a man who would one day leave his cell only to go to his death? Has anyone attempted, during your captivity, to humble your spirit or break your will or corrupt your heart? Have you requested anything that has not been granted you? Would it not appear that some benevolent power has been watching over you? Three years spent as you have spent them, monsieur, is not a punishment; it is an opportunity—for education: Let us suppose that nature has intended that you should become a man, for you are, would you not then have sorely missed those three years?"

"But surely," cried Sainte-Hermine somewhat impatiently, "I have been sentenced to something. What is my punishment?"

"To join the army as a simple soldier."

"And that, monsieur, is not punishment; it is debasement."

"What rank did you hold among your stagecoach robbers?"

"What do you mean?"

"I am asking you what rank you held with the Companions of Jehu."

Hector bowed his head. "You are right," he said. "I shall be an ordinary soldier."

"And be proud of it, too, monsieur. Marceau, Hoche, Kléber—they all started out as ordinary soldiers. Jourdan, Masséna, Lannes, Berthier, Augereau, Brune, Murat, Bessières, Moncey, Mortier, Soult, Davout, Bernadotte, now marshals of France, almost all began their careers as simple soldiers. Begin as they did, end up like them."

"Orders will be given to keep me in the army's lowest ranks."

"You will force the hand of your officers with brilliant feats."

"By force I will serve a government with which my family could not agree. Nor can I."

"You must admit, monsieur, that when you were attacking stagecoaches in the Vernon Forest, you'd not yet even had the time to realize with what you'd agree or disagree. You were simply following family traditions, not making a reasoned decision. Since you have been in prison, since you have been studying the past and contemplating the future, you must now know that again an old world is collapsing and a new one is rising from its ruins. Everything that defined the world of your fathers has died, violently, inevitably, providentially. Everywhere, from the throne down to the lowest ranks of the army, from the highest magistrates to the lowest village mayors, you see nothing but new faces. Your own family attests to this recent division in our history. Your father and two brothers belonged to the past, you belong to the new world. Your own thinking surely must confirm that."

"I am obliged to admit, monsieur, that there is a great deal of truth in what you are saying. Just as Louis XVI and Marie-Antoinette represent the old regime that they were born to, Bonaparte and Josephine, both of less noble birth, epitomizea new era for France."

"I am delighted not to have been mistaken. You have indeed become the intelligent man that I foresaw three years ago."

"Might I, in order to eradicate traces of my past, enlist under a name other than my own?"

"Yes. Not only may you enlist under a different name, but you may also choose the branch in which you are condemned to serve."

"Thank you."

"Do you have a preference?"

"None. Whichever path I follow, I shall simply be as dust borne by the wind."

"Why let yourself be carried away by the wind when you might stand against it? Would you like me to give you some advice, monsieur, concerning the branch in which you might wish to serve?"

"Please do, monsieur."

"We are going to embark on a bitter war with England, a naval war. Since you have the choice, become a sailor."

"I was thinking of that," said Hector.

"There are precedents in your family. Five of your ancestors bearing the same name, starting with Hélée de Sainte-Hermine, vice-admiral in 1734, have occupied high-ranking posts in the navy. Even your father's brother was a ship's captain, as you know better than anyone since you served under his orders as apprentice pilot and midshipman until you were fourteen. So when you again stand on the deck of a vessel, you will have already completed half of your naval training."

"Since you are so well versed in what has happened in my family over the last century and a half, can you tell me, monsieur, what has become of my uncle? Having been in prison for the last three years, I have been out of touch with everyone."

"Your uncle, a loyal servant of the king, resigned his commission when the Duc d'Enghien was killed and withdrew to England along with two of your cousins."

"When must I be at my post?"

"How many days do you require to put your affairs in order?"

"My affairs will quickly be in order, as I assume my fortune has been confiscated."

"Your entire fortune still belongs to you, and if your steward has not been pilfering from you, you will find your income for the past three years, three hundred thousand francs, somewhere in a drawer. Not a bad beginning for a sailor."

"Clearly, monsieur, from all you are telling me, I owe you a great deal, and yet I have neglected to thank you. Put the blame on the emotion I feel in this strange situation, and please do not think that I am ungrateful."

"I am so far from thinking you ungrateful that I would like to give you one further piece of advice. I have been keeping it for last because it's the best."

"Please tell me, monsieur."

"Do not join the imperial navy."

"Where then would you have me enlist?"

"Sign on with a corsair. A new law has just granted corsair ships—the ones called 'privateers' by the English—the same status as government vessels. Forced to serve as a simple sailor, it's unlikely you would ever adapt to the rigid discipline maintained on a vessel of the imperial fleet. On a corsair ship, where the distance between ranks is more readily bridged, you might easily become the captain's friend and perhaps even purchase a share in the vessel. He would then be free to assign you whatever rank he wants, under which you might move eventually from the unofficial navy to a government vessel, where your time of service could be calculated from the first day you first served as apprentice pilot on your uncle's ship."

"But, Monsieur Fouché," said Hector, surprised to find such kindness in a man who did not have the reputation of being very kind, "what have I done to deserve such attention from you?"

"Well, I have no idea, and I hardly recognize myself," said the Minister of Police. "However, on occasion, I do enjoy aiding men who have demonstrated their intelligence in difficult situations. They seem always to manage to perform with flying colors and yet to keep their honor intact. I do not know what will become of you, but some day you will thank me, for then you will have more to thank me for than you do today."

"Monsieur," said Sainte-Hermine with a bow, "from today onward I count myself in your obligation for everything, even for life itself."

"The day you join up, don't forget to send me the name of the ship, the number that falls to you in the crew, and the pseudonym you choose when you enlist. You do still intend to serve under a different name?"

"Yes, monsieur. The name Sainte-Hermine is dead."

"For everyone?"

"For everyone, and especially for the woman who was to make it her own."

"Until it comes back to life with the rank of commandant or general, right?"

"But by that time I hope that the person to whom we allude will have long, and happily, forgotten me."

"And if she asks me how you died, since I must know everything in my role as Minister of Police, what shall my answer be?"

"Tell her that I died with all the respect that I owed to her and in all the strength of my love for her."

"Monsieur is free to go," said Fouché, opening the double doors.

The gendarmes stepped aside. The Comte de Sainte-Hermine bowed and left the room.

XLIX
Saint-Malo

ON ONE OF THOSE MANY GULFS along the coast of France, from Calais to Brest, between Normandy and Brittany, between the Cape of La Hague and Cape Tréguier, opposite the old French islands of Jersey, Guernsey, and Aurigny, rising up on a rock like the nest of some aquatic bird, is the little town of Saint-Malo.

In former times, back in those primitive days lost in history's mist when Brittany was still called Armorica, that rock, bathed by the Rance, rose far from the water, from which it was separated by forests and prairies. The islands around and opposite Saint-Malo must then have been a part of that land. Until the cataclysm of 709 B.C., which must have swallowed up a sizable portion of land that perhaps had once extended as far out into the sea as the Cape of La Hague or Cape Tréguier.

Incursions into Brittany by Norman pirates early in the ninth century made Charlemagne weep on his deathbed and forced the Bretons in the area to take refuge on the rock of Saint-Malo. Between 1143 and 1152 Jean de Châtillon moved the bishopric to Saint-Malo, and that is when the town began to take on new life.

Daughter to the savage ocean, Saint-Malo developed rapidly under the protection of its brave seamen and under the seigniorial jurisdiction of the bishop and chapter. The population grew and thrived under organization that safeguarded community principles and the peoples' rights. It became safe haven, though its prosperity was shaky as is often the case with growing towns.

The town increased the number of ships in its harbor by offering tax exemptions and enlarged the volume of its commerce by granting immunities and privileges that had traditionally been reserved for dukes and kings. During times of war it enriched its coffers with the frequent capture of enemy vessels, whereas during peacetime solid business deals and lucrative transactions buoyed the town's prosperity. Saint-Malo formed, as it were, an independent republic within the Breton nation. (As such, it provided asylum to the young Count of Richmond of the House of Lancaster, who later would become king under the name Henry VII. Pursued unrelentingly by Edward IV, first sovereign from the House of York, in 1475 he took refuge in the Saint-Malo church.)

One curious detail: At night, when the tide was low, ships in Saint-Malo were guarded by a pack of twenty-four bulldogs imported from England.

That practice was begun by the chapter and the community in 1145, and it continued until 1770, when a young officer challenged the four-legged sentinels by attempting to force his way past them after curfew had rung. He was devoured by the animals. The council found it fit to have them poisoned.

It would be a long and glorious story to tell of all the boats that slipped out of the Saint-Malo shipyards and pushed waves before them in their mission to seize English, Portuguese, and Spanish ships in their iron claws. Not another nation has in its annals as many glorious combats to record as does this small town whose walls one could circle on foot in one hour. As for those ramparts, the people of Saint-Malo entrusted their protection to nothing else.

Since 1234, Saint-Malo seamen have sailed the oceans. Matthew Paris, seeing them pounce swiftly on English vessels, called them the "light brigades of the sea." Praises for those hardy Breton sailors reached Saint Louis's ear, and along with some Picards and Normans he dispatched them to do battle with Admiral Dubourg and the English navy. The English admiral was soundly beaten, and his vessels were forced to return to their home ports. And when Saint Louis, motivated by holy madness, undertook the last crusade on April 1, 1270, ships from Saint-Malo, faithful to his call, sailed around Spain to await him on the appointed day at Aigues-Mortes.

Fortune protected Saint-Malo ships well until the Battle of the Ecluse on June 24, 1340, which they lost to the English and Flemish. The citizens of Saint-Malo afterward patched things up with their enemies and joined them in supporting the efforts of the Duc Jean de Monfort to take the French throne. The duke's efforts failed when he was chased from his lands and forced to take refuge in England instead.

Saint-Malo meanwhile submitted to King Charles V, but that did not prevent the Duke of Lancaster from trying to take the town. He placed great hope in artillery, a recent invention, although it proved to be no match for the tactical wiles of the townspeople, whoe slipped behind Lancaster's lines in the middle of the night, killed many of his men, burned down part of his camp, and, according to Froissart, made of the failed Lancaster and his whole army historical objects of ridicule.

Once Duc Jean again gained possession of his duchy, he too attempted to conquer Saint-Malo. He set up a crippling blockade that cut off the town's food supply and shut down the aqueduct that brought the town its water. He then took away the rights and privileges the townspeople had long been granted. His extreme measures strengthened their resolve against him, and just as they had borne their allegiance to King Charles V, they now aligned themselves with King Charles VI, under whose patronage they built up a formidable fleet of ships that enabled them to ravage the coasts of England.

October 25, 1415 knelled the fatal hour of Agincourt. France was all but lost. Saint-Malo, though, fell to the Duc de Bretagne. Dressed in white robes, the inhabitants welcomed him with ermine-decorated flags.

Victorious England extended its dominion throughout France. Its flag flew over Notre-Dame; it flew over all the Norman fortresses. It flew everywhere except above Mont-Saint-Michel, where the three fleurs-de-lis protested our defeat. When an English fleet, equipped by Cardinal Bishop Guillaume de Montfort, tried to blockade the valiant citadel, ships from Saint-Malo, although fewer in number, did battle with the English vessels. The struggle was hot and desperate, but the English ships were boarded and their crews were slaughtered. The cry of victory at Saint-Malo awakened France. She lifted up her head in surprise and began again to breathe more freely, for not all had been lost in her northwest territory.

News of the victory prompted Charles VII to break out of his habitual lethargy, for a moment, and on August 6, 1425, he rendered an edict exempting Saint-Malo's ships for three years from any taxes, old or new, owed to the crown. These exemptions were increased twofold when François I de Bretagne forbade his farmer general from collecting any port or harbor taxes whatever. Nor was he allowed to exact or accept any contributions, except those granted by the dukes, in support of the captaincy or for the upkeep of fortifications. In 1466, with Saint-Malo's immunities and tax exemptions as models, Louis XI used similar principles to build up Paris's population, which had diminished during the so-called commonwealth wars.

In 1492, at about the same time that Christopher Columbus was discovering America, seamen from Saint-Malo, as well as from Dieppe and Biscay, were discovering Newfoundland and some of the lower coasts of Canada. The Basques called the area they found *baccalaos,* which gave us the word "*baccalat,*" for cod, as it continues to be known in Italy, Spain, and the south of France. Jacques Cartier, the Christopher Columbus of Canada, would be the first to bring back to Saint-Malo that precious fish, which would stimulate a business soon to enrich a third of Europe.

In 1505, Princess Anne, daughter of François II, who at seven was betrothed to the Prince of Wales—a betrothal cut abruptly short when he was strangled on his uncle Gloucester's orders—and who married two French kings in succession, Charles VIII and Louis XII, appeared briefly in Saint-Malo. She continued work on the castle there despite opposition from the chapter. To demonstrate just how little she respected the wishes of her adversaries, she had workmen carve on the fortress wall overlooking the town her unambiguous sentiments: *"Quic en groingne! Ainsi sera. C'est mon plaisir"* ("Let them grumble! So be it. Such is my will").

The same year in which the people of Saint-Malo got a town hall, that is, the freedom to govern themselves, Jacques Cartier was born, and during his lifetime (1491-1557) a great age of exploration would grow and flourish, with the seamen of Saint-Malo participating in every major expedition. They went with Cartier to Canada. They went with Spain's Charles Quint to Africa when he restored Moulay Hassan, the king of Tunis, to his throne. They manned their ships to go to India in the wake of the Portuguese, just as they'd follow Cabral across the Atlantic to Brazil.

They participated in their country's wars, too. During the bitter War of 1512 between France and England, the people of Saint-Malo, with Monsieur de Bouillé leading them, attacked the English as they were setting up a base on Cézembre Island. Those that Bouillé's men did not hack to pieces, they forced to flee.

And when François I went to war with Spain, whom did he call upon to strengthen Admiral Annebaut's fleet? Of course, on the people of Saint-Malo, whose ships he chartered. Actually, several captains refused to join the admiral, because they wanted to make war against Spain on their own account and anywhere on the high seas. That is how it happened that a part of Charles Quint's fleet, returning from America, was captured by ships from Brittany and Saint-Malo that had traveled as far as the Gulf of Mexico to seek out the enemy.

And when Henri II, who had succeeded his father François to the throne, was quarreling with Edward VI, he picked up his pen and wrote to Saint-Malo, enjoining them to "prepare their ships as soon as possible, hurry to sea, attack the English, and do all possible damage"—with the promise that "they will not be required to give up any of their take, nor pay any tithe or any other fees."

In 1560, the people of Saint-Malo received a letter from the new king, François II, who forbade them to dispatch any fishing boats, because he required every vessel in their fleet to block the path of the Calvinists out of Anjou. Alarmed by the death sentence that had been pronounced on the Prince de Condé, the Calvinists were gathering at points along the Breton coast in hopes of getting passage to England. While Catholic seamen from Saint-Malo were cruising back and forth along the coast of Brittany to prevent the Huguenots from reaching England, their Calvinist counterparts were engaged in the expedition that Admiral Coligny had sent to Florida under the command of Captain Ribaut.

The Battle of Jarnac, won by the Duc d'Anjou, brought temporary peace to France in 1569, and Charles IX took advantage of the period of relative calm to visit Brittany. Guillaume de Ruzé, Bishop of Saint-Malo, accompanied him; and that is the only time the bishop ever came to visit his bishopric. In their festival finest, armed with harquebuses and led by four hundred children, the citizens of Saint-Malo came out to greet Charles IX. The next day, Corpus Christi, the king himself took part in the processions, and at noon the town launched a naval combat, purely for the entertainment of His Majesty. Showered with gifts, he returned home by way of Cancale and Dol.

And that is not all. The next year, when the inhabitants of Saint-Malo learned that His Very Christian Majesty was having severe financial problems, they discovered the amount of the royal debt and paid it off in full. Those kinds of subjects we don't see any more!

When the Saint-Bartholomew's Day massacre took place in 1572, the people of Saint-Malo refused to participate. Not a single Calvinist was killed in Saint-Malo. But the following year, however, when the English under Montgomery and the French Huguenots took Belle-Isle, Saint-Malo's seamen, paying all expenses themselves, did not hesitate to take to their ships, and they chased off Montgomery at the cost of sixty of their own.

The people of Saint-Malo joined La Ligue and supported French Catholicism and the monarch as enthusiastically as they did everything. So, the news that Henri III, the last of the Valois dynasty, had been assassinated and that the king was now the Huguenot and Bourbon Henri IV plunged the city into doleful silence. Although the governor of the château, Monsieur de Fontaine, demonstrated willingness to welcome the heretic king, the people of Saint-Malo took up arms and barricaded the town, with the vow that town and inhabitants would submit to no monarch until "God gave France a Catholic king."

And no sooner had Henri abjured, realizing that without money he could not come to Brittany, than Saint-Malo promised to furnish him with cannons, gunpowder, balls, and money, as much as the king should require to come to Brittany and put down the Duc de Mercoeur. Further, Saint-Malo contributed twelve thousand crowns toward the costs of the expedition. Yet these were the very same men who had just killed the governor of the château, De Fontaine, on the ground that he had betrayed their interests by welcoming Henri IV to the city and to the castle. Saint-Malo now became one of the new king's most zealous supporters and began a war of their own upon the Ligue's garrisons, which they had been supplying up until then.

Henri IV wrote to the people of Saint-Malo to commend them for being "providers of the most legitimate, open and loyal navigation that one could hope for," and he intervened with Elizabeth on their behalf against English pirates.

Let us not confuse pirates with corsairs. Saint-Malo was already a maritime power at the outset of the seventeenth century. In 1601, two of their ships, the *Croissant* and the *Corbin*, rounded the Cape of Good Hope, on their way to India. In 1603, three other of their ships set out "for trade and discovery of lands in Canada and areas adjacent." In 1607, the Comte de Choisy, nephew of the Duc de Montmorency, in preparation for a voyage around the world with a fleet of five ships—the *Archange*, the *Choisy*, the *Affection*, the *Esprit*, and the *Ange*—outfitted his expedition in Saint-Malo, for he believed the seamen there to be the best that he could possibly find.

When the assassination of Henri IV placed Louis XIII on the throne, he wasted no time in confirming the privileges his father had conferred on the town of Saint-Malo. He had two of his warships outfitted in Saint-Malo to protect the crews on the fishing boats off the coast of Newfoundland.

Richelieu, too, called upon these faithful townspeople when he decided to besiege La Rochelle, which was supplying and supporting the Huguenots. He needed a navy that could measure up to Buckingham's fleet, but he had only thirty-four whaling boats. The people of Saint-Malo provided twenty-two more. Eight thousand inhabitants in a small port city by themselves accomplished almost as much as did all of the rest of France. As for their expenses, just as for their blood, so often spilled for France, they said the king owed them nothing. Saint-Malo was granted an admiralty.

In 1649, to populate their new colony in Canada, the government put a large number of prostitutes on board ships that departed from Saint-Malo. On their arrival in Canada, within two weeks each one had found a spouse, to whom she brought a dowry that comprised a bull, a cow, a boar, a sow, a rooster, a hen, two kegs of salt meat, some weapons, and eleven crowns.

So well known was the value of men from Saint-Malo that the French fleet's flagship normally recruited its crew in Saint-Malo. Louis XIV changed that custom into law.

By the end of the seventeenth century there were one hundred and fifty ships based in Saint-Malo. Sixty of them were less than one hundred tons; the other ninety were from one hundred to four hundred tons.

By then as well some of France's great seamen had begun to appear. From 1672 until 1700, in the annals of Saint-Malo, one must enter the names of Dufresne des Saudrais, Le Fer de La Bellière, Gouin de Beauchesne, the first man from Saint-Malo to round Cape Horn, Alain Porée, Legoux, sieur de la Fontaine, Louis-Paul Danycan, sieur de la Cité, Joseph Danycan, Athanaze Le Jolif, Pépin de Bellisle, François Fossart, La Villauglamatz, Thomas des Minimes, Étienne Piednor, Joseph Grave, Jacques

Porcher, Josselin Gardin, Nouail des Antons, Nicolas de Giraldin, Nicolas Arson, and Duguay-Trouin. As brilliant as they were in their own day, they are as obscure in ours. Except for one: Still as bright as Jupiter remains Duguay-Trouin.

In 1704, during the War of the Spanish Succession, so disastrous for France, Saint-Malo nonetheless captured eighty-one ships, and their sale produced two million four hundred twenty-two thousand six hundred fifty pounds and two deniers. Saint-Malo began trade with Mocha, and farther east, in India, opened trading posts in Surat, Calicut, and Pondicherry. Saint-Malo conquered Rio de Janeiro and in another ocean took possession of Mauritius, which was named Île de France. The town expanded, ramparts were built; and when Duguay-Trouin died, his equivalent was born in Mahé de la Bourdonnais, who would govern Île de France and Île Bourbon in a way that made up for the defeats we suffered in Asia.

During Louis XIV's fateful wars, brought to an end by the shameful treaty of 1763, Saint-Malo's trade suffered enormously. In spite of hopes encouraged by the reign of the new king Louis XVI, Saint-Malo's economic activity continued to decline, and during the revolutionary storms between 1794 and 1795 it was practically destroyed. In 1790, Saint-Servan, up until then a suburb of Saint-Malo, broke away, taking with it half of Saint-Malo's population. By the end of 1793 all that was left of the erstwhile maritime glory in Saint-Malo were two or three fishing boats and not a single corsair.

The departure of the proconsul Le Carpentier in 1793 allowed Saint-Malo a little economic breath, and in the next year they were able to put five small corsair ships to sea. Between 1796 and 1797, they had as many as thirty, although some of them were armed only with blunderbusses and light guns. In 1798, Saint-Malo outfitted twenty-eight new corsair ships, and they maintained about the same number of ships until the peace of 1801 was signed with England.

But as we have seen, the peace lasted only a historic moment, and, as of 1803, hostilities had broken out afresh to demonstrate again the deep and ancient hatred the two countries shared. It was a period that would produce new seafaring heroes, men like Le Même, Lejolif, Tréhouart, and Surcouf.

The name Surcouf brings us back to our story.

L

Madame Leroux's Inn

ON JULY 28, 1804, at about eleven in the morning, in spite of the heavy clouds hanging so low over the rooftops that they seemed to be coming in from the sea rather than the sky, a young man about twenty-five or twenty-six years of age hardly seemed to notice the weather. He was walking out of the village of Saint-Servan, where he had stopped on the road from Châteauneuf just long enough to enjoy a simple lunch. As he walked through the granite rocks on the Boisouze path, a path that has since been replaced by the imperial highway, the pouring rain coursing down over his leather hat and seaman's jacket did not prompt him to move any faster. He walked with a light step, his bag on his back; with his walking stick he swatted the tops of flowers as he passed, and droplets of water rose into the air like so many diamonds. The sea was roaring both behind and in front of him, but he seemed to give no more thought to it than he did to the lightning flashing above his head. He reached the site of a jetty and even there the spectacle of the storm raging before his eyes, terrifying though it must have been, could not draw him out of his thoughts.

It was the Sillon jetty, which looks out over the Rocabey area. A narrow jetty, constructed between the open sea of the English Channel and the inner bay, it links Saint-Malo to Saint-Servan. It stands about thirty feet high and is only about eight feet wide, and with every blast of wind from the sea, whenever storms coincide with high tide, waves roll over it to crash loudly on the other side into the inner bay. With the wind and the tides tormenting the Channel into wild rebellion like that, rare was the human being who would dare to venture out onto the narrow causeway. There were stories not only about men but also about horses and carriages being swept away into the bay by those torrents of water; so it would have been wise to wait until the battle between sky and sea had calmed a little before attempting to cross the Sillon. But the young man did not alter his pace and started out over the causeway. Twice before he reached the farther end, the sea, like a monster with two heads opening up its jaws on either side of the jetty to devour him, crashed giant waves down upon him. Yet he reached the other end of the Sillon, all the while walking at the same deliberate pace. When he got to the château, he walked close to its walls, which, though they could not protect him from the rain, at least sheltered him from the rough wind and sea.

Only by wading through knee-deep water was our traveler able to reach the drawbridge and get down into the town. Once he got his bearings, he turned quickly to the left and soon, as he expected, found the square, on which the Café Franklin sits today. He appeared to know where he was, and he started down the street that runs from the Place au Beurre to the Rue Traversière. Only he got lost in the maze of streets, no one of them more than two meters wide, until he spotted a sailor who had found shelter in a doorway. "Say, comrade," he asked, "can you tell me where I might find Madame Leroux's inn?"

"À La Victorieuse?" the sailor wondered.

"Yes, À La Victorieuse," the traveler answered.

"Are you familiar with the anchorage, comrade?" asked the sailor.

"Only by name."

"Good God," said the sailor.

"Is it not safe?"

"It's a good harbor, but to venture down there you will need well-lined pockets."

"In any case, tell me where the inn is. And if you can come have supper with me this evening, we shall drink a bottle of their best wine and eat some lamb from the salt meadows."

"With pleasure," said the sailor. "Never turn down a comrade's invitation. Who shall I ask for?"

"René," replied the traveler.

"Very well. What time?"

"Oh, at about five, if you can. And now I would like to point out that you still have not answered my question."

"Which question?"

"I asked for directions to Madame Leroux's inn."

"About twenty yards from here, in the Rue Traversière; you'll see the sign. But don't forget, to be welcome at À La Victorieuse, you first have to empty a bag of gold on the table and say, 'Give me something to eat and drink, for I can pay, as you can see.'"

"Thanks for the advice," replied the traveler, setting off once more.

He followed the man's directions, and about twenty yards away he was standing in front of a large building. Above the door a painted sign showed a frigate and displayed these words: "À LA FRÉGATE *VICTORIEUSE.*"

The traveler hesitated a moment. Never had he heard such a din, such a raucous mixture of shouting, cursing, blaspheming, swearing. The corsair *Niquet,* one of Surcouf's rivals, had returned to port several days earlier with two excellent takes, and all the seamen had received their shares just the day before. If they had not yet had enough time to spend their piasters, they were making up for it now, feverishly, as the appalling rainstorm had pulled all the crews out of the streets and into the inns.

There was really no reason for the traveler to hesitate before entering, for nobody even noticed him. The patrons at the inn were much too busy with their own affairs to wonder about those of a stranger. Some were drinking, some were smoking. Others were playing backgammon or cards. Twenty-five or thirty players were crowded around two billiard tables, while fifty or sixty spectators were standing on chairs, benches, and stoves to watch. In the midst of the clamor, one could still hear the sound of coins ringing out as they hit the marble tables, but it was difficult to follow a train of thought. In their half-drunken state the seamen were shouting their every thought aloud, as much to themselves as to anyone else, who was paying no attention in any case.

The traveler ventured into the fog of smoke that commingled with the effluence of wine on the men's breath and vapor from their their steamy, rain-soaked clothes. He kept asking and looking for Madame Leroux, but no one bothered to answer him. Evidently she reigned over a kingdom of madmen. Then he caught a woman's eye and began to make his way over to her. Seeing a new face, one unskewed by a drunken smile, she likewise worked her way through the crowd toward him.

Madame Leroux was a petite but chubby woman about thirty years old. As a rule, she wore a captivating smile, spoke honeyed words, and displayed pleasant mannerisms, but she knew perfectly well, when necessary, how to alter her professional demeanor in order to repel any advances, either amorous or financial, that her clients might try out on her. Then she would place fists on her hips and seemingly grow larger, while her voice would roar like thunder; her hand might strike like lightning, too. It goes without saying that she approached the traveler in her most pleasant manner.

"Madame," he asked, in the same decorous tone and with the same courteous gestures he'd have used to greet a grand lady from the Faubourg Saint-Germain, "three days ago, did you not receive two trunks and a wooden crate addressed to the Citizen René?"

"Yes, yes. I certainly did, Citizen," Madame Leroux replied. "Your room is ready, and if you would like to follow me, I would be delighted to show you there myself."

René nodded and followed Madame Leroux up the spiral staircase to room number 11, in the middle of which his two trunks and the wooden crate stood waiting for him. Beside the window, the thoughtful hostess had placed a table along with paper and ink; for surely a man who owned two such elegant trunks and a wooden crate so carefully nailed shut had letters to write.

"Will the Citizen take supper below, or does he prefer eating in his room?" asked Madame Leroux.

René remembered the advice of the sailor he had met a few steps from the Rue Traversière. He dug carelessly into his pocket and pulled out a handful of louis, which he placed on the table. "I would like to be served here," he said, "and nicely served."

"You will be, monsieur. You will be," said Madame Leroux with her most charming smile.

"Well then, my dear Madame Leroux, please make me a good fire, for I am soaked to the bone. Then a good supper for five o'clock, two places. A good fellow will be coming, asking for René; please show him my room. And be sure we have some good wine."

Five minutes later, a splendid fire was burning in room number 11.

Scarcely was René alone again when he stripped off his soaking clothes. Then he pulled from his bag a complete outfit similar to the wet one lying on the floor. He dressed with the greatest care but was sure to stay within the bounds of a seaman's tastes.

By then, the summer storm had disappeared. The pavement dried, the sky again was blue, and nature, except for a few tears still dripping from eaves, was smiling once more, no longer angry, ready to welcome her children to her breast. Suddenly, a series of cries shattered the afternoon air. At first they sounded like people in pain, moaning, only to be followed by joyous bursts of laughter. René opened his window and looked down on a scene he'd not have dreamed in his wildest imagination. A seaman who had received two thousand piasters as his share from the corsair's take had somehow managed to spend half of it already, and, ridding himself of the rest, he had been heating the piasters red-hot in the stove and then throwing them toward the onlookers gathered at the door. They of course had pounced on the coins and, unsuspecting, had burned the skin from their fingers when they picked them up; thus, the cries of distress. Others, however, waited for the coins to cool and then painlessly put them in their pockets; hence, the shouts of joy.

In the midst of all those onlookers, René recognized the sailor he had met that morning, although there was still an hour or so before dinner would be served. At first René had thought that he would pay a visit to the illustrious Surcouf that very day, but fearing the time to be too short, he had put off the visit until the morrow. As it was, René was not at all unhappy for the opportunity to gather some information about the extraordinary man he had come to see from an ordinary sailor. So he motioned to his guest, and the man started to work his way through the compact crowd. René had plenty of time to pull the bell cord and have some cigars brought up, along with a rope of chewing tobacco and a decanter of brandy.

They arrived barely a minute before the sailor, whom René greeted warmly, shaking his hand and showing him a chair near the table.

Looking around the room, the good fellow found it a bit elegant for a simple sailor like him. The brandy, the cigars, and the rope of tobacco confirmed his suspicion that the newcomer too had gotten some money from a corsair's take. "Ah, sailor," he said. "It appears that it was not a bad campaign. Two sailor outfits, what luxury! During the ten years that I've been on a privateer, whenever my clothing got wet, I just let it dry on my back. I have never had money enough to own two outfits."

"There you are mistaken, comrade," René replied. "I have just left my parents' house, and I am nothing more or less than a young man of means. The campaign I shall embark on will be my first. However, I am eager to learn. I do not fear danger, and I am resolved either to make my fortune or die trying. I have been told that two or three ships are currently being outfitted as privateers: the *Leth*, captained by Niquet; the *Saint-Aaron*, captained by Angenard; and the *Revenant*, captained by Surcouf. Which of these three ships would you choose?"

"Well, I'll be damned. No joke. I've already chosen."

"Ah! You are going back to sea?"

"I signed on yesterday."

"On which of the three ships?"

"On the *Revenant*."

"It sails the fastest?"

"Nobody knows, since it has not yet been at sea. With Surcouf, though, it has to sail well or give the reason why. Surcouf could sail a barge."

"So, do you have confidence in Surcouf?"

"Oh, yes. This won't be the first time I've sailed with him. Out with *La Confiance* we played some good tricks on the English. Yes, we really took it to that poor John Bull!"

"Could you not tell me some of those good tricks, comrade?"

"Oh, there are plenty to choose from."

"Go ahead, I'm all ears."

"Wait until I get a fresh chaw," said the old sailor.

He went about the operation with all the attention it requires, then poured himself a glass of brandy and tossed it back. He coughed twice, and began: "At the time we were near the island of Ceylon. Our campaign had begun badly. Just when we were getting under way in Sainte-Anne, a canoe overturned and all three men aboard it got devoured by sharks—in those regions you don't stay long in the water without getting eaten.

"We were off to the east of Ceylon, and we set our cruise from the Malaysian coast to Coromandel, up the Gulf of Bengal. There we had many fortunate encounters, that it was a real blessing. In less than a month we captured six magnificent ships, all heavily loaded, and all of them around five hundred tons.

"Once we had sent off the captured ships and some men to sail them, we still had one hundred and thirty Brethren of the Coast aboard our own. With a ship like *La Confiance,* with a captain like Surcouf, we had no reason to expect our successes to end there.

"From time to time we would meet British cruisers. When we had to flee before them, our national pride was somewhat hurt. But because *La Confiance* sailed so fast, we could feel pride even in flight, for we realized how easily we could escape the English. We had been sailing for about a week without seeing another sail until one morning the lookout shouted: 'Ship ahoy!'

"'Where?' cried Surcouf, who had heard the shout from his cabin and rushed to the deck. 'How big is it?'

"'Big enough so that the *Confiance* couldn't make one mouthful of it.'

"'All the better! What is its course?'

"'No way to tell, for it's sailing into the wind.'

"Immediately, all eyes and all glasses focused on the same point. We could see a tall pyramid outlined in all its whiteness against thick fog. In those latitudes, fog rolls down from the tall coastal mountains during the night and often still hides the coastline in the morning.

"We figure the ship could just as easily be an ocean-going warship as a vessel belonging to the East India Company. If it is a warship, well, too bad—we'll have our fun. And if it happens to be a merchant ship, we'll capture it.

"We are scarcely two leagues apart, and although it is difficult to judge the strength of a vessel when it's facing you, we are already beginning our observations—"

At that moment came the announcement that the table was ready and supper awaited René and his guest. Whatever may have been the pleasure with which the old sailor was narrating and his new friend was listening, the announcement had its desired effect. Both stood up, putting aside the rest of the story until later.

LI

The Fake English Ship

⁓·⁓

MADAME LEROUX HAD BEEN completely won over by the handful of gold she saw gleaming between her guest's fingers. So as not to disturb him, she had arranged for supper to be served in the room next to his. The table, laden with oysters and set with glasses of three different shapes and shiny silverware next to each plate, as well as offering two bottles of Chablis, both uncorked, presented an inviting picture. The old sailor stopped at the door and laughed at the sight of it: "Ah," he said, "if you expect to eat like this every day while you're at sea, you are sorely mistaken, my young friend. Although on Surcouf's ships they do set a good table, we eat beans more often than roast chicken."

"Well, my friend, when we need to eat beans, we shall eat beans, but in the meantime, since we have oysters, let's eat oysters. But first—you know my name, only I don't know yours, and it would be easier to converse if I did. So, what is your name, my friend?"

"Saint-Jean, at your service. On board ship they called me Grand-Hune, because I was a topman. Whenever we fought, that's where my post was."

"Very well, Saint-Jean. A glass of Chablis? This Chablis has not crossed the equator, I guarantee."

Saint-Jean held out his glass as René poured. Then eagerly he began to drink. "Damn!" he said when he'd finished. "And I thought it was just cider. Pour me another glass, comrade, so I can offer it my apologies for behaving so cavalierly with the first."

René did not need to be asked twice. His intentions were to get Saint-Jean to talk and to speak as little as possible himself. After the Chablis came the Bordeaux, and after the Bordeaux, the Burgundy, and after the Burgundy there was Champagne. Saint-Jean, pure of heart, put up no resistance.

Over dessert, René said, "I believe it is time to tell the rest of your story, how Surcouf managed to finish his cruise on an English ship instead of on the *Confiance*."

"When we changed tack so we could heave to, the two ships were no more than two leagues apart. I was at my post on the maintop with a spyglass. I immediately informed the captain that the other ship's guns were hidden, that it was superbly fitted out, and that its sails were trimmed English-style. We still needed to know what kind of ship it was and how strong, but while the captain and I are talking, the position of the *Confiance* becomes problematic, because the wind, weak at first, now stiffens so much that soon we are moving along at four knots. So, in order to remove all doubts and to find out all we can about the enemy, we get rid of our small sails and begin to luff at two points to the wind, to move closer to the other ship. Immediately it performs the same operation; if it were not larger than us, one might think it was our shadow. The distance between us keeps us from evaluating each other, so the *Confiance*, after sailing along at the same speed for some time, bears away three points to port. But the mysterious vessel repeats the same maneuver, and once again we find ourselves in an oblique position and we're still unable to learn everything we need to know about the ship's armament, for numerous bundles and kegs are hiding its guns from one end to the other.

"You will discover, my friend," Saint-Jean noted, "that the one good fairy not invited to Surcouf's baptism was Patience. Furthermore, the whole crew was as worked up as the captain, and as ready for battle: Too bad for that unknown ship, as we're assuming it's no stronger than we are, if we come to do battle with it!

"The best way to take advantage of the *Confiance*'s superior construction is to get in close. But such a maneuver is extremely dangerous at the beginning of combat, so we tack once more and haul up in order to keep our retreat open should it become absolutely necessary. Finally we begin to draw windward of the unknown ship and are able to gain on it. A great cry of joy rings out as we realize that.

"Surcouf came to sit near me. 'Damn it,' he said, 'we shall soon know if this ship is playing fair and if it truly wants to come alongside. An old sea wolf I am and I'm not easily fooled. I know every trick those merchant ship brigands hold. I have seen many formidable-looking ships, under the command of captains at the peak of their careers, who have tried to frighten their pursuers by pretending they too were eager to fight!'

"Surcouf was so convinced he was right that he did not hesitate setting the course of the *Confiance* so that we would pass to the windward of the enemy ship. That was serious business, for if he were mistaken we risked receiving a broadside point-blank or even being boarded.

"Surcouf slid down a rope all the way to the deck, then hurried over to the lieutenant and the second in command. 'Confound it, gentlemen!' he said, stomping his feet. 'I have made a serious mistake. I should have let the English ship draw closer first and made them pursue us at different speeds so I could be sure of their strength and speed.'

"Surcouf spat out his cigar in exasperation. Then, after a moment trying to collect himself, he said, 'I've just learned a useful lesson.'

"Then he picked up his spyglass again and stared at the other ship for about five minutes. With the palm of his hand he pushed the copper tubes back together. Calling out to the crew, he shouted, 'All hands on deck!'

"We gathered around him. 'By God,' he said, 'there is no longer any doubt. You are men and not children, so what good would it do to hide from you what I've learned? Take a look at that English ship. It has a figurehead, spritsail braces with simple pulleys, and new pieces above the first reef of the foretopsail. Well, it is indeed a frigate.'

"'A frigate, damn it!'

"'And do you realize which frigate it is? It's that rascal *Sibylle*, by God! We will have our hands full trying to be rid of it. Still, I'm not an idiot. If I can manage to get the *Confiance* closer to the wind, I'll be curious to see if they can catch us. Ah!' he said, clenching his fists and his teeth, 'if only I had not put half of my men on the ships we captured and sent to Île de France. Then, by God, even if there were nothing to be gained, I would treat myself to a little conversation with the English ship so we could have a little fun. But, with the crew as it now is, I cannot allow myself that pleasure, because it would mean sacrificing the *Confiance* with no hope of success. It would be better to fool the English. So, what trick can we come up with? What bait might we use?'

"Surcouf went aft and sat down. He put his head in his hands and began to think. Five minutes later, he had come up with the plan he was looking for. It was about time, for less than a league now separated us from the *Sibylle*."

"'Bring up the English uniforms!' he shouted. In one of the ships he had recently captured, we had found twelve boxes of English uniforms that were on their way to India. Thinking they might be of use some day, Surcouf had kept them.

"We all immediately understood what Surcouf was intending, and smiles replaced the anxious looks on our faces. We carried the boxes up and laid out the English uniforms between decks. Each sailor went down a hatch dressed in our national uniform and came back up in a red one. In less than five minutes everybody on deck was an Englishman.

"About thirty of our crew put their arms in slings, and others wrapped bloody cloths around their heads—we got the blood from a chicken. We nailed planks to the ship's sides to make it look as if we had been patching bullet holes. With hammers we smashed the boards covering our ship's boats. Finally, our one true Englishman, our head interpreter, dressed in a captain's uniform, took possession of the bridge and the megaphone, while Surcouf, dressed as a simple sailor, stood beside him, ready to tell him what to say.

"Our ensign, a good fellow named Bléas, wearing an English officer's helmet, stood near Surcouf. 'At your orders, Captain,' he said. 'I hope you like my disguise.'

"'You are superb,' said Surcouf, laughing. 'But now the time for masquerades and jokes is over. Give me your fullest attention, Bléas, for the mission I am assigning you is extremely important. You are the nephew of the *Confiance*'s outfitter, so you have a vested interest in what happens. In addition, you speak English admirably. Moverover, I have absolute faith in your courage, intelligence, and levelheadedness.'

"'Captain, I can only repeat what I have already said: I am at your orders.'

"'Thank you. Bléas, you will get into the skiff and board the *Sibylle*.'

"'In ten minutes, Captain, you will see me on her deck.'

"'Not so fast,' said Surcouf. 'Things are not so simple. When you've been in the skiff for five minutes, I want it to take water.'

"'I'm happy for the skiff to take water, Captain, and I'm willing to go down with it, even if it means being eaten by a shark while trying to swim to safety. But what I would really like to understand is how all that could possibly help save the *Confiance*.'

"'Do you think I would allow harm to come to you, Bléas?'

"'Not at all, Captain.'

"'Then don't ask for explanations.'

"'For me that is all well and good. But how about for the men who will be with me?'

"'They will play their parts better if nothing has been explained to them. As proof that I think you are in no danger of death, neither you nor your men, here are a hundred doubloons for you and twenty-five for each of your companions. Don't try to be frugal with that money. It is in addition to your pay, designed to combat any problems your captivity might cause. But never fear. I promise that you will be out of prison before you've had the need or opportunity to spend much of the money, even if I should have to give up fifty Englishmen in exchange for you. At present, I don't need to add that on top of those hundred doubloons and your shares of our captures, there will be a generous reward for you and your men.'

"'That will not be necessary, Captain.'

"'Bah! Enough of that. Gold brings good luck. So, do you understand?'

"'Perfectly.'

"'And don't start swimming away.'

"'But are we then simply to let ourselves drown?' cried Bléas in surprise.

"'No, but when water is up to your ankles, head toward *La Sibylle* and call out for help in your best English. Do we understand each other?'

"'Yes, we understand each other.'

"'Well, then, give me your hand, and climb into the skiff.'

"Then he turned to the skiff's commander: 'Kernoch, my good man, you do trust me, don't you?'

"'Hell's bells! Do I trust you? Absolutely.'

"'Well, don't worry, but I need you to take this marlinspike, and when you are halfway to the frigate, punch two or three holes in the skiff's hull so that it starts taking water.'

"Leaning over toward Kernoch, Surcouf took something from his pocket and whispered a few words in the man's ear before he slipped a roll of paper into the skiff commander's vest pocket. 'No reason for that,' said Kernoch, 'but very well.'

"'Aren't you going to give me a kiss?'

"'What do you mean? With great pleasure,' the sailor replied. And stuffing his wad of tobacco, as big as an egg, far back in his mouth, he planted on each of Surcouf's cheeks one of those fat kisses that country people call nanny kisses.

"A moment later the skiff left our ship.

"The *Confiance*, close to the wind, struck all but its topsails, bore up, recognized the English flag with a cannon shot, came round to port, and hove to. The *Sibylle*, not completely trusting our nationality, kept us within range, dumped into the sea some of the fake bundles obstructing some of the gunports, and, evidencing a mighty array of cannons, hove to on our port side.

"Their captain asked us where we were coming from and why we had kept so much sail as we drew near. Our interpreter, repeating what Surcouf was telling him to say, answered first that it had taken some time for us to identify the *Sibylle* because of its disguise, and then that we had approached them so quickly because we had some good news for the captain."

"'What news?' the captain himself asked through his megaphone.

"'The news of your promotion,' the interpreter replied coolly. In dictating this answer, Surcouf showed how much he understood the human heart, for the man to whom one announces good news rarely doubts its veracity.

"Immediately doubt disappeared from the captain's face; yet, shaking his head, he said, 'It is strange how much your ship looks like a French corsair.'

"'But it is indeed a French corsair,' the interpreter answered, 'and quite a famous one. We captured it on the Gascony coast, but since Bordeaux corsair ships are the fastest on all seven seas, we decided to continue our voyage in it instead of our own. Our intention is, God willing, to pursue and capture Surcouf.'

"During the conversation between our interpreter and the English captain, the men in the skiff began suddenly to call out in distress, for their boat was indeed beginning to take water and sink.

"We promptly hailed the frigate and asked it to send help to our men, for our own boats, we said, were even more damaged by grapeshot and cannonballs than the sinking skiff and thus were incapable of putting to sea.

"The first duty, the most imperious law of the sea is to save those in danger, be they friends or enemies. And so the *Sibylle* put longboats to sea to help Ensign Bléas and his sailors.

"'Save our sailors,' the interpreter shouted. 'We ourselves will make a tack and then come back to pick up our men and the skiff.' To complete the maneuver, the *Confiance* lowered its foresail, raised its topgallant and jib, set the spanker, and moved away from the frigate.

"Surcouf's idea was brilliant. Now that he was free to maneuver, he was jubilant: 'Do you see those good Englishmen?' he said. 'How can we not love them? See how they are helping our men climb aboard? Now Kernoch is collapsing and, my word, Bléas is fainting. Oh, those charming rascals, I shall never forget how well they have played their parts. Our friends are safe, and so are we. Get ready for our next tack! Full sail! Close to the wind! Close—haul the sails! And you, cabin boy, light a cigar and bring it to me.'

"The wind from the open sea was blowing strong. Never had the *Confiance* conducted itself more nobly than on that occasion. Swift as it sailed, one would have thought it aware of the danger from which it was helping us to escape. We were proud of sailing such a ship. In admiration we watched its boiling wake streaming out behind us.

"As soon as the *Sibylle* realized our trick, it released a volley, pulled up its boats, and started after us. But we were already out of range. The chase lasted until evening. In the night, we slipped their company. From its gallant masts to its keel, the English ship disappeared from our sight."

As Saint-Jean came to the end of his tale—from which we have removed many picturesque details that might have rendered it unintelligible, for René had not ceased pouring rum, eau-de-vie, and brandy into his guest's glass—the old sailor's head dropped to the table. Snoring heavily, he'd slipped into the capricious kingdom of sleep.

LII

Surcouf

➤⋮➤

RENÉ LEARNED that Surcouf normally signed up crew members every morning from eight to ten. So at seven-thirty René was pulling on the clothes he had been wearing the day before. They had dried during the night, and since they showed he had traveled a long way, he thought them more appropriate for his introduction to Surcouf than new clothes from a tailor. At eight o'clock he reached the Rue Porcon de la Barbinais, then followed the Rue de la Boucherie to the Rue de Dinan. At the end of that street, next to the ramparts opposite the gate with the same name, stood Surcouf's house, between courtyard and garden.

About a dozen sailors, earlier risers than René, were already waiting in the antechamber. Each man was to enter in turn, and so there would be no question about the order of admittance, a sailor sitting by the door was distributing numbers which he would call as each turn arose. René was number sixteen.

The walls of the antechamber were decorated with weapons from many different countries. The skin of a black Java panther served as the background for a collection of poisoned Malay daggers, arrows that had been dipped in the most horrible poisons, and sabers whose wounds, even if only skin-deep, were always lethal. On another wall a lion skin from the Atlas Mountains framed a collection of Tunisian kandjars, flissas from Algiers, pistols with sculpted silver handles, and Damascus swords curved like crescents. On the third wall a prairie bison skin displayed a collection of bows, tomahawks, scalping knives, and rifles. Finally, the skin of a Bengal tiger flaunted sabers with gilded blades and jade hilts, as well as some damascened daggers with ivory and carnelian handles, not to mention rings and gold bracelets. The weaponry represented all four parts of the world on the four walls of Surcouf's waiting room.

While René was examining Surcouf's trophies with much admiration, including a long display on the ceiling of a twenty-foot-long caiman and the coils of a boa almost twice that length, three or four of the men hoping to enlist had gone through, but meanwhile ten others had joined René in the anteroom.

Now and then they heard gunshots. Two or three of Surcouf's officers were amusing themselves by shooting at iron plates that had been placed at various distances in the immense garden. One could see the traces of bullets where they'd flattened against the plates. Nearby the antechamber, too, was an arms room where three or four young men, midshipmen or ensigns on the corsair ship, were working out with sword or saber.

Although René was wearing the clothing of a simple seaman, as soon as Surcouf saw him he knew that he was dealing with a man whose condition was more elevated than his clothing indicated. He looked René up and down. His gaze paused on the young man's unwavering eyes. He examined René's well-formed body; he noted the fine, elegantly shaped beard. He peered at his hands to complete his observations. But René's hands were neatly gloved. The gloves were old, it is true, but they had been cleaned with an eraser, and it was easy to see in the man wearing them, if not luxury itself, at least aspirations to luxury. So, when René gave him a military salute and stopped two paces away, Surcouf responded by doffing his hat, something he would not normally do for an ordinary seaman.

As for René, he had taken in the imposing figure of Surcouf with one glance: about thirty-one years old; short blond hair, with a neatly trimmed curtain beard on the chin; a powerful neck, strong shoulders. He was not very tall, but his very presence bespoke Herculean strength.

"What would you want of me?" asked Surcouf with a slight nod.

"I know that you will soon be going to sea, monsieur, and I would like to enlist in your service."

"Not as an ordinary sailor, I presume?" Surcouf asked.

"As a simple sailor," René replied with a bow.

Surcouf looked at him carefully, and with astonishment. "Allow me to tell you," Surcouf went on, "that you appear no more cut out to be a sailor than a choirboy is to shine shoes."

"That is possible, monsieur, but there is no job, however difficult, that cannot be learned quickly if one has the will to learn it well."

"But strength is also required."

"Even if strength is lacking, monsieur, much can be done with skill. It seems to me that great strength is not essential to reef in the main-topsail or the fore-topsail, nor for throwing grenades from the main-top or stays onto the deck of an enemy ship."

"In our profession," said Surcouf, "there are some maneuvers that do require great strength. Suppose you are needed to assist with a cannon. Do you think yourself strong enough to lift a cannonball of forty-eight up to a cannon's muzzle?" With his foot he rolled a ball of forty-eight over toward René.

"I think that would be easy," René answered.

"Go ahead! Try!" said Surcouf.

René leaned down, and with one hand he picked up the ball, as if he were lawn-bowling, and threw it over Surcouf's head into the garden. The cannonball rolled about twenty yards before it stopped.

Surcouf stood up, looked at the ball, and sat back down. "That is re-assuring, monsieur. On the *Revenant,* there are not more than five or six men, me included, who are able to do what you have just done. Would you permit me to look at your hand?"

René smiled, removed his glove, and extended his fine, delicate hand. Surcouf examined it.

"By God, gentlemen," he shouted to his officers in the room close by, "come see something curious." The officers hurried over.

"This looks like a girl's hand," Surcouf went on, "and it has just tossed that ball of forty-eight over my head, and it landed where you see it now."

If René's hand had seemed like a woman's in Surcouf's powerful clasp, it looked like a child's in Kernoch's colossal grip. "Come now, Captain," said Kernoch. "You are joking, surely. Is this a hand?" And with a gesture of disdain, brute force scoffing at its inferior, he tossed the hand aside.

Surcouf had made a movement to stop Kernoch, but René, himself stopping Surcouf, asked, "Captain, will you allow me?"

"Go ahead, my boy," said Surcouf, always interested in the unexpected, as is every superior mind.

Gathering himself up, René leaped out of the window into the garden. A few feet from the ball he had thrown lay another, one that had no doubt been used in a similar exercise. Placing one ball in the palm of his hand and balancing the other on top of it, with his arm partially extended he carried both of them back. When he reached the window, he put one ball in each hand, then leaped up onto the sill, slipped under the window bar, stepped down into the room, and presented one of the cannonballs to Kernoch: "A keg of cider for the crew," he said, "for the man who can throw the ball the farthest."

René had accomplished his feat with such ease and grace that several of the men reached out to touch the cannonballs to be sure they were truly made of iron.

"Ah, Kernoch, my friend, you cannot refuse a proposal like that," Surcouf observed.

"And I don't refuse," said Kernoch, "and provided that my patron saint James does not abandon me. . . ."

"Go ahead," René said to the Breton giant.

Kernoch collected himself; concentrating all his strength in his leg and right arm, with one motion he released both like a spring. The ball flew through the window and dropped ten yards away, then rolled three or four more before coming finally to a stop.

"That is what a real man can do," said Kernoch. "Let the devil try to beat it."

"I am not the devil, Monsieur Kernoch," said René. "But I do believe you will be the person treating the crew."

With the ball in his hand, René began simply to swing his arm back and forth. On the third swing he tossed the projectile. It fell three or four yards beyond the first and rolled another ten yards farther.

Surcouf let out a jubilant cry and Kernoch an angry one. All the others remained speechless in surprise.

René, though, had grown suddenly horribly pale and had to lean against the fireplace. Surcouf eyed him with concern. From a little cupboard he pulled out a small flask of eau-de-vie and handed it to René. "Thank you," said René, "but I never drink eau-de-vie." He walked over to a tray on which there was a carafe, a glass, and some sugar. He poured a little water into the glass and drank it. A smile reappeared on his lips as color returned to his cheeks.

"How about another attempt, Kernoch?" asked a young lieutenant.

"I don't think so," Kernoch replied.

"Might I do something else to please you?" asked René.

"Yes," said Kernoch. "Make the sign of the cross."

René smiled and crossed himself, adding the first words of Sunday prayers: "I believe in God the Father omnipotent, creator of heaven and earth."

"Gentlemen," said Surcouf, "please allow me a few moments alone with this young man."

Everyone withdrew. Kernoch was grumbling; the others were laughing.

Alone with Surcouf, René became as calm and unassuming as he had been before. Whereas another man might have alluded to the victory he had just won, he simply waited for Surcouf to speak.

"Monsieur," said Surcouf, laughing, "I don't know what else you can do beyond what you just did before my very eyes, but a man who can leap through a window four feet high and throw a cannonball of forty-eight will always be of use on a ship like mine. What are your conditions?"

"A hammock on board, the normal food, and the right to be killed for France. I desire nothing more, monsieur."

"My dear sir," said Surcouf, "it is my custom to pay for services rendered."

"But a seaman who has never sailed or a sailor who doesn't know his job can render no services. On the contrary, it is you who would be rendering me a service by teaching me how to do the job."

"My crew gets a third of my take. Does it suit you to enter my service on the same conditions as those of all my sailors, best and worst?"

"No, Captain, for your sailors, seeing that I know how to do nothing, for

I've everything to learn, would accuse me of stealing money I have not earned. In six months, if you agree, we will have this conversation again. That is enough for today."

"But, my dear sir," said Surcouf, "you surely know how to do more than perform gymnastics like Milon de Croton and throw weights like Remus? Are you a hunter, for example?"

"Hunting was one of the pleasures of my youth," René replied.

"So you can shoot pistols?"

"As well as other men."

"Are you skillful with the sword?"

"Skillful enough to get myself killed."

"Well, on board we have some excellent shots, and there's an arms room where any crewmember can practice with sword or saber when he is not on watch. You will do as your mates, and after three months you will be as skillful as any man of them."

"I hope so," said René.

"The only thing left to decide is your pay. And we shall not wait six months for that. Rather we'll come to a decision as we eat—I hope you will do me the pleasure of dining with me today."

"Oh, to be sure, Captain, I thank you for the honor."

"While we are waiting, would you like to watch some shooting? Kernoch and Bléas are equally skilled with the pistol, and once they've begun a contest, neither one gives in easily." Surcouf motioned René over to the other window.

Kernoch and Bléas stood twenty-five paces from their target: an iron plate with a vertical white chalk line dividing it in two. Unconcerned by the presence of two more spectators, the two sailors continued their challenge. Although they were not exceptional, both men were remarkably skillful, and their each good shot won their audience's applause.

When Kernoch placed a bullet right on the white mark, René applauded along with the others. Still holding a grudge, Kernoch took the second pistol from Bléas and, without a word, handed it to René.

"What would you like me to do with this, monsieur?" René asked.

"You displayed your strength a few minutes ago," said Kernoch. "Now, I trust, you will not refuse to show us your skill."

"With pleasure, monsieur, though you don't leave me much of a chance since your shot struck the line. Still, your bullet, as you must have noticed, hit slightly more to the right than to the left."

"So?" said Kernoch.

"So," René replied, "I shall have to place mine exactly in the middle."

René seemed not even to have taken time to aim, so quickly had he pulled the trigger. And the bullet struck the line indeed exactly; one would have thought that the silver spot spreading out on both sides of it had been measured with a compass.

The sailors looked at one another in surprise, while Surcouf burst out laughing. "Well, Kernoch," he asked his foreman, "what do you say to that?"

"I say that by chance that can happen once, but had he need to do it again. . . ."

"I shall not do it again, as what I've done is mere child's play. I would, however, propose something else."

Looking around the room, René spotted some sealing wafers on a desk. He took five of them and, placing his hand on the window bar, he leaped nimbly down into the garden, where he arranged the five wafers on the iron plate like the five of diamonds. Then he vaulted back with the same agility through the window, picked up the pistol, and obliterated the five wafers with five shots. Not a trace of them remained on the iron plate.

Handing the pistol to Kernoch, he said, "Your turn."

Kernoch shook his head. "Thank you," he said. "I'm a good Breton and a good Christian. There's the devil at work in all this and I want nothing more to do with it."

"You are right, Kernoch," said Surcouf; "and so the devil cannot play a nasty trick on us, we will take him along with us on board the *Revenant*."

Surcouf then opened the door to the next room, where the ship's fencing master was at work. Surcouf, adept at all physical exercises, wanted his seamen to be equally skilled, and so had hired a fencing master for his crew. The man gave lessons both in saber and épée.

Surcouf and René watched for a moment as one man attacked and another parried. Surcouf thought the parry to be poorly executed, and René opined, "I would have countered with a quarte parry and riposted with a direct attack."

"Monsieur," said the fencing master, twisting his moustache, "that would be a good way to be skewered like a weakling."

"Possibly, monsieur," René said. "But in that case I would have been too slow in both my parry and my riposte."

"Would monsieur care to take a lesson?" the fencing master asked Surcouf, laughing.

"Be careful, my dear Bras-d'Acier," said Surcouf. "Monsieur here may give you a lesson. He has already provided two lessons and if your student is willing to lend him his foil, he might soon teach you a third."

"Chasse-Boeuf," said the fencing master, "give your foil to Monsieur, and he will try to put into practice the advice he just gave you."

"That you will not see, Monsieur Chasse-Boeuf," said René. "It is impolite to touch a fencing master; I shall be content to parry."

With the student's foil in hand, René performed the customary salute with admirable grace and assumed the guard position. And an unusual combat began. Master Bras-d'Acier called to his aid all the resources at his disposal, but to no avail. Using the four basic parries, without even trying to counter, René constantly evaded the master's foil. What's more, Bras-d'Acier deserved his name. With an arm of steel, for a quarter of an hour he went through the entire fencing repertory: feints, direct attacks, disengagements. He complicated even already-complicated attacks. But it was all in vain. The tip of his foil inevitably passed to the right or left of his adversary's body.

Seeing that Bras-d'Acier had no intention of asking for mercy, René performed his departing salute with courtesy to match his opening one. As Surcouf led him to the door, René promised to be on time for dinner, at five o'clock.

LIII

The Officers on the Revenant

THE SAME DAY, at five in the afternoon, René was shown into the captain's living room, where Madame Surcouf was playing with a two-year-old child.

"Excuse me, monsieur," she said, "but Surcouf has been kept by unexpected business and could not be here as promptly as he intended. He asked me to do the honors of the house while we wait for him. Please be indulgent of a poor provincial woman."

"Madame," said René, "I knew that Surcouf had been happily married for three years to a charming woman. I would that I'd not have waited this long to meet his wife, dare I say, if the title of sailor, assuming Monsieur Surcouf agrees to grant me that title, has not turned my wish into an indiscretion. I have always admired his courage, madame, and today I admire his devotion. No man has paid his debt to his country more fully than Monsieur Surcouf. Although France could expect much from him, she had nothing to claim from him. And to leave behind such a lovely child, whom I ask permission to kiss, and especially to have to leave the child's mother, requires much more than courage. It requires devotion."

"Ah, truly," said Surcouf, who had heard the end of the sentence and seen, with both paternal and conjugal pride, the future sailor kiss his child and greet his wife.

"Commander," said René, "before seeing Madame and this charming child, I would have believed you capable of any sacrifice. But, now that I have seen them, I doubt, unless you confirm it, that your love of country can be so strong that it could ever truly supersede the heart of your heart."

"Well, madame, what do say to that?" asked Surcouf. "In the three years you have been the wife of a corsair, have you ever heard a sailor turn a compliment like this new man I have hired?"

"You are joking!" cried Madame Surcouf. "Monsieur surely has not been taken on as an ordinary sailor, I hope."

"As the most ordinary of sailors, madame. Although in a drawing room I may have the advantage over the good men of your husband's crew by an accident of education, even the most ignorant among them will have the advantage once I am on board."

"I had told you five o'clock, monsieur," said Surcouf, "because I wanted to be able to introduce you to all the guests who are part of the *Revenant*'s staff as they arrive."

The door opened at that very moment, and Surcouf obliged: "First of all, here is our second in command, Monsieur Bléas."

"I have the honor of knowing Monsieur Bléas by reputation," said René. "He is the man who, on board the *Confiance*, sacrificed himself along with Kernoch to board the *Sibylle*, the ship you recognized too late as an enemy. Such devotion gives honor both to the man who makes the sacrifice and to the man for whom it is made."

"I hope, Commander," said Bléas, "that you are disposed to introduce Monsieur to me, for until now I know him only as one of the best pistol shots I have ever seen."

"Alas! Monsieur," said René. "Unlike you, I have no glorious past on which to lay praise. My name is simply René, and all I ask of Monsieur Surcouf is that he be willing to welcome me as a sailor on board the *Revenant*."

"I'm not the person to ask," said Surcouf with a laugh. "For that, you must ask our crew master," and he pointed to Kernoch who was just entering the living room.

"Come over here, Kernoch! I'm sorry you were not here a moment ago when Monsieur René was talking so enthusiastically about a certain skiff master on board the *Confiance*, a man who sacrificed himself along with a young ensign whose name I have forgotten, to board an English vessel. Once on board he simulated an attack of nerves to divert the Red Coats, while the captain of the *Confiance*, who had thrown himself like a hare into a leopard's claws, made away at full sail."

"My word," said Kernoch, gesturing toward René, "if Monsieur had been there, everything would have been much simpler. You could have given him one of our Lepage pistols, shown him the English captain, and told him, 'Blow off that gentleman's head for me.' In no time he'd have picked up the pistol and shot the Englishman dead, and that would have caused a good deal more commotion on board than my attack of nerves. . . . Ah! Lieutenant Blaise, you were not there this morning when Monsieur René gave us a lesson in pistol shooting. I am sorry you missed that, but if he sails with us, as we have been led to hope, you will surely see how well he wields that little instrument. As for the way he manages a foil, here comes your friend Bras-d'Acier—he can give you all the information you need."

"You are mistaken, Kernoch," said the fencing master. "For Monsieur did me the honor of parrying every thrust I attempted, yet he never once troubled himself to riposte."

"Indeed, you have guessed my weakness, Monsieur Bras-d'Acier," said René. "I am much better trained for defense than I am for attack. My fencing master, an old Italian named Belloni, used to claim that one could disconcert one's opponent far more by parrying three successive thrusts than by touching him once. So, if it is all the same, why touch when one can simply parry?"

"Now," said Surcouf, "the only men left to introduce you to are these two latecomers. They are, I believe, the two best grenade throwers in the world. Although they may be late for dinner, they are always quick to take up their positions, one on the fore-topsail and the other on the main, when there is fighting to be done. . . . And now, Monsieur René, if you would offer your arm to Madame Surcouf, we will go into the dining room."

A chambermaid was waiting for that announcement to take away the little Surcouf, who, like a well-brought-up child, withdrew at the first request.

The sumptuousness of provincial tables is well known, and Surcouf was often cited for the excellence of his table. His dinners would have satisfied Homeric heroes, for here you could eat like Diomedes and drink like Ajax. As for Surcouf, he would have challenged Bacchus himself. It goes without saying that the dinner was raucous.

René, drinking only water, was the target of so much mockery that he begged for mercy, which was granted by everyone except Master Bras-d'Acier. Tired finally of such persistence, René asked Madame Surcouf to excuse him for what he was about to do and asked her permission to drink to her health. Permission was granted.

"And now, madame," he said, "do you have a cup worthy of a true drinker; a cup that holds two or three bottles, perhaps?"

Madame Surcouf obliged, and a servant brought a silver bowl embla-zoned with a coat of arms from the peerage of England. René poured three bottles of Champagne into the bowl.

"Monsieur," he said to the fencing master, "I shall have the honor of emptying this cup to Madame Surcouf's health. Please note that you are the one forcing me to do so, for I told you the truth at the beginning of the meal: Normally I drink only water. Now, once I have emptied this cup, you, I trust, will in turn refill it and empty it as I shall have done, not to Madame Surcouf's health but to her husband's glory."

Applause thundered for his speech. The fencing master, however, grew quiet, and his eyes grew wide.

With a sad eye and a disdainful smile René contemplated his challenge for a second. He lifted the cup to his lips and the table went still, with every guest agog at the young sailor and eager to see how far he would carry this folly, for even the most inveterate of drinkers would consider quaffing three bottles of Champagne without a pause to be folly. Impassively René began to drink, and his lips never left the cup's silver edge until not a single drop of the effervescent wine was left. To prove it, he placed the cup upside down on his plate. Then he sat back down, and placing the cup before the fencing master, said, "Your turn, monsieur."

"Nicely done," said Kernoch. "Your turn, Master Bras-d'Acier."

But the fencing master felt unequal to the challenge. When he tried to back out, Kernoch got to his feet and declared that if d'Acier would not make a good-faith effort to empty the cup, he himself would be forced to do so. Without hesitating, Kernoch broke the wires around the cork of a bot-tle of Champagne and poured it in the silver cup. Bras-d'Acier then asked to be allowed to drink the three bottles one at a time, and everyone agreed. He had barely finished the first, however, when he fell back and cried for mercy, for he couldn't drink another drop. Five minutes later he rolled off his chair to the floor.

"Allow me first to take care of our would-be Saint-Georges," an-nounced Kernoch, "then I'll be back to sing a little song sure to make us all forget any chill this little incident has brought upon us."

In those days a dinner, even in big cities, rarely ended without some of the guests singing to the glory of the master or mistress of the house in praise of their profession. So Kernoch's proposal was greeted with enthusi-asm, and during his brief absence the other guests kept shouting: "Kernoch! A song! A song!" They shouted even more loudly when he reappeared.

Kernoch was not the kind of man who needed to be asked twice. He sig-naled that he was about to begin and, with a pleasing voice and the appro-priate mien, he launched into song:

Le Brig Black

Mer jolie et bon vent,
Quand
Le temps favorise
La nuit notre vaisseau,
Ho!
Si la brise
Frise
L'eau,
Cric! Crac! et sabot
Cuiller à pot!

(The Black Brig

Fine seas and good breeze,
When
The weather favors
Our ship at night
Ho!
If the breeze
Skims
The seas,
Crick! Crack! Dash
In a flash!)

"All together now," cried Kernoch. And all the guests, except for Bras-d'Acier, whose snoring they could hear in the next room, joined in the chorus:

Si la brise
Frise
L'eau
Cric! crac! et sabot
Cuiller à pot!

The song was typical forecastle poetry, the kind of music sure to be a great success at a seaman's dinner. The room called for encores, and it seemed that the bravos and applause would never end. There was, though, another thing that created almost as much note as the crew master's couplets, and that was René's demeanor after he'd emptied the cup with which he challenged the fencing master. For his face had neither paled nor reddened, and his speech was slurred no more than that of a man after he drinks a glass of water on arising in the morning.

All eyes had turned toward Surcouf, for a song from him would double the value of his hospitality. Knowing what his guests wanted, he said, "Very well. I'll sing you the sailor's song I used to sing when I trained cabin boys."

A murmur circled the table, and several voices called out, "Shhhh! Silence!" Silence there was. And Surcouf began:

> "Cabin boy, pick up the rope at the foot of the mast
>   And tie me a square knot."
> "One, two, it's done! . . . May the devil come fast!
>   Master, a soldier or city boy I'm not
>   I can twist and untwist your rope to the last
>   I'm learning my job and my lot."

Surcouf sang all the verses with as much success as Kernoch. But the eyes of the lovely hostess betrayed her curiosity about their youngest guest. She marveled at his calm demeanor, and wondered if he maintained it simply by his nature or by sheer will. She wondered, too, what was his nature and his background, his heritage. Finally she could wait no longer and asked, "And how about you, Monsieur René? Will you be the only one not to sing a song from his own country?"

"Alas, madame," said René. "I am a man without a country. I was born in France, and that is all I am allowed to remember. Even if I searched my memory, I am not sure that I would be able to find a song still residing there. All the joys of my youth and every flower of my adolescence have been destroyed by three long, sad years of winter. However, let me dig into my memory, and if I come upon some snowdrops, to honor your request I shall gather them. You will please excuse me to your guests, madame, for my want of knowing any songs about their glorious profession, although I'm sure none shall be lacking after I complete one campaign. In the meantime, may this please you."

His voice as fresh and pure as a young girl's, he sang:

> Were I a ray of sun
> With love I would glow
> Envelop you with my light
> But I would pale near your eyes.
>
> If I were the fortunate mirror
> Reflecting you in your boudoir

In me you would see your own image
In my heart accept this lovely mirage.

He rendered the next four verses as successfully and poignantly as the first two, and when he had finished, Madame Surcouf said, "Gentlemen, when the nightingale has sung, all other birds fall silent. Let us now go into the living room, where coffee awaits us."

René stood up, offered his arm to Madame Surcouf, and accompanied her to the living room. Scarcely had he released his arm and bowed to her than Surcouf came over to him. Taking René's arm, he led him to a window, René responding with all the deference of a subordinate to his superior.

"I believe it is time, my dear René," said Surcouf, "for us to put an end to this charade. Tell me what you want from me, and why you wanted to see me. You are too charming a companion for me not to try, inasmuch as possible, to please you."

"I have never wanted anything else, and I want nothing more now, than being taken on by you, Captain, as an ordinary sailor and part of your crew."

"But what can have inspired such caprice? It is useless to try to hide that you are a young man of means. You have the education of a man who could aspire to the highest government positions. Are you unaware of the company you will find yourself in and the kinds of services you will be called upon to perform?"

"Monsieur Surcouf, a man like me, who leaves aside all pride, finds that there are no companies unworthy of me. As for my service, it will be difficult, I am sure. But you know that I am strong, and you have seen that I am clever with my hands. I drink only water, and even when I am forced to drink such quantities of wine that would make another man lose his head, you have seen that it has no effect on me. As for danger, I believe I can say the same thing of it as I say for wine. I have lived too long waiting for death each day not to be familiar with it. Having been given the choice of the branch I wanted to serve in and of the captain I wanted to serve under, I have decided to become a sailor, and as you are one of the bravest and most loyal officers I know of, I have chosen you as my master."

"I must warn you, monsieur," said Surcouf. "A sailor, even an ordinary sailor who enlists with us, does so under particular conditions, and once they are noted on the contract, such conditions are always observed."

"I wish to share with my companions their service and life. I have not shown, nor do I feel, that I deserve to be relieved of any of the tasks incumbent upon me as an ordinary sailor. As I am sure you can understand, I would however be reluctant not to have my own hammock."

"That request is so easy to grant that it is impossible to refuse. But I can propose something better: Would you care to be my secretary? That way you would have not only a hammock but an office as well."

"I gratefully accept, provided that the position leaves me free to pursue ordinary seaman's work and to fight when necessary."

"I would be happy to have you give up your work as a seaman," said Surcouf, laughing, "but I am not so stupid as to relinquish your aid when we have to fight."

"May I ask another favor? Which is to fight with my own weapons, that is, with weapons I am used to."

"When we enter combat, we bring all the weapons up on deck, from which each man chooses as he pleases. You may bring your own up with you. So the favor I grant is nothing."

"One final request. If we happen to land on the coast of Coromandel or Bengal, will you allow me, at my own expense, of course, to hunt for a tiger or panther? For I have often heard about such hunts but have never had the opportunity to participate. Also, if ever you have any expeditions in which you fear for the life of one of your officers, entrust it to me. No life depends upon my own, and nobody will miss me."

"In that case," said Surcouf, "on those days we make captures, you will allow me to treat you as an officer. Our takes are divided in the following way: one third for me, one third for the officers, and one third for the soldiers."

"Will I be allowed to use my share as I wish?" asked René.

"That is only fair," Surcouf replied.

"And now, Commandant, allow me another question," said René. "Do you have any weapons you can always depend upon?"

"Yes. I have a rifle, a double-barreled shotgun I've baptized with the name *Foudroyant*, and my bottle-breakers, with which you already are acquainted."

"What are your bottle-breakers?"

"My pistols. At sea, so my men can practice their marksmanship, I have bottles tied to the studdingsails' outriggers. All the sailors have the right to join in, and whoever manages to break a bottle, for all the pitching and rolling, wins a crown if he is using a gun and five francs if with a pistol."

"I will request permission to participate, with the right to use my prizes as I wish."

"Of course. And now, putting aside your modest requests, I would like to advise you, my dear René, to think seriously about the conditions to which you are agreeing, whether by vocation or by compulsion from a force beyond you. I would like to make something of you, in spite of your reluctance. Now, have all the conditions been set? Do you have anything else to request? Do I have anything else to propose?"

"Nothing, Commandant. And I thank you."

"Kernoch, who is now your friend, will teach you the practical part of your job. I myself will take responsibility for higher studies. At the moment, though, Madame Surcouf is looking for you, with a cup of coffee in one hand and a glass of liqueur in the other."

René walked toward Madame Surcouf and, after greeting her politely, said, "Please excuse me, madame, but I never drink coffee or alcohol."

"People say it is like Champagne," said Kernoch, joking, as he broke into the young seaman's apologies. "If you drink only a little, it goes to your head."

"I would be sorry," said René, "if Madame Surcouf saw anything in my coarse victory other than the wish to rid myself of Bras-d'Acier's mockeries, for that would have spoiled one of the most charming meals I have had in my entire life."

"And since it is now dessert time," said a voice behind him, "you no longer fear, I trust, that your meal will be spoiled."

"Well," said René, "Master Bras-d'Acier has come back to life! Allow me to congratulate you, monsieur. I thought you would be out until at least tomorrow morning."

"By the sword of Saint-Georges, Captain, you will not allow one of your officers to be thus insulted without demanding immediate satisfaction! Swords! Swords!" With that cry the fencing master hurried back into the arms room, where he had taken his siesta, and returned almost immediately with an épée in each hand.

Madame Surcouf uttered a small cry, and several men stepped in front of Master Bras-d'Acier. "Monsieur," said Surcouf himself, "I command you to return to your quarters immediately. And stay there until we sail."

"Excuse me, Commander," said René, "but we are not on board your ship. Rather we are in your home, where by your invitation you have made your guests your equals, at least for the time being. If you now send this gentleman away, you will be forcing me, on a point of honor, to leave as well, and to kill him under the first streetlamp we find. If, on the other hand, you allow what began as a comedy to end as a comedy, we shall be able to present to Madame Surcouf the strange spectacle of a duel to the death in which nobody will be killed."

"But. . . ." said Surcouf, unconvinced.

"Please allow me, Commander," said René. "I give you my word of honor that not a single drop of blood will be spilled."

"Well, since that is your will, gentlemen. Do as you please."

Once Surcouf had given his permission, the guests moved to either side of the living room so as to leave the area in the middle free.

Master Bras-d'Acier, for whom duels were sacred, first took off his jacket and his vest, then held out the handles of the two épées to René. René noticed that Bras-d'Acier, in his hurry to grab two weapons for the duel, had in error not picked up two épées but rather one épée and a foil. René quickly chose the foil, and the sight of the young man holding a foil with its buttoned point aroused laughter from both sides of the room.

Master Bras-d'Acier, looking around the room to discover the cause for such mirth, soon realized too that René was holding a foil, not an épée.

"As I was saying, monsieur," said René, "you must not yet be fully awake. But in any case, you have fulfilled my wishes. En garde, please, and spare no effort." The young man himself assumed the on-guard position.

"But," all those watching cried, "you cannot defend yourself with a foil when this gentleman is attacking with an épée."

"That is how it is," René replied gravely. "Otherwise, tomorrow you would force me to meet this gentleman outside with equal weapons, and then, so as not to appear a mere braggart, I should have to kill him, something for which I would never be able to console myself. So come on, Master Bras-d'Acier; you can see that I am waiting for you. Let us fight until the first scratch, if you will. And so that I shall not be accused of trickery, with Madame's permission, I will do just as you have done."

Throwing his seaman's jacket and vest on a chair, René stood before them in his shirt, made of the finest batiste, its brilliant whiteness a stark contrast to the ecru of his opponent's shirt. Quickly he reassumed the on-guard position, the point of his foil lowered and his body poised so elegantly that the spectators could not help applauding, as if he had already made a thrust.

Annoyed by the applause, the fencing master began his attack, and the same spectacle they had provided that morning by sunlight was played out again that evening in torchlight. Bras-d'Acier called upon all the feints, thrusts, and ripostes in the fencing repertory, and all his attacks were parried by René with utter sangfroid and exasperating simplicity. Then, one fine feint was so skillfully delivered by d'Acier that the point of his épée, though it did not scratch René's skin, did rip open his shirt and left his chest partially bared.

René began to laugh. "Go pick up your épée, monsieur," he said to his opponent, and at the same moment his foil caught Bras-d'Acier's weapon so cleanly and with such force that it was thrown ten paces behind him.

While the fencing master was retrieving his weapon as he'd been invited to do, René dipped the button of his foil into a bottle of ink. "Now," he announced to d'Acier, "I shall make three thrusts, and they will mark a triangle on your chest. In a real duel, any one of these three would be fatal. When we are good friends once again, and I hope that will be soon, I shall teach you how to parry them."

No sooner had he said it than he did it. After delivering three lightning-quick thrusts, René stepped back. The button of his foil had left three black spots on the right side of the fencing master's chest. They formed a triangle as perfect as if it had been drawn with a compass.

René placed his foil down on a chair, put back on his vest and jacket, picked up his hat, and extended his hand to his opponent, who refused to take it. He shook Surcouf's hand and kissed that of his wife, at the same time begging her pardon for twice having wandered beyond propriety in her presence, first by drinking down three bottles of champagne and then by staging a duel. Then, with a gracious smile and an elegant bow to the rest of the guests, he left the room.

Scarcely had the door closed behind him and Bras-d'Acier gone back to the arms room to get dressed than everyone began to sing the praises of the captain's new recruit aboard the *Revenant*.

"Why in the world would such a coxcomb enlist as a simple sailor?" cried Surcouf.

"I know," whispered Madame Surcouf into her husband's ear.

"You know?"

"He is disappointed in love."

"What makes you say that?"

"When his shirt was torn, around his neck I could see a golden chain with a medallion, and on the medallion was a diamond memento."

"About love," said Surcouf, "you may have guessed correctly. But what could make a man of such distinction enlist as a sailor?"

"Ah," she said, "that I do not know."

"Yes, that indeed is the secret," said Surcouf.

The following day René was awakened by Surcouf and Master Bras-d'Acier. Night, and Surcouf especially, had brought counsel to the fencing master. He had come to apologize to René.

LIV
Getting Under Way

It was the end of July. The walls of Saint-Malo overlooking the inner and outer harbors, as well as the rock in Saint-Servan, were aswarm with spectators eager to watch the seaport pageantry. All the ships in the harbor were decked out with flags, as was every house looking out over the port. Moving slowly from within the inner harbor was a fine, stately four-hundred-ton brig towed by four longboats, each with a dozen oarsmen, all of them singing a corsair song to the rhythm of their oars. Their voices drowned out the noise of the crowd.

> The corsair on his sailing ship
> Demands victory or death.
> Heave ho! Long live France!
>
> Leaving Saint-Malo
> Our long oars slap the water.
>
> Leaving Saint-Malo
> Our long oars slap the water.
> Heave ho! and good luck.
>
> Once at sea, sailors, keep a look out!
> The best ships are the biggest ones.
>
> Once at sea, sailors, keep a look out!
> The best ships are the biggest ones.
> Heave ho, our barge!
>
> Our barge moves right along
> Faster than a flying fish.

As the longboats and ship were slipping through the narrow channel that separated Saint-Servan from Saint-Malo, above the bowsprit onlookers could see a beautifully sculpted skeleton clothed in a shroud and holding up his tombstone. The brig was the *Revenant*, and Captain Surcouf had paid for the ship himself. It was built for the high seas, the theater of the brave captain's exploits, and it was about to reappear like a revenant, a ghost, in the Atlantic and Indian Oceans.

As soon as the spectators, scattered as they were, either anchored to the rocks or perched on the ramparts or crowded at every window, found the longboats close enough, they would shout: "Long live the *Revenant!* Long live its crew!" And the rowers, standing up and raising their oars, would answer, "Long live Surcouf! Long live France!"

As the brig passed before their excited eyes, the people of Saint-Malo could count the sixteen twelve-pound cannons whose necks protruded from the ship's portholes, they could see the large thirty-six-pound "smasher" mounted on pivots in the bow and, with more surprise, the two twenty-four-pound cannons extending from the captain's cabin. The oarsmen had again sat down, and as they pulled the ship past Surcouf's house, they continued to sing:

> We hook it, now it's caught,
> But I've set sail for Paris.
> Heave ho! you landlubbers!
>
> Freebooters with official papers
> Have left me high and dry and in prison.
> Freebooters with official papers
> Have left me high and dry and in prison.
> Heave ho! What misfortune!
> With one shoe off and one shoe on,
> I've come back on board.
>
> With one shoe off and one shoe on,
> I've come back on board.
> Heave ho! the best corsairs!
>
> The meanest corsairs
> Don't cruise against the English.
>
> The meanest corsairs
> Don't cruise against the English.
> Heave ho! But notaries,
>
> Judges and lawyers
> Are bigger pirates than anyone!

They had come opposite the Dinan gate, near where Surcouf's house stood. At its windows were the corsair's wife, his child, his relatives, his friends. They looked impatient, their faces darkened by frowns, for the embarkation was scheduled for exactly twelve noon. Yet here it was, nearly eleven o'clock, and not one of Surcouf's crew members had yet gone on board. He had sent his second in command, Bléas, to find out what his men at this late hour might be doing at Madame Leroux's and in the Rue Traversière. Bléas had indeed found out and was whispering to Surcouf that just as Caesar had been blocked by his creditors in Suburre when he was about to leave for Spain, Surcouf's crew was being blocked by Jews who had lent them money. The crew members had promised to use their advances to repay the money they had borrowed, and the Jews were holding them to that pledge. Surcouf was about to intervene when René asked the captain for permission to go in his place, to see if he could not find some way of settling things amicably between the debtors and creditors.

Scarcely do sailors receive their advances in the pay houses than their wives and creditors fall upon them to secure as much of it as they can. And we must say, at that critical moment the wives are worse than the creditors. Their cries, tears, and moans compete with the threats of the moneylenders, but usually their noisy recriminations manage to drown out any demand from the Jews. So, greedy though the moneysellers may be, the women are usually the first to take claim of the seamen's pay. Besides, the miserable money vultures realize that not only public sentiment but judges, too, always rule first in favor of the wives; so, although they may tear out their usurious hair, they usually allow, if begrudgingly, that family debts take precedence over their own. However, as soon as the last woman has been paid, with renewed fury those cormorants fall upon their prey. If the first sailors cornered give in and pay up, they set the stage for like-minded behavior from their mates. Some with curses, others with deep sighs, the seamen follow suit nonethess, and the money slips from their grasp. But sometimes a creditor may be unreasonable regarding family outlays and therefore unwilling to settle for half of the sum he is owed, though even just half will yield him a substantial profit. Or sometimes the first debtor, recalcitrant and near revolt, ignites riot among his comrades, and if an armed force has to intervene, angry sailors and implacable creditors will curse and blame each other with epithets worthy of Homeric heroes.

And that is what had just transpired. René landed right in the middle of a veritable riot. When the sailors caught sight of him, though, they realized that help was coming. Someone shouted, "It's the captain's secretary!" And he was greeted with thundering bravos.

René was carrying a sack, which seemed to be full of gold, and the sight of that was enough to plead his cause with the creditors. He climbed up on a table and gestured for silence. Everyone fell quiet immediately. And what a silence it was! One could have heard one of Descartes's atoms spin by.

"My friends," he said. "This is first time our captain is fitting out his ship in his native city, and on this occasion he does not wish for there to be any quarrels between his sailors, from wherever they may hail, and his fellow townspeople."

Among the faces staring up at him, René noticed Saint-Jean, the sailor who in exchange for dinner had given him all he needed to know about Surcouf. "Come over here, Saint-Jean," he said. Then turning to both the sailors and the creditors, he asked, "Do you all know Saint-Jean?"

"Yes, we know him," they all answered.

"He's an honest man, is he not?"

"Yes!" all the sailors answered together. "Yes, yes, yes!"

"Yes!" the Jews answered, though not quite so loudly or enthusiastically.

"I am putting him in charge of settling all your accounts. He will pay each creditor five percent interest, no matter what the date of the debt. Those who have loaned money for one month or two weeks or seven days will receive exactly the same amount as if they had made a one-year loan."

The Jews began to grumble.

"You can take it or leave it," said René, pointing to the sack. "There is the money, and here is my pocket. Once the money is in my pocket, you will see neither the sack nor its contents again. Going once, going twice, going three times. . . ."

"We agree!" the Jews shouted.

"Saint-Jean, take care of the accounts, and hurry it up. The captain is getting impatient."

Saint-Jean, a skilled accountant, ably made rapid calculations. Fifteen minutes later it was over. The amount the Jews had at first been demanding totaled was fifty-two thousand francs. In the end, with twenty thousand, everything was paid off, and the Jews, smiling through their bushy mustaches and pointed beards, admitted that they would like nothing better than to see all their debts settled in the same way.

René had a group receipt, drawn up by Saint-Jean, and he counted out the moneylenders' twenty thousand francs, on the condition that every debtor would be free to leave. The doors were opened, all barriers lifted, and the sailors, in a whirlwind of noise, raced toward the Dinan gate, where they were to gather for their departure. With embarkation set for noon, they had a quarter hour to spare.

The wrinkles disappeared from Surcouf's brow on seeing the arrival of his entire crew.

"My word," he said to René. "I knew you were a match in wrestling with Hercules, shooting with Junot, measuring swords with Saint-Georges, and drinking with General Bisson, but I did not know that in diplomacy you were the equal of Monsieur de Talleyrand. How in the devil did you manage?"

"Well, I paid for them," René answered simply.

"You paid for them?" Surcouf asked.

"Yes."

"How much did you pay?"

"Twenty thousand francs. It was a great bargain; they were asking fifty."

"Twenty thousand francs!" Surcouf repeated.

"Is it not customary," said René with a laugh, "for the newcomer to pay for his welcome?"

"Really," Surcouf muttered to himself, "he must be Tsar Peter's grandson, trying, as his grandfather did, to learn how to become a sailor."

Then, speaking aloud to his crew, he said, "You faithless curs, perhaps you think you owe something to me for having saved your hides from your creditors. You are mistaken. Once I have paid my advances, you, as any member of my crew shall know, have no right or reason ever to expect another cent from me. No, it was your new comrade René, who says he is paying for his welcome. Twenty thousand francs is a little expensive, but what can I say? That is the idea he got into his head. I trust that you will be grateful, and if ever he is in any danger, you will do whatever is necessary to help him. And now, let us go on board!"

Just opposite his house, Surcouf had had a pier built, with steps leading down to water level at low tide. As the tide was already coming in, the lower steps were already covered. With the beating drum summoning them on board, the sailors marched down the steps six by six and climbed into the rowboats that would take them to the *Revenant*. On each trip a rowboat could take twelve men. An hour later all one hundred forty sailors were on board. René had been among the first, and he was being continually thanked by his comrades. Last came the officers. As they climbed aboard the *Revenant*, fife and drums played.

Then, in an instant, everyone was at his place: The captain was on the bridge, the topmen had gone aloft, the signal officer was standing near his chest of flags. The roll was called. The crew was made up of one hundred forty-five men, and Surcouf intended to increase that number to one hundred eighty in their first ports of call. Only Bras-d'Acier was missing. He had sent word to Surcouf that since René was on board, there was no need of a fencing master.

When the boats had been tied to the stern, a cannon was shot and a tricolored flag hoisted to the gaff peak of the mainmast, giving the signal for departure. Since the wind could not reach the brig where it was, the oars-men had to tow it farther out to catch the sea wind. The sailors continued rowing, while Surcouf, an excellent pilot in those parts, guided the helms-man. The sailors picked up the cadence of both their oars and their songs.

When they got as far as the Roche aux Anglais, the ship stopped. Every-one could hear Surcouf's voice. He was shouting to his crew, but he also wanted to be heard by all those spectators who had come to bid them good-bye: "Good weather, good sea, good wind! Let's pick it up and sail quickly out to sea! Set the sheets, hoist the topsails and topgallant-sails on the jib halyards, and set our course."

The sails dropped down along the masts, then gracefully began to catch the wind. The ship started out through the Petite Conchée Channel, and two hours later, in Saint-Malo, all that was left of the *Revenant* was a white dot far distant from the shore. Then it too disappeared.

LV

Tenerife

⤜⋅⤛

SOME MILES OFF THE COAST of Morocco, opposite the Atlas Mountains and between the Azores and the Cape Verde Islands, rises the queen of the Canary Islands, whose peak, reaching the height of 3,700 meters, is usually hidden by clouds. The air in this delicious zone is so pure that at times you can spot the mountaintop from thirty leagues away, and from the island's peaks you can clearly see an ordinary ship an amazing twelve leagues away.

There, in the shadows of the gigantic volcano, in the archipelago that the ancients called the Fortunate Islands, Surcouf stopped. From there he could train his eye on the route from the two Americas to Spain, and on the route from India to Europe, from Europe to India. He stopped to take on water, purchase fresh supplies, and buy a hundred bottles of the Madeira wine you could still find in those days. In our time, that Madeira, favored child of the sun, has completely disappeared; it has been replaced by an al-coholic beverage called Marsala.

From Saint-Malo to Tenerife, except for the inevitable gales in the Bay of Biscay, the weather was favorable and the crossing good, if one can call a crossing good for a corsair ship when it encounters not a single ship to capture. In evading an English frigate, though, the men were able to judge how well the Revenant sailed; running free, they could do twelve knots.

The good weather allowed Surcouf ample time for his customary shooting practice. He broke a great number of bottles, as did René, who rarely missed. The sailors themselves never came close to the level of their captain's shooting skill, and they openly applauded the young man's abilities, but what the officers especially admired were the beautiful weapons he used to perform his feats of marksmanship.

René's weapons included a shotgun with an ordinary barrel, which he used for small prey, and a rifle of the same caliber but with a grooved barrel for hunting large animals or for shooting men, who in some countries must be numbered among the dangerous animals. Two wooden boxes each contained a pair of pistols, one a set of dueling pistols, the other a pair of double-barreled pistols for fighting under fire.

In addition, René had a boarding axe that was custom-made to fit his hand; undecorated and cast in burnished steel, it was so sharp that with one blow its blade could cut through a metal rod as thick as a man's finger as if it were a reed. But his favorite weapon, a weapon on which he lavished special care and that he wore hanging from a silver chain around his neck, was a Turkish dagger, slightly curved. Thanks to the superb temper of the blade, he, like Damascus Arabs, could slice through a flowing silk scarf with it.

Surcouf seemed to be delighted to have René on board, and especially to have him serving as his secretary, as it afforded him the opportunity to talk with René as much as he liked. Surcouf had a dark, rigid personality, and as a rule he was not very communicative with his men. In order to maintain order among such a heterogeneous group of seamen from so many different countries and backgrounds, he engaged them in a variety of shipboard activities. He had set up two arms rooms, one on the quarterdeck for his officers and the other in the forecastle for those sailors who demonstrated an aptitude for fencing. He had organized shooting practice for them, the senior officers practicing on the ship's starboard side and the subordinate officers and common sailors on the port side.

Only Surcouf's second in command, Monsieur Bléas, was allowed to enter his cabin for any reason at any time. Any other officer, even the lieutenant, needed a serious reason to do so. Surcouf, however, had extended the privilege of open access to René, but not wishing to create jealousy among his companions, he rarely took advantage of it. Instead, he'd wait until Surcouf came to see him.

The captain's cabin was elegantly decorated in military style. The copper of the two twenty-four-pound cannons, which could be pulled in completely when no enemy was in sight, gleamed like gold, so well polished were they by the Negro, Bambou, who took particular pleasure in seeing his reflection in them. On the wall hung a cashmere tapestry from India, and the cabin was decorated with weapons from countries around the world. For a bed Surcouf used a simple hammock, made of striped canvas, that hung in the space between the two cannons. More often than not, though, Surcouf simply stretched out fully clothed on the large sofa, which also occupied the area between the two guns. During battle, any furniture endangered by the recoiling cannons was removed, and the cabin was given over to artillery men.

On deck, Surcouf rarely spoke to anyone except the lieutenant on watch. When he appeared, everyone hurriedly moved aside to allow him space to walk. Often, so as not to put the sailors to that trouble, he would simply stand at the taffrail.

When he was in his cabin, Surcouf would call Bambou by striking a drum. The vibration could be felt all over the ship, and the nature of the drumbeat told everyone what sort of mood Surcouf was in.

In the earthly paradise they had been enjoying for a week at the foot of the Tenerife peak, Surcouf added dancing to the pastimes of hunting and fishing. Every evening, beneath that beautiful sky alive with stars, many of them unknown in Europe, with sweet aromas rising from the trees and a cool breeze beginning to blow in from the sea, on grass as fine as a carpet, peasant women dressed in picturesque costumes would come down from the villages, from Chasna, Vilaflor, and Arico.

On the first evening it had been difficult to come up with music to accompany the dancers and their beautiful partners, until René had said, "Find a violin or guitar for me, and I shall see if I can remember anything from my earlier itinerant days."

To find a guitar in a Spanish town, all you have to do is reach out your hand. The next day René had ten violins and as many guitars to choose from. He picked up the nearest at hand, and as soon as he began to play people recognized that he brought to the instrument a master's touch. The following day, the fife player and drummer who sounded the retreat each evening joined the orchestra, and under René's direction they added high notes here or a drumroll there to the strains of René's Spanish instrument.

Sometimes René would entirely forget the dancers, and, carried away by his memories, he'd move into some sad improvisation. Then the dancing would stop, and everyone would grow silent. And listen. The extempore melody might run minutes long or merely for a few measures, and when René had finished, Surcouf would whisper, "My wife was right. He was surely disappointed in love."

At last, one morning the call to battle stations awakened René. A ship had been spotted at the latitudes of the Cape Verde Islands, about two or three leagues away, and by the cut of her sails it was definitely an English ship. At the cry of "Sail ho!" Surcouf had rushed to the deck and given the order to get under way. Ten minutes later, under a cloud of sails thickening by the second, to the noise of men reporting to their battle stations, the *Revenant* was out to sea and heading for the English ship. By then, René too had appeared on deck, his rifle in hand, his double-barreled pistols in his belt.

"Well," said Surcouf, "it looks like we are going to have some fun."

"Finally," said René.

"It looks, too, like you are eager to join in."

"Yes. But I would like you to show me a place where I'll be in no one's way."

"Well, stay near me, and each of us will have a sailor to recharge our guns."

"Bambou!" Surcouf shouted. The Negro came immediately.

"Go get me Foudroyant," he ordered, referring by name to one of his guns; Badin was the name of the other. "And bring along Monsieur René's shotgun as well."

"That is not necessary," said René. "I am carrying the death of four men in my belt and another man's death in my hands. For someone working as an amateur, I think that is not too bad."

"What is the English ship doing, Monsieur Bléas?" Surcouf asked as he loaded his gun. Bléas was standing at the stern taffrail, and with his spyglass he was watching the English ship's movements.

"It is changing tack and trying to escape, Captain," the young officer answered.

"Are we drawing closer?" Surcouf asked.

"If so, it is so little that I cannot be sure."

"Ahoy!" shouted Surcouf. "Hoist the topgallants and the studdingsails! Be sure there's not a single sail larger than a handkerchief that is not picking up the wind."

The *Revenant,* leaning gracefully and widening the foaming circle that its hull was pushing out before it, demonstrated, like a thoroughbred, that it had felt its master's spur. The English ship, for its part, was also under full sail and could see the advantage the corsair ship had over it.

Surcouf ordered a cannon shot, inviting the other ship to show its colors, while he had his tricolored flag raised to announce his ship's nationality. The English flag went up, and the English ship, now only half a cannon shot away, opened fire with its stern guns in hopes of dismasting the corsair or at least damaging it enough to slow its course. But the volley caused little damage and wounded only two men. A third volley came, accompanied by an indescribable, sinister howl that René, still untutored in the havoc of combat at sea, did not recognize.

"What the devil has just flown over our heads?" he asked calmly.

"My young friend," Surcouf replied just as calmly. "That is bar shot. Are you familiar with the novel by Monsieur de Laclos?"

"Which one?"

"*Les Liaisons dangereuses.*"

"No."

"Well, Laclos is the man who invented those hollow balls that almost took your head off. Do you find such details unpleasant?"

"No, of course not. When I dance, I like to know the name of the instruments in the orchestra."

Surcouf climbed to the bridge. Only then realizing just how close the ships were, he asked, "Is the thirty-six-pounder ready?"

"Yes, Captain," the gunners answered.

"What projectiles are you using?"

"Three bunches of grapeshot."

"Ready to fire! Helm to port!" And when he saw they were in the enemy ship's wake, he shouted, "Fire!"

The gunners obeyed, and the grapeshot, sweeping the English ship from one end to the other, covered its deck with dead men and debris.

Swinging the helm to starboard and leaving the wake, Surcouf shouted, "Steady as she goes!"

Now that they were within shotgun range, Surcouf pulled off two shots with Foudroyant, and two men fell to the deck from the top of the mainmast.

He dropped Foudroyant and reached out toward René: "Quick, your gun!"

René asked for no explanation and obeyed. Quickly bringing the gun to his shoulder, Surcouf fired. He had just seen, in the enemy captain's cabin, an English gunner about to light a long twelve-pound cannon that was aimed at him and his officers. But before the man could ignite the wick, he was dead. With that feat, Surcouf had saved his own life and the lives of several on his staff.

They had sailed within pistol range, and René killed the next gunner who took up the wick and was now following on the heels of his dead mate. René's other three shots, to the main and foretop, sent three more of the enemy to death.

The two ships, now no more than ten paces apart, were lying athwart each other. Surcouf shouted, "Fire on the port hand!"

Grenades rained down onto the English ship's deck from the mast tops of the *Revenant*, and the topmen, twenty yards apart, exchanged blunder-buss fire. Just as the English ship was about to fire its starboard battery, it took a terrible broadside from the *Revenant*—a broadside that broke up all its railing, loosened five or six of its cannons, and cut the base of the main-mast. The topmen who had been aloft were thrown into the sea.

In the midst of the infernal racket, Surcouf made his voice heard: "Let's board her!"

Fifty voices took up the cry, and they were about to board the enemy ship when another cry rang out: "They've struck!"

The enemy had struck its flag. The combat was over. Among the cor-sairs, two men had been killed and three wounded. The English ship counted twelve dead and twenty wounded.

Surcouf brought the English captain on board. He learned that the ship he had just captured was the *Liverpool Star*, armed with sixteen twelve-pound guns. Given its limited value, Surcouf was content to demand a ran-som, six hundred pounds sterling, which he distributed to his crew as an encouragement bonus. He kept nothing for himself. In the event that the enemy ship might encounter a weaker corsair vessel on the way back to England and thereby attempt to exact revenge for its defeat, Surcouf or-dered Monsieur Bléas to go on board, dump the cannons into the sea, and soak their powder.

The *Revenant* then continued on its way toward the Cape of Good Hope. The seamen were proud of the fight, pleased with the week's stay in Tenerife, and delighted to be crossing the line with a companion as gener-ous as René, who would not fail, when the time came, to pay handsomely for his baptism.

LVI

Crossing the Line

THE DAY BEFORE Surcouf was expecting to cross the equator, or rather, at three in the morning on that lovely September day, the lookout shouted, "Sail ho!"

Immediately Surcouf came out of his cabin. "What is its course?" he asked.

"It's coming from the northwest, heading southeast, which is our direc-tion too."

Scarcely had he spoken his words than Surcouf had climbed nimbly from the quarterdeck onto a strut. From the strut he reached the mainmast topsail.

When they heard the words "ship ahoy"——magic words on any vessel—— the crewmen on duty scurried up onto the yardarms and topsails to evaluate the strength of the ship they would be dealing with. It seemed to be traveling the same path as the *Revenant,* although it was probably coming from the Gulf of Mexico. The *Revenant* slowed and turned so that it would pass within cannon reach on the windward side of the English vessel, for Surcouf wanted to be able to assess its capabilities but still retain maneuverability, whether he wanted to attack or retreat. In fact, both vessels, being still some distance apart, had about two hours to observe and study each other.

Around daybreak, when the sky was just beginning to brighten, the English ship realized by virtue of the superior speed of the *Revenant,* the shape of its sails, and its tall masts, that it was crossing paths with a corsair. Immediately the ship fired one of its cannons and raised its flag. While the colors of Great Britain, like an ominous flame, rose through the ship's rigging and began to flutter in the wind from the mizzenmast horn, the ball ricocheted over the water's surface. Barely touching the tallest waves, it flew over the pirate ship and splashed into the sea on the other side.

Surcouf followed the cannonball with a scornful eye that invested it only with insignificance. Although he was not sure the British vessel was a merchant ship, he had decided to attack it in any case. With a whistle he commanded silence, which he followed with this order: "Every man aft!"

The entire crew, now numbering about a hundred and fifty men, gathered around the hatchway dome. Surcouf wanted to prime the crew without first consulting his officers about the advisability of attacking the unknown ship, for he knew the general opinion would have been to avoid such a formidable undertaking as they could see that the decks of the English ship were covered with uniforms. They did not yet know that the ship was carrying a double crew and soldiers on board.

"Despite its imposing looks," said Surcouf, "it is not a warship. I can guarantee that it is a ship of the English Company. To be sure, we are not strong enough to demolish her with our cannons, but we are man enough to board her. So arm yourselves for boarding. In recompense for the perils you will be facing in this assault, I will grant you the devil's share for one hour."

With joyous shouts every man hurried to his combat position and armed himself to the teeth. The quartermaster distributed boarding sabers, battle-axes, long pistols, and daggers, so useful in hand-to-hand combat. The topmen were carrying copper blunderbusses and barrels of grenades aloft, and the petty officers were preparing dangerous grappling irons.

Meanwhile, the ship's two doctors and their helpers were preparing a station beside the main hatchway to take care of the wounded. The pharmacy chest was made ready, with its flasks and medicines; its cloth strips, compresses, and balls of bandages; the inevitable tourniquet; and the surgical kits with their somber display of shiny, polished instruments. Finally, they made space for an operating table and mattresses that lay ready for the poor fellows who would, sadly, need them.

A long, shrill whistle blast gave the order for every man to take his post and prepare for battle.

As for the English captain, trusting in his strength, he completed a tack to return to the attack. At the same time, he sent one of his officers to extend the invitation to any of the passengers, including the women, who might want to climb to the poop deck to watch them capture or sink a French corsair.

Surcouf, noting his opponent's maneuver, turned to meet him. He had the tack to his port side and the English ship to starboard. He passed so near the ship that he could read her name, the *Standard*. When the corsair was near her midsection, the English ship fired a broadside, to which Surcouf did not riposte. The damage amounted to no more than a few holes in the sails and some cut ropes, all of which could quickly be repaired.

Seeing that the enemy decks were covered with fighting men, Surcouf had pikes distributed to a dozen sailors, whom he positioned in the middle of the deck, with orders to strike indiscriminately either the advancing enemy or any of the *Revenant*'s retreating sailors. The mast platforms held as many men as space allowed, all of them well supplied with grenades; the copper barrels of their blunderbusses reflected the morning sunlight. The best sharpshooters on board the *Revenant* had meanwhile settled in on the spars and in the longboats, positions from which they could shoot at the English officers as well as if they were in a redoubt.

By then, the enemy's poop deck had begun to fill with elegant ladies and handsome gentlemen eager to enjoy the spectacle, some with the naked eye, some with spyglasses, some with opera glasses.

"Do you realize," Bléas said to Surcouf, "that all those skirts and dandies perched on the poop deck are laughing at us? See how they bow and make little hand gestures as if to say to us: 'Have a good trip, gentlemen, for we shall sink you. Do try not to get too bored down there at the bottom of the sea.'"

"That is just posturing!" Surcouf replied. "Don't let those elegant puppets upset you, because within the hour you'll be seeing them bow down before us, humble and submissive. Just watch that imprudent gunner take a dive."

Indeed, a handsome, bare-headed young man, his blond hair blowing in the wind, had at that moment slipped through the rails to load his cannon. Surcouf took aim and fired, but the bullet went through his hair without even grazing him. He raised his hand disdainfully, no doubt thinking he had time before Surcouf could reload. But Surcouf was using Foudroyant with its two barrels. He shot a second time, and the young man folded up like a tree snapping in the wind. With his arms wrapped around his cannon, the wounded man began slowly to slide down its barrel until, losing his grip, he dropped into the sea and disappeared.

Surcouf watched every move, and the man's death made a great impression on him. "Everybody facedown!" he shouted, after a moment of silence during which he tried to dispel his emotion.

It was high time. Smoke blew from the enemy ship's entire length, but it was Surcouf's lucky day. Thanks to the order he had given, not one of his men was hit. As soon as Surcouf saw he was on the enemy's quarter, he bore up so he could cross behind the other ship and board aft on the port side with the wind. To prevent being boarded, the *Standard,* like a bull constantly whirling around to show its horns, made another tack, which obliged the *Revenant* to come about now on a starboard tack and, hugging the wind, pass by its opponent a third time.

Every maneuver of the *Revenant* led to only one conclusion for the Englishmen: The corsairs were determined to board them. The English captain readied the helm to come about, but the *Standard,* whose mainsail had been furled for shooting, stayed close to the wind and could not tack. Unable to move as it intended, it was forced to bear away, and the *Revenant* momentarily found itself beneath the ship's stern, which rose high above it like a fortress. Surcouf's lower sails were already furled, but to decrease his speed still more so as not to sail past the enemy, he backed his sails. As the *Revenant* moved slowly alongside the enemy vessel, Surcouf shouted "Fire!" and they let fly a broadside of balls and grapeshot.

The two massive ships met to a horrible cracking sound. Their yards and pulleys intermeshed, they came so close together that their cannons were touching. At the same instant, orders to fire arose on both ships, and the volleys from both clouded the air. The *Revenant,* lying lower in the water than the *Standard,* also lay below the line of fire from the enemy guns, whereas the broadside from the *Revenant* had slammed into the other ship's railing just a foot above the deck and mowed down everything it hit. Panic had taken hold of the English ship.

Surcouf's attack had been bold and completely unexpected. The English thought the corsair had been rendered hors de combat by their earlier broadside, and they could not imagine that Surcouf, with a crew a third the size of their own, would consider boarding them. They had all gathered at the taffrail to watch the *Revenant* go down in defeat and to savor its crew's last moments. Now their astonishment, or rather their terror, knew no bounds: Grappling hooks clattered down along the deck, and the heavy anchor hanging on the starboard side of the *Standard*'s bow caught onto the pirate ship's chase-port, as if to provide the corsairs a convenient bridge between the two vessels. And twenty-five men were lying dead or wounded in their blood.

"Your turn, Bléas!" Surcouf roared. "Board them!"

"Let's board them!" the crew shouted in unison, leaping onto the enemy ship.

Surcouf ordered the two drummers to beat the charge. Electrified by the sound, the corsairs, with axes or sabers in hand, daggers between their teeth, lips curled in fury, eyes bloodshot, their feet landing on anything to help them, appeared at the *Standard*'s broken railings.

From the platforms of the *Revenant*, Guide and Avriot were tossing grenades down onto the enemy deck. When they seemed to pause for a moment, Surcouf shouted up to them: "Keep going, Avriot! Keep going, Guide! More grenades, keep them coming!"

"Right away, Captain," the topman Guide yelled down from the top of the mizzenmast. "The two men throwing grenades from the yardarm have just been killed."

"Then throw the two bodies down on the English. They shall have the honor, dead though they may be, of being the first on board the enemy ship!"

Strong arms tossed the two bodies down; they described an arc as they fell. They landed on a group of officers, who scattered.

"Forward, my friends!" Bléas shouted, taking advantage of the officers' retreat.

Three men leaped down from the bridge connecting the two ships. Forward of them was the Negro Bambou, who had wagered his share of the take that he would indeed be the first to land on the English deck; René and Bléas followed. Armed with the lance he used so deftly, with two thrusts Bambou killed two Englishmen. René swung his axe two or three times, and any man he struck was soon lying at his feet.

But suddenly he paused. Standing motionless, he gazed with astonishment and terror at a passenger with a bullet through his chest as he was being carried across the deck by his two daughters. One was supporting his head, and the other was kissing his hands; neither was giving a thought to the risks they were running. They walked straight through the horrible carnage, then disappeared through the hatch. René had been unable to take his eyes off the wounded man's pallid face, in which he could see the final throes of death, and even after he was gone, René was still staring at the hatch. In fact, Bléas had to shove him aside to shoot an Englishman who had an axe raised above René's head. Only then did René come out of his strange abstracted state and throw himself once more upon the enemy.

Standing on the *Standard*'s bulwark, Surcouf could take in the entire scene being played out on its deck, which seemed always to be blanketed by red uniforms. No matter how many were felled, the gaping holes in the English ranks would fill back up. His men were working wonders, but seemingly in vain. Kernoch, brandishing a tamper, was using it as a club, and every time the giant Breton swung it, a man paid with his life. But despite such displays of stamina and courage, the corsairs had reached no farther than the base of the mainmast.

Surcouf gave orders to pull two sixteen-pound guns out through portholes. He had them loaded with grapeshot, and before the English could realize what was in store for them, he had the guns aimed at the stern. "Leave some space on the catwalks!" Surcouf shouted in a raspy voice.

Everyone who recognized his intention moved toward the port or starboard side, to leave an open passage for the iron whirlwind that was to come. Scarcely had they moved aside when, in a deafening explosion, the two cannons vomited their grapeshot. Wounded and dead bodies lay everywhere on the stern and the poop deck.

Surcouf's tactic, so disastrous in its effect, might have caused the English to lose their courage, but their captain rallied them, and another fifty fresh men poured forth from the hatches. Unfortunately for the *Standard*, though, Avriot and Guide had just received two new basketfuls of grenades, which they promptly began tossing down onto the deck. One exploded at the base of the bridge, and the English captain fell facedown.

"The captain has been killed!" Surcouf yelled. "The captain has been killed! Will somebody who speaks English tell them to strike their colors?"

René leaped forward and, raising his bloody axe, shouted out, "The captain of the *Standard* is dead. Lower the flag!" He delivered the order in such good English that the flag officer, thinking the order had been given by the *Standard*'s second in command, immediately obeyed.

The combat, however, had not come to an end. The second in command, learning that the captain was dead, leaped to the bridge to take control of the vessel; he appealed to those Englishmen who were still unhurt to defend His Majesty's ship on their honor and bravery. Despite the horrible butchery on board the *Standard,* because the ship was transporting soldiers to Calcutta, there were still as many men able to bear arms among the losers as among the winners. Fortunately for the corsairs, they still held the deck, and they pushed the new captain along with the few men following him down between decks, then closed the hatches on them. Furious at the defeat he was suffering, but refusing to give up the fight, the new captain aimed two eighteen-pound cannons at the gun deck, whereby he planned to collapse the upper deck and bury in the debris Surcouf and his staff.

Hearing the sound of the rolling cannons, Surcouf guessed the intention. He opened up the hatch and leaped down among the English guns. Immediately he espied a young midshipman who, in courageously defending himself, had taken serious wounds and was bleeding profusely in several places. Surcouf rushed to help him, but the young man misunderstood the Breton's generosity and, leaping at his throat, tried to stab the corsair with his dagger. Bambou, seeing that his master's life was in danger, ran the midshipman through with his lance, and the poor fellow breathed his last. The same lance thrust would have killed Surcouf if the point had not hit one of the buttons on his uniform.

Finally, the men in the battery had no choice but to surrender, as had their mates on deck. "No more killing!" Surcouf shouted. "The *Standard* is ours! Long live France! Long live the Nation!" His men cheered loudly, and the carnage came to an end.

Then another shout rang out: "How about an hour for the devil's share you promised us?"

"I did so promise," Surcouf said, turning toward René. "And the promise will be kept. Remember, however, that all passengers are exempt from pillage and the women are spared any violence. I shall watch over the men's interests. René, you will protect the women's honor."

"So be it, Surcouf," René replied.

Hurrying toward the women's cabins, he ran into the ship's surgeon. "Monsieur," René asked him, "one passenger, an older gentleman, was grievously wounded. Could you tell me where his cabin is?"

"They took him to his daughters' cabin."

"And where is it?"

"A few more steps and you will hear the poor girls sobbing."

"Is there then no hope of saving him?"

"He has just expired."

René leaned against a cabin door for support, passed the back of his hand over his eyes, and gave a sigh.

At that moment a band of bloodthirsty drunken men plunged into the 'tween-deck. Howling and singing, knocking over everything in their path, they began kicking open cabin doors. A woman's voice cried out in distress, and René remembered the two lovely girls sobbing over the loss of their father.

René leaped toward the sound of the cry and came to a door that muffled a woman's pleas for help. The door was locked from the inside, but René still had his axe. One blow, and the door splintered.

Inside, a sailor was clutching one of the girls in his arms, intending to do her violence. The other girl, kneeling beside the body of her dead father, with her arms raised to the heavens, was begging God, who had just made orphans of them, not to add to their sad calamity by abandoning them to their shame.

"You rascal," René shouted to the loutish sailor. "In the captain's name, release that woman."

"Me? Release this woman? She's my share of the booty. I'm keeping her, she's mine."

René grew pale, paler than the dead man lying on the bed. "The women are not part of the booty. Don't make me tell you a second time to unhand her."

"Don't worry," said the sailor, gritting his teeth, and with that he pulled a pistol from his belt and fired point-blank. Only the primer burned, but already René's left arm had whipped out like a spring. In a flash, the sailor fell dead—stabbed to the heart by the dagger that always hung from René's neck.

So as not to frighten the terrified girls further with the sight of blood, René kicked the sailor's body out of the cabin. Then he stood blocking the door. "You can be reassured," he said, his voice as sweet as a tender woman's. "Nobody else can get in."

The two girls threw themselves in each other's arms. After a moment, the older girl turned to the young man: "Oh, monsieur," she said, "why cannot my father still be here to thank you! He could do that better than us two poor children, still quaking at the danger we have just faced."

"Thanks are not necessary, mademoiselle," René answered. "By doing what I did, I have fulfilled both my duty and my heart's wishes."

"You are then our protector, monsieur, and I hope you will be so until our journey's end."

"Alas, mademoiselle, I am a poor protector," René replied. "I am only an ordinary sailor, like the man who was dishonoring you, and my power amounts to no more than my strength. However," he went on with a bow, "if you are willing to place yourself under our captain's protection, I dare promise that no harm shall come either to you or to your fortune."

"You will please tell us when and how we should appear before him."

At that very moment René heard Surcouf's voice. "Here he comes now," he said to the two sisters, at the same time that he heard Surcouf say to one of his men, "And you are telling me that René is the man who killed this sailor?"

René opened what was left of the door. "Yes, Captain," he said. "I did."

"What was he doing, René, that you had to kill him?"

"You can see what condition this poor girl is in," he said, pointing to the younger girl's torn clothing.

"Oh, monsieur," cried the girl, throwing herself at Surcouf's feet. "This gentleman has saved more than our honor!"

"Are you French, mademoiselle?" Surcouf asked.

"Yes, Captain. This is my sister," and her voice broke as she added, "and this is our dead father."

"How did your father die?" asked Surcouf. "Was he fighting against us?"

"Oh, good God! Would my father ever fight against Frenchmen?"

"Well then, how did this great misfortune happen?"

"We boarded this ship in Portsmouth. We were going to Rangoon, in India, where we have a business establishment. The commander of the *Standard* invited us to come up on deck to watch, he said, the spectacle of a pirate ship he was going to sink. A bullet struck and killed my father, but he was only a spectator."

"Please excuse me, mademoiselle," said Surcouf, "if I keep pressing you with questions. I am doing so not simply out of curiosity, but also in hopes of being useful to you. If your father were living, I would never have even dared enter your cabin."

The two girls looked at each other. These were the miserable pirates that the English captain, Mr. Registon, was promising to hang for his passengers' amusement? Nothing was clear to them any longer; for not even in high society had they ever encountered more courtesy than they had received just now from these two corsairs.

Surcouf's eyes were too keen and his mind too sharp not to realize the cause of the lovely young Frenchwomen's astonishment. "Mesdemoiselles," he said, "the time is ill chosen to ask all these questions, but I wanted to reassure you as quickly as possible regarding the new situation you find yourself in as a result of our victory."

"Oh, monsieur, we are the ones who should apologize for being so slow to respond. We beg you, please, to ask us anything you want, for you seem to know better than we do ourselves what will be in our best interest."

"One word from you would have been enough to send us away, mademoiselle," said Surcouf, "and one word is enough to keep us here. You say

that you were on the way to Rangoon. That is in the Pegu Kingdom, beyond the Ganges. I cannot guarantee that I can take you that far, but I can
say that I will take you as far as Île de France, and from there you will
surely be able to find a way to the Burmese empire. If this great misfortune
puts you in need of money, you will do me the honor of letting me know."

"Thank you, monsieur. My father surely had some bills of exchange
representing considerable sums."

"Is it indiscreet to ask your father's name?"

"The Vicomte de Sainte-Hermine."

"The Vicomte de Sainte-Hermine who served in the Royal Navy until
1792, when he resigned his commission?"

"Exactly, monsieur. His convictions would not allow him to serve under
the Republic."

"He belonged to the younger branch of the family, I believe. The head
of the family was a Comte de Sainte-Hermine, who was guillotined in
1793. His two sons also died for the Royalist cause."

"You know our family history well, monsieur. Could you possibly tell
us what happened to the third son?"

"Did he have a third son?" Surcouf asked.

"Yes, but he disappeared in the strangest manner. The very evening the
contract was to be signed for his marriage to Mademoiselle Claire de Sourdis, the very moment in fact that they were to sign the contract, he was suddenly nowhere to be found. And he has never been seen or heard of since."

"I must say that he is completely unknown to me."

"We were raised together until he was eight years old. Then he joined
my father on his ship and stayed with him until '92. He left us when his
family called him back. We have never seen him again. Were it not for the
Revolution, he would be a seaman like our father." The girl tried to
smother a sob.

"Go ahead and cry, mademoiselle, and don't be ashamed," said Surcouf.
"I am sorry to have come between you and your sorrow for a moment. I shall
accompany the *Standard*, or rather, I shall choose a captain to take it as our
prize, to Île de France. There it will be sold. But from Île de France to Rangoon, you will surely find, as I have the honor of saying to you, a thousand
opportunities to arrange a crossing." Surcouf bowed respectfully and left.

René followed him, but just as he was about to step through the doorway, he thought that the younger of the two sisters wanted to say something to him. He stopped, and when he reached out his hand toward her, the
girl unthinkingly clasped it and brought it to her lips. "Oh, monsieur, for
the love of God," she said, "please ask the captain not to allow our father's
body to be thrown into the sea."

"I shall ask him, mademoiselle," said René. "But I would also like to ask something of you and your sister."

"Oh please, what is it?" they answered together.

"Your father looks very much like a relative of mine whom I loved very much and whom I will never see again. Please allow me to kiss your father."

"Oh, with all our hearts, monsieur," the two girls replied.

René went over to the body, kneeled to the floor, leaned down, kissed him respectfully on the forehead, and then, trying to hold back a sob, walked out.

The two sisters were astonished as they watched him leave. A son's good-bye to his father could not have been more loving and more respectful than René's good-bye to their father the Vicomte de Sainte-Hermine.

LVII

The Slave Ship

WHEN SURCOUF AND RENÉ CAME back up on deck, there were scarcely any traces of the combat left. The wounded had been carried down to the makeshift hospital, the dead had been thrown into the sea, the blood had been washed away.

René told Surcouf about the two girls' request that their father's body not be tossed into the sea, but rather that it remain on ship until they made their first landfall. The request was contrary to all maritime rules; yet in certain circumstances similar favors had been granted—that is how Madame Leclerc, Pauline Bonaparte, had brought her husband's body back from Saint-Domingue, for example.

"So be it," said Surcouf. "Since the *Standard*'s captain has been killed, Monsieur Bléas will take command of our prize. He will have the captain's cabin, and if there is another officer's cabin available, that is where we shall put the Sainte-Hermine sisters. Their father can then remain in their cabin, sealed up in an oak casket."

When René told the sisters the news, they insisted on thanking Surcouf immediately.

The elder sister, Hélène, was almost twenty years old; Jane was seventeen. Hélène was blonde, her fairness comparable only to a new flower that had been brought back from Japan just three years earlier by the Jesuit Camelli, thought it has since become common in larger greenhouses under the name *Camellia*. Her blonde hair shone like gold, and when the sun softened its outline, it assumed a lustrous, iridescent hue, like a halo of the kind that perfume forms around a flower. Her plumpish hands were luminously pale, but tinged with pink under unusually transparent fingernails. Her waist was like a nymph's, her feet like a child's. If Jane's beauty was less conventional than her sister's, she was the more attractive. Her tiny, mischievous mouth was as fresh and pert as the bud of a rose. Her nose, with its playful flare, was neither Greek nor Roman, but completely French. Her eyes shone with the dark fire of sapphires. Her skin favored the color of Paros marble that has long been warmed by the Attican sun.

Surcouf had already had someone clean the cabin of the *Standard*'s second in command so that it could accommodate the two sisters, and he invited them now to say their good-byes to their father, as it was important in those latitudes to seal up the body promptly in a casket. The casket would remain in the room where the body lay. Surcouf asked René to supervise the removal of the girls' things to the new cabin and to help them in any way he could.

Hélène and Jane went into their old room. René remained just outside the door, so as not to disturb them while they expressed their painful grief. An hour later, still sobbing, their eyes drowned in tears, they came back out, but Jane could scarcely walk, and she seized René's arm for support. Her sister was carrying their jewel box and their father's purse. They both appreciated René's discretion in allowing them to mourn their loss in private, but only Hélène, the stronger of the saddened two, was able to thank him. Jane was still sobbing too much to speak.

René helped them arrange their new room, and then left them alone, for he intended to take care of preparing their father's body himself. Within two hours, the carpenter had built an oak casket, and they had laid the body of the Vicomte de Sainte-Hermine inside. When they were sealing it up, the girls heard the first hammer blows. They guessed what the men were doing and hurried back to their former cabin to see their father one last time. But they found René waiting at the door. He had suspected that filial piety might prompt them to return, and he wanted to protect them from further pain. He drew them into his arms, one on either side of him, and led them back to their new room. Embracing each other, they collapsed in tears on a sofa. René placed Jane's hand in Hélène's, then kissed them both respectfully and left the room.

All their actions had been so chaste, yet they had rapidly come to know each other somehow intimately but in such terrible circumstances that neither Hélène nor Jane, nor even René, was fully aware of the close bond they'd developed, as close as that between a brother and his two sisters.

The next day, the two ships were sailing together toward Île de France. Forty corsairs from the *Revenant* had gone on board the *Standard*, with Bléas as commander of the captured ship. Thinking it important that the girls have a friend or at least a sympathetic heart on their journey, René had received permission to join Bléas.

Two days after the combat with the *Standard*, the *Revenant* spotted a sloop and gave chase. The sloop at first tried to flee, but the order to "Strike your sails for the *Revenant*," reinforced by a cannon shot, encouraged the sloop to strike its sails.

As the *Standard* passed near the sloop on the port side, René, who was standing on the poop deck with the two young women, witnessed a disturbing scene. Two men were lying near death, despite the efforts of a young black man to help them drink a brew prepared by some sorcerer with skin the color of ebony. A short distance away were five young black women, nearly naked, exposed to the rays from a burning sun that would have killed European women. One of them was trying to feed an infant she held in her arms, but in vain, for the child was nursing at a dried-up breast. When sailors from the *Revenant* climbed on board, four of the women got to their feet and ran away. The fifth attempted to run as well, but she was too weak and, fainting, she collapsed on the deck and dropped her child. An officer picked up the child and laid it beside its mother.

The officer was looking for the ship's captain. By the size of the ship's masts, he had determined it to be a slave ship. And indeed, down in the hold, he discovered eighty poor blacks lying chained in the closed, virtually airless space. Fresh air could reach the hold only through the hatch, which was usually covered. The odor from the hold was noxious, nauseating.

As the longboat was leaving the sloop, whose flag indicated it was American, Surcouf signaled for René and Bléas to return to the *Revenant*. The command worried the girls, but René explained that the sloop's captain was probably a slave trader, and since trading slaves was illegal without special authorization, they were probably going to assemble a war tribunal on board the *Revenant* to judge the captain.

"And if he is found guilty," Jane asked in a quavering voice, "what will be his fate?"

"Well," said René, "he runs the great risk of being hanged."

Jane let out a small cry of horror. René had no time to console her. Since the longboat was already at the hull of the *Standard* and since the sailors were waiting with oars raised, and since Bléas had already climbed down, René barely had time to grab the rope ladder and drop into the craft.

The other officers were already gathered in the wardroom when Bléas and René arrived. The American captain was then brought in. He was a tall man, and his bulk evidenced almost superhuman strength. He spoke only English, which is why Surcouf had summoned René to the council. For his cry "The captain is dead, lower your flag" had left no doubt in the mind of Surcouf or any Englishman who'd heard it that René spoke English as well as he spoke his mother tongue.

The captain had brought along with him papers showing that he was an American trader, but he could produce no document to show that his was one of the eight American ships authorized as slave traders by the European powers. When he confessed that he had no such authorization, they read to him the particulars of the crime he had committed by removing the black people in his hold from their lands and families by force or by trickery. The captain admitted his guilt. He was sentenced to death: a cruel and humiliating death, for slave traders are hanged from the yardarms either of their own ships or the ships of their captors.

Once the judgment was pronounced, they granted the captain, who had listened to his sentence without the slightest expression of feeling, an hour to prepare for his death. They left him in the wardroom with a guard at each door, for they feared that, in order to escape a shameful death, he might throw himself into the sea.

He asked for paper, pen, and ink so he could write to his wife and children. His request was granted. As he began to write, he appeared to be calm, but he'd written barely a dozen lines when little by little his emotions began to show, as if until then a cloud had been veiling his features. Soon he could no longer see to write, as the tears, in spite of himself, were pouring from his eyes and blurring the words of his farewell letter.

He asked to speak to Surcouf, who came immediately, as did René to serve as interpreter.

"Monsieur," the captain said, "I began to write to my wife and children to say farewell. But since they were unaware of the shameful profession I had undertaken for love of them, I thought that a letter in which I told them about the cause of my death might increase rather than assuage their pain. I would like to make a request. In the secretary in my cabin you will find the sum of four or five thousand francs in gold coins. For my sloop and my eighty prisoners I had hoped to get forty-five or fifty thousand francs. That would have been enough to set myself up in business and put behind me the blot I have allowed to stain my life. God has not permitted that to happen. My sloop and my prisoners indeed belong to you, but the five thousand francs you will find in my drawer are mine. I beg of you, and this is a seaman's last wish, to please send those five thousand francs to my wife and children. Write only this: 'From Captain Harding, who died accidentally while crossing the line.' My conduct, as reprehensible as it may be, might be excused by tender hearts, for I acted as I did to provide for my large, beloved family. From now on, at least, I shall no longer have to watch their suffering or witness their want. Never would I have killed myself, but since I am to be killed, I accept my death, not as a punishment, but as a kindness."

"Are you ready?"

"I am."

He got to his feet, shook his head to force the last tears from his eyes, and on a sheet of paper he wrote his wife's address: "Madame Harding, in Charlestown." He handed the address to Captain Surcouf. "I have asked for your word, monsieur," he said. "Will you promise?"

"By the faith of a seaman, monsieur," Surcouf replied, "what you desire will be carried out."

Surcouf gave a signal. A drumroll began. The time had come. Confronting death, the captain regained his calm. Again displaying no emotion, he removed his tie, lowered his shirt collar, and, with a firm step, he followed Surcouf from the wardroom to the deck and the site of the execution.

A deep silence reigned on deck, for executions have a sobering effect on all seamen, even pirates. A rope, noosed at one end and held by four men at the other, was hanging at the mizzenmast. Not only was the entire crew of the *Revenant* on deck, but the two other ships had hove to, and their decks and yardarms were crowded with onlookers as well.

The American captain placed his own head in the noose, then turned toward Surcouf: "Do not make me wait, monsieur," he said. "Waiting is suffering."

Surcouf stepped over to the captain and pulled the rope from around his neck. "You have truly repented, monsieur," he said. "That is what I was hoping to see. Give yourself to God, for you have already undergone your punishment."

The American captain placed his trembling hand on Surcouf's shoulder, looked around vacantly, and collapsed to the deck in a dead faint.

What sometimes happens to the strongest of men happened to him. Strong when facing pain, he grew weak at the prospect of joy.

LVIII

*How the American Captain Got Forty-Five Thousand
Francs instead of the Five Thousand He Was Asking For*

⁂

THE AMERICAN CAPTAIN SOON REGAINED HIS SENSES. Never had Surcouf really intended to carry out the death sentence. He had recognized in the captain those kinds of superior qualities that are especially prized by men of war, and he had simply wanted to make a lasting impression on the slave trader's mind. That goal having been clearly achieved, Surcouf meant now not only to spare the man's life but also to reverse his ill fortune.

Surcouf set their course for Rio de Janeiro, one of the largest slave markets in South America, which lay eighty or ninety nautical miles to the southwest. As soon as Surcouf cast anchor in the bay he summoned Captain Harding to the *Revenant*.

"Monsieur," he said, "when you thought you were about to die, you made one request, asking me to convey to your widow the five thousand francs in your secretary. Today I can do something even better. As we are in the best port for trading in Negroes, I authorize you not only to sell the eighty you still have aboard your ship but also to keep the proceeds."

Harding looked up in surprise.

"One moment, monsieur," said Surcouf. "In exchange, I shall require something of you. One of my men, my secretary, really more a friend than a servant, would like to have your little sloop, though I'm not sure why."

"You can give it to him, monsieur," said Harding. "It belongs to you, as does everything I owned."

"Yes, but René is a very proud man. He would not accept a gift either from you or from me. He would like to purchase your ship. So take into consideration what you were just saying, that the ship no longer really belongs to you, and attach a reasonable price to it for a man who, being disinclined simply to take it from you, is quite willing to buy it from you."

"Monsieur," Harding replied, "your conduct in this whole business is a model for my own. Please set the value of my sloop yourself, and I shall sell it for half of that amount."

"Your sloop, monsieur, is worth between twenty-eight and thirty thousand francs. René will give you fifteen, and you will give him papers confirming your ship's nationality and its right to sail under the American flag."

"But won't that make for problems," Harding replied, "when the authorities notice that the owner is French?"

"Who will notice?" asked René, who was attendant in his capacity as interpreter and Surcouf's secretary.

"It is quite difficult," said Harding, "to speak English so well that nobody will notice, especially when it is a Frenchman trying to speak with an English tongue. This is the only man I have ever met," he said, pointing to René, "who might get away with it."

"Well, monsieur, since I am the one buying the ship," René said, "there is no longer anything standing in the way. Have your consul prepare a bill of sale, and take ashore all your possessions. Here is a voucher allowing you to draw fifteen thousand francs on the establishment David and Sons, in the new part of the city. Please give me a receipt."

"But," said Harding, "you can give me the money when the contract has been signed."

"You will need the time to be sure that this draft can be paid upon presentation. We would like to leave this evening, Monsieur Surcouf and I, or, at the latest, tomorrow morning."

"What is the buyer's name?" asked Harding.

"Well, you may put down whatever you like," René said with a laugh. "Fielding from Kentucky, if you think that would be suitable."

"And when will you be free?" asked Harding, rising to his feet.

"Tell me when you would like me to be at the consulate, and I shall be there."

They checked with Surcouf, who decided that they would not leave port until the next day. So they agreed to meet at four in the afternoon. By five o'clock, the *New York Racer* had been officially sold to John Fielding from Kentucky. By six, Captain Harding had received his fifteen thousand francs. At seven, two hundred sailors and soldiers of the English navy, preferring to remain in Rio, were transferred to the British consul on the condition that England in turn would release an equal number of French prisoners. Finally, as day was breaking the following morning, the three ships set sail, all three showing national colors, on course toward the Cape of Good Hope.

On the *Standard,* both Hélène and Jane were delighted to see René again. Abandoned to their own devices as they were, they would never have been able to arrange their voyage to Rangoon and to their father's establishment along the Pegu River. Neither knew India; but, while in London, Hélène had met an officer in the Indian Army stationed in Calcutta, and, before her departure, arrangements had been made for the marriage of Hélène de Sainte-Hermine to Sir James Asplay on her arrival in India. Jane had planned to continue to operate the trading post with her father until she too was married. At that point, depending upon whether the newly married couples wanted to live with their father or whether he preferred living with one or the other of them, or with both of them alternately for six months of the year, they had intended to decide whether to keep or sell Rangoon House.

Of course, the family's plans had been undone by the death of the Vicomte de Sainte-Hermine. They needed a new plan by which to chart their future, but since the girls were so broken by their father's death, they were incapable of coming up with an appropriate one themselves. So it was fortunate that at the same time they had lost their father's love they had found in René a brotherly affection.

Thanks to the superb weather, their passage from Rio de Janeiro to the Cape of Good Hope was like a stroll. Slowly the three young people grew very close to each other, to Hélène's great satisfaction; for she found René charming and hoped that once she herself had been reunited with her promised husband, Jane would not be long in finding a suitable mate, a man like René, perhaps.

Both young women were musicians, though since their father's death neither had touched a piano. Still, with René, often they would listen to the sailors' chants as the ship made its effortless way in the peaceful trade winds. One night, one of those beautiful nights which, as Chateaubriand said, are made up not of shadows but by the absence of day's light, a clear voice rose from the quarterdeck, singing a sad Breton song. The first enchanting notes prompted Hélène to put her hand on René's arm to ask for silence, and they listened to the sad legend of a girl who, during the Terror, saves the lord of her village by taking him on board an English vessel. Only when the sentinel calls out, "Who goes there?" she is unable to answer because she does not speak English; she is shot, but gets back to the village and dies in her lover's arms. When the lament ended, the girls, with tears in their eyes, begged René to ask the singer for the words. René, however, said that was not necessary, for he was certain he could remember the words; and as for the music, all he needed was the piano, some lined paper, and a pen.

They all went back to Hélène's room. René put his head in his hands, thought for a moment, and began to write. Without a pause, he wrote out all the notes of the melody. Then, placing the paper on the piano, with a voice even sweeter and more expressive than the sailor's, he offered a beautiful rendition of the same sad ballad.

As he repeated the last couplets, René put such expression in the phrases "I love her! I love her! I love her still!" that one might have thought he was singing his own story with those simple words, that his own melancholy too lay in love forever lost. His sad voice echoed in the girls' hearts, his plaintive notes awakening the most tender of their emotions and uniting their hearts with his.

The ship's clock was striking two when René went back to his own cabin.

LIX
Île de France

THE SAME DAY, at five in the morning, the sailor on watch called out, "Land ho!" They were within sight of Table Mountain.

The winds had been favorable and the ships had been sailing along at twelve or thirteen knots. They'd rounded the Cape of Good Hope. At Needle Cape, though, they'd encountered a gale that pushed the three ships rapidly toward the east; they soon were out of sight of any land. They had set their course toward Île de France, and later that same day they could see the Piton des Neiges off in the distance. Île de France, as Mauritius was then called, was the only refuge the vessels would have in the Indian Ocean.

It was in 1505 that Dom Manuel, King of Portugal, decided to establish a viceroy or a governor general on the coast of India. He entrusted the position to Dom Francisco d'Almeida, who was massacred five years later by the Hottentots near the Cape of Good Hope just as he was preparing to leave for Europe.

During those early years of d'Almeida's government, Dom Pedro Mascarenhas discovered the islands later named Île de France and Île de Bourbon, but no one can recall any Portuguese settlement on either of the islands during the entire time they were in Portugal's control, that is, throughout the sixteenth century. The only benefit native inhabitants realized from European visitors amounted to a few herds of goats, monkeys, and pigs that had been turned loose on the islands. In 1598, the island now called Île de France was taken over by the Dutch.

Little by little, the Dutch gained control of all the Portuguese and Spanish conquests in the Indian Ocean, and consequently of Cerne Island and other Mascarenes. Admiral Cornelius Van Neck was the first to land on Cerne Island in 1598. His fleet had set out from Texel on May 1, its flagship the *Mauritius*, which name was later given to the island. The Dutch put two longboats into the bay to reconnoiter and take soundings in order to determine if the waters could receive large vessels. One of the longboats reached the port, where, the sailors discovered, the water ran deep enough that it might hold up to fifty ships. When the sailors returned to the flagship that evening, they brought with them several large, exotic birds and many smaller ones they had been able to catch by hand. They had also found a freshwater river that came down from the mountains and promised an abundant water supply.

The island appeared not to be inhabited, but because he was carrying so many sick men on board, the admiral was reluctant at first to spend time exploring it. Still, he landed a sizable detachment, with orders to take precautions in the event of a surprise attack. For several days he dispatched boats to other parts of the island to determine if anyone was living there. In their explorations the crews discovered only peaceable quadrupeds that fled before them and great numbers of birds so oblivious of any danger that they did not move even to escape capture. However, a flying bridge, a capstan bar, and a mainyard bore witness to some maritime disaster that had taken place on the coast of Cerne Island.

After giving thanks to God for bringing them to such a fine port and safe harbor, the admiral named the island Mauritius, in honor of the Prince of Orange who was then Stadhouder of the United Provinces.

It was one of the most picturesque islands imaginable. On every side of it there were mountains covered with trees of the lushest green. The mountain peaks were often hidden in the clouds, and the trees grew so thickly on the rocky soil that it was impossible to cut one's way through them. Most of the trees had very dark wood, as dark as the most beautiful ebony, but there were other bright red or dark, waxy yellow woods as well. The numerous palm trees offered healthful refreshments; the palm heart tasted a bit like a turnip and could be prepared in the same way. And the plentiful wood supply enabled the sailors to build comfortable huts. The fresh, salubrious air helped the sick men regain their health. As for the sea, fish swam in such abundance that the Dutchmen always pulled their nets in full. One day, they caught a ray so big that it fed the crew of one of the ships for two days. The tortoises were so huge that one stormy day six men took refuge under one shell.

The Dutch admiral had some men nail a plank to a tree, on which were carved the arms of Holland, Zeeland, and Amsterdam, along with this inscription, in Portuguese: "Reformed Christians." He also had a palisade built around a field eight hundred yards in circumference, where they planted various seeds and cuttings to test the soil. On their departure they left behind some poultry, so that ships stopping in the future might find food other than what the island alone provided.

On August 12, 1601, Hermansen sent a yacht, *Le Jeune Pigeon*, to Mauritius in order to take on water and provisions. A month went by with no news of the ship. When finally it returned, it brought along a Frenchman. He had a story to tell.

Several years before, he had traveled out of England on a ship that had set sail for India, along with two others, one of which was lost near the Cape of Good Hope. Every soul went down with it. The crews of the remaining ships became so decimated by disease that they had no choice but to burn the lesser of the two ships. Only the typhus and scurvy continued to spread quickly among the skeleton crew until there were not enough sailors to man the ship.

It ran aground on the Timor coast near Malacca. Only the Frenchman, four Englishmen, and two Negroes had survived. The castaways, impoverished though they were, managed to get a junk and together they made plans to return to England. The trip began well enough, but the Negroes, more alarmed the farther they sailed from their home country, plotted to take over the ship. When their plan was discovered, fearful of being punished and in despair, they leaped into the sea.

Surviving several storms, the rest of the crew ended up on Mauritius. Even if they could have worked together, they would have been in danger, but they could agree on little and worked together at less. After a week on the island, the Frenchman proposed they stay there until heaven sent them help. But the Englishmen, determined to continue their trip, insisted on taking again to the sea. Strong in their majority, they proceeded with their plans—and left the equally determined Frenchman alone on the deserted island.

Living on fruit and tortoise meat, he survived there almost three years, till heaven did send help. His clothing in tatters, he was almost naked. His physical strength had not diminished; he was indeed as strong as the sailors on the Dutch ship. But he had lost some of his mental faculties, as was evident in any attempt at sustained conversations.

It appears that the Dutch visited Mauritius in the year 1606, but they did not establish any permanent base there before 1644. Although it is difficult to know exactly who made the first settlements, they were probably set up by pirates, who infested the Indian Ocean during the sixteenth century. All that we know for sure is that in 1648 Van der Master was governor of Mauritius, and later, according to the voyager Leguat, when he arrived on Rodrigues Island, it was Lameocius. In 1690, when Leguat, on his way back from Rodrigues, was detained in Mauritius, Rodolphe Déodati, from Geneva, occupied the post of governor.

From 1693 until 1696, a few Frenchmen, tired of unhealthful conditions in Madagascar, came to the Mascarenes with both black and yellow women, whom they married as there were no white women in their company. Flacourt took possession of one of the Mascarenes in the king's name, and the French flag flew where Portugal's had flown before. Flacourt named the island Île de Bourbon, a name it has kept. On his departure, he left behind a few men and women with one of his protégés, Payen, in charge. These new settlers found the soil fertile, and they put their energy into growing crops. They lived on fish, rice, tortoises, potatoes and other vegetables, but forbade any use of beef in order to increase the size of their herds. In their little corner of paradise they lived peacefully and happily.

Four English pirates—Avery, England, Condon, and Pattison—after amassing a great fortune in the Red Sea along the coasts of Arabia and Persia, joined the French settlement on Bourbon, as did some of their crews. The king of France pardoned them, and one of the pirates, who had arrived in the Mascarenes in 1687, was still alive in 1763.

While Bourbon, pleased with its new name, was prospering in the hands of Frenchmen, Mauritius was going into a decline under the Dutch, who began to lose interest in the colony after their settlement on the Cape of Good Hope. They abandoned Mauritius in 1712. On January 15, 1715, Captain Dufresne, taking advantage of the Dutch withdrawal, landed on Mauritius with about thirty Frenchmen and changed its name to Île de France.

The two islands flourished. Their good ports, fertile soil, and healthful air encouraged the settlers to consider founding a true colony. In 1721, Monsieur de Bauvillier, governor of Île de Bourbon, sent the Chevalier Garnier de Fougeray, captain of the *Triton*, to Île de France. He took possession of the island on September 23 in the name of the king of France and planted a mast forty feet high, on which he flew a white flag with a Latin inscription. On August 28, 1726, Monsieur Dumas, a resident of Île de Bourbon, was named governor of the two islands, although they each had separate governments, with Monsieur Maupin heading that of Île de France.

But the true father, founder, and lawmaker of the colony was Monsieur Mahé de La Bourdonnais, who, though somewhat forgotten by history books, has found his place in novels. When he arrived to take control of the government in 1735, he discovered that the courts on Île de France were subordinate to those on Bourbon, so he acquired letters of patent conferring on them power equal to that of the courts on the neighboring island for everything related to criminal laws. For the eleven years of Monsieur de La Bourdonnais's tenure as governor, however, the patent proved to be useless, as not a single case came to trial on the island. The only real problem on Mauritius was runaway slaves. So Monsieur de La Bourdonnais organized a kind of police force made up of subservient blacks, whom he set against the refractory ones.

La Bourdonnais was the first to plant sugar cane on Île de France. He also established cotton mills and began indigo production; their products found outlets in Surat, Moka, Persia, and throughout Europe. The sugar mills he established in 1735 were generating an annual revenue of sixty thousand francs fifteen years later. He brought manioc from Brazil and Santiago to the island, and when the plant failed to please or interest the colonists, he by decree forced each of them to require each of his slaves to set out three hundred manioc plants.

Essentially everything on Île de France begins with Monsieur de La Bourdonnais. It was he who drew up the road system. Using yoked oxen to drag stones and wood down to the port, it was he who had the seafront houses built. It was he who built the arsenals, batteries, fortifications, barracks, mills, quays, offices, shops, and an aqueduct about six hundred yards long that brought fresh water to the port, to the hospitals, and to the coast. Before him, the inhabitants of Île de France had known nothing about shipbuilding. Whenever they had had problems with their fishing boats, they had to seek recourse from any ship's carpenter who happened to be in port. He encouraged the colonials to help him build a navy, for which the island had an abundance of wood. They cut down trees in the forest, seasoned the timber, shaped it suitably, and in two years the shipbuilding was ready to begin.

In 1737, Monsieur de La Bourdonnais prepared pontoons for careening and unloading ships. He built dinghies and launches for transporting material. He constructed new lighters for carrying water and invented an apparatus by which they could raise dinghies and launches out of the water to more easily repair them. Thanks to his new apparatus, a ship could have any holes plugged and then be repaired, cleaned, and returned to the water in the space of an hour. He constructed a brig, and it turned out to be an excellent ship. The next year, he built two more and started work on a vessel of five hundred tons.

He was doing too much good for calumny not to besmirch his name. He went to Paris to defend himself. It was easy: In one breath he was able to dispel the clouds hanging over his reputation; and then, since there was discussion of France soon breaking with England and Holland, he developed a plan to arm ships and attack trading centers belonging to the two enemy powers. The plan was approved but never implemented. La Bourdonnais left Paris in 1741 with the title of commander and a special commission to captain *Le Mars,* one of the king's ships.

Peace was concluded in 1742, however, and Monsieur de La Bourdonnais returned to Île de France. New accusations were leveled against him, and again he left for France. In Pondicherry he met Monsieur Poivre, who was taking back to France pepper trees as well as cinnamon trees and several trees used for dying.

This is the same Monsieur Poivre who in 1766 was named by Monsieur le Duc de Choiseul to be intendant of Île de France and Île de Bourbon. He began cultivation of the rima, the breadfruit tree from the Society Islands. To both of the islands under his care he introduced nutmeg, cinnamon, pepper, and cloves. Today, Île de Bourbon alone harvests four hundred thousand cloves, considered in Asia to be of better quality than cloves from the Moluccas. He also introduced the ampalis, the large-fruited mulberry from Madagascar, rosewood, the bayberry tree, China tea, bloodwood, Indian coral trees, cinnamon plants from Ceylon and Cochin China, several varieties of dates, coconuts, mangoes, allspice, oaks, pines, grapes, European apples and peaches, avocadoes from the Antilles, velvet apples from the Philippines, sago palms from the Moluccas, soapwood from China, some Jolo maran trees, and the mangosteen, reputed to be the best fruit in the world. Such were the gifts to Île de France from its governor, or rather, from the governor's intendant Monsieur Poivre.

After a brilliant succession of governors, each of whom contributed further to the building of the splendid, flourishing colony, General Decaen received the governorship from the hands of Monsieur Magallon-Lamorlière. He received it along with a war with England. So it was that now Île de Bourbon and Île de France were the only ports of refuge for French vessels in the Indian Ocean, and that is where pirates like Surcouf, L'Hermitte, and the Dutertres would send the ships they captured; that too is where they would head to undergo repairs. So it was rare not to see sailing in those waters two or three English ships, waiting for the corsairs to appear so they might get their booty back.

"Land ho!" When Surcouf heard those words, he'd hurried onto deck. He was quite surprised when he climbed to the crosstrees on the *Revenant,* for he saw that the sea was empty from Port Savanne all the way to the Pointe des Quatre-Cocos. Of course, he could not be sure that, hidden by land, there were no English ships sailing, waiting, in the Baie de la Tortue or the Baie du Tamarin.

This was Surcouf's fourth trip to the island that Suffren called the Cythera of the Indies, and he easily recognized Île de France through the mists that always surround forested islands. He could see the Montagne des Créoles and the mountain chain around the principal port that led up to the Morne des Bambous. Surcouf and his crew found themselves just off the entrance to the main port.

When a ship comes to Île de France simply to dock or take on food and water, the captain sometimes hesitates in his choice between the main port and Port Louis. But when, like Surcouf, one comes to make repairs or sell a prize, there is no hesitation. On entering the port, a ship is driven along by prevailing winds that for nine months of the year are strong enough to bend the trees on the island from east to west, just as the trees in the south of France are bent by the mistral from north to south. While it is simplicity itself to enter the port when the trade winds prevail, it is next to impossible to leave, because the ship is then sailing into a headwind.

Surcouf, once he was sure that the sea was clear, marked the Pointe du Diable, and now that he knew his path, he sailed northeast to avoid the shallows. Leaving behind him the great forests near Savanne, he beheld to his left the Montagnes Blanches and the Morne de la Faïence as well as the Flacq. When they came abreast of L'Île d'Ambre, he turned west-north-west to round the Cap Malheureux. Tacking back and forth between the Pointe au Vaquois and the Pointe aux Canonniers on the windward side of the island, they thus came to Port Louis.

Already, the signal peak had announced the arrival of a frigate, a brig, and a sloop. So already the hill behind the hospital church, the Chien-de-Plomb, and the entire Pointe aux Blaguers were covered with curious on-lookers gazing through their spyglasses. The ships cast anchor at the Pavilion, where the health officer, alerted by signals, made his inspection. Along with the health officer came a flotilla of small boats bringing fruits and drinks of all kinds.

Once clearance was given, Surcouf, who had of course been recognized and greeted by all the people in the flotilla, gave the order to move on so they could anchor at Chien-de-Plomb. But well before he could get there, his name had been passed from boat to boat to all those people watching from shore, and it had reawakened among them memories of France. As the *Standard,* the *Revenant,* and the *New York Racer* docked, the throng as one welcomed them joyously with bravos and cheers.

LX
On Land

~≈:≈~

EVERYONE KNOWS HOW EASY IT IS to land on Île de France. In the deep, well-sheltered port, you can step from your ship onto the Quai du Chien-de-Plomb as easily as you might step across a small stream. Ten steps farther on, you will reach the Place du Gouvernement, where you can walk beneath the palace windows and pass the intendant's building with its magnificent, one-of-a-kind tree. Walking up toward the Champ de Mars, you will follow the Rue du Gouvernement, and just before you reach the church on your right, opposite where the theater stands today, you will find the Grand Hôtel des Étrangers, as did the group now appearing at the hotel door.

Surcouf, with Mademoiselle Hélène de Sainte-Hermine on his arm, was followed by René, escorting Jane, and then Bléas and two or three lower-ranking officers. The two young women chose the hotel's best apartment, and they sent immediately for a seamstress to make them mourning clothes. Their great loss still pained them deeply, but the circumstances in which their loss had taken place, with the sea offering them a vision of eternity, as well as René's kind presence and his conversation, so instructive, so captivating, so varied, had afforded the girls' wounds a kind of balm that, although it could not completely heal them, did assuage the pain.

When René asked them what they would like to do, they answered that they would not venture out in public until their black garments were ready. On board ship, mourning weeds did not seem necessary, but in a city they felt ashamed not to appear in clothing that expressed their bereavement and reflected their sadness. They did say, though, that their first visit would be to Les Pamplemousses.

So the reader will have guessed, hearing the name Les Pamplemousses, they were planning a pilgrimage to the setting in Bernardin de Saint-Pierre's novel *Paul et Virginie*. Although that charming idyll, so like a translation of *Daphnis and Chloe* from Greek, had been published fifteen years earlier, it maintained a poignant presence in the girls' minds. It was one of those novels that leave a mark on society, the kind of novel that some readers adopt fanatically while others toss it aside scornfully, and both are ready to defend vehemently what is a matter of taste.

We remember that unfavorable reception *Paul et Virginie* met when it was read in Madame Necker's salon. Monsieur de Buffon had been bored, Monsieur de Necker had yawned, Thomas had fallen asleep. And Bernardin de Saint-Pierre, doubting his own talents, nearly decided not to have the novel published.

Moreover, he decided to burn the manuscript, for its very existence was a cruel reminder of the great disappointment he had experienced in Madame Necker's salon. It had been condemned by the greatest minds of the day.

Such was the situation when it happened that Joseph Vernet, the painter of seascapes, came to visit him. Remarking his friend's sadness, Vernet inquired as to the cause, and when Bernardin told him, Vernet insisted that he read the novel aloud to him.

Vernet listened attentively but betrayed neither appreciation nor distaste. He remained worrisomely silent to the end, while Bernardin became increasingly distraught until finally his voice was quavering. He read the last word. With apprehension, he looked up at his judge. "Well?" he asked.

"Well, my friend," said Vernet, embracing him, "what you have written is quite simply a masterpiece!" Judging not scientifically or intellectually, but with his heart, Vernet got it right, and posterity has agreed with him.

The seamstress promised the Sainte-Hermine sisters their mourning garments for the following day. The day after that, the girls decided, they would undertake their pilgrimage.

René meanwhile did his best to make their excursion into the country one that would rival a royal tour of the Fontainebleau or Marly forests. For the girls he had two palanquins made of ebony and silk. For himself he bought a Cape horse, and for Bléas and Surcouf he rented the best he could find. He asked the proprietor of the Hôtel des Étrangers to hire twenty Negroes, for he would need eight to bear the palanquins and twelve more to carry their provisions. They would dine along the Rivière des Lataniers, and the evening before René sent on ahead a table, a tablecloth, and chairs. For those who preferred fishing to hunting, he'd hired a lovely fishing boat furnished with all necessary equipment. René himself, since he wasn't sure which of the sports he would participate in, would simply sling his gun over his shoulder so as to be prepared for whatever his two lovely companions should prefer.

On the day of the excursion the weather was beautiful, as is usually the case at those latitudes, and in order to escape the day's heat, by six in the morning everyone had already gathered in the lower room of the Hôtel des Étrangers. The palanquins and their bearers were waiting outside. Nearby three horses were snorting. Four Negroes balanced metal boxes filled with food on their heads; the eight others would spell their companions. René allowed Bléas and Surcouf to choose their horses, and since, like most seamen, they were mediocre riders, they chose the two least spirited ones. So the Cape horse was left for René. Bléas, who was not a bad horseman, was hoping he might finally get the better of René, but although the Kaffir (that's what they called the Cape) seemed disinclined to allow its rider to mount, once René was in the saddle the horse must have realized that he would not be easy to throw.

Such excursions, frequent on Île de France, have their own unique character. Since the roads were very poor in those days, women usually traveled by palanquin and men on horseback. The Negroes, who ordinarily wore little, on special occasions assumed a kind of blue jacket, like a bathing garment, that hung down to their knees. Eight men lifted the palanquins and placed the poles on their shoulders. Holding a large stick to help them maintain their balance, they started off at a rapid pace. The four Negroes carrying the dinner baskets also set off, all four swaying in unison to the rhythm of a Creole song that was more melancholic than gay.

The route they took was delightful. To the right were the Montagnes du Port, running off to the northeast where they are not as tall. Then, suddenly, beneath the Pieter Both up rose the Montagne du Pouce, which no one had ever climbed. Beyond that was the Enfoncement des Prêtres, a spectacular high plateau hidden back in a valley, its green amphitheater a pleasure to see. After they crossed the Rivière des Lataniers, they came to Terre-Rouge.

Everywhere there were bamboo groves, and black trees, and bushes of sweet-smelling cassis. At every moment bands of multicolored parrots were flying by; monkeys were hopping about, as were hares, so plentiful that you could fix them with a stick. There were flocks of doves, and tiny quail that are found only on the island.

They came to some land that had once been cultivated, but the fields of wheat, corn, and potatoes that had grown there in times gone by had given way to a wide carpet of flowers marked here and there by small, brightly colored mounds that appeared to be altars. And they could still see the ruins of two small huts that belonged to the story of Paul and Virginie.

There was only one opening in the mountains to the north, and through it, to the left, they could see the peak called the Morne de la Découverte, the peak from which signals were sent to incoming ships. Above the bamboo groves, in the midst of the wide plain, rose the steeple from the Pamplemousses church, and beyond it stretched a forest all the way to the tip of the island. Or they could look directly out over the Baie du Tombeau, just to the right of the Cap des Malheureux, and then out onto the open sea, where lay a few tiny uninhabited islands in the middle of which the peak called Point-de-Mire rose like a bastion from among the waves.

The pilgrims first visited the stone that covered Paul and Virginie's tomb, which was sometimes guarded by the old priest who had made of this place a paradise of flowers and greenery. Each of them prayed on the sepulcher, but the two young women found it difficult to pull themselves away. Less enthusiastic about idyllic romance than by the prospect of bagging game on the island, the men left to hunt, with some of the bearers as guides. René, however, remained behind to look after the sisters. Jane had brought along Bernardin de Saint-Pierre's book, and on the heroine's very tomb, René read aloud three or four chapters.

The day was beginning to heat up, and as the open plateau offered no shade, the two girls and their cavalier were forced to leave. Focusing so much on the purpose of their excursion, they only now paused to appreciate the countryside. A traveler in Armenia who happened upon the Garden of Eden would be no more surprised than one who came upon this beautiful area called Les Pamplemousses. Everything the three companions saw was a marvel, and no matter the countless number of wonderful sights, each one in itself enthralled them.

For the first time they saw silvery sugarcane, its knotty, fibrous stalks rising nine or ten feet up in the air with long, pointed, fluted leaves. Complementing the cane fields were those of coffee plants, whose fruit, according to Madame de Sévigné, was as popular as Racine's plays. For the past one hundred seventy-two years coffee had been one of Europe's sensuous delights, just as for the past two hundred years Racine had provided intellectual delights for all those who loved poetry. What especially awed the three young people was nature's abundance, for there were delicious fruits hanging from every tree, and within easy reach were almonds, avocados, and rose apples for the picking.

Beside the Rivière des Lataniers, the Negro retainers were just finishing preparations for the meal. Never had any drink seemed more refreshing than the three glasses of water drawn from the Lataniers for René and his charming companions. The huntsmen had not yet come back, but ten minutes later, some not-too-distant gunshots announced that they were on their way. Although it was only ten in the morning, after several hours in the pure, fresh air, our travelers were starving.

Besides, the table was appetizing. The sailors had explored the ocean waters and come back with huge quantities of shellfish, including a multitude of those little oysters to be served, just as in Genoa, still attached to rocks from the sea. Branches laden with fruit stood at each corner of the table. The proprietor of the Hôtel des Étrangers, commissioned to prepare the fare at the center of the meal, had provided half a lamb, a quarter of young venison, and perfectly roasted lobsters. And there were varieties of fish we know nothing about in Europe, plumper and tastier than anything on our tables. The best wines available on the island were meanwhile chilling in the riverbed.

The hunters came back with a young stag, two or three hares, and a number of grouse and quail. The cooks would prepare the fresh game for dinner, because the pilgrims were so enjoying themselves that they had all cried out, "Let's stay here all day long!"

They agreed that they'd first eat, then rest in the shade by the river until two o'clock. After that, by horse and palanquin, they'd visit the spot on the coast where the *Saint-Gérain* had wrecked, for thus would their pilgrimage be complete: They would have seen where Paul and Virginie were born, where they were wrecked, and where they were buried. For now, though, they gazed upon a bounty of rare fruits, plump fish, and enticing meats. With curiosity piquing their appetites, lunch lasted until two o'clock.

The bearers, too, had eaten well, nor had they been spared the arrack. Hoping such prodigality would continue with dinner, they were ready promptly after lunch to begin working again. So the party started back toward the coast, leaving the hill and its papaya trees behind. Sometimes the Negroes had to hack their way through thickets with their axes, but generally they walked along at a rapid pace, and however bad the roads were, the girls were able to ride smoothly in their palanquins.

In less than three quarters of an hour they arrived opposite the Île d'Ambre, or rather just opposite the passage where the *Saint-Gérain* slipped between that small island and the larger Île de France.

Although the coast bore no signs of the catastrophe that ends Bernardin de Saint-Pierre's pastoral novel, emotions ran higher here than they had back by the tomb. Their hearts pounding, the sisters stared out at the scene of the catastrophe and one of them asked the naval officers how it might have happened—then suddenly they heard a strange, loud noise and saw a wild flurry of activity at the water's surface.

The reason soon became clear. Two great massive sea creatures were struggling together out in the waves: a medium-sized whale, doing battle with its mortal enemy the swordfish. It was as if two gigantic gladiators had waited until the very moment the party of pilgrims had arrived to begin their duel.

The battle was long, unrelenting, and vicious on both sides. The huge cetacean, rising up on its tail, displayed a mass the size of a church tower. Its two blowholes spouted streams of water high into the air, but little by little their height became less and less, and soon they were tinged with blood. Finally the two columns looked like pink rain, and it appeared that the smaller of the two sea combatants would likely be the winner. For the swordfish was so agile that it seemed to be everywhere at once, and continually it dug its sword into the sides of the whale. Finally, gathering its strength for one supreme effort, the whale raised itself out of the water and then fell back on top of the swordfish. It must have crushed its enemy, for the swordfish did not reappear. The whale, meanwhile, thrashed the water for a moment, then began to stiffen as it went into convulsions. With a loud cry it expired, and were it not for its mammoth echo it would have sounded very much like the cry of a dying soldier.

LXI

The Return [1]

Monsieur Leconte de Lisle, about whom the Academie is apparently thinking at this very moment, and who must have lived on Bourbon, on Île de France, or in India, charmingly describes a young woman's excursion by palanquin in a short poem entitled "Le Manchi":

> *Tu t'en allais ainsi, par ces matins si doux,*
> *De la montagne à la grand-messe.*
> *En ta grâce naïve et ta rose jeunesse,*
> *Au pas rhythmé de tes Hindous.*

> (And thus would you go, on mornings sweet,
> From the mountain to high mass apace,
> With youth's innocence and rosy grace,
> To the rhythmic steps of your Hindu bearers' feet.)

But let not the reader think that the songs accompanying the "rhythmic steps" of those carrying the palanquin had anything in common with Leconte de Lisle's poetry. Nothing is less poetic than those primitive songs, and nothing is less melodious than their music. When man, in his primitive state, has embraced an idea in a few words and, to express it, has found a simple melody in a few notes, he repeats those words and notes endlessly. The words suffice the demands of his mind and the notes meet his musical needs. Thus Hélène and Jane's palanquin bearers, instead of inventing song out of the young women's beauty, instead of singing about Hélène's

black eyes and raven hair or the blonde, blue-eyed Jane, were content to repeat with little variation a few or two lines ending with an exclamation
similar to the lament of a baker as he kneads his bread:

> *V'là la maîtress arrivée*
> *En montant . . . hein!*

(This is our mistress,
Coming up . . . Oh!)

If the road descends instead of climbs, they need only to change the refrain:

> *"V'là la maîtresse arrivée*
> *En descendant . . . hein!"*

(This is our mistress,
Coming down . . . Oh!)

Sometimes an amorous poet, one who has perhaps been separated from
his beloved, will go beyond the set limits of a particular song or elegy by
adding four new verses to the commonly repeated original four. Then another poet, in the same spirit, will add four verses more. A third poet, another four. In time, then, the original simple lament becomes a poem to
which many people have contributed, like Homer's rhapsodies.

Or a poem may assume a different goal. It becomes a dance song, perhaps, and inevitably in these islands it ends up as a *bamboula,* a black cancan, more elegant but also more lascivious than our own in France.
Ordinarily, slaves dance their cancan near the table while the masters eat.
Often at the table there may be girls from twelve to fifteen years old, an
age in the colonies that would correspond to eighteen or twenty in Europe. The girls at table enjoy watching the dances. The bamboulas unfold
before their eyes and gladden their hearts without troubling their imaginations in the least.

Back by the river after the Sainte-Hermine sisters and their escorts had
finished their dinner, the bearers accompanying them put together an orchestra and formed a big circle around the table. Some of the Negroes became chandeliers, each of them holding above the head a twisted branch,
similar to a grape branch, that burns best when green. The torches lit up a
space thirty feet in diameter, which became a stage for singing and dancing.

A black woman stepped into the space to sing this simple, perhaps too simple, song:

> *Dansé, Callada,*
> *Ziʒim boum boum;*
> *Dansé, Bamboula,*
> *Toujou con ça!*

> (Dance, Callada,
> Zizim boum boum;
> Dance, Bamboula,
> Always like that!)

All the black men and women in the circle repeated the singer's four lines of verse and danced along with her as she moved in place.

Then the woman began to sing again:

> *Yon jou dimanche de bon matin*
> *Moin déceune en ville bien pomponné,*
> *Moin contré youli béqué bien malin,*
> *Qui dit moin belle moune me yon ti bouqué*

> (One Sunday morning early
> I go to town all dressed up,
> I meet a tricky white man
> Who tells me I'm as pretty as a little flower.)

Dancing as they had before, her companions joined her in the chorus:

> *Dansé, Callada,*
> *Ziʒim boum boum;*
> *Dansé, Bamboula,*
> *Toujou con ça!*

Then all the blacks invaded the open space and danced together.

The commotion rose to such a pitch that the picnickers had to reach out and clutch the dancers in order to bring their feverish bamboula to an end. They returned to their places, the singer joining them, and the circle reformed. It had been empty only for a moment when Bambou, Surcouf's Negro, entered it and in his Martinican accent began to sing:

Zizim, trala la la la,
Zizim, trala la la la,
Zizim, trala la la la,
Zamis vini dansé bamboula.

Travail la pas fait moin la peine,
Pioché la pas fait moin la peine,
Quatre piquets la pas fait moin la peine,
Car doudou moin yo voyé si loin.

(Work doesn't make me suffer,
The pickaxe doesn't make me suffer,
Four stakes can't make me suffer,
But my beloved is so far away.)

Although Bambou sang his verses in Martinican Creole, the local Negroes had no trouble understanding them, and they energetically joined in the song and dance at each refrain. René understood what the words meant, and two or three times he asked the girls if they might prefer to withdraw, but they found the spectacle, new to them, fascinating, and they chose to stay.

Soon night had completely fallen, and René gave the orders to make ready for the return journey. The women climbed into the palanquins, the men onto their horses. The signal for departure was given, and they were on their way when an unplanned spectacle provided a worthy sequel to the magnificent day. Two or three hundred black men and women who had appeared earlier like predators at the smell of fresh game, and who had enjoyed the excess from the hunt, decided now to show their gratitude by leading their hosts home. Each of them had cut a branch of the same torch wood by whose light the escaped slaves had brought Paul and Virginie back home, and in a procession of flame the travelers started back toward Port Louis.

Nothing could have been more picturesque than that line of moving flames. It lit up the lovely countryside for the travelers as they passed. They could survey plains dotted with huge trees, and if sometimes a mountain blocked their view, a gaze upward, just above its peak, was rewarded with the Southern Cross in all its scintillating beauty. Sometimes the mountains and forests would open up, and they could look out over the endless sea, calm as a mirror, its surface reflecting the silvery moon. The flames from the torches flushed out all kinds of game, from stags to wild boars to hares, to the joyous cries of the travelers. The torches, spread out as they were as in a great basin, would come together to surround the animal, and when the animal ran, the torches, trying to follow, would form a long river of flowing fire. Once the animal had escaped, the errant torches would, like soldiers, come back to take their places at the front of the procession.

As they were passing through the Malabar camp, the strangest thing happened. Île de France, being the rendezvous for many different peoples of India, had attracted a number of people from Malabar: exiles from the Indian coasts who had been bathed by the Sea of Oman before they'd gathered here to form a community where they lived and died among themselves. Light still shone in a few of the houses, but every door and every window opened, and the lovely olive faces of the women, with their big black eyes and their silken hair, appeared. They all were dressed in long cotton or cambric robes, their arms agleam with silver or gold bracelets and their toes decorated with rings; they looked like Greek and Roman women come back to life, to view the parade of flame in the night.

From the Malabar camp they started up the Rue de Paris, then turned into the Rue du Gouvernement, where the proprietor of the Hôtel des Étrangers was waiting respectfully on his doorstep to greet his guests. The two young women were in great need of rest. Even though riding in a palanquin is generally not uncomfortable, it can be fatiguing for the unaccustomed. Hélène and Jane quickly said good-bye to René and thanked him for the lovely day he had arranged.

When they got back to their room, Hélène's face, which had brightened somewhat during the day, once again grew sad. Turning to her sister, she said with a voice that reflected both sadness and shame, "Jane, I think it is time to pray for our father."

Jane's eyes filled with tears, and she threw herself into her sister's arms. Then she knelt down at her bedside, crossed herself, and whispered, "O Father, please forgive me!"

But to what was she alluding? To some new feeling growing in her heart, perhaps, that in this strange and beautiful new locale was enchanting her out of memories of her father.

LXII

The New York Racer

≈:≈

AT DAYBREAK THE NEXT MORNING René went into Surcouf's room. The captain was already awake but still in bed.

"Well, my dear René," Surcouf said, "you invite us to a picnic, and you regale us with a feast fit for a nabob. I agreed to a picnic, but I warn you that Bléas and I are going to pay our share of the day's costs. We insist."

"My dear commander," said René, "I was just coming to request a favor that would make me the debtor more. For it, I would do anything to please you."

"Speak, my dear René. Unless it is something absolutely impossible for me to grant, I can guarantee it before you even ask."

"I would like you to send me, on whatever pretext, to explore the coast along the Pegu River. You will be tied up here on Île de France or nearby for several months at least. Grant me six weeks of leave, and then I will join you wherever you happen to be."

"I understand," Surcouf said, laughing. "I have made you the guardian of two lovely girls whose father we unintentionally killed, and now you would like to carry out the duties of a guardian to the end."

"There is some truth in what you are saying, Monsieur Surcouf. However, I can see through your words and read your thoughts. I tell you, though, that the feelings that drive me to undertake the voyage are not the feelings of love. It is a trip I promised myself when I purchased the slaver. I do not know what will happen to me, but I would not like to have been near as we are to the coasts of India without having participated in one of those splendid tiger or elephant hunts that enables one to be completely alive because death is so near. The trip would also allow me to take the two orphan girls to their home, but no one will ever know the real cause of my real interest in them. You talk of love, Captain. I am not even twenty-six years old, and yet my heart is as dead as if I were eighty. I am a man condemned to kill time, my dear Surcouf. Since that is the case, I would prefer killing time while doing extraordinary things. My heart is dead to love, but I would like to feel it come alive with other sensations. Allow me to seek out those sensations; help me discover them by granting me a leave of six weeks or two months."

"But how are you going to get there?" asked Surcouf. "Sailing in your walnut shell?"

"Oh! That is another reason I have come," said René. "You know that I had the boat transferred to me as if I were an American. I have all the necessary papers for proving the boat's nationality, and I speak English well enough to defy Englishmen and Americans the world over to say that I am not from London or New York. And America is at peace with the whole world. I shall be sailing under an American flag. Everyone will let me pass; if they do not, I shall simply present my proof and I'll not be retained. What do you have to say to that?"

"But surely you are not going to ask your two beautiful passengers to travel aboard a ship that has carried a cargo of slaves?"

"My dear commander, in two weeks you will no longer recognize the *New York Racer*. From the outside, nothing will look different. Just another coat of paint, nothing else. Assuming you grant me my leave, the ship will become a jewel inside, thanks to the magnificent woods and splendid fabrics I caught a glimpse of yesterday."

"Well," said Surcouf. "You have your leave, my friend. All you had to do was ask."

"Then all that remains for you to do is to point out the best ship outfitter you know in Port Louis."

"I know just the person, my young friend," said Surcouf. "Furthermore, if your expenses are greater than you expect, a word from me will guarantee you unlimited credit."

"I would like to be able to thank you for that additional service, my dear captain, but if you give me the man's address, I shall ask for nothing more."

"So, are you a millionaire?" cried Surcouf, no longer able to resist asking.

"Somewhat more than that," René answered nonchalantly. "And now, if you will tell me what time suits you," he added, getting to his feet, "and if ever you yourself need to have recourse to my purse. . . ."

"I shall not hesitate, I promise. If only to see how deep it is."

"So," asked René, "what time suits you, my dear captain?"

"Immediately, if you like," Surcouf replied, jumping out of bed.

Ten minutes later the two companions were walking down the main street. They turned onto the Quai du Chien-de-Plomb and entered into the shop of the best shipbuilder in Port Louis.

"Ah!" cried the builder. "It's dear Monsieur Surcouf." For Surcouf was as well known in Port Louis as he was in Saint-Malo.

"Yes, Monsieur Raimbaut, and I'm bringing you a good customer, I believe."

Surcouf pointed out to the shipbuilder René's ship bobbing up and down opposite Trou-Fanfaron. "There, Monsieur," he said, "is the sloop belonging to one of my friends. It needs to be refurbished outside, and inside it requires a complete makeover. I thought of you, and I am bringing you my friend."

The shipbuilder thanked Surcouf, stepped outside, and shaded his eyes with his hand as he looked at the ship. "I need to see it up close," he said.

"Nothing easier," René replied. He shouted out to a sailor who was standing on the bridge: "Ahoy there, on the sloop! Bring the boat over."

Immediately the launch slipped down the hoist, and two sailors stepped down into it. Soon the three men were in the boat and shortly after reached the sloop. As if he were going aboard his own vessel, Surcouf climbed up first, followed by René and then Monsieur Raimbaut.

With his measuring stick Monsieur Raimbaut calculated every dimension and asked René what changes he would like to see. René replied that there was nothing to change but much to beautify. The captain's apartment afforded space for two small bedrooms in front, near the entrance hatch, as well as a dining room, while the back of the apartment offered a bedroom large enough for two beds. With a curtain in the middle the bedroom could be divided in two.

"This room, Monsieur Raimbaut," said René, "must be paneled with teak wood. Cashew will be sufficient for the two front rooms. I would like the dining room to be done in ebony with gold tones. All the ornaments must be made of ungilded copper so that they can be polished daily. Prepare your estimate; you and Monsieur Surcouf can decide together on the price. I shall pay half today and half on delivery, but my ship must be ready to sail in two weeks."

"I hope that sounds good, Father Raimbaut," said Surcouf.

"Too good," the builder replied. "Because there is work enough for a month."

"That's no affair of mine," said René. "I must have my sloop in two weeks. As far as costs are concerned, you may do your calculations up on deck with Monsieur Surcouf."

Just as they came back up on deck they saw a carriage stop opposite the *Standard*. Two young women got down, called for a boat, and went on board the ship Surcouf had captured. "Who are those women who have come to see us so early in the morning?" Surcouf wondered.

"The two Sainte-Hermine girls are going to pray beside their father's casket. Let us not trouble them as they fulfill their pious duty. Once they are back up on deck, we can pay our respects."

They waited several minutes. Then, since the sloop was moored right next to the quay, they simply jumped from the ship to the jetty, where they signaled to the boat that had taken the girls to the *Standard*. They were soon climbing up the starboard ladder, and as they were stepping onto the deck, they heard a scream: "Help! Help me! A shark!" cried a sailor swimming nearby.

Everyone gasped. The man was hurrying toward the ship, and behind him, in his wake, the shark's dorsal fin was slicing through the water. People were shouting: "Hang on!" "Wait!" "We're coming!"

René waved his arms decisively, and commanded, "Nobody move! I'll take care of it!"

At that moment the Sainte-Hermine girls, hearing the shouts, appeared on deck. They watched as René put his hand to his chest to be sure the dagger he usually carried around his neck was there on its silver chain. He threw off his jacket and vest, and climbing up on the rail, he shouted, "Courage, my friend! Keep swimming!" And dove into the water.

Jane paled and let out a cry. Hélène, dragging her along, managed to reach the poop deck, where Surcouf reached out his hand to help them up. They got to the rail just in time to see René resurface.

Holding the dagger between his teeth, René dove a second time, then reappeared, this time between the sailor and the shark, no more than three meters from the monster. He dove a third time, toward the creature. Suddenly, the shark made a convulsive movement and began to thrash its tail as if it were in pain. The water around it began to redden. A joyous shout arose among the crew. René reappeared a meter behind the shark, but only long enough to take a breath. Scarcely had he disappeared than the shark began thrashing its tail again and during one of its convulsions turned over, belly up. Its white stomach had been sliced open; the cut was a meter long.

Without awaiting anyone's orders or counsel, the sailors, meanwhile, had launched a boat and were rowing rapidly toward René. He had replaced the dagger in its sheath, and leaving behind him the shark blinded by its pain, he was swimming back toward the ship. In his path he met the boat. Two sailors reached down and helped him out of the water, and when he was in the boat, they hugged him and, raising their caps in the air, they shouted, "Long live René!"

Their words were repeated by everyone, including the seamen aboard the *Standard* and the two girls, who were waving their kerchiefs.

As for the sailor who had so unwisely gone swimming despite his comrades' warnings, he was thrown a rope and hoisted back on board.

René received a hero's welcome on the *Standard*'s deck. Up until then, some of his companions had been jealous of this young man, who was not only handsome, rich, and educated but also clearly superior in whatever pursuit he undertook. Now that they had seen him risk his life to save a poor devil like them, however, their enthusiasm knew no limits, and jealousy was ousted by admiration and gratitude.

René, though, hurried away from these accolades and climbed to the poop deck, where he found Jane half unconscious. Hélène, with tear-

streaked eyes, was administering smelling salts, while Surcouf was trying
to revive her by slapping her hands. Just when René reached them, Jane
half awakened and, unthinking, seized his hand and kissed it. Then, with a
cry, she hid her face in her sister's breast.

"How about that!" said Surcouf. "You must either be the devil himself
or be tired of life to keep trying things like that."

"My dear commander," said René, "I had heard that Negroes in Gondar,
whenever they are attacked by sharks, dive beneath them and slice open their
stomachs with a knife. I merely wanted to see if that was in fact possible."

At that moment, Monsieur Raimbaut, who had been absorbed in his calculations and, true merchant that he was, had seen nothing of what had
happened, climbed up to the poop deck and handed a paper to René. René
glanced at the total, eight thousand five hundred francs, then passed the estimate on to Surcouf. While the two sisters, and especially Jane, gazed in
wonder at the brave René, Surcouf studied Monsieur Raimbaut's bill with
the greatest attention. Then, handing the paper back to René, he said, "If
we subtract five hundred francs, the figure seems reasonable."

"But," asked René, "will the ship be ready in two weeks?"

"I guarantee it," Monsieur Raimbaut replied.

"Then please give me your pencil, Monsieur," René said to him.

Master Raimbaut did as he was bade, and René wrote on the back of the
bill:

To the bearer, Monsieur Rondeau will pay Monsieur Raimbaut the sum
of four thousand francs, and two weeks from today, if the sloop is finished, an additional four thousand five hundred francs.

Surcouf raised his hand to interrupt, but René paid him no attention. He
went on writing:

Monsieur Raimbaut will distribute five hundred to his workers as a
bonus.

René,
Sailor on board the *Standard*.

LXIII

The Guardian

CAPTAIN SURCOUF, RENÉ THE SAILOR, and the two sisters returned to the Hôtel des Étrangers in the same carriage. Two hours later a servant came to ask René if he would receive the Sainte-Hermine sisters or if he preferred to visit them in their room. René thought the latter alternative to be the more appropriate, so the servant went on ahead to tell the sisters that René was coming. The girls welcomed him, but with a little embarrassment.

"Since I am the elder," said Hélène, smiling uneasily, "I suppose I should be the first to speak."

"Permit me to be a little surprised at how solemn you are, Mademoiselle."

"You should use the word 'sad,' Monsieur, rather than 'solemn.' The situation of two orphans three thousand leagues from home, two orphans carrying their father's dead body with them and still having another thousand or twelve hundred leagues to cover before they reach their destination, is certainly not a joyous one, as I am sure you will agree."

"It is true that you are orphans," said René. "And you do have another thousand leagues to cover, that is true as well. But you have a faithful, respectful brother who has promised to watch over you and who will keep his word. I thought that we had agreed that you need not worry over a single detail, and that you would leave all your concerns in regard to your safety to me."

"And so far we have done exactly that, Monsieur," said Hélène, "but we cannot continue to take advantage of the great kindness you have not hesitated to show us."

"I thought I had obtained the favor of watching out for you until such time as we reach Rangoon, that is, until you are once again settled on your land. I have made my arrangements with that in mind. But if you prefer distancing yourselves from the guardian whom Surcouf has chosen for you, I am ready to resign my commission from that honorable position. Delighted as I was to be chosen, I should be in despair if that were an imposition."

"Oh, Monsieur René! . . ." cried Jane.

"Of course," her sister interrupted, "we are, and would continue to be, happy to know that we are protected by a man so good, so generous, and so brave as you, but it is not suitable for us to retain you only for our own benefit. All that we ask is that you commend us to a captain who is leaving for the Burmese empire. He then could put us ashore at some point along the coast, and from there we could arrange an escort to take us to the Pegu River."

"If indeed you prefer that arrangement to what I propose, Mademoiselle, I have no right to insist. From this moment on, to my great regret, I shall say nothing more. But it pains me to give up the plan I have been preparing since the day I met you, and which, for the past two months, has soothed me with happy dreams. Think about it. I await your orders and shall act accordingly." René got to his feet and, picking up his hat, prepared to say good-bye to the two sisters.

Instinctively, without thinking, Jane rushed to place herself between him and the door. "Oh, Monsieur," she said. "May God keep you from thinking that we are ungrateful for all that you have already done and all that you would yet do for us. But my sister and I are a little frightened when we see how great an obligation we are contracting with a stranger."

"A stranger!" René exclaimed. "You are more cruel than your sister, Mademoiselle. She had not dared pronounce that word."

Jane began again. "My God!" she said. "How difficult it is for a girl, for a child of my age, for whom a mother and father have always done the thinking, to express my own opinions! Oh! Even if my sister should scold me, I shall not let you leave us with such a poor opinion of our hearts."

"But, Jane," said Hélène, "Monsieur knows perfectly well that—"

"No, Hélène," said Jane. "No. He knows nothing. That was clear to me when I saw the way he stood up to take his leave. That was clear to me when I heard the change in his voice as he offered to place us under the protection of another."

"Jane! Jane!" Hélène repeated.

"Oh! Let him think what he wants," cried Jane, "as long as he does not think we are ungrateful!"

Then, turning toward René, she continued: "No, monsieur. What came from my sister's mouth were social proprieties. From mine you will hear the truth. And here is the truth: My sister is afraid, and this is not the first time we have talked about this, that your being away from your post for two months might hurt you in the eyes of Monsieur Surcouf. She fears that your own interests might be compromised by the kindness you are showing to us. She would prefer for us to lose our entire fortune rather than for you to lose a promotion you so richly deserve."

"Please allow me first to respond to that portion of Mademoiselle Hélène's fears. Monsieur Surcouf himself made me your guardian, just as my own heart has made me your brother. He encouraged me to purchase the little sloop, with which I'd hoped to take you to Rangoon under the flag of a neutral country so as not to expose you to the kind of dangers you experienced on board the *Standard*. This morning, you yourselves observed Monsieur Surcouf as he settled the price of the improvements I've contracted for the sloop. You will be more comfortable, more at home, and safer on the *New York Racer* than you would be on any ship, no matter what size."

"But, sir," Hélène said timidly, "just so that we might enjoy a more comfortable passage, can we permit you to spend eight or ten thousand francs more than you would have spent if we were not passengers?"

"You are mistaken, Mademoiselle," René insisted. "You are not the ones going to India, I am. Seeing Île de France or Île de la Réunion is not the same as seeing India. I am a keen hunter. I have promised myself that I would hunt panthers, tigers, and elephants. I am keeping that promise, that is all. Whether or not you accept my offer to take you to your settlement, I will still go to India, for I have heard that the areas along the Pegu River have more tigers than anywhere else in the Burmese kingdom. Also, allow me to remind you, my dear sisters, you have one final, painful duty to fulfill. So far, I am the one whom you have entrusted with this pious task. Will you not grant me the sweet sadness of finishing what I have begun? By tearing me away from you prematurely, will you take from me a memory that would stand surely among those dearest to me for the rest of my life?"

With her hands clasped and tears in her eyes, Jane was meanwhile praying, her aspect more eloquent even than René's words. And when Hélène reached out her hand to René, Jane seized it first and kissed it passionately.

"Jane! Jane!" Hélène murmured. Jane lowered her eyes and fell back into her chair.

"To continue to refuse such sincere offers," said Hélène, "would be almost an outrage to friendship. Therefore we accept, and we promise to remember your brotherly protection forever."

Hélène rose and bowed gently to René as a way of ending their affecting visit. René said good-bye and left the room.

From that moment on, René had only one thing in mind: preparing the *New York Racer* for sea. In exchange for its old cast-iron cannons, Surcouf proposed five copper cannons from the *Standard*. While fifteen men would be enough to sail the sloop, and the crewmen from the *Standard* and the *Revenant*, with Surcouf's permission, volunteered, it was unfortunately an American ship, which could not be manned by a French-speaking crew. So René hired ten Americans and found among Surcouf's two crews five men who did indeed speak English. In addition, Surcouf proposed that his first mate, Kernoch, serve as René's pilot, for Kernoch, who had twice sailed to the mouth of the Ganges, knew the waters.

The sailors wanted to show René how grateful they were for his generosity and loyalty to them in the shark incident. They knew that René intended to go tiger or panther hunting, and they also knew he had only a sin-gle-shot rifle and an ordinary shotgun. So when they found an English shotgun with a grooved barrel at the best gunmaker's in Port Louis, they all chipped in to buy it for him. They presented it to him the evening before he was to leave. On the barrel they'd had these words engraved: "Given by Surcouf's sailors to their brave comrade René."

Nothing could have pleased their comrade more, for more than once he had regretted not having armed himself fully and properly for his journey. He was proud to be leaving Île de France with such an exceptional gift and appropriate piece.

On the agreed-upon day, Master Raimbaut turned the ship he had so handsomely redecorated with the island's magnificent woods over to René. The two girls' rooms, which René himself had planned, were especial mod-els of taste and elegance. After their father's casket had been carried from the *Standard* onto the *New York Racer* and placed in a tiny chapel draped in black, René went to the hotel and told Hélène and Jane that he was now awaiting only their orders to set sail. They too were ready to leave.

They ordered a mass for the dead, and the next morning at ten, led by Surcouf, the two young women entered the church. Everyone knew that a mass was being said for a former French ship's captain, and all the authori-ties of Île de France, along with every captain, every officer, and every sea-man on every ship passing through or based in Port Louis, were in attendance at the service, which was augustly military.

An hour later, René, Surcouf, and the two sisters were on their way to the port, where they had planned a luncheon aboard the *New York Racer*. In the name of his two passengers, René had invited Bléas and Kernoch as well. All of the ships anchored in the port were dressed with flags, as if for a holiday, and the *New York Racer*, the smallest and the most elegant of them all, had hung every pennon to be had from its mast, both yards, and peak. Still, the mood at lunch was sad, despite everyone's effort to be gay and despite the lively strains of patriotic music that General Decaen, the is-land's governor, had ordered the garrison's band to play nearby on the quay.

Then it was time to leave. They raised their glasses in one last toast to René and his lovely passengers. Surcouf kissed the hands extended to him by the two sisters; he embraced René. A cannon signaled their departure.

The *New York Racer* began to move, pulled by two launches from the *Stan-dard* and the *Revenant*, for the crews wanted to provide their comrade one last service. The launches and ship wended their way out of the port, with a crowd of spectators following them as far as they could along the quay.

When the sloop reached the Passe de la Bête, only a thousand feet away, the launches stopped. Leaving the quay, the sloop unfurled all her sails; all that was left to do was to trim them to catch the wind. While the sloop was reeling its cables back in, the sailors on the two launches raised their voices in a farewell toast, shouting: "May the trip go well for Captain René and the Sainte-Hermine sisters."

The ship sailed along the Baie de la Tombe and disappeared from sight behind the Pointe aux Canonniers. Soon its wake disappeared too.

LXIV
Malay Pirates

SIX DAYS LATER, with smooth sailing and without ever seeing another ship, they once again crossed the equator. The only thing the two lovely passengers had to endure was the stifling heat inside the ship. René had furnished their rooms with bathtubs, however; so thanks to his foresight, they were able to pass the hottest hours of the day in some comfort.

In the evening, they could enjoy the deck, where the cooling breeze brought with it sweet sea smells and relief from the day's heat. At a table there they would take their evening meal, and thanks to everyone's skill at catching fish and to supplies that had been readily available in the Seychelles and the Maldives, the food they ate was as fresh as any on land.

From the evening into the night, too, those steamy latitudes offered marvelous displays on the ocean's stage. In the seas near India, sunsets are simply magnificent; scarcely has the solar orb disappeared into the ocean than it seems to cast itself like dust or golden sand across the sky's blue canvas.

So life aboard ship in the middle of the ocean is not as cheerless as one might think. The more the eye observes the sea, the more it discovers, for the ocean holds thousands of marvelous creatures that are invisible to the untrained eye. While countless of the sea's creatures live deep in its waters, they also swim to the surface to breathe, and the observant ocean voyager will be amazed by their variety in habit, shape, and color.

For more than a week they had been sailing with light winds. Then, around eight o'clock one evening, while the moon still hung bright and serene in a clear sky, clouds suddenly began to creep up over the horizon. They soon reached high into the sky, which quickly assumed the appearance of a deep, dark quarry. The moon struggled hopelessly against the clouds, although from time to time a few faint rays broke through the sky's dark veil. Other clouds turned inky and greenish like copper as they got crisscrossed by bolts of lightning. A few drops, as large as five-franc coins, began to fall onto the deck. Thunderclaps boomed in the distance. The sky went totally black, the wind whistled. The sloop had never been moving faster.

Suddenly, in front of the ship, spread out over the water's surface was a wide, silvery sheet that soon proved to be a mass of living creatures, mostly jellyfish, brought by the waves to the surface. Swimming at different depths, those tossed onto the surface looked like cylinders of fire, while the creatures in the rollers just beneath them resembled sea snakes five or six feet long. As they contracted or expanded they all produced beams of light, as if they were afire. Then, seeming to lose their phosphorescence, their vibrant reds, pinks, oranges, greens, and azure blues turned to the color of seaweed. Noting the interest of his passengers in the display, René managed to catch a few of the creatures and put them in a jar filled with seawater. The gleam from the jar was bright enough for them to read and write by for an entire evening.

Each evening, seated on the poop deck or at the window in one of the sisters' rooms, René would spend hours studying those gold and silvery masses forever moving in the depth of the sea. The rougher the sea and the darker the night, the more brilliant they seemed to be. Sometimes he'd see huge creatures, fifteen or twenty feet in diameter, and in the light of their phosphorescence he'd espy a variety of other animals, particularly sea bream and bonita, which lacked phosphorescent properties. Schools of fish swimming through these waters looked to be on fire. The sloop itself left a fiery wake. It seemed no longer merely to be cutting through the surface of the water, but rather to be plowing lava, and as the prow furrowed into it, it was as if flaming lava were rolling out from port and starboard.

Eleven days of sailing took them near the Maldives. One morning, with the wind blowing lightly from the southeast, the sailor on watch called out, "Ship ahoy! A pirogue!"

Kernoch rushed up on deck; René, holding a spyglass, was already there. "Where is it?" Kernoch asked the watch.

"To leeward."

"Is it an outrigger?"

"Yes."

"Is everything ready?" Kernoch asked the first mate.

"Yes, Captain," he answered.

"Are the cannons loaded?"

"Yes, Captain. Three with balls, three with grapeshot."

"And how about the long gun?"

"The master cannoneer awaits your orders."

"Have him use a third more powder than the usual charge and twenty-four pounds of balls. Have the gun cases brought up on deck."

"Master Kernoch! What's got into you?" asked René.

"Would you hand me your spyglass, Monsieur René?"

"Of course," said René, handing it to him. "It is an excellent English spyglass."

Kernoch looked at the pirogue. "Yes, indeed," he said. "There must be seven or eight men on board."

"Does that little toy boat worry you, Kernoch?"

"Not particularly. For it's not the remora, when I see it, that worries me. What worries me is the shark."

"And what shark might be using this remora as a pilot?"

"Some Indian prau would not be sorry to capture a fine ship like the *New York Racer*—or to demand a ransom of several thousand rupees for our lovely passengers."

"Well," said René, "God help me, but I think your outrigger, if outrigger it is, is sailing straight for us."

"You are not mistaken."

"What will it try to do?"

"It is coming to scout us out, to count how many cannons we have and how many men, and to see how we'd be hard or easy to digest."

"Good Lord! But do you realize that in five minutes your outrigger will be within rifle shot?"

"Yes, and I think that if you would like to give them a proper greeting, you should not waste any more time before getting your guns."

René called out to the sailor who acted as his personal servant and whom everyone on board called the Parisian. Like anyone who has grown up in the fine city of Paris, François was good at anything, knew a little about everything, and feared nothing. He could dance a jig wild enough to make the American crewmen die laughing, he could kickbox, and when necessary he could handle a sword. A dyed-in-the-wool Bonapartist, François found it humiliating to be in company with so many Englishmen, but, as his master had told him, it was really none of his business; and that was answer enough for him.

"François," said René, "go to my room and get my carbine, my double-barreled gun, and my pistols, and bring powder and bullets for each."

"So, we are going to have a little chat with those rascals, Captain?" François asked.

"Parisian, do happen to speak Malay?"

"Not Malay," he answered. And he went down through the bow hatch, whistling "Let us watch over the Empire's safety."

Five minutes later, he came back on deck with the guns, and since the outrigger was quickly drawing nearer, René immediately began loading his rifle. A beautiful weapon made by Lepage, it had an exceptional range for the day: at seven or eight hundred paces it could kill a man. The shotgun with the grooved barrel was loaded with bullets rather than grapeshot, as were the two pistols. René jammed both pistols into his belt, picked up his rifle, and handed the shotgun to François to hold for him.

The pirogue was still approaching but was slightly over two hundred yards astern. René took the megaphone from Kernoch: "Ahoy there! Come about for the *New York Racer.*"

In response, one of the men in the outrigger climbed up on the bow and made an obscene gesture. To which, René grabbed his rifle barrel with his left hand, put the gun to his shoulder, and pulled the trigger, almost without aiming. The man jerked backward and fell into the water. Angrily, the pirogue's crew began shouting death threats.

"Kernoch," said René, "do you know who Romulus was?"

"No, Monsieur René. Did he live in Saint-Malo?"

"No, my dear Kernoch, but he was a great man anyway, and like all great men, he was quick to anger. In anger he one day killed his brother. However, since it is a terrible crime to kill one's brother, and since terrible crimes have to be punished, he was. It happened when he was passing his men in review; a storm blew up—and he disappeared! . . . Get the pirogue in your sights, Kernoch, aim with the long gun, and make it simply disappear like Romulus."

"Gunners," shouted Kernoch, "are you ready?"

"Yes," they answered.

"Well, then, when you have the pirogue in your sights, fire!"

"Wait!" René cried. "François, go tell the women not to be afraid. Tell them we are just testing our cannons."

François disappeared a moment down through the hatch, then returned to say, "They said they would be fine, and that with you, Monsieur René, they would never be afraid."

The twenty-four-pound gun was on a swivel, so they had been able to follow the pirogue's path. They shot when it was still almost two hundred yards away. It was as if René's order had been followed to the letter. Where the pirogue had been there were now just a few pieces of floating debris and some dying men, who disappeared one by one in the jaws of sharks.

Then the sailor on watch called out, "The prau!"

"Where?" asked Kernoch.

"To windward."

And indeed, they could see it, about sixty feet long and four or five wide, moving like a serpent. They counted thirty oarsmen and added forty or fifty fighting men, not including those who were probably lying down, hidden, on the bottom of the prau. As soon as it emerged from the straits, the prau headed directly for the sloop.

"Is everything all set?" Kernoch asked.

"We await your orders, Captain," the chief gunner replied.

"A third more powder than usual and twenty-four pounds of lead," Kernoch reminded him.

As the wind, stiffening, was making maneuvering easier, he said, "Make ready to come around when I give the order."

"The same direction?" asked the first mate.

"Yes, but at a lower speed. We do not want to look like we are fleeing before such miserable enemies."

They reefed their sails, and the sloop lost a third of its speed. "Are you sure you can get the ship to tack with these sails?" Kernoch shouted to the mate.

"It will turn like a top. Relax, Captain."

They could now see the Malay men more clearly. The chief was standing at the curved bow; he was gesturing threateningly with his gun.

"Don't you have a few words for him, Monsieur René?" Kernoch asked. "I do not like the way the man is acting one bit."

"Wait until he is a little closer, my dear Kernoch. We don't want to lose our reputation; with those kinds of people, it is important for each shot to count. François, have the pikes brought up on deck so that we can repulse them if they should try to come aboard."

François went back down through the hatch and re-emerged with two sailors, each carrying an armful of pikes. They set them on the starboard side, as that is where the pirates would try to board.

"Send two men aloft with blunderbusses, my dear Kernoch," said René, and when the order was carried out, he added, "Now watch the somersault that man shall perform."

He pulled the trigger. Indeed, the man standing in the bow, no doubt their leader, stretched out his arms, dropped his gun, and toppled over backward, a bullet through his chest.

"Bravo, my dear Monsieur René. And now I've got a little surprise for them."

As René handed his rifle to François to be reloaded, Kernoch whispered a few words to the two strongest crew members, and then: "Prepare to come about!" he shouted to the first mate.

"Ready to come about!" the mate said to the helmsman.

Kernoch left the bridge for a moment to speak to the chief gunner: "Listen, and let us be sure we understand each other, Valter," he said. "We are going to come about."

"Yes, Captain."

"Your gun will swing completely around. You must take advantage of that moment. You will have only a second to fire."

"Ah, yes. I understand," said the gun-layer. "A good trick, Monsieur Kernoch, if I say so myself."

Another man had stood up in the prau's prow, and another shot sent him to the ocean's depths.

Meanwhile, the ship was bearing off. Then suddenly an explosion was heard, and from one end of the prau to the other men were dropping like flies. "Bravo," said René. And in English, he shouted, "Yes! Another shot like that, Master Kernoch, and it will all be over."

The prau was in serious difficulty. More than thirty men had been knocked to the bottom of the boat. A few among those that were unhurt were hurriedly throwing the dead bodies into the sea while the rest made ready to continue the battle. It seemed less than a minute before their bullets and arrows were raining down on the sloop. They caused little damage, but twenty oarsmen had meanwhile regained their seats and the prau continued to move forward.

Kernoch had been making adjustments for the surprise he had in the works for the Malays. It was ready. He had wrapped four twenty-four-pound cannonballs in a net that he'd suspended from the end of the fore-yard on the starboard side. The apparatus would work like a crusher by dropping vertically on the prau, which was now barely a hundred yards from the sloop as it maneuvered to arrive athwartship.

"Fire on the starboard side!" Kernoch shouted. The three sixteen-pounders, loaded with grapeshot, boomed in unison and made three huge gaps among the oarsmen and the other survivors.

Master Kernoch judged that the time had come to finish them off, and he called out to the helmsman: "Bear away!"

The distance between the prau and the sloop narrowed rapidly amidst a flurry of gunshots. Then a strange whistling cut through the air. The cannonballs wrapped in netting dropped straight down on the prau and smashed it, like boulders breaking a caiman's back. Forty or fifty survivors thrashed in the sea, their only hope of salvation the ship they'd set out to attack.

Once the Malays managed to board the *Racer*, the battle truly began. The terrible, vicious, hand-to-hand combat, with pikes inflicting ghastly wounds, soon had the deck carpeted in blood. In the midst of it all, despite the noise, René thought he heard the women's cries.

Pale, frightened, their hair streaming, Hélène and Jane rushed up on deck. Two Malays, who had broken a window and leaped into their quarters, were pursuing them with daggers in their hands.

Jane threw herself into René's arms crying, "Save me, René! Save me!" The words were barely uttered when the two pirates collapsed, one on the deck, the other down the stairway.

René placed Jane in her sister's arms, discharged the other shots in his pistols at two heads coming over the rail, grabbed a pike, entrusted the two young women to François, and threw himself back into the fray.

LXV

Arrival

⁂

THE COMBAT NEARED ITS END. Of the hundred pirates who had attacked the sloop, only ten had survived, and most of them were wounded and near death. The sea would finish the job that fire had started.

"All sails set!" cried Kernoch, the hero of the day, thanks to his inventiveness, for who knows what would have become of the sloop if more of the Malay pirates had been able to climb aboard. "Head north!"

The topsail was unfurled, and the vessel, obeying the wind as a horse obeys the spur, started forward in a northerly direction by the compass. In the water behind the sloop a few men were still afloat on some debris from the prau; others were struggling with little hope of reaching a spar before being pulled down by sharks into the depths of the sea. The *Racer* was still about two hundred leagues from the coast.

René returned to the young women who were sitting on the steps of the little stairway leading up to the poop deck. Leaning on his bloody pike, with his hair blowing in the wind and his shirt slashed by knives, he cut a figure as handsome as a hero out of Homer. On seeing him, Jane let out a cry of joy, a cry nearly of admiration. Her arms outstretched, she said, "You have been our savior for the second time!" René responded to her innocent invitation not with a hug and a kiss, but rather with a gentle clasp of her hand, which he pressed to his lips.

The expression in Hélène's eyes thanked him for his reserve toward her sister as she said, "Though my gratitude may be less expressive than Jane's, it is no less great, you may be sure. God is good even in the pain he inflicts upon us. He has taken a father from us, but he has given us a brother, a protector, a friend, and, how shall I say, a man who himself is able to place limits on our gratitude when it seems to have overstepped its bounds. What would have become of us without you, sir?"

"Someone else would have stepped into my place," René answered. "It would have been impossible for God not to send you help. Had I not been available, He'd have sent an angel to serve as your defender."

François, who had gathered up René's weapons, brought them to him. "Put everything in my room, François," said René. "Fortunately the time for using such miserable instruments of destruction has passed."

"Oh, good sir," said the Parisian, "don't dismiss your weapons so lightly. When you need them, you use them effectively. Those two men know what I mean." He pointed to the two Malays who had broken in upon the girls and pursued them up on deck; their bodies were being thrown into the sea.

"Hurry up, my men," said René to the sailors who were cleaning the deck. "Hurry up, and make sure not a single drop of blood is left. Captain Kernoch says that I may give you three bottles of arrack so that you can drink to his health and the health of these young ladies. He also allows me to give you triple pay for what you have done today. Come, my ladies, let's go up on the poop deck or back down to your quarters. Before you go down, though, the ship's carpenter should check things out, so I should think you'd prefer the upper deck. Or you may use my room until yours are ready."

"Let's go up to the poop deck," said Hélène.

All three climbed the stairs. They looked out over the vast plain of the sea. God's creation almost always affords consolation for the ill deeds man has done.

"When you think," said René, putting his hand to his forehead in dismay, "that a few moments ago men were out there tearing each other apart with knives, daggers, and blades of all kinds. Yet for the least of those men I would risk my life if he were in danger just now!"

Hélène sighed deeply and sat down on the bench beside René and Jane.

"But have you no family in France?" he asked abruptly. "I could carry them news about you and ask them to take you under their protection."

"The story of our family is a very sad one. For death seems always to intervene. First our aunt left us, ahead of her husband, the father of three boys. Their first son was shot, and the second guillotined in horrible circumstances. As for the third, he remains a mystery. My father did everything he could to discover what became of him, but it was as if a veil had been thrown over the young man's life. The very evening he was to sign his marriage contract, he disappeared, like one of those legendary heroes whom the earth swallows up and who are never seen again."

"And did you ever meet that young man?" asked René.

"Yes, indeed. I remember the occasion. We were both quite young. He served for a time under my father when he was a ship's captain. He made for an attractive apprentice in his sailor's hat and uniform, his dagger at his side. He was about twelve or thirteen years old, so I must have been six or seven. My sister is younger and knew him less well. My father had thought of uniting our families by even tighter bonds: I remember that we used to call each other not only 'my little cousin' but also 'my little husband' and 'my little wife.' It is one of those childhood memories that we'd best forget, especially as there is no reason to remember, for the heart has not really been implicated, after all. When we learned about the great misfortune that had befallen our cousin, we tried to find out where he was. But all our efforts were in vain, and my father assumed the poor child was lost. Then came those three great catastrophes, the deaths of Cadoudal, Pichegru, and the Duc d'Enghien. My father grew sick of France. He decided to concentrate all his efforts on the large piece of land he owned on the far side of the world, where it was said that all you had to do was plant rice to make a fortune. In London we met Sir James Asplay, who has been living in India for seven or eight years, in Calcutta, so he is almost a neighbor, for we are only about three hundred leagues apart. He has studied the soil in India; he knows what it can produce. He is also a great hunter, and he dreams of one day establishing an independent kingdom some sixty leagues in circumference. As for me, I am like Hamlet. I am not so ambitious, and even if my kingdom were no larger than a walnut shell, I would be happy there as long as my sister was happy too." Hélène gently pulled her sister's head to her and kissed her tenderly.

René had listened attentively to her narrative. Now and then a sigh would escape from his breast, as if he had memories linked to her own.

He got to his feet; he paced back and forth on the poop deck. Finally he came back and sat back down beside them. He hummed a little song written by Chateaubriand that was popular at the time:

> *Combien j'ai douce souvenance*
> *Du joli lieu de mon enfance!*
> *Ma soeur, qu'ils étaient beaux ces jours*
> *De France!*

Ô, mon pays sois mes amours
     Toujours.

(How sweet my memories
Of my childhood home!
Dear sister, how lovely were those days
          In France!
Oh, my country, I shall love you
          forever.)

The three of them fell into a silence befitting their thoughts, and only God knows how long they might have sat like that, silent, if François had not announced that dinner was being served, but not in the dining room, as it had been damaged during the fighting. Instead, they would be eating in Monsieur René's room.

The Sainte-Hermine sisters had never been to René's room, and they were astonished by the furnishings and decor. Himself an excellent artist, René had painted in watercolor many of his favorite country scenes and notable places. Between two of the paintings was a collection of valuable weapons, and opposite the weapons a display of musical instruments, which both of the girls, being gifted musicians, were eager to study. Among the instruments was a guitar, which Jane knew how to play. Hélène was an accomplished pianist, but since her father's death not even the thought of putting her fingers to the keys had occurred to her, although there was a piano in the girls' quarters.

So now there was another bond between the sisters and René: music. René too had a piano in his room, but rarely ever did he play those noisy pieces written by the grand masters of the day. He preferred sweet, plaintive melodies that complemented the feelings in his heart, pieces like Grétry's "Une fièvre brûlante" or Weber's "Dernière pensée." More often than not, though, the strains he played on the piano echoed the sad song of memory in his heart, a song that was his alone. Then his hands would discover such melodious chords that he was no longer simply playing music. He was speaking a language.

Often, during the night, the young women had heard haunting harmonies, but they had always assumed it was the wind whistling in the ropes and rigging. or maybe the work of nature on the elements that travelers in early days thought to be songs of the sea gods. Never would they have guessed that the cadences they heard, so vague and so sad, were coming from the fingers of a man and the cold keys of a piano.

After lunch, so as to escape the burning equatorial sun on deck, they all stayed in René's room, and on the piano the young man's fingers awakened a sad melody that Weber had just composed in Vienna. Like the melancholy poetry written by André Chénier and Millevoye, Weber's music was still new and just beginning to be known in the world, a world that in the tumultuous wake of revolutions had much to lament. As René surrendered to the poignancy in the music, the song grew more languorous beneath his fingers, and, reduced to simple chords, it was all the more sorrowful.

Even after he had finished Weber's melody, René's fingers continued instinctively to wander over the keys, and from the composer's memories he moved on to his own. In improvisation was where the young man's soul truly shone. Those who read music as if it were a painting or a book would see in these affecting measures not the sunlight on a lovely valley or fertile plains but the cloud that darkens them into a desolate world, a place where brooks moan instead of murmur or where flowers weep instead of spreading perfume. The girls found the music so moving and unusual that tears came unnoticed to their eyes.

When René's fingers stilled, Jane rose from her seat and knelt beside Hélène: "Ah, sister," she said, "is not such music as sweet and pious as a prayer?" Hélène answered with only a sigh and held Jane gently to her heart. It was clear that for the past few days the young women had been experiencing new depths of emotion for which they were not totally prepared.

Days passed, though the three young people hardly sensed their passing.

Then one morning the watch called out, "Land ho!" René surmised that they had reached Burma; further calculations proved he was right. In amazement, Kernoch watched him do his calculations, for René, who had never sailed before, was able to execute tasks that he himself had never been able to master. They took their bearings and headed directly for the mouth of the Pegu River. The coast was so low that it was barely distinguishable from the water.

The call "Land ho!" had brought the two girls up to the deck, where they found René, spyglass in hand. He handed it to them, but unaccustomed as they were to maritime horizons, at first they could see nothing but the endless sea. As they drew nearer the coast, however, they could distinguish what seemed to be islands, their mountain peaks visible, because of the pure air, at a greater distance than usual.

The sloop raised a new flag to the top of the mast and fired twelve cannon shots. Immediately from the coast a fort's cannons answered. Kernoch requested a pilot, and in a short while a small boat appeared at the mouth of Rangoon River and approached the *Racer*. The pilot climbed on board.

Asked what language he spoke, he replied that he was from neither Pegu nor Malacca, but rather, to escape from paying tribute to the King of Siam, he had fled from Junchseylon to Rangoon and become a pilot; he spoke a little English, he said. So René could address him directly as to whether the Pegu River was navigable for boats drawing approximately nine or ten feet of water. The pilot—his name was Baca—answered that they would be able to sail about twenty leagues up the river, up as far as a little settlement that belonged to a French nobleman. The post, he said, was made up of only a few huts, and the settlement was called Rangoon House. There was no doubt that it was the property of the Vicomte de Sainte-Hermine.

The little ship was clearly American, but the authorities examined it carefully nonetheless. Unlike the merchant ships that generally came to trade in the region, it underwent three inspections before it received authorization to continue upriver. It was late in the day when they arrived in Rangoon, and sailing up the Rangoon River, which connects with a branch of the Irrawaddy, they finally reached the Pegu. Arising on the south slopes of five or six hills, the Pegu River ends up in the Rangoon River after flowing for twenty-five or thirty leagues between the Irrawaddy and the Sittang. They stopped in Siram, the first town on the river, to buy fresh supplies. They found chickens, doves, fish, and game from the swamps and rivers. If the wind continued to blow from the south the little ship would be able to sail upriver and reach Pegu in two days. If the wind changed and blew from the opposite direction, however, it would be necessary to tow the ship all the way with the longboats, and the journey would take twice the time.

The Pegu River had been about a mile wide at the point where the sloop had entered it with sails unfurled. But soon it had begun to narrow, and now, squeezed in by jungle on both sides, it was no wider than the Seine as it passes between the Louvre and the Institute. They could sense that hidden away in those jungles, ten or twelve feet tall, about the height of the poop deck—the ship's mast rose about five or six meters above the tops of the trees—lurked all kinds of dangerous animals. From the deck, they could see wide expanses of marshland; on the right the marshes extended all the way to the uninhabited banks of the Sittang, and on the left all the way to a string of towns watered by the Irrawaddy.

René quickly realized that navigation on a river so swallowed up by jungle was not without risk. He made the decision to stand watch himself, and he had his rifle and his double-barreled shotgun brought up on deck. When evening came, the two young women came to sit beside him on the poop deck. Eager to find out how hunting calls would sound in such vast solitudes, he asked for his horn. From time to time loud noises rose from the jungle, and they imagined horrible battles being fought tooth-and-claw among its denizens. But who were its denizens? Tigers, probably, and caimans, and long boa constrictors able to smother an ox in their coils, then crush its bones and swallow it whole.

The silence was at once solemn and frightening, broken as it was from time to time by cries alarmingly unfamiliar to human ears, and the young women repeatedly stopped René's hand before he could raise the horn to his lips. When, finally, he did, the fanfare rang out, sonorous, vibrant, rousing. The blare reverberated out over the jungle, weakened, and then died out in the distance of a land still unnamed by God or man. And the silence that followed was overwhelming, as if the jungle and its every creature were holding their breaths in uncomprehending awe of a sound their ears had never heard before.

The fair wind held, and they kept moving with no need for towing. Then another sound shattered the silence: the sailor on watch called out, "Ship ahead!"

Everything seemed dangerous in that land. René first reassured his two companions, then picked up his gun and walked to the balcony of the poop deck to see for himself what the situation was. The sisters prepared to go down to their room at the first signal from René. The night was bright, for the moon was full, and in the moonlight they could all see an object that did indeed look like a boat.

It seemed to be maneuvering without a pilot, as if it had yielded entirely to the pull of the current. The closer it got, the more clearly René could see what appeared to be not a boat but an uprooted tree. Seeing nothing particularly dangerous in an uprooted tree, he called the two girls up to the balcony. The tree was only about twenty yards from the sloop when René saw something gleaming like two burning coals in its branches. Although he had never seen one in the flesh, he quickly realized that in the tree floating directly toward them crouched a panther. It had perhaps been trapped when a windstorm had uprooted the tree and dropped it into the river, where the panther was now caught in the current with no way to reach shore.

"If my little sister Hélène would like a lovely rug," René said, "all she has to do is say the word." He pointed to the animal.

The panther had taken notice of the travelers; its fur was beginning to bristle and its jaws were snapping together—it was clearly less threatened by them than they were by it. René put his gun to his shoulder.

"Oh, don't kill it! The poor creature!" Hélène cried, stopping him, for a woman's first reaction is always one of compassion.

"Indeed," René murmured, "it would be like murder."

The tree and the sloop bumped together. They could hear branches scraping along the hull, when suddenly the helmsman let out a horrible cry.

"Get down!" René shouted, with a voice demanding instant obedience. His gun barrel had been resting on his shoulder, but it quickly dropped into his left hand and he fired two shots in rapid succession.

Famished because it had been trapped on the tree for so long, the panther had leaped up on the rail, to the horror of the helmsman, who had turned to see the ferocious creature gathering itself to pounce on him. His cry had alerted René and earned two bullets for the panther.

With one leap, René was between the helmsman and the panther, his second gun at the ready. But the panther was already dead. One of the bullets had gone right through its heart.

LXVI

Pegu

AT THE SOUND OF THE SHOTS, the entire crew rushed up on deck. For they all thought they were being attacked again by Malays; the one good thing about fear lying in the past is that it can prepare you for the future.

Kernoch, who had gone below to get a little rest, was one of the first back on deck. When he saw the helmsman and the panther lying close by each other, he first thought them both to be dead. Still he went to the helmsman's aid, expecting his flesh to have been torn by the panther's claws in the struggle, but he did not have a single scratch.

The ship's butcher carefully skinned the panther. Its hide, as René had said, was to go to Hélène. But Jane begged her sister for it, and Hélène obliged.

The wind was still fair, and they continued heading slowly upriver.

The two girls, still a-tremble, in time retired to their room. They were beginning to feel less enthusiastic about the exotic country they would be living in. René stayed with them until three in the morning. Even so, hardly a moment passed that they did not imagine the fierce face of some wild, bloodthirsty animal at their window. They spent the night in the grip of terror, and when day finally came, they went to look for their young protector.

René was already on deck, and as soon as he saw them he called out, "Come quickly. I was just going to wake you so that you could see the beauty of these two pagodas at daybreak. The closer pagoda is called Dagung; you can identify it by its golden spire and parasol. We sailed right by it during the night."

The girls were impressed by the two monuments, especially by Dagung, because it is stood so high above the surrounding countryside. The pagoda had been built on a terrace made of rocks, and the terrace itself was quite high, the stone stairway up to it having more than a hundred steps. In the light of the rising sun, as René had said, the temple was indeed splendid, golden, aloft on its pedestal. Yet the forests that surrounded it had held all sorts of terrors during the night, and the jungles along the river were no more reassuring. Throughout the long night they had heard the cries of alligators; they sounded like children being massacred.

From time to time the forest was broken by huge rice paddies, which were worked by a special category of people called *Karens*. People of simple customs, with a language different from Burmese, they are hard workers, primarily farmers. In fact, they never live in cities, but in villages, and their houses are built on stilts. Just as they never fight among themselves, they also stay out of government quarrels.

The Pegu River was so full of fish that all the sailors had to do was drop a few lines and in minutes they'd have enough for the entire crew's dinner. Some of the crewmen decided they'd like to try panther meat. The cook did prepare some cutlets, but although the animal René had killed was only a year and a half or two years old, even the strongest teeth were unable to pull the meat from the bone.

Two days later, with no further incident except a fight between a caiman and an alligator, they reached the town of Pegu. Still bearing the scars of the revolutions it has suffered, most of the town's fortifications have been destroyed. What remains of them rises thirty feet above water level; the tide itself can rise ten feet. Ships drawing more than ten or twelve feet cannot go beyond Pegu, because at low tide they would touch bottom a league farther upriver.

The authorities decided that the sloop should remain in customs, where it would become the responsibility of the *chékey*, a lieutenant attached to the Ministry of War. The travelers were escorted to a building that looked like a palace; in fact it was called the palace for foreigners, the rare visitors to Pegu normally being housed there. René decided, however, that he would prefer to stay on board the sloop, which he could use as his base to make all the necessary arrangements for reaching the Vicomte de Sainte-Hermine's property in Betel Land, as the region was known.

The arrival of the sixteen-cannon American sloop aroused considerable interest in Pegu, for America had begun to develop a worthy reputation among traders in the Indian seas. So it was that the day after the *New York Racer* reached Pegu, the first person to pay a visit was the emperor's interpreter. He had been charged with presenting to the ship's owner a gift of fruit from the *shabunder,* whose job it was to supervise the port and collect customs duties. He also informed René that the next day the *nak-kan* and the *Serodogee* would be coming to offer their respects. Anticipating such visits, René had purchased cloth and weapons as gifts for such local dignitaries before he left Île de France, and he gave the *shabunder* a double-barreled gun, which elicited delight as well as gratitude. René also gave him a tour of the sloop, since the man's position, similar to that of the port commissioner in England, warranted him detailed knowledge of the ship.

Accompanied by two slaves carrying a silver spittoon, the commissioner chewed betel continually throughout his visit, but not without offering some to René. Like a true follower of Brahma, René chewed some of the savory leaf; but as soon as his guest was gone, like a man who wants to keep his teeth white, he quickly rinsed out his mouth with water and a little arrack.

The following day, René welcomed aboard the *nak-kan* and the *Serodogee.* In the Pegu kingdom, where there are no secrets, the title *nak-kan* means "the king's ear," not unbefitting an official whose role is similar to that of a police commissioner; the *Serodogee* is the king's secretary.

Both men were accompanied by spittoon-carriers, but, although they were constantly chewing betel and spitting, their conversation enabled René to gather more accurate information about the property his two lovely passengers had inherited. He learned that with betel alone, if they wished to continue growing it, they could earn at least fifty thousand francs a year by sending it all to India. In addition, they could earn approximately the same amount by growing rice and sugarcane. The settlement lay about fifty English miles from Pegu, but the journey there took you through forests filled with tigers and panthers. What's more, René learned, the bandits from Siam and Sumatra who infested the forests posed a greater danger than the wild beasts.

René's visitors were dressed similarly, one in violet and the other in blue, their long gowns being elaborately decorated with gold, especially on the sleeves. Both government officials sat on their haunches throughout the visit, with the king's secretary serving as the interpreter. René presented the secretary with a gold-embroidered Persian carpet, and to His Majesty's ear he gave a handsome pair of pistols made in Versailles.

Since our arrival in Pegu, we have mentioned betel so often that the reader might think it important for us to give some details about this plant which Indians love even more than Europeans do their tobacco.

The betel plant creeps and climbs like ivy. Its leaves resemble those of a lemon tree, only they are somewhat longer and more pointed. The fruit of the betel plant looks much like a plantain, and generally people prefer the fruit to the leaf. Usually it is grown like grapes, and like grapes it needs support. Sometimes cultivated along with the areca palm, the plants can be trained to grow into lovely bowers. Betel grows commonly throughout the East Indies, especially along the coasts.

Indians chew betel leaves at any time of the day, and even at night. Because the leaves are bitter if chewed alone, betel chewers typically wrap the leaves around areca nuts and a little chalk to sweeten them; the wealthy might also add some Borneo camphor, aloe wood, musk, or ambergris. Prepared this way, betel is so tasty and sweet-smelling that Indians appear to be unable to live without it. Anyone who can afford it uses it regularly. (Some Indians chew areca nuts with cinnamon and cloves, but that is considered inferior to areca and a little chalk wrapped in betel leaves.) Once they begin to chew, they also begin to spit; taking its color from the areca nut, the spittle is red. Because Indians use betel so habitually, their breath always smells sweet, and indeed the scent can perfume an entire room. But chewing ruins their teeth. They turn black as they begin to rot, and finally they fall out. Some Indians have chewed so much betel that they have lost all their teeth by the time they reach twenty-five.

If two Indians are parting for some time, it is customary for them to exchange betel in a silk purse. Among Indians one cannot imagine a proper good-bye without receiving betel from a person whom one sees frequently. Nor would one even think of speaking to a man of any social standing, or to one's own peer, without first perfuming one's breath with betel. Women too use betel; they call it the love plant. Betel is chewed at mealtime, it is chewed during visits with friends or associates, it is exchanged with greetings as it is with farewells, it is carried at all times. Betel plays an important role at all hours of the day and night, in the lives of the East Indies peoples.

Scarcely had the two betel chewers left the *Racer* than rumors were spreading about the rich American shipowner who showered local officials with gifts of pistols, carpets, and double-barreled guns. Soon, too, sounds of wild music were drawing near to the sloop. René immediately summoned the two young women. He had spared them the boring official speeches, but he wanted them to enjoy the music.

René and the two sisters climbed up to the poop deck, from which they could watch, and hear, the approach of three boats, each carrying an orchestra composed of two flutes, two cymbals, and a kind of drum. The musicians were seated in the bow of their boats on a little platform that had a cloth stretched out above it, so they were separated from the rowers, who were sitting two by two on benches behind them. A flag was flying from a mast in the stern, which was decorated with a row of cow tails, the cow tails being religious talismans from Tibet. The flutes sounded very much like oboes, and the music was simple but not unpleasant. René asked the musicians to repeat two or three pieces so he could copy down the principal melodies. Each boat he rewarded with twelve *talks* (one *talk* is worth three francs and fifty centimes).

From the day of their arrival in Pegu, René had been trying to work out how they might best reach the property owned by the Vicomte de Sainte-Hermine. The only alternatives seemed to be by horse or by elephant. In addition, according to the port commissioner, they would need an escort of at least ten men.

However eager René may have been to continue their journey to Betel Land, it was clear that they would have to wait, because Pegu was preparing for a large religious festival, and nobody would be willing to leave town before fulfilling his religious duties. Once the festival was over, the *shabunder* promised that he would arrange for René to rent either horses or elephants and that the expedition would be fully equipped for tiger hunting. René would be able to keep the animals for a month, or even two or three, as he wished. For the horses and the guide, the price would be twenty *talks;* for the elephants and their mahouts, thirty.

After René had promised the *shabunder* that he would not rent horses or elephants except through him, the *shabunder* offered René a window in a house that stsood along the stairs up to the grand pagoda so that he might more closely view the religious procession. René accepted, and he was quite surprised to find, when he arrived there with the two girls, that the *shabunder* had provided carpets and chairs.

Throngs of men and women attended the ceremony. Between sunrise and ten in the morning more than thirty thousand people appeared, each carrying an offering according to his means and zeal. Some were dragging along a tree, its branches bent down by the weight of gifts—betel, jams, and pastries—for the priests; others led crocodiles or cardboard giants holding up pyramids laden with all sorts of gifts or, bringing up the rear, cardboard elephants decorated with wallpaper and wax. Many bore fireworks. All were dressed in their finest, their clothes usually made of local silk every bit as good as our own, and perhaps even better.

The Burmese women dressed as freely as Europeans, which is to say they were not veiled. Sad to say, they owe that privilege not to liberality, but to oppressive indifference. Men consider them to be inferior beings, placed by Nature somewhere between the men themselves and the animals. In a court of law, depositions by women rank as nothing more than information, and they are not even taken inside the courtroom. In marriage, Burmese women may be sold by their husbands to strangers. In such cases, women are not deemed to have been dishonored; they are simply obeying their husbands. Obedience thus becomes a reason to enslave women in this fashion. A second reason to the same effect is the necessity to help their families.

There are courtesans in Rangoon and in Pegu, and we have no hesitation in raising this matter in order to criticize the law that keeps so many women in houses of prostitution. It is not out of laziness or corruption that Burmese girls turn to this loathsome profession. Among the Burmese, debtor's laws are similar to what they were in the Rome of the Twelve Tables. A creditor becomes the master of his debtor and of the debtor's family so long as he fails to pay his debts. He and his family can be sold as slaves; and since the proprietors of brothels pay the highest prices, if the debtor's wife and daughters are attractive, that is where the creditor will sell the poor creatures. They could be called the daughters of bankruptcy.

In former times there existed a class of prostitutes who were called wives of the idols. If a woman had made a vow to have a son, and instead of a son had a daughter, she would take the girl to the idol and leave her there. To defray the girl's expenses to the idol, she would become the idol's wife and be sold by him for the benefit of passing strangers. The locals referred to such girls as *valasi* (the idol's slave); foreigners called them bayadères, a word that means both dancer and courtesan.

LXVII

The Trip

THE DAY AFTER the pagoda celebrations ended, the *shabunder,* good to his promise and at René's request, had three elephants and their mahouts waiting on the quay beside the sloop. Unable to trust his Anglo-American crew sufficiently to leave the ship under their control, he decided to put Kernoch and his six Bretons in charge; he knew they would keep their guard up because of the visceral hate between the two peoples, and loyal Bretons could always be counted on in the event of a struggle. So the only crewman who would accompany the party out of Pegu was the Parisian, his faithful François.

Two elephants with their palanquins, large enough for four people, proved to be sufficient for him and for the two young women. For added protection, as the *shabunder* had advised, René hired ten guards, with each man and his horse costing him five *talks* a day for as many days as he wanted. He also required two additional horses, for himself and François, as at times they would no doubt prefer to be on horseback rather than in the palanquin. Since they could not be sure of finding any villages on the way, two pack horses were loaded with food, which they expected to be able to supplement with fresh game. The guide said the trip would take three days.

Without qualms Kernoch, assured that he could count on the Burmese authorities should he experience any problems with the crew, stayed behind in Pegu while René's little caravan started off toward the east. That evening they camped beside the freshwater stream they had been following and that had brought them near the edge of the forest through which they'd be traveling the next day. They drew extra water in case they'd not come across more during their journey.

The palanquins, removed from the elephants' backs and placed on the ground, became tents when canopied over by mosquito nets. There the young women could sleep protected. A large fire was lit to keep snakes and wild animals away. The guide claimed that the elephants would do the work of sentinels, that they would instinctively raise an alarm at the approach of any danger. René, however, was not entirely convinced, for he had not yet seen proof of elephants' sense and intelligence, so he decided to stand watch himself. He took the first half of the night and entrusted the second half to François.

Before that, however, he made friends with the two giant pachyderms. He brought them armfuls of fresh branches and an apple-like fruit they were especially fond of. These intelligent animals can quickly distinguish between those who bring them food because it is their duty, as in the case of the mahouts, and those who, like true friends, offer them what might seem superfluous but is in fact extraordinarily important because it goes beyond what is simply necessary. At first the elephants looked at René distrustfully, as if they did not understand why a stranger would be paying such attention to them, but they did enjoy what he offered. He was careful, too, not to create jealousy; he made certain he gave the second elephant as much as the first. Then he had the two girls give the elephants two or three sweet, freshly cut stalks of sugarcane. Carefully the elephants took the cane from the girls' hands and lifted it to their mouths in obvious delight. Before leaving Pegu, René had packed a small stock of cane for just this purpose, to ensure that the elephants would consider the two girls and him to be friends.

The night was uneventful, although several panthers did come to drink from the stream and a few caimans ventured out of the jungle to see what they might find. The elephant on duty—elephants know as well as men when one watchman is enough—called attention to them. At midnight the first elephant knelt down and went to sleep, while its comrade arose to take over the watch. If the elephants, like René and François, had divided the night up into shifts, they actually trusted each other more than did René François.

At daybreak the two elephants, sounding a kind of fanfare, invited everyone to get up. The girls had slept well, safe in the knowledge that René was watching over them. They breathed in the scented morning air.

René came over to them with an armful of leaves for the elephants. Hélène and Jane had been a little fearful of getting too close to the mammoth creatures, but the affectionate look in the elephants' eyes allayed their misgivings at least a bit. Taking the leaves from René, they held them out to the elephants, who seemed virtually to coo with satisfaction as they began eating them. When they had finished, the elephants demonstrated their thanks to René as well, for they had seen that the treat had come at his initiative and that he did out of kindness what the girls did out of fear. Still, the elephants felt that something was missing. And they looked around for it: their sugarcane. René gave some to the girls, who fed it to the elephants, and they crunched away at it with joy.

Everyone had only a light breakfast, for they were planning to stop twice that day: first, at about eleven, near a lake where they would wait out the hottest hours of the day; then, in a clearing suitable for a camp, about seven o'clock, for the night.

The two girls climbed back up on their elephant, who seemed pleased by such honor as they bestowed on him. René and François got on their horses. François led, with René just behind him, along with the girls. The guide rode in front, and the ten guards, also on horseback, formed a column on either side of the party. The second elephant, carrying only his mahout, walked behind the first. The forest was so dark and menacing that, although René was not concerned for himself, he could not help feeling somewhat afraid for his two friends. He called for the guide, who spoke a little English.

"Is this the part of the forest," he asked, "where we might expect to be attacked by brigands?"

"No," the guide answered. "The brigands are in the other forest."

"What are the dangers we run here?"

"Wild animals."

"What kinds of wild animals?"

"Tigers, panthers, and enormous snakes."

"Fine," said René. "Let's keep moving." Then, turning to François, he said, "Go to the canteen and bring me two big pieces of bread."

François brought back both halves of a loaf of bread, and as soon as the elephants saw it, they assumed it was meant for them. The second elephant moved up closer to René, who found himself nearly wedged between the two giants. Leaning out of their palanquin, the girls watched in terror. Another step, they thought, and René and his horse would be crushed between the two elephants.

Smiling reassuringly, René held up the two pieces of bread for the elephants to see. Their trunks, rather than threatening him, sought to gently enfold the young man. Like a coquette playing hard-to-get so as to increase the value of the favor she will be granting, René made the elephants wait eagerly a few moments before suddenly giving them each a piece of the bread for which they were now longing. Thus was another stone added to the temple of friendship that René was constructing of him with the two monstrous quadrupeds.

"What did our guide tell you a moment ago?" asked Hélène.

"To anyone but you, I would say that he told me the forest was full of game, and that we had no need to worry about what we would eat between here and Betel Land. But you are a trusted companion, and I must answer that he told me to sleep with one eye open unless there are good eyes watching over us as we sleep. You may sleep well, knowing that I shall be watching over you."

From the moment they had gone into the forest, it was as if they had entered a church. The travelers' voices had dropped lower and lower, until they were speaking barely above a whisper, as if they were afraid someone would hear them. It was so dark that it could have been six in the evening, the green canopy above them so thick that they could hear no birdsong, as if it were indeed night; yet neither could they hear a single strange note of the concerts generally played by nocturnal animals as they hunt, mate, eat, and drink in the night's dark forest.

The travelers were awed by nature's power. For even in the darkest depths of this forest, where no daylight seemed ever to penetrate, brilliant flowers sometimes bloomed, their perfumes filling the air. Other plants, wanting sunshine to unveil their vibrant colors, reached up toward the source of light, wrapping themselves around the first branches, slipping between others, until finally reaching the peaks of the trees, where they'd unfold in the greenery like rubies and sapphires set in emerald. At first you might think they had flowered from the gigantic trees because the blooms are so huge, so sturdy; but if you look for their stems, you will find them to be a vine as thin as a kite string. In forests like these, mystery is everywhere.

The forest's mystery can prompt thoughts as dark as death, and thoughts of death. For death surrounds you on every side. Behind that bush, a tiger lurks. On that branch, a panther watches. That slightly undulant stalk that stands maybe six or eight feet high ends at a serpent's head; the rest of its body is lying in coils, but in a trice it could strike and reach you from fifteen or twenty feet away. The lake, its surface as smooth as a mirror, hides caimans, crocodiles, and alligators—perhaps a gigantic *kraken;* never has anyone been able to pull it from the mud, but its huge mouth can open up and swallow both horse and rider at once. With its deep forests and fabulous beasts, India may be the most fertile and the most lethal quarter in the universe.

Such were René's thoughts as he rode beneath the dark canopy of silent trees, through which the sun struggled almost in vain to cast its fiery arrows. Suddenly, as if a curtain had been raised, they passed from the darkest dusk into the brightest light. They found themselves across from a lake, and to reach it they had only to cross a meadow that spread before them, its grasses swaying, every blade beckoning, as it might in a dream. It looked like a bit of paradise lost. Banks of flowers as yet unnamed in any botanist's book spread such sweet perfumes, you'd think you might die from their sweetness. Their feathers ruby, emerald, and sapphire, fabulous birds crisscrossed the sky with strange and startling cries. And off in the distance lay the lake, like an azure carpet.

They exclaimed delight, so great was the contrast between the dismal forest and this open field, the shining lake. They gratefully breathed in the fresh air.

The procession started out across the meadow. The grasses rustling just ahead of them indicated several reptiles were nearby. The guide remained alert, and once, with a swing of his stick, he killed a snake marked by black and yellow diamonds. In Burmese they call it the checkerboard snake. Though barely a foot long, its bite is deadly, and, the guide explained, depending on when you are bitten, you die either as the sun sets or as it rises.

Intact, unbitten, they reached the lake. It was here they had planned to stop for lunch, so in the meadow René had killed several fowl that resembled partridges as well as a small gazelle, no bigger than a hare. François, a good Parisian, had learned how to cook during street demonstrations and he prepared the game quite nicely.

René took his usual good care of the elephants. When he noticed them extending their trunks toward a tree's flower-laden branches just out of their reach, he asked François if his Paris upbringing had also taught him how to climb trees. François answered yes, and armed with a little sickle he cut off some of the branches with the large white and red flowers somewhat like fuchsia. The elephants watched, their anticipation keen, while with their trunks they caressed René's hands. Then they enjoyed their lunch.

So did the travelers, and afterward they made themselves comfortable for their siesta. They had bidden farewell to their fears. The weather was lovely, the countryside was beautiful. It was almost impossible to think that danger might threaten them.

LXVIII

The Emperor Snake

FRANÇOIS HAD BEEN EXPLORING the jungle, where he had flushed two or three peacocks. Thus he had gotten the idea of shooting two peacocks and using their beautiful tail feathers to make fans for the two sisters. So, after their meal was over, he asked René's permission to pursue his idea; but when René mentioned that where there were peacocks there were also tigers, the carefree Parisian street boy quickly decided he would rather hunt the latter. Taking his cutlass and one of René's double-barreled guns, he set out, though he had not gone ten steps before René had second thoughts about allowing such an amateur hunter going off alone to bag a tiger. He called out to François to wait for him.

Everything was quiet, and the two girls should be safe from danger, but still, before leaving, René wanted to take some precautions. He gave each of the elephants a chunk of bread, then led them to opposite sides of a tree whose immense, leafy branches began twenty feet above his head. Pointing to the two young women, he said to the two giants as if they could understand him, "Watch over them."

The girls laughed at Reneé's concerns. That did not prevent him from giving them all sorts of advice, however. Most importantly, he told them, if some animal were to put them in danger, they should take shelter between the elephants' legs, for they would be as safe there as in an unassailable fortress.

His desire keen not to kill peacocks but to stand face to face with a tiger, René said good-bye to the girls and quickly caught up with François. They disappeared into the underbrush.

The underbrush soon turned into dense jungle. The growth got so thick that they would have to hack their way through it, and to that end François pulled out his cutlass. At the same time, René spotted a path. An animal had recently passed there, and the fresh bones told René that it was a large carnivore. As he started down the path, he called out to François, who followed him.

By several twists and turns, the path led them to the animal's lair. It was a tiger's den. Neither one of the jungle's royal couple was there, but two little tigers, about the size of large house cats, were playing and growling at each other in the lair. At the sight ot two such strange creatures, the cubs, though not yet very strong, prepared to defend themselves. Quickly René reached out, grabbed one by the scruff of the neck, and tossed it to François, saying, "Take it away! Take it away!" He himself picked up the other cub, then hastened to make his way out of the leafy tunnel, where it would have been impossible to defend himself.

The tiger cubs were meanwhile squealing and yelping as if to call their mother to their aid. She replied. From a distance of about four or five hundred yards her terrible roar brought René and the Parisian to a halt, for less than half a second.

"We must get out of the jungle! Out of the jungle!" René shouted. "Or we are done for!" François did not need to be told twice. Stepping up his pace, he got clear of the jungle in record time and ran into the scrub brush with the little tiger, which he hoped to deliver to the Jardin des Plantes in France, still in his grasp.

He and René heard a second roar, this time from not more than a hundred yards away. Twenty yards to the front of them stood a tree and a bush. "Let the cub go," René shouted, turning his own loose. "You take the tree; I'll take the bush."

They had just reached their shelters when a third roar rolled over their heads like thunder. The next moment the tigress with a flying leap landed in the scrub, not twenty paces away. For a heartbeat she seemed to hesitate between maternal love and vengeance. Maternal love won out. Meowing like a cat, though her meowing was terrifying, she crawled toward her kittens.

François had her in profile in his sight. He raised his gun and fired. Taken by surprise, the tigress twisted in the air and fell back to the ground. The shot had smashed her left shoulder.

The tigress easily determined where her enemy stood, as smoke from the gunshot still enveloped François in smoke. She leaped, and despite her wound she bounded toward him. She was quickly narrowing the distance between them when François fired his second shot.

The tigress took the shock, then fell. With a direful roar she struggled to get back on her feet. But she couldn't advance: with her good front leg she began pawing at the ground and with blood streaming from her mouth she was chewing at the grass.

"I got her! I got her, Monsieur René," François shouted, like a child who has just killed his first rabbit, as he started down the tree in anticipation of clubbing the tigress to death.

"Stay away, man!" René screamed. "And reload your gun."

"Why, Monsieur René? She's dead, isn't she?"

"And how about the male, you idiot? There, just listen." A terrifying, blood-chilling roar alarmed their human ears.

"Reload your gun; reload your gun, and get behind me," said René. François, however, was trembling so much, no less from excitement than from fear, that he was spilling more powder on the ground than he was putting in his gun barrel. René handed him his gun and took François's, which he loaded for him; then they exchanged weapons again.

"He is no longer roaring," François whispered.

"And he will not roar again," said René. "Since his mate does not answer, he realizes that she is either dead or caught in some trap. So instead of showing himself as she did, he will first study the situation. Stay alert and keep your eyes open."

"Shhh!" François whispered in René's ear. "I heard some branches snapping."

Within an instant, René had touched his companion's shoulder. He pointed at the tiger's huge head visible at the end of the jungle path, down low to the ground; it had first run to its den and, finding it empty, was now creeping silently through the underbrush. François nodded that he saw it.

"In Phillip's right eye," René said aloud. And he pulled the trigger.

For a few seconds, there was too much smoke for them to see what had happened. Then: "Since I am alive," René said calmly, "the tiger must be dead." And indeed, as they soon saw, the tiger was writhing in agony, near death.

"What did you mean when you said: 'In Phillip's right eye?' Is the tiger called Phillip?"

"No," René replied. "We call Phillip a tiger, because we cannot trust him."

Both tigers were too severely wounded to be feared, so the two hunters could simply wait and let death do its work. Although the tiger had been shot only once, it was the first to die, for, as the excellent marksman had announced it would, the shot went through the animal's right eye and directly into the brain, so that it was killed almost immediately. It took another quarter of an hour for the twice-shot tigress to breathe her last.

René and François had hoped that their three shots might have prompted some of their men to come find out what had happened to them. They'd hoped in vain. So, pleased with their kill, they decided to return to the lakeside and come back for the tigers with a horse. François, however, had no intention of leaving behind his prize catch. He slung his loaded gun over his shoulder and picked up the two tiger cubs by the scruff of the neck.

Once René had reloaded his own gun, they started back toward the lake, about a kilometer away.

They had not taken a hundred steps when a deafening cry, loud as ten trumpets, echoed through the forest. A second cry followed. Puzzled, René and François looked at each other. It was a cry that did not recognize; what could it be?

Suddenly René understood. "Ah!" he cried. "The elephants are calling for help!"

René was running so fast that soon François could not keep up with him. His sense of direction keen and correct, René reached the shore just twenty yards away from where he had left the two young women. He froze at the sight before him.

All the guards had scattered. They were hovering in the distance while the two sisters, still seated at the base of the tree, and apparently paralyzed by terror, were holding on to each other for life itself. The two elephants had remained at their posts, and with their trunks raised they were holding an enormous serpent at bay. Wound around one of the tree's lowest branches, the snake had fixed its eyes on Hélène and Jane as prey; its scaly head swung just fifteen feet above them. The girls seemed to be hypnotized by its stare.

The men in the escort had fled because, armed as they were with only cutlasses and pikes, they had no means of fighting this formidable opponent. The elephants, though, were as determined to protect their precious charge as they were prepared to fight. When they spotted René, they broke into joyous trumpeting.

With one glance, René knew what he needed to do. He threw down his gun, and rushing over to the two girls, he picked them up as easily as if they had been children and carried them over to François, who had just arrived at the lake. "There," he said with a sigh of relief.

Then, picking up his gun, he announced: "And now, Master Python, it's just you and me! We shall see if bullets made by Lepage are as effective as Apollo's arrows."

The serpent's hissing sounded like the wind in a storm at sea. A foul-smelling slobber dripped from its mouth, and its bloodshot eyes glared like lightning bolts when it pulled back its huge head. The python's neck, though its thinnest measure, was as big as a barrel. Its coils were hidden among the branches and leaves of the massive tree.

René steadied himself. This was the kind of opponent you dare not miss with your first shot. He aimed into the serpent's open jaws and squeezed both triggers. The tree shook with the monster's thrashing. Snapping branches as it went, it was pulling itself back up into the tree. It was soon lost in the foliage, but the tree kept shaking as if it were victim to a tempest.

François hurried over to René with a loaded gun. "Get as far away as you can with the girls," René told him, "and leave me your cutlass."

The elephants still had their trunks raised in the air, and their small eyes still seemed to be able to see the serpent. They had also started stomping their feet, in an effort, perhaps, to provoke the snake.

Finally it reappeared. Its hideous head, now a bloodied mass, was sliding down the trunk toward the ground. Two more shots rang out. They reached their mark.

Perhaps the python had lost its strength or maybe it was blinded by its four wounds, but it appeared to have lost all control of its sinuous movements and it fell like a dead weight at the base of the tree. Had Rangoon's pagoda collapsed onto its granite base it would not have shaken the earth more or with mightier noise than did the falling python.

The snake seemed to be unconscious as well as uncoiled. Then, suddenly, as if a mechanical spring had been released, it started slithering off. Not yet powerless, but blind, it passed within the reach of one of the elephants, and the pachyderm stepped with all its weight on the snake's bloody head. The press of three or four thousand pounds applied by all the elephant's strength was crushing the serpent's prodigious effort to free itself, but nonetheless it managed to begin wrapping its long body around the elephant. Seeing the danger its comrade was in, the second elephant rushed to help and knotted its trunk around the serpent's body. Soon it too was wrapped in the python's coils, and the three creatures in their formless mass for a moment looked like a gigantic parody of the statue of Laocoön and his sons.

The elephants trumpeted with pain. René, a mere pygmy next to these three antediluvian mammoths, had only a man's advantage: his reason. He could think, so he could be the victor.

With François's cutlass in hand, he found his moment when, thanks to a supreme effort by the elephants, a length of the python's body was not wrapped tight against their bodies. René lifted the newly sharpened blade, and with one blow, like a giant out of Homer or a hero from *Jerusalem Delivered*, he cut the snake in two. Even with its backbone severed, the serpent continued to writhe, until finally it weakened and fell from the elephant onto the ground.

Half suffocated, one of the elephants dropped to its knees. The other remained on its feet, but it was tottering and panting loudly and painfully. René ran to the lake and filled his hat with water, which he then poured little by little into the mouth of the elephant still standing. The elephant on its knees needed some time to clear its lungs. He had called the two mahouts

to attend to them while he hurried back to the young women he had left in
François's care.

They were deathly pale. He hugged them as he would two sisters, but as
he embraced Jane, her lips brushed against his. He quickly pulled away.
Jane could not stifle her sad sigh.

LXIX
Brigands

THEY ALL NEEDED a few moments to recover from the excitement. René
led the two girls to a little grassy mound where they sat down together.
Prudent and protective, he kept the reloaded gun beside him. Gentle and
caring, he took a gold-inlaid crystal bottle from his pocket and administered smelling salts to his young friends.

Once they had fully regained their senses, Hélène responded to René's
questions about what had happened and why they had let the serpent get so
near without even trying to flee. She said that as they were certain they had
nothing to fear with two giants watching over them, once lunch was over
they had allowed themselves to fall asleep. After some while, from deep
within her sleep, Hélène sensed that something was not right. First it was a
strange, sickening odor, then it was the cries of terror she thought she
heard. But only when the elephants began stomping on the ground did she
have the strength to open her eyes. And she saw the monster's hideous head
hanging twenty feet above her, its jaws spread wide, its eyes staring right at
her. The horrible smell was the snake's fetid breath.

She had awakened her sister, who had tried to get up and run, but she
had not even been able to stand up. In terror Hélène remembered reading
in Levaillant's travelogue about the power serpents have to mesmerize
their prey; about how, without even moving, they can draw birds out of
trees and attract animals they want to eat. Levaillant himself had nearly
been the victim of a serpent's gaze, and only by firing a shot had he been
able to break the spell. Hélène had sought to do the same by crying out for
help, but like in a nightmare, her voice failed her. With René nowhere in
sight, she'd thought she and her sister were doomed.

Then everything had gotten confused in her mind. The next thing she
remembered was being snatched up by someone, or something, and being
carried off. Then she saw she was in René's arms. Away from the serpent

and the hypnotic power of its gaze, she had recovered most of her faculties, but so great had been her terror that she had closed her eyes and seen nothing of René's battle with the python.

Now that she and her sister were again safe and sound, again in the debt and embrace of the man who had vowed to protect them, Hélène had no words to describe the profound gratitude she was truly feeling.

Jane had listened without saying a single word. Her body was trembling, and occasionally her hand would squeeze René's while the tears slipping out from under her eyelids coursed down her cheeks.

But François, too, had a tale to tell: of his two little tiger cubs, of how with two shots he had killed the tigress and the tiger Monsieur René had downed with just one shot. Thus he brought René's attention back to the tigers and the two magnificent pelts they didn't want to lose. René offered ten *talks* to any of the men who would agree to retrieve them, either by horseback or on stretchers made with their lances. The escort soldiers preferred to use stretchers, and since they all wanted to go, René doubled the amount so that everyone could share in the bonus, whether they were needed or not.

The elephants also did some retrieving. With their trunks they picked up François's cutlass and gun, which were still lying on the recent battlefield, and brought them to René, who had saved their lives with them. The elephants laid the weapons down at René's feet. They perhaps understood their debt to René; they caressed him delicately with the tips of their trunks.

With their weapons at hand, René and François led their men to the site of the pelts, where René was pressed to tell the story of the battle he and François had fought against the jungle's royalty. He did so more simply and with more modesty than a hunter from Saint-Denis would relate how he shot a rabbit in the Vésinet forest.

They carried the tigers back to the camp in triumph. The men who had stayed behind had meanwhile measured the serpent's body: it was forty-six feet long and more than three feet in circumference. It represented an event so violent, one could imagine only that the eyes of God, in some outland far from civilization, had ever witnessed its equal.

It was time again to get under way. The girls climbed back into their palanquin. René and François mounted their elephant as well—to the animal's honor, it appeared—while the guides led the two horses by their bridles. They had traveled for two or three hours when they found themselves again in a forest as dense as the one they had left that morning. Again they shuddered a bit at the thought of the terrors lurking in the shadows, except that now the travelers knew the dangers were not just imagined but real.

They quickly began setting up a camp for the night. They cut down small trees to make posts about six feet high, which they drove into the ground to form an enclosure about fifteen feet in diameter. They lay the palanquins on the ground, as that is where the girls preferred to sleep. For supper they prepared two gazelles René had shot on the way. He had also collected their blood for the cubs to drink instead of tiger's milk; the cubs did not object. Finally, to keep wild animals away, outside the fence they lit fires that could be fed from inside; a fence only six or seven feet high provided only limited protection against tigers and panthers, but fire, as we know, would keep wild animals away.

Compared to the day before, night was calm. Through the cracks in the palisade they could see eyes glowing like burning coals, and their hearts would begin to pound when not far off some wild animal would roar. Yet all that was trivial compared to what they had experienced during the day, and the sentinels did not fire even once. François and René stayed on watch in turn; so did the two elephants.

At six the next morning they broke camp. It was the day they planned to reach the girls' home. Their journey would continue through a part of the forest where the dangers posed by its beasts were fewer than those presented by brigands. The brigands' lair was located in the same cluster of mountains in which lay the Pegu River's source, and, when pursued, they took refuge in the village of Tungu. The girls' home was also situated in those mountains, on the banks of the Sittang River, which afforded the settlement its value, as produce could be sent downriver all the way to the sea.

They set out with not only René and François riding on their elephant but also a small arsenal. The possibility that they might encounter brigands from whom they'd have to protect the two young women had prompted René to devise a battle plan. It involved the elephants, and René was certain that his allies would not abandon or disappoint him.

At eleven they found a suitable place to make a halt. In fact, they were in the ruins of an old village that had been sacked by the very brigands now roaming and pillaging the countryside in groups of twelve or fifteen. They had made the area their territory. So, like an army general, René had given orders to everyone in his party about what to do in the event of an attack. But an unexpected incident disrupted his well-laid plans.

They were seated at lunch when they heard gunfire scarcely a half kilometer away. The shots seemed to be coming from the banks of the Sittang, where, it appeared, another party of travelers was being attacked. With dispatch, René had six men climb onto the elephant, while he himself leaped on one horse and ordered François to mount the other one, and they hurried off in the direction of the shots. On reaching the river, they saw one boat being attacked by another three.

The boat under attack carried two English officers, easily identifiable by their red coats and golden epaulettes, along with an escort of ten or twelve men; but like René's men, they were armed only with pikes. The bandits, on the contrary, had several guns, of poor quality though they were, and each of the three boats held about ten men. Two of the boats were edging close to the Englishmen's boat to enable the bandits to board it; from the third boat two dead men were thrown into the river. Clear as it was that the Englishmen's weapons were superior to those of the bandits, it was even clearer that without help, the two officers and their escort would be overwhelmed by the bandits' superior numbers.

"Hang on, Captain!" René called out in excellent English. "Try to move over this way. Anyone who aims a gun at you is a dead man." In proof, two gunshots rang out and two bandits fell. René and François exchanged guns, and with two more shots two more bandits dropped.

"Reload them," René told François as he pulled his pistol from his belt, for a bandit was preparing to leap from his boat onto the other. There was a pistol shot; he fell into the river.

Emboldened by such effective aid, the two Englishmen also began to shoot, and three more bandits fell.

Meanwhile, the elephant, comprehending the threat, had lumbered into the river, in spite of the mahout and the six men on its back, and had overturned one of the boats. As the bandits from the sunken boat resurfaced, the elephant stunned them with its swinging trunk while the men on its back stabbed them with their pikes.

The reinforcements had helped the English officers regain the courage they had nearly lost. Since they were shooting almost point-blank, every shot they fired was another man killed. In less than ten minutes, either shot by René and François as well as the Englishmen or clubbed by the elephant or stabbed by the pikemen, the brigands had lost half their numbers. At their chief's order they beat a hasty retreat.

It was the last order their chief gave, for in the next instant he himself fell dead. His command had told René who the leader was, and René's pistol had made him pay.

From then on it was a rout. Three or four more shots followed the fleeing brigands and added three or four more victims among their ranks.

The Englishmen's boat drew up to the bank, and René greeted the officer as he stepped out: "Sir, I am sorry not to have someone to introduce me, so I am forced to introduce myself."

"You introduce yourself in such a way, sir, that you need no one to vouch for you," the Englishman said, shaking his head. "Now, may I ask where we are? How far are we from Rangoon House? For that is where we are headed."

"About two or three leagues from the Vicomte de Sainte-Hermine's land, and about a quarter of a league from our convoy, which I left when I heard the first shots. If you would like to join us and finish your trip by land, we too are going to the Vicomte's settlement, and I can offer you either a horse or an elephant."

"I shall take the horse," said the English officer. "That is more appropriate. I must add that I am delighted to meet a fellow Englishman five thousand leagues from home. Especially one who is so courageous and who can shoot so well."

René smiled at the man's mistake. He handed him his own horse and called out to François. "François, take care of my weapons and follow with the elephant."

With that, he leaped on the second horse, and gesturing in the direction they would be taking, he galloped off. In less than five minutes they were back in camp and found the convoy safe where they had left it.

Except that Jane had been so worried, she had not been able to stay in the palanquin. She had climbed down with her sister, and when the two girls had heard hoofbeats, they had started toward the horsemen.

Both men dismounted with the elegance of perfect squires, and René, taking the English officer's hand and greeting the Sainte-Hermine sisters, said, "Miss Hélène, I have the honor of introducing Sir James Asplay." Then, turning to the Englishman, he said, "Sir James Asplay, I have the honor of introducing Miss Hélène de Sainte-Hermine and her sister Miss Jane."

Leaving them dumbfounded, René stepped back so as not to interfere with the first moments of their reunion.

Jane left René with a searching look that seemed to mix an apprehension or fear with tender love before she turned and followed her sister. While Jane still had the prowess to choose her words, she was no longer able to command either her heart or her eyes.

René was cleaning his guns with a cambric handkerchief when Sir James came up to him and said, "Sir, I did not yet know in how many ways I am obliged to you. Miss Hélène has just been telling me about them, and she tells me, too, that she does not wish to be deprived of your company much longer." René respected the wish and joined the girls.

Two hours later, when night was falling, a whole pack of dogs began to bark as the caravan entered the domain belonging to the Vicomte de Sainte-Hermine. They arrived without the Vicomte's remains. Realizing how painful it would be for the two girls to travel with their father's coffin during the course of the three-day trip, he had arranged for it to be transported separately by another escort. The dead would arrive in Betel Land three days after the living.

LXX
The Steward's Family

FOR ABOUT AN HOUR AND HALF, the path that the convoy had been following had become increasingly more passable, and René and his escort realized they were nearing a well-populated settlement. The path had brought them to a portcullis, at the base of which was a drawbridge. Through the portcullis bars they could see the outlines of several huts on both sides of an avenue that led up to a large building, apparently the manor house of the small village. A great uproar had arisen among the village's canine population when René had sounded on his hunting horn the customary return from a fox hunt.

Sir James had not heard a flourish played so well since he had left England, but the dogs had not heard a fanfare ever before. The villagers—except for the patriarch, who did recognize the instrument that had troubled the night's tranquility—were more accustomed to hearing the roars of wild animals, and at the sound of the horn they all rushed out from their huts into the avenue, as did the dogs from their kennels.

At the manor, the household awakened with a start. Doors opened, windows squeaked on their hinges, and a dozen servants of all colors—Negroes, Hindus, and Chinese—appeared, each of them carrying a resin torch. An old man moved forward from the house alone. A torch illuminated the face of a man sixty-eight or seventy years old. He wore his white hair long and had a full white beard; apparently neither scissors nor razor had touched them since he had come to India. His large black eyes sparkled from beneath thick silvery eyebrows. He held himself erect; his step was firm. He stopped ten paces from the gate.

"Greetings," he said, "to any strangers who request hospitality. But we are not in France, and the strangers will surely allow me, before I open the gates of a house that is not my own, to ask them who they are."

"My father should have been the one to answer," Hélène replied, "but death has sealed his lips, and he is unable to say what I shall say in his name. Blessings unto you, Guillaume Remi, unto you and your family."

"Heavens!" the man cried. "Can it be, instead of my dear master, my young mistresses? I have long been awaiting this moment, though I thought I'd not see them before I died!"

"Yes, Remi, it's us," the two girls said together. Hélène continued: "Please open up quickly, my good Remi, for we are exhausted by our three-day journey. And we bring you guests who would be even more fatigued than we, had not their courage and devotion given them strength."

The old man ran to the door, shouting, "Jules! Bernard! Come quick! Open the gates for the honorable lords who have come to see us."

Two strong young fellows about twenty-two or twenty-four years old hurried to the gate, while the old man continued to shout orders: "Adda, tell Friday to light the ovens, and tell Domingo to kill some of our plumpest fowl. What is there to eat, Bernard? What do we have in the storeroom, Jules?"

"Relax, Father," the two young men replied. "We have enough food for a regiment, and I see no more than a company."

René and Sir James had dismounted and were helping Hélène and Jane climb down from their elephants. "Jesus!" Remi cried when he saw the young women, "how lovely! And what are your earthly names, my dear angels from God's heaven?"

Jane and Hélène each gave her name. "Mademoiselle Hélène," said the old man, "you look just like the Vicomte your father. And you, Mademoiselle Jane, you are the spitting image of your mother. Ah! my dear master," the old man continued, as tears began to roll down his cheeks. "Never shall I see you again! Never shall I see you again! Never again!

"But that is not everything," he went on. "The dead, even those whom we have loved dearly, must not make us forget the living. We were told that you were coming: by the postman from Pegu, with his little bells, whom we had never seen before. He brought us a letter from your father, my children! Your father alerted us that he was on his way and that you were coming too. On the letter was written 'one hundred francs to the bearer.' I gave the man two hundred, one hundred of your father's money and one hundred of my own, so pleased I was to have such news. You will find your rooms ready; they have been ready for six months.

"So long as they remained empty, my heart was empty too. God be praised! Here you are, and the emptiness has been filled."

The old man, with his hat in his hand, led the column toward the large manor house, its windows now opened. They entered a large dining room paneled with ebony and an acacia the color of gold. The parquet was covered with exquisite mats that had been woven by the black women of the household. The table was set with heavy, brightly colored porcelain, purchased in Siam; the service glistened in contrast with the tablecloths, which had retained the ecru color of unwashed linen, and the napkins made of aloe fibers. The spoons and forks had been carved from a very hard wood as sturdy as metal. English knives purchased in Calcutta completed the table service.

There is no explaining how much patience and will had been necessary to gather together all these things in so isolated a place. But devotion has such resources, and gratitude such ways! Moreover, ever since the letter announcing the arrival of the Vicomte and his two daughters, the steward had kept the table set, so that if the guests arrived at any time of day or night they would know that they were expected. The steward had had the glassware wiped and the porcelain dusted daily.

The rest of the furniture as well as the beds, mirrors, and tapestries had been made in England and come via Calcutta. Remi's sons had made several trips to India, on this side of the Ganges, and with chartered boats they had brought back to what they called the big house all the furnishings along with other necessities and even some luxuries.

Guillaume Remi was a carpenter, and he had taught each of his sons a trade. One was a cabinetmaker, another a locksmith, the third a farmer. The third son, Justin by name, was out tracking a tiger when the Sainte-Hermine sisters arrived. The tiger had killed one of his buffaloes, and he had gone to wait for it to return for the dead animal's remains. A hunter as well as a farmer, Justin usually provided game for the household. All three sons could be hunters or soldiers, were expert marksmen, and could serve any country in the world as excellent soldiers.

Adda, Remi's daughter, escorted the two girls to their rooms, which added but one more surprise to all the others. For they had been expecting to discover some hut made of mud bricks or straw, not a house in which the appointments were so complete, they might constitute luxury.

The two young men were led to their apartments by Jules and Bernard. Jules, who had done an apprenticeship in Calcutta and could speak English, served the captain, while Bernard, who spoke only French plus some Sumatran and Malaysian patois, placed himself at René's disposal. But let us understand each other: by the words "served" and "placed himself at someone's disposal," we are not saying that Jules and Bernard in any way behaved like servants. Favored with an innate pride and fully aware of their own worth, they offered the guests a host's courtesy rather than a servant's obsequiousness. René and Bernard became fast friends on that very first evening; it took the somewhat haughtier Englishman a little more time to warm to Jules.

When supper was served, the travelers entered the dining room to find the table set with only four places. Guillaume Remi was standing at the wall with his two sons and daughter.

"Adda," Hélène said, her voice sweet, "not counting a place for your brother who is off hunting, there are still four places missing on this table."

The girl looked at Hélène in astonishment. "I don't understand, Mademoiselle," she said.

"One place for your father," Hélène continued, more insistently, "between my sister and me, one for you between these two gentlemen, one to my right and another to Jane's left for your two brothers, and also a fifth place should your brother the hunter return. I think, too, that I can speak for Monsieur René, who will surely agree that he would not be displeased to see his friend François seated at his table. Today François killed a tiger with no more emotion or pride than an experienced hunter. A man who has killed a tiger, in my opinion, has the right to sit at any table, even if it's an emperor's table."

"But, Mademoiselle," said the old man, stepping forward, "why would you wish to erase the distinction between servants and masters? Even if you so order, we will still know who we are."

"My friends," Hélène said, "among us there are neither servants nor masters. At least that is what my father told me scores of times. When we come here requesting hospitality, you arise from your table and welcome us into your house—you have demonstrated hospitality: now honor us with your company. We do not intend to change your custom or your schedules, but for this evening, please do us the honor of eating with us."

"Since Mademoiselle so wishes," said Remi, "we shall obey." He struck a drum used for summoning servants, and four Negroes appeared.

"Give your orders," Remi said to Hélène. She asked that five more places be set and indicated where they should be placed.

The two sisters moved their chairs to either side and the old man sat down between them. His two sons took their places to Hélène's right and Jane's left. The two men also moved to make space, and René, polite like the true Frenchman he was, showed Adda to her chair. Then they called François, who at first refused the invitation. When he saw there was no getting out of it, however, he bravely took his place opposite the setting for the absent hunter.

It was only then, in the glow of the candlelight at the table, that the French party noticed how truly beautiful Adda was. An involuntary cry of admiration escaped from the lips of the two sisters. For Adda was a Hindu

Venus. Her eyes were large and black. Her skin was slightly swarthy, her smooth hair was as black as a crow's feathers. Her satiny, cherry-red lips and pearly-white teeth would have inspired a portraitist, as would her arms and hands a sculptor. She was wearing a Bengali silk sari, its soft folds clothing what they did not hide; like the sculpted drape on a marble goddess, the silk fabric revealed all the mysteries of love that modesty entrusted to it. Adda had the grace not only of a woman but also of some wild animal, the swan as well as the gazelle, yet with that, it was clear she was consummately French in spirit and character. She superbly blended the two races.

The four black servants had just removed the first course when the dogs again started barking. Everyone paused. "Don't pay any attention to that," said Remi. "Justin is back."

He'd barely spoken than the dogs were barking even more ferociously. "Has he killed the tiger?" René asked.

"Yes," Remi replied. "And he has the pelt with him. That is why the dogs are so excited."

At that moment the dining room door burst open and the eldest of the three brothers, a handsome young man of Herculean size with tawny beard and hair, appeared. He was dressed in a long, old-style Gallic smock that came down to his knees and was belted around the waist. With the tiger's head resting on his own, and with the two front legs crossed over his chest, he resembled an antique standard-bearer like the ones we see in Le Brun's paintings of Alexander's battles. His own broad forehead splattered with drops of the animal's blood, he made an entrance as unusual as it was unexpected. Everyone stood up.

After greeting them all from the doorway, he walked over to Hélène, kneeled, and solemnly said to her, "Mademoiselle, please accept this carpet for your feet. I wish it were even more fitting for you."

LXXI
The Garden of Eden

IN 1780, about twenty-five years earlier, the Vicomte de Sainte-Hermine, captain of the ship the *Victoire*, had been charged with a special mission to the King of Pegu, who had just gained Pegu's independence from the Emperor of Ava. The purpose of the vicomte's mission was to obtain for

France seven or eight leagues of land that lay between the Metra River and the sea in order to establish there, on the west coast of the new kingdom in the Gulf of Bengal, a French enclave. In exchange, Louis XVI was offering weapons, money, and even French engineers to help the King of Pegu consolidate the new kingdom.

The king's name was Maderagee-Praw. An intelligent man, he accepted France's proposal. And to show Sainte-Hermine proof of his devotion to France and his esteem for the vicomte personally, he invited the captain to choose a tract of land in some uninhabited part of his kingdom where he might set up his own commercial operation.

On board the *Victoire* there was a keen-witted carpenter, the son of one of the Vicomte de Sainte-Hermine's longtime servants. The only book this carpenter had ever read, but one that he had read and reread, was *Robinson Crusoe*. It had so affected him that whenever their ship came to shore on some deserted island, he would beg the Vicomte de Sainte-Hermine to let him take his carpentry tools and a gun, some powder, and ammunition, and stay on there to live out his dream. The carpenter was Remi.

Monsieur de Sainte-Hermine had no personal wealth. Recognizing the value of the land the king was offering to him, he decided that he would at least see if he could find a suitable piece of property. It would prove to be the fulfillment of Remi's dreams.

Sainte-Hermine likely took the same path his daughters would follow years later, though, at the time, one of his daughters had not yet been born. When he reached the spot that we now know in 1805 as Betel Land, the vicomte saw its commercial advantages immediately. From there you could reach Rangoon and Siriam by the Pegu River, while the Sittang River offered a route to the Mergui archipelago and the Tabaluayn River took you to Martaban and Siam's entire western coast. Furthermore, the land was protected by nature herself. A peninsula, it was almost completely surrounded by branches of the Sittang River, and its link to the mainland was only a hundred meters wide. The land had probably already been cultivated, for betel does not grow naturally in Burma, and betel was growing everywhere.

That peninsula, about two leagues long and a quarter to a half league wide, was the piece of land Monsieur de Sainte-Hermine chose. He carefully made drawings of the land, with measurements, and he told the King of Pegu that if he so truly esteemed him, the king would grant him the parcel of land shown in the drawings and at the same time fulfill all the vicomte's personal wishes.

The piece of land looked so small on paper and appeared to be such a tiny part of his kingdom that the king saw no problem in granting the Vicomte de Sainte-Hermine his wish. He acknowledged the concession and placed upon it his royal seal, and Monsieur le Vicomte de Sainte-Hermine found himself the owner of a substantial parcel of land in the kingdom of His Majesty Menderagee-Praw.

Remi had followed the vicomte's negotiations with all the pangs of covetousness. When the papers were signed, sealed, and initialed, Remi was summoned by Monsieur de Sainte-Hermine. "Well, Remi," he said. "I hope you are pleased!"

"Just as I always am when good things happen to you, Captain," Remi replied.

"But I am not the person to whom good things are happening just now."

"What do you mean?" Remi was beginning to understand. He blushed and started trembling. "Oh, my God! Captain," he cried, "is it possible?"

"Well, by God, yes. You will be the sole owner of this land, since you will be my representative. I cannot tell you when I shall return or even if I shall return, but if I do not return, and if the land is not claimed by my children, it will be entirely yours. If I do come back, or if my heirs come in my place, we shall divide any past and future profits fifty-fifty. I am leaving you five thousand francs, ten guns, three barrels of powder, three hundred pounds of lead, and all the tools, for after all the tools belong to you. Should you want a slave, even two or four, they are yours for the asking."

"I need no slaves," said Remi. "But you know that whenever you return, if you return, you will have not a quarter of the profits, or even half, but everything."

"Fine," said the vicomte, "we shall deal with that when the time comes." He shook Remi's hand and left him there in the middle of the forest from which the carpenter planned to get the materials for the houses he expected to build.

It was ten in the morning. Remi found himself alone with God and he felt the rich vigor of nature, and he contemplated his land. He said proudly to himself, "I am king over all I survey."

At the same moment he heard a roar. The animal, a tiger perhaps, might have been answering him, as if to say: "Fine! But even though you are king, I am master." Remi had not expected to take possession of his new empire without some protest from the denizens, so the roar did not disturb him.

He set to work. Choosing a tree with branches near the ground, he built a kind of hut around the trunk so that during his first night in the forest he would be protected from any surprise attacks by wild beasts. He also left an opening in the roof so, if necessary, he could climb into the upper branches, in which, using two planks, he built a seat for himself and a shelf for five loaded guns. As evening fell he ate some of the food the vicomte had left for him. He was absolutely delighted. For the first time in his life he was his own master; he was like Augustus, the master of the universe.

If he had forgotten the roar he'd heard that morning, a movement in the tall grass sixty yards away provided a quick reminder. Remi kept on eating, but his eyes never left the tall grass. They widened when he saw the panther.

Remi was not familiar with the habits of the big cats. So he decided, wisely enough, to put himself out of harm's way. Slowly, carefully, he put his foot on the lowest branch of the tree and placed his hand on the third; he began to climb. When he reached the planks, he was about twenty-five feet off the ground. He sat down. He was calm, he felt safe, as if he'd been enclosed in a fortress.

But the panther had caught his scent. And unfortunately, unlike Remi, it had not had its supper. It began to move slowly forward, low to the ground like a cat stalking a bird. About twenty yards from the tree, gathering its savage strength, the panther made a powerful leap that carried it to a branch about two meters below Remi's seat.

Remi reached for the carpenter's axe hanging from his belt. When the panther extended its front paw to climb the tree, Remi took advantage of the moment to swing his axe and chop it off. The paw bounced from branch to branch as it fell to the ground.

The panther, screaming with rage and pain, raised its second front paw, and Remi swung his axe again, with equal strength and skill. The second paw tumbled through the branches to join the first, while the panther, screaming again, lost its balance and dropped the twenty feet to the ground.

Remi picked up one of the five loaded guns, and before the panther could recover from its fall, he splintered its head with a bullet. He climbed down from the tree, found his knife, and skinned the cat properly. He hung the skin on a tree and nailed the two paws to his door, as he had seen tribesmen do with wolf paws. Then he went back to his supper, saying, "When things are far away, they seem dangerous and mysterious, but when we see them up close, they prove to be nothing at all!"

The other panthers must have understood. Although Remi could hear them roaring during the evening, through the night, and even at dawn, not a single one dared to come near the hut.

Little by little, the hut changed its shape. What had begun with walls of branches had a month later become a veritable small fortress with squared logs set one against the other. An attic made from wooden planks had been added, as well as a ladder to climb up to it. Six boards served to build a primitive bed, and a solid four-legged table, along with a stool, completed the furnishings.

One morning Remi found himself greeting a caravan. Evidently the Vicomte de Sainte-Hermine, upon reaching Pegu, had attended to everything he thought a poor, lonely man in the middle of nowhere might need. He had sent rice, wheat, maize, a horse and mare, a cow and calf, a boar and a sow, a rooster and six chickens, as well as a huge watchdog, its mate, and a pair of cats. There was also a mill that Remi could set up to grind grain. The men who led the caravan asked Remi only for a receipt, as the Vicomte de Sainte-Hermine had paid them in advance. Remi added a tip of a few *talks* to that amount before sending them back to Pegu.

At first Remi was overselmed by so much wealth. How would he ever house all those creatures? Fortunately the vicomte had also sent nails, locks, and any number of other goods Remi would never be able to find in the wilderness. Because it would be impossible for him to build a true shelter for all the animals in twenty-four hours, or even in a week, he instead constructed a palisade around his hut, one tall and solid enough so that nothing could leap across or slip through it. He had finished it by the second day; it was about a hundred yards in circumference and consequently about thirty-three yards in diameter. He untied the animals once they were inside the palisade and closed the gate behind them.

The rooster perched himself on one of the gateposts and immediately assumed his sentinel duties. Dutifully, too, the hens started laying on the day they arrived. The dogs and cats quickly demonstrated their domesticity, the dogs posting themselves on either side of the door to the hut while the cats climbed up into the attic.

The attic was beginning to look like an arsenal. It housed ten guns that were kept always loaded, with about fifty cartridges waiting nearby, all ready to play their role as messengers of death. The view from the attic was perfect, and ideal for a watch. In the walls, Remi had drilled loopholes through which he could shoot in any direction without being exposed to enemy fire.

During the day the animals often roamed in the meadow outside the palisade, although the chickens liked to stay near the house and scratch in the dirt. When evening came, the animals instinctively came back inside the fence. The rooster's nervousness and the dogs' barking were sure signs that a tiger or panther might be prowling not far away, but neither ever appeared, not by night or day.

Remi was discovering that his many animals involved a lot of work for one man alone. The thought sometimes crossed his mind—a thought he attributed to his own weakness—that a woman would not be useless in his little colony. Not only could she help him in his labors, but she could share with him the joy of seeing his colony grow. One night, tormented more than usual by such thoughts, which surely must have been sent by the devil,

Remi awoke an hour before daylight. But not just because of the devil. The rooster was crowing, and the dogs were barking. And there seemed to be gunshots coming from the river.

Remi grabbed a gun and filled his pockets with ammunition. Followed by his dogs, he hurried down to the river. But already the fight had ended. Three bodies lay near the bank; they were clearly dead, and had probably been attacked by brigands coming up the Sittang River from the west coast of Siam.

Remi looked around and called out, but nobody answered. When the dawn was breaking, though, he thought he saw a human creature kneeling, silent, as stiff and motionless as a statue. Nor did the figure move when he approached. It was a young Hindu girl, about twelve or thirteen years old, and she was kneeling beside the body of a man about forty. He had been shot in the chest.

Alone for the past two months in this wilderness, with his unkempt beard and hair, Remi looked very much like a brigand himself. But the girl did not appear to be afraid. She simply pointed to the dead man, then bowed her head and wept.

Remi allowed her time to express her sorrow. Then he motioned to her to follow him.

She rose but did not move. She called out three times; three times she received no answer. She paused, but did not hesitate. With animal-like grace she placed her hand in Remi's, and, resting her head against his shoulder, she fell in with his footsteps.

Three quarters of an hour later, as they approached the palisade, the animals pressed themselves against the gate and in joyous noise welcomed them as they moved aside to let the couple pass. The dog barked, the pig grunted, the cow mooed, the horse whinnied, the cat meowed, the rooster crowed, each animal greeting her as if Eve were entering the Garden of Eden. Only the man kept silent, but as he opened the door to his house, his heart was pounding as it never had before.

LXXII

The Colony

REMI CLIMBED UP to the second story several times with armloads of the fern-like plants that were growing profusely around the house, and over the ferns he spread the panther skin. Then he built two stools like the one on the ground floor. The second floor thus became a bedroom for the new Eve.

Remi found the young Burmese woman enchanting. She was wearing a long sky-blue robe with embroidery around the neck and on the cuffs of her wide sleeves; a silk braid served as a belt around her waist. On her feet, small as a child's, were sandals of woven straw. Her hands were slightly darker than her face and delicately shaped. Her eyes glimmered with intelligence, and they were filled with gratitude, as if they were saying, "Since misfortune has brought me to you, what can I do for you?" Remi, meanwhile, was as eager to do all he could for her, to help her forget her misfortune.

They were soon able to communicate about the necessities of daily life in a vocabulary that mixed Burmese with French words. It took no words, though, for Remi to learn that her people had been farmers, as she began immediately to look after the animals. She pointed out that the pigs should be penned separately, and the same day a sty was built. She noted that the calf no longer needed its mother's milk, although it still enjoyed drinking it, either out of laziness or gluttony. With long, thin grasses, she wove baskets so tight that they could hold the cow's milk as well as could a wooden bucket or porcelain bowl. She gathered the eggs, and she separated the layers from the brooders so that they would always have both fresh eggs and young chicks running around the courtyard. Most important of all, she discovered that the climbing plant growing virtually everywhere on the property was betel. Also familiar with corn and wheat, she showed Remi how best to cultivate them both.

Remi thoroughly enjoyed his new activities, for they allowed him proximity to the girl, who had now been there about two months. Remi set up the mill that the caravan had delivered, and he taught her how to bake bread, which they enjoyed with the butter and cheese made with the excess milk. She made nets and ropes from aloe fibers, so they were able to add fish to their food supply.

Although their life had become more and more comfortable, Remi realized one day that their farm had grown too large to be managed without servants. So he decided to go to Tungoo, about fifteen leagues away, to see if he could purchase some Negro slaves or hire some servants. He also wanted to find out if he could sell the betel Eve had harvested and prepared; he would be able to furnish as much as anyone wanted.

One morning, then, instead of turning the horse out to pasture, Remi saddled it, put on its bridle, and swung up onto his mount. But the mare, accustomed to the company of her mate, became alarmed and wanted to go along too. Acknowledging her plight, he saddled and bridled her as well, then opened the gate. Only Eve was standing there, blocking the gate, and when Remi tried to ride through, she raised her arms, began to weep, and, using two of the few French words she knew, she cried, "With you! With you! With you!"

Remi was already worried about leaving Eve alone for two or three days. He feared that in his absence some harm might come to her, for she would never be able to defend their little settlement if it were attacked. He reasoned, too, that if he had to lose one or the other, he would prefer losing his house and animals to losing Eve.

Judging his guns and powder to be his most important possessions, since with guns and powder he could get back anything that was taken from him, he hid them under some rocks. As for the animals, he saw no cause for worry, since they were mostly herbivores and could find their own food. So, with nothing holding him back, and with twenty-five louis from his treasury in his pack and Eve at his side, he was content to leave his little farm to God's protection.

A compass was Remi's guide to Tungoo, but a compass could not take them across a branch of the Sittang. Remi tried to find a ford, until his young friend indicated to him with gestures that a ford would not be necessary since she knew how to swim. At the riverbank she and Remi took each other's hands and together they led their horses into the deep stream.

That same evening they reached Tungoo and Remi realized again how valuable Eve was to him. She spoke Burmese and served as his interpreter. She remembered items that their little, new settlement required, and that he'd have forgot. She had prepared the betel, which was determined to be of excellent quality, and they had supply enough to pay for all their purchases. Indeed, the buyer committed himself to taking all that Eve could prepare in the next three months, and he would come himself to pick it up. From that day on their settlement was known as Betel Land.

They purchased four Negroes, two men and two women. And they hired two young men who were skilled in growing rice as well as two women to help Eve take care of the animals and prepare the betel. In addition, they purchased two buffaloes, male and female, of course, to pull the plowshare Remi would make from teakwood instead of iron.

It took them three days to get back home, because the men, women, and animals could not move as fast as the horses. They crossed the river without incident, and soon they were back within sight of their little home. The dogs saw them coming and ran out to meet them, as did many of the other animals. But not the rooster—he remained perched on the fence—or the chickens, which singlemindedly continued to parade their chicks single-file. Nor did the two cats move from either side of the door, where they sat as gravely as two Egyptian gods. Nothing had happened while their masters were gone.

Remi found everything to be intact both inside and out. Thankful, he raised his arms to the heavens, but Eve thought the gesture was meant for her, and she threw herself innocently into his arms. As Remi held her tight in his embrace their lips met. It was their first kiss.

In that moment, Remi lost all his misanthropy. Notably, he stopped reading *Robinson Crusoe*, although he did name one of the Negroes Friday.

Now that Remi had the Negroes and other help, he divided up the work, with each individual having certain tasks. A daily routine set in.

Remi used his own skills to make a plow and then a harness. With the buffaloes in harness, Remi plowed approximately ten acres. He planted wheat. He harrowed the ten acres and the wheat began to grow.

Eve and one of the black women took care of the animals and the house. One of the two men Remi had hired to help with the farming cut irrigation channels in a swampy area to make a paddy-field. The second of the hired men, who had the skills of a huntsman and fisherman, was charged with supplying the household with food. Game and fish being so plentiful, he had time left over to help the black woman who so adeptly attended to the betel. In betel lay Remi's great hope for the success of his enterprise.

Thanks to the help of the new workers, the little colony was taking on quite a prosperous look. Before, the Negroes had always been whipped; they refused to work hard because they were being forced to do it. But now that they were well fed and treated more like servants than slaves, they worked willingly from morning to evening. And everyone at Betel Land wore a smile on his face, except for the master of the house. True, Remi was no longer a misanthrope, but what he was now was even worse. He was in love.

As for Eve, she already loved Remi with all her heart and in all her innocence. Her simplest words and slightest touch made that very clear to him. The fact that she loved him afflicted his heart. If Eve had not loved him, or even if she had never told him she loved him, he would have been strong enough to resist the love he felt for her. But resisting her love as well as his own was beyond his capabilities.

A question will no doubt come to the reader's mind: "Why. . . ?" I will answer even before it is stated. Because Remi was a good man and an excellent Christian. He was the legitimate son of Mathurin Remi and Claudine Perrot, and not for anything in the world would he have wanted, or allowed, their eldest son to sire a line of illegitimate children.

The conflict between temptation and his conscience was at its peak when one evening the dogs began to bark, not in anger or in alarm, as at the approach of some danger, but in a friendly way, as if they were welcoming a member of the family. Remi opened the door. And the person he greeted was indeed a brother.

He was a French Jesuit. Bearing the message of Christ, he was on his way to China, where for his faith he would probably meet his death.

"Father, you are doubly welcome!" Remi said joyously. "For you are bringing us more than we can ever give you."

"What could I be bringing you that is so important, my children?" the man of God asked.

"You are bringing salvation to this young woman and happiness to me. She is a pagan, and I love her. You will baptize her this evening; you will marry us tomorrow."

The neophyte's religious instruction did not take long. The brother asked her if she recognized any other God than Remi's God, and she said no. Asked if she wanted to live and die in the same religion as Remi, she said yes.

That evening Remi announced to all his workers that the next day would be a holiday. Then he led the Jesuit father to the top of a small hill. On it stood a cross. It was where Remi went to pray every morning and evening. "Father," he said to the man of God, "this is where you will bless us tomorrow, and I give you my word that within a year from the time you give us your blessing, a chapel will be built on this spot."

The following day, in the presence of the four Negroes and the two Peguans, Remi and Eve were united in marriage. Eve's baptism took place just before the marriage, so that even if Eve, with her limited knowledge of our religion, and thus without intention, had been inclined to sin, she had no time to, neither in action nor thought, between the two ceremonies.

The Jesuit left that very day. Following ancient practice, on leaving he blessed the master, the mistress, the servants, the animals, and the home.

The animals had not been waiting for his blessing to reproduce. The buffalo cow had birthed a calf, the mare a colt. The cat family had grown by six kittens, and the dog family by ten puppies. There were so many piglets that they'd lost count; they had turned some of them loose in the forest, where they became wild. Their calf had meanwhile developed into a handsome yearling bull.

Three months after their visit to Pegu, the betel merchant, as he'd promised, arrived. With him came two or three other merchants eager to learn how much product Betel Land could provide each year. The merchant who had made the agreement with Remi paid the sum they had agreed upon. But since the land had produced three times more betel than was expected, Remi's enterprise, it turned out, brought him not three but more than nine thousand *talks*, for the other two merchants, suspecting that they too might do business with Remi, had come with bags full of the little gold ingots that the Burmese use for money.

The merchants proposed a contract with Remi. They promised to make annual payments of fifteen thousand *talks*, twelve thousand for betel and the rest for corn, rice, and wheat. If the harvest of one of the cereals proved to be poor, Remi would recompense them with the equivalent in betel. The merchants agreed further to send to the settlement two buffaloes, four more black men, and two more black women, as well as two more Peguans, one a locksmith and the other a cabinetmaker.

Nine months and a few days after the good Jesuit left, with one of the black women performing her duties as midwife perfectly, Eve gave birth to a son. They named him Justin. He was baptized by Remi himself in the new chapel he had built on the site of his marriage to Eve. His good faith to the promise he'd made to the Jesuit surely brought him good fortune, for each of the next two years brought another son: Bernard, and then Jules. Then three years went by. Adda was the name they gave to their fourth child, a daughter.

The settlement continued to flourish. The cultivated fields extended for leagues. Eighteen servants and slaves were now working there, not counting ten black or mixed-race children who had jobs appropriate for their age, except for the very youngest, who spent their time playing with the kittens or chasing the chickens. Remi's eldest son was being trained for farming, fishing, and hunting. Bernard, the second son, was apprenticed to the locksmith, and the third, Jules, to the master cabinetmaker, both tradesmen having been sent as promised by Remi's business partners.

In view of the colony's growing prosperity, Remi decided to build a large house for Monsieur le Vicomte and all around it smaller houses for Remi and the other employees or servants.

He drew up plans for the vicomte's house; he had free rein for that, but everyone joined in when the building began. The two apprentices were already skilled enough to work alongside their masters as woodworker and locksmith, while Remi devoted his carpenter's art to sculpting joists and verandas. When the time came that Eve was covering the walls with cloth from Prome, Pegu, and even Calcutta, they began building the rest of the village, which would number from fifteen to eighteen houses.

It took them two years to finish the enormous task. The colony was prospering enough that they were able to invest between fifteen and eighteen thousand *talks* from their annual revenues, which is about sixty thousand francs, in the construction and were thus able to finish more rapidly than they'd expected.

Remi's three sons had become strong, handsome young men, and all three were skilled in handling weapons. Twice the little colony had been attacked by brigands. But thanks to the three brothers and the four blockhouses at each corner of the village, the welcome the brigands received made them never want to try again.

Justin especially had become the terror of all bandits, both men and animals. If ever news came of a tiger or panther anywhere within two or three leagues of the settlement, Justin would throw his gun over his shoulder, put his father's axe in his belt, and head into the forest. He'd not return until the tiger or panther was dead. That evening, when he came into the dining room and found there the people they had been awaiting for so long, the pelt he wore on his back and over his head came from the thirteenth tiger he had killed.

A year before, a great misfortune had befallen the loving family and had pained all the servants and slaves as well. Remi's wife, the mother of three handsome sons and a beautiful daughter, had died.

LXXIII

The Vicomte de Sainte-Hermine Is Buried

NOW THAT WE HAVE SEEN how the Vicomte de Sainte-Hermine's settlement had been founded on Betel Land, we need not explain to our readers the effect that patriarchal family had that night on the two sisters, James Asplay, and René, except to say the family had brought to the early part of the nineteenth century the customs and qualities of Hebrews in Biblical times. Abraham was no more venerable than Remi, Rebecca no more beautiful than Adda. David and Jonathan were no prouder than Bernard and Jules. Nor was Samson, who killed a lion by tearing its jaws apart with his bare hands, any more courageous than Justin.

As the two girls went to their room and the two young men to their apartment, they could only marvel at what they had heard and seen in this setting of modest grandeur.

The following day, when Adda came to see how Hélène and Jane had slept, she asked if her father could come see them. They agreed, of course, and when the old man slowly came up the stairs and solemnly entered their room, he was holding a little notebook in his hand. He had come to give an account of his stewardship.

"Mesdemoiselles," he said, "the first thing that should be done when a debtor and creditor meet after twenty-four or twenty-five years is that the debtor should state what he owes and open the accounts."

The girls looked at each other in surprise. "Our father never said anything about that," Hélène answered. "If he had an opinion, he would probably say that he was in your debt rather than you in his. The only advice he gave us was to sell the settlement and to divide the proceeds with you."

Remi began to laugh. "I cannot accept such conditions, Mademoiselle. That would be placing too high a price on the service I have given to my honorable master. No, Mademoiselle. If you are not too tired, you will come with me and judge for yourself the extent of your wealth. Your sister of course has the right to accompany you, and if you would like these two gentlemen to come along as well, I would be delighted to present my accounts before the largest number of witnesses possible."

The two sisters looked questioningly at each other and agreed that they should go alone. They wished the good steward the best possible outcome, and they feared that a man, no longer a stranger when he is your fiancé, might oppose the generosity Hélène intended to show to her steward. "We shall go alone, my venerable friend," she said. "Just lead the way, please."

The old man walked slightly ahead of them, then opened a small door and motioned to them to come in. The little room was the only one in the house to be built of stone, and it had bars on the windows. The only furnishings were two small iron barrels, one about a foot tall and the other maybe three feet tall. Standing on two iron bars that had been set into the wall, both barrels were also chained to the wall, and they were further protected by two iron rings.

The old man pulled a key from his pocket and opened a padlock. He lifted the cover from the taller barrel to reveal a treasure of gold ingots about the size of one's little finger. The girls held each other tightly as they gazed in wonder at the barrel's brimful contents.

"Mesdemoiselles," said the old man, "in this barrel there must be more than a million francs."

The girls gave a start. "Whose gold is it?" Hélène asked. "It cannot be ours."

"And yet that is the simple truth," said the old man. "I have been the steward of your property for about twenty years. Most years it has earned between fifty and fifty-five thousand francs. I have not calculated exactly what is here; for that, we would need special scales. But even after the expenses of the farm have been accounted for, I'd guess that you would still have approximately nine hundred thousand francs."

The girls looked again at each other while the old man took a second key from his pocket and opened the smaller barrel. It was half full of rubies, carbuncles, sapphires, and emeralds, which, like gold ingots, served as currency for trade in Burma. The old man scooped up a handful of the precious stones; when he poured them back into the barrel they fell in a cascade of flames.

"What is all that?" Hélène asked. "Did you find the treasure of Haroun al-Rachid?"

"No," the old man answered, "but it seemed to me that gold might not carry the same value in France or England as it does here. However, these precious stones, as rough as they are, would be worth twice as much as gold in France. In themselves, at the current rates in this country, they should be worth at least three hundred thousand francs."

"Why are you showing us all this?" asked Hélène with a smile, for although Jane was listening, she was completely indifferent to all the details and apparently lost in thought.

"My purpose is to show you, my dear mistresses, that just as the people, the animals, and the crops on this farm belong to you, so do the gold and precious stones."

"My friend," Hélène answered, "I know what arrangements were made between you and my father. 'Remi,' he told you as he left, 'since you wish to remain here, I shall allow you do that. With the few resources I can leave with you, I would like you to set up a commercial operation. And when I or one of my heirs return, you will divide up equally between you and me whatever money it earns.' Unfortunately, my dear Remi, it is I, the heir, who has returned, but I come in my father's name both to request his share and to honor his terms. Half of what you own belongs to my sister and me, but the other half is yours."

Tears coursed down the old man's cheeks. "No! That surely is not what your worthy father intended. Or when he made that agreement with me, he never thought the operation would prosper as it has. Remember that we are only simple farmers. We would be delighted if you would allow us to continue to earn our living in your service, and I would ask only that you guarantee the right of my children and grandchildren to continue to do so after I am dead."

Hélène looked severely at Remi. "You are forgetting, Remi," she said, "that by being too generous with us you are being unfair to your children. Your children have worked as you have, not as long, of course, but according to their age and strength, and have participated in building up this wealth. Must I be the one to defend their rights?"

Remi tried to insist, but just then a Chinese gong sounded three times to announce that lunch had been set on the table. Hélène let Jane go on ahead

while she took Remi's arm. The door to the little room closed securely behind them, they proceeded down to lunch.

Not even a king's table had ever been more sumptuously set. Peacocks
from India, golden pheasants from China, and Burmese guinea-fowl lay in
magnificent array on the table, and heaped in stunning arrangements were
exquisite fruits: mangoes, guavas, royal bananas, pineapples, durian, avocadoes, jackfruit, and rose apples. For drinks they had palm wine and
grapefruit juice, which were served as cool as iced liqueurs, for they had
been stored deep in the ground.

Since the plantation had no orchard, the three brothers had gathered
fruits in the forest, but to find mangoes, Justin had traveled more than two
leagues upriver and discovered something else as well: tiger tracks, in the
jungle along the Sittang River.

The news had the five young men ecstatic. They planned a tiger hunt for
a few days later. They decided, moreover, to hunt with elephants, so that
the women could join them. Actually, it was Jane's idea that they hunt with
elephants, and everyone had readily agreed. Hélène, though, had looked
sadly at Jane and murmured, "Poor sister!"

Jane was not without courage, but her proposal for the hunt came less
from courage than from fear. For nothing frightened her more than the
thought of René going off on such a dangerous hunt and she being left behind in anguish for the three or four days he was gone. René tried to dissuade her from joining the hunt, but all he managed to do was to make her
sadder. So Hélène suggested that for the time being they put off the hunt,
especially as they were expecting the vicomte's body to arrive at any moment, and they needed to attend to funeral arrangements before they could
plan for a hunt and fun.

As they were leaving the lunch table, Hélène summoned Sir James and
René for a stroll outside the house. She told them what had transpired with
her father's steward and how, in spite of the old man's reluctance, she had
insisted that the arrangement between him and her father be followed rig-
orously. Both men agreed with her decision.

"So," said Hélène, with a smile, "now Jane has become a rich heiress
without even realizing it, for she did not hear a word of our conversation.
Still, even with riches, it will not be easy to find a husband for her in this
wilderness."

"She should have taken the same precautions we took, my dear Hélène,"
said Sir James, "and brought a husband along from Europe."

They both looked at René, but the young man remained impassive, except for a vague smile, more sad than joyous, on his face.

At that moment their attention was distracted by the three brothers.

They were redirecting a stream so that it would flow into a small pond, which they had excavated in the shade of a magnificent baobab, before reaching the river. The pond would provide the girls a lovely place for bathing. Like all of the excellent family's activities, it was designed to please their guests and improve their sense of well-being.

Back to the house Jane was sitting in the doorway and absentmindedly watching Adda train two little Burmese horses for the riding pleasures of Hélène and Jane. In the lower part of the country, between the Arakan River and Tenasserim, where the ground is swampy and often flooded, as well as in the delta formed by the many branches of the Irrawaddy, the horses are small, weak, and of poor quality, but when you reach the drier ground around Henzada, you will find a breed of horses that, though small, is elegant and untiring. Since, in Burma, the elephant is the preferred mount of important people, and since water buffalo or oxen are used to draw the traditional carts short distances, the horse is something of a luxury.

On the plantation there were five or six horses. No one other than Remi's sons and Adda, however, took the liberty of riding them, although it would be more accurate to say that no one else dared to ride them. Adda, who'd had no benefit of the niceties of European civilization, had no concept of saddles designed for a woman's use, and so she rode like a man. Beneath her skirt, pulled tight and slit down the sides, she wore pants that came down to her ankles. Her body lithe and uncorsetted, she could bend with the horse's every movement. With her hair flying in the wind, she resembled those women about whom Phaedra speaks, those women who held Thessalian lances near their flowing braids as they rode into the wind.

As much as the two young European women openly admired Adda's grace and mastery, they said they could never ride like that. Adda had a solution to the problem: René or James would draw a picture of French saddles, and her brother the woodworker would make them.

It was then that they saw a procession coming out of the forest. From the belvedere they could descry an elephant, four horses, and about ten men. The elephant was draped in black cloth. The girls had no doubt that their father's body had arrived.

The gong was struck to bring everyone together. Then the doors were flung open and together they all waited for the funeral procession to arrive. When the elephant bearing the coffin came into the courtyard, the two sisters fell to their knees, and all their friends and all the servants followed suit.

The *shabunder* of Pegu had agreed to take charge of details for the funeral. He had entreated two Jesuit missionaries to take advantage of the escort and the transport that would coduct them safely through the forest where wild animals posed great danger. In exchange, the missionaries would say the prayer for the dead over the coffin of the Vicomte de Sainte-Hermine.

The coffin was carried to the little chapel. For want of candles, resinous wood was burned for twenty-four hours to simulate as much as possible the atmosphere of a chapel of rest. The mass for the dead was solemnly said, and the vicomte's body was laid to rest beside Eve in the family vault.

For several days the entire colony grieved in the sad memory of the vicomte's violent, untimely death. And Jane was able to weep unchecked, without having to offer a reason for her tears.

The two Jesuits continued on their way to China.

LXXIV

Tigers and Elephants

FOR A FEW DAYS AFTER the Vicomte de Sainte-Hermine's funeral the young people sought out no amusements, nor did they speak further of the hunt they'd planned.

Still, for a hunt involving elephants, preparations had to be made. Jules the woodworker had to build howdahs about a meter tall with space enough for four or five people. Bernard the locksmith had to make five or six lances of the sort that the Bengali use to hunt wild boars.

René, meanwhile, had spared no effort in strengthening his friendship with the two elephants. Every day he himself led Ali and Omar, as he had named them, out of their stable and devoted time to them. He let them pick him up with their trunks. He had them bend their legs, which he then used as steps to climb up on their huge backs, and afterward he'd have them place him gently back on the ground with their trunks. Both elephants came whenever he called their names. He could stir them up or calm them down at will; they were aggressive or submissive by his command, and never did they fail to carry out the orders he gave.

Some eight or ten days after the funeral the howdahs were ready, as were the lances. Yet the hunting party went unmentioned for a few more days. It was Jane who finally spoke up: "Monsieur René, what about that tiger hunt?"

René bowed to Jane and her sister and said, "My ladies, you may give the orders whenever you wish."

They decided upon the following Sunday. As the site of the hunt was only two hours away, they planned to leave at four in the morning so as to be there before daylight, around six o'clock.

At four o'clock on the following Sunday everyone was ready. They tied down the howdahs by using heavy chains, which they wrapped several times around the elephants' bodies. To the howdahs they strapped chests full of ammunition and food, as well as large jugs of water. Then they checked their weapons. Justin and his brothers had only regular-issue guns with bayonets, so René gave to Justin his grooved single-shot rifle, which Justin had admired and on several occasions, at René's invitation, fired; Justin had been especially pleased with how straight it shot.

The party left the settlement with Justin on horseback, while Sir James, Jules, and Hélène traveled in the howdah on Omar's back, and Jane, Bernard, and René on Ali's. Each howdah had room enough for a servant to hold a parasol.

Sir James lent Jules one of his Manton guns. René tried to lend one of the two double-barreled pistols in his belt to Bernard, who refused the weapon as he wasn't familiar with it. They also had two lances in each howdah.

The elephant drivers, or mahouts, sat on the animals' heads, where they were protected by the large ears. Instead of the iron hook they normally used to guide their elephant, the mahouts had lances so that they could also protect themselves should the need arise.

The hunters had hesitated to hire beaters because of the danger they'd surely encounter, but twelve men had volunteered anyway. They were being led by François, who chose to carry nothing other than his ordinary gun and the famous cutlass that had severed the boa with one blow. A pack of about a dozen dogs, trained to hate tigers, accompanied the party.

As Sir James had participated in tiger hunts several times around Calcutta, he was named leader of the expedition.

The party covered approximately two leagues without spotting anything. When they reached the jungle where Justin had seen tiger tracks, however, the dogs became nervous, the elephants started walking with their trunks raised, and Justin's horse began to shy, prick up its ears, and sniff the air. François shouted encouragement to his men, but they were hesitant to go into the jungle, even after he set the example himself. The dogs, though, bravely followed him.

"Careful!" Sir James shouted. "The tiger cannot be far away."

He had scarcely spoken when one of the dogs cried out in distress. And immediately they heard a deep, harsh growl. Whoever has not heard a lion roar or a tiger growl has not heard either of the two most frightening sounds in nature. It is a sound that chills the senses as it penetrates deep into the body, not just through the ear, but through the very pores.

The alarming growl was echoed by two, then three more, but they came from different directions. The tiger was not alone.

Guns were cocked. The dogs were barking more heatedly, as if now they were not only smelling the animal but also seeing it.

"Tiger coming!" François shouted.

And out of the jungle exploded a magnificent royal tiger in all its furious glory. In one bound it covered twenty meters and landed at least seven or eight feet clear of the thick jungle, but it had hardly touched the ground than it sprang back into cover.

All the hunters' animals made noises of fear. Except for Justin's horse; it seemed more angry than afraid. Its nostrils steamed when the big cat appeared, and its eyes flashed like lightning bolts. Had it not been restrained by a bridle, it would likely have rushed into battle.

Who can imagine a more beautiful sight than that of Justin, secure on his mount, without a saddle, without stirrups, without a blanket, and the horse even more attentive to his master's hand, voice, and knees than to the bridle. All eyes were fixed on him. Hatless, his chest half uncovered, his sleeves rolled up above his elbows, he clutched his horse's mane with one hand and his lance with the other.

Suddenly, driven by the beaters' shouts, the sound of water buffalo horns, and the barking dogs, a second tiger emerged from the jungle. It did not bound out like the first, but crept out on its stomach, like a fleeing animal. It had covered ten yards when it found itself facing the elephants, and, readying itself to spring, it crouched even lower.

The girls shouted, "Tiger! Tiger!" The elephants took a defensive position. The hunters were set to fire. And like lightning , Justin flew by them on his horse.

On reaching the confused tiger, he let out a cry and encouraged his horse to jump directly over the fierce beast. With all his strength he threw his lance and pinned the tiger to the ground. He reined in his horse a few steps beyond. "I leave the others for you, gentlemen," he said. "I have mine."

As he guided his horse to its place behind the elephants, the tiger, with a horrible roar, tried to get back on its feet. But the lance, as if it had been propelled by a steel spring, had not only cut all the way through the beast's ribs but also buried itself five or six inches into the ground. When finally the tiger managed to get to its feet, the shaft of the lance still in its body, in a rage the wounded animal spun around and, taking the shaft between its teeth, broke it. That was its swan song, and it came with a long sigh. Then, coughing up blood, and still pinned to the ground, the tiger expired.

As if the tiger's last lament had been a call, a call for combat or perhaps for vengeance, the first tiger reappeared sixty yards away and covered twenty of them in one bound. It was now so close to the hunters that another bound could take it to either of the elephants. But it had no time, for it had barely landed when two shots rang out together. The tiger rolled to the ground. Sir James, situated to the side of the tiger, had shot it in the hollow beneath its shoulder, while René, directly in front of it, had blasted its forehead. The tiger was stone dead.

But already three more tigers, perhaps in response to the deadly detonations, had leaped out of the jungle, roaring wildly. As if they understood what had just happened and feared that if they stopped moving for a moment the hunters would add them to the kill, they began to run in a circle in order to reconnoiter the enemy they were facing.

The hunters had too much experience to waste their shots, and they waited for the tigers to break from their feverish circle. Then one of them did. It leaped at René's elephant, but it was careful to come in from the side so as not to be trampled. So when René quickly took aim with one of his pistols and shot, he hit the animal in the thigh. It was only a minor wound and it made the tiger angrier still. With eyes flaming and teeth bared, it dug its claws in the elephant's side and tried to climb up to the howdah. The elephant, however, shook it off, and the tiger landed a few yards away. By then René had been able to aim his pistol a second time, and this time he shot the tiger in the neck. The elephant walked over to the tiger, and raising its trunk to protect itself from the tiger's claws, the elephant tried to crush the tiger under its huge feet. But the tiger slipped aside, and once more it leaped, this time clawing at the elephant's chest. Bernard, on the far side of the howdah, tried vainly to take aim at the animal, but fortunately, although neither hunter was now able to see the tiger, the mahout, with one leg caught by the tiger's claws, was able to plunge his lance into the tiger's chest. The big cat's grip loosened. It dropped to the ground, and immediately the elephant stepped forward to crush the last life out of it.

In the other howdah, Sir James, Hélène, and Jules were in even greater danger. While one tiger was attacking their elephant from the front, a second had leaped onto the elephant's rump, where, unfortunately for the tiger, it was open to a shot from René. He aimed and fired, but even though the bullet went through the beast's heart, the tiger at first did not even loosen its grip. It twisted its head, it bit at the wound; then it fell to the ground, dead.

The head of the other tiger was not more than a few feet from Hélène when Sir James managed to set the two barrels of his gun directly against the animal's fierce flesh and pulled the triggers. Lead, wad, and flames tore into the tiger. It too fell dead.

They could all finally breathe again.

François, his beaters, and the dogs came out of the jungle. Two of the beaters had been in the path of the last three tigers, and one of the men had had his head crushed while the other had had his chest ripped open. They had died so quickly that they'd had no time to cry out, or if they had, their cries had been drowned out by the horns, the barking, and the shouts of the other beaters. When François's men saw the five tigers lying on the ground, not more than forty or fifty yards apart, they quickly forgot their two dead friends. For among Bengalis and the Burmese, five dead tigers is easily the equivalent of two dead men.

Adda, on her little Burmese horse, similar to Justin's, came to meet the procession. Then she rode back to the settlement to announce that the four guests and her three brothers were safe and sound, though two dead men were being carried back to the plantation on stretchers.

The two elephants, Omar and Ali, who had been wounded, though not severely, had earned new respect from the two girls, and Hélène expressed her wish to buy them to help guard and protect the house. René told the two sisters that from that moment on they could consider the elephants to be their own property. He would take responsibility for making the necessary arrangements with the elephants' owner by using the *shabunder* as intermediary.

That evening Jane came down with a fever, which everyone attributed to fatigue after the day's events. Her sister stayed by her side. René and Sir James went off to talk, and later, when they asked Adda how Jane was, she told them that she had heard Jane weeping in the sisters' room, but as she did not want to be indiscreet, she had not gone in. James saw that René was deeply concerned about the girls' unhappiness, especially Jane's, and he promised to find out the next day the cause behind her great sadness.

In that torrid zone, nights were pleasantly cool. The two men walked for a long time, until one in the morning. Through the muslin cloth hanging over Jane's window, they could see a candle flickering in her room like a star lost in vapor.

The next morning, René was saddened but not surprised when Sir James brought word that Hélène was asking him to pay a visit to Jane, whose condition was growing worse. As the young man and the two sisters had grown to be so close, it would have been inappropriate for René to refuse. René asked Hélène to accompany him, but she answered that she thought that she would be in the way. Apparently, Jane wished to speak with him privately.

René knocked softly on her door. A thin, quavering voice said, "Come in."

LXXV

Jane's Illness

IN THE ROOM all the shutters were closed, so the interior was cool and dark with a faint breeze drifting in through the louvers. Jane was lying on the chaise longue. As René came in, she stood up and reached out her hand.

"You asked to see me, dear sister," said René. "Here I am." Jane motioned to a chair placed near the head of her chaise longue, then with a tired sigh lay back down.

"Yesterday," Jane began, "as we were coming back to the plantation, my sister expressed her desire to keep the two elephants that have taken such good care of us. You answered that we should consider them ours, and then you expressed your intention of leaving in a few days."

"That is true," said René. "Circumstances pressure me to leave soon. My captain granted me leave, by special favor, only for the time absolutely necessary to bring you to your home and to see you settled. That has been done. Thanks to God, you and your sister have arrived here safely. Your sister has found the protector she was expecting, and the first priest coming through on the way to China or Tibet will bless their marriage."

"Exactly," said Jane. "My sister would have preferred that you be here for the wedding."

René looked sadly at Jane, and, taking one of her hands between his own, he said, "You are an angel, Jane. Only powerful reasons can keep me from answering you as I would wish to."

"So you refuse?" Jane asked with a sigh.

"I must," René said.

"You must admit that you are not telling me the real reason you have to leave."

René looked her in the eyes. "Would you like me to tell you, no matter what the reason is?" René asked.

"Whatever it is," Jane replied, "I want to know. Sometimes the truth is the most painful medicine, but it is always the most effective one. I am waiting!"

"Jane," said René, trying to be strong, "unfortunately, you are in love with me." Jane uttered a tiny cry.

"And unfortunately, I cannot be yours." Jane put her hands over her face and burst into tears.

"I would have preferred not to have said what I have just told you, Jane," René continued. "But I felt that in all honesty I had to."

"That is enough," said Jane. "Please leave me."

"No," said René. "I cannot simply leave you like this. You must know what is keeping us apart. You can then be my judge and your own."

"René," Jane said, "you see how weak I am. I was not strong enough to deny that I love you. And now you tell me that there is some impediment to our union, some insurmountable impediment—well, then, go on. You have injured me. Now cauterize the wound."

"Allow me to touch you with a brother's hands, Jane, and not with the hard hands of a surgeon. Forget that the veil has been torn and that through the rent I was able to see what you were trying to hide. Give me your two hands, and lay your head on my shoulder. I do not want you to stop loving me, Jane. God forbid! But I would like you to love me differently. You were born in 1788, my dear friend. You were two years old when a young cousin named Hector de Sainte-Hermine joined your family to sail with your father and learn the seaman's life. He was the third son of your father's eldest brother, the Comte de Sainte-Hermine. Perhaps you do not remember him, but certainly your sister would."

"I too remember him," said Jane. "But what does that young man have to do with the insurmountable impediment that keeps us apart?"

"Let me tell you the whole story, Jane. When I finish, you will no longer doubt my loyalty.

"That boy left with your father and undertook three sea voyages. He was beginning to enjoy the life of a sailor when the Revolution broke out. His father summoned him back home near the end of 1792. You surely remember his departure, Jane, because it was so painful for him. He wept hot tears, it was that difficult for him to leave you. He called you his little wife."

A thought flashed into Jane's mind. "Impossible!" she cried, looking at René in horror.

"Hector," René continued without a pause and without any indication that he had noticed Jane's surprise, "went back home, only to see his father beheaded, his eldest brother shot, and his second brother guillotined. Faithful to the oaths he had sworn, he followed their path. Then peace came. We all thought everything was over. Hector felt free again, and he viewed the world anew, as if scales had fallen from his eyes. He could venture forth, he could fall in love, he could place hope in the future."

"And he fell in love with Mademoiselle de Sourdis," said Jane, her voice breaking.

"And he fell in love with Mademoiselle de Sourdis," René repeated.

"But then what happened?" Jane asked. "How could he leave at the very moment the marriage contract was being signed without anyone knowing why or how? What became of him? Where is he?"

"As they were signing the contract, one of his friends appeared and asked that he carry out a promise he had made. His word had been given, and he chose to jeopardize his happiness and risk his life rather than to hesitate a single instant and compromise his honor. He dropped the pen with which he was about to sign his marriage contract, and he slipped out of the room. He ran to where he could hear the voices of his dead father and brothers. Eventually he was captured. Thanks to the intercession of a very powerful man, instead of being shot as he requested, he was imprisoned in the Temple. Three years later, when the Emperor, who thought he was dead, learned that he was still alive, he deemed three years in prison to be insufficient punishment for a man who had dared rebel against him; so he sentenced Hector to become a simple soldier or a common sailor, with no hope of promotion.

"Hector, having begun his military career in the navy with your father, asked to be allowed to become a sailor. His request was granted. Then, because Hector thought that he would have greater freedom as a freebooter than in the regular navy, he went to Saint-Malo and hired on with Surcouf on the brig *Revenant*. You know how by chance the *Standard*, on which you, your sister, and your father were sailing, met the *Revenant*. You watched the battle. That is where your father died. . . .

"But, as I was saying, Hector was a member of Surcouf's crew. He heard the name the Vicomte de Sainte-Hermine, he saw that he was dead. He heard you express the wish that your father's body not be thrown into the sea. He spoke to Surcouf, and Surcouf agreed to keep his body on board. In addition, Surcouf authorized Hector to follow you everywhere, never to let you out of his sight until you and your sister were settled on your plantation.

"Now, my dear Jane, you know everything. There is no need for me to tell you the rest. But I need for you to keep all this an absolute secret, even from your sister.

"That child who learned the first principles of a seaman's life from your father and who was so sad to leave you when he was summoned back to his family in 1792; that child who saw his father beheaded, his eldest brother shot, and his second brother guillotined; that young man who, despite the terrible things that had happened to his father and brothers, followed in their footsteps; who, believing the war was over, declared his love to Mademoiselle de Sourdis; who, because of that infamous marriage that never took place, promised himself he would never give his love to another; who was captured while fighting against the Emperor; who, instead of being shot, spent three years in the Temple prison; that man whose life, in the end, the Emperor spared, on the condition that he become an ordinary soldier in the army or a simple sailor in the navy; that young man, Jane, was the Comte de Sainte-Hermine, your cousin—me!"

Dropping to his knees beside Jane's chaise longue, he took her two hands in his and covered them with kisses and tears. "Now," said René, "you can decide for yourself. Can I, without failing in all the duties of an honest man, be the husband of any other woman than Mademoiselle de Sourdis?"

Jane tried to smother her sobs. She threw her arms around her cousin and with icy lips placed a kiss upon his forehead, then fainted dead away.

LXXVI

Delayed Departure

WHEN JANE FAINTED, René's first inclination was to pull some English salts from his pocket for her to breathe. But he thought better of it. Returning her immediately to her senses would be returning her merely to a world of pain. Perhaps, if he let nature do its work, while she was unconscious she might regain the strength she would need when she awoke, as the day draws its strength from night shadows and morning tears.

Soon Jane did indeed sigh. She was beginning to regain her senses; René, who was holding her closely, could feel her heart beating on that shadowy threshold between life and death. She opened her eyes, and without really knowing where she was, she murmured, "How peaceful I feel!"

René said nothing. Now was not the time to dispel illusions or interfere in any way with those first vague hints of her return to her senses. On the contrary, with his own potent magnetism he strove to prolong her tenuous, transitory state, hovering as she was between life and death. It was almost as if her soul were suspended above her body, but little by little it returned and her thoughts came back to her, and, with those thoughts, awareness of her situation.

As is the case for those who have done nothing to bring misfortune upon themselves, her despair was both sad and sweet. It soon turned to resignation. Tears continued to stream from her eyes, but not violently, and she was no longer sobbing; rather, her tears were like the sap that flows from a young tree in the springtime when an axe has cut it inadvertently.

She reopened her eyes, and she saw the young man sitting beside her. She said, "Ah, René! You have stayed beside me. How good of you. But you are right. For you as well as for me, this situation cannot continue. Only please stay a moment, so that I might draw strength from you against myself. You will see that I shall do whatever is possible when reason and will are working together. As for your secret, have no fear. It will remain as deeply buried in my heart as the dead are buried in their tombs.

"Believe me, René, that despite all that I have suffered and shall yet suffer, I would not wish never to have known you. When I compare all my suffering these recent times with the path of my life before I met you, and with whatever course it may take after you have departed from it, I prefer my present life, however painful it may be, to the colorless life that lies behind me and the aimless life that yet awaits me.

"For now, let me remain in my room along with my memories of you. Please go back downstairs. Tell them that I shall not be coming down, that my sickness is not serious, that I am merely tired. Say that you have advised me to stay in my room. Send up some flowers, and come see me if you have a moment. I shall be grateful for anything you can do for me."

"Must I obey?" René asked. "Or should I stay, in spite of what you are saying, until you've had time to gather your strength?"

"No. Obey me. Only when I say to you 'Don't leave!' must you not heed my words."

René rose to his feet. He kissed his cousin's hand with a brother's tenderness, then stood for a moment watching her, before he went to the door. There he turned and looked back once more. Then he left.

Hélène was the only one to realize how seriously Jane was ill, and she attributed her illness neither to her fatigue nor to the dangers she had faced. She understood the real cause.

A kind and gentle spirit, Hélène was more rational than she was passionate, and she was not marrying for love. She had met Sir James in society, and while she found him attractive and noble in three ways—in mind, in birth, and in his heart—in reality she did not love him so much that her life's happiness depended on their life together. His feelings for Hélène were roughly the same. He had come from Calcutta as agreed, but he'd done so more like an honorable man keeping a promise than like a lover eager to rejoin the woman he loves. Had it been necessary, he would have traveled around the world as promptly as he had covered the four or five hundred leagues from Calcutta to Betel Land, and if, at the end of the journey, he had not found Hélène waiting, he would have been surprised, because any well-born woman is as much a slave of her word as is a man, but he would not have been in despair. In that way, their two hearts were made for each other, and in their life together they were likely to be comfortable, content.

But that was not the case with Jane. A free spirit with a passionate mind and a burning heart, Jane needed to love and to be loved. Appearances mattered little to her. She had not cared that René wore the suit of an ordinary sailor. She had not wondered if he was rich or poor, noble or common. He had simply materialized as her hero, her savior when she was struggling against a rapacious pirate's arms and kisses. She had seen René leap into the sea to save a poor sailor who had been given up for lost by his comrades when he fell prey to a shark; she had seen him fight and conquer the monster, the terror of every seaman. She had seen an honor-bound René, simply to protect her and her sister, undertake a fifteen-hundred-league journey during which he had faced Malay pirates, tigers, serpents, and bandits. She had seen him dispense gold as generously as a nabob. What else did she need to see or know? And he was young, handsome, distinguished. She had told herself that Providence and not chance had brought them together, and she had loved him as a person of her eager, romantic nature falls in love for the first time. She loved him with all her heart. And now she had to abandon all hope of being loved in return, a hope she had nourished from the first day they met up to this very moment. But now she had been forced to see the failure of that hope in her own heart and in René's. And what would become of her now, in this wilderness four thousand leagues away from France? What good could come of a burning heart destined to live in unhappy solitude and to fade away in despair's sunless winter? How fortunate her sister was! She loved and she was loved. Yet a love like that shared by Hélène and Sir James would never have satisfied Jane.

A woman who has never been beautiful has never been young, but a woman who has never been loved has never lived. In her despair Jane ripped to shreds her tear-soaked cambric handkerchiefs, in the corner of which she had dreamed of one day sewing René's initials with her own.

The day passed in that fashion. Her indisposition gave her the excuse for not coming down. Hélène suspected that Jane's illness had not been caused by fatigue or fear in the wake of the dangers she had faced, and she took the unusual step of sending up to find out if Jane would see her. Jane agreed, and almost immediately she heard her sister's steps in the corridor.

Jane swallowed back her tears and tried to smile, but scarcely had she seen her dear sister, from whom she never hid anything, than she began to sob again, and opening her arms to Hélène, she cried, "Oh, sister, how miserable I am! He does not love me, and now he is leaving."

Hélène closed the door, locked it, then threw herself into Jane's arms. "Oh!" exclaimed Hélène in answer to her sister. "Why did you not tell me about your love when there was still time to combat it?"

"Alas," Jane replied. "I have loved him from the moment I first saw him."

"How egoistical I was!" said Hélène. "I was thinking only of my own feelings instead of watching out for you, as was my duty as your older sister and second mother. I was counting on the man's loyalty!"

"Oh, don't accuse him," Jane cried. "The heavens are witness that he has never consciously done anything to make me love him. I loved him because he was the most handsome, the most chivalrous, and the bravest of any man I've known or heard of."

"And has he told you that he did not love you?" Hélène wondered.

"Oh, no! No, he understands how much that would have hurt me."

"Is he married, then?"

Jane shook her head and answered, "No."

"Is he just being considerate, perhaps?" asked Hélène. "Does he think you are too rich and noble to be the wife of a simple naval lieutenant?"

"He is nobler and richer than we are, sister!"

"Well, there must be some secret in all that," said Hélène.

"More than a secret. There is a mystery," Jane replied.

"A mystery you cannot tell me about?"

"I swore."

"Poor child. At least you can tell me what I can do to help you."

"Get him to stay as long as he possibly can. Each day he remains here will be one more day added to my life."

"And you plan to keep seeing him until he leaves?"

"As much as possible."

"So you are sure of yourself?"

"No, but I am sure of him."

The window was open, and Hélène stepped over to close it. Looking down, she saw Sir James in the courtyard talking to four or five dust-covered men who clearly had come a long way. They were talking loud and seemed in high spirits.

Catching sight of Hélène, Sir James called out: "Ah, Hélène, my dear, please come down. I have some good news for you."

"Yes, go down quickly, Hélène," said Jane. "And come back up as soon as you can to tell me what the news is. Alas!" she murmured. "Nobody has any good news for me."

Jane had not long to contemplate further her unhappy destiny, for Hélène had soon returned. "You understood why we let those priests who said prayers for the dead over our father's body leave Betel Land without asking them to stay and bless our union, don't you?" Hélène asked.

"Yes," Jane replied. "You thought it would be an impiety to have the same priests first chant a mass for the dead, then proceed to a wedding mass."

"Well, God is now rewarding us. Father Louis, an Italian priest living in Rangoon, takes a journey through the kingdom every two or three years looking for pieties he might render, and Sir James Asplay has just learned from these Peguans seeking jobs as farm laborers that in three or four days Father Louis will be here. Ah, Jane dear, how lovely it would have been if four of us could have been made happy on the same day!"

LXXVII
Indian Nights

LIFE BECAME FOR JANE a succession of extreme emotions and contrasting sensations. When René was with her, she felt alive with all of life's resources at her call; when he was gone, she languished, and her heart seemed scarcely to beat.

René, who truly loved her with all the love of a relative or friend, did not minimize the seriousness of her condition. Nor did he escape the girl's captivating influence, for he was young and high-spirited, and Jane was beautiful and passionately in love. With longing glances, the little pressure of her hand, her sighs, she made the blood of the young man she loved race a bit more. For René, his attraction to her in their long, impassioned conversations was both sensual and painful. Trying not to fall in love when one is twenty-six years old and in the fullness of life and youth, when the sky and earth and air are all intoxicating you with the Orient's heady excitements and every breeze is whispering the imperative "Love," is like fighting against all the powers of nature.

It was as if René was every day setting himself in the way of an overwhelming temptation, yet daily he left the same field of battle as the victor. Surely he was put to the test in trying to remain as impassive and strong in the face of that pretty peril as much as he was in the face of less delectable dangers in the jungle's depths or on heavy seas.

The bedrooms on the second floor of the house opened onto balconies that looked out either to the west or east. On one of those balconies René and Jane would spend the best part of every night. For adornment Jane preferred flowers to diamonds, pearls, and other precious stones that rarely left their hiding place in a jewelry box, and there, on the balcony, without realizing and certainly not calculating the seductive power of its perfume, she would weave necklaces with the lovely, sweet flower called the *mhogry*.

The mhogry, which resembles jasmine or lilac though its fragrance is more like tuberose or mock orange, has a calyx that is white, pink, or yellow and rests on a long corolla, through which one can pass a thread. A necklace of the mhogry envelops its wearer in alluring perfumes.

There, on the balcony, too, they could behold the prodigiously splendid Indian nights. In the Indies sunrises and sunsets alike are breathtaking. The sky vaunts all the colors that a skillful fireworks artist would bring to the flames in a pyrotechnic display. On lovely fall and spring days, to the extent that it is possible to distinguish fall and spring from the rest of the year, when the full moon rises, it looks more like our pale sun in the West. If the sun is made of fire, the moon is made of gold, and its diameter is enormous. When the moon reaches its zenith, by its light one can read, write, and hunt as if it were daylight. The nights are splendid in their variety. Sometimes they are so dark that you cannot see two steps ahead; other times you'd think it was day, except the light is coming from the starry sky, from the infinite number of constellations, many unknown in Europe, that are spread out over the firmament. The stars seem closer in the Indies, more numerous, more brilliant than in our hemisphere, and the moon, instead of weakening their light, seems to reinforce it with its own.

The wind also lends a magic to the night. It rustles in the tops of the tallest trees and in the thick grasses. From the flowers it receives a thousand heady scents as they surrender their perfumes to the breeze. It is as if nature were burning incense on the altar of that universal God whose name might change but who himself is unchangeable.

With the night breeze wafting over them, the two young people would sit together, side by side, on the balcony. Jane's hand resting in René's, they'd sit sometimes for hours in silence. Intoxicated by the night, Jane might dreamily sigh over René's name and wonder at her bliss.

"René," Jane said one such evening as she gazed languorously up at the sky, "how happy I am. Why could God not simply grant me this happiness? I would not ask for more."

"Well, Jane," René answered, "in that question is where our weakness lies, for we are but poor inferior creatures. Instead of trying to imagine a God of the universe who has established a cosmic harmony among all celestial bodies, we have created God in our own image, a personal God. We ask him to explain, not nature's great cataclysms, but our little individual misfortunes. But we pray in fact to a God, if he does exist, whom our human minds cannot fathom and whom human tools cannot measure. We pray as did people in ancient times: they would pray to their household god, a small statue a cubit tall, always visible and available. We pray as the Indian prays to his fetish, as the African prays to his grigri. If an event is painful or unhappy, we ask, 'Why did you do this? Why did you not do that?' We ask, yet our God never answers, because he is too distant, and he is not concerned with our petty passions in any case. Then we are unjust toward him, for we blame him for our misfortunes, we make our errors his, and if we are no less unhappy, we are now also blasphemous and sacrilegious.

"Dear Jane, you ask why God cannot simply allow us to continue here together, as if we in our insignificance could make of time something like eternity. Yet we are nothing but tiny atoms caught up in a nation's cataclysms, our lives poised between a world that is coming to an end and a world that is newly beginning, as we are pulled one way by collapsing royalty and another way by a rising empire. Ask God why Louis XIV weakened France by sacrificing so many men to his wars, why he ruined the treasury with his lavish marble and bronze caprices. Ask God why Louis XV undertook such disastrous policies so that he could say—and it was not true when he said it—'The Pyrénées no longer exist.' Ask him why, influenced by a woman's whims and bent under a priest's yoke, Louis XV made Holland wealthy and ruined France by revoking the Edit de Nantes. Or why he continued his grandfather's ruinous work by consorting with the likes of the Duchesse de Châteauroux, the Marquise d'Étioles, and the Comtesse Du Barry. Ask him why Louis XV, against all counsel, followed the advice of a corrupt minister and why, ignoring history's proof that alliance with Austria invariably brings misfortune to the fleur-de-lys, he brought an Austrian princess to the French throne. Ask God why he gave to Louis XVI bourgeois instincts instead of royal virtues, why he allowed the king to take an oath he did not intend to keep; why he allowed him to seek foreign help against his own subjects; why he brought him to such an ignoble end, his august head lowered to the level of a scaffold designed for vulgar criminals.

"There, dear Jane, in the tumult of history is where you find our story's beginnings. Thereby you can understand why I did not remain with your family even though I had found in my uncle a father and two sisters in my cousins. Thereby you can see why my father died too on a scaffold still red with the king's blood. Why my eldest brother was shot, why my second brother was guillotined. And why I myself, in order to keep my sacred promise, had to follow a path, without conviction or enthusiasm, that, at the very moment I was about to attain true happiness, bereft me of all hope. I was thrown into the Temple for three years and then delivered to the false clemency of a man who, by granting me life, condemned me to misfortune. If God answers you, if God answers your question 'Why can I not keep living like this? I would not ask for more,' he will say, 'Dear child, I have had nothing to do with the infinitesimal events of your two lives. Chance brought you together, and necessity forces you apart.'"

"Then you don't believe in God, René?" Jane cried.

"Yes, I do, Jane. I do believe in God. But I believe in a God who has created countless worlds, who has drawn their myriad paths in the ether. And because of that, he has no time to be concerned with the misfortunes or happiness of two little atoms inching their way over the surface of this terrestrial globe. Jane, my poor friend, I spent three years reflecting on these mysteries. I descended into the unfathomable depths on one side of life, and I came out on the other, not knowing how or why we are alive, how or why we die—knowing only, or so I tell myself, that God is a word, a very useful word for naming what we seek. When I die I shall learn who God is, unless death is more silent than life."

"Oh, René," Jane murmured, leaning her head on his shoulder, "such philosophy is too weighty for someone as weak as I am. I prefer believing. Believing is easier, and not so hopeless."

LXXVIII

Preparations for a Wedding

THOUGH STILL A YOUNG MAN, René had endured much suffering; hence, his world-weariness and his indifference to danger. At the age of twenty-two, an age when life normally opens up before a man like a garden bursts into bloom with flowers, it had closed for René. He had suddenly found himself in the Temple, where four prisoners had just committed suicide and almost all the others waited only to ascend the scaffold. From his point of view initially, God was unjust: God was punishing him for following the example and precepts his family had set for him in their devotion to royalty. He had spent much time reading and reflecting upon God's justice, and man's, before he came to realize that devotion outside the law can sometimes be criminal, and that the only devotion truly acceptable in the eyes of God is devotion to one's country. Furthermore, he had begun to think of God primarily as the creator of all those worlds and universes spinning harmoniously in space by the thousands rather than as a personal God who, after noting the birth of each man in his registers, then determines each man's destiny. And if René was mistaken, if against all probability, even against all possibility, God was indeed unjust and blind—if the lives of his human creatures were not composed materially of accidents and not subject to chance's whims, but unfolded instead by some implacable divine design—then he would fight against that God; and despite God he would be an honest man.

René's period of trial was long, and he had come out of it purified and infrangible, like well-tempered steel. His childhood beliefs had fallen one by one at his feet, as in a battle the poorly jointed pieces of one's armor might drop by bits to the ground. But then, like Achilles, he no longer needed armor: adversity had become his mother, and she had dipped him in the Styx. No longer did he trust that God would, or would not, protect him from any dangers he might encounter; he now entrusted his protection to his own strength, his own skill, his own sangfroid. The qualities that nature had generously bestowed upon him he brought to his moral and physical education as he perfected the habits of his mind and body. He became responsible for his own destiny. So he no longer had need or reason to blame God for the petty events or serious trials in his life. He did no evil, because he detested it, was horrified by it, for he knew evil well, and he did good without need of any reward. For by doing what was right he was merely performing his duty as an individual to the society that sustained him and his fellow human creatures.

Of such a man, Jane had correctly said to her sister, "I cannot trust myself, but I trust him." And taking advantage of the little time René could remain in Betel Land, she sought out his company as much as possible every day. In the morning they would take long horseback rides around the plantation, and only when the bell rang for lunch or the heat forced them back would they come home. Then, later in the afternoon, they would ride off again. If sometimes they went farther than was prudent, Jane had no fear, for René's gun was hanging at his saddle and his pistols were in their holsters. In fact, for some time now Jane seemed to have become completely indifferent to danger, as if she was seeking it out rather than trying to avoid it.

In the evening the two would meet on the balcony, where they would talk philosophy and broach all sorts of topics they would never have thought of discussing a month earlier. Whereas Jane had never had a particularly inquiring mind before, she now became curious. Often she'd return their conversation to the mysterious subject of death, and her ideas, if no more conclusive than Hamlet's, had become more clearly defined. Her mind came to such questions fresh; in time she was able to see and appreciate some of what René was thinking.

In appearance Jane seemed hardly different: a little paler, perhaps, a little sadder, and her eyes seemed sometimes feverish, but that was all. Regularly, near the end of their evenings together on the balcony, she would fall asleep with her head resting on René's shoulder. René would meanwhile sit motionless in the bright moonlight, his heart bleeding for this beautiful child who seemed to be destined for a life of sadness and misfortune. He might nod off, and then, though he'd never allow himself a tear when he was awake, a tear would slip from his eyes. At that moment, looking up at the heavens, he'd wonder if what we suffer on this earth might buy happiness for some in another universe.

Thus they passed their days and nights. Each day Jane grew paler and sadder.

Then one morning Father Louis arrived. If his arrival had been eagerly awaited by some, by others it had been dreaded. Unable to hide her feelings, Jane ran to her room, threw herself down on the bed, and burst into tears.

Father Louis knew he was expected. One of the Peguans at the settlement had been sent back to the city in order to serve as his guide. Fearlessly, in God's protection, Father Louis had set off with that man alone. He arrived on a Tuesday, and it was decided that the wedding would take place the following Sunday. That way, they'd have four days to prepare for the couple to receive their wedding blessing.

In the excitement over the father's welcome arrival, only René had noticed that Jane had disappeared. Attentive, even more concerned than a lover would have been, he went up to her room. Pushing open the door as a brother might do, he found her hopelessly sobbing on the bed where she had collapsed. Jane knew, and René understood, that the day assuring Hélène her happiness would also be the day of her own undoing, for once Sir James Asplay and Hélène were married, they'd have no reason to beg René to extend his stay, nor would he have any cause to further delay his departure.

René took Jane in his arms and carried her over to a window, which he opened. He smoothed back her hair and kissed her gently on the forehead. "Courage, my dear Jane," he whispered. "Courage!"

"Oh, courage is an easy word to say," she answered with a sob. "You'll be leaving me, and someday you'll be reunited with the woman you love, and I shall never see you again."

Without speaking a word—What could he say? She was right!—René hugged her to his breast. He could barely breathe. His heart ached, and from his eyes fell unaccustomed tears.

"How good you are," she said, touching his eyelids with her fingers and bringing them to her lips as if she wanted to drink his tears.

Jane was indeed truly unhappy, but René was perhaps even more unhappy than she. For he knew that he was the cause of her misery and he had no words or way to console his friend. Try as he might, his imagination could come up with nothing but words too banal to be acceptable. His mind was equally helpless. Sometimes only a heart can console another heart.

They remained silent, both of them lost in thought, both of them think-ing about the same thing: impossible love. In their poignant silence they were able to communicate their sympathies for each other more effectively than if they had exchanged banal words.

Each of the few days before the wedding found Jane sadder and more deeply in love with René, who was not insensitive to the sad yearning in Jane's love for him. If it had been determined that he were not to spend his life with Claire, the only other woman René might have chosen—for the attraction was strong—was Jane.

The preparations for the wedding only intensified Jane's pain. By tap-ping a tree called *tsy-tchou*, Bernard had been able to make a varnish as transparent and hard as the famous Japanese lacquer. The slaves had made candles from wax pods deposited by the *pelatchong* worm in the *caula-tchou* tree. They had gathered huge bunches of a particular jungle fruit that's used for making the alcohol in a drink that the Negroes and lower-class Hindus love. The activity and excitement could not help but remind Jane that, no matter how dearly she loved her sister, all this preparation was to ensure Hélène the kind of happiness she herself could never expect to at-tain. It broke her heart.

On Saturday evening, Jane experienced convulsions. René saw her rise from the table and leave the room. Assuming that she'd gone upstairs to her bedroom, he followed her. He found her lying unconscious on the fourth step of the stairway. He picked her up and carried her.

In her room, René administered smelling salts as they would ordinarily bring her back to her senses when she fainted; but they had no effect. Jane was lying in René's lap, her breast against his. Her hands were as cold as marble, her heart seemed to have stopped. His mouth was only a few cen-timeters from Jane's own, and he instinctively felt that by breathing into her lungs he could bring her back to life, yet he feared that if he placed his lips on hers, she would start, as if she had received an electric shock. He did not dare to run the risk; perhaps he was not as sure of himself as Jane thought.

Seeing Jane so pale, so near death, René felt his own heart break. Tears escaped his eyes and fell onto Jane's face. They were like dew fallen upon a wilted flower. Jane raised her head and opened her eyes.

"When you are gone, when you are gone," the child lamented, "what will become of me? Oh, I would rather die!" Her exclamation was followed by violent sobs.

René made a move to get help, but Jane clung to him, sobbing and say-ing, "Don't leave me alone. I do not mind dying, but I want you to be here."

Taking her in his arms, René held her gently to soothe her pain.

After a while René and Jane retired to the balcony, where they sat together until two the next morning. The household, still busy with wedding preparations, was awake most of the night too. The three brothers had cut down some trees in full blossom, which they were using to build an arbor from the house to the chapel. As it was to be a surprise for Hélène and Sir James, they had been working at night. They were planting the last tree when René led Jane back to her room.

"Those poor flowers were supposed to live throughout the springtime," said René. "Now they will be dead in three days!"

"I know someone who was to live more than just one spring," Jane murmured, "but who will be dead before they are."

LXXIX
The Wedding

AT DAYBREAK OF THE WEDDING DAY, René was about to ask after Jane at her bedroom door when he saw Hélène go into her room. The good-hearted young woman, regretting that she had not paid much attention to her sister the evening before, had come to beg Jane's forgiveness and to assure her that she had not abandoned her out of indifference. The two girls embraced. They held each other tightly for about a half hour, then separated.

When René heard Hélène return to her own room, he tiptoed to Jane's bedroom door. He could hear her sobbing and, between sobs, repeating his name. Quietly, he called out to her: "Do you need anything, Jane? May I come in?"

"Oh, yes," said Jane. "Yes, I need to see you. Do come in."

He opened the door to find her seated on her bed, in a long batiste dressing gown. Beside her lay a bag of rubies, sapphires, and emeralds; some of the stones were spread out over the sheets. From among them she was choosing the largest, most beautiful stones and placing them in a small perfumed pouch made of Spanish leather and embroidered with two letters, a "C" and an "S."

"Come," she said to René. "Come sit down here beside me." René pulled up a chair and sat down by her bed.

"My sister has just left," she said. "She is so happy. The only thing that saddens her is that I have been unable to hide my tears. She asked me when you were leaving; I told her that it would be tomorrow, for you are leaving tomorrow, are you not?" she asked, her voice attempting to simulate strength.

"You asked me to wait until the day after her wedding."

"And you were extremely kind to agree. Please believe that I am grateful to you, dear René. She asked me if I wanted her to try to keep you here several days longer. But I told her you had already made your decision, and besides, it's time to get it over with."

"Get it over with, my dear Jane? What do you mean by that?"

"I mean that I am suffering. I mean that I am making you suffer, that there is no way out of our situation, that even if you delay your departure by three, four, or five days, we shall still then have to part. You do not ask for a reprieve from death unless you are happy to be alive."

René sighed and did not otherwise answer, for he shared Jane's opinion. He was surprised, though, that she'd had the courage to explain herself so clearly.

Jane poured the rest of the jewels out onto her bed and continued sorting through them, again taking great care to choose the most precious of the stones. René hardly dared ask her what she intended to do with the stones she selected. There was something unutterably sad in her every gesture.

Daylight was beginning to brighten the room. The household had begun to awaken. René and Jane could hear footsteps in the hall. Jane reached out her hand to René, indicating that it was time for him to go back to his own room. René kissed the proffered hand and left.

He was now as morose as Jane had been. He pulled off his dressing gown and put on a morning coat, then went downstairs.

The horse that Justin normally rode without saddle or bridle was grazing freely in the meadow beside the house. Holding out a handful of grass and whistling gently, René made his approach. The horse took the grass from René's hand, and in that moment René sprang onto its back. The horse bucked wildly. Once René got his legs around it, however, the horse was all his, and no amount of prancing and bucking could throw its rider.

Up until that morning, no one but Justin had been able to mount *L'Indomptable*, the untamable, as the horse was appropriately called. Someone threw open a window and shouted, "Good God, René! Nobody dares ride that horse. You'll be killed."

In less than five minutes, though, the untamable had been tamed; the horse became as gentle as a lamb. Wrapping a portion of the mane around one hand, René used it as a bridle to guide the horse as he rode over to Jane's window. There, despite the horse's resistance, he got it to kneel down. But scarcely had he released the pressure on its neck than the horse leaped up and dashed madly off.

Keeping both hands behind his back, René did nothing to slow it down. But the horse was following a narrow path, and it suddenly took a sharp turn. In the path in front of them was an old black woman. With his knee and hands René got the horse to move to the right, but not quickly enough to avoid brushing the old woman's shoulder and knocking her down.

The woman screamed. Immediately, René too was on the ground. He helped her back to her feet. Any other man might not have bothered, for an old black woman is of little importance, especially in India, and a white man might even have considered it his right to knock her down and continue on his way. But not René; he was a good man. From his pocket he pulled out a little gold ingot, worth perhaps fifteen or twenty francs. The old woman tried to kiss his hands.

The accident had not been serious. When René was certain that the old woman could walk with no difficulty, he whistled for *L'Indomptable*. Leaping on its back, he started back to the house.

Justin was waiting to congratulate René; he had seen René spring without hesitation onto the difficult horse's back and in minutes tame it. René was still talking with Justin when the old black woman reappeared, this time in the courtyard. She asked the servants some questions. Then she disappeared into the house.

"Who is that woman?" René asked.

Justin shrugged. "She is a witch," he said. "Only what could such scum be doing here? With one shot we could be rid of her!"

Then, noticing that René was still wearing a pair of pants and his white jacket, whereas Sir James was already in uniform, Justin said, "You are going to be late, Monsieur René. The ceremony is to take place at ten o'clock."

René pulled out his watch. It was quarter till nine. "Good," he said. "I have plenty of time."

But he did go back up to his room. As he was walking through the living room, he was surprised to see the old woman leaving Jane's room. He could not imagine what she was doing there, but when he asked her, she shook her head as if to say she did not understand and went on her way.

René decided to ask Jane herself, only the bedroom door was locked. He knocked softly and asked if he could come in, to which Jane responded, "Impossible. I'm getting dressed."

René proceeded to his own room, where he quickly changed from his white pants and jacket into his elegant lieutenant's uniform. When he came back downstairs, he found the priest in the dining room.

Ever since they had learned the priest was coming, Adda had been busy making him a chasuble so that he would not have to officiate in his black robe, which would surely sadden the occasion. Thanks to an aquatic plant used in India to dye priests' robes golden, and adding to that her painting and embroidery skills, she had made a chasuble that would have been considered a work of art even in Europe. Certainly Father Louis had never been dressed so magnificently; his face radiated joy.

At ten o'clock the candles on the altar were lit. Everyone was ready, but Jane was so feeble that the priest invited her to take someone's arm to walk to the chapel. She chose René's.

The arbor of flowering trees, extending from the house to the chapel, was a great surprise, and the trees seemed to have magically taken root. The marriage medallion and the wedding ring had been brought from Europe. As there was no mayor in Betel Land, it was to be strictly a church wedding, not a civil one. After the customary questions and the couple's affirmative responses, the priest slipped the ring on Hélène's finger.

And at that very instant, with a sigh, Jane collapsed on the chair opposite her. René quickly held out some smelling salts. Realizing that her own personal sadness would affect painfully everyone else there, she tried to pull herself together as she pretended that she'd simply knelt down for a moment. Only Hélène and René were aware of what had really happened.

Jane tried to take part in the marriage feast, but her strength failed her. She got up from the table and left the room. René glanced at Hélène, who motioned for him to stay. But then, five minutes later, she said, "René, will you go see how Jane is, please? You have served as a doctor for everyone, and except for that poor child who has been so ill, you have done miracles."

René got to his feet and hurried upstairs. He found Jane stretched out on the floor of her room, as she'd been unable to reach her bed or chaise longue. Lifting her by the shoulders, he dragged her over to the window and helped her into an easy chair.

He checked her pulse. Her arteries seemed to be boiling instead of beating. She would go from absolute prostration one minute to great exaltation the next, and then, when the fever left her, she would drop abruptly back into a torpor that was even more frightening than her fiery flush. It seemed that some serious accident had occurred in this beautiful human machine, which seemed no longer to respond to ordinary rules and remedies but rather to be subject to unpredictable, erratic whims beyond her will or repair.

"Oh," said René in despair, "are you trying to kill yourself, my dear Jane?"

"Oh," Jane replied, "if I had the time, I would not kill myself. I would simply die."

LXXX
Eurydice

⁂

THERE WAS NOTHING René could say. The despair he sensed in Jane's young heart roused all his pity. Her suffering had reached such a degree of intensity that René decided not to leave her side that day. He'd give her whatever support he could.

Dinnertime came. Hélène's heart was joyful, but all signs of joy disappeared from her face when she went up to Jane's room to see if she would be coming down. She found Jane in such a state of torpor that she could not imagine anything to distract a mind so stricken. She begged René to stay with Jane, for she understood that only the cause of her sister's pain could, if not make it cease, at least numb it.

René too was overwhelmed. No longer having words to speak to Jane, he could only sigh as he watched over her, and hold her hands. The language in touch between the two of them expressed more than any words they might have exchanged.

If René had thought that delaying his departure might heal Jane, of course he would have done so, even though what was taking him away was moral necessity, which for some is a force that pulls more strongly than any other. Jane herself had seemed to come to accept his departure, however. For the past week, she had been counting the days until Monday, if with dread, because once Monday had come and gone, time would cease to exist for her. It was as if her life had been tied to a clock that had been wound up for a week; once the week was over, the clock, and her life, would stop.

News of Jane's illness had spread all over the plantation, and everyone was saddened by the decline of their lovely young mistress. Everyone also held the same opinion: that the snake charmer had cast a spell on her. That is what they called the old black woman whom René had knocked down with his horse and whom he had later seen outside Jane's room. René had heard all the rumors circulating among the household servants about the woman, and he also remembered Justin's words: "With one shot we could be rid of her!"

Of course, René should have known better than anyone what was really causing Jane's illness. Still, when he went down to dinner—at Jane's request, so that he might make excuses for her—he asked Justin about the woman. He learned from Justin that they called her the snake charmer because of an uncommon gift that enabled her to handle without harm even the most venomous of serpents. Her talents did not stop there, however. It was claimed that she also knew the particular properties of poisonous plants and could put them to deadly use so that one might kill a person in minutes while another might cause an animal to waste slowly, painfully away. What connection could there be between Jane and a woman like that, René wondered.

He intended to ask Jane herself when he went back up to the sick girl's room, but the words dared not leave his mouth at the sight of the innocent angel. As he gazed at her, a vague terror crept over him. He began shivering, as if with unwanted premonitions. His heart suddenly tightened. He let out a little yell that made Jane start.

He rushed over to her. Like a father with a child he fears losing, he pulled her close to his breast, kissed her forehead and her hands. His caresses being as full of tenderness as they were devoid of any sensuality, Jane did not misinterpret them. Even so, unaccustomed as she was to them, she found them sweet, and she began to revive. Her heart beat more strongly, and her cheeks lost their pallor. It was her way of thanking her friend René for his sweet attention.

Night fell. The two young people went out onto the balcony as usual. The night itself might have been conspiring to bring Jane peace, for never had a more luminous sky lit up the shadows in the land. The starry sky belied distinctions between night and day, its diffuse light bathing every reach of their eyes in its glow. The breeze carried with it a delicate, somewhat pungent, odor that seemed to stimulate the blood and dilate the lungs; it brought all the senses strangely, more intensively, alive. Such power is found only in the burning air of Asia, and especially India.

René believed in the eternity of matter, for he had seen that sand could be divided into a thousand grains but never be completely destroyed. He did not believe in the soul, because not in any form had the soul ever appeared to him, and he believed only in what he could see and touch. Bichat had resolved that question, and René had closely studied Bichat's great book on death and life when was in prison. As he explained his philosophy of materialism to Jane, tears coursed down her cheeks in two pearly streams.

"So, René," she said, "you believe that once we part it will be forever, and that we shall never again see one another?"

"That is not what I am saying, Jane," René replied. "Chance has brought us together once, and should you go back to Paris or I come back to India, chance might bring us together again."

"I shall never return to France," Jane said sadly, "and you will never come back to India. Just as our hearts have been kept apart in this world by the power of your love for another woman, so will our bodies be kept apart for all eternity by the earth itself. You were telling me a moment ago, René, that you believe only in what you can see and touch. Yet I am forced to believe in your love for Claire de Sourdis, however invisible and impalpable that love may be."

"Yes, but the object of my love is indeed palpable and visible. I also believe in your love for me, Jane, although I cannot see it. For I can feel it: it surrounds me like the clouds in *The Aeneid* that hid the gods."

"That's right, René," Jane said, wiping her eyes with her handkerchief. She left it for a moment over her eyes; then, getting to her feet, she went on: "René, I have been cruel and self-centered; I am making you miserable because of my own misfortune. I shall see you tomorrow, René, and tomorrow we shall part. Please don't let me lose my courage for that crucial moment. I shall need all my strength, and perhaps you will need all yours too."

"Are you going back to your room, Jane?"

"Yes. I need to pray. I know that praying cannot heal me, but prayer is like opium: it dulls the senses. Only promise me one thing."

"What is that, Jane?"

"That you will not slip away without saying farewell. I shall need a long, consoling farewell. I shall have to fall asleep on your shoulder as I usually do, but this time I shall have to fall asleep thinking I shall never wake up."

René was reluctant leave Jane as he was assaulted by emotions he could not fully understand. He escorted Jane to her bedroom door, where he held her closely for a moment against his breast. Then he went back to his own room, although on his way he paused two or three times because he thought that Jane was calling him back.

Unable to fall asleep, he walked over to his bedroom window, to breathe in some of the night's cool air. The first chill of morning seemed already to be hovering just above the ground, and the white glow that had given the night its translucency was beginning to fade into a grayish fog. He breathed deeply in. That's when he thought he heard Jane's door open.

Thinking she might be ill, René ran to his own door, but he didn't open it as he didn't want to appear to be spying on her. He returned to the window. The night had lost most of its luminous glow, but still it was impossible not to recognize her.

Wrapped in her dressing gown, Jane was walking hesitantly, as if she were barefoot, toward the meadow. His first thought was that she was sleepwalking and that she had left the house without realizing it. But he soon changed his mind. For she was not walking ghostlike, as if in a trance; rather, she was taking her steps gingerly and trembling with pain whenever she stepped awkwardly on a pebble or some sharp stone. Once she looked up toward his window, but he had time to step back, so she did not see him.

Jane's strange venture was not only unusual, it was also unwise. The odor from the meats that had been grilled for the wedding feast still hung in the air, and it could have attracted some wild animal that, hidden in the bushes, could easily pounce on her without warning. René felt around in the dark for his loaded rifle. When he found it, he moved back to the window.

To his alarm, he saw a dark shape moving toward Jane, but in the want of light he was unable to make it out. Jane, however, was not fleeing; instead, she seemed to be greeting it. It, man or woman, René could not tell. Then, suddenly, Jane gave a sharp cry. She fell to one knee. She began rolling on the ground as if she were in great pain, while the dark shape started moving toward the woods.

Convinced that Jane had been murdered, René put the gun to his shoulder. The mysterious shadow had not taken ten steps when he pulled the trigger. A second sharp cry rang out, no less painful than the first. The obscure shape crumpled to the ground, jerked convulsively two or three times, then lay still.

René threw down his gun. He ran down the stairs and out the door, which Jane had left wide open. He saw Jane's body outlined against the grass. He rushed to her, picked her up, and carried her back to the house.

The gunshot had wakened everyone. At the thought of an attack, each man had grabbed the first weapon he could find as he rushed from his room. Justin and two or three slaves were waiting at the door with torches when René arrived with Jane in his arms. He had not even noticed the snake hanging from her foot, its poison fangs still buried in the wound.

"It's a checkerboard snake!" Justin shouted, grabbing the reptile and smashing its head against the wall. "Someone needs to suck the poison out!"

"I'll do it," said René, carrying Jane up to her bedroom. "Go look, and ask around. Sometimes Negroes have secrets to counteract snake venom."

"That's right," said Justin. "Three or four of you get your horses and go looking for the snake charmer. Bring her back here, fast!"

René had placed Jane on her bed. With her eyes closed and her hands folded on her breast, she appeared to be already dead. Her foot was as white and as cold as marble; from two tiny needle-like pricks oozed a little drop of blood. René applied his lips to the wound and began to suck the blood. His lips could feel a slight trembling in her foot.

By then the whole household had gathered in Jane's room. When René finally looked up, exhausted, he saw Hélène. Even paler than her poor dying sister, she was standing in front of the others with her equally pale husband, Sir James.

"Sir James," said René, "go quickly to my medicine chest and get a flask of ammonia and a scalpel." Sir James ran to René's room and almost immediately returned with the items he'd requested.

Around the wound a bluish circle as large as a five-franc coin had already appeared.

René poured a few drops of the ammonia into a glass of water. Then he took the scalpel and, like an experienced surgeon, cut an "x" in the wound; foul, black blood gushed out. Once again he set to sucking at the wound and alternately pressing it with his thumbs until at last the blood began to run red. He poured a dozen drops of the ammonia water over it. The pain was intense; Jane drew up her leg.

"God be praised!" cried Hélène. "She is not dead."

"She will not die until tomorrow, at the same time she was bitten today," Justin whispered.

Seeing some sign of life in Jane, however faint, René had her drink the glass of ammonia water. It was then that the men who'd gone to look for the snake charmer returned. They had found the witch's body lying not twenty yards from the spot where Jane had been discovered.

"Ah!" said René. "When I heard Jane's cry and saw her fall, I thought she was being slain. I had my gun in my hands; I took a shot. I killed the woman."

"Oh, poor man," Justin whispered. "You have killed the only person who might have been able to save her."

"My poor dear child!" cried René, hugging Jane against his breast and sobbing.

"Don't pity me," murmured Jane, so quietly that nobody else was able to hear. "Did you not hear Justin say I still have twenty-four hours to live?"

"And?" René wondered.

"So, dear love of my life," Jane murmured, "I still have twenty-four hours to tell you openly how much I love you! Then let death be welcome. For I have been counting on it; I just never expected it to be so indulgent."

At that moment the priest came in, though nobody had thought to alert him. Through her half-open eyelids, Jane discerned his presence.

"Leave me alone with this saintly man," she said. Then, she whispered to René, "Come back as soon as he is gone. I don't want to waste one minute of the twenty-four hours I still have left."

Everyone left the room.

Once all the witnesses to this sad event were outside Jane's room, they could give some rein to their pent-up grief. Hélène nearly passed out in her husband's arms, and he had to half-carry her back to her bedroom. What had happened had been so little expected that it had paralyzed even Hélène's tears.

René went out onto the balcony, where their two chairs were still standing side by side, just as he and Jane had left them. Sitting in his chair, René rested his head against Jane's and let himself sink into a pain deeper than any he had experienced before.

He could see now that Jane had calmly arranged her death to coincide with the exact time that he would be leaving her. And that woman she had summoned—that woman who had paid with her own life for her sordid love of money; that woman who had made him a participant in this sad dance of death—was she not like the Nubian slave whom Cleopatra, herself intent upon death, asked to bring an asp in a basket of figs?

Jane had set the schedule for her death. The evening before, she had made him promise that he would not leave without telling her, because she wanted to have the opportunity to say her farewells. But they would not be ordinary farewells; they would be eternal. And she had taken measures. She knew that everyone on the plantation, humans and animals alike, detested the witch, and she was afraid that if the woman entered the courtyard at night, she'd be greeted by barking dogs and cursing servants. So Jane had decided to go out herself to meet the witch, and to go barefoot so that it would be easier not only for her to steal through the house but also for the snake to inject its poison into her foot.

And now, rather than lamenting the limited time God was granting her to spend with René, she was grateful to have twenty-four hours to declare to him the magnitude of her love.

Her confession with Father Louis had been short. "I love René," she'd confessed, and that was her only sin. The priest left her at dawn; he had been with her no more than a half hour. To René he said, "Go be with the saintly child. She loves you, and you will have no trouble consoling her about her death."

When René went to her bedroom, she awaited him with open arms. "Sit down here beside me, my love," she said. "You know of course that you cannot leave me before I die."

"First show me your foot," said René. "I would like to see how things are progressing."

"What's the use? Has not my sentence already been pronounced? Now I have only twenty-three hours to live. I ask for neither appeal nor reprieve. I am happy."

"What did the priest say to you?"

"Many good, unconvincing things. He tried to give me hope. He told me that we are surrounded by spirits, as diaphanous as the air in which they float. So we cannot see them, but they are the souls of those who have loved us. They move around us, touch us. They whisper unintelligible words in our ears when we are awake; they speak to us while we sleep. They know things we do not know, for they understand fate's secrets. Still, sometimes they are able to convey to us, in part, certain revelations; we call them premonitions. 'It is true that we believe only what we see,' he said, 'but many proofs have made us realize how weak and how powerless our senses are. Before microscopes were invented, for more than six thousand years our eyes had never seen a fraction of the creatures now made visible by that instrument. The first person who looked into the world of the infinitesimally small, realizing that it was limitless, went mad. Well,' said the priest, 'someday perhaps someone will invent an instrument with which we can see myriad transparent things, just as we now can see what is immeasurably small. And then, by means other than with words, we shall be able to communicate with those sylphs we know only in poetry.'

"Well, my dear René, the thought that when I am dead my soul will never leave you, that I shall be able to follow you, to go where you go, to be part of the very air you breathe, in the wind that blows through your hair—absurd though the idea may be—gives me infinite joy. Did not Shakespeare say, 'There are many things in heaven and on earth that human philosophy has not even dreamed of?'"Jane's voice had grown faint; she let her head fall on René's shoulder.

"Are you in pain?" the young man asked.

"No, not really. But I am getting weaker. My foot is cold, the foot I shall use to take my first step into the tomb. The chill will rise little by little, and when it reaches my heart, I shall go from my own bed to an eternal one."

René could sense that she was falling asleep, so he stopped speaking, in the hope that from sleep she would draw strength for one final combat. It was a tormented sleep, interrupted by convulsive movements and unintelligible words.

Hélène came upstairs, and, finding the bedroom door slightly ajar, she looked in, to see how her sister was. Jane was asleep, her head still resting on René's shoulder. Hélène drew near and kissed her sister on the forehead.

"My God, Hélène," said René. "With all these people in the house, does nobody know what can be done? If not to heal her, at least to relieve the poor child's suffering?"

"Oh, do you think I haven't asked everyone, even the least witting? They all have told me the same thing: that death will not be painful, but that it is inevitable. My dear René, please tell her that though I am leaving her alone with you, it is not out of indifference but because I do not want to steal from her any moment of her last happiness with you." Bending down over her sister once more, Hélène kissed her a second time and tiptoed out of the room.

As Hélène was leaving, Jane's eyes opened. She stared into space for a moment, then sighed. "Oh, my dear René," she said. "I have just had the most beautiful dream! I saw, as clearly as I see you now, a lovely angel from heaven in all its light come down to my bedside. It kissed my forehead, it said 'Come with us, my sister, we are expecting you,' then it kissed me again and flew away."

To tell her the truth would be to destroy her illusion, so René said not a word.

"And now, my love," Jane went on, "let me raise a question. When I decided the other day not to survive your departure, you saw me sorting through those precious stones and putting some in a separate pouch?"

"Yes, Jane. And I was going to ask you what you were doing, but I thought that would be indiscreet."

"I saw that you were holding back," said Jane. "But since it was not yet time to tell you, I said nothing."

"The pouch," said René, "was embroidered with two initials, a 'C' and an 'S'."

"Those two initials were intriguing, were they not?"

"They are the initials of Claire de Sourdis."

"That's right," said Jane. "And the little pouch is destined for Claire de Sourdis, my *cousin*. Some day, when you have made Napoleon forget the mistake you made, when you have regained a position worthy of you, Mademoiselle de Sourdis will become your wife. Then you will say to her: 'Out there, in a country with hot breezes and burning passions, I met two young women, my cousins. First I saved their honor, and then their lives. Far from you, although you were always in my mind, I devoted my life to them. One of them, the younger, had the misfortune of dying. I loved her tenderly as a friend and brother, but she did not have my heart. My heart belonged only to you. She died for the love of me, for hers was one of those loves that kills when it cannot give life. But before she died, she took up this pouch and put in it a part of her personal fortune. It holds enough precious stones to make three complete necklaces, one of rubies, one of sapphires, and one of emeralds. She herself picked out the stones from a collection ten times larger. She herself embroidered your initials on the pouch. Finally, as she was dying, she asked me to present it to you in her place. You cannot refuse it, because it is given to you by a hand from the tomb. But do not be jealous: I never loved her. And besides, there is no reason to be jealous of the dead.'"

René began to sob. "Oh, say nothing more, Jane," he said. "Say nothing more."

"Whenever you see one of those necklaces, you shall have to think of me."

"Oh, Jane, Jane," René cried. "How can you think that I shall ever forget you?"

"I am thirsty, René. Give me some water." Water was the only thing she asked for that morning, and she asked for it two or three times.

René handed her a glass of water. She gulped it down. Her face clouding over, she seemed weaker still as she asked, "Has no one come to ask how I am? It seems that Hélène is being careful to honor my request to be alone with you."

Realizing that Jane honestly felt that Hélène was unconcerned about her, René was sorry to have hidden her visit. "Don't blame Hélène," he said. "She came up while you were sleeping."

"Ah," said Jane with a smile, "I was not mistaken. It was Hélène I saw in my dream, thinking she was an angel from heaven. Dear Hélène, she has almost everything one needs to pass for an angel, except wings."

"Jane," said René, "I shall not leave you even for a moment. But you are causing great pain for those who love you by not inviting them to spend some of this precious time with you, as you will be leaving them forever."

"You are right, René. Call everyone."

René laid her head gently back on the pillow, then went to get Hélène. He returned quickly, and Jane said to him, "Come sit down here beside me. Only you have the right to remain by my side until I die. Later tonight I shall say that I want to sleep, and everyone will leave. Then you will take me out to the balcony where we have spent so many delightful hours. You will hold me in your lap and I shall be able to say farewell to the sky, to the stars, to all creation, and to you."

They could hear people coming up the stairs to pray at Jane's bedside. First her sister Hélène appeared, then Sir James Asplay, followed by the priest. Behind them came old Remi, his three sons, Adda, and then François. Behind him followed the Burmese servants and the Negroes. They all knelt down.

René stayed by the dying girl's bedside. The priest stood in the middle of the room, with the others on their knees around him, as he made a touching farewell to the girl who had experienced so little of life: love's mysteries, the joys of marriage, the delights of motherhood. He then contrasted such earthly pleasures with the divine happiness reserved for God's chosen.

Father Louis had barely finished when Jane fainted away for the second time that morning. The priest ushered most of the company from the room, saying, "I think that we are fatiguing her unnecessarily. To enter heaven, there is no one who needs fewer prayers than this chaste child."

Only René, Hélène, and Sir James remained with Jane. René held some smelling salts to her nose. She started, moved instinctively, opened her eyes, and smiled at them. For she saw that at her bed she was surrounded by those who loved her, and in the chapel her dear father was awaiting her. She reached out her hand to Hélène, who threw herself into her sister's arms.

"You know, dear Hélène," Jane said, "that I could not keep on living. I consulted the poor old woman, whose death I caused, about the best way to end my life. She told me about the checkerboard snake. So I shall die because I wanted to die. Don't pity me. If René had left me today, I would have died a slow, sad, painful death. Only now I am the one leaving him, as I choose. Misfortunes we impose upon ourselves are always bearable. It's those that destiny imposes upon us that we have trouble resigning ourselves to. You can see how calm and happy I am. Except for my pallor, one might think that our roles were reversed, for you are the one who's weeping while I am the one who's smiling.

"My dear Hélène, so that I may die as I have dreamed of dying, I must die as I am at this very moment, resting on René's shoulder. His hands must be the ones that place my hands together on my breast for all eternity. You still have many long years of happiness before you, my dear Hélène; I have only a few minutes. Leave me alone with him, dear sister, and he will come tell you when everything in this world is over for us. May God grant that we meet again in the next!"

Hélène kissed Jane one last time. Sir James squeezed her hands. The strong lines of his face could not conceal his throbbing pain; a tear rolled down his cheek. He put his arm around Hélène's waist, and, holding her tightly, as if he feared that death might try to tear her from his grasp, he led her from the room.

Time passed; night came. But it came so brightly that in the bedroom it might have still been dusk.

"It might be about time," said Jane. "I can feel the chill rising as I descend toward the grave. I feel no pain, but I can sense that it is impossible to go on living." She pointed to her waist: "From here down," she said, "I am no longer alive. Carry me out onto the balcony. That is where I want to say my farewells; that is where I want to die."

René picked Jane up and carried her to the balcony. As they sat together, she in his lap, Jane seemed to breathe more easily and come a bit more back to life.

The night was as brilliant as the night before. René could see the path Jane had taken on the far side of the meadow. In his mind's eye he could still see the old black woman, and he could still hear Jane cry out as she fell to the ground. He could see the old woman crumple when he shot. The images racked his memory; he broke openly into sobs. He hugged Jane to his breast, crying, "Oh! Jane! Dear Jane!"

Jane smiled. "You were wise not to cry out to me like that yesterday," she said. "Otherwise I would not have been able to bring myself to die."

For a moment she fell silent. Then, her eyes seemed to dilate, as if they were taking in both René and the heavens. "Hold me closer, René," she said. "It feels like you are letting me slip away."

"Oh, no!" René cried. "No, I am holding you as tightly as I can."

"Then death must be pulling me away. Save me, René! Save me!" Her grip around René's neck tightened, she buried her face against his chest. René bowed his head over hers.

Some while later he felt her tremble. He raised his head; he saw Jane's face, twisted now in pain.

"Ah!" she cried. "It is gnawing at my heart, it is gnawing at my heart." She pulled René's head down to her and placed her lips on his.

"Adieu!" she said. "Adieu!" Then, in an almost inaudible voice, she added, "Perhaps we shall see each other again." And collapsed.

Stunned, René looked at her. Her eyes were open, as if she might have been still alive. He placed his hand on her heart; it had ceased to beat. He moved his cheek down near her lips; she had breathed her last, and her last breath had borne away her soul.

Still he gazed at her, waiting for some faint word, scarcely perceptible movement, to show that she was still alive. But no. She was dead, undeniably dead.

He carried her back to her room. He laid her on the bed and placed her hands together over her heart. Then he struck the gong.

Everyone rushed up, led by Hélène and Sir James. "It is over," René said, and they all burst into tears.

Hélène walked over to the bed. As she reached out to close Jane's eyes, René halted her. "Oh, no," said René, gently pushing Hélène's hand aside. "You know that she asked me to do that."

Once he had completed his sacred duty, René rushed from the room, saying, "Stay with her body. As for her soul, I am taking that with me."

Now, at least, one of them knew the answer to the great mystery they had so often explored in their discourse under the night stars.

Death had smitten Jane, and the tropical climate demanded that she be buried quickly. The priest stayed with her. Hélène spent the rest of her wedding night in her husband's arms weeping for her sister, while old Remi, with Adda and his three sons, made the funeral arrangements. Jules and Bernard built her a teakwood casket. Justin decorated the chapel with flowers. Adda wrapped the body and laid it among fresh branches on a mattress and pillow made of aloe fibers.

At five that afternoon again the gong was struck, sadly to announce that the funeral would begin. Everyone on the plantation gathered by the courtyard gate, near the steps where the casket was waiting. More prayers were said, and then four girls carried the casket to the chapel.

René had turned the two elephants loose. As if they understood the misfortune that had befallen René and the two young women they had protected, they remained observant of the proceedings. Indeed, they seemed to be grieving too. Like two stone giants, they stood mute and motionless on both sides of the chapel door.

Jane was laid in the vault where Eve and the Vicomte de Sainte-Hermine were already resting. As is often the case with primitive peoples, the religious ceremony was followed by a feast to which even the plantation's humblest slaves were invited.

The day after the funeral, René announced that he was leaving. Whatever Hélène's obligations to him, and although he had rendered great services to the two sisters, he knew that his presence at the settlement would only be a source of sadness, a painful reminder of loss, for Hélène knew all too well that Jane had died of her love for René.

As she was thanking René profusely for all his services, Hélène took the opportunity to mention the great personal expense he had undertaken to bring them to Burma. René merely smiled at her and courteously kissed her hand, and she realized it was useless to insist that he allow her to pay him back. Anticipaing his refusal, she proffered him a small chest that Jules had made and that she had filled with precious stones. From under his shirt René pulled the pouch Jane had embroidered. He raised it to his lips, then opened it to show Hélène the precious gems it held.

So, after emptying the chest onto the table, he chose just one stone—a beautiful sapphire—from among all the ones Hélène had wanted to give him. "The sapphire is a stone of sadness," he said. "I shall use it to make a ring that will never leave me."

Hélène proposed, in addition, a kiss. "Oh," he said. "That I can easily accept. It is a sister's gift to her brother." And he kissed her on both cheeks.

The next day everything was ready for his departure. He would use the same escort that had accompanied them on their journey to Betel Land. The elephants, however, would be left behind, as Jane had requested that they stay at the plantation. Sir James, hoping for better success than Hélène had had, asked how much they might pay for the elephants, but René dismissed the offer with his reply: "Jane asked for them, I gave them to her, and they are hers." At Sir James's insistence, René did accept his best Manton gun, on the condition that Sir James take one of his in exchange.

At daybreak the following day the escort was waiting in the courtyard. But René was not, and when they checked his room, they found it empty. They were about to begin a search when René came out of the chapel. He had spent part of the night beside Jane's casket.

René had final more visit to make, to Omar and Ali. They thought at first that he was coming to take them with him, but they soon realized that was not to be the case. They were not enough like courtesans to hide their pain.

Since there were no women on the return trip, they agreed to make only one stop between Betel Land and Pegu; they would camp overnight at the lake. René and François were riding small Burmese horses, which can gallop forever without tiring, but the men on foot were even more astonishing in keeping up with them at a tireless pace. Around noon they paused to rest for a moment during the heat of the day, in the deepest part of the forest. The three brothers had supplied René with large quantities of betel, some of which he distributed among his men, with the promise of more that evening and again the next day.

They reached the lake at about five o'clock. When they made camp they saw what looked like huge logs floating on the lake's surface, though in fact they were caimans of all sizes. Undeterred, the Negroes and Hindus, who had only to shed their knee-length blue sarongs as they wore what passed for swim attire underneath, made for the water. René and François meanwhile kept their guns at the ready, their eyes moving from the lake to the edge of the thick forest.

LXXXI

Return to Pegu

SUDDENLY ONE OF THE SWIMMERS SCREAMED and disappeared beneath the water. It was clear that a caiman had come up under him and, grabbing one of his legs, had dragged him to the bottom of the lake.

The anguished cry of terror sent all of the other swimmers hurrying for shore. Just behind the last man one of the reptilian monsters was churning up the water in determined pursuit. The man had barely touched shore when the caiman's head rose out of the water and the creature began pulling itself up onto land. It was no more than ten yards behind the Negro when he reached René.

"Well, what's the matter?" René asked with a laugh.

"That caiman want to eat my body," the Negro replied, and it seemed he was right as the animal was making directly for the man.

"So," René wondered, "now caimans are attacking people on dry land?"

"Master, he already taste human flesh, I think. Now he coming for me. But now me hunt him."

"But, my poor man, you have no weapons," said René.

"Me not need," said the Negro, who then turned to his companions to announce, "No, me not need weapons. Me need dat tree over der."

Instead of crawling back to the water, the caiman had stopped, perhaps to debate whether it should proceed since the man now stood among others of his kind. Yet the man was walking back toward the caiman, and he got so close that the caiman obliged by opening its jaws, so that the man could throw himself more readily into its mouth. The two jaws snapped together, but on nothing except air, and made a sound like that of one plank striking flat against another.

The caiman gave chase to the man. It was leaping four or five feet at a time, but the African quickly reached the tree he had pointed out to his friends. With the caiman gaining on him by the yard, the Negro made a great leap and climbed up the willow-like tree with the agility of a monkey. But he was not out of danger, as René soon saw, for like a giant lizard the caiman was climbing clumsily up after him.

The Negro slid out onto one of the horizontal branches, and the caiman, its hunger stimulated by frustration and all its physical effort, set out on the branch behind its prey. The man looked to be doomed, and everyone watching shared the shiver of fear. He had reached the end of the branch. And he simply dropped to the ground.

His friends rushed over to join him, and together they grabbed the end of the branch and began shaking it violently. The caiman, despite its hard head, realized that it had climbed into a trap. It started moving desperately, but it was clearly at a disadvantage in a quaking tree. It hung on with all four legs in its losing attempt to keep its balance on the unsteady branch until finally it slipped down under the branch like a saddle under a horse's belly. Then it fell to the ground, where it lay motionless. It had fallen on its head and broken its neck.

The men leaped on it, and an hour later, seated around a large fire, the guards were eating caiman meat instead of the caiman eating them.

Night was coming on rapidly. René had the men cut down trees and gather wood as they would need a huge fire to keep the caimans and wild beasts at bay, especially with the smell of roast meat in the air. Ten minutes later they had enough wood for the night, and René had them stack it so they could easily feed the fire whenever it began to die down. To keep up their spirits, he passed around more betel and invited everyone to sleep peacefully. He and François would take all the night watches themselves.

Once the fire was lit, the lugubrious concert of the jungle night began: tigers roaring, panthers mewing, caimans crying like sobbing children. From everywhere, it seemed, came a threatening voice, as if the forest, water, and jungle had been taken over by an army of demons preparing to tear each other apart. The air came to life last. Around eleven o'clock bats as large as owls started flying back and forth above the flames, their cries adding shrill notes to the frightful symphony as they flew through the dense smoke, which might have risen from the mouth of hell.

You needed a heart protected by those three layers of steel that Horace wrote of in order not to tremble at the chaos of noise. François, though he was a brave man, felt his courage beginning to fade when he saw two points of light bobbing in the darkness of the forest barely thirty yards away. He reached out to touch René's arm.

"Silence," said René. "I can see them." He had already raised his gun to his shoulder, and, as quickly as if he were doing target practice, he fired.

The shot was answered by a terrible roar that, like a signal, summoned countless other roars from everywhere around their bivouac except the lake. The threat was serious.

"Throw more wood on the fire," René ordered. François obeyed.

The Burmese and Indians woke up with a start, and in English René asked them, "Who among you can climb a tree and strip off all its branches?"

One Burmese man stepped forward. With François's cutlass in hand, he climbed up the closest tree with the speed of a monkey. Instantly branches were falling to the ground, for the man knew it was important not to delay.

Fortunately, the tree was full of resin, and when they threw the branches on the fire the flames leaped up to create a veritable rampart between their bivouac and the forest.

But the roars from the area where René had shot had not stopped. Either the wounded tiger was not ready to die, or, as is often the case, it was attended by its mate. René reloaded his gun and put François in charge of holding the four guns that made up his arsenal. Then, picking up some firebrands, he threw them into the branches of another tree rich in resin. The tree caught fire, and in an instant flames were rising from the base to the summit. Burning like a gigantic fir at festival time, the tree lit up the countryside for fifty yards around.

Down by the lakeshore René spotted two caimans trying to slip up on the men unawares, although the fire was beginning to give them pause. As René drew closer, he could see that the heat had begun to make their skins shrivel. Their big stupid eyes opened with surprise. They were the size of five-franc coins, and that was all René needed. He put a bullet through the eye of the closer caiman, not ten yards away. The animal jerked convulsively and fell backward just a few feet from the water. The Negro who had demonstrated his experience with caimans grabbed a firebrand and jammed it like a spear into the monster's mouth. The caiman, bellowing, dove into the water to put out the fire. The second one turned away and sank back into the lake.

The tree was still in flames, and burning branches, falling, were setting fire to the tall grasses and other trees nearby. The blaze grew even larger. The wind from the lake pushed the flames before it. They could hear the cries of animals that the flames surprised in their sleep. They could hear serpents hissing as they tried to flee, trees shaking as they thumped against them.

"Come, my friends," said René. "Now I think we can sleep in peace." And in the middle of the circle of flames, he lay down. Five minutes later he was sleeping as peacefully as if he had been back in his ship's cabin.

LXXXII

Two Captures

RENÉ WOKE UP AT DAYBREAK. François had remained on watch all night, but not a single animal, not even a caiman, had disturbed him. René gave the signal for breaking camp, after he'd distributed a swallow of arrack and some betel to each of his men.

Fortunately, the horses had been fettered, for they had been panicked by the sight of the fire and its reflection in the lake behind them. The animals who lived in the lake's dark depths cannot have had any idea what was happening to their habitat, which, mirroring the forest ablaze over a distance of a half league, looked like a lake of flames throughout most of the night. By dawn all the animals in the nearby forest had fled. René and his men could no longer hear tigers roaring, snakes hissing, or caimans wailing. Everything was quiet, except for the distant crackling of the dying fire.

All the men looked admiringly at René. It is unusual to be brave at night; many's the man who'd willingly face danger during the day but who will tremble after nightfall at the approach of a danger unseen, no matter how slight it would be by the light of day. René, though, was made of different stuff; fear held no sway over him.

They started out. While none of the men admitted his anxiety, they all walked at a resolute pace to get them out and away from the cursed forest. At about two o'clock they reached the forest edge; they could breathe more easily.

They could also stop to have dinner, for even the bravest among them would have considered it foolhardy even to pause inside the dark forest. Only now, back out on the plain, in full daylight, did they realize how long, and with what determination, they had walked with nothing to eat. From a pack on one of the horses, they drew a leg of antelope that had been smoked and roasted. They sat down joyously, and with their meat they drank a glass of arrack.

From that point they had only a two- or three-hour walk over the open plain. Few bushes grew there, and during the day wild animals were scarce. Without further incident the convoy made its way back to Pegu.

René's sloop was still bobbing at anchor just where he had left it. He called out, and immediately a boat put out from the *New York Racer* to come for him.

That same evening, in the presence of the port commissioner, René cleared up his accounts with the man who'd supplied the slaves, guards, horses, and elephants for the expedition to Betel Land.

There was nothing left to keep René in Burma. Chance alone had brought him there, and now that he had fulfilled his family duties toward the Sainte-Hermine sisters, he had no further reason to stay. So the very next day he hired the same pilot who had brought the sloop up the Pegu River. Knowing that sooner or later René would need him to travel back down the river, the pilot had waited patiently for René to finish his business in Betel Land and return to Pegu; he had meanwhile eaten all the rice he wanted for three or four pennies a day.

The date was May 22, 1805. And René had no idea what had happened in France since he had left the port of Saint-Malo on the *Revenant* a year earlier.

Like many of us who may have few reasons to regret having left our home country for a time, René nevertheless felt the hold of the motherland on him, and with it a certain nostalgia for what was then France. And what had France become? When René had left, Bonaparte was planning to invade England. Had he carried out his plan? Or had it been abandoned? Once he got back to Île de France and found Surcouf, he'd no doubt learn more of the situation and Napoleon.

The *New York Racer* moved quickly downriver with the current, and in only three days they'd traveled from Pegu to Rangoon. On the fourth day they were at sea, and René set his course for the northern tip of the island of Sumatra. Ten days later they were passing Aceh, in the north of Sumatra, and then facing the wide expanse of ocean, empty of even a rock, from Aceh east to the Chagos archipelago.

At daybreak the following day, the sailor on watch called out, "Ship ahoy!"

René hurried up on deck with his spyglass: near Cape Juzu were three ships, two of them sailing together toward the Chagos islands, and the third one heading directly toward them. Their shape indicated that the first two were merchant ships, but, as René well knew, even merchant ships were now armed like government warships.

He turned his attention to the third ship. There was no mistaking it. Its speed and maneuverability said that it had to be an armed corsair ship. René handed the glass to François, saying simply but firmly, "Look for yourself."

François peered through the spyglass; reacted excitedly. René smiled as François handed back the glass, saying, "By my faith, I would swear that's what it is."

The solitary third ship fired a cannon shot and raised its colors through the smoke. "You see," said René, "they have raised the Republican flag."

The other two ships together returned fire and unfurled the British flag. "Full sail!" René shouted. "Set our heading for the battle."

The three ships were about two leagues away from land, where the wind was nearly still, so they were soon hidden in their own clouds of cannon smoke. Farther out to sea, though, the wind was blowing from the northwest and it set the speed of the *New York Racer* at five or six miles per hour.

Picking up the full force of the wind, René races toward the increasingly thicker cloud that has enveloped the three ships. The incessant booming of the cannons echoes like thunder off the Malay shore. The three ships have been battling for nearly an hour when René can at last order his men to their battle stations. The cannoneers are in position, their wicks are lit; the sloop sails into the cloud of smoke.

René makes out the name *Louisa* under the poop taffrail of one of the ships, but he has little concern for the ship's nationality or that of the crew. He knows that it is fighting a French ship, and that is enough! "Fire on the starboard!" he shouts as the sloop comes alongside the enemy ship.

Moving past the enemy ship, which has no idea where this new line of attack can have come from, the *Racer* fires two shots from the cannons forward and aft, both loaded with balls. One shot strikes the base of the mizzenmast, and with a horrible cracking sound the mast topples over onto the *Louisa*'s deck.

Through the ever-thickening smoke, René hears a familiar voice rise above all the clamor, shouting: "Let's board 'em!"

René's bowsprit gets tangled in the rigging of the other enemy ship, but no matter—using his megaphone, he echoes the cry that rang out a moment before: "Let's board 'em!"

Through a gap in the smoke he sees an English officer on the ship's bridge. He passes his gun from his right hand to his left, takes aim and fires. The Englishman tumbles off the bridge and falls to the deck.

"Let's board 'em, my friends! Let's board 'em!" he shouts once more, and he is the first to clamber out onto the bowsprit. Eight or ten of his men, with François at their head, climb out along the shrouds and onto the bowsprit, then follow their leader along the bridge hanging over the other ship's deck.

The English are astonished enough to see men dropping down on them as if from the sky when suddenly René's voice thunders in perfect English: "Strike your colors for the *New York Racer!*"

The second in command begins to raise his arm to countermand the order, but his arm drops to his side and his words never leave his throat. The bullet from a pistol has gone into one temple and exited out the other.

The English strike their colors, and René's voice again calls out, in French this time: "It's over, my friends. The English ship has surrendered."

Then he stops to listen. All is quiet.

He waits a moment for the wind to lift the smoky veil still hanging over the *Louisa* and hiding her from the sister ships. Slowly the smoke begins to rise; it creeps up around the masts, hovers, thins.

Both of the English ships have surrendered. On the deck of the other René gets sight of the French captain, the new master of the enemy ship, standing with one foot on the English flag. René has not been mistaken. It is Surcouf.

The two men together raise up a joyous, triumphant cry. They are too far apart for the reach of their arms, so they embrace each other with the call of their names.

LXXXIII

Return to Chien-de-Plomb

NEITHER SURCOUF NOR RENÉ could immediately leave the ships they had just captured. But once all the formalities had been completed and the officers had given their word, once François had gone aboard the *Louisa* as its captain and Édeux, Surcouf's second in command, had taken over the English three-master the *Triton*, Surcouf and René both put their skiffs in the water for a visit.

They met halfway between their two vessels, and René leaped from his skiff into Surcouf's and threw himself into the corsair's arms. They decided to spend the day together and then have dinner that evening. Each vaunted the cooking on his own ship, but Surcouf found René's menu more appealing.

While they dined on board the *New York Racer*, René gave Surcouf a short version of his trip to Burma. He told him about the hunts, the attacks that came by day and by night, his combat with the Malays, and the duel with the boa. He related the circumstances surrounding Jane's death, but he did not reveal the cause behind it. He spoke of the return to Pegu from Betel Land, and of the forest fire he set to ward off the attacks by tigers and caimans.

Surcouf trembled with delight. "That's the advantage of going on land," he said. "You can have some real fun. I've had three or four nasty encounters with some English ships that let themselves be captured like idiots, although today I was thinking that this time I had thrown myself into the lion's jaws when fortunately you appeared and pried them open. Would you believe it? I was so busy with those two ships that I didn't even see you coming. And I have the reputation for having the best eyes among all the captains from Saint-Malo, whether they be Breton or Norman! So you can imagine how astonished I was to hear the music from your sixteen-pounders blending in with our own. Let me add, though, that I did recognize your voice the moment you spoke, even if you were speaking English. But do you know what we have captured?"

"I have no idea," said René. "I was not fighting to capture anything; I was coming to your aid."

"Well, my dear man," said Surcouf, "we have captured enough pepper to spice up the entire ocean from the Cape of Good Hope to Cape Horn. Three million francs worth of pepper, my friend. And a million of that is for you and your men."

"A million for me? But why? You know I wasn't fighting for your pepper."

"Sure, but how about your men? It is possible to refuse a million for one's self, but not for eighteen or twenty poor devils who are counting on that money to salt and pepper their soup for the rest of their lives. You can split up your share among them, if you want—five hundred thousand francs is no mean sum! But you will surely give them at least their own share."

"You mean that *you* will be giving it to them!"

"It doesn't matter whether you do it or I. They don't care where the million francs come from, only that they come.

"But to answer your other question, when you asked what was happening in France—if there was fighting on land or on sea. I have no idea, because the sound of cannons doesn't reach all the way to the Indian Ocean. The only thing I know is that the Holy Father, may God protect him, went to Paris to crown Napoleon emperor. I have not heard one word about invading England, but if I could give a bit of advice to His Majesty the Emperor, well, I'd say he should stick to his soldiering and leave sailoring to us."

As for Surcouf himself, he too had had a one-on-one battle with a shark, and he'd demonstrated that no less than René, he could maintain his equanimity in whatever perilous situation he might find himself.

Several days after René had left with the two sisters for Pegu, Surcouf too had set off, but to hunt down enemy vessels, and he'd made port on Mahé Island. There a pirogue had struck a sleeping shark, and the shark had overturned the pirogue somewhere between Praslin and La Digue. All the men in the pirogue, except for their leader, became the shark's prey, and they were all part of Surcouf's crew.

The incident had a profound effect on the *Revenant*'s crew, especially on the only man who had escaped the shark's jaws. He made a vow to the Madonna. But busy as they are, whether on deck or at their little leisure, sailors have a short memory.

While Surcouf was in port, an old friend living on Mahé Island invited him and some of his officers to the settlement he had founded several years before on the west side of the island. They left the *Revenant* in a longboat and quickly covered the distance. They had a fine day, until they began the trip back to the ship.

The longboat started back first, only now it was filled with fresh supplies for the campaign the *Revenant* was about to undertake. Manning the boat were one officer and Bambou, the captain's Negro, to whom Surcouf had given the gun and the game bag he normally carried himself.

Their host had meanwhile put the plantation's pirogue at his guests' disposition, and three of them—Surcouf, Ensign Joachim Vieillard, and Millien, the second surgeon—left shore with their host at the helm. Propelled by four strong Negroes, the pirogue skimmed over the limpid waters of the lagoon, a home for exceptionally huge, hungry sharks, and they could already see the *Revenant*'s newly painted guns gleaming in the setting sun when suddenly, in the pirogue's wake, one of those marine monsters appeared. It sensed the presence of human flesh, and it got so close to the pirogue that their host gave it a violent blow with his paddle.

But the animal was driven by instinct, and it did not back off. It picked up speed, and when it came alongside the boat, they could see it was even longer than the pirogue. Then, turning, and rolling on its side, it tried to take the boat, as it had no doubt decided its contents to be worthy fare for its gluttony. Its thrashing tail almost overturned the pirogue, and the crew and passengers were beginning to fear the worst. The shark kept coming at them, no matter that they struck it repeatedly with their oars and paddles.

It was during one of these assaults by the shark, its gaping mouth now reaching as high as the rails on the pirogue, that Surcouf reached into a basket and took out a fresh egg, a gift from their host, which he threw at the shark. The projectile slipped neatly into the shark's mouth, and the shark seemed to savor it. It closed its jaws with their triple rows of teeth. It disappeared underwater.

The danger had passed. The host, his guests, the negro crew, they all laughed about the attack and the egg that had satisfied the monster's hunger and saved their lives. They joked that the next time they would serve the shark an omelet.

Surcouf's recent combat with the two English merchant ships was his fourth since leaving Île de France. His crew had been reduced to only sixty-eight men. He'd decided, he said, to return to the French colony, unless René disapproved. René wanted nothing more.

On May 26, the *Revenant* and the *New York Racer,* along with their prizes, crossed the equator. On June 20, as dawn was breaking, the lookout called, "Land ho!" As the sun neared the horizon, they could see the mountains more and more clearly, and the next day at dawn found them between Flacq and the Îles d'Ambre. They recognized the bay where the *Saint-Géran* had foundered.

The surroundings seemed quiet. Surcouf, at the head of his little flotilla, set his course for Île Plate and sailed between the island and Point-de-Mire. Once through those waters, he headed for the Pavillons harbor. Just as he reached the Baie du Tombeau, Surcouf was met by the pilot boat. The pilot announced that there were no longer any English vessels cruising around the island, probably because of the preparations both France and England were making for war.

Surcouf, René, and their two prizes entered Port Louis with no difficulty. They cast anchor beside the Quai du Chien-de-Plomb.

LXXXIV

A Visit to the Governor

SURCOUF AND RENÉ, each bringing back a huge prize, were greeted joyously by the inhabitants of Île de France.

Of all our colonies, Île de France was perhaps the one most attached to the mother country. A French poet—a prose poet, to be sure, but Chateaubriand was also a prose poet—had given the island a poetic allure with his novel *Paul et Virginie* and made it even more assuredly a daughter of France. Its brave colonists, adventurous, full of fantasy and feeling, stood in great admiration of the tumultuous events we had lived through since the Revolution and the great wars we had undertaken with Bonaparte. They loved us not only for the benefits they gained in commerce with our vessels and enjoyed in the merchandise we sold them, but also because it is in their nature to value and honor grandeur.

For approximately sixty years now Île de France has been called Mauritius as for three generations it has belonged to England. Yet at heart, the island is still as French as it was when the white or tri-colored flag flew over Port Louis and Port Bourbon. If today the names of all those Breton and Norman heroes have been nearly erased from our memory, even though we ourselves can only vaguely remember names like Surcouf, Cousinerie, L'Hermite, Hénon, and Le Gonidec, there is not a child living in Port Louis who can not only recite their names but also cannot recount their exploits, to which the activities of pirates in the Gulf of Mexico pale by comparison.

On Île de France, our seamen would be welcomed as warmly during disastrous times as they were during prosperous ones. Many a time, on their signature alone, the famous banker Monsieur Rondeau would advance them the means to repair any losses or construct new ships, in amounts as high as two hundred or two hundred fifty thousand francs. It is true that our brave seamen always stuck together, and if any one of them had been unable to meet his commitments, ten others would inevitably have joined together to aid him.

By now René felt impervious to danger. He had thrown himself totally into learning as much as he could about being a seaman, and he appreciated fully what good advice Monsieur Fouché had given him about launching his naval career. He knew that if he had been placed as second in command on a government ship and had achieved half of what he had done in that position on Surcouf's ship or even as captain of his own little sloop, he would have won the praise of his superiors along with a lieutenancy on a ship in the imperial navy.

René had discharged his duties with tremendous accomplishment under the seasoned eyes of a man who had not the slightest streak of jealousy in his heart. Surcouf, who had been offered command of a frigate, was known and admired by all French navy officers, and a recommendation from him could place René as a midshipman on the vessel of his choice. René wanted now to return to Europe and take service under one of those illustrious captains commanding a ship like the *Tonnant*, the *Redoutable*, the *Bucentaure*, the *Fougueux*, the *Achille*, or the *Téméraire*. For that, he needed a recommendation from Surcouf. Surely Surcouf would not refuse.

Surcouf knew the governor of Île de France, General Decaen. He went to visit the governor and asked if the next day he would give audience to a brave lieutenant who wished to return to France so that he might join the battle for the waters off Spain or in the North Sea. With characteristic enthusiasm, Surcouf told the governor how bravely René had comported himself when they captured the *Standard* and how he had nobly given up his share of the prize so that he could take to Burma two French girls whose father, a passenger on board the *Standard*, had been killed.

General Decaen replied that he would be pleased to receive the brave man Surcouf was recommending, and the next day at the appointed time René appeared at the official residence. The doorman, however, hesitated to let him in. Noting his reluctance, René asked what the difficulty was.

"Are you sure that you are Monsieur Surcouf's second in command and the captain of the *New York Racer*?" the doorman asked.

"Perfectly sure," René replied.

The poor doorman's hesitation was not surprising. Since among corsairs uniforms are not absolutely necessary, René had chosen to dress in the current fashion and with his customary elegance. It was difficult in any case for René to hide the social class into which he had been born and raised, but on Île de France he saw no reason even to try. So he looked like he might be going to visit the Comtesse de Sourdis or Madame Récamier.

General Decaen, too, was expecting to greet an old sea wolf, a sailor with a crewman's cut, shaggy sideburns and beard, when before him stood a handsome young man with a pale complexion, gentle eyes, curly hair, and the trace of a moustache. And instead of being rigged in the probably colorful but not particularly well-cut battle uniform, he was impeccably dressed, right down to his kid gloves. The governor had gotten to his feet when René's name had been announced, but, stunned by the man's appearance, he'd got no farther.

René, on the other hand, approached the governor general with the ease of a man accustomed to society's best drawing rooms. He bowed gracefully to greet the general.

"What?" said the general in astonishment. "Are you the man our good corsair Surcouf was talking about?"

"Heavens, General," René replied. "You alarm me. If Surcouf promised you anything other than a poor fellow about twenty-four or twenty-five years old, with little experience as a seaman since he has been aboard ship only a year, I am ready to withdraw and confess that I am not worthy of the interest that, on Surcouf's recommendation, you have been kind enough to show me."

"No, monsieur," the general replied. "On the contrary, my surprise, far from offending you, should be seen as tacit praise for you and the way you present yourself. Up until now I'd thought that one could not be a corsair without cursing at every other word, wearing one's hat cockeyed, or walking with bowed legs like a man unaccustomed to dry land. Please excuse me; I was mistaken. And please do me the honor of telling me to what good fortune I owe the pleasure of your visit."

"General," said René, "you can do me a great service. You can help me get myself killed honorably and appropriately." René sat down and began twirling his rattan cane, its knob topped with an emerald.

"Get yourself killed, monsieur?" exclaimed the general, trying to repress a smile. "At your age, with your fortune, your elegance, and the success you have no doubt already had, and are destined yet to have, in the world? Surely you are joking. . . ."

"Ask Surcouf whether or not, when facing the enemy, I do whatever I can to expose myself to death."

"Surcouf told me, monsieur, incredible things about your courage, your skill, and your strength. That is why, when I first saw you, I doubted that you could be the person he'd spoken of. Not only did he speak of your courage when facing men but also your bravery in the face of wild animals, and that is sometimes more difficult still. If I am to believe Surcouf, at your age you have already completed Hercules's twelve tasks."

"There is no great merit in all that, General. A man who has no fear of death and who indeed would welcome it is practically invincible, except for some stray bullet. Then, too, I was dealing with tigers, and cruel as the tiger is, it is also cowardly. Whenever I found myself face to face with a tiger, I would simply stare at it until I'd forced it to avert its gaze. Any creature that averts its gaze, man or animal, is already beaten."

"Truly, monsieur," said the general, "you delight me. And if you would do me the honor of dining with me, I would like to introduce you to Madame Decaen. I would have you shake my son's hand as well, and perhaps you could tell him about some of your hunts."

"I am pleased to accept, General. Rarely is a poor devil of a sailor so fortunate to associate with a man of your distinction."

"Poor devil of a sailor!" the general repeated with a laugh. "A sailor whose share of the take will be five hundred thousand francs! Allow me to say to you that your wealth surely does not make you a poor devil."

"That reminds me of something I forgot to mention, General. Since I am not a professional corsair, my custom is to give my share of the prize to charity. So, of those five hundred thousand francs coming to me, I have distributed four hundred thousand among my men. As for the last one hundred, allow me to offer them to you for benefit of any poor Frenchmen who might like to be repatriated or any poor widows of men lost at sea. Will you accept?"

Before the general could answer, however, René bent over a table, took a sheet of paper, and he wrote the following note in an aristocratic hand to match his aristocratic style:

Monsieur, please pay to the bearer, on the basis of this note alone, the sum of one hundred thousand francs to General Decaen, governor of Île de France. He knows how he is to use this sum.
                    Port Louis, June 23, 1805
                    to Monsieur Rondeau, Banker
                    Rue du Gouvernement, in Port Louis

General Decaen read the note and in astonishment he said, "But I should at least wait until you have sold the ship you captured before I cash this."

"There is no reason to wait, General," René said nonchalantly. "The credit I have with Monsieur Rondeau is three times what I am asking him to pay you."

"Would you please give him some advance notice?"

"That is not necessary. You see that the note is made out to the bearer. Besides, he has a copy of my signature; it was sent to him by my banker in Paris, Monsieur Perrégaux."

"Since you have been back on the island, have you seen Monsieur Rondeau, or have you sent word of your return?"

"I have never had the honor of meeting Monsieur Rondeau, General."

"Would you like to meet him?"

"With pleasure, General. It is said that he is a true gentleman."

"He is charming. Would you like to have dinner with him in our home?"

"If he is a friend of yours, I would be delighted," said René, and immediately he rose to his feet as Madame Decaen had just come in.

"Madame," the general said, "allow me to introduce Monsieur René, Captain Surcouf's second in command. He is the man who recently fought the English so valiantly, and probably saved our Saint-Malo friend's life and liberty. This evening he will do us the honor of dining here along with Monsieur Rondeau, his banker, on whom he has just given me a draft for one hundred thousand francs that may be used to assist sailors' widows and poor Frenchmen hoping to repatriate. You, madame, will be in charge of that pious task. Please thank Monsieur René, and give him your hand to kiss, I beg of you."

Madame Decaen, though quite surprised by her husband' request, held out her hand. René bent forward and barely touched her hand with his lips and his fingers. Then he stepped back and, bowing, prepared to take his leave.

"But, monsieur," said the General, "you are forgetting that you have something to ask me for."

"Oh," said René, "now that I shall have the honor of seeing you again today, please allow me not to importune you further with this visit." With a bow to the astonished general, then another to a more astonished Madame Decaen, he left the room.

The governor and his wife looked at each other in wonder at such a singular curiosity as Monsieur René.

Shortly thereafter General Decaen went to see Surcouf and asked him to come to dinner with his second in command and Monsieur Rondeau the banker. Surcouf accepted, of course, and the governor told him what he had forgotten to tell René: that dinner would be served between three-thirty and four o'clock.

Scarcely had General Decaen left than Surcouf burst into René's room.

"What happened, my friend?" he asked. "Monsieur le Gouverneur has just asked me to dinner with you and Rondeau."

"Something perfectly normal happened. The governor is a true gentleman, and he realized he would please me greatly by inviting you."

LXXXV

A Collection for the Poor

WITH MILITARY PUNCTUALITY, at precisely three-thirty Surcouf and René appeared at the governor's mansion.

René would have preferred to wait until quarter to four, as the custom among society was to allow guests some latitude, but Surcouf would not hear of it. He pointed out that at home he normally had dinner at three-thirty, and he did not like guests to keep him waiting. So, at precisely three-thirty by Surcouf's watch, they were knocking on the governor's door.

They were led into the drawing room, where they remained alone for a moment. It seemed that Madame Decaen was still dressing, the general was finishing his correspondence, and their son, Alfred Decaen, was out riding with his servant. "You see, my dear man," said René, putting his hand on Surcouf's arm, "I was not such a bumpkin after all. We still had a good quarter of an hour before anyone could have accused us of not showing the proper courtesy to our hosts."

Shortly, though, the general joined them. "Pardon me, gentlemen," he said, "but Rondeau, who is a model banker, asked if he could come at four. That is when he closes his offices, you see, and in the ten years he has been practicing his profession he has always been the last person in the office to lay down his pen. While we wait, would you prefer to remain here, or would you perhaps like to take a stroll in the garden?—

"My son, I see, is just now dismounting his horse, and he will need a few minutes to get ready for dinner." The general opened the window: "Hurry! Hurry!" he shouted to his son. "We shall be waiting for you on the terrace by the sea."

The general and his two guests went out into the garden and walked down shaded paths to the terrace. The panorama was magnificent; they could see from the Bête-à-Mille-Pieds all the way to the Baie de la Grande-Rivière. At both ends of the terrace long tents had been set up, one to serve as an armory, the other as a shooting gallery, which offered all sorts of targets—metal plates, silhouettes, and paper circles—to test one's shooting skills.

By chance they first went into the armory with its trophies, pistols, masks, and foils.

"Here you will be in your element, Monsieur René," the general said. "For Surcouf has told me that you are more than a first-rate marksman. You are truly superior, he says."

René's lips quivered. "General," he said, "my captain Surcouf looks at me with a father's love. To listen to him, I am the best horseman, the best marshal, the best shot with a pistol since that famous mulatto Saint-Georges. I won't even mention that Surcouf tried to have me go up against Saint-Georges so that he could celebrate my triumph. Unfortunately, a friend's eyes are like telescopic lenses, for they magnify merely your good qualities. Conversely, with the lenses turned around, to your friend's eye they make your faults seem smaller. I shoot like many men, perhaps a little better than most, but my superiority goes no further than that. And as far as fencing is concerned, I have surely lost a great deal of my skill, for since I've been on ship I have not even picked up a foil."

"Because there has not been anyone good enough to pick up another foil and face him! Don't be so modest!"

"What, not even you, Monsieur Surcouf?" the general asked. "And yet you have the reputation of being quite a fencer."

"In Saint-Malo, General, in Saint-Malo! But even there, the one time I saw this man with a foil in his hand was time enough to cost me my reputation."

Just then Monsieur Decaen's son appeared at the armory. "Come over here, Alfred," the general said, "and take a lesson from Monsieur Surcouf. You claim to be a good fencer, and Monsieur Surcouf has quite a reputation. So I hope he will do me the service of proving to you that you are indeed a conceited fop."

The young man smiled, and with a young man's confidence he took two foils and two masks from the wall and handed Surcouf one of each. "Monsieur," he said, "I trust you will do my father and me the service he has requested. I would be eternally grateful."

Surcouf had no choice but to accept the challenge. He took off his hat and jacket, put on the mask, and saluted the general. "I am at your orders, General," he said. "And at your son's orders."

"Gentlemen, you may expect to see something like the duel between Entelle and Dares," said the general with a smile at the moment Monsieur Rondeau arrived.

"Ah! Just in time! Gentlemen, let me introduce Monsieur Rondeau. He has the reputation of being one of the better shots on the island; here everyone is skilled with weapons, even our bankers. My dear Monsieur Rondeau, this is Monsieur Surcouf, whom you have known for a long time, and Monsieur René, whom you have not yet met, but with whom, I believe, you have business dealings. . . ."

"Ah," said Monsieur Rondeau, "is this Monsieur René de—

"Just René, monsieur," René replied. "But that does not prevent him from calling himself your servant, if you will so allow."

"What do you mean, monsieur?" said Monsieur Rondeau, putting his hands in his vest pockets and puffing out his chest. "I am your servant, and up to three hundred thousand francs or even more."

René bowed. "But we are delaying these good gentlemen," he said.

"Gentlemen, you may now cross swords," pronounced the general.

Surcouf and Alfred Decaen both took the guard position. One stood as rigid as a statue—needless to say, it was Surcouf—and the other was poised with all the grace and confidence of youth. Neither had the obvious advantage, although their styles were totally different. Surcouf was serious, a little stiff, and he preferred simple parries, whereas Alfred, his foil constantly in motion, his hands and feet always moving, attacked frequently, parried with counters, broke off with no reason, and purposelessly placed his foil in quarte or tierce position. After ten minutes, the young man had touched Surcouf once while Surcouf had touched him twice. Alfred bowed to Surcouf, declared him the winner, and handed his foil to the banker.

Monsieur Rondeau took off his coat, moved his wallet from his coat pocket to his pants pocket, and took the guard position. He and Surcouf were perfectly matched. When each touched the other twice, Surcouf took off his mask and handed his foil to René.

"My dear Surcouf," said René, "you know how much I hate to fence when there are people watching, especially people as skilled as these. Please excuse me from following you and allow me instead to rest on the reputation you have made for me. I could only destroy it by trying to build on it."

"Gentlemen," said Surcouf, "although we are good friends, I have seen René fence only once, and on that day as well he gave the same reasons to keep from fighting. Let us grant him his request and not offend his modesty. Besides," he added, "I believe I hear the bell calling us to dinner."

Monsieur Rondeau's face broke into a triumphant smile, his face brightening like a poppy when its petals open. "Since Monsieur does not want to do me the honor of crossing swords with me," he said, "we shall put it off for now."

René bowed, and Surcouf hung the foil and the mask back up on the wall.

The bell for dinner had indeed rung, and Madame Decaen had come down the stairs to meet them. The young man ran up to Madame Decaen, threw his arms around her, and kissed her like a schoolboy who had not seen his mother since early that morning. They all greeted one another and exchanged compliments, then waited to see who would be Madame Decaen's escort.

"Monsieur René, will you give your arm to Madame Decaen?" asked the general. René bowed, offered his arm to their hostess, and together they walked to the dining room.

After the first course, which was accompanied by the usual clangor of forks and spoons and china, Monsieur Rondeau sighed with contentment and turned to René. "Monsieur René," he said, "yesterday, at the theater, I went to the *Café de la Comédie* to get some ice cream. A group had formed around a man there, a sailor who had just come back from Burma, and he was saying such outrageous things about his captain that I could hardly listen without laughing."

"What was the man saying, Monsieur Rondeau?" asked René.

"He was saying that with one blow of the man's own cutlass, the captain had cut a python in two. The python, he said, was squeezing the life out of two elephants."

"And that made you laugh, Monsieur Rondeau?"

"It did, sure."

"I daresay that if you had been there, you would not have laughed."

"Do you think me timid, Monsieur René?"

"That is not what I am saying, monsieur. But there are spectacles that can intimidate the bravest among us. The very man who was telling that story yesterday had just killed a tigress and borne away her cubs by the nape of the neck; and yet, at the sight of the dreadful serpent, he started quaking like a child. Still, I can assure you that he is not a coward."

"If not a coward, at least a joker," said Monsieur Rondeau. "For he added that the snake was forty-seven feet long."

"Well, he is the one who measured it. I did not," René replied calmly.

"So you are his captain?"

"Yes, monsieur. That is, if the man's name was François."

"Yes, that's right, that is the name I heard. And the snake was suffocating two elephants?"

"I cannot confirm that it was suffocating them, monsieur, but I do know that their bones were beginning to crack even though the snake itself was already dying. I had already put two bullets in its head." Madame Decaen was looking at her guest with great astonishment, while Alfred regarded him with curiosity.

"But," said Surcouf to Monsieur Rondeau, "if you had heard the name

René you'd have had more reason to believe the seaman's every word. For right here, near the Quai du Chien-de-Plomb, with the whole population watching, Monsieur René fought a shark whose final moments turned out as bad as those of the python."

"What?" said Monsieur Rondeau. "You are the man who ripped open the stomach of the shark that was after a sailor?"

"Yes, monsieur. But, as you know, that is the easiest thing in the world to do, unless you want a sharp knife and a little skill."

"The man told still another story," Monsieur Rondeau went on; good man though he was, he seemed to be eager to make himself look ridiculous. "He said that scarcely twenty yards away from a tiger that had just leaped from the jungle, the captain took his aim, but before he fired he announced: 'In Phillip's right eye!' Actually I'm not sure if he said the right or the left eye, but the seaman had no idea what his captain was talking about, nor do I."

General Decaen began to laugh. "General," René said, "please be so kind as to tell Aster's story to Monsieur Rondeau. If I told it, he would never believe me."

"My dear Monsieur Rondeau," said the general, "Aster was a great archer in Amphipolis, but when he was mistreated by Phillip, he left his land. He took refuge in Methone, which was soon besieged by Phillip, and in that Aster saw an opportunity to get revenge. To be certain that Phillip would know the vengeance had been his, on an arrow he wrote: 'Aster to Phillip's right eye.' And indeed, not only did Phillip lose his right eye, he almost lost his life. So he sent another arrow back to the city, and on it were written these words: 'Once Methone is taken, Aster will be hanged.' The king of Macedonia took Methone as surely as he kept his word to Aster. That's the story, Monsieur Rondeau, and I guarantee that even if it is not true, it is historical."

"Good God! That man's skill could rival yours, Monsieur René."

"Very well," said René. "I see that you are serious about getting me to fence, Monsieur Rondeau, and that you are not willing to grant my desire to abstain. So, after dinner I shall place myself at your disposal, and if you agree to the terms I shall propose, I promise that you will tire of the game before I."

The conversation then turned to other things, but as soon as dinner was over, Madame Decaen and Alfred, eager to see Monsieur Rondeau put in his place, suggested that they should have coffee and drinks in the armory. So they did, and Monsieur Rondeau, whose stomach was beginning to protrude more than his pride might have liked, was not the last to arrive.

"So what are you proposing, Monsieur René?" the general asked.

"Did you not tell me, General," said René, "that Madame looks after the poor?" He bowed toward Madame Decaen, and continued: "Well, if either of us receives five hits without touching his opponent, that person will pay a thousand francs."

"Oh!" said Monsieur Rondeau with a loud laugh, "I believe I can accept the wager, monsieur." So he took a moment to pick out a foil, then rubbed the blade on the sole of his shoe, whipped it through the air a couple of times, bent it, and, once it was in his hand, assumed the guard position.

René picked up the closest foil, bowed, and also went on guard. "To you the honor of the first move, monsieur," he said.

Monsieur Rondeau made three quick attacks, proving that his eye was sure and his hand quick. But René blocked all three attacks with simple parries. "Now it is my turn," said René.

Again they took the guard position, and then it was like a burst of light. "One, two, three," René counted, and with each attack the foil button hit Monsieur Rondeau. René turned to the spectators, and they all spoke together: "Three times."

"Your turn, monsieur," said René. "But I warn you that this time, I will parry your first two attacks and will riposte directly. I'm telling you ahead of time, because you might think me more skilled than I really am and so might confuse your parries."

Monsieur Rondeau pinched his lips and said, "I'm ready, monsieur." And he made two attacks that René parried.

As he had promised, René riposted with two direct hits. There was no contesting the second riposte, for René's foil had broken on the banker's chest.

"Madame," said René, bowing to Madame Decaen, "Monsieur owes you one thousand francs for the poor."

"I demand a revenge match," said Monsieur Rondeau.

"With pleasure," said René. "On guard!"

"No, no. Not with the foil. I admit you are my master with the foil. Let us see what you can do with pistols."

"Just one shot apiece, right?" said René to Monsieur Rondeau as Alfred hurriedly opened two boxes of pistols. "There is no reason to make the good people of Port Louis think the island is under attack."

"Fine, one shot apiece, monsieur," said Monsieur Rondeau. "What shall our target be?"

"Just a minute," said René. "That will be easy."

Alfred had loaded four of the pistols. "That's enough," said René, and with one of the pistols in hand, and without even aiming, he fired. The bullet struck right in the middle of a palm tree about twenty-five paces away.

"Can you see the hole the bullet made?" he asked Monsieur Rondeau.

"Perfectly well," he answered. He picked up a pistol.

"Do we agree that the closer bullet will be the winner?" René asked.

"We agree," said Monsieur Rondeau.

The care with which the banker took his aim showed how seriously he was taking the revenge match, and his bullet struck the tree not more than an inch away from the first ball. "Well," he said with a swagger, "for a banker, that was not a bad shot."

René in turn picked up a pistol, aimed, and shot. "Gentlemen, go look and choose the winner," he said.

The general, Surcouf, Alfred, and especially Monsieur Rondeau hastened to inspect the target. "Ah," said Monsieur Rondeau, with not a little satisfaction, "if I'm not mistaken, I do believe that you missed the tree completely."

"You are mistaken, monsieur," said René.

"What? I am mistaken?"

"Yes. You are looking at the wrong place. Look in the first hole."

"Yes, and then?"

"Can you feel a bullet?"

"Yes, I can feel it."

"Pull it out."

"Here it is."

"Now, dig again."

"Dig again?"

"Yes, keep digging."

Monsieur Rondeau paused in surprise. "Can you not feel a second bullet?" René asked.

"Yes, I do."

"Well, I placed my second bullet on top of the first. The surest way of winning this match was to put another bullet in the same hole as the target."

Everyone was quiet for a moment. Even Surcouf was surprised to see such skill.

"Would you like another revenge match, Monsieur Rondeau? This time with guns?" René asked.

"Ah, no. I don't think so."

"I was going to propose something easy."

"What was that?"

"Shooting one of those bats flying around above us out of the air."

"You can shoot bats?" asked Monsieur Rondeau.

"Even with a pistol," René replied. And with the fourth pistol, which still had not been discharged, he shot and killed a bat whose bad luck had brought it near the armory.

That evening René had again not found the opportunity to tell the governor of Île de France what service he required of him.

LXXXVI
Departure

AT ELEVEN THE FOLLOWING MORNING René went to see the governor for the third time. On this occasion he was greeted as a friend rather than as a guest, for his frank, open, generous nature had pleased the governor. He welcomed René with open arms and told his doorkeeper not to allow them to be interrupted.

"This time, my dear René, we shall not be disturbed. I have not forgotten that I can do you a service and acquit a debt by so doing. What is your request?"

"As I told you, General, I am looking for an opportunity to get myself killed."

"You keep repeating the same joke, my dear René," said the general, shrugging.

"I am not joking for one second," René went on. "I am already bored nearly to death with life. And what if someday I become so despondent that I blow my brains out—would that not be a useless, ridiculous death, and would I not be crazy for doing so? But by dying for France, I can die usefully and gloriously, and I would be called a hero. Make me a hero, General. That surely is no more difficult that anything else."

"What must I do?"

"First you must give me news of France. People have been talking about a general coalition against France; at least that's what they were saying in Calcutta. Do you know what the situation is, and can you tell me?"

"I believe we are still in Boulogne, building flat boats and looking across the Channel at London through the fog."

"But you believe war is inevitable, do you not, General?"

"I not only believe it, I am sure of it."

"General, I myself have never sung my own praises, though you have no doubt heard something of my reputation from my friends, and perhaps even from my enemies. But do you think that a man such as I, who fears neither God nor the devil, who speaks four languages, who is ready at the slightest signal to brave water or fire, can be useful to my country?"

"Do I think so! By God, yes, I do. And if that is how you want me to help you to sacrifice your life, I am at your service."

"If I stay here with my twelve-gun sloop, General, I shall not be good for anything. No one will know me when I die, and as I said a moment ago, my death will have been for naught. But if I can manage to use what talents God has granted me, then I can make a name for myself, gain a position, and achieve a long-sought goal."

"And how can I help?" asked the governor.

"This is what you can do: You can write that the good you have heard about me and the reputation for courage I made for myself in India compel you to send me back to France with your recommendation—"

"To the minister?" the general cut in.

"Oh, no! Far from that. Rather to the first good sea captain I might meet. With a recommendation from you, there is not a captain who would not accept me as a first-class midshipman. I have the right to hold such a rank, for I have served as second in command under Surcouf and have myself captained an armed sloop all the way to India. I realize that my ship is insignificant, but if was able to do with a sloop what one normally does with a brig, then with a brig might I not do what can normally be done with a corvette, and with a corvette what can be done with a true ship of the line?"

"What you are asking is simple, my dear René," said the general. "I would like to do something more significant for you. First of all, I shall give you the order, based on the services you can provide, to return to France. And also I shall give you letters for three first-rate sea captains, all good friends of mine: Lucas, who captains the *Redoutable;* Cosmao, captain of the *Pluton;* and Infernet, commander of the *Intrépide.* Wherever you might meet them, you may go aboard, and ten minutes later you will have your place in the officers' mess. Is there anything else I can do for you?"

"No, thank you. By doing what you have said, you will fulfill my every wish."

"How do you expect to get back to France?"

"I need help from no one, General. My little sloop, with which I can defy the best sailing English ship, is completely mine. It is an American ship, and consequently neutral; and although I speak English too well to be an American, only Americans would know that. In two or three days I shall set off, leaving my share of the take to the eighteen men who accompanied me to Burma. You yourself will receive the money, and as each member of the crew returns to Île de France, either together or separately, you will give each his share. Only one man should get more, and that is François, for he followed me all the way to Pegu; he should get two shares instead of only one."

"You will come back to say farewell, will you not, Monsieur René?"

"I shall have that honor, General, and I shall bring you the calculations I have done for what each man's share should be. I would have too many regrets if I were to leave without presenting my respects to Madame Decaen and my friendship to Monsieur Alfred."

"Would you not like to see them now?" the general asked.

"I would not wish to disturb them," René replied, then bowed to the governor and left.

When René returned home he found Rondeau the banker waiting for him. Amidst all the events of the day before, he had not forgotten that his job was to make money, so he had come to ask René to work with him with a proposal that would enable him to distribute to the crewmen their shares before he left Port Louis. Certainly advancing the men their money now would be simpler than expecting them to return to Port Louis to collect their share of the amount that the captured ship would command when it was sold, as well as their percentage of René's own share, which he would be distributing among them.

First, René and Rondeau agreed that the crew would get all of the five hundred thousand francs that were due to them. Then, from his own share of five hundred thousand francs, one hundred thousand francs would first be taken out for the poor, and the remaining four hundred thousand would be divided up among his eighteen men, except that François would have a double share.

Monsieur Rondeau asked for an initial payment of twenty thousand francs, for which sum he would disburse the million francs immediately. René agreed. He gave the banker a draft for twenty thousand francs to be taken from funds he had available at home. He then sent the one hundred thousand francs for the poor to Madame Decaen immediately; Monsieur Rondeau could pay his debt of two thousand francs to the general's wife as he wished. Finally, René sent word to his men to come see him the following day.

René's eighteen men gathered at noon the next day. René first told them that they would receive their share of the proceeds from the captured ship before it was sold; that is, five hundred thousand francs. He added that from his own share he was giving one hundred thousand francs to the governor for use in helping old sailors no longer able to work as well as seamen's widows and orphans. René's crewmen were due even more amazement when they learned they would also be sharing their captain's remaining four hundred thousand as a token for their loyal devotion, which would be doubled in the case of François, who had accompanied him all the way to Betel Land. In closing, René announced that they would be leaving for France in two days, and he advised them to save as much of their money as possible for their wives. That would not be difficult since, in addition to what they had earned from earlier captures, they would now be receiving more than sixty thousand francs apiece.

Each man received his due either in French gold or English banknotes, which they protected with their hands over their pockets, as if they were afraid that by some strange chance the gold or notes might escape them. They had filed in quietly, but they were leaving noisily. Not only did they have francs in their pockets but they also shared the prospect of returning to France on a neutral ship, which meant that they could hope to reach home without any danger beyond the normal perils of sailing. In the face of such good fortune they could freely demonstrate their joy. And they did, as loudly as they could.

The memory of that avalanche of men rolling from the Place du Théâtre down to the quay was kept alive for years in Port Louis. Events were often dated from that day when the crew of the *New York Racer* received their dividends.

As he had promised, two days later René visited the governor's house to bid a painful farewell to the general's fine family. They had welcomed him as a son and brother, even as they suspected, with some poignancy, that beneath his elegant perfection and the simple name René lay a mystery he dared not reveal. He brought the young Alfred Decaen his double-barreled pistols, which he asked him to keep as a souvenir, and to demonstrate their accuracy, he split four bullets on a knife blade placed about twenty paces away.

The governor's letters were ready. Their praises went beyond anything René could have imagined. As was his right by his authority as governor, General Decaen recommended that the young captain of the *New York Racer* be made a commander on the first ship he might board. At the end of the visit the governor asked when the *New York Racer* would raise anchor and promised to come bid farewell to the ship's crew and captain.

They were scheduled to raise anchor at precisely three o'clock. Already at noon the Quai du Chien-de-Plomb was crowded with people.

René had not issued an order to his men, but he had asked them all to be on board by two o'clock and added that he would be grateful if they'd be in such state as to allow them to perform every maneuver smoothly. He wanted to provide the people of Port Louis a spectacle unheard of in a seaport: a sober crew, each man of which had sixty thousand francs in his pocket. His friendly request produced what the strictest orders might not have.

René had told his crew how great an honor it was for the governor to come see them sail. So, on their own, without even telling René, they had ordered six boats to tow the sloop from the quay. Brandishing banners, each boat bore, in addition to oarsmen, a band of musicians.

The governor had his own rowboat tied to René's sloop. As they left the quay, a salvo boomed out and the musicians sang "The Departure Song." At the governor's signal, in answer to the salvo, sixteen cannon shots rang out from Fort Blanc. The ship slipped gently out into the channel about a quarter of league away, where it could catch the wind in its sails. Then it stopped, but only long enough for the governor's boat to pull up alongside them and for him and his family to deboard the sloop. In the bowboat they returned to Chien-de-Plomb, along with six boatloads of musicians.

The *New York Racer* set sail toward the south and soon disappeared in the first mists of the evening.

LXXXVII

What Was Happening in Europe

NOW WE THINK IT IS TIME to bring the reader up to date on what was happening in Europe. The governor had been unable to do the same for René because he himself did not know, distant as Île de France was from the scene of the events.

We remember where we left Napoleon. After the victory of the Pyramids that had awed Egypt, after the victory at Marengo that had subjugated Italy, frightened Germany, stitched Spain to a corner of Bonaparte's imperial coat, and incorporated Holland into the French Empire, Napoleon had transferred his dreams of universal empire, which had been dashed at Saint-Jean-d'Acre, to the cliffs of Dover. Little did he suspect that the very man who had destroyed his fleet at Aboukir was once again to get in the way of his plans, this time in the English Channel, just as he had done in Egypt. That man was Nelson.

Let us then present to our readers a picture of that unusual Englishman whose brutal victories raised him for a brilliant historical moment to the same level of genius as the man he was destined to combat, although he lived barely long enough to accomplish his mammoth task: the task of saving England from perhaps its greatest danger since William the Conqueror. Let us see who this Nelson was and by what providential series of events he came to occupy, in the modern world, the same position that Pompey had held against Caesar in the ancient one.

Nelson was born on September 20, 1758; so at the time we are speaking of, when René set sail for France, he was nearly forty-seven years old. He grew up in Burnham-Thorpe, a small village in Norfolk County, where his father was a pastor; his mother died young, leaving eleven children. One of his uncles, a naval officer related to the Walpole family, took him as a midshipman aboard the sixty-four-gun vessel *Redoutable*. By strange coincidence, a life filled with strange coincidences, Nelson would be killed by a bullet from a French ship of the same name that would also be armed with sixty-four guns.

Nelson's first voyage took him to the Pole, where his ship was trapped in ice for six months. On an expedition off the ship he encountered a polar bear, which he fought bare-handed. The white monster would have crushed him with its paws if one of his comrades, seeing his plight, had not come running up with his gun and shot it into the bear's ear.

When he sailed to the Equator, Nelson got lost in the forests of Peru, where he fell asleep under a tree and got bitten by a serpent. He nearly died, and for his entire life his skin bore two tiny spots to remind him of the snake that had bit him.

In Canada, Nelson fell in love for the first time. Quite foolishly, so he'd not have to leave behind the woman he loved, he decided to resign his commission as commander. His officers took him by surprise, tied him up like a thief or a madman, threw him over a horse, and carried him back to the ship. They released him only when they'd gotten back to sea.

(Suppose that Nelson's resignation had been accepted and that Bonaparte had taken Saint-Jean-d'Acre. Then neither Aboukir nor Trafalgar would ever have happened, and our navy, instead of meeting destruction by the English, would have continued victoriously forward in our conquest of the entire world. Only Nelson's arm held us back.)

On his return to London Nelson married a young widow named Mrs. Nesbitt, whom he loved with all his characteristic passion. When he went back to sea, he took along her son from an earlier marriage.

Horatio Nelson was captain on board the *Agamemnon* when Toulon was surrendered to the English, and it was he who was dispatched to Naples to deliver to King Ferdinand and Queen Caroline the news that our main military port had been taken.

Sir William Hamilton met him at the king's palace, then took him back to the embassy. He left Nelson in the drawing room while he repaired to his wife's room. "Milady," he said, "I'm bringing you a little man who is unable to brag of being handsome. But unless I am sadly mistaken, some day he will be the glory of England and the terror of France."

"What makes you think so?" Lady Hamilton asked.

"The few words we exchanged. He is in the drawing room. Go do the honors of the house, my dear. I have never before had an English officer in my house, but I'd not have this man stay anywhere else but here." And there, at the English embassy, situated where Via Chiaia meets the river, Nelson did stay.

That was in 1793. Nelson was thirty-four years old, small of stature, as Sir William had noted, with pale blue eyes and an aquiline nose, which also set apart men of war like Caesar and Condé to make them look aptly like birds of prey. Nelson's strong chin marked a man as tenacious as he was obstinate, but his hair and beard were unprepossessingly pale blond, thin, and patchy.

There is nothing to indicate that Emma Lyonna had any better an opinion of his looks than did her husband. The ambassador's wife, a striking beauty, had a profound effect on Nelson, however. He left Naples not only with the reinforcements he had sought at the court of the Two Sicilies but also madly in love with Lady Hamilton.

That love was Nelson's shame, if not Emma Lyonna's, for by that time she had long forgotten what shame meant.

Was it shame that drove Nelson at Calvi, where he lost an eye, and on the Tenerife expedition, where he lost an arm? Did he hope thus to cure himself of his love for Emma, or did he act out of ambition or simply in his pursuit of glory? Nobody knows, but on both occasions he gambled so recklessly with his life that it was difficult to believe he harbored much care for it.

Nelson's position was critical. He was charged with blockading the French fleet in the port of Toulon and with attacking it if it left port. But the fleet had indeed slipped past his guard and had taken Malta. Further, it had advanced to Alexandria, where it had landed thirty thousand men.

And that was not all. Hammered by a storm and suffering severe damage as well as being low on food and water, Nelson was unable to continue his pursuit of the French. He had to take refuge in Gibraltar.

He was lost. He might have been accused of dereliction, as he had been sailing for a month in the Mediterranean—nothing more than a big lake really—in his search for a fleet of thirteen warships and eighty-seven troopships. Not only had he been unable to locate them, he had not even been able to learn where they had gone.

In order to take on supplies in Messina and Syracuse as well as wood in Calabria, for the repair of his ship's broken masts and spars, he needed the authority of the Two Sicilies. However, the court of the Two Sicilies had signed a peace treaty with France that required strict neutrality: a condition that disallowed granting Nelson his request. It was also a condition that Ferdinand and Caroline, who detested the French and hated France, ignored. Nelson left Naples with the grants he'd sought, but not before he had seen Lady Hamilton again, after five years. So he also left crazier and more in love than ever.

Swearing now to win a great victory or get killed trying, Nelson pursued opportunity. He won; he also very nearly got killed.

Never since the invention of gunpowder and the use of cannons has a naval battle brought to the seas so horrific a disaster. Of the thirteen warships in the French fleet, only two were able to extricate themselves from the flames and escape to Malta. One ship, the *Orient*, had exploded. Another ship and a frigate had been sunk; nine were captured. Nelson had conducted himself like a hero. Throughout the entire battle he had defied death, but death had eschewed him.

He did receive a painful wound, however. A cannonball from the *Guillaume Tell* hit one of the *Vanguard*'s spars, on which Nelson was climbing, and when he looked up to see the cause of the terrible cracking sound, the broken spar struck him in the forehead. It tore the skin off his cranium and pulled it down over his good eye. Like a bull struck with a club, he dropped to the deck. He was covered with his own blood.

Convinced that it was a mortal wound, Nelson asked the chaplain to bless him and to convey his farewells to his family. But the surgeon discovered, on examining Nelson's skull, that it was intact. He pulled the skin back away from Nelson's eye and tied it down with a black cloth. The next minute, Nelson was picking up the megaphone he had dropped and shouting: "Fire!"

Nelson's hatred for France was like the breath of the Titans. The destruction in the battle at Aboukir Bay was immense.

A light ship carried the news of Nelson's victory over the French fleet to the court of the Two Sicilies. All over Europe there was an enormous cry of joy; it echoed even into Asia, so feared were the French and so execrated was the French Revolution. In Naples especially, the court of Ferdinand and Caroline, for so long mad with anger at the French, went crazy with happiness over England's victory.

Nelson's feat had stranded thirty thousand Frenchmen in Egypt, Bonaparte among them. Bonaparte—the man of Toulon, of the 13th Vendémiaire, of Montenotte, of Dego, of Arcole and Rivoli; the victor at Beaulieu, at Wurmser, at Alvinzi and of Prince Charles—had grown accustomed to winning. In less than two years he had counted one hundred fifty thousand prisoners, won one hundred seventy flags, taken five hundred fifty large-caliber cannons, six hundred smaller ones, and five sets of bridges. Bonaparte thrived on ambition; he imagined revolutions and empires as great as those in the Orient. He was the adventuresome captain who, at twenty-nine, already more accomplished than Hannibal or Scipio, had tried to conquer Egypt and surpass Alexander and Caesar. And now he'd been halted, wiped out, stricken from the list of combatants. At the momentous game of war, he had met a player who was more fortunate or more skillful than he. On the grand chessboard of the Nile, whose pawns are obelisks, whose knights are sphinxes, whose rooks are pyramids, where the bishops are named Cambyses, the kings Sesostris, and the queens Cleopatra, he had been checkmated!

One can measure by the gifts the sovereigns of Europe sent Nelson the terror they had felt when the names France and Bonaparte were pronounced together. And now, with France brought low and Bonaparte in Egypt, they were mad with joy. These were their gifts; we have copied the list from a note written by Nelson himself:

From George III, the dignity of becoming a peer of Great Britain and a gold medal.

From the House of Commons, for Nelson and for his heirs, a title, Baron of the Nile and of Burnham-Thorpe, with a pension of two thousand pounds sterling beginning on August 1, 1798, the day of the battle.

From the House of Lords, a similar pension, under the same conditions, beginning on the same date.

From the Irish Parliament, a pension of one thousand pounds sterling.

From the East India Company, a one-time gift of ten thousand pounds.

From the sultan, a diamond buckle with a victory feather, worth two thousand pounds, and a rich pelisse valued at a thousand pounds.

From the sultan's mother, a diamond-studded box, valued at twelve hundred pounds sterling.

From the King of Sardinia, a tobacco pouch decorated with diamonds, also valued at twelve hundred pounds.

From the island of Zante, a sword with a golden hilt and a cane with a golden knob.

From the city of Palermo, a tobacco pouch and a golden chain on a silver platter.

There was also, from Nelson's friend Benjamin Hallowell, captain of the *Swiftsure*, a typically English gift, and to fail to include it here would be a serious omission. When, as we have said, the *Orient* exploded, Hallowell pulled its mainmast onto his own ship, and from the mast and its iron fitments, he had his ship's carpenter and locksmith make a casket. On it a plaque provided this certificate of authenticity:

I certify that this casket is made entirely with wood and iron from the ship *L'Orient*, a large part of which was saved by His Majesty's ship under my command in Aboukir Bay.

Ben. Hallowell

Accompanying the casket was this letter:

To the honorable Captain Nelson.
My dear lord,
    I am sending to you, along with this letter, a casket carved out of the mast of the French ship *L'Orient*, so that, when you abandon this life, you may rest in your own trophies. The hope that such a day is still distant is the fervent desire of your obedient and loving servant.

Ben. Hallowell.

Of all the gifts he received, let us hasten to say that Hallowell's touched Nelson the most. He received it with obvious pleasure. He placed it against the wall in his cabin, just behind the chair where he sat to eat. Eventually an old servant, saddened by this constant reminder of death, was allowed by the admiral to move it to the tween-deck.

When Nelson left the horribly damaged *Vanguard* for the *Fulminant*, the casket came with him but remained on the forecastle for several months. One day, while the officers from the *Fulminant* were admiring Captain Hallowell's gift, they heard Nelson shout up from his cabin: "Admire it all you want, gentlemen, but it was not made for you."

At the first opportunity, Nelson sent the casket to his upholsterer in England and asked him to line it with velvet. After all, given his profession, he might need it at any moment, and he wanted it to be ready when he did.

Nelson was killed seven years later at Trafalgar. The casket was ready.

LXXXVIII
Emma Lyonna

⁂

BY GOD'S JUSTICE, to punish the victor at Aboukir Bay and Trafalgar, the name Emma Lyonna would forever remain linked to Nelson's.

As soon as Emma Lyonna received Nelson's letter, for it was to her that he announced his victory when he sent the news by fast boat to Naples, she ran to Queen Caroline's apartments with the open letter. Queen Caroline glanced at it eagerly and shouted, or rather squealed, with joy.

Without consideration for Garat, the French ambassador, Caroline issued orders to set in motion preparations to welcome Nelson to Naples as a triumphant victor. No doubt Caroline thought she had nothing more to fear from France, although it was Garat who had read Louis XVI his death sentence and who had been sent to Naples by the Directory as a reminder to Caroline and Ferdinand of the pitfalls of monarchy.

Nor did Caroline want to be outdistanced by other sovereigns, for she recognized that she owed Nelson more than most, doubly threatened as she was by the presence of French troops in Rome and by the proclamation of the Roman Republic. So she had her lover, Prime Minister Acton, obtain the king's signature on a royal warrant naming Nelson the Duke of Bronte, after one of the three Cyclops who made thunder, along with an annuity of three thousand pounds sterling.

When Ferdinand presented the royal warrant to Nelson, he also gave him the sword that Louis XIV had given to his son Philip V when he left to reign over Spain, and that Philip V in turn had given to his own son, Carlos, when he left to conquer Naples. The sword, according to King Charles III's instructions, was to be passed along only to defenders or saviors of the Kingdom of the Two Sicilies. In addition to its historical value, which was not negligible, it was valued at five thousand pounds sterling, or one hundred twenty-five thousand francs in our currency, as its hilt was studded with diamonds.

As for the queen, she had decided to give Nelson a gift that all the titles and favors of the kings of this earth could never equal. She had decided to give him Emma Lyonna, the object of his most ardent dreams for the past five years. Consequently, on the morning of the day Nelson was to make his triumphant return to Naples, she had said to Emma Lyonna, as she brushed aside the beautiful lady's chestnut brown hair to kiss her forehead, as purely white as that of an angel: "My dear Emma, in order that I may rule Naples and you may rule Nelson, the admiral must be ours. And in order for him to be ours, you must be his." Emma had lowered her eyes, and without an answer, she had seized the queen's hands and kissed them passionately.

Let us consider how Marie-Caroline, which was the full name of the queen, could make such a request, or rather give such an order, to Lady Hamilton, the wife of the English ambassador.

Emma was the daughter of a poor Welsh peasant. She had no idea when or where she had been born, and of her early childhood she could remember only an arduous journey when she was three or four years old. She could remember a poor canvas dress, and as she walked barefoot in rain and fog along mountain paths, her freezing hand would cling to her mother's skirts. When she grew too tired or if they had to cross a stream, her mother would carry her.

She could remember being cold and hungry on that long journey. Whenever they passed through a city, her mother would stop at the door of some rich man's house or at the baker's. With a plaintive voice she would ask for some coins, which were usually refused, or for a loaf of bread, which usually was not.

Their destination was the little town of Flint, which was where Emma's mother and her father, John Lyon, had been born. Lyon had left County Flint with his wife to look for work. They had ended up in Chester, where John Lyon had died young and poor. His wife had returned to her home-town with her three-year-old child to see if it would be hospitable or cruel.

She could remember herself on a hillside. She was taking care of a small herd of four or five sheep. They would drink at a fountain, and she would look at herself in the water, at her forehead crowned with wreaths of wild-flowers.

Later a little money reached the household by way of the Count of Hal-ifax; part of it was for the mother's comfort, part was for her daughter's ed-ucation. Emma was enrolled in a boarding school for young women, their uniform a straw hat, a sky-blue dress, and a black apron. She stayed there two years. Then her mother came to get her. There was no more money; the Count of Halifax had died, and he'd not included the two women in his will.

She took a position as a child's maid in the home of a certain Thomas Hawarden, whose widowed daughter had died young and left three chil-dren in her father's care. She was walking the children along the shore one day when she had an encounter that would change her life.

A famous London courtesan, Miss Arabell, and her current lover, a tal-ented painter named Romney, had stopped there, as the painter wanted to sketch a Welsh peasant girl. Curious, the children in Emma's charge tiptoed over to see what the painter was doing; Emma followed. The painter turned around, and his eyes fell first on the thirteen-year-old Emma. He gasped in surprise. The painter had never seen a woman or child so beautiful.

He inquired after her, and Emma's education, though limited, allowed her to respond politely. He asked how much she was paid to take care of the Hawarden children, and she replied that she was given her clothes, food, and lodging, and in addition the sum of ten shillings a month. Immediately the painter entreated her: "Come to London," he said. "I shall give you five guineas for each sketch you let me make of you." And he handed her a card that read: "Edward Romney, 8, Cavendish Square."

Miss Arabell meanwhile had pulled a small purse from her belt. It contained a few gold pieces, and she tried to give it to Emma. The girl took the painter's card and put it carefully in her bodice, but she refused the purse. When Miss Arabell insisted, saying that she could use the money for her trip to London, Emma answered: "No, thank you, ma'am. If I go to London, I shall go with the money I've already saved and that I shall continue to save."

"Out of the ten shillings you are making a month?" Miss Arabell laughed.

"Yes, ma'am," the girl replied simply. And that was all there was to it.

No, that was not all there was to it. Six months later, Emma appeared in London at Cavendish Square, only to discover that Romney was traveling. Emma was able to find Miss Arabell, however. Now the mistress of the prince regent, Miss Arabell had reached the height of her profession as a courtesan. She took Emma on as a companion.

For two months Emma stayed with Miss Arabell. She read every novel she could get her hands on, and when she went to the theater, she'd return home and repeat the lines of all the characters on stage. She'd mime the dancers in every ballet she'd see. What for others was a mere diversion became for her an occupation.

She had just turned fifteen, and she was in the prime of her youthful beauty. Her body was supple and its every movement by nature evoked the grace of the most skillful dancers. Her face, in spite of life's vicissitudes, still retained the immaculate complexion of childhood and reflected virginal modesty. It openly expressed any emotion; in melancholy it darkened, in joy it dazzled. It was as if her soul's candor could be read in the purity of her face, so much so that a great poet of our time, not wanting to tarnish in any way her luminous beauty, said when speaking of her first lapse: "She fell not into vice, but into imprudence and goodness."

England's war against its American colonies was raging at the time, and press gangs were active. When the brother of one of Emma's friends was caught and impressed into the navy, his sister, Fanny, sought Emma's help. Certain that no one could resist Emma's beauty or refuse her requests, Fanny begged Emma to use her powers of persuasion, and seduction, on Admiral John Payne. Emma could sense her vocation as a temptress opening up before her. She gaily put on her most elegant dress and went with her friend to see the admiral. She got what she wanted, but at a price, for John Payne also made demands. Emma paid for her friend's brother's freedom, if not with her love, at least with her gratitude.

As John Payne's mistress, Emma Lyonna had her own house, her own servants, and her own horses. But her good fortune came and went with the brilliance and speed of a meteor. John Payne's squadron left, as did the gilded life of Emma's dreams.

Emma, however, was not the kind of woman to kill herself, like Dido, for an unfaithful Aeneas. One of the admiral's rich, handsome friends, Sir Harry Fatherson, offered to keep Emma in the manner to which she had indeed grown accustomed, and having already taken her first step down vice's pathway, she did not object. For an entire season she was the queen of parties, hunts, and dances, but when the season ended, she found herself again abandoned. Discarded by a second lover, for a second time debased, she fell into such misery and circumstances so dire that her only recourse seemed to be the Haymarket sidewalks, there to join those poor creatures who have to beg love from passersby.

Fortunately, the procuress to whom she had turned on entering the business of public depravity was struck by her distinction and modesty. So, instead of prostituting her in the manner of the other women in her house, she took Emme to visit an eminent doctor who frequented her establishment.

He was in fact the famous Doctor Graham. Part mystic, part sensualist, and all charlatan, he professed the material religion of beauty to the young people of London. When Emma appeared before him, he had found at last his Venus Astarte.

He paid dearly for the treasure, but for him the treasure was priceless. He laid her down on Apollo's bed. He covered her with a veil more transparent than Venus's own when Vulcan had kept her captive before Olympus. He announced in all the newspapers that finally he possessed the unique, the supreme specimen of beauty that he had so far been lacking to prove his theories.

Such an appeal to lust and science drew disciples in that great worldwide religion of love to Doctor Graham's offices in droves. It was a total triumph. No painting or sculpture had ever produced a masterpiece to match the doctor's love goddess; Apelles and Phidias were vanquished.

Artists flocked to see her, among them Romney, now back in London, who recognized at once the girl he had seen in County Flint. He painted her in all sorts of poses: as Ariadne, as a bacchante, as Leda, as Armide. In the Imperial Library we have a collection of engravings showing the enchantress in all the voluptuous poses that sensual Antiquity could invent.

And that is when young Sir Charles Grenville, of the illustrious family of Warwick the kingmaker, curious to see what the excitement was all about, first beheld Emma Lyonna. He was dazzled by her beauty, and he fell head over heels in love. The young lord made Emma glorious promises, but she replied that her gratefulness bound her to Doctor Graham, and she resisted Grenville's every attempt to seduce her. This time, she vowed, she would leave a lover only to follow a husband.

Sir Charles gave his gentleman's word that he would become Emma Lyonna's husband as soon as he came of full age. In the meantime, Emma agreed to an elopement. They lived together as husband and wife, and Emma bore three children who, on their father's word, would become legitimate upon his marriage to her.

Emma Lyonna also made great progress in music and drawing, thanks to the best teachers in London. She perfected her English; she learned French and Italian. She could recite poetry like Mrs. Siddons, and she had marvelous stage presence in performing the art of pantomime.

They had been living together three years when a cabinet change cost Grenville his job, from which he derived most of his income. Unable to significantly reduce his expenses, he wrote to his uncle, Sir William Hamilton, to ask him for money. His uncle did not respond initially, but eventually he answered that he would soon be coming to London and that he would take advantage of that opportunity to "study" his nephew's affairs.

The word "study" had alarmed the young couple. They both desired and feared Sir William's visit, and when, suddenly, he did come to see them, they discovered that he had already been in London for a week. Sir William had used that week to gather information about his nephew, and all the evidence led to the same conclusion: that his nephew's dissolute life and poverty were accountable to a prostitute with whom he had already had three children. Emma left her lover alone with his uncle, who then gave him no other alternative but to leave Emma Lyonna immediately, unless he cared to give up his inheritance, his only fortune. He allowed his nephew three days to make up his mind.

The young couple's only hope lay in Emma. Only she might be able to obtain from Sir William Hamilton forgiveness for her lover, by showing that he was worthy of pardon. So, instead of wearing the clothes appropriate to her elevated social station, Emma donned a homespun dress and straw hat of the sort she might have worn as a girl. Her tears, her smiles, her radiance, her voice, they would do the rest.

When she was announced to Sir William, Emma threw herself at his feet. Whether by design or by accident, the cord on her hat came loose, and her lovely chestnut brown hair fell down over her shoulders. Emma had no rival when it came to expressing suffering.

The old archeologist, who up until then had warmed to nothing but Athenian marble and the statues of Greater Greece, for the first time gazed upon a living beauty to rival the cold, pale perfection of goddesses sculpted by Praxiteles and Phidias. Love, which he had never been able to comprehend in his nephew, entered violently into his own heart, and he made not the slightest effort to defend himself against its control.

Sir William accepted everything: his nephew's debts, Emma's low birth, social scandals, the publicity, the art, the venality of caresses, everything, even the children born out of wedlock if out of love. His only condition was that Emma surrender herself to him in compensation for his own total abandonment of dignity.

Emma had triumphed even beyond her greatest expectations. But she too had her conditions. While the promise of marriage had been enough to win her affection with Sir Charles, she would go to Naples with Sir William only as his lawful wedded wife. As we said, Sir William agreed to everything.

In Naples, Emma's beauty had its usual effect. Not only did it astonish, it dazzled.

An enthusiastic antiquarian, a well-known mineralogist, and the British ambassador, as well as a foster brother and friend of George III, Sir William attracted to his home the finest society in the capital of the Two Sicilies—men of science, politicians, and artists alike. It did not take long for Emma, an artist herself, to learn all she needed to know about politics and science, and soon, among the habitués at Sir William's salon, Emma's judgments were law.

There was no end to Emma's triumphs. No sooner had she been presented at the court than Queen Marie-Caroline announced that Lady Hamilton was a close friend, and Emma became the queen's favorite. They were inseparable. Not only did the daughter of Marie-Thérèse appear in public with the Haymarket prostitute, as they'd ride together through Toledo and Chiaia streets in the same carriage and the same style dresses, but sometimes they'd pass evenings together, with Emma striking Antiquity's most ardent and voluptuous poses for the benefit of the queen. Then Marie-Caroline would tell Sir William, proud of the attention the queen lavished on his wife, that she would not give Emma back to him until the following day because she could not do without her friend.

And now Nelson was returning to Naples in triumph as the defender of old royalty. His victory at Aboukir kindled hope anew in the hearts of all those kings who were trying so desperately to keep their wobbly crowns on their heads. At any cost, Marie-Caroline, an ambitious woman eager for wealth and power, intended to preserve her crown. So it is not surprising that she'd seek help from her friend, who held such fascination for the victorious admiral. It is not surprising that she said to Lady Hamilton, the very morning she would again see Nelson, now the keystone of despotism: "That man must be ours. And in order for him to be ours, you must be his."

Was it very difficult for Lady Hamilton to do for her friend Marie-Caroline, with Admiral Horatio Nelson, what Emma Lyonna had done for her friend Fanny Strong with Admiral Payne?

What a glorious reward for the poor pastor's son from Burnham-Thorpe, for the man who owed his grandeur to his own courage and his renown to his own genius! Surely it was a glorious balm for his wounds to see all of Naples welcoming him—the king, the queen, the court. And what a reward for his victories, that magnificent woman whom he absolutely adored!

LXXXIX

In Which Napoleon Sees That Sometimes It Is More Difficult to Control Men Than Fortune

NELSON RECEIVED a true hero's welcome in Naples. The French ambassador was furious at the effrontery. He demanded his passports and left.

Because the king did not want to give France the satisfaction of attacking him first, he set an army of sixty-five thousand men against Championnet, who had a mere twelve thousand. Ferdinand was beaten so badly that he fled back to Naples, but Championnet followed with the zeal typical of Republican generals at the time. Five or six thousand lazzaroni tried to do in Naples what the king's sixty-five thousand men had been unable to do in the field. They stood up to the French, and they managed to defend the city for three days—long enough to get the king, along with the queen and royal family, as well as the British ambassador and his wife, safely out of the city. They went to Sicily.

With a passport from the king, Cardinal Ruffo left Messina in an attempt to take back Calabria and then Naples. He succeeded and did not stop in fact until he reached the borders of Rome. The French were beginning to lose their reputation of invincibility.

Ferdinand returned to Naples. He had compiled a list of one hundred Republicans to be sentenced to death without trial, among them the former admiral Caracciolo. While Caracciolo had resigned as admiral in Ferdinand's naval forces, he found himself, as a citizen of Naples, where the revolutionary fever of France had spread, compelled to enlist in the Republican cause. That was the only grievance the king had against him.

No court would have dared find him guilty of high treason, yet Nelson, for but a kiss from the seductive Emma and a smile from the queen, accepted the role of executioner. His men captured Caracciolo in his hideout and brought him in chains on board the British ship *Foudroyant*. There, against the laws of humanity as well as war, a Neapolitan admiral was found guilty by an English admiral and on the very next morning was hanged like a thief from the yardarm of a ship's mizzenmast.

One would have thought that on Nelson's return to London he would have at least received a public reprimand for his shameful complicity with the Neapolitan Bourbons. On the contrary, he was welcomed triumphantly for his victories at Aboukir and Naples. All the ships in the Thames flew his colors, the government hailed him as the country's savior, the people greeted him with enthusiastic ovations.

He had returned to England with Lady Hamilton, and not far from London he bought a country house called Merton. There he hid his love, his glory, his remorse. He had a daughter with Emma Lyonna; at her baptism she was given the name Horatia.

The Baltic wars called Nelson back to the seas. As vice-admiral he led the attack that forced open the port in Copenhagen and burned the Danish fleet. When he received orders to cease fire by signal from the admiral in command, Nelson put his glass to his blind eye and responded, "I don't see anything." It was a response worthy of Alaric or Attila, and by any civilized standard it deserved to be punished. In London, however, his response earned him only more glory; in the rest of Europe it was received with a gasp of horror.

Again Nelson returned to England in triumph. The king made him a lord. For in Nelson Great Britain had found its great hopes; he was the nation's one true counterbalance to Napoleon.

And Napoleon was continuing his duel with England. For the last eighteen months, all along the coasts of Holland and France, he had been making preparations to invade England. In ports from Dunkirk to Abbeville, five or six hundred armed launches waited, ready to transport the troops encamped near Boulogne. In one day they would be able to land on British soil an army as invincible as that of William the Conqueror.

Although England made fun of Napoleon's boats, calling them nutshells, she was keeping a careful eye on the troops amassing across the Channel and her squadrons were constantly sailing back and forth in the Channel to block the way to London. For that reason, Napoleon did not want to invade until he had also assembled a fleet of seventy or eighty warships that could sail into the Channel and draw the English fleet into combat. Little did he care whether they would win or lose, as long as they occupied the enemy long enough for him to land one hundred fifty or two hundred thousand men on British soil.

At that particular historical moment, though, the French warships were blockaded, some in the Escaut, some in Brest, others in Cadiz and Toulon. And there was no way that they could assemble in any sufficient number except by artful subterfuge or sheer audacity. But none of our admirals, not in France or Holland or Spain, had the necessary genius to execute such heroic or desperate maneuvers to bypass Fortune's obstacles.

Though brave of heart, our admirals were timid of spirit, and imagination failed in the face of an order like: "If you cannot be victorious, let yourself be beaten. But fight in any case." They failed to comprehend the need to keep the English fleet away from London at all costs; they failed to see that by occupying English ships even five hundred leagues away from the Channel, they would be enabling Napoleon to implement more readily his plans for the invasion of England.

Of course, the English knew as well as Napoleon what he needed to do. They knew that he was desperate to bring his scattered ships together. Indeed, he dreamed of getting two squadrons out of Toulon and Brest and sending them, manned with forty or fifty thousand combatants, on two different routes toward the West Indies. The two squadrons would surely attract the attention of the English command, and while the English fleet was at full sail to the West Indies, Napoleon would perhaps have the opportunity to set up his movable bridge across the Channel and do what only two other men, Caesar and William the Conqueror, had been able to do before him.

The sheer immensity of the plan caused Napoleon to lose patience with it. He returned to a simpler plan, one just as likely to succeed in luring all the English squadrons away from the Channel. By his order, Admiral Villeneuve, to whom Napoleon would be giving the command of the combined Spanish and French fleets, had sailed out of Toulon with thirteen warships and several frigates. In Cadiz he had joined forces with the Spanish squadrons, led by Admiral Gravina, and then crossed the Atlantic to join Admiral Missiessy's squadron of six ships in the Antilles. Napoleon now placed Admiral Ganteaume, who was commanding the French fleet in Brest, under orders to take advantage of the first storm severe enough to prevent the English admiral Cornwallis from maintaining his watch off Brest so that Ganteaume could join Villeneuve, Gravina, and Missiessy in Martinique. After harassing the English possessions in the Antilles, the assembled fleet was then to sail rapidly toward France so as to encounter the English squadrons as they were heading out to the open sea to aid their colonies. Somewhere near Europe, by plan, the French were to engage their enemy and then, whether victorious or vanquished, make all speed to the Channel to assist in the invasion of England.

The storms came, but unfortunately the winds died down before Ganteaume was able to leave Brest. So Villeneuve sailed back into European waters with orders to engage Cornwallis long enough to allow Ganteaume the opportunity to get his fleet out of Brest. That accomplished, the two French fleets could join in battle with the English fleet, whatever its strength and numbers, near the Channel. But that had yet to be accomplished.

"The English," Napoleon cried, making a fist like Ajax, "do not realize what is hanging over their heads. If I can be master of the Channel for even twelve hours, England is dead." Napoleon uttered that proclamation in Boulogne. He was standing before one hundred eighty thousand men who had soldiered with their general Bonaparte across the continent. They had not lost their taste for victory.

Time was of the essence. Napoleon knew that it was only a question of days before Austria would declare war and all of Germany would revolt. He had no doubt that Villeneuve had neared Brest, but after a difficult night battle fought not only in darkness but also in fog, Villeneuve had lost two Spanish ships to English hands. Then, in spite of his orders to open Brest, join forces with Ganteaume, and sail to the Channel, he had gone to port at Ferrol, where he was unnecessarily taking on supplies.

Napoleon was furious. He could feel fortune slipping through his fingers. He wrote to Ganteaume, still trapped in the Brest harbor: "Find a way to get out. If you manage to leave port, in one day we can avenge six centuries of inferiority and shame. Never, for any greater result, will my soldiers on land and on sea have risked their lives."

He also wrote to Villeneuve: "Leave, and do not waste a single moment. Leave, and with my squadrons united, sail up to the Channel. We all are waiting. Everything is ready for the invasion, and in twenty-four hours it will be over."

On top of Napoleon's impatience with his admirals came his stupefaction when he learned that Villeneuve was now trapped in Cadiz. Napoleon resorted to epithets like idiot and coward, declaring that Villeneuve was not fit to command even a frigate. "He's a man blinded by fear," he said.

To the Minister of the Navy, Decrès, who was Villeneuve's friend, Napoleon wrote: "Your friend Villeneuve will probably be too much of a coward to get out of Cadiz. Send Admiral Rosily to take command of the squadron if it still has not left port. And summon Admiral Villeneuve back to Paris to explain his conduct."

Minister Decrès did not have the heart to announce to Villeneuve the misfortune that had so gravely befallen him, for it afforded him no way to redeem himself. The minister wrote only that Rosily was coming, but he did not explain why. Nor did he advise Villeneuve to set sail before Rosily arrived in Cadiz, although he hoped that would be the case. In his embarrassment, caught between his friend, whose mistakes he recognized, and the Emperor's legitimate anger, the minister made the mistake of choosing neither side, and thus left everything to chance.

Villeneuve was able to read between the minister's lines. What hurt him the most was the reputation for cowardice that he knew he would gain but did not deserve. He knew, too, that the French navy was in a sorry state—indeed, he knew better than most how disastrously weak it was—and that any fleet facing Nelson in all his foolhardy courage might as well consider itself beaten before the battle even began.

Gravina meanwhile exchanged half of his ships, which were barely seaworthy, for the best that he could find in the Cadiz arsenal. We now had better ships, but the personnel remained the same. By then it was September 1805.

During the eight months they had been at sea, our crews had gained some experience. Some of the captains were excellent, but among the officers too many had come from the merchant marine and therefore were lacking in the skills and spirit of navy men. What they were lacking even more were naval tactics to respond effectively to the new methods of attack the English were employing. Instead of forming the customary battle line and moving forward systematically, with each vessel choosing as its adversary the ship opposite, Nelson attacked rapidly and unpredictably, without following any set order. His ships would fall upon the enemy fleet and cut its formal battle line in two. Fearless of the ensuing confusion, during which it was scarcely possible in the heavy smoke to distinguish friend from foe, he would fire until his adversary either struck its colors or sank.

Fearing that his invasion of England might fail, Napoleon wrote a letter to Monsieur de Talleyrand in which he talked about new plans, plans that were then still the stuff of imperial dreams:

It is over. My fleets are nowhere in sight on the Ocean. If they are able to reach the Channel, there is still time. I can climb into a boat, invade England, and cut the coalition knot in London. If on the other hand my admirals are weak and maneuver badly, I shall lead my two hundred thousand men to Germany. I shall take Vienna, I shall chase the Bourbons out of Naples, and once the continent is pacified, then I shall return to the Ocean and win a maritime peace.

Napoleon was at La Malmaison on September 18, the day he learned of the Austrian emperor's manifesto against France. France answered in kind. With that rapidity of execution characteristic of him, Napoleon came to terms with the failure of the Boulogne expedition and turned his attention instead to his plans for wars on the continent, which he had been considering seriously for nearly two weeks.

Never had he disposed of so many resources. Never had he seen such a huge battlefield open up before him. Emperor and general, he was for the first time as free as Alexander and Caesar had been. Those among his companions at arms who'd been so misguided by their jealousy—Moreau, Pichegru, Bernadotte, etc.—had removed themselves from the lists by their foolish or guilty conduct. With him now were officers eager to yield to his will and respect his judgment; excellent men who brought to him the very qualities necessary to carry out his plans.

His army was tired of France at peace. For ten years it had breathed the glory of war, and now it had waited for four years to return to the fields of battle and honor. Ten years had shaped his men for this; they were prepared to undertake the most difficult marches and to engage in the most serious endeavors. The army was splendidly confident; one might say that France had never seen one better.

Napoleon needed to move his forces quickly to the middle of the continent. That was the difficulty.

XC

The Port of Cadiz

By OCTOBER 17, 1805, the Emperor had already sent back to Paris two cannons and eight flags that he had taken at the battle of Gunzburg. Within the next three days he had entered Munich, besieged Ulm, and fought the battle of Elchingen, which would make Marshal Ney a duke. On the very day of that battle, and the day before Napoleon sent forty more flags to the Senate, a sloop flying the American flag entered the port of Cadiz where Admiral Villeneuve's fleet still lay at anchor.

Once in port, the sloop took its bearings and upon inquiry learned that the *Redoutable* was moored at the base of the fort. Since the sloop could not easily maneuver its way to the fort, it let down its best skiff, and the captain ordered the oarsmen to take him to the *Redoutable*.

When they drew near, the ship's watch officer hailed them. They answered that they were from the *New York Racer* and that their captain was bringing Captain Lucas news from India and letters from the governor of Île de France.

Immediately Captain Lucas was summoned. He came up on deck and motioned to the officer on the skiff to climb aboard. The officer, of course, was none other than René. He climbed quickly up the ladder and onto the deck.

Captain Lucas welcomed him politely, but was careful to maintain the formality befitting his superior position, for, especially in the navy, hierarchy is absolute. He asked his visitor if he would like to speak with him alone; the answer being affirmative, he invited René to accompany him to his sitting room.

As soon as the two men had entered the captain's cabin and the door was closed, René handed Lucas the governor's letter. Lucas did no more than glance at it.

"My friend General Decaen recommends you to me in such glowing terms," he said to René, "that it's I who must ask what I might do for you."

"Captain, in three or four days you will be waging a great naval battle. I have seen but minor skirmishes at sea, and I admit that I would like to lend myself to a matter of more moment, in European waters, so that I might add some luster to my name, which is known now only in the Indian Ocean."

"Yes," said Lucas, "yes, we will indeed soon be waging a major battle in which, you can be sure, one will in one way or another add luster to one's name, whether one dies or lives. May I ask you, not just for the matter of the facts themselves but rather in the manner of friendly conversation, what your naval background is?"

"My background , Captain, dates from barely two years ago, when I first served with Surcouf. I took part in that famous combat during which, with a one-hundred-man crew and sixteen cannons, he captured the *Standard*, which was carrying forty-eight cannons and a crew of four hundred fifty. Since then I have captained that little sloop with which I sailed to Burma. On my voyage back to Île de France, I had the good fortune of coming upon Surcouf, who was engaged in combat with two English ships. I sailed to his aid and captured one of the ships. It was carrying sixteen cannons and sixty crew members, though I myself had only eighteen men."

"I know Surcouf quite well," said Lucas. "He is one of our boldest corsairs."

"He gave me a letter for you in case we should meet," said René, handing the captain of the *Redoutable* the letter Surcouf had written on his behalf. Lucas read it carefully from beginning to end.

"Monsieur," he said to René, "for Surcouf to praise you so highly, you must truly be an exceptional man. He writes that of your share of the prize, five hundred thousand francs, you gave four hundred thousand to your men and one hundred thousand to the poor on Île de France. From that I take it you must have a large personal fortune and consequently a true vocation for the sea. You entered service, Surcouf tells me, as a simple corsair, with the ambition of advancing more rapidly than you could have in the imperial navy. Unfortunately, all I can offer you on board the *Redoutable* is a third lieutenant's position."

"That is more than I hoped for, Captain, and I gratefully accept. When may I begin my duties?"

"Whenever you like!"

"As soon as possible, Captain. I can already smell the powder, and I am sure that within three or four days I shall see the great battle for which I left the other hemisphere. My ship's tonnage is too small for it to be useful to you. I shall go back on board and send it to France; then I shall return."

Lucas got to his feet, and with a charming smile he said, "I shall be waiting, Lieutenant." René shook both his hands effusively, then left for his sloop.

When René got back on board the *Racer,* he called François to his cabin. "François," he said, "I shall be staying on here in Cadiz. I entrust my sloop to you for the journey back to Saint-Malo. This portfolio contains my will and testament; if I should be killed, you will find that it includes you. In addition, I am leaving in your care this bag of precious stones. If I am killed, you will take the bag in person to Mademoiselle Claire de Sourdis. She lives with her mother, Madame la Comtesse de Sourdis, in the Hôtel de Sourdis, which on one side opens onto the quay and on the other into the Rue de Beaune. Enclosed in the bag is a letter explaining where the stones come from, but do not take them to her, and do not open my testament, unless my death has been proven beyond all doubt.

"I have already, at the end of the ship's papers, added your name as the current owner. I'm asking you to take good care of the ship for a year. In the drawer of my secretary you will find twelve rolls of gold, each containing one thousand francs; three of them are to help you get through the year. If you are stopped by the English, you can present to them the ship's American registry. If they ask what has happened to me, you can say that I met Nelson's fleet and joined one of his ships.

"Farewell, my dear François. Embrace me, take my weapons, and try to make it safely to Saint-Malo. As soon as you arrive, be sure to take news of Robert to Madame Surcouf and her family."

"That means," said François, wiping his eyes with the back of his hand, "that means you do not love me enough to take me with you. And I would have followed you to the ends of the earth and even farther. Good God! It simply breaks my heart to leave you!" And the good man burst into tears.

"I'm the one leaving you," René continued. "Because I believe you to be my one true friend, the only man on whom I can depend. For this portfolio contains securities worth half a million francs, and in the bag are stones worth three hundred thousand more. Knowing that all these matters are in your hands, I am as confident as if they were in my own. Let us shake hands like good men. Let us love each other like two brave hearts. Let us embrace like true friends! Take me to the *Redoutable*. You will be the last man that I bid farewell."

François realized that there was no changing René's mind. René gathered his weapons; he was now carrying only his rifle, his double-barreled shotgun, and his grappling axe. Then he called everyone on deck and, after announcing the decision he had made, he invited his men to recognize François as their captain.

Every man lamented the news. René guaranteed all of them their current conditions of sail: their regular pay, and one year in the Saint-Malo harbor on board the *New York Racer*. They all promised him their absolute devotion as he climbed back down to the skiff along with François and six oarsmen.

Ten minutes later René was standing before Captain Lucas, where he and François said their farewells. One of the greatest recommendations for a man is the esteem his inferiors hold for him. René had that and more: He was greatly loved. His men's sadness and François's tears evidenced for the captain the depth of feeling among the sloop's crew for his new third lieutenant.

As René and François were breaking their farewell embrace, Captain Lucas took down from the wall a lovely meerschaum pipe, which he presented to François. Not knowing how to express his gratitude, François began again to sob and left without saying a single word.

"I like his way of showing what he thinks of people," said Lucas. "You must be a fine fellow if they love you like that. Come now. Let us sit down and have a chat."

Setting the example, the captain sat down first. His eyes fell on the only three weapons René had left: the grooved-barreled rifle, his shotgun, and the axe.

"I am sorry to have given away my weapons to friends on Île de France," René said, "so that I might have something to offer worthy of you. All I have left are these three things. Choose."

"They say that you are an excellent shot," said Lucas. "So you keep your guns, and I shall take the axe. I hope I prove myself worthy of it during our next battle."

"If you don't mind my asking, when will the next battle take place?"

"Well," said Lucas, "it may not be immediately. The Emperor has sent word to Villeneuve that we are to set sail with the combined French and Spanish fleets for Cartagena, there to join Rear Admiral Salcedo. Then we are to proceed to Naples and land troops for General Saint-Cyr's army. 'Our intention,' the Emperor added, 'is that wherever you may find the enemy, even if he is stronger, you will attack without hesitation. Be sure to be decisive with the enemy. As you must surely realize, the success of these operations depends essentially on how quickly you are able to leave Cadiz. We are counting on you to set sail as soon as possible, and in this important operation we recommend the greatest boldness and diligence.' The Emperor is not bothered by exaggeration when addressing Villeneuve, for in his eyes the admiral is one of those men who need spurs rather than a bridle. At the same time he has ordered Vice Admiral Rosily to take command of the combined fleet if it is still in Cadiz upon his arrival from Paris. He is to make the *Bucentaure* his flagship and send Villeneuve back to the capital to account for the campaign he has just completed."

"Good lord!" said René. "The situation is indeed serious."

"And the war council," Lucas continued, "is now with Admiral Villeneuve. The admirals and squadron leaders, Rear Admirals Dumanoir and Magon, and captains Cosmao, Maistral, Devillegris, and Prigny, represent the French ships. They will be consulted about the state of each ship in their command and about their hopes and fears in the event of battle."

Suddenly Lucas, who had been walking up and down as he spoke, stopped and faced René. "Do you know what the Emperor is saying?" he asked.

"No, Captain. I am completely out of touch. I have been away from France for two years."

"The English, he says, will become less of a threat to France once we find two or three admirals who are willing to sacrifice their lives. While some among us are not admirals, in two or three days we need to prove to His Majesty that, if there are no admirals who are *willing to die,* there are at least some captains who *know how to die.*"

Their conversation was interrupted by an officer who announced, "Captain, there is a signal summoning all captains to the flagship."

"Fine. Order the skiff," Lucas replied. Once the skiff was ready, he climbed down into it, and like the captains of five or six other ships who had not been called to the original war council, he headed for the *Bucentaure.*

René, meanwhile, was shown the third lieutenant's cabin, which was larger and more comfortable than his captain's quarters on board the *New York Racer.* He had just carried in the two or three chests he had brought with him when Captain Lucas came back on board. René dared not appear without being summoned, but after their earlier conversation, he was certain that the captain would do him the honor of a second meeting. He was not mistaken.

Five minutes later, the captain had summoned him, and now René was waiting respectfully for his superior to speak.

"Well," Lucas began, "it'll be tomorrow or the next day. The admiral said: 'If the wind is favorable and allows me leave port, I shall do so tomorrow.' Evidently he had been informed that Nelson had just sent six of his ships to Gibraltar. So he summoned Admiral Gravina, and after a brief conversation, he called all the ship captains together to order them to prepare for sailing. That was why I was called to the flagship."

"Will you be assigning me to some particular service?"

"As you are still unfamiliar with my ship and my crew," said Lucas, "you should begin by getting to know them; then we shall see. Other than that, you have the reputation of being an excellent shot, so I suggest you take a place on one of the high decks, somewhere that you'll be able to look out over the deck of any vessel we encounter. Shoot as many gold epaulettes as you can, and if we board them, follow your inspiration. I shall carry your axe, and I am pleased to have it. I have asked that my own cutlass be delivered to your cabin. It is too big for me," said Lucas, with a joking reference to his own height, "but it should suit you well."

Both men bowed, and René returned to his cabin. There he found a handsome Damascus steel sword from Tunis. Its wide, curved blade had been so superbly tempered that, with a quick flick of the wrist, you could slice through a silk scarf floating in the breeze.

As the fleet prepared to leave, the admirals, to some surprise, discovered that in the two and a half months they'd been in Cadiz harbor, a number of their men had deserted ship. In particular, the Spanish ships had lost as much as a tenth of their crews. The officers spent an entire day trying to round up as many of the fugitives as possible in the streets of Cadiz, but many of them had already left the city. Finally, on the morning of October 19, at seven o'clock, the combined force began to move.

Nelson, who lay about sixteen leagues west-northwest of Cadiz with the greater part of the English fleet, knew what was happening. He knew, too, that if Villeneuve could reach the straits first, he might escape. Nelson set out to block Villeneuve's passage.

It is difficult to set sail from the port of Cadiz; six years before, it had taken Admiral Bruix three days. On October 19, 1805, a beautiful day, the calm and the contrary currents soon stopped Villeneuve's fleet, and only eight or ten ships were able to get through the pass. The next day, the twentieth, a light breeze from the southeast made the going easier for the fleet. During the night, clouds had rolled in, announcing a storm from the southwest, but the combined fleet needed only a few hours of a good breeze to bring its ships out into the wind off Cape Trafalgar. Then, even if a storm should blow up, if it was blowing from the east to the southwest, it would still be favorable to Villeneuve's plans.

By ten o'clock the last of the French and Spanish ships were out of Cadiz. That is when Villeneuve, deciding there was no turning back, wrote this dispatch to Admiral Decrès:

> The entire fleet is under sail. . . . The wind is to the south-southwest, but I think it is just the morning wind. I have received the signal that there are eighteen sails. So it is quite probable that the citizens of Cadiz will soon be able to send news about us. . . . My greatest desire, Monsignor, as we set out, is to conform to His Majesty's intentions and to do my best to eradicate the displeasure he has shown about the events of our last campaign. If this campaign is successful, it will be difficult for me not to believe that all is as it should be, that everything has been calculated for the best in His Majesty's service.

The English fleet was a few leagues off Cape Spartel, guarding the entrance to the straits.

XCI

The Little Bird

TWO MONTHS EARLIER, Nelson had assumed his military career was over. He had retired to his magnificent country house in Merton with Lady Hamilton, whose husband, Lord Hamilton, had died, so now only one obstacle stood in the way of Emma's marriage to the celebrated admiral: Mrs. Nesbitt, his wife.

Nelson had no plans of going back to sea. Tired of triumphs, saturated with glory, overladen with honors, mutilated in body, he longed for solitude and tranquility. To that end, he was in the process of moving any papers and effects of importance from London down to Merton. The enchanting Emma Lyonna's future seemed to be assured.

And then a thunderbolt struck.

On September 2, just twelve days after Nelson had come home, he heard someone knocking loudly on their door in Merton—at five in the morning. Nelson thought immediately that it had to be a messenger from the Admiralty as he jumped from his bed and went to greet the early-morning visitor.

It was Captain Blackwood, who had indeed come from the Admiralty with the news that the united fleets of France and Spain, so long pursued by Nelson, were now blocked in the Cadiz harbor. Recognizing Blackwood, Nelson cried, "I am willing to wager, Blackwood, that you are bringing news about the combined fleets and that I am to be given the assignment of destroying them": which was exactly the case.

All of Nelson's retirement plans evaporated into thin air. He could see nothing more than that little parcel of earth, or rather of sea, where the French and Spanish fleets lay immobilized. Beaming with joy, buoyed by the confidence drawn from his many victories, he kept repeating to the captain: "Blackwood, you can be sure that I shall give Villeneuve a lesson he will never forget."

His first intention had been to leave for London to prepare for the campaign without telling Emma anything about his new mission, at least not until the last minute. But she too had been awakened by the knocking, and she'd observed how intense his conversation with Blackwood had been.

Afterward she led him to his favorite spot in the garden, a place he called his bridge. "What is the matter, my friend?" she asked. "You don't want to tell me what's bothering you."

Nelson tried to smile. "I am the happiest man in the world," he replied. "What more could I want, surrounded by my family and blessed with your love? Truly, I would not give sixpence to have the king as my uncle."

Emma interrupted him. "I know you well, Nelson," she said. "And you will never be able to fool me. You know where the enemy fleet is. Go and destroy it. Go finish up the business you have started so well. Destroying the fleet will be your reward for the two long, tiring years you have had to endure."

Nelson kept his gaze fixed on his mistress. Although he said nothing, Emma could read in his eyes an indescribable expression of gratitude. She went on: "However difficult your absence will be for me, you must proffer your service to your country as you always have and leave immediately for Cadiz. For your services will be gratefully accepted, and after Cadiz your heart will regain its serenity. You will win one last glorious victory; then you will return home happy to find rest and dignity."

Nelson, silently, continued staring at her for several more seconds, until his eyes filled with tears. "Good Emma! Brave Emma!" he cried. "Yes, you have read my heart. Yes, you have guessed my thoughts. If there were no longer an Emma, there would be no Nelson. You have made me what I am. Today I shall go straightaway to London."

The *Victory*, alerted by telegraph, was in the Thames that very evening, and the next day preparations for sailing were under way.

Nelson and Lady Hamilton had another ten days together before his departure. He spent the last five almost exclusively at the Admiralty, but on the eleventh, they went back to their dear country home in Merton for one last visit. They spent the next day there, alone, together, and that night as well.

One hour before daylight Nelson got up. He went into his daughter's room. A religious man, he bent over her bed and prayed silently with great devotion and many tears.

At seven that morning he bade farewell to Emma. She accompanied him to his carriage. There he held her tightly. She was weeping, but she tried to smile despite her tears as she said, "Do not go into battle unless you see the little bird."

In order to take the full measure of a man, we should not measure him only at the peak of his grandeur but also at his low, more vulnerable points. Here is the story of Nelson's little bird:

The first time Emma saw Nelson after he came back from the battle at Aboukir as the "Hero of the Nile," she had felt suddenly faint as she kissed him. Nelson had her carried to his cabin, and she was just beginning to regain her senses when a little bird flew in through the window and lit on Horatio's shoulder. As she opened her eyes, though perhaps she had never really closed them, Emma asked, "What is that little bird?"

Nelson smiled and laughingly answered, "It is my protective spirit, madame. When a tree was cut to make the mast for one of our ships, in its branches was the nest of a Bengalese finch. Each of my victories has been preceded by a visit from this little bird, whether I was on the high sea off England, India, or America. It is my good omen, so perhaps there is some victory awaiting me today if this little bird has come to visit me." Indeed, the little bird might have come to announce his greatest victory, that over Emma Lyonna. Then he added more darkly, "But I do know that the day I enter battle without seeing this little bird, on that day misfortune will befall me."

And that is why Emma said, "Do not go into battle unless you see the little bird."

Nelson reached Portsmouth the next morning. On September 15 he was at sea. Nelson was eager to make good speed, but bad weather forced the *Victory* to remain within sight of the British coast for two whole days. The delay allowed Nelson time to send his mistress two little letters filled with his love for her and their daughter, but they also hinted at a sense of foreboding.

Finally the weather improved. Nelson was able to leave the Channel, and by September 20, under full sail, he had joined the English fleet, its twenty-three ships under the command of Vice Admiral Collingwood, off Cadiz. On the same day, he celebrated his forty-sixth birthday.

On October 1, he wrote to Emma about his meeting with Collingwood, although he first mentions one of those nervous attacks he had on occasion been experiencing since the day he'd been bitten by a serpent. Here is the letter:

October 1, 1805

My dearest Emma,

What a relief it is for me to pick up my pen and compose a few lines to you. For this morning at about four o'clock I had one of those painful spasms that completely unnerve me. I think that one of those attacks will kill me some day. However, it is over now, and all I feel is great fatigue. Yesterday I wrote for seven hours. The incident was probably due to fatigue.

I joined the fleet rather late on the evening of September 20, and I was unable to communicate with it until the next day. I believe that everyone, including the fleet's commander, was glad to see me. When I explained my battle plan to the officers, it was as if they had received a revelation, and they leaped with enthusiasm. Some of them were even shedding tears. My plan was new, unusual, and simple. If we are able to carry out our plan against the French fleet, victory is assured. "All your friends around you have total confidence in you!" the officers shouted. Perhaps there is a Judas among them, but the majority are certainly delighted that I am in command.

I've just now received letters from the king and queen of Naples in answer to my letters of June 18 and July 12. Not one word for you! Truly, that king and queen would make Ungratefulness itself blush! I am attaching copies of their letters to mine, which at the earliest opportunity will leave for England to tell you how much I love you.

Still no little bird. But there is yet time.

My mutilated body is here, but my whole heart is with you.

H.N.

By October 20, exactly one month after Nelson had joined Collingwood's fleet, Admiral Villeneuve had received from the French government his orders to leave Cadiz, sail through the straits, land troops on the

Naples coast, and then, once he had swept the Mediterranean clean of English ships, proceed to the port of Toulon. The combined fleets, made up of thirty-three ships, eighteen French and fifteen Spanish, first came into sight of the British at seven on the morning of the twentieth, a Sunday.

Battle seemed to be imminent, and that morning, Nelson wrote two letters. The first was to his mistress:

My dearly beloved Emma, I have received word that the enemy fleet is leaving port. We have very little wind, so that I can not expect to reach them before tomorrow. May the god of battles crown our efforts with glorious success. In any case, victorious or dead, I am sure that my name will become dearer to you and Horatia, and I love both of you more than my own life.

Pray for your friend,

Nelson

Then he wrote to Horatia:

Victory, October 19, 1805.

My dear angel, I was the happiest man in the world when I received your little letter of September 19. I am so pleased to hear that you have been a good girl and that you love dear Lady Hamilton, for she adores you. Give her a kiss for me. The combined enemy fleets are leaving Cadiz, they tell me. That is why I hasten to answer your letter, my dear Horatia, to tell you that are always in my thoughts. I am sure that you are praying to God for my safety, for my glory, and for my early return to Merton.

Your father sends you his blessing, my dear child.

Nelson

The next day he added this postscriptum to Emma's letter:

The morning of October 20

We are near the entrance to the straits. I have received word that we can see forty sails off in the distance. I imagine that there are thirty-three gunships and seven frigates, but since the wind is cold and seas high, I believe they will return to port before nightfall.

Finally, as the combined fleets came more clearly into sight, he wrote in his journal:

May the great God, before whom I prostrate myself in adoration, grant England, in the general interest of oppressed Europe, a grand and glorious victory. And may he also allow the victory not to be obscured by any mistakes on the part of those who will fight and triumph. As for me personally, I remit my life into the hands of the one who gave life to me. May the Lord bless the efforts I shall undertake in faithful service to my country. I entrust and give to him alone the holy cause for which on this day he has deigned to name me the defender. Amen! Amen! Amen!

Having made that prayer, in which we find that blend of mysticism and enthusiasm that on occasion appears beneath the seaman's rough exterior, he wrote this last will and testament:

> October 21, 1805,
> Within sight of the combined forces of France and Spain,
> About ten miles away

Considering that the eminent services rendered to the king and the nation by Emma Lyonna, widow of Sir William Hamilton, have never been rewarded either by the king or by the nation,

I bring the following to your attention:

1) That in 1799, Lady Hamilton obtained information contained in a letter from the King of Spain to his brother the King of Naples, in which he informed him of his intention to declare war on England. Thanks to that information, the minister was able to send orders to Sir John Jervis to attack the Spanish arsenals and the Spanish fleet if the opportunity arose. If those things were not done, it was not Lady Hamilton's fault.

2) That the British fleet, under my command, would never have been able to go back to Egypt the second time if, through the influence of Lady Hamilton on the Queen of Naples, orders had not been given to the governor of Syracuse to allow our fleet to take on all needed supplies in Sicilian ports. Thus I got everything I needed and was able to destroy the French fleet.

Consequently, I leave to my king and to my country the care of rewarding her for her services and providing her an appropriate living.

I also entrust to the benevolence of the nation my adopted daughter Horatia Nelson Thomson, and I request that from now on she bear the name Nelson.

These are the only favors I ask of the king and of England, at the moment when I shall risk my life for them. May God bless my king and my country, along with all those who are dear to me!

> Nelson

Nelson's precautions in the face of battle to guarantee his mistress's future offer some proof of the admiral's premonitions of his own death. To authenticate further the last requests that he had recorded in his journal, he summoned from the *Euryale* Captain Hardy as well as Captain Blackwood, who had come to Merton at the behest of the Admiralty seven weeks before, to serve as witnesses. He had them sign the testament, and indeed their two names can be found in the logbook alongside Nelson's.

XCII
Trafalgar

AT THAT TIME, predictably and consistently, the French employed only one plan of attack in their naval battles. Without fail, they would move toward the enemy, if possible with the wind, in one long line, and each ship would attack the one opposite it in the enemy line and do battle until either one or the other had been destroyed. Let chance measure the strength of each ship.

The French navy embraced other principles, too, that made combat less dangerous for its enemies than for itself. Official instructions published under the navy's auspices stated, for instance, that the first and primary objective of any naval combat was to unrig or dismast the enemy. Thus the English general Sir Edward Douglas would remark, "We always noticed that in our dealings with the French, our ships always took more damage in their riggings than in their hulls."

Our objective to unrig made the English artillery only more effective. Already their cannons could fire every minute, whereas ours fired every three, and they could cover our decks with corpses before we managed to hit anything at all. While we were aiming to hit the masts and rigging, which often took five or six attempts, a seventy-four-gun English ship could shoot three thousand pounds of iron per minute into an enemy's hull. And when those three thousand pounds of iron hit, they would crush the ship's hull, tear loose our cannons, and kill every Frenchman in their path.

"England owed its absolute mastery over the seas to that hail of shot," Nelson wrote to the Admiralty. Certainly it was what he owed his victory to five years before at Aboukir.

Nelson had also dispensed with the custom of fighting in lines. He would align his ships in the shape of a "V," with his own ship at its head. Like a Macedonian wedge, his ship would tear through the enemy line at a strategic point, all the while shooting in both directions. Once it broke through, it would turn back, with one column following it. The other column would mirror the maneuver, and the ships that had been surrounded would be destroyed before help could come to them.

In the council meeting he had held two days before the battle, Admiral Villeneuve had said, "Every effort of each ship must aim to support any ships that are attacked by drawing near the flagship, which will set the example. A captain must take counsel more from his own courage and his love of glory than from any signals the admiral might send, for the admiral, caught up in battle and surrounded by smoke, may not be able to send signals at all. *Any captain not fired upon will be considered as not being at his post,* and any signal sent to remind him of that fact will be a dishonorable blemish for him."

Nelson had said: "Once I have divided my fleet into two squadrons, I shall engage in two different battles. One will be offensive, reserved for Collingwood; the defensive battle I shall reserve for myself. Villeneuve will probably be sailing over an area five or six miles wide. I shall thrust our ships at him and break his fleet into two parts. I shall then leave to Collingwood the advantage of numbers and the responsibility of superior forces.

"The English fleet is composed of forty vessels, and the Franco-Spanish fleet has forty-six. Collingwood, with sixteen ships, will attack twelve enemy ships. I, with the twenty-four remaining ones, shall contain the other thirty-four. Not only shall I contain them, but I shall throw myself at the center, where their ships are gathered around their flagship. Thus I shall be able to isolate Villeneuve from his squadron, and I will prevent him from sending orders to the vanguard.

"As soon as I have explained my intentions to the commander of the second column, complete control and absolute command will be in his hands. He will attack as he sees fit and pursue his advantages until he either captures or destroys the ships he has surrounded. *I shall see to it that no other enemy ships come to interrupt him.* As for the captains of each ship, if during the combat they are unable to see or completely understand their admiral's signals, they must be reassured. They cannot do wrong if they can maneuver their ships alongside an enemy ship."

Nelson's simple exposition of his naval tactics roused a long, enthusiastic shout that echoed through the council room on the *Victory,* where the squadron captains and officers were gathered. Later, Nelson wrote to the Admiralty:

It was as if there was an electric shock. Several officers were moved to tears. They all approved of our plan of attack. They found it innovative, unexpected, and easy to understand and carry out. From the first of the admirals to the last of the captains, they all cried out: "The enemy is done for if we can make contact with them."

The admirals were indeed going into combat, but whereas Nelson could already taste victory, Villeneuve was setting out with little confidence. Among his many good, devoted men, most of them willinghearted and highly skilled, he could sense an unease, a presentiment of destruction, which may have been only his own fear. For he remembered Aboukir. Since then, his letters had frequently mentioned our officers' lack of experience at sea, our captains' lack of experience in battle, our soldiers' lack of experience in combat, and our fleet's general lack of unity.

The wind that had allowed Villeneuve and Gravina to get under way had suddenly dropped. Hindered by the inexperience aboard some of the Spanish ships, which had fallen to leeward as they were reefing in, the combined fleet was able to move only very slowly away from the coast.

Nelson's frigates had meanwhile alerted him that the French and Spanish fleets had left port, and he was already advancing to engage in battle when the strong winds dissipated. The sea went calm. Night fell before the adversaries could enter into combat.

Fires blazed here and there in the night, and from time to time cannon shots marked the distance between the ships. Villeneuve knew that it would be useless to try to hide his movements from the enemy; and he needed to gather his fleet into a more compact formation. The next morning at about seven, the admiral signaled for his ships to form their normal battle line, with their frigates on the starboard side.

Observing their maneuvers, Nelson realized that the long-awaited battle would take place that very day. In preparation for the battle, he had his furniture tied down, and Lady Hamilton's portrait was removed from the wall and stowed between decks, where it would be safer.

The joint fleet was moving rapidly and resolutely forward in close battle ranks; the distance between the enemy fleets narrowed with each wave. A light breeze from the west-northwest barely filled out the topmost sails as the English ships rose and fell on long swells that indicated a storm was imminent. The English fleet was moving at about a league per hour. It was sailing in two columns, for such was Nelson's plan.

The *Victory*, Nelson's ship, sailed at the head of the first squadron. Behind it were two ninety-eight-gun vessels, the *Téméraire* and the *Neptune*, bronze battering rams designed to open the first hole through the enemy lines. The *Conqueror* and the *Leviathan*, each with seventy-four guns, followed the *Neptune* and preceded the *Britannia*, a vessel with one hundred cannons, flying

Rear Admiral Northesk's flag. The *Agamemnon*, one of the first ships Nelson had captained, followed in the wake of the *Britannia* and led four seventy-four-gun ships: the *Ajax*, the *Orion*, the *Minotaur*, and the *Spartiate*.

Whereas the English ships carried two thousand and forty-eight cannons, the French fleet had one thousand three hundred and fifty-six, though the Spanish brought one thousand two hundred and seventy more. They were now within normal cannon range. Villeneuve, by a precaution normally taken at sea but not appropriate on this occasion, had given the order not to fire until they were at close range. Since the two English lines were massed so close together, however, each French shot would have struck its mark with no waste of fire.

Around noon, and about a quarter of an hour ahead of Nelson's northern column, the column to the south, led by Admiral Collingwood, reached the middle of our line, where the *Santa Ana* lay. The *Belleisle* and the *Mars* followed. Both the *Tonnant* and the *Bellerophon* sailed on the heels of the *Mars*, while a cable-length behind came the *Colossus*, the *Achille*, and the *Polyphemus*. A little to the right, the *Revenge* was followed by the *Swiftsure*, the *Thunderer*, and the *Defence;* the *Dreadnought* and the *Prince*, both of them difficult ships to maneuver, lay between the two lines; they belonged, however, to Collingwood's squadron.

Admiral Villeneuve's flag flew from the mast of the *Bucentaure*, and Admiral Gravina's flag flew above the *Principe de Asturias*, a ship with one hundred and twelve guns. Rear Admiral Dumanoir was on board the *Formidable;* Rear Admiral Magon was on board the *Algesiras*. Two magnificent three-deck Spanish ships, the *Santisima Trinidad*, with one hundred and thirty-six cannons, and the *Santa Ana*, with its one hundred and twelve guns, were also flying admirals' flags: the first the flag of Rear Admiral Cisneros, the second of Rear Admiral Alava.

A number of ships, hindered in their progress by the calm and the heavy swells, had not yet reached their battle stations and for the time being lay in a second row behind Villeneuve's battle line. They were the *Neptuno*, the *Scipion*, the *Intrépide*, the *Rayo*, the *Formidable*, the *Duguay-Trouin*, the *Mont-Blanc*, and the *San Francisco di Asís*.

The three principal ships in the battle line were clustering around the flagship *Bucentaure*. In front was the *Santissima Trinidad*. The *Redoutable* followed in its wake, and, still maneuvering itself into position on the leeward side, the *Neptune* lay between the *Bucentaure* and the *Redoutable*. When Captain Lucas discerned that the point of convergence for the two English columns, one led by the *Victory* and the other by the *Royal Sovereign*, wold be the *Santa Ana*, he maneuvered the *Redoutable* so that it would lie between the *Bucentaure* and the *Santa Ana* at the moment of collision.

Beside him on the upper deck stood a young officer nobody knew. He was armed with a cutlass and rifle; he went by the name René. He and Lucas could see Nelson standing on his own upper deck with another man. It was Blackwood, captain of the *Euryale*.

Nelson summoned an officer attached to his general staff. "Mr. Pasco," he said, "transmit this watchword to the entire fleet: *England expects every man will do his duty!*"

Nelson was dressed in his blue uniform. On his chest he was wearing the decorations of the Order of Bath, the Order of Ferdinand, the Order of Merit, the Order of Malta, and finally the Ottoman Crescent—all to the surprise of Captain Hardy, who shared with Blackwood the admiral's trust and affection.

"For the love of God, Admiral," Hardy admonished him, "change your uniform. Your chest bedecked with decorations will become everyone's target."

"It is too late," Nelson replied.

The two captains then begged him at least to consider his rank as general in chief and not lead the vanguard into the middle of Villeneuve's amassed ships. "The *Leviathan*," Hardy said, "is right behind you. Let it go first and draw French fire."

"I'd be willing to let the *Leviathan* pass me," Nelson replied with a smile, "if it can." Then he leaned toward Hardy and said, "Meanwhile, crack on more sail!"

At that command, Blackwood prepared to leave the deck of the *Victory* and return to his own ship. Nelson bade him farewell from the top of the ladder to the poop deck. He squeezed Blackwood's hand tenderly while the captain congratulated him on his approaching victory. "How many ships captured or sunk will be enough to mean it is a great victory?" he asked Blackwood with a laugh.

"Perhaps twelve or fifteen," Blackwood replied.

"Twelve or fifteen would not be enough," said Nelson. "I shall not be content with fewer than twenty." Then his brow darkened, and he said to his friend, "Farewell, Blackwood. May all-powerful God bless you. I shall never see you again."

It was not Nelson, however, who had the honor of firing the first shots. The *Royal Sovereign*, at the head of Collingwood's line, was sailing at an angle that enabled it to cross the Franco-Spanish battle lines before the *Victory*. Captained by Collingwood, it pounced on the *Santa Ana;* coming alongside, starboard side to starboard side, it raked the three-deck Spanish ship with grapeshot and shrouded it in smoke.

"Good Collingwood!" shouted Nelson, pointing to the gap at the center of the enemy line. "Look, Hardy! See how he throws his ship into the fray, not looking ahead, behind, or to either side. Now the path is open. Let us all catch the wind."

At the same time, Collingwood, in the midst of the thundering guns, was shouting to his squadron captain Rotheram, "Ah! How happy Nelson would be if he were here!"

It would not be long before Nelson was there. Already cannonballs from the seven ships at the heart of the Franco-Spanish fleet's battle line were flying over his head, ripping his sails, and digging furrows on the deck.

The first man to fall on board the *Victory* was a young man, Nelson's secretary. He had been standing by the admiral and Hardy when he was cut in half by a cannonball. Knowing Nelson's fondness for the young man, Hardy had the body carried away immediately to spare the admiral's feelings.

At about the same moment chain shot dropped eight men to the deck, their bodies cut in two. "Oh!" cried Nelson. "They cannot keep shooting with such intensity for long!"

As he'd spoken, wind from a ball passed close to Nelson's face and nearly asphyxiated him. He reached out and latched onto the arm of one of his lieutenants; wobbly for a moment, he tried to catch his breath. "It was nothing," he said as he regained his composure. "It was nothing."

The cannonballs were coming from the *Redoutable*. Contrary to the custom of the day, Lucas was aiming low rather than for the masts and rigging. "My friends," he had said to his cannoneers before the battle, "aim low! The English don't like to be killed."

So far the *Victory* had not fired a single shot. "We have three ships within range. Which of them should we board?" Hardy asked.

"The nearest one," Nelson replied. "You may choose for yourself." Since the *Redoutable* had been the enemy ship causing them the most damage, Hardy ordered his helmsmen to steer the *Victory* toward her and to come up along the French ship, port side to port side.

"I think it's time," said René to Lucas, "that I go take my place on the top." As René climbed up through the shrouds toward the mizzen top of the *Redoutable*, she and the *Victory* began vomiting volleys of grapeshot at each other. They crashed together with such force that one seemed to have ripped open the other, and that is indeed what might have happened if the wind had not caught in the *Redoutable*'s mass of sails and driven her, along with the *Victory*, backward.

The action of the wind on the two vessels created a gap in Villeneuve's battle line, and the ships just behind Nelson slipped through it. Some moved to the right, others to the left, and the combined fleet was effectually separated in two parts.

It was noon. The battle was under way. The English had raised the banner of Saint George. The Spanish had unfurled the banner of Castille, which was hung with a long wooden cross beneath it, and as our tricolor rose above the prow of each French ship each crew had shouted seven times "Long live the Emperor!"

The six or seven ships surrounding Villeneuve had all opened fire on the *Victory*. When neither the *Redoutable* nor her two hundred fire-spitting cannons can stop it, the *Victory* passes within pistol range of the *Bucentaure*'s stern. A British sixty-eight-pounder is loaded with one round shot and a keg of five hundred musket balls, and the carronade tears into the French ship's stern. As the *Victory* drifts past, her fifty guns, loaded with double and triple projectiles, rip into the *Bucentaure;* they dislodge twenty-seven cannons and mow down the cannoneers.

Still locked together, the *Victory* and the *Redoutable* continue to drift. The *Redoutable* begins to burn. From the mizzen-top and its batteries, the *Redoutable* answers the English fire. Muskets have replaced heavy artillery, and our sailors have gained the advantage. In a short time the quarterdeck and catwalks on the *Victory* are strewn with bodies. Of the ship's one hundred and ten able riflemen at the outset of the action, only about twenty can still do battle. The tween-deck is covered with the wounded and dying, with more still to come. Confronted by these bleeding heaps of wounded, their legs broken, their arms separated from their bodies, the surgeons look at each other helplessly. The *Victory*'s chaplain is overwhelmed by the horror of it all and flees from this "butcher's stand," as he would still describe it ten years later. He runs up on deck, into the midst of the tumult. Through the smoke he sees Nelson and Captain Hardy on the quarterdeck. The chaplain is running toward Nelson with his arms outstretched when he sees Nelson fall to the deck.

It was exactly fifteen minutes until one.

A musket ball from the mizzen top of the *Redoutable* had struck him. It had entered his body through the left shoulder and, unhindered by his epaulette, it had smashed the spinal column.

As it happened, he had been standing at exactly the same spot where his secretary had been killed, and he'd fallen facedown in his secretary's blood. He tried to get back up on one knee, by supporting himself with his good arm. Hardy, just a few feet away when he'd heard his admiral fall, hurried to his side and, with the help of two sailors and Sergeant Secker, got him back to his feet.

"I hope, Milord," he said, "that you are not seriously wounded."

But in the face of his captain's hope, Nelson replied, "This time, Hardy, they have finished Nelson off."

"Oh, I hope not!" the captain cried.

"Yes, indeed," said Nelson. "When I felt my body weaken, I knew that my spinal column had been broken."

Hardy had ordered the men to take the admiral immediately to the surgeons. They were carrying him there when Nelson noticed that the ropes to the tiller had been cut by grapeshot. He told Captain Hardy, who ordered a midshipman to replace them with new ones.

With his pocket handkerchief Hardy covered Nelson's face and decorations so that his sailors would not realize it was their admiral who had been wounded. As soon as Hardy and his men got him down between decks, Mr. Beatty, the ship's surgeon, rushed to his aid.

"Oh, my dear Beatty," said Nelson. "All your science cannot save me now. My back is broken."

"I hope your wounds are not as great as Your Lordship thinks," the surgeon said just as the chaplain reappeared.

"Reverend," Nelson cried out to him, his voice filled with pain but still strong, "remember me to Lady Hamilton, remember me to Horatia, remember me to all my friends. Tell them that I have made my last will and testament and that I bequeath Lady Hamilton and my daughter Horatia to my country. Remember what I have just told you, don't ever forget. . . ."

Nelson was carried to a bed. With difficulty, the surgeon's assistants removed his uniform and covered him with a sheet. While they were busy attending to him, Nelson said to the doctor, "Doctor, I'm done for! Doctor, I'm dying!"

Mr. Beatty examined his wounds. Assuring Nelson that he could do his examination without hurting him, he probed the wound and discovered that the ball had indeed gone through his chest and reached his backbone. "I am certain that the shot went all the way through my body," said Nelson.

The doctor looked at his back. There was no exit wound. "You are mistaken, Milord," he said. "But please try to tell me what you are feeling."

"It feels like there's a pool of blood rising inside me whenever I take a breath," said the wounded man. "I have no feeling in the lower half of my body. . . . It is difficult for me to breathe, and although you don't seem to agree, I still believe that my back is broken."

The symptoms gave no cause for hope. But beyond the surgeon, his two assistants, Captain Hardy, and the chaplain, nobody on board the *Victory* knew how serious their admiral's condition was.

Everyone on the *Redoutable* knew, however. As Nelson was falling to the deck, the French crew heard a loud voice from the mizzen top shouting, "Captain Lucas, let's board them! Nelson is dead!"

XCIII
Disaster

⁂

LUCAS STARTED UP through the shrouds of the *Redoutable*. At twenty feet, he could see that the *Victory*'s deck was indeed empty. Immediately he called for his assault division, and within a minute they were swarming over the decks, up on the poop deck, on the railing, and up in the shrouds. They opened fire.

Those of the *Victory*'s cannoneers still standing left their positions to repulse this new attack from the French ship. Under a hail of musket balls and grenades, they pulled back in disorder into their gun batteries.

The *Victory*'s speed saved her. The *Redoutable* was unable to stay on her long enough for Lucas's men to climb over her railings. Captain Lucas gave orders to cut the slings off the mainyard so it could be dropped to make a bridge between the two ships. In the meantime, though, Ensign Yon and four sailors, using the anchor hanging out over the English ship's chain wales, managed to reach the *Victory*'s deck. The assault division noted the path they had taken and, led by the *Redoutable*'s second in command, Lieutenant Dupotet, rushed after them.

The *Victory* was about to offer the strange spectacle of a flagship in the midst of its own victory being captured by a vessel with twenty-six fewer guns. Only just then a frightful volley raked the deck of the *Redoutable*, and at the same moment the man who had climbed down through the rigging from its mizzen top dropped into the tumult on the deck like a meteorite.

The mighty English *Téméraire* had also broken through Villeneuve's battle line and had thrown itself under its enemy's bowsprit. Its volley felled two hundred men. Then, falling back alongside the French ship, the *Téméraire* once again raked it with a broadside. The second broadside brought down the flag. But to no avail, for immediately a man unknown to most of Lucas's crew rushed to the flag chest, pulled out a new tricolor, and hung it from the yard.

Then a third enemy ship joined the first two in their attempt to crush the *Redoutable*. The English *Neptune* came in from the stern and delivered a broadside that brought down both the mizzenmast and the foremast. Again the French flag fell under the hail of iron. Still, the mainmast was standing, and the same man who'd hung the flag from the yard now tacked the tricolor up to the gallant yard. Then he ordered avenging fire on the *Téméraire*. The ensuing volley dismasted the ship and killed fifty men.

Another volley from the *Neptune* demolished one of the *Redoutable*'s side walls, crippled its rudder, and opened gaping holes at the water line. The ocean was gushing into the hold, and by now every man of the general staff had been wounded. Ten out of the eleven ensigns lay dead or dying. Of six hundred and forty-three crew members, five hundred and twenty-two were out of action, three hundred of them dead and two hundred and twenty-two wounded.

The next ball from the *Neptune* smashed the mainmast. It came down, and the flag came down with it. The flag-hanger man looked for a place to fly a third tricolor, but the ship was as flat as a pontoon. Lucas stopped him, his voice calm: "It's no use, René. We are sinking."

The *Bucentaure* was in a similarly sorry state. Its bowsprit had gotten caught in the *Santisima Trinidad*'s gallery, and the crews were trying in vain to free it. Neither of the two ships was able to maneuver, and both of them were being pounded mercilessly by the *Victory* and four other English ships. As the two ships, which together had two hundred and ten guns and almost two thousand combatants, continued firing at the five English vessels, Villeneuve managed in his desperate situation to find the resolve he had not shown in combat.

He stood tall on the poop deck of the *Bucentaure,* his figure lit up by the artillery fire from the six warring ships. Trapped as the flagship was, he was suffering murderous broadsides from behind and from the right, and he was unable to use his port guns. His officers were falling around him, one after the other. After an hour of fighting, or rather of agony, Captain Magendi fell wounded, then Lieutenant Dandignon, who'd replaced him, was also struck down, and now Lieutenant Fournier seemed only to be waiting his turn. The main mast and shortly thereafter the mizzenmast crashed chaotically onto the deck. The flag got hung back up on the foremast.

The light wind failed to disperse the thick clouds of smoke rising from the burning ships, so the admiral could no longer even see what was happening to the rest of the fleet. At one point, when the smoke thinned for a bit, he discovered that the twelve ships in the van were lying motionless. On the only mast he had left, he had signals raised ordering them to change tack and come back to the battle.

Then night began to fall, and Villeneuve could see nothing more. At three o'clock, his third mast collapsed into the massive debris already on the deck.

That is when Villeneuve tried to launch his boats. The boats on the deck had been smashed by the falling masts, however, and those on the sides were riddled with bullet holes. The two or three they did put in the water sank immediately.

Throughout the battle, his hopelessness continuously being compounded, Villeneuve had rushed from deck to deck without hesitating to expose himself to the ship's most vulnerable sites, as if he were asking nothing more of fate than a ball from a cannon, biscaien, or musket. But fate had reserved suicide for him.

Admiral Gravina's flagship, abandoned by the seven other Spanish vessels, surrendered after four hours of fighting. The remainder of the Spanish squadron allowed itself to drift with the wind toward the coast near Cadiz.

Meanwhile, on board the *Victory,* the crew was growing more jubilant. Every time a French ship struck her colors, they shouted "hurrah," and with every cheer, Nelson, for the moment forgetting his wounds, would ask, "What is happening?" The explanation afforded him great satisfaction.

Suffering from a terrible thirst, Nelson kept asking for water, and the motion of a paper fan helped to cool him, but his foremost concern appeared to be Captain Hardy's safety. The chaplain and surgeon tried to assure Nelson on that point, and they sent message after message to inform Captain Hardy that the admiral wished to see him. The longer that Hardy failed to appear, the more impatiently Nelson would shout, "You are not willing to bring me Hardy. He must be dead."

Finally, an hour and ten minutes after Nelson had been shot, Captain Hardy came down between decks. When the admiral saw him, he cried out with joy, shook his hand affectionately, and said, "Well, Hardy, how is the battle going? How has the day gone for us?"

"Very well, Milord," the captain replied. "We have already captured twelve ships."

"I hope that none of ours has stricken its colors?"

"No, Milord. Not one."

Reassured on that point, Nelson turned to his own situation. "I am a dead man, Hardy," he sighed. "I'm sinking fast. Soon all will be over for me. Come closer, my friend." Then he whispered, "I would like to make one request, Hardy. When I am dead, cut some of my hair for my dearest Lady Hamilton, and be sure to give her everything that's mine on board."

"I have just talked with the surgeon," Hardy answered. "He still hopes to save your life."

"No, Hardy, no," Nelson replied. "Don't try to fool me. My spinal column has been crushed."

As Hardy's duties called him back up on deck, he shook the wounded man's hand and took his leave.

Nelson asked for the surgeon, who was working on Lieutenant William Ruvers. His leg had been blown off. The surgeon had his assistants take care of the lieutenant's bandages while he attended to the admiral.

"I just wanted news about my old friends," said Nelson. "As for me, Doctor, I no longer need you. Anyhow, I have told you before that I've lost all feeling in the lower part of my body. It is already icy cold."

"Milord, let me check you," the surgeon said to Nelson. He felt Nelson's lower limbs, and it was true that they had already lost all feeling; he could find no life in them.

"Oh," Nelson continued, "I know what I'm talking about. Scott and Burke have already checked my legs, and I had no more feeling then than I do now. I am dying, Beatty. I am dying."

"Milord," the surgeon said, "unfortunately there is nothing I can do for you." As he made that final pronouncement, he had to turn to hide his tears.

"I knew it," said Nelson. "I can feel something rising in my chest."

Then, placing his hand on his chest, he whispered, "Thank God, I have done my duty."

Unable to do anything further to relieve the admiral's suffering, the surgeon returned to the other wounded men. Soon, though, Nelson again had the company of Captain Hardy, who had just dispatched Lieutenant Hill with the terrible news of Nelson's fatal wound to Admiral Collingwood.

Hardy congratulated the admiral, now undeniably in death's clutches, for having won such a complete, decisive victory. He announced that as best he could judge, fifteen French ships were already in the hands of the English fleet.

"I would have bet on twenty," Nelson whispered. Suddenly, remembering the direction of the wind and its indications of a coming storm, he shouted, "Drop anchor, Hardy! Drop anchor!"

"I suppose Admiral Collingwood will take command of the fleet," the captain said.

"No, at least not while I am still alive," said the wounded man, propping himself up on his good arm. "Hardy, I'm telling you to drop anchor. That's an order."

"I shall so order, Milord."

"On your life, you must, and within five minutes." Then, his voice dropping, as if he were ashamed of how feeble he'd become, he said, "Hardy, please don't throw my body into the sea."

"Oh, no! Of course not. You can rest easy on that score, Milord," Hardy replied with a sob.

"Take good care of Lady Hamilton," Nelson said, his voice weaker all the time. "Take care of my dearest Lady Hamilton. Give me a kiss, Hardy!" At the admiral's bidding, and weeping, the captain kissed him on the cheek.

"I die content," said Nelson. "England is saved."

Captain Hardy stayed by the side of the illustrious admiral in mute admiration. Then, kneeling down, he kissed his forehead. "Who is that kissing me?" Nelson asked, his eyes already clouded with death's shadows.

The captain answered, "Me; Hardy."

"May God bless you, my friend!" the dying man said, and Hardy went back up on deck.

Nelson sensed the presence of the chaplain nearby. "Ah, Reverend, I have never been a serious sinner," he said. After a moment of silence, he continued, "Reverend, please remember that I am bequeathing to my country and to my king Lady Hamilton and my daughter Horatia Nelson. Never forget Horatia."

He was thirsty again. He cried out, "Water, water . . . Where's the fan? . . . Give me some air . . . Rub me."

He had directed his last plea to Reverend Scott, the chaplain, who had earlier given him some relief by rubbing his chest. Nelson's voice was faltering, the pain was intensifying. He needed to gather all his strength to say one more time, "Thank God I have done my duty."

Nelson had spoken his last words.

Summoned by Nelson's servant who'd told him that his master was near death, the surgeon came back to the bedside and took the dying man's hand. It was already cold. He checked for a pulse; there was none. He touched his forehead. Nelson opened his one eye; it closed immediately.

Nelson had just breathed his last. It was twenty past four. He had lived for three hours and thirty-two minutes with the fatal gunshot wound.

The reader might be surprised at all the details I have supplied about Nelson's death. But it seems to me that one of the greatest warriors the world has ever known should be accompanied all the way to death's door, if not by an historian, at least by a novelist. These are not details I found in some book. They come from the official account of his death, signed by both the ship's surgeon, Mr. Beatty, and Reverend Scott, the chaplain.

XCIV

The Storm

PERHAPS THE STORY of the Battle of Trafalgar should end with Nelson's death. But it would be unjust to obscure the names of the many other brave men who also died while doing all they could for their countries.

We left Villeneuve in despair on the *Bucentaure*'s splintered deck, where he found himself without a launch seaworthy enough to take him to one of the undamaged ships that lay far from the battle or even to one of the ten vessels in the vanguard that had exchanged a few shots with Nelson's line, actually engaging in battle. Had he been able to reach another vessel in the fleet, he could have returned to the fray with reinforcements; and the day, though still lost, would not have been the frightful disaster that it turned out to be. But he was chained to the *Bucentaure* like a living person to a corpse. Exposed to all dangers without being able to respond to any one of them, he had no choice but to strike his colors. An English cutter took him on board the *Mars*.

Rear Admiral Dumanoir had repeated Villeneuve's signals to change tack and rejoin the battle. They were addressed to ten ships, including the *Héros*, whose captain had been killed at the beginning of the battle, the *San Agostino*, the *San Francisco*, the *Mont-Blanc*, the *Duguay-Trouin*, the *Formidable*, the *Rayo*, the *Intrépide*, the *Scipion*, and the *Neptune*. Only four of them—the *Mont-Blanc*, the *Duguay-Trouin*, the *Formidable*, and the *Scipion*—obeyed the signal from the squadron leader, however, and those four had to use their ship's boats to help them change tack.

The rear admiral had sent a signal for them to tack "wind ahead," which would allow them the possibility, by bearing up, of joining the fight when they found their positions opportune. Dumanoir himself was on board the *Formidable*. With the other three ships he started down from north to south, along the battle line, in the hope that they might gain positions by which to catch the English in a crossfire. But it was three o'clock, already late. And there were disasters almost everywhere: the *Bucentaure* had been captured, the *Santisima Trinidad* had been taken over and manned, the *Redoutable* was in splinters. On every side English ships were attacking vessels that had fallen to leeward. The four ships had barely set course before they were raked with artillery fire, which wreaked great damage and reduced their ability to fight back. Disheartened, they moved away from the battle.

Fighting was furious at that end of the French line where Collingwood had attacked. Two ships, the *Santa Ana* and the *Principe de Asturias*, merit a historian's honorable mention. After two hours of battle, the *Santa Ana*, the first ship in the rear, had lost all three of its masts but had given the *Royal Sovereign* almost as much as it had received. It struck its colors, but only after Vice Admiral Alava had been seriously wounded.

The *Fougueux*, the ship nearest to the *Santa Ana*, tried valiantly to help its neighbor by preventing the *Royal Sovereign* from breaking through the line. But when it was abandoned by the ship just behind it, the *Monarca*, it lay open to attack by two enemy ships. Still, the *Fougueux* crippled them both, and then, in hand-to-hand combat with the *Téméraire*, it repulsed the English in three attempts to board. Of its seven hundred men, the *Fougueux* lost four hundred, among them its commander, Captain Beaudoin, who was replaced by Lieutenant Bazin. When the English made their fourth attempt to board, they succeeded in storming the forecastle. Bazin was wounded in the fray, and at the end of it had only a few men left. Trapped on the quarterdeck, covered with blood, he had no choice but strike his colors.

At the very place where the *Monarca* had backed away from battle, the *Pluton*, under Captain Cosmao, had slipped in and stopped the forward progress of the *Mars* as it was preparing to break through the French line. The *Pluton* poured shot after shot into its enemy and was about to board it when a larger ship appeared and started firing into the *Pluton*'s stern. With a skillful maneuver, by turning sideways the *Pluton* was able not only to escape but also to fire several murderous volleys at its new adversary. Then, windward of its first adversary, the *Pluton* cut down two of the masts on the *Mars* and put it out of action. The dutiful *Pluton* had no time to pause; it sailed to the aid of embattled French ships that fought outnumbered because they'd been abandoned by vessels less scrupulous than the *Pluton*.

Behind the *Pluton*, the *Algesiras* was performing equally valiantly. Captained by Rear Admiral Magon, it was giving battle comparable in every way to the one that had just been fought with such courage by the *Redoutable*.

Rear Admiral Magon was born on Île de France to a family from Saint-Malo. Young, handsome, brave, he was born, too, to be a leader of men. After he'd raised the tricolor, he gathered his crew around him and promised to honor the first man among them to board the enemy ship with a magnificent baldric, which had been given to him by the Company of the Philippines. Every man was eager to have the prize.

A rival of the captains of the *Redoutable*, the *Fougueux*, and the *Pluton*, Rear Admiral Magon pushed the *Algesiras* forward to block the path of the English ships that were trying to break the line. In his maneuvers, he met the *Tonnant*, a former French ship that had become English after Aboukir, commanded by a valiant officer named Tiller. When Magon got within pistol range, he fired his guns; then, coming about, he rammed his bowsprit into the enemy ship's rigging. With the two ships now entangled, Magon called by name his bravest sailors as he prepared to lead them in boarding the *Tonnant*. They had all gathered on the deck and the bowsprit of the *Algesiras* when fearsome enemy grapeshot caught them broadside and wounded Magon in one arm and thigh.

Magon's officers persuaded him at least to have his wounds bandaged so that he could continue fighting, but as he was being helped below deck, he caught sight of Captain Tiller leading a column of men about to board the *Algesiras*. Pulling away from the sailors at his aid, he grabbed a boarding axe and repulsed the Englishmen. Three times they came at him, and three times he pushed them back. His ship's captain, Letourneur, was killed as he fought beside the unyielding Magon, and when Lieutenant Plassant took the captain's place he was wounded in turn. Magon, who stood out in his brilliant uniform, was hit once more. His strength ebbing, he handed over command to Monsieur de La Bretonnière and headed down between decks with the help of two sailors. By now, though, the side wall of his ship was gaping open, and a ball from a biscaien struck Magon full in the chest. He fell at the same time as the foremast, it too toppled by a cannonball.

Its deck empty of any soldiers or officers to defend it, the *Algesiras* was stormed by the English, while nearby four other French ships—the *Aigle*, the *Swiftsure*, the *Berwick*, and the *Achille*—were also engaged in fierce battles.

After locking yards with the *Bellerophon* and fighting for almost an hour, the *Aigle* was able to pull away from the opponent it had been about to board and turn toward battle with the *Belleisle*. Its captain, the brave Commander Courège, was killed at three o'clock, but the ship continued the combat. It struck its colors at three-thirty as it lay under fire from both the *Revenge* and the *Defence*.

The *Swiftsure* lost two hundred and fifty men as well as its commander and captain, both of whom were standing on the bridge when they were killed. Lieutenant Lune, who took their place, was felled at the same post of honor. Overwhelmed by two enemy ships, the *Bellerophon* and the *Colossus*, the *Swiftsure* ultimately surrendered.

The *Berwick*, commanded by Captain Camas, whom James in his *Histoire navale* calls the valiant Captain Camas, suffered tremendous losses in its battle with two enemy ships, first the English *Achille* and then the *Defence*. Yet even with its three masts cut at the base, Camas continued to maneuver his two batteries. He had counted fifty-one dead and two hundred wounded when he himself was killed. Lieutenant Guichard lived only a few minutes longer, and the *Berwick* became an English prize.

The *Achille*, which first attacked the *Belleisle*, soon found itself surrounded by the *Polyphemus*, the English *Swiftsure*, and the *Prince*. It was being pounded by their one hundred and ninety-six guns, but Captain Deniéport, despite a thigh wound, still refused to leave his bridge. He was killed at his post. Then the foremast came down under the heavy fire; it crashed to the deck in a mass of flames that spread everywhere.

Covered with flames, all its officers wounded or killed and with no allied vessel nearby, the *Achille* was left with a midshipman in command. His name was Cochard, and he kept fighting though all hope was gone. Fearing an explosion, the English ships moved away from the burning ship, so Cochard and what remained of the crew could concentrate on fighting the fires instead of firing at the enemy. The young officer's last act was to nail the flag up on the gaff. Then the *Achille* blew up.

While Admiral Dumanoir and his four ships were moving away from the combat, one vessel, the *Intrépide,* under the command of Captain Infernet, was boldly sailing back into the heat of the battle. Its flag was the last French flag still flying. Infernet pushed back the *Leviathan* and the *Africa,* came under fire from the *Agamemnon* and the *Ajax,* fought hand to hand with the *Orion*—he tried to board it twice and repulsed an English attempt to board him—and surrendered only when a sixty-gun enemy ship, the *Conqueror,* brought down his last mast. Of his crew of five hundred and fifty-five men, three hundred and six were out of action.

The lowering of the *Intrépide*'s flag was the battle's last sigh. The day was over; France had lost, utterly.

The names of several men should go down in history for their display of personal honor in the midst of general defeat. Villeneuve, until the end, had done everything he could at the risk, or in the hope, of getting himself killed; Rear Admiral Magon sacrificed his life for France; Lucas, with a crew of only one hundred and thirty-six survivors, had fought like a lion, and from the top of one of his masts an unknown hand had fired the shot that killed Admiral Lord Nelson. The *Achille* had warred as remarkably as the *Vengeur* in 1794, and Infernet and Cosmao had been magnificent in every way.

Seventeen French and Spanish ships had been captured by the English, and one had blown up. We mourned the loss of six or seven thousand men, counting both the dead and the wounded. It was a defeat unequaled in our history, but the vanquished still retained the glory of their courage and devotion.

The English had carried off a resounding victory, but it was a cruel and bloody victory too. And they paid dearly for it; for with Nelson dead, the English navy had literally been decapitated. Indeed, for the English, losing Nelson was worse than losing an army.

Nightfall and the storm finished off the English victory. The severe structural damage to six of our ships attested to how valiantly they had fought, but as the sun set and the wind rose that day they could barely remain afloat on the heavy swells. Collingwood had taken command of the floating debris. Instead of coming to anchor as Nelson had insisted, he'd spent the rest of the day manning the seventeen surrendered ships, most of them dismasted and taking on water. The storm took him entirely by surprise.

For the next two days it raged. The sea, the wind, the lightning, the shoals—all those scourges of the sky and the sea—created more anxiety than the battle itself. For sixty hours the furious sea toyed with the three fleets. It made no distinctions between the vanquished and the victorious.

Some of the ships captured by Nelson broke loose from their towlines. They drifted off, and the waves ran them aground in the shoals of Cape Trafalgar. When Collingwood realized that the wind was tearing away his trophies one by one, he set the *Santisima Trinidad* on fire and pushed three other ships—the *San Agostino,* the *Argonaute,* and the *Santa Ana*—into its flames. For a moment the sea seemed to grow calmer, and the wind to die down, in the face of the largest funeral pyre ever mounted at sea.

The vanquished fared better, once the battle was over, than the victors. Admiral Gravina and his eleven ships found protection from the storm in the port of Cadiz. But the English ships, far from any shelter, suffered only more damage. Many of their ships dismasted and all of them forced to fight the storm for their own survival, they were often unable to tow their even more crippled prizes. That is why they now decided to set adrift some of the ships they had captured, and why their prisoners cheered the sea's rage.

The Englishmen in charge of the *Bucentaure,* once they realized Collingwood was going to leave them alone with their prisoners, put the ship back in the hands of what was left of its French crew. The crew, blessing the storm that delivered them from the prospect of imprisonment on their own ship, managed to raise several makeshift masts, hang up some pieces of sail, and, driven by the storm, make for Cadiz.

The *Algesiras,* which bore the remains of brave Rear Admiral Magon, just as the *Victory* did Nelson's, also owed its deliverance to the storm. Although severely damaged by the combat during which it had so gloriously fought, it still rode the waves better than the other ships, thanks to its recent construction. But its three masts were gone. The mainmast had been broken fifteen feet above the deck; the foremast now stood only nine feet tall, and the mizzenmast five. The ship towing it, itself having trouble maneuvering, had cast off the towline, and the Englishmen on board the *Algesiras* considered themselves lost. They fired cannon as a call for help, but the English fleet was too occupied by the storm to respond. At a loss, they sought out the French officer who had been second in command, Monsieur de la Bretonnière, and begged him, with the help of his crew, to man the ship so that they could all, French and English alike, be saved.

As soon as he heard the proposal, Monsieur de la Bretonnière realized how he and his compatriots might benefit. He asked for permission to confer with his officers and crew, who were being held below deck, and it was granted. When he told his officers what the English had pled of him, they immediately grasped the advantage of the situation, thanks to that quick intelligence that is one of the great qualities of the French; for the *Algesiras* was carrying thirty or forty armed Englishmen against their two hundred and seventy Frenchmen who, though unarmed, were ready to do anything necessary to get back their ship. Together, Monsieur de la Bretonnière and the officers went down into the hold to present their plan to the prisoners. First Monsieur de la Bretonnière would enjoin the English to surrender. Then, if they refused, at a signal the Frenchmen would rush them; while the English with their weapons would certainly make many victims of the French in a fight, superiority in numbers would win out in the end. The prisoners responded with enthusiasm.

Captain La Bretonnière went back to the Englishmen with his companions' answer. Since the *Algesiras* had been abandoned in such dangerous circumstances, he said, all prior engagements in regard to status were now broken. The French were in essence now free. If, however, their guards felt obligated by honor not to cede without a fight, then, the captain assured them, the French were willing to do so, unarmed. They only awaited the signal to begin the battle.

In fact, two of the crew were so eager to fight that they leaped on the English guards, who greeted them with two bayonet thrusts. One was killed outright and the other was seriously wounded. That caused an angry uproar, but La Bretonnière was able to contain it.

He then allowed the English officers some time to reflect. They deliberated only briefly, however; they agreed to surrender to the French on the condition that they be freed as soon as they reached French soil. Monsieur de la Bretonnière set one final condition. They would have to permit him time to request their freedom from the French government, which, he guaranteed them, he would get.

Cheers rang out all over the ship. The officers and sailors went to their posts. From storage, the carpenters pulled some topmasts, which they attached to the stubs of the main, fore, and mizzen. They found some sails. They started toward Cadiz.

All night long the storm Nelson had predicted raged. The next day it was even stronger and more terrifying. The *Algesiras* fought the entire day against the storm, and although they had no pilot, a seaman familiar with the Cadiz coast helped them make their way. They managed to reach the entrance to the harbor, but once there, they dared not try to enter.

Only one bow anchor and a thick cable kept the ferocious wind from driving the ship to its death on the rocks. If the anchor were to give, the *Algesiras* was lost, because she lay only two or three cable lengths from the deadly shoals off Diamond Point. They anxiously waited for night to end.

During the night they heard cries of distress even through the furor of the storm. When finally dawn broke, they knew why. The *Bucentaure* had been smashed against the rocks. But the *Indomptable* was anchored nearby; scarcely involved in the fighting, it had suffered little damage and benefited from good anchors and solid cables.

All day long the *Algesiras* fired its distress cannons. A few small boats did try to bring help, but they were inevitably swamped by the high seas. One that was finally able to reach the ship brought a small kedge anchor.

Once again night fell over the sea, with the *Algeciras* and the *Indomptable* anchored just a few cable lengths apart. The storm intensified, and all the lanterns on deck of the *Indomptable* were burning. The ship fired its distress cannons; its two anchors had pulled loose. Lanterns burning, like a flaming specter, with all its crew on deck, it drifted past the *Algesiras* by just a few feet. The men on board the *Algesiras* heard it crash on the rocks off Diamond Point. The sea swallowed up the crew's desperate cries. Fifteen hundred men had been on board; fifteen hundred men perished together.

The *Algesiras*, held in place by its tiny anchors, survived another night. The dawn came almost by surprise. And the sea began to calm. The French sailors guided their ship into Cadiz harbor, where it ran aground on a mud flat. It would float off at the next high tide.

Let us now look at what happened to the *Redoutable*, Captain Lucas, and Lieutenant René.

We have said that Captain Lucas fought for three hours before striking his colors. Out of a crew of six hundred and forty-three, there were five hundred and twenty-two out of action, including all of the officers and ten out of the eleven midshipmen. Three hundred men had been killed; two hundred and twenty-two were seriously wounded. Captain Lucas himself had suffered a slight thigh wound.

The ship had lost both its mainmast and its mizzenmast. Its stern had been demolished; it was little more than a gaping hole where the *Tonnant*'s cannons had battered it. Almost all of its guns had been damaged, some when the ship was boarded, others by cannonballs, and still others by the ruinous explosions first of an eighteen-pounder and then of a thirty-six-pound carronade. There were holes, too, in both sides of the ship; it looked like little more than a carcass.

When the deck planks had no longer been strong enough to resist, enemy balls had fallen onto the between-deck and killed many of the wounded men lying there as they awaited the surgeons' care. Fire had broken out near the tiller and deprived the ship of any way to maneuver. The ship had sprung major leaks, but the pumps had been broken during the fighting.

Although the *Victory* and the *Téméraire* had both been attached along-side it, neither had been capable of manning the *Redoutable*. At about seven in the evening, the English ship *Swiftsure* brought a towline to Captain Lucas and took over the *Redoutable*.

During the night, René went to the captain and proposed that they slip through one of the openings and swim to shore, approximately a league away. Lucas was an excellent swimmer, but, because of his thigh wound, he feared he would not be able to reach shore. René said he would take care of everything; he'd help the captain in the water and swim for both of them, he said. But Lucas refused categorically and insisted that René leave on his own.

René shook his head. "I came all the way from India to find you, my commandant," he said. "And I shall never leave you. But if we get separated, then it will be each man for himself. Where shall we meet? In Paris?"

"You can always find out about me at the Ministry of the Navy, my dear friend."

Then René whispered to him, "My dear captain, I have two rolls of fifty louis here on my belt. Will you accept one of them?"

"No, thank you, my brave friend," said Lucas. "In fact, in one of the drawers in my cabin, if my cabin is still there, I have about thirty louis, and I was about to offer you a portion of that. As soon as you get to Paris, don't fail to ask about me. My rank guarantees that these bulldogs will have to treat me with some consideration, but they may not have the same consideration for you."

The next day, the captain of the *Swiftsure* sent a cutter to collect Captain Lucas along with his second in command, Monsieur Dupotet, and Ensign Ducrès. Captain Lucas was told he could have another officer join him on board the *Swiftsure*. He asked for René.

The whole day was given over to rescuing the crew, for they could see the ship was sinking. Fortunately, they had time to take off one hundred and nineteen men. Two others fell as they were being transferred; one of them drowned.

They set sail for Gibraltar. The next day they had reached one of Hercules's columns.

René had kept secret the fact that he spoke English. So his captors spoke freely around him, and he listened to everything they said. That is how he learned that they were going to divide up the prisoners and send them to England on two different frigates, as one frigate alone could not carry an additional sixty or seventy men. A few days later, he learned further that, given the importance the English attached to Captain Lucas, he would be taken to London separately, on a ship of the line, which would leave on the same day as the frigates. They would form a small squadron made up of two frigates, a corvette, and a three-masted merchant ship for the return to Europe. I say "return to Europe" because Gibraltar is more African than European.

Captain Lucas would be traveling on the *Prince;* it had not participated in the battle, so its rigging and its crew were intact. René, along with about fifty of his companions, was to sail on board the merchant ship *Samson.* Before leaving René, Lucas told him how much he admired him for the courage he had shown on the fateful day of October 21. Their farewells were the farewells of two good friends, not those of a commander with an officer of inferior rank.

The ships traveled together as far as the Bay of Biscay, where a storm drove them apart. The *Prince,* a good-sailing ship, stayed close to the coast and was able to round Cape Finisterre. Captain Parker, on the *Samson,* however, had less control over his vessel, so he took it farther out to sea, according to the maxim that says in a storm, there is no danger greater than the coastline.

Finally the storm abated. When the sun had returned and they could determine their latitude, they realized that they were some thirty or thirty-five leagues west of Ireland, and they set their course to the east. The experienced seamen among them knew, though, that the calm seas would not last long, and Captain Parker, who had never had the responsibility of a true warship, was worried about their plight.

He had been quick to recognize René's sea knowledge, so he approached the French lieutenant on deck, where prisoners were allowed to walk in small groups. In his poor French, the captain haltingly opened a conversation. Pointing to a mass of black clouds rising in the west, he said, "We shall have dinner late today, Lieutenant. But I have asked the cook to make the wait worthwhile." As the dark clouds continued to rise, he added: "That is a spectacle we have to keep our eye on. It should keep us busy."

"Yes," René answered. "There is just one thing I would ask. I hope it does not keep us too busy."

René's fears, we must say, were not misplaced. What they saw was an ominous sight indeed. The heavy, dark clouds building up in the southwest soon looked like a chain of mountains rising into the air. You could see in detail those celestial Alps: the peaks with sharp ridges, the steep paths to reach them. From the highest peak in those fantastic Andes, as from the top of a volcano, came one last puff of smoke, like the final belch of a dying eruption. The sight was sublime, the smoke rising from a hidden Andean blaze and, buffeted by the wind, moving across the deep blue of the sky. For the sky was magnificently blue everywhere except in that area where it seemed to have been invaded by the black smoke from a volcano.

"In any case," the captain said lightly, "if something comes from that black chaos, it will not happen immediately. And we shall have plenty of warning, so we can dine and even digest our food at our leisure."

"Meaning no disrespect, sir," said an old salt who ordinarily would not have dared to speak to his captain, "a southwest wind is faster than your teeth and your stomach, however good they may be."

"I agree with your sailor," said René. "I don't think the storm will allow us to dine at our leisure. If I were asked my opinion, I would suggest that we get ready for the storm, for it will fall on our ship as suddenly as a hail-storm or lightning bolt."

"But, Captain," said a midshipman sitting on the topgallant rail, his collar up, his gaze fixed on the dark mass that occupied everyone's mind, "there's no wind at all, and the waves are barely lapping against our hull. What's the hurry?"

"Mr. Blackwood, if your uncle were in your place, he would see more clearly than you. Furl the topgallant sails and strike them immediately."

As Blackwood gave the order, the old sailor, like a prophet of doom, said, "That's good! But it's still not enough."

The captain smiled at him and went on, "As soon as you have struck the topgallants, take in three reefs and furl the mainsail." The order was executed promptly.

They could see that now the wind was rising on the horizon, for it was beginning to wrinkle the water's surface, and the dark mass in the southwest was spreading over the sky like an immense ink blot. The light breeze had become a brisk wind; it carried a threat.

"And now, old man, what would you do?" the captain asked the sailor who seemed to be so full of advice.

"If it were me," said the old sailor, "meaning no disrespect, I would take down even more sail, leaving almost nothing up."

"Bring down the foresail and the fore-topmast staysail," the captain shouted, and again the order was speedily executed.

The waves were high, the thunder rolled.

"Dinner is ready, gentlemen! Dinner is ready," shouted a midshipman appearing in the hatchway, a towel over his arm. He let the towel float in the wind for a moment, and noted, "Well, well. We've got a little wind up here. Down below we couldn't even feel it."

"Yes," the captain replied, "but you'll be feeling it below soon enough."

"What's the weather like up there?" one of the officers below deck called out to the midshipman.

"Well, I've seen better," he answered.

"Isn't the captain coming down for dinner?" another man asked.

"No! He will stay on deck with that young prisoner so commended to us by Captain Lucas; the one they say killed Nelson."

"If there is any danger," the second lieutenant said, "I'll reward him handsomely for that deed! I swear, I'll send him to the bottom of the sea ten minutes before I end up there myself."

"My dear man, you're being unfair," one of his colleagues said. "Even if he is the one who killed Nelson, he was just doing his duty as a Frenchman. Would you deserve to be thrown into the sea if you had killed Lucas? I know that all the Lucases in the world are not worth one Nelson, but Lucas too is a good, brave captain. Did you not see his gleaming uniform the three different times he tried to board the *Victory*? Did you not see his boarding axe shining like a rainbow through the fire and smoke? If you should ever find yourself facing Lucas, in good weather or bad, salute him respectfully and walk on by. That's what I would do."

The discussion was lively in the officers' mess, but on the bridge there was dead silence. The wind had abruptly dropped. The ship, uncontrollable, began to roll heavily through the waves. As it plunged sluggishly into a trough, the water would rise up over its sides, and then, as it struggled to pull itself back up, the water would pour off the upper deck back into the ocean in a myriad of glistening little waterfalls. Then suddenly the lantern on the bridge would rise up almost vertically toward the sky.

"It's a rough night, Captain Parker," the first lieutenant said. His rank gave him the right to speak.

"I've seen wind changes announced by a lot fewer signs," the captain replied with confidence.

"But," growled the old sailor, for his forty years at sea gave him rights that the others recognized, "along with these changes there are signs the oldest sailor could not miss."

"Gentlemen, what do you think?" said the captain. "Now there's not a breath of air and we have struck all our sails, even the mizzen topsail."

"Yes," said the old salt. "And what's more, the *Samson* isn't doing too badly for an honest merchant ship. There aren't many square-rigged ships not flying King George's flag who could catch the wind better and leave it in their wake. But there are times when a seaman has to think. Do you see that grayish light bearing down on us? Who can say where it's coming from? From America, from the pole? One thing sure, it's not coming from the moon."

The captain went over to the hatch. He heard the young officers laughing and clinking their glasses together. "Enough drinking and laughing!" he shouted. "Everyone on deck!"

Instantly they rushed up on deck. As soon as the officers and crew saw the state of the sky and sea, they turned all their thoughts to getting ready for the approaching storm. No one spoke, for each man was putting all his strength and energy into the task that awaited him.

Fifteen minutes earlier, a pale, sinister fog had begun to form in the southwest, and now it was bearing down on the ship with the speed of a horse galloping to finish first in a race. The air had lost the warmth of the east wind; little gusts from the southwest were whistling through the rigging, precursors of the coming storm.

They heard a loud roar. First the ocean's surface had begun to ripple, then it was covered by white foam, and a moment later the wind in all its fury smashed against the heavy mass of the motionless vessel.

The storm was gathering its strength. The captain unfurled a few sails to gain maneuverability and run before the wind. But the merchant ship did not respond to the current needs or to the captain's efforts. Slowly, heavily, it began to turn away from the east, but its flanks were still open to the full force of the storm. Fortunately for all those whom Providence had placed on the defenseless ship, the storm's full violence did not strike immediately. For a minute the few sails they had unfurled flapped on their yards, filling out and then collapsing, until the hurricane struck with all its strength.

The sky was so black that the men had to feel their way around the deck. Themselves as dark as specters, they could see each other only when flashes of lightning were reflected off the white frothy waves. The white streaks of light were brief, and startling, and afterward the plunge back into darkness made the night seem darker still. They had done everything humanly possible to counteract the effects of the storm. Now they could do nothing but wait. They counted the minutes.

Thrown against the masts or railings by the ship's pitching and rolling, bruised, stung by ropes that the wind turned into lashing whips, exhausted by fear and fatigue, the sailors were losing hope. They now clung to the windward side of the *Samson*, their backs bent to protect themselves from the huge waves crashing over the quarterdeck. Each man lost in his own thoughts, nobody said a word. Except for an occasional curse, a few laments, and several cries to heaven, some in prayer and some with blame.

The sea was playing with the ship as a giant might play with a kite, striking it from behind, from the front, from aft on the port side and aft on the starboard side; indeed, from all sides at once. The ship would rise to the top of the moving mountains, hover, and then crash down into an abyss from which it seemed impossible ever to return.

With enormous force one wave had barely struck the ship aft on the port side when another struck opposite, and in scarcely an instant the foresail became useless. The gale had caught the sail and ripped its strong canvas as simply as if it were flimsy muslin. Torn off its yard, the sail left only shreds on the mast. Then the rudder tiller snapped. The ship began to list to starboard, and the waves crashing over it kept it from righting itself.

"What shall we do?" the captain asked René.

"Tiller to windward! Tiller to windward!" René replied.

"Tiller to windward!" Captain Parker shouted, his voice loud enough to be heard above the noise of the storm.

The old sailor had already replaced the tiller with a spare, and he took over the helmsman's job. Quickly and confidently he obeyed the order as he watched the sails to see the ship's response. Twice the mainmasts dipped down toward the horizon and twice they gracefully rose back up. Beaten down a third time by the raging waves, the ship listed again. This time it did not right itself.

"What shall we do?" the captain again asked René.

"Chop down the masts!" said René.

"Go get an axe," Parker shouted to the second lieutenant, who acted as fast as if he had come up with idea himself.

At the foremast, ready with the axe, the lieutenant shouted: "Shall I chop it down?"

"Wait. Old Nick," the captain shouted to the helmsman, "is the ship responding?"

"No, Captain."

"Then start chopping!" Parker said, calmly but firmly.

One swing was enough. Under the tension of its weight, with one blow of the axe the mast cracked painfully. With the rigging crashing down around it, like a tree uprooted, it dropped the short distance into the sea.

"Ask if the ship is righting itself," René whispered to the captain.

"Is the ship righting itself?" he shouted to the helmsman.

"Captain, it did move a little, but the gale is still too strong."

The second lieutenant was already at the base of the mainmast; he realized how important his job was. "Shall I cut it?" he asked.

"Cut it!" the captain's somber voice called out.

The axe struck, and a terrible cracking sound followed. It struck a second time, then a third. The mast, the sails, the rigging, all crashed into the sea, and the ship righted itself immediately. Though still wallowing, it was now being driven along by the wind.

"It's righted itself!" the crew shouted with relief. Up until then they had been able to do nothing but wait in their own silence.

"Cut everything off, so that nothing can hinder the ship's movements," the captain shouted, emotion in his voice. "But be ready to furl the topsail. Let it hang for a moment until the ship can get out of this difficult situation.

But meanwhile, chop away! Go at it, men. With whatever you have, knives or axes, cut loose everything!"

With newfound strength and courage, the men began cutting away all the spars and rigging still attached to the ship. And the *Samson* rose lightly over the foam, like a bird whose feathers were skimming the water's surface.

The wind, though, was roaring like thunder. Only one sail was left, the topgallant, and as it filled out in the raging gale, it presented the danger of ripping out the one remaining mast, the mizzen. René placed his hand on the captain's shoulder and pointed to the sail. Parker understood immediately, and the words that he uttered were more like a prayer than an order: "The mast cannot hold much longer, my good men. If it falls on the bow, that will surely do us in. A couple of men will have to go aloft and cut the sail from the yards."

The second lieutenant, to whom the order seemed to be addressed, took a step backward. "The mast is bending like a willow tree," he said. "And it already is split at the base. It would be risking death to go aloft with the wind the way it is."

"You are right," said René. "Give me your knife."

And before the second lieutenant could ask why, René had grabbed the knife and was climbing up through the shrouds, where the yarns were so taut they seemed to have reached their breaking point. The experienced eyes on deck saw at once what he was trying to do.

"It's the Frenchman! It's the Frenchman," ten voices rang out. With that, seven or eight experienced sailors, ashamed to see a Frenchman doing what they had not dared to do themselves, started up through the ratlines toward the heavens streaked with lightning.

"Back down," the captain shouted through his megaphone. "Everyone back down except the Frenchman." The sailors could hear his words, but they were both too eager and too ashamed to ackknowledge them.

René had reached the top. He chose a rope holding the billowing topsail at its base to the lower yard and severed it with his razor-sharp knife blade. The sail was asking for nothing more than to be released, and it whipped out from the mast like a flag unfurled. At the same moment, the violence of the hurricane lifted the ship up on the crest of a huge wave, and when it fell back down heavily under its own weight, the ensuing shock broke a lanyard in the lower rigging. The mast responded with a frightening crack. It began to lean.

"Come down!" the captain shouted through his megaphone. "Come down through the stays. Down through the stays! Your lives depend upon it! Everybody down!"

Only René obeyed. He dropped down to the poop deck like lightning following a wire down into a well.

The mast tottered for a moment. Leaning in one direction, then in every other, it soon yielded to the ship's rolling movements. It broke like a match-stick and dropped into the sea. Everything disappeared: ropes, yards, stays. A few of the men crashed down onto the deck, the others lost in the waves.

"A lifeboat! A lifeboat!" the captain cried, but in an instant they were gone. The men, masts, and rigging had disappeared in the heavy fog that blanketed the ship.

Once the captain realized that there was no way to save the men who had fallen into the sea, he put the wounded sailors in the surgeon's care. Then he turned to René, whom he found utterly calm, almost serene, as if he had played no part in, or even witnessed, the *Samson*'s catastrophe. While he was checking to see if René had been hurt in any way, a sailor informed him that there were already four feet of water in the hold.

Apparently, so much water had washed over the ship, in those waves sailors call "sea packages," that the hold was half full before anyone had even thought to look. "In other circumstances," said the captain, "that would be nothing to worry about. But you know how sailors hate to man the pumps, and exhausted as they are already, I hardly dare impose such a detestable duty on them."

"Captain," said René as he shook his hand, "are you willing to trust me?"

"Absolutely," the captain replied.

"Well, then, below decks I have sixty-eight men who have done nothing but wait out this storm while your crew has been working so hard to save them, as well as themselves, of course. Now let my men work so that yours may rest. Let me have them back for four hours, and in four hours there will not be one drop of water left in the hold. My men in those four hours will have done for your crew something of what your crew has been doing for them for the past two days."

The captain took advantage of a calm in the storm to gather his men to-gether on deck. "My friends," he said, "I have some bad news. There are four or five feet of water in the hold. If you let it keep rising, by tomorrow morning the ship will sink. But if you agree to man the pumps, there is still a chance we can escape the greatest danger we have faced up to now."

What Captain Parker had predicted happened. More than half the crew flopped down to the deck as they said they'd rather sink than man the pumps. The other half said not a word, but it was easy for Captain Parker to see that they would put up considerable resistance if he insisted. "My good men," said the captain, "I can understand how tired you are and how much you hate to pump. So here is Lieutenant René. He is grateful for the care you have given him and his men during our trip, and he has a proposal to make."

René had acquired some prestige among the English crew, for the rumor had spread that he had been the man who killed Nelson. Their admiral Lord Nelson had long been fighting the French, the weather, and sometimes even God, so the man who killed him could be no ordinary man.

The old helmsman was the first to raise his hat and wave it in the air. "Lieutenant René," he said, "is an accomplished seaman. There's nobody braver, and we will be happy to listen to his proposal."

The crew, now hardly paying any attention to the storm, cried with one voice: "Let's hear what Lieutenant René has to say. Hurrah for Lieutenant René!"

He greeted them with tears in his eyes. To the great astonishment of the entire crew, for they had never heard him speak a word of English, he addressed them in as pure an English as if he had been born in Suffolk County. "Thank you! During a battle we are enemies, and after the battle we are rivals. But in danger we are brothers."

They shouted their agreement, and he continued: "This is what I am proposing: You have sixty-nine prisoners aboard. They have been below decks resting for the past two days while you have been up here working for them. Although you were also working to save yourselves, although you had no thought of them while you were fighting the storm, through me they are asking to be allowed to work for you."

The English sailors were listening carefully, but they didn't understand. "Give them their freedom for four hours. During that time they will man the pumps for you. In four hours the ship will be saved, you will all drink a glass of gin together, and they will return to their posts as prisoners, happy that you will have fond memories of them as they will of you. On my honor, I answer for everything."

The Englishmen were mute with astonishment. Never would such an idea have occurred to any of them. So chivalrous was the proposal that the prisoners be allowed to save their enemies' ship that they could not fully grasp it immediately.

Captain Parker anticipated their reaction. He threw his arms around René's neck and cried, "My good men, Lieutenant René answers for them, and I answer for him."

Then there was such a hullabaloo that it would be hard to imagine. Meanwhile, the captain had whispered an order to René, and the first group of about twelve prisoners came up through the hatchway. They were as surprised to be brought up on deck in the midst of a storm as they were to see the ship no longer with any masts or rigging, just as had been the case with the *Redoutable*. Then they saw their lieutenant: he was smiling at them and extending his hand.

"My good friends," he said. "For the last two days these good companions have been fighting the storm. You could appreciate its fury although you did not see it with your own eyes. They have saved us and the ship, but they are completely exhausted. And now there are five feet of water in the hold."

"We'll man the pumps," said the mate from the *Redoutable*. "In three hours it'll be gone."

René repeated in English what the mate had said, and Captain Parker ordered up a keg of gin.

"Well, then, my friends," said René, speaking to the Englishmen. "Do you accept?"

They cried out in unison: "Yes, Lieutenant! Yes, we agree!" They and their prisoners, who just a few days before had been mercilessly drawing each other's blood, now threw themselves into each other's arms like brothers.

"Tell your men they can go rest," René whispered to Captain Parker. "And you should do likewise. Just tell me where you expect to make land, and for the next four hours I shall take charge of everything, even steering the ship."

"We must nearly be in Saint George's Channel, and the wind and the swells are no doubt pushing us toward the little port in Cork. Set one of the spare masts with whatever sails you can find and set our course toward Cork, between ten and twelve degrees longitude," the captain advised. "A glass of gin!" he added, setting the example and clinking his glass against René's.

Ten minutes later René's men were in the hold. The victors were asleep, the vanquiushed were working. Four hours later, not a drop of water lay in the hold, and the prisoners took themselves back to prison.

The following day, what was left of the *Samson* was dropping its anchor in the gulf, about two cable lengths from the little town of Cork.

XCV
Escape

THE NEXT DAY, the English realized that they could not possibly keep the French prisoners on board the ship, as it would be too easy for them to dive into the water and swim ashore. Once on land, they would as easily find sympathy from the Irish, who would never turn in a French prisoner. There had always been a special kind of pact between the two countries, perhaps because they equally hated England. So the officers on board the *Samson* decided to jail their captives in the town prison.

As the prisoners were climbing down the ladder alongside the ship, one of them said to René in an accent that left no doubt of his Irish origins, "Take me with you into your cell. You won't be sorry."

René regarded the man; he seemed trustworthy. When René was asked with whom he'd share his cell, he selected the Irishman and he let six other men prisoners choose for themselves. Each cell held eight men.

René was aware that once the *Samson* left Cork, they would be delivered to one of the pontoon prisons off Portsmouth, and he knew how horrible conditions were there. Still, he did not force the issue with the Irishman. Nor did he plan to, for he'd not set himself above his comrades and thus arouse unnecessary mistrust. He assumed that sooner or later the man would explain himself. He was not mistaken.

Their cell was on the ground floor of the prison. The barred window looked onto a courtyard, which was enclosed by a wall sixteen feet high. Two sentries stood guard day and night. Scarcely had their door been locked when the Irishman, after first examining the courtyard through the window, came over to René and said in English, "We need to get out of here unless we want to end up on the pontoons off Portsmouth."

"Yes," René replied. "So now we need to find the means. I have the money, and if money can be of use, I can make it available to my good comrades."

"Money is a good thing," said the Irishman, "but there's something better yet." He showed René eight sail needles fixed in eight stretcher rods. "When I saw that we were going to be taken," he explained, "I thought about the future and I said to myself, 'There is no prison you can't escape from if you are courageous and strong.' So I set aside a packet of needles, I broke eight stretcher rods, and I found a file in the locksmith's shop. That's what's in my baggage."

"I can see eight daggers," said René, "and I see a file for cutting through the bars, but I don't see any rope, which we need to scale the walls."

"You have said that you have money. I am Irish, and I know my country and my countrymen. It will take at least six weeks before our ship is repaired and ready to go back to sea. In that time, Ireland will certainly give us one of those nights during which no English sentry is going to be willing to freeze to death when he can simply open the guardroom door and spend the night next to the stove. As for my countrymen, for them being a Frenchman is the same as being a liberator, a friend, a brother, and an ally;

so from them there is nothing to fear and everything to hope for. You said you have money. Money is not absolutely necessary, but it does make things easier. Surely we'll be able to find some good fellow, maybe even the jailer himself, who will happily throw us a rope from the other side of the wall. All we need to do is wait and be ready. Let me work on the jailer, and within a week we'll be out of here. That doesn't mean we'll be saved, but we'll be closer to being free. . . . People have seen us talking; our comrades might be a little suspicious. Tell them what we were talking about, without going into details, and make sure that they don't breathe a word. Give them enough to keep their courage up."

While René was doing what the Irishman bade, the cell door opened and their jailer appeared. "So, how many of you are there?" he asked, and counted. "Eight; so we shall need eight mattresses. We don't expect you to sleep on the straw after all. If you were Englishman or Scots, I might say otherwise."

"Bravo, Father Donald!" said the Irishman. The jailer gave a start, for he'd just heard someone address him by name in perfect Irish.

"He has not forgotten," the Irishman said to his friend, "that he is a distant cousin of the brave General MacDonald, under whom I served in Naples and Calabria."

"So, you are Irish?" asked the jailer.

"Indeed I am, and I come from Youghal, only ten leagues away. Doesn't Father Donald remember that I used to come play with his two sons, James and Tom? It is true that that was a long time ago, twenty years. They were good kids. What has become of them, Father?"

The jailer wiped his eyes with the back of his hand. "They were conscripted to serve with the English. James deserted, and he was shot. As for Tom, he was killed at Aboukir, the poor boy."

The Irishman looked at René as if to say, "As you can see, it won't be as difficult as we thought." To Donald he exclaimed, "The dirty English bastards! Will we ever get even with them!"

"Ah, if only we could," Donald said, holding up a clenched fist. "I'm longing for the day."

"Are you a Catholic?" René asked. The jailer answered by crossing himself.

René walked over to him, took some gold from his pocket, and handed it to the jailer, saying, "Here, my friend. Here is some money so you can have masses said for your sons' souls."

"You are English," said the jailer. "I never accept anything from an Englishman."

"I'm a Frenchman, and a good Frenchman, my good man, as your fellow countryman can attest. If masses are said in the next world, I have sent plenty of Englishmen there to serve as choirboys and attend the priests who say them."

"Is that true?" the jailer asked his fellow countryman.

"As true as the Holy Trinity," the man replied.

The jailer turned around and extended his hand to René. They shook hands.

"Now," René asked, "will you accept the money?"

"Anything from you, sir, since you are not English."

"So much for that," said the Irishman. "Now that we are friends, and good friends, we need to treat each other like comrades. Good bread, good beer, and a nice warm fire when it's cold."

"And meat with every meal," René added. "Here is money for the first week." He handed the jailer five louis.

"Well, is this man an admiral?" the jailer asked the Irishman.

"No," he answered, "but he is rich. He captured some ships in the Indies and he joined us on the eve of the battle."

"What battle?" the jailer asked.

"The Battle of Trafalgar, where Nelson was killed."

"What?" the jailer cried. "Nelson has been killed?"

"Yes, and if necessary I could show you the hand that killed him."

"That's enough for today. Tomorrow we shall talk again."

"Good night, Father Donald. And don't forget: good bread, good beer, and fresh meat."

The prisoners could not complain about their jailer. That very evening, they could see that Donald was conscientiously keeping his promises. They could also see that two sentries were walking back and forth in the little courtyard beneath the barred window of their cell.

A week went by, and there was no further communication between the Frenchmen and the jailer. On the other hand, the jailer never visited their cell without whispering with his fellow countryman. "Everything is going well," the Irishman would tell René afterward.

The weather was getting colder and colder. There were times when the wind gusted so bitterly cold that the sentries would take refuge in the warm guardroom until the wind died down. That's when the Irishman would file away at the bars. There were three bars, and he had already filed through the one in the middle at its base.

The weather turned from bad to worse, and one evening the Irishman told René, "Give me a hundred francs." René pulled five louis from his pocket and handed them to him.

The Irishman disappeared with the jailer. He came back an hour later.

"Let's pray that the weather's so bad tonight that you'd not put the devil himself out in it," said the Irishman. "If so, we are free."

Supper came, more plentiful than usual, and all eight men were able to stow some bread and meat in their pockets for lunch the next day. At about nine that evening, driven by a north wind strong enough to dehorn all the oxen in the county, snow began to fall. At ten o'clock, the prisoners listened intently, but they couldn't be absolutely sure that the sentries had left the courtyard. It could be that the sound of their footsteps was being muffled by the snow that was already covering the paving stones. They opened the window a crack and peered carefully out. It was important to be sure the English sentries seemed to have deserted their posts for the warmth of the guardroom.

The Irishman picked up a stone in the corner of the room and threw it across the courtyard and over the wall. From its other side a rope appeared. It dangled toward the courtyard.

"Now all we have to do is finish filing through this bar," said the Irishman.

"Fine, but let's not waste any time," said René, and, grabbing the bar with both his hands, with one jerk he ripped it out of the stone in which it was set. "This will be my weapon," he said. "It's all I need."

The Irishman was the first to slip through the window's other two bars. He checked the courtyard for the sentries, but they were nowhere to be seen. He tied the rope to a crampon on the wall. It grew taut; someone was holding the other end on the other side of the wall. Clenching one of the broken stretcher rods with its embedded needle between his teeth, he climbed up to the top of the wall and disappeared on the other side.

René followed, just as skillfully and quickly. When he reached the other side, the Irishman was holding the rope's other end. Their liberator had already disappeared.

When the last of the other six men cleared the wall, they tossed the rope back into the courtyard.

It was one of those nights in northern climes when you cannot see four feet in front of you. Certain that no one was pursuing them, the Irishman asked that they wait a moment while he got his bearings. He listened.

"The sea is over there," he said, pointing east. "Actually, it's not really the sea, because the sound isn't loud enough; it's Saint George's Channel. That's the way they will go looking for us, so we have to go in the opposite direction. We'll go north until we get to Limerick. I know the countryside, and I'm pretty sure I won't get lost. It would help if we had a compass."

"I have one," said René, pulling from his pocket a little compass he always carried with him. It had been very useful when he was in the Indies.

"Well, then," said the Irishman, "let's be on our way!"

First they had to get out of Cork. Fortunately it was not a walled city, though it was a garrison town. They had not gone a hundred paces before they heard the cadenced steps of an English patrol. The Irishman ordered silence, and silently all eight of the prisoners backed into a tiny street. They were huddling in a large doorway when the patrol, nearly brushing against them, marched by. They all held their breath. They heard one of the English soldiers say, "The captain could surely have let us stay in the guardhouse. Even a Frenchman would have to be the devil himself to try to escape on a night like this."

As the footsteps faded in the distance, the fugitives left their hiding place and set off in the opposite direction. Ten minutes later they were out of Cork, and on their faces they could feel the bite of the same bitter cold north wind that Hamlet complains about on the parapets of Elsinore Castle. The escapees paused for a moment.

"We are on the road to Blarney," said the Irishman. "I have some friends there if it's a place you would like to stop to sleep. I think, though, it might be wiser to keep going to Mallow. The road is deserted, and we won't pass a single house."

"Do you know anyone in Mallow?" René asked.

"In Mallow, there are ten friends for every one of us."

"Well, then," said René, "let's go to Mallow. That will give us a day's head start over those who will try to follow us tomorrow morning."

They reached Mallow at six in the morning, about an hour before daylight. The Irishman walked straight to a house he apparently knew and knocked at the door. When he heard the question "Who goes there?" from a window on the second floor, he responded with a question of his own: "Does Farrill still live here?"

"Yes," the voice replied. "I'm Farrill. Who are you?"

"I'm Sullivan."

"Wait, wait. I'm coming down to open the door."

The door opened, and the two men threw themselves into each other's arms. Farrill urged his friend to come in, but the Irishman, who had asked the other fugitives to hide against the wall, said: "We are not alone. I have some friends, and we need hospitality until tonight."

"Whether there were ten or a hundred of you, you would get what you need. Not the way Farrill would like to provide it, but as his means allow. Come in, whoever you are."

The prisoners came to the door. "Sir," said René, "we are French prisoners, and we escaped from Cork prison last night. Sullivan, our comrade, vouches for you, and we trust we can place ourselves in your hands."

The door was open. Farrill motioned them in, and they all slipped in without anyone seeing them. When the door had closed behind them, Sullivan alerted René that he was not to offer anything to Farrill in exchange for his hospitality, because such an offer, whatever it might be, would hurt Farrill deeply. Although Farrill was obviously not rich, his hospitality was everything the Irishman had promised. If not opulent, it was at least cordial and sufficient, and it included several big bottles of good Dublin beer for them to drink.

As they had covered six and a half leagues, they spent the day sleeping and eating, recovering from their fatigue. That evening at seven, the fugitives set out once more, this time for Bruree, about seven leagues farther on. The shoes of two of the fugitives had been in such a sorry state that Farrill had gone out during the day to buy two new pairs. So nothing could slow them down, at least not bad shoes.

At about five in the morning they reached Bruree. Sullivan had been careful to stay on the right bank of the little river, the Maigue, on which the village lies. There he knew a man who was no less hospitable than the good Farrill had been, and things happened much as they had the day before. The fugitives were able to drink, eat, and sleep, and that night they set off for Askeaton.

Because they were taking a difficult path that cut across the countryside rather than a road easy to follow, Sullivan's friend insisted on accompanying them as their guide. Not only was Sullivan unfamiliar with the route, he also didn't know anyone in Askeaton. So he gratefully accepted his friend's offer, for both himself and his companions.

On the way to Askeaton, their guide's magic words "they are Frenchmen!" opened arms and doors to the fugitives. Housewives' faces broke into smiles, in spite of the additional expense, which in a country as poor as Ireland was surely onerous.

Their guide took them to his brother-in-law's when they reached Askeaton. Their conversation didn't take long, and by the end of it they had made plans for the following day. René had offered to buy a ship to sail back to France, which, he figured, they would have ample time to load with any supplies they might need. But Sullivan shook his head. He didn't trust the people in the port as much because, unlike the Irish who lived farther inland, they often had to deal with the English. Aside from that, all along the coast soldiers were looking for the fugitives, for the news had spread far and wide that eight Frenchmen had escaped from Cork prison. So Sullivan thought it best to take a ship by surprise, in whatever state it happened to be, and they could always stop elsewhere, if necessary, to take on supplies.

They didn't cover more than four leagues that night. They stopped in

Loghill, where they asked about the ships at anchor on the River Shannon. They learned of a sloop at Foynes, but it was too far out in the pass. Their guide suggested a small ship masted like a sloop that was lying at anchor between Tarbert and the opposite island; it would not be difficult to seize.

They decided to make their move between three and four in the morning. They untied a rowboat that some trusting soul had left along the bank, and once they'd rowed up next to the sloop, they climbed aboard. They surprised the occupants, three men and a woman, who began screaming at the sight of the eight men. Sullivan explained, in excellent Irish, that if they didn't shut up, necessity would force him and his companions to shut them up. The sail needles he displayed at the same time persuaded the poor devils to put up no more resistance.

In mere minutes, the fugitives had raised the anchor and unfurled the sail. The wind was blowing from the north, so the little sloop sailed out into the Atlantic Ocean as majestically as a big sailing ship. When they'd gotten about a league from shore, they put the three men and the woman in the same rowboat they had used to get out to the sloop. René gave them twenty louis, and he promised that if he made it safe and sound to France, he would send them a draft on the Bank of Dublin for double the value of their boat.

The good people put little faith in René's promise. But, since nobody had forced him to give them the twenty louis, and as they had some hope of getting the draft, they set out for the Shannon in good spirits. They arrived back so quickly at the spot where their boat had been moored that they were not quite sure whether their adventure had been real or a dream.

XCVI

At Sea

ONCE THE FUGITIVES WERE MASTERS of the sloop, their first order of business was to determine what supplies it contained. It was carrying a load of peat, it turned out, but otherwise it had on board only a hundred potatoes, eight cabbages, two jars of butter, and ten or twelve bottles of drinking water: barely enough food for five or six days, if they were careful. The ship's owners had brought no bread on board, and they probably had none at home either, the general situation in Ireland then being as it is today.

"Let's see," René said. "It seems to me that the wise thing to do would be to start rationing immediately. We had a good supper last night, and we ate well this morning; so we won't need to eat until this evening."

Several voices were raised in protest. "Come now," René continued. "Let's be reasonable and agree on one thing: Nobody will be hungry until eight this evening."

"Agreed," said the Irishman. "Nobody will be hungry before eight. Those who are can tighten their belts or sleep, and while they sleep, they can dream about eating."

"For now, don't you think the most urgent thing to do is build a fire?" asked one of the sailors.

"Ah, that at least we can do," Sullivan said. "We certainly won't run out of peat. The sun's not out, and it doesn't look likely to be out soon; and the snow is falling, which will provide us a good source of water if we can find a tarp to collect it. But first, let's give ourselves the pleasure of warming our fingers."

They lit a fire in a brazier and kept it burning from morning till night, then from night till morning, when it was even more necessary. For in January and February, the nights along the English coasts and in the Channel are unbearable.

Not only was it cold, it was also near impossible at night to see well enough to navigate. The men had found an old rusty compass, but it worked so badly that they were often sailing off course. They had searched in vain for a distance log to learn how far they had come. Further, there were no instruments to determine what the wind direction was or in which direction they should sail. And there was neither oil nor candle to light the binnacle. All they knew was that they needed first to sail south and then toward the east, but to guide them they had no instrument other than René's pocket compass, and they had no light to see by other than that poor peat fire they had so scorned at first.

Since René had the most experience at sea and since the men trusted his courage, he was unanimously chosen to be captain. The sea was high, the wind was strong and variable, and the ship's sails were in tatters; so René ordered his men to gather together all the sails they could find. Sullivan found a chest, and in it he found sails in somewhat decent shape and a candle. It burned through the night, and by its light the sailors were able to work at mending the large sail.

At eight, every man received his two potatoes, his two cabbage leaves, his chunk of butter, and his glass of water.

Even with Sullivan's find there was not enough sail. They decided to sacrifice the foresail by cutting it up into pieces in order to repair the main sail. They lost more time than they would have wished in repairing the sail, but once it was raised, they could move much more rapidly and surely.

The candle had been replaced with pieces of oak that they burned in clay pots filled with peat. By their readings of René's compass, they were now nearly certain they were on the right heading. They were being careful in rationing their food, by René's order, but still on the fourth day it became apparent that if they kept eating as they were, they had barely enough left for two or three days. They conserved their water as best they could, yet they needed some of it to boil the cabbage. The potatoes, at least, they were able to cook directly in the peat fire.

On the fifth day they sighted a sail on the horizon. René summoned his companions and pointed to the ship. "It is either an English ship or one of our allies," he said. "If it is English, we'll storm aboard and capture it. If it is from a friendly nation, we will ask for help, they'll give us what we need, and we'll continue on our way. We took the *Standard* sloop the *Revenant*. They had four hundred and fifty men; we had but one hundred and twenty. They had forty-eight guns; we had only sixteen. And we were not even hungry. Up with the helm, Irishman, and let's have at 'em."

Each man picked up his needle dagger, and René hoisted his iron bar. But whether it was friend or enemy, merchant ship or armed for war, it fled, and the little sloop was forced to give up the chase.

"Doesn't anyone have a drop of water to give me?" a sailor asked, forlorn.

"Yes, indeed, my good man," said René.

"But what about you?" the man asked.

"Me?" René answered with a smile that would have made an angel jealous. "I'm not thirsty." And he gave his own ration of water to the sailor.

They made it until the evening of the fifth day, and then they distributed the last of the food. Each man had one potato, one leaf of cabbage, and a mere half glass of water. As we know, when ship crews are in distress, the most pitiless suffering is thirst. A thirsty man has no pity even for his best friend.

By the next day, our fugitives were almost crazy from thirst. Each man kept to himself as much as he could; faces were pale and haggard. Suddenly, one of the sailors let out a cry and leaped into the sea.

"Heave to and throw out a rope!" René shouted, then dove into the water after the sailor.

Two seconds later he surfaced with a grip on the man. René had to fight him, but finally got the rope around his waist and got it knotted.

"Pull him in," he called out.

After they'd pulled the sailor back on board, René noted, "And now it's my turn."

Already they had thrown out three ropes. René grabbed one and a moment later was back on board the ship.

Delicate and thin though he was, René seemed to be the only man on board not suffering from hunger and thirst.

"Ah!," said the Irishman. "If only I had some lead to suck."

"Do you think gold would serve the same purpose?" René asked.

"I have no idea," the Irishman answered, "because I've always had more lead than gold."

"Well, try this in your mouth." René held up a twenty-four-franc gold piece bearing the effigy of Louis XVI.

"Oh, that's good, and it feels so cool," said the Irishman.

"Do you hear, Monsieur René?" the other six sailors asked, their mouths open, their arms outstretched.

"Here," he said, giving each of them a gold coin. "Give it a try."

"How about you?" they asked.

"Oh, my thirst is not unbearable. I'll keep that for a last resort."

That day sucking gold proved to be an effective substitute for that unusual form of refreshment favored by thirsty sailors, sucking lead. They may have spent the day complaining, but they did it with gold louis in their mouths.

At first light the next day the sky grew brighter in the south. René, who'd been at the helm all night, stood up and shouted, "Land ho!"

His cry was magical. Immediately the seven others were on their feet.

"Helm to starboard!" shouted one of the sailors. "It's Guernsey. The English always cruise back and forth around the French islands. Helm to starboard!"

They turned the tiller and, steering away from the islands, headed for Cape Tréguier.

"Land ho!" René shouted once more.

"Ah!" said the sailor. "That I do recognize. It is Cape Tréguier. Now we have nothing to fear. Let's keep as close to the coast as we can. In two hours we'll be in Saint-Malo."

At the helm, the Irishman followed his instructions. An hour later on their right they passed the Grand-Bé rock, the peninsula where Chateaubriand's tomb lies, and soon they were moving under full sail into the Saint-Malo harbor.

The sloop being of English construction, it had first been identified as a foreign ship. But as soon as they saw the clothes the crewmen were wearing, the port officials quickly guessed the truth: that the men must be sailors fleeing England's prisons or pontoons.

When they reached the jetty, the deputy naval officer came to meet them in an armed launch. It did not take them long to identify themselves, and René took responsibility for providing all the details of their escape while a clerk recorded them. René and the four sailors who knew how to write signed the official statement.

That done, René asked if there were information about an American ship back from Île de France called the *New York Racer,* captained by a man named François. As it happened, René was told, the ship had arrived just ten or eleven days before and was anchored near the shipyard. René explained that the ship belonged to him, though temporarily it had been put in the name of Surcouf's quartermaster, and he asked if he might be allowed to visit it. Now that his identity had been confirmed, they said, he was free to go wherever he chose.

The officer had meanwhile realized what a sorry state the poor fugitives were in, for he'd overheard two or three of them say they were dying of hunger and thirst. He had sent for eight cups of bouillon, a bottle of wine, and the port surgeon, who arrived along with the nourishment the fugitives so badly needed. The surgeon warned them to be careful since they were so exhausted. He had them take the bouillon only a spoonful at a time, with no bread, and allowed them only very small glasses of wine. A quarter of an hour later, somewhat restored, they all tried to give back to René their gold louis, but he would not hear of it. They were in his service, he said, until they found something better.

René then told the authorities that he and his companions had stolen their sloop from some poor Irishmen, and he asked that its value be appraised so that he could reimburse the owners. Reimbursement would be easier than he'd originallythought, for he had discovered in one of the ship's cabinets the ship's papers with the owner's address.

With their sloop at anchor in the outer harbor, René and his companions, who had regained their strength, climbed into a rowboat. "Now, my lads, let's move!" said René, less to his companions than to the rowers. "Straight to the *New York Racer.* There'll be two louis for the rowers."

"Say," said one of the rowers, "that's Monsieur René. He's the man who paid the debts of all my friends serving on the *Revenant* with Monsieur Surcouf. Hurrah for Monsieur René!"

The other rowers, hoping their enthusiasm would earn them double pay, joined in the shouts of "Hurrah!" at the top of their lungs.

When the crew on the *New York Racer* heard the shouting, they ran up on deck. René recognized his friend François standing on the poop deck while looking through his spyglass to see who was coming.

Suddenly François shouted, "Comrades, it's the boss. Hurrah for Monsieur René!" Immediately they decked out the ship with flags, and without even asking permission of the port commissioner, they fired eight guns.

The sailors climbed up into the rigging, and, waving their hats, they were shouting, "Hurrah for Monsieur René!" On the top rung of the ladder, François was waiting with his arms outstretched, as if he were about to leap into the sea so he could embrace his captain all the more quickly.

One can imagine the cheers René heard when he stepped on board. He paid off the rowers to their satisfaction while his seven companions told the crew of the *New York Racer* how they had escaped, and how René had given them his own water, and how he had kept up everyone's courage, and how he'd declared them his men until they found something better. Then, so that the rowers too might join the celebration, for hadn't they returned René to his ship, the seven sailors asked René if they might share their rations with them.

"My good men," said René, "you don't need to share your rations, for you can all share my dinner. The day of my return is a day of celebration, and every sailor on board my ship is an officer the day I return from an English prison."

René passed around more refreshments to his companions, then summoned the cook and composed the dinner menu himself.

That day, all foods tempting, good, and delectable that could be found in Saint-Malo ended up on the table of the crew of the *New York Racer* and its captain.

XCVII
Monsieur Fouché's Advice

RENÉ ARRIVED IN SAINT-MALO on January 11, 1806, the very day that the Kingdom of Naples was invaded and that Masséna entered Spoleto.

Months earlier, while the unfortunate Villeneuve was losing the Battle of Trafalgar, the Emperor had crossed the Rhine and begun his campaign by taking the Donauwerth Bridge and crossing the Danube. Then, while he was preparing to take Ulm, Marshal Soult took Memmingen and Marshal Ney was winning the battle of Elchingen, which would give him his first title of duke.

Ulm surrendered. General Mack and the thirty thousand men in his garrison marched out to meet the Emperor and laid down their arms at his feet. Then, led by the imperial guard and the first eighty grenadiers, each carrying a flag taken from the enemy, he entered Augsburg. He occupied Vienna, won the battle of Austerlitz, and concluded an armistice with the Emperor of Austria, who had allowed the Russians to leave the Austrian states so precipitously that Junot, carrying a letter from Emperor Napoleon to Emperor Alexander, a letter in which Napoleon was asking for peace, was unable to catch up with the Russians.

Between December 12 and December 29 Napoleon was staying in the Schönbrunn Castle, where he decreed on the 27th that the Naples dynasty had ceased to reign.

On January 1, 1806, he abolished the Republican calendar. Perhaps so people would forget certain dates? In that case, he was not successful; not only were the dates not forgotten, they did not even revert to their old Gregorian designations. The French people continued to refer to the two dates the Emperor may have most wanted them to forget as Offenburg and the 18th Brumaire.

As the news of Napoleon's victories reached France, it was greeted by such enthusiasm that memory of the Trafalgar disaster began to fade. To ensure that Trafalgar would not sit like a stain upon his reputation amidst all his other triumphs, Napoleon had ordered that the disaster be blamed on the ocean storm rather than on the English victory. So the only news France had of Trafalgar was what the newspapers had been allowed to print, and René was perhaps the only Frenchman to have returned from the calamitous battle.

On the day following his arrival in Saint-Malo, the maritime prefect, addressing René as captain, invited him to the prefecture, and René was quick to accept. The magistrate was naturally eager to have precise information about the Trafalgar catastrophe, but of course he was also aware of the Emperor's orders, unlike René. The prefect explained to René the Emperor's position on the matter, but he also said he would like to know the truth. Since René had received no orders directly from any superior, he asked for the magistrate's discretion, and shared with him what he had seen of the battle with his own eyes.

In exchange, the perfect told René that Commander Lucas had been a prisoner in London on his own recognizance for eight or ten days but had then been granted his freedom, in recognition of the splendid courage he had demonstrated in his command of the *Redoutable*. Because it had been from the *Redoutable* that Nelson's fatal shot had been fired, the English did not want it said that they were keeping Lucas prisoner out of revenge. Freed, Lucas had arrived back in Paris just the day before; the maritime prefect had indeed received a telegraph confirming it. Upon René's request, the prefect said he would find out Lucas's address and send it to him.

With obvious signs of his esteem, the prefect then dismissed René. He had learned everything he could from him.

In Saint-Malo, René had become something of a legend. The people's admiration of him, already abundant, knew no limits when René's action regarding the stolen sloop became public knowledge. Its value was determined to be eleven hundred francs, and René had arranged for a draft of two thousand five hundred francs, payable by the head banker at O'Brien and Company in Dublin, to be sent to the sloop's owner, a poor coaster named Patrick operating out of the town of Loghill. Great was his family's astonishment to learn that he was to appear in Dublin at O'Brien and Company, where he would be paid more than twice what his sloop was worth.

René had meanwhile learned all the details of François's trip back to Saint-Malo. His return had taken so long because near Cape Finistèrre he had been pursued by an English brig, which he had successfully escaped by changing course and sailing toward America. Sailing at eleven or twelve knots during the pursuit, the *New York Racer* had truly earned its name. François told René that if he had suffered the misfortune of being captured, he would have shot himself. René knew his friend well enough not to doubt it.

Nor was René surprised, in light of François's devotion to him, to find everything in its place on the ship, with his portfolio still in the secretary drawer, his testament in the portfolio, and the precious stones in their little bag. With the resources René had left him, François had already paid the crew and kept all accounts current; the most scrupulous auditor would not have found even a quarter of a centime's discrepancy in the books. René begged François to stay on as his front man captain aboard the *Racer* until some decision had been made about René's future.

After he'd seen the prefect, René made his second visit in Saint-Malo, and that was with Madame Surcouf, to whom he gave glowing reports of her husband. Then he prepared for his journey. From his well-furnished wardrobe on the sloop he chose only what was necessary for the moment, and, as he did not want to draw attention to himself by taking a seat in the mail coach, he booked a place on a diligence. With Captain Lucas and the Emperor both back in the capital, René had two reasons for returning to Paris as soon as possible.

When he reached Paris, René took lodgings in the Hotel Mirabeau, then in Rue de Richelieu (it would later be moved to Rue de la Paix). He had scarcely written his name on the hotel register and gotten to his room when Fouché's secretary paid him a visit. The Ministry of Police requested his presence as soon as he could manage it. As there was nothing to keep him from going that very day, and as he was indeed burning with desire to know what future Fouché had in store for him, he asked the secretary to wait, dressed rapidly, and joined him in his carriage.

As soon as René was announced, he was admitted. "His Excellency awaits Monsieur René," said the secretary as he stood by the open door to the minister's study.

Fouché greeted him with his usual sardonic expression, which in its familiarity René found more welcoming than off-putting. "Well, how is the captain of the *New York Racer*? You are back!"

"Your Excellence uses a title that demonstrates he already knows how everything has gone for me."

"That's my job," said Fouché. "And I would like to compliment the way you have taken care of business. Are you pleased with the advice I gave you?"

"Of course. A man with Your Excellency's perspicacity can give only good advice."

"Good advice isn't everything, Monsieur René. It must also be followed. In that regard, I congratulate you. Here is a copy of Monsieur Surcouf's letter to the Ministry of the Navy, which recounts the struggle for the *Standard* and its capture. In it Surcouf speaks of a certain sailor named René who conducted himself in such a way that Surcouf had not a moment's hesitation in naming him ensign first class. My interest in Monsieur René prompted me to request a copy of this letter from my colleague Monsieur Decrès. Here is another letter, sent to the same ministry, announcing Surcouf's arrival in Île de France and reporting the leave he gave Ensign René to take two young women and their father's body to Burma on a ship he'd purchased flying the American flag. Here is a third letter, this one reporting the ensign's return to Île de France after encounters with various monstrous animals; evidently we are speaking about tigers as big as the Nemean lion and serpents as long as the Python. On his way back from Burma, this Monsieur René happened upon the combat raging between Surcouf and two English ships. René captured one of them, thus leaving Surcouf free to take the other, and Surcouf, being Surcouf, lost no time in doing so. Afterward, leaving his share of the prize to the poor of Île de France and to his men, René asked for permission to take part in a major naval battle that, he'd learned, the Emperor had ordered to stop the English. With letters from General Decaen, governor of the island, and with leave from Surcouf his commander, he set sail again on his little ship the *New York Racer*. He reached the Bay of Cadiz three days before the Battle of Trafalgar. He went aboard the *Redoutable* and introduced himself to Captain Lucas, who took him on as a third lieutenant.

"When the battle began, Captain Lucas was attacked by three ships, but he set his sights on the *Victory,* and he nearly took it. Without the intervention of the *Téméraire,* which wiped out one hundred and eight of his men with one broadside, he would have surely captured the English flagship. Meanwhile, Nelson was dying from a bullet fired from the *Redoutable*'s mizzen top. It is said that the shot was fired by a third lieutenant named René, who did not have a set battle station and had received permission to go where he wished. Consequently, he had chosen, along with the topmen, the most dangerous place." Fouché paused for a moment and stared at the young man. "Is it true, monsieur, that Third Lieutenant René killed Nelson?"

"I cannot swear to it, Monsieur le Ministre," René replied, "although I was the only man with a gun at the mizzen top. For a moment I could pick Nelson out because of his blue uniform, his crosses, and his epaulettes. I did aim and fire, but there were men shooting from the maintop and the foretop as well, so it is impossible for me to swear that I was the one who rid France of its dangerous enemy."

"Nor can I swear it," said Fouché, "but, to anyone who asks, I repeat and shall keep repeating what has been told and written to me."

"No doubt Your Excellency already knows how my odyssey ended as you want no detail as to how it was begun."

"Yes. As a prisoner, you were first taken to Gibraltar and then to England on board the *Samson* with Captain Parker. During a terrible storm, you and your men manned the pumps and saved the ship, which otherwise would have surely sunk. Then you were imprisoned in Cork, but you escaped with seven companions. You stole a small sloop in the Shannon River. You sent its owner back to shore while you returned to Saint-Malo. As you thought it necessary to compensate the ship's owner, you sent him a draft for two thousand five hundred francs to be drawn on the O'Brien bank in Dublin."

"I must say, monsignor," René observed, "that you are marvelously well-informed."

"You understand, monsieur, that it is quite rare for a sailor to buy an American sloop with his own money, give up his share of a capture to his men and the poor, travel two thousand leagues to join the desperate fight at Trafalgar, and escape after a week in prison. Then to remember, after coming back to France, that from a poor coaster he'd appropriated a miserable ship worth eleven hundred francs, which represented the poor man's entire fortune, and which René more than doubled in his remittance to the owner from whom he had *borrowed* it. You generously repay all your debts, monsieur, beginning with the ones you contracted with me. Since my earlier advice was so well heeded, would you like to stash somewhere in your mind the advice I am going to give you now?"

"Please tell me what it is, monsignor."

"You now call yourself Monsieur René, and that is how you will be received by the Emperor. In my report there will be no mention of the Comte de Sainte-Hermine. The Emperor has nothing against the sailor René, so he will put no obstacles in your path and may even help you advance. But if he sees the slightest connection between René the sailor and the Comte de Sainte-Hermine, he will not be pleased. You will have accomplished so much for nothing, and from nothing you will likely have to start again. That is why I sent for you as soon as you reached Paris. The Emperor will no doubt be back on the twenty-sixth. In the meantime, go see Captain Lucas at the navy ministry. The Emperor will want to see Lucas immediately upon his return. If Lucas offers to introduce you to His Majesty, accept; you could ask for no one better to introduce you. I have no doubts that if you follow my advice and keep the Comte de Sainte-Hermine a secret, you will make the military fortune of Third Lieutenant René."

René took leave of His Excellency the Minister of Police. He still had no idea why Fouché was taking such interest in him. Fouché might have wondered the same thing, and, if asked, he might have answered honestly enough: "I don't know, except that some men can prove to be so appealing that even the worst-tempered among us cannot resist them."

René went directly to Lucas's hotel. He found the captain completely recovered from his wounds and generally pleased with the way the English had treated him.

"If we embark on another campaign, I hope you will come sail with me, my dear René," he said to the young man. "You can try to deliver to Collingwood a duplicate of the bullet you sent Nelson."

Captain Lucas, himself uncertain about the date of Napoleon's return to Paris, learned from René that he would be coming back incognito on the twenty-fifth. Lucas thought for a moment. "Come see me on the twenty-ninth," he said. "Perhaps I will have some good news for you." The news would be delayed a few days.

Napoleon returned to Paris on the twenty-sixth. He had spent a few days in Munich to celebrate Eugene Beauharnais's marriage with Princess Auguste de Bavière, but he had allotted only one day to the other European cities on his homeward journey. In Stuttgart he accepted the congratulations of his new allies. In Karlsruhe he took care of family alliances. He knew all the while that Paris was impatiently awaiting his return, for Paris was eager to express its joy and admiration.

France was deeply satisfied with the way public affairs were progressing now that the citizenry had relinquished much of its involvement. As if reliving the first heady days of the Revolution, France wanted to celebrate the remarkable achievements of its armies and leader. The campaign had lasted only three months instead of three years, the continent had been disarmed, France had extended its borders far beyond all expectations. New glory had gilded French feats of arms, and the prospect of peace promised renewed prosperity. Indeed, the acclaims after Marengo were nothing compared to what followed Austerlitz, which was for the Empire what Marengo had been for the Consulate. Marengo had secured the consular power in Bonaparte's hands, and Austerlitz guaranteed Napoleon the imperial crown he'd placed on his head. And in the streets of the capital the people would welcome back Napoleon with exultance and thanks, shouting "Long live the Emperor!"

The Emperor sent word to Lucas on the morning of the third that he would receive the captain on the seventh. The meeting was scheduled for ten in the morning, so Lucas asked René to have breakfast with him at nine, and then accompany him to the Tuileries. There, René, who did not have an audience with the Emperor and did not want to request one, would wait in the antechamber in the event that Napoleon expressed a desire to meet him.

It is safe to say that René dreaded any such meeting. Twice he had met Bonaparte's piercing gaze, first at Madame Permon's house and later at the Hotel Sourdis on the evening the marriage contract was to be signed, and the man's eyes terrified him. They seemed able to take the measure of everything they looked upon and then to etch it in his imperial memory. Fortunately, René had all he needed to meet the gaze in Bonaparte's eyes: a clear conscience, for that no man could perturb.

On the morning of the seventh, at ten minutes till ten, Captain Lucas and René passed through the Tuileries gates. René accompanied Lucas as far as the antechamber; then the captain went on ahead.

An intelligent man, Lucas told the Emperor the entire story of René's selfless, courageous actions without ever mentioning his name. But he found that the Emperor already knew as much about his third lieutenant as he did, so he ventured the information that the young hero was at that moment in the antechamber, should the Emperor wish to meet him.

The Emperor nodded his assent and rang a bell. An aide-de-camp opened the door. "Bring in Monsieur René, third lieutenant on board the *Redoutable*," Napoleon said.

Napoleon took one look at the young man as he came in, and his eyes registered surprise. "What?" he said. "Do you come to the Tuileries out of uniform?"

"Sire," René replied, "I came to the Tuileries not to have the honor of meeting Your Majesty, for I never expected I would be received, but rather to accompany the captain, with whom I expect to spend a part of the day. Besides, Sire, I am a lieutenant without really being a lieutenant. Captain Lucas did indeed name me to the rank three days before the Battle of Trafalgar, for his third lieutenant had died a few days earlier, but my nomination was never confirmed."

"I thought you held the rank of a second lieutenant," said Napoleon.

"Yes, Sire, but that was on board a corsair."

"On board Surcouf's *Revenant,* right?"

"Yes, Sire."

"You contributed to the capture of the English ship the *Standard*?"

"Yes, Sire."

"And with a great deal of courage."

"I did my best, Milord."

"I've heard about it from General Decaen, the governor of Île de France."

"I had the honor of being presented to him, Sire."

"He told me about a trip you took in the Indies."

"Yes, I did go about fifty leagues into the interior."

"And the English did not harass you?"

"It was in a part of the Indies they do not occupy, Sire."

"Where was that? I thought they occupied all of the Indies."

"I went to the Kingdom of Pegu, Sire, between the Sittang and the Irrawaddy."

"You had some terrifying hunts in that part of the Indies, I am told."

"I met and killed several tigers."

"Was killing a tiger for the first time an exciting experience?"

"The first time, yes, Sire. But not after that."

"Why is that?"

"Because the second time I forced the cat to avert its gaze, and from that moment on I realized that the tiger is an animal that man was meant to dominate."

"And when you stood facing Nelson?"

"Facing Nelson, Sire, I hesitated for a moment."

"Why was that?"

"Because Nelson was a great man of war, Sire, and because I thought that perhaps he was a necessary counterweight to Your Majesty."

"Ah! But you fired at him nonetheless: a man who may have been sent by Providence?"

"I thought that if indeed he had been sent by Providence, then Providence would turn the bullet aside. Besides, Sire," René continued, "I have never boasted, or even claimed, that I killed Nelson."

"If, however. . . ."

René cut in: "One does not boast about such things; they are the kinds of things one hardly dares to admit. If I had needed to kill Gustavus-Adolphus or Frederick, I would have done so for the good of my country, but I would have never gotten over it."

"And if you were among my enemies, would you shoot me?"

"I shall never be among them, Sire!"

"Very well."

He seemed to have concluded, but then turned to Lucas. "Monsieur le Commandant," he said, "this very day I am declaring war on both England and Prussia. In a war against Prussia, which has only one outlet to the sea, you will have little to do; but in a war against England . . . well, for that I shall have plenty for you to do. You are, I believe, one of those men about whom I was speaking in a note I sent to Villeneuve, men who know how to die and who sometimes even wish to die."

"Sire, I never lost sight of Villeneuve at Trafalgar. No one can dare tell you that he did not promptly and religiously do his duty."

"Yes, once he reached Trafalgar. I know. But up until then he caused me a great deal of pain. It is his fault that I ended up in Vienna instead of London."

"Don't be too much dissatisfied, Sire. You have lost nothing by a change of direction."

"I've lost no glory, that is true. Yet today, as you can see, although I have been to Vienna, I must start afresh, as once again I must declare war on England and Prussia. There appears to be no other way, now, than to defeat England on the continent by defeating the kings whom England subsidizes in her alliances. I shall see you before war begins, Captain Lucas. And before you go, here is a cross of an officer of the Legion of Honor. I hope you will accept it, and never forget that the cross I am giving you is my own."

Turning to René, he said, "As for you, Monsieur René, please leave your name with Duroc, my aide-de-camp. Since Captain Lucas seems to be your friend, we shall do our best to keep you together."

"Sire," said René, stepping forward with a bow, "since Your Majesty has not recognized me, I would be able to continue to act under the name people have recently known me as and under which I was introduced to you. Were I to do so, I would be deceiving the Emperor, and even at one's risk of rousing the Emperor's anger, one should never deceive him. Sire, for everyone else, my name is René; but for Your Majesty I am the Comte de Sainte-Hermine." Again he bowed before the emperor, and waited.

The emperor remained motionless for a moment. His brows furrowed; his face first expressed surprise, then turned severe. "What you have just done is noble, monsieur, but it is not enough for me to forgive you. You will leave your address with Duroc and go back home. There you will wait for my orders, which will come by way of Monsieur Fouché. Unless I am mistaken, Monsieur Fouché is one of your defenders."

"Not because of anything I have done, Sire," said Sainte-Hermine with a bow, and, leaving the room, he went to wait for Captain Lucas in his carriage.

"Sire," said Lucas, "I have no idea what reasons Your Majesty might have to hold a grudge against my poor friend René. But I swear on my honor that he is one of the bravest and most loyal men that I know."

"Good Lord!" Napoleon said. "I can see that! If he had not revealed his true identity, when nothing demanded it, he would have been a lieutenant on board a frigate."

Alone again, Napoleon stood motionless for a while with a worried look on his face. Then, throwing his wrinkled gloves violently down on his desk, he said, "I have the worst luck. That is exactly the kind of man I need in the navy."

As for René, or the Comte de Sainte-Hermine, if you prefer, all he could do was obey the orders he'd received. And that is what he did. He went back to the Hotel Mirabeau on Rue de Richelieu. And waited.

XCVIII

A Relay Station in Rome

ON DECEMBER 2 Napoleon won the Battle of Austerlitz. On the twenty-seventh he declared the Naples dynasty defunct. On February 15 Joseph Napoleon entered the city of Naples, which had been abandoned for the second time by the Bourbons, and on March 30 he was proclaimed King of the Two Sicilies.

Along with the new King of Naples, or rather the future King of Naples, the French army had invaded the Roman states. Deeply irritated by the French military actions, the Holy Father had summoned Cardinal Fesch to complain of what he called a territorial violation. The cardinal had consulted with Napoleon, who had responded:

Holy Father, you are the sovereign of Rome, it is true. But Rome is a part of the French Empire. You are pope, but I am emperor, an emperor like the Germanic emperors of old, like Charlemagne. And for you I am like Charlemagne in more ways than one, in power and in kindness. Therefore, you will obey the laws of the Empire's federated system by opening up your territory to my friends and closing it to my enemies.

To that typical Napoleonic response, the pope's eyes, normally gentle, had cast daggers. He'd then replied to Cardinal Fesch that he recognized no sovereign above himself, and that if Napoleon wanted to renew the tyranny of Germany's Henry IV, he would revive Gregory VI's resistance.

With disdain Napoleon had observed that, it being the nineteenth century, he had little fear of the pope's spiritual weapons but that he would not be providing the pope any pretext for their use in any case, as he had no intention of interfering in religious matters. He would take military action only against temporal sovereigns, and meanwhile leave the pope secure in the Vatican, where he would remain the respected Bishop of Rome and head of all the bishops in Christendom.

That discussion, with little give-and-take, took the whole month of December 1805. During that time, to demonstrate further the seriousness of his intentions regarding the Roman states, whatever stand the pope might take, Napoleon had General Lemarois initiate military occupation of the three provinces along the Adriatic coast: Urbino, Ancona, and Macerata.

Eventually Pius VII set aside his threats of excommunication and agreed to discuss a compromise even with the following conditions:

The pope, as independent sovereign over his states, proclaimed and guaranteed as such by France, would nonetheless contract an alliance with France, and whenever France was engaged in war, the pope would bar its enemies from the Roman States;

French troops would occupy Ancona, Ostia, and Civitavecchia, but their expenses would be paid by the French government;

The pope would commit to dredging and improving the silted-in port of Ancona;

The pope would recognize King Joseph and banish Ferdinand's consul as well as any persons who had slain Frenchmen, and any Neapolitan cardinals who refused the oath of loyalty; further, the pope would relinquish his ancient right to choose the King of Naples;

The pope would agree to extend the Italian concordat to all the provinces of the Kingdom of Italy that had become French provinces;

The pope would name French and Italian cardinals without delay, and he would not insist that they make the trip to Rome;

The pope would designate the plenipotentiaries charged with preparing a German concordat;

And finally, to reassure Napoleon as to the spirit of the College of Cardinals and to ensure the influence of France in accordance with its newly expanded territories, the pope would increase the number of French cardinals so that they occupied at least one third of the total seats.

Two of the conditions were of particular repugnance to the Holy See. The first was the stipulation that it close its borders to any enemies of France; the second, that it increase the number of French cardinals.

Napoleon then ordered the invasion of the other Vatican states. Two thousand five hundred men were gathered in Foligno, and two thousand five hundred more, under General Lemarois, in Perugia. General Miollis, an old Republican soldier of impeccable character, a cultivated mind, and unswerving loyalty, was to take command of both brigades, which were to join up with another three thousand men to be sent by Joseph out of Terracina. With eight thousand soldiers, then, Miollis was to invade the capital of the Christian world.

By whatever means he found necessary, General Miollis was to enter the Sant'Angelo castle and take command of the papal troops, and to leave the pope in the Vatican with his honor guard. He was to take over the police and to use them to chase off any brigands hiding in Rome. He was to send all the Neapolitan cardinals back to Naples. In answer to any questions, he was to say that he had come with purely military intentions in order to expel any enemies of France from the Roman territories. Although he was to maintain the utmost respect for the head of all Christianity, he was also to use the ample funds allotted to him to make a show of his own position and thus make apparent to the Romans that the true head of government in Rome was the French general in Sant'Angelo, not the old pontiff in the Vatican.

It had long been customary for the pope to provide asylum to the brigands who continually devastated the Neapolitan states. Such brigands were not just a passing phenomenon; they were a permanent scourge on the land. In the Abruzzi, Calabria, and the Basilicata, banditry was a profession passed down from father to son; one man might become a brigand the same way another might become a carpenter, tailor, or baker. For eight months of the year these gentlemen of the highways plied their trade, but through the winter they stayed safely in their homes, and nobody would ever consider disturbing them there. When spring returns, they did too, each brigand to his particular spot, and among the most enviable were those spots closest to the border with the Roman states. Sometimes, in extraordinary circumstances, like those facing Naples at the moment, the Neapolitan government might attempt to apprehend the bandits, but the Roman government never did. So the brigand had only to cross the border to find inviolable asylum. He might find more than sympathy, too. Among the clerical party in the papist states, there was a great commotion to try to save the brigand Fra Diavolo, who, having been pursued like a stag by the indefatigable Major Hugo, had just been captured.

It was during such circumstances that a young man about twenty-six or twenty-eight, of medium height, wearing an unusual uniform that did not belong to any regiment, showed up at the relay station to hire a horse and carriage. He was carrying a small double-barreled English carbine over his shoulder. A pair of pistols in his belt indicated that he was aware of the dangers one might risk on the road between Rome and Naples.

The stationmaster said that he had a carriage but he couldn't rent it because it had been placed with him to be sold on consignment. As for horses, there were plenty to choose from.

"If the carriage suits me and is not too expensive," the traveler said, "I might be willing to buy it."

"Well, then, come take a look."

The traveler followed the stationmaster. The carriage was a small open cabriolet, but since the weather was warm, that would be more an advantage than an inconvenience. And as the young man was traveling alone, with one trunk and a grip, he'd have room enough.

They discussed the price; the traveler haggled, mostly because he thought he should and not out of any real concern for the cost. The price was set at eight hundred francs.

The traveler asked that the cabriolet be brought to the gate and harnessed. While he himself watched the postilion chain his trunk to the back of the cabriolet, an army officer was also watching, although with feigned indifference.

The officer made the same request as the young traveler. "Do you have horses and a carriage for hire?" he asked the stationmaster.

"I have nothing left but horses," the stationmaster replied matter-of-factly.

"What have you done with all your carriages?"

"I've just sold the last one to that gentleman there."

"The law stipulates that you must always have a carriage at the disposal of travelers."

"The law!" said the stationmaster. "What do you call the law? We haven't known laws here for a long time." He snapped his fingers like a man who doesn't mind at all being without what most people consider society's moral safeguard.

With a curse the officer expressed his disappointment.

The young traveler glanced over at him. He saw a handsome man about twenty-eight or maybe thirty, his face stern, his eyes light blue. He appeared to be both stubborn and quick to anger. He stamped his feet as he spoke aloud to himself: "But good God! I've got to be in Naples by five tomorrow, and I'm not looking forward to riding sixty leagues on horseback!"

"Monsieur," said the traveler with that courtesy by which people of a certain class can recognize each other, "I too am going to Naples."

"Yes, but you are in a carriage," laughed the officer bitterly.

"And that is how I can offer you a place beside me."

"Excuse me, monsieur," said the officer, bowing politely and changing his tone, "but I do not have the honor of knowing you."

"But I know you. You are wearing the uniform of a captain in General Lasalle's third regiment of hussars, one of the bravest in the army."

"That is not reason enough for me to be so indiscreet as to accept your offer."

"I understand your reluctance, monsieur, and I shall put you at ease. We shall each pay half of the cost of the horses."

"Well," said the captain of hussars, "there's still the carriage, and we must come to some agreement about it."

"I don't want to offend your sensibilities, monsieur, and I would very much like to have you as a traveling companion. Since neither one of us will need this old carriage once we get to Naples, we shall sell it or, if we are unable to sell it, burn it. If we do sell it, since I paid eight hundred francs for it, I'll take four hundred francs and you'll take the rest."

"I accept your proposal on the condition that you allow me to give you your four hundred francs immediately. The carriage will then belong to both of us, and we'll share any loss half and half."

"In order to please you, monsieur, I am willing to accept your entire offer, but I think we're making things a little bit too complicated among fellow countrymen."

The officer walked over to the stationmaster. "I'm buying half of your carriage from that gentleman," he said, "and here are my four hundred francs."

The stationmaster just stood there with his arms crossed. "The gentleman has already paid me, so the money should go to him rather than to me."

"Couldn't you say that a little more politely, you rascal?"

"I speak the way I speak. Take it as you wish."

The officer started to reach for his sword, but then simply put his hand on his belt. He turned to the young traveler. "Monsieur," he said, and the politeness in his voice stood in sharp contrast with the words he had just spoken so harshly to the stationmaster, "would you please accept the four hundred francs I owe you?"

The traveler bowed and opened a little leather case with a metal latch that he was carrying over his shoulder along with his gun. The officer poured the gold he was holding into the case.

"Now, monsieur," he said, "whenever you are ready."

"Don't you want to tie your suitcase up beside my trunk?"

"No, thank you. I'll keep it behind me. It will protect my ribs from this jolting old carriage. Plus it contains a pair of pistols that I would not mind having close at hand. On your horse, postilion, on your horse!"

"Would the gentlemen not like an escort?" asked the stationmaster.

"Ah, do you think we are nuns on the way back to our convent?"

"As you wish. You are completely free."

"That's the difference between you and us, you rotten pope-lover!" Then, to the postilion, the officer shouted, *"Avanti! Avanti!"*

The postilion started off at a gallop, and the young traveler instructed him: "Take the Appian Way! Not through the San Giovanni Gate."

XCIX
The Appian Way

IT WAS ABOUT ELEVEN THAT MORNING when the two young men, leaving the Pyramid of Sextius off to their right, appeared in their cabriolet on the Appian Way, its paving stones still intact after two thousand years of travel over them.

The Appian Way, as we know, was to Caesar's Rome what the Champs-Elysées, the Bois de Boulogne, and the Buttes Chaumont are to Haussmann's Paris. In the golden days of antiquity it was called the Grand Appia, the queen of highways, the Elysian path. It was the meeting place, both in life and in death, for all who were rich, noble, and elegant in the incomparable city.

All along the Appian Way trees of all species, and especially the magnificent cypress, give shade to splendid tombs. For the Romans, a people for whom death held an attraction nearly as strong as it does for the English, and among whom suicide was rife, particularly during the reigns of Tiberius, Caligula, and Nero, took great care in choosing the place where their bodies would sleep throughout eternity. Rarely would a Roman leave the plans for his tomb to his heirs; that was a pleasure he reserved for himself, and often he would oversee its construction. So most of the funerary monuments we still see today bear either the letters V.F., for *Vivus fecit* ("he built this while he lived"), or V.S.P., for *Vivus sibi posuit* ("he erected this for himself while he lived"), or V.F.C., for *Vivus faciendam curavit* ("he saw to the construction of this while he lived").

According to a widespread religious tradition during Cicero's time—a time when many beliefs were beginning to disappear: when, said the Tusculum lawyer, one oracle could not look at another without laughing—the soul of an unburied man was forced to wander for one hundred years on the banks of the Styx. Therefore, to refuse a body burial was to commit a sacrilege, which could be atoned for only by sacrificing a sow to Ceres.

But it was not enough just to be buried; one had to be buried appropriately. The pagan's representation of death was more attractive than our own. Instead of a fleshless skeleton with a naked skull, empty eye sockets, and an evil sneer, death for the Augustan Romans was a lovely woman, the pale daughter of Sleep and Night, with long strands of pale hair, cold white hands, and a wintry embrace. Death came, when called, like some unknown friend out of the shadows, and moving slowly, silently, leaned down over the dying man to close his eyes and seal his lips with one doleful kiss. Deaf, mute, insensate, the corpse would then lie in wait for the flames on his funeral pyre to be lit, and, its flames consuming the body, the spiritual would be separated from the material, the latter becoming ashes while the spiritual became a god, a shade. Invisible to the living yet also among the living, like our ghosts, the shade would now regain possession of its five senses and return to its old habits, tastes, and passions. That is why a warrior was buried with his shield, his javelin, and his sword; why a woman lay among her needles, her diamonds, her golden chains and pearl necklaces; why a child might wake to find the toys he loved most, some bread and fruit, and, in an alabaster vase, a few drops of milk from his mother's breast, had he not had the opportunity to be weaned.

So, if the location of the house they'd be occupying during a short lifetime commanded the attention of the Romans, just imagine how much greater their concern when planning for the home in which they would spend eternity. It had to be properly situated; it had to be designed to suit their tastes, custom, wont, and wishes. For the shades were sedentary gods, with no freedom beyond their tombs. Men of simple tastes, men with pastoral thoughts, wise men and philosophers, might have their tombs constructed in their gardens or in the woods, thus to pass eternity among nymphs, fauns, and dryads and to be forever soothed with the soft sounds of rustling leaves, lulled by the babble of streams flowing over pebbles, cheered by the songs of birds hidden in boughs. A much greater number, though, and indeed the immense majority, wanted movement, excitement, action, a stir, and they would pay exorbitantly for land along the highways—the Latin Way, the Flaminian Way, and especially the Appian Way—where travelers from every country passed by with news of Europe, Asia, and Africa.

Over the course of two thousand years, the Appian Way gradually ceased to be an imperial road, and the highway to Naples now ran past houses as grand as palaces and tombs more imposing than monuments. But still the shades within them could catch the passing panoply. What's more, they could speak to passing travelers through the mouths of their tombs; for each man had his epitaph.

In an epitaph a man's character survives the grave. So says a modest man:

> I was, I am no longer.
> That is all my life and all my death.

The rich man announces:

> Here lies
> STABIRIUS
> He could have occupied a rank in
> all the decuries of Rome;
> he refused.
> Pious, valiant, faithful,
> He came from nothing; he left thirty million sesterces,
> and he would never listen to the philosophers.
> Stay healthy, and imitate him.

To be sure to attract the attention of passersby, Stabirius, the rich man, had a sundial engraved above his epitaph!

The man of letters entreats:

> Traveler!
> However eager you are to reach the end

of your voyage,
this stone asks you to look,
and to read what is written here;
here lie the bones of the poet
MARCUS PACUVIUS,
That is what I wanted to tell you.
Farewell!

The discreet man whispers:

My name, my birth, my origins,
what I was, what I am,
I will not reveal.
Mute for all eternity, I am a few
ashes, bones, nothing!
I came from nothing, and that's where I've returned.
My fate awaits you. Farewell!

A contented man declares:

While I was in the world, I lived well.
My play is over, and yours too soon will end.
Farewell! Applaud!

On the tomb of a poor child taken from the world at the age of seven, a father, perhaps, rues:

Earth! Rest lightly upon her!
She rested lightly on you!

To whom did those shades, all of them so eager to hold on to life, want to speak from their tombs? To whom were they calling from their sepulchers, the way courtesans today might tap at their windows to catch the attention of passersby? What kind of world was it that they sought to share even as it rushed so hastily, so joyously, by without a care or eye for them?

It was a world that celebrated youth, beauty, elegance, wealth; a world that entertained the aristocracy of Rome. A fashionable meeting place, the Appian Way was like the Longchamp of antiquity, except that on the Grand Appia, people would meet all year long rather than for only three days.

By about four in the afternoon, the day's intense heat would have passed and the sun, less scorching, would be dropping toward the Tyrrhenian Sea. The shadows of the pines, the green oaks, and the palm trees would be lengthening from the Occident to the Orient, and the Sicilian oleander would be shaking off the day's dust in the first breezes wafting down from a chain of blue mountains, where the temple of Jupiter Latial commands the landscape. Indian magnolias would lift up their ivory flowers, like perfumed bowls ready to gather in the evening dew. The sacred lotus from the Caspian Sea, which would have fled the burning noonday sun to seek shelter deep down in the lake, would begin to rise back up to the surface, and, opening its calyx wide, it would breathe in the coolness of the evening hours. And then, beneath the Appian Gate, would begin to appear what one might call the vanguard of the handsome crowd, the *Trossuli,* the little Roman Trojans. In turn, the residents from along the Appia would themselves come out and, sitting on chairs they'd carried out from the atrium, or leaning on horsemen's mounting posts, or lighting on the circular benches set in front of the resting places of the dead to afford a respite for the living, they would watch the passing parade.

Never did Paris, in rows up and down the Champs-Elysées; never did Florence, rushing to the Cascine; never did Vienna, hurrying to the Prater; never did Naples, crowded into Via Toledo or Chiaia—never did anyone anywhere see such a variety of actors, such a throng of spectators!

C

What Was Happening on the Appian Way
Fifty Years before Christ

FIRST TO APPEAR are men on Numidian horses, the ancestors of the horses our gentlemen ride today. The horses, without saddles or stirrups, are draped in golden cloth or a blanket made of tiger skins. Some of the riders will stop to watch the parade; others will continue on their way, and they will be preceded by runners wearing short tunics, with a mantle rolled on their left shoulder, and light shoes. Around their waists they wear belts that can be tightened or loosened according to their speed. Still other horsemen gallop blind over the stones of the Appian Way, as if they were racing for a prize, while alongside them bound huge, magnificent dogs with silver collars. Woe be to the man who gets in the way of that yapping, whinnying whirlwind! For he will be torn apart by dogs and trampled by horses in the swirling dust. Bleeding and broken, he will be carried away, while the young patrician who rode over him will look back without slowing down and, laughing loudly, will keep riding on.

Behind the Numidian horses come the light chariots. Called *cisii,* not unlike tilburies, they are built for speed, which they gain from three mules harnessed in fan formation. While the mules on the right and left, shaking their silver bells, gallop and leap, the mule in the middle trots invariably in a line straight as an arrow. Next come the *carrucae,* taller carriages, of which the modern *corricolo* is only one variety, or rather descendant. The members of the elegant set riding in the carrucae rarely handle the reins themselves; for that they have Nubian slaves who wear their country's colorful costumes. Behind the cisii and the carrucae follow the four-wheeled carriages, the *rhedae,* which are furnished with purple cushions and rich carpets, and the *covini,* covered carriages so tightly closed that their passengers can engage each other undetected as they travel through the streets of Rome and on public promenades.

Then there are the matrons and the courtesans. In stark contrast to each other, the matron, dressed in her long stole and wrapped in her thick *palla,* sits as stiff as a statue in her *carpentum,* a strangely shaped chariot that only patrician women are permitted to use, while the courtesan, draped in gauze from Cos, a fabric that might have been woven from fog, reclines casually on her litter, which is borne by eight porters in magnificent *paenulae.* To the right of the courtesan might be her freed Greek woman, her messenger of love, an Iris of the night who takes a moment of respite from her sweet commerce to fan the air her mistress breathes with peacock feathers. On the courtesan's left might be a Liburnian slave carrying a velvet-covered step to which is attached a long, narrow carpet of the same cloth, so that the noble priestess of pleasure will be able to descend from her litter and walk to her chair without having her feet, bare and covered with jewelry, ever touch the ground.

For once they have crossed Campo Marzo, once they have passed through the Capena Gate, once they are on the Appian Way, while many may continue riding on in their carriages or on horseback, many others stop, and, leaving their horses in the care of their slaves, they walk the grounds among the tombs and grand houses, or they rent chairs or stools at half a sesterce per hour.

Ah! That is where you can admire true elegance! That is where the arbiter of style reigns! That is where you can view true models of good taste and study the latest fashion for the cut of a beard, the fall of the hair, or the shape of a tunic, that knotty problem Caesar resolved—he wore his long and loose—but style has changed more than a little since Caesar! That is where serious discussions are granted the weight of winter rings, the composition of the best rouge, the most unctuous fava pomade for firming up or softening your skin, the benefit of lozenges made with myrtle and mastic and soaked in old wine to help your breath smell good! All the while they listen while they toss little balls of amber back and forth from one hand to the other, thus to refresh and perfume the air at the same time. They nod approval, with their eyes they agree, and sometimes their hands applaud the most extravagant theories. They smile; their teeth are white as pearls. Their veils thrown back over their shoulders, they bare their heads, and in contrast to their jade-black eyes and ebony eyebrows, their magnificent hair shimmers fiery blond, golden blond, or ash blond, depending on whether they have treated it with a soap made from beech ashes and goat fat (they order it from Germany) or with a mixture of vinegar lees and mastic oil. What is easier still is to visit the taverns near the Minucius Portico, just across from the Temple of Hercules and the Muses, where poor girls from Gaul sell their hair for forty sesterces to a shearer who then sells it for half a talent.

This spectacle is looked on with envy by the half-naked man of the people, by the starving Greek who would do anything for a meal, and by the philosopher with his worn-out cloak and empty purse, there to compose his text for a speech attacking luxury and wealth.

And all those elegant people—reclining, sitting, standing, moving back and forth, leaning first on one leg, then the other, raising their arms for all the world to see that they've removed their hair with pumice, laughing, declaring their love, gossiping, rolling their *r*'s, humming songs from Cadiz or Alexandria—have forgotten the dead who are listening and calling out to them from their tombs, unheard. The fashionable crowd prefers voies like their own, and they simply continue making small talk in the language of Virgil or making puns in the language of Demosthenes. They especially like to speak Greek, because Greek is the true language of love, and a courtesan who is unable to say to her lovers in the language of Thais and Aspasia "my life and my soul" is a woman good only for Marsic soldiers with their leather sandals and shields.

And yet it is to give opinion, joy, and spectacle to these vain, foolish crowds that Virgil, the gentle Mantuan swan, the poet who was Christian in his heart if not by upbringing, sings of country pleasures, curses Republican ambitions, attacks the impiety of civil wars, and composes the greatest poem of any since the epics of Homer, only to burn it because he finds it unworthy not only of posterity but also of his contemporaries! He writes for all those giddy young people, for the false-hearted women and young men of means who have left their health in brothels and their purses in taverns, for the idle and lazy and vain: all of them, above all, Italian, but cantankerous like the English, proud like the Spanish, and quarrelsome like the Gauls. They spend their lives strolling beneath the porticos, holding forth in the baths, clapping in the circus, these young men of means and false-hearted women, yet it is for them that Virgil writes. And it is for them that Horace flees the Battle of Philippi, throwing down his shield so that he can run all the faster back to them. It is for them, for their attention and praise, that Horace composes what he calls trifles—his odes, his satires, and his *Ars Poetica*—as he walks otherwise absentmindedly through the Forum, on the Campo Marzo, along the Tiber. These are the people that the poet Ovid misses so painfully when he is in exile among the Thraces, there to pay for the easy pleasure of having served for a short time as the lover of the emperor's daughter or perhaps for the bad luck of having learned the secret of young Agrippa's birth. To these people he addresses his poem *Tristia,* as well as his *Epistulae ex Ponto* and *Metamorphoses.* They are the reason that he begs Augustus and later Tiberius to allow him to return to Rome, so that he can again be with them on the Appian Way. He longs for them, and it is them he sees when, far from home, he closes his eyes and in his mind's eye again looks out over all of Rome, over the Gardens of Sallustus and the poor Subura quarter, over the majestic Tiber, where Caesar nearly drowned while fighting Cassius, over the muddy Velabrum and its nearby sacred woods, the refuge of the Latin she-wolf and the cradle of Romulus and Remus! For these same people, too, so as to keep their love, which is as changeable as an April day, Maecenas—descendant of the Etrurian kings and friend of Augustus; voluptuous Maecenas, who when he walks leans on the shoulders of two eunuchs, both of them more man than he—pays poets to sing, painters to finish their frescoes, actors to cavort on stage, Pylades the mime artist to make a thousand faces, and the dancer Bathyllus to redefine grace. It is for these people that Balbus opens a theater, that Philippus builds a museum, and that Pollion constructs temples.

For them, Agrippa freely distributes lottery tickets worth twenty thousand sesterces; for them he imports cloth from the Hellespont that's embroidered with silver and gold and furniture inlaid with ivory and mother-of-pearl. For them he builds baths where, from sunup to sundown, they can be shaved, perfumed, and massaged, as well as provided with free food and drink. For them he digs thirty leagues of canals and constructs seventy-seven leagues of aqueducts; he brings more than two million cubic meters of water per day to Rome, to its two hundred fountains, one hundred and thirty water towers, and one hundred and seventy pools. And it is for them as well that Augustus turns a city of bricks into a city of marble.

He brings obelisks from Egypt; he builds forums, basilicas, and theaters. For them the wise Emperor Augustus melts down his golden table service; from the spoils of the Ptolemies he keeps a murrhine vase from his father Octavius and he keeps one hundred and fifty million sesterces (thirty million of our own francs) as his heritage from his uncle Caesar, after his defeat of Antony and conquest of the world. For them he rebuilds the Flaminian Way all the way to Rimini. For them he summons philosophers and buffoons from Greece, dancers from Cadiz, gladiators from Gaul and Germany, as well as boas, hippopotami, giraffes, tigers, elephants, and lions from Africa. It is for all of them, and when he is dying he says, "Romans, are you pleased with me? Did I play my emperor's role well? Yes? In that case, applaud!"

Since Augustus's time almost two thousand years had passed when our two travelers were journeying over the Appian Way. What had once been death's favorite domain was itself now dying. Between Capena and Albano lay no more than a long series of ruins, ruins in which only the eye of an experienced archeologist could read antiquity's mysteries.

CI

An Archeological Conversation between a Navy Lieutenant and a Captain of Hussars

※∶≋

THE TWO YOUNG MEN WERE SILENT for some time. The younger of them, the one who had first purchased the carriage, surveyed the mammoth letters of ancient history along the road with fascination. The other man, a little older, looked disinterestedly at the ruins his traveling companion seemed find so absorbing.

"And to think," said the officer nonchalantly, almost disdainfully, "that there are people who know the name and history of each of these stones."

"That is true, there are people like that," his companion replied with a smile.

"Just imagine, yesterday I was dining with Monsieur Alquier, our ambassador, for whom I had a letter from the Grand Duke of Berg. During the evening a scholar showed up, an architect, and I must say, he has a lovely wife."

"Visconti?"

"Do you know him?

"Well, from the description you gave, who wouldn't?'"

"So you live in Rome?"

"I came to Rome for the first time yesterday and this morning I left with you, but that does not keep me from knowing Rome as if I had been born there."

"So you have been interested in learning about the Eternal City, as they call it?"

"In my leisure time. I love antiquity. In those days men were giants, and Virgil was right when he said in one of his superb verses that some day, when the plow opens their tombs, we shall be astounded at the size of their bones."

"Oh, yes, I remember," said the young captain, yawning at the memory from his school days: *mirabitur ossa sepulcris.* "But," he continued with a laugh, "were they really taller than we are?"

"We just now happen to be passing by the place that proved it."

"Where are we?"

"We are near the Circus of Maxentius. If you stand up, you can see a mound."

"It is not a tomb?"

"Yes, but in the fifteenth century it was excavated. It was the tomb of a man missing his head, but even without it, he was more than six feet tall. His father was a descendant of the Goths, his mother of the Alani. He had started out as a shepherd in the mountains, and had become a soldier under Septimus Severus, then a centurion under Caracalla and a tribune under Heliogabalus; he ended his career as emperor, after Alexander II. On his thumb, instead of rings, he wore his wife's bracelets. With one hand, he could drag a loaded chariot, and merely by squeezing a stone he could crush it into dust. He could bring down thirty fighters, one after the other, without even breathing hard. He could run as fast as a galloping horse; indeed, he could circle the grand circus three times in fifteen minutes, and each time around he'd fill a bowl with his sweat. He'd eat forty pounds of meat a day, and he could empty an amphora at one go. His name was Maximin. He was killed near Aquileia by his own soldiers, who then sent his head to the Senate. The Senate had it burned before the people in the Campo Marzo. Sixty years later, another emperor, Maxentius, who claimed Maximin as an ancestor, had his headless body brought back from Aquileia. As he was having this circus constructed for horses and chariots, he also built his ancestor's tomb. Since the bow and arrow were the dead man's favorite weapons, he was buried with an ash bow from Germany and six arrows made with reeds from the Euphrates; the bow was eight feet long, and the arrows five. Maxentius drowned while defending Rome against Constantine."

"Yes, I remember Le Brun's painting in which Maxentius is trying to swim to safety. That round tower there, with the pomegranates growing the way they do in the hanging gardens of Semiramis, is that his tomb?"

"No, that is the tomb of a charming woman whose name you can read on the marble. In the thirteenth century it was used as a fortress by the nephew of Pope Boniface VIII. The woman was Caecilia Metella, the wife of Crassus and daughter of Metellus from Crete."

"Ah," said the officer. "So she was the wife of that fellow who was so miserly that when he went out with the Greek philosopher he had purchased, he would put an old straw hat on the wise man's head to protect him from sunburn and then take it back on the way home."

"That didn't stop him from loaning thirty million to Caesar, whose creditors in Rome were preventing him from taking up his administrative functions in Spain. Caesar went on a loan but he came back with forty million and all his debts paid. All that's left of Crassus's story are those thirty million he gave to Caesar and this monument raised in honor of his wife."

"Was she really worthy of a tomb like this?" the officer asked.

"Yes, for she was a noble, witty woman. She was an artist and a poet, and at her house would gather the most elegant, the richest, and the wittiest people of Rome, among them Catalina, Caesar, Pompey, Cicero, Lucullus, and Terentius Varro. Can you imagine what such a gathering must have been like?"

"It must have been more enjoyable than spending the evening with our ambassador Monsieur Alquier. Her tomb has been ransacked, it appears."

"Yes, by order of Pope Paul III. He found the urn containing her ashes, and he had it taken to the corner of a vestibule at the Farnese Palace. That is where it must still be today."

If the hussar officer had at first been listening somewhat distractedly to his companion's explanations, the more the younger man had spoken, the more attention the captain had been paying to him. "I must say," he noted, "there's something I don't understand. How can written history be so boring, yet the stories you tell be so engaging? I have always stayed as far away from old ruins as I would from a nest of vipers, but now I'd be ready to turn over these stones one by one if they would agree to tell me their stories."

"And all the more so because the story of the stones we're approaching is particularly unusual," said his guide. Their carriage had passed Caecilia Metella's tomb, and they were now nearing ruins that time had brought to a terrible state of deterioration.

"Go on, tell me. I am as curious as the sultan in *One Thousand and One Nights*, who each night had the lovely Scheherazade tell him one of her wondrous tales."

"That is the villa that belonged to the two Quintilian brothers. They tried to assassinate Emperor Commodius."

"Wasn't he Trajan's grandson?"

"Yes, and Marcus Aurelius's son. But as emperors come and go, they are all different. When Commodius was twelve, finding his bath too hot, he ordered that the slave who'd overheated it be burned, and even after the bath had cooled down, he refused to get into it until the slave had been roasted. The more ferocious the young emperor became in his tastes, the more capricious became his wishes. The result was numerous conspiracies against him, including the plot hatched by the owners of the villa whose ruins we are now passing. The brothers, like all the conspirators, wanted simply to assassinate Commodius, but it was not easy to kill a man of his size and strength.

"The emperor did not want to be called Commodius, the son of Marcus Aurelius, but rather Hercules, the son of Jupiter. He spent his life at the arena, where he often proved himself to be more skillful than any of the gladiators. From a Parthian he had learned how to use a bow; from a Moor he had learned to throw the javelin. One day at the arena, just opposite where the emperor was seated, a panther grabbed a man and would have devoured him had not Commodius rescued him with his bow. His aim so true, his arrow missed the man and killed the panther. Another time, realizing that the people's love for their emperor was beginning to cool, he spread the word that he would kill one hundred lions with one hundred javelins. The circus was filled with spectators, as you might expect. One hundred javelins with gilded points were brought to his imperial loggia; one hundred lions were let into the arena. One by one, Commodius threw each of the one hundred javelins, and he killed one hundred lions."

"Surely not!" said the young officer.

"I did not make that up," said his companion. "That comes straight from Herodius; he was there, he saw it happen."

"In that case," said the hussar, "what can I say?"

"Furthermore," his companion went on, "the emperor was six feet tall, and as I said, he was very strong. With a stick he could break a horse's legs; with his fist he could stun an ox. He once encountered a huge, corpulent man, and drawing his sword, he cut him in half with one swing. So you can see that it was not easy or reassuring to plot against a man like that.

"However, the two Quintilian brothers had made their decision and remained firm in it. They did take precautions, though: they buried all their gold and silver, along with all their precious stones and jewelry. Then, in a narrow, vaulted passageway leading from the palace to the amphitheater, they lay in wait.

"Fortune appeared to be with the conspirators, for Commodius appeared alone. The two brothers pounced on him, and their accomplices surrounded him. 'Here,' said one of the brothers, striking him with a dagger, 'here you are, Caesar; here's what I'm bringing you from the Senate.'

"A frightful battle followed, but Commodius was only lightly wounded. Hardly affected at all by the conspirators' thrusts, with each thrust of his own he knocked a man down. Finally, laying hold of the brother who had struck him, he placed his hands around the man's neck and strangled him. As he was dying, the elder brother cried out to his brother, 'Run, Quadratus, all is lost!'

"Quadratus ran; he leaped to his horse and galloped off. The emperor's soldiers immediately set off after him. For the man fleeing it was a matter of life or death; for the soldiers an enormous reward was at stake, and they were gaining on Quintilian. Fortunately, he had prepared a ruse as a last resort.

"Though it is unusual, we have to believe it because the honest Dio Cassius is the one who tells the story. The fugitive was carrying with him a small flask of hare's blood, for the blood of the hare, unlike that of any other animal, does not decompose or coagulate. Quintilian drank all the blood in the flask and fell from his horse, as if he'd had an accident. The soldiers found him lying in the road, apparently vomiting blood. They concluded he surely must be dead, and after removing all his clothing, they left his body lying there. They reported back to Commodius that his enemy had killed himself in a fatal fall from his horse. Meanwhile, Quintilian had gotten back to his feet and returned home to find some clothes, then gathered up what gold and jewels he could, and fled."

"And what of Commodius?" the hussar asked. "How did he die? A butcher like that who can kill one hundred lions in one day is an intriguing man."

"Commodius was poisoned by Marcia, his favorite mistress, and strangled by Narcissus, his favorite slave. Pertinax took over the empire, and six months later he lost it along with his life. Then Didius Julianus bought Rome and the whole world, but Rome was not yet accustomed to being bought."

"She got used to that later," the officer interjected.

"Yes, but this time Rome rebelled, although it is true that the buyer had neglected to pay. Septimus Severus took advantage of the rebellion, had Didius Julianus killed, and assumed the throne. Everyone breathed easier."

As they would find no relay station until they got to Velletri, five leagues away from Rome, the postilion asked permission to rest the horses. The two travelers granted it happily, as they had arrived at one of the most interesting places in the countryside around Rome.

CII

In Which the Reader Will Guess the Name of One of the Two Travelers and Learn the Name of the Other

THE TRAVELERS WERE at the very spot where the destiny of Rome had been decided. When the young hussar learned that they were on the battlefield where the Horace and Curiace brothers had fought, the young hussar raised his hand to his calpac in salute. Both men rose to their feet in their cabriolet.

Before them the Albano road cut through a long chain of hills including, at the far left, the Soracto, green today, but covered with snow in the days of the Horace brothers. At the chain's highest peak rose the temple of Jupiter Latiaris. They could see, too, the white peak of a small hill, Albano, where stood in ruins Domitian's vast villa and grandiose dreams. To their right, descending toward the Tyrrhenian Sea, lay the chain of hills that formed the amphitheater in which a succession of peoples had fought and died: the Falisci, the Aequi, the Volsci, the Sabine, the Hernici. The amphitheater held two thousand five hundred years of memories, and it had stood at the center of world history for twenty centuries, from the days of the Republic and down through a long line of popes. Behind the travelers, though linked to them by the chain of tombs and ruins they had passed, was Rome and the Valley of Egeria, where Numa would come to consult his oracles. And beyond Rome stretched the wide sea with its bluish islands, like clouds on the road to eternity.

The horses had rested. The carriage started again to move.

Near the tomb of the three Horaces a little path led off to the right through the russet ground cover so typical of the Roman countryside, its coloration like that of a lion skin. Barely visible, the path disappeared into the rolling hills, where it still afforded the traveler on foot a shortcut between Rome and Velletri.

"Do you see that path?" said the young man as he continued in his role as guide, while his companion, now hanging on every word, showed impatience at any pause in the narration. "It was probably on that path that Milo's gladiators abandoned the litter they were escorting and attacked Clodius, who was engaged with some farmers harvesting grain. Clodius took a lance through the chest that came out through his right shoulder. He hid in those ruins, which were farm buildings in those days. The gladiators found him hiding in an oven, finished him off, and dragged him down the highway."

"Tell me," said the hussar officer, "how Clodius could have had such influence over the Romans, since he was nearly ruined financially and had so many debts."

"It was simple. First of all, he was so handsome that he'd been given the nickname Pulcher, for beauty, and you will remember how important beauty was to ancient peoples. While the loss of his army when he fought the gladiator Spartacus outside Capua might have harmed his popularity, it didn't, thanks to his four sisters. One had married the Consul Metellus Celer; a second, Hortensius the orator; the third, Lucullus the banker; and the fourth, Lesbia, was the mistress of Catullus the poet. Gossip in Rome held that he was the lover of all four of his sisters, and certainly incest, as we know, was not uncommon during the last days of Rome. So Clodius, through his four sisters, reaped the benefits of four vital worldly forces: through Metellus Celer's wife, he could tap consular power; through Hortensius's wife, he had the advantage of one of Rome's most eloquent voices; through Lucullus's wife, he had access to coffers of the wealthiest banker in the world; and finally, through Lesbia, Catullus's mistress, he enjoyed the regard that a great poet's celebrity can provide. Furthermore, he had won the support of the wealthy Crassus, who sought in Clodius's huge popularity his own uses. He was also a good friend of Caesar, not only sharing his debauchery but even attempting to seduce his wife. Pompey held him in great favor, as he had deployed his brother-in-law Lucullus's legions to Pompey's great benefit. And Cicero, too, embraced him, for Cicero loved his sister Lesbia, and Clodius had no objection to his being her lover.

"That was what caused his death. I have said that he pursued Mussia, she who was Pompey's daughter and Caesar's wife. In order to see her, on the occasion of the Feast of the Good Goddess, he disguised himself as a woman and entered her house, although, as you know, the presence of men and even of male animals at lesbian orgies was absolutely prohibited. A servant recognized Clodius and denounced him. Mussia helped him escape through secret passages, but that did not prevent the news of his illicit deed from spreading, and there was a great scandal.

"He was accused of impiety by a tribune and required to appear before his judges. Crassus told him not to worry, and then bribed the judges both with money and with some lovely patrician girls who were willing to sacrifice themselves for Clodius as they renewed the fable of Jupiter and Ganymede for the corruptible gods of justice. Which only magnified the scandal. As Seneca said, 'Clodius's crime was not as bad as his absolution.'

"Clodius had come up with an alibi in his defense. He claimed that on the evening before the Feast of the Good Goddess he was a hundred miles from Rome, and consequently he could never have covered thirty-five leagues in five hours to attend the festival the next day. Unfortunately, Terentia, Cicero's wife, was madly jealous. She knew that her husband loved Lesbia, and she had actually seen him conversing with Clodius on the very evening in question. Even the wily Cicero could not find a way around the ultimatum she delivered to him: 'If you are in love with Clodius's sister, then you will not bear witness against him, and I shall know where your affections and loyalty truly lie. If you are not in love with Clodius's sister, then you have no reason not to bear witness against the brother.'

"Cicero, deathly afraid of his wife, bore witness against Clodius. And Clodius never forgave him. Out of that flared the hate that brought tumult and riots to Rome for more than a year. The end came when Milo repaid Cicero by having his gladiators kill Clodius.

"Still, the people remained unusually faithful to their idol even after his death. A senator conveyed Clodius's body back to Rome. Fulvia, his wife, raised his funeral pyre in the Curia Hostilia, and from it the people of Rome took firebrands and burned down a whole neighborhood."

"My dear man," said the officer, "you are a veritable walking library, and I am pleased to be traveling with a second Varro—you see, I too know a little about Roman history." Clapping his hands, the officer applauded himself for having come up with the Latin scholar's name. "Go on, go on," he said. "What is *that* tomb? I would be happy to stump you for once." And he pointed to a monument rising on their left.

"Not this time," his guide replied. "For I happen to know a great deal about that one. That is the tomb of Ascanius, the son of Aeneas. He was separated from his mother when he had the misfortune of losing hold of her dress during the rape of Troy, but he was able to catch up with his father, who bore Ascanius's grandfather Anchises and the household gods with him. Their flight from Troy would end with the founding of Rome. At the same time, curiously enough, Telemachus, the son of Ulysses, was leaving Troy by another gate, and he would found Tusculum. His tomb is not more than two leagues from here. Ascanius and he belonged to enemy races, one Asiatic, the other Greek, and both came to Europe, where they were rivals, and their two peoples remained hostile to each other. The duel the fathers had begun in Troy was continued by their sons in Rome. From the house of Alba emerged the Julia family, which gave birth to Caesar, while from the house of Tusculum came the Portia family, which was the family of Cato; and you know how bitter was the struggle between Cato and Caesar. After more than a thousand years, the Trojan duel ended in Utica. There Caesar, a descendant of the vanquished Trojans, exacted vengeance for Hector by defeating Cato, a descendant of the victors. The tomb of Ascanius used to be the first one you'd reach coming from Naples and the last you would pass on the road from Rome."

The elder and less knowledgeable of the two travelers reflected quietly for a few moments. After turning the thought over in his mind, he said, "You must have been a history professor."

"No, not at all," his companion replied.

"How then have you learned so much?"

"I'm not really sure. By reading books here and there, I suppose. But these are things you don't consciously learn; you simply remember them as you enjoy them. For if you enjoy history, if your mind enjoys its interesting details, then the events and actors invade your brain, and your brain gives them shape—you begin to see men and events in a different light."

"I declare!" said the young officer. "If I had a brain like yours, I would spend my entire life reading."

"I don't wish that on you," the young scholar replied with a laugh. "Nor would I wish you the conditions I was studying in . . . I was sentenced to death. I spent three years in prison, and daily I expected to be shot or guillotined. I had to find some way to pass my time."

"Indeed," said the officer, glancing at his companion more carefully, hoping to read his past in the deep lines on his face, "you must have had a hard life."

The man smiled at him in sadness. "The fact is," he said, "I have not always slept on a bed of roses."

"You surely belong to a noble family?"

"I am more than noble, monsieur. I am a gentleman."

"Were you sentenced to death for political reasons?"

"For political reasons, yes."

"Would you prefer that I not ask you these questions?"

"I don't mind, but I will only answer what I can, unless I prefer not to."

"How old are you?"

"Twenty-seven."

"It's strange, but you seem both younger and older than that. How long ago did you get out of prison?"

"Three years ago."

"What did you do when you got out?"

"I went to war."

"At sea or on land?"

"At sea against men, on land against wild beasts."

"What does that mean?"

"At sea I was a corsair, on land I was a hunter."

"At sea, whom were you fighting?"

"The English."

"On land, what were you hunting?"

"Tigers, panthers, and boas."

"So you went to India or Africa?"

"I was in the East Indies."

"Where in the Indies?"

"In a place little known in the rest of the world; a place called Burma."

"Did you participate in grand naval battles?"

"I was at Trafalgar."

"On which ship?"

"The *Redoutable*."

"Did you catch sight of Nelson?"

"Yes, up close."

"How did you get away from the English?"

"I did not get away. I was taken prisoner; they took me to England."

"Was there an exchange of prisoners?"

"No, I escaped."

"From the pontoon prisons?"

"From Ireland."

"And where are you going now?"

"I have no idea."

"What is your name?"

"I have no name. When we part, if you give me a name, I shall be as obliged to you as a godson is to his godfather."

The officer looked at his traveling companion in surprise. He sensed that the younger man hid a painful mystery behind his apparently carefree life as a vagabond. He appreciated what he had been told, and he did not hold what he had not been told against the man.

"How about me?" he said. "Don't you wonder about me?"

"I am not curious. But if you would like to tell me who you are, I would not be ungrateful."

"Oh, my life has been as prosaic as yours has been strange and romantic. My name is Charles Antoine Manhès. I was born on November 4, 1777, in the little town of Aurillac, in the Cantal. My father was state's attorney in the civil court, so you see I do not belong to French aristocracy. What was your title, by the way?"

"I was a count."

"When I was in school in my little native town, and this explains why my education has been neglected, the administrators in my department saw military promise in me and sent me to the school of Mars. I began to study artillery in particular, and I learned so quickly that I was made an instructor at the age of sixteen. When they disbanded the school, I took a test and did well enough to be assigned to Cantal's Third Battalion and later to the Twenty-sixth Regiment. I went to the front with the Army of the Rhine and Moselle, for four years, and then spent the years VII, VIII, and IX with the Army of Italy. I was seriously wounded at Novi; I was six weeks recuperating before I went back to my regiment near the Genoa River. Have you ever gone through lean times?"

"Yes, sometimes."

"Well, I can tell you what that's like, too, because that's the way it has always been with me. My friends chose me lieutenant, and I was made Chevalier of the Légion d'Honneur on June 6 of last year. After the Austerlitz campaign I was made captain. Today I'm a captain and aide-de-camp to the Grand-Duc de Berg, and I'm taking news about the Emperor's entrance into Berlin to his brother Joseph in Naples. I am to give him, too, all the details about the Iéna campaign, in which I participated, and when I get back, they have promised I shall be promoted to major. That would be nice for a twenty-seven-year-old. There, that's my whole story. But perhaps more interesting is the fact that we've reached Velletri, and I am dying of hunger. Let's go eat."

The nameless traveler had no difficulties with that proposal. He too leaped down from the cabriolet with the soon-to-be major Charles Antoine Manhès and went into the hotel named the Birth of Augustus.

Of course, archeologists would have to confirm it officially, but the hotel was purported to have been built on the ruins of the house in which the first Roman emperor had been born.

CIII

The Pontine Marshes

꙳꙳꙳

THE TRAVELERS DID NOT ENJOY a good meal, but it would have been wrong of them to complain of ill treatment at the Birth of Augustus when Augustus himself, even when he was emperor, would take for his meal only two dry fish and a glass of water.

One could fill a book with tales about Augustus, even from his conception and birth, which destined him, the son of a miller and an African woman, to rule over the world. Did not Antony say of him: "Your natural ancestor was African, your mother turned the crudest millwheel in Arcia, and to sift through the flour your father used hands that had been blackened by the money he handled in Nerulum"?

There had been omens. His mother Atia had fallen asleep on her litter in the Temple of Apollo, it was said, and while she slept, the marble serpent that coiled around the statue of Apollo as the god of medicine separated itself from the altar, snaked over to the litter, and stole into it, there to wrap itself around Atia and hold her in its coils until she'd been impregnated. Divinity struck again when the boy Augustus was one day going to school. An eagle swooped down from the sky and took from his hand the piece of bread he was carrying, only to return it to him a moment later—after it had been soaked in ambrosia from Olympia. And when a bolt of divine lightning hit the house of Atia and her son, it became sacred.

The evening that the travelers arrived, Velletri was holding a celebration. Peasants from near and far had filled the streets. There was dancing; for always in Italy half of the people danced even while the other half wept. That night in Velletri they were not worrying whether French soldiers were marching in Rome or stationed in Naples or besieging Gaeta. They were not worrying that the twenty-four-pound French cannons were booming on the other side of the Pontine Marshes in the attempt to breach Gaeta's walls. Napoleon had written to his brother: "Press on with the siege." And Joseph had obeyed.

The peasants smiled at the two Frenchmen. Girls reached out their hands to them, inviting the two young travelers to dance with them. Nor did the girls turn their heads aside when French lips sought to kiss their Italian own. If ever any one of those merry peasant girls found herself alone with a Frenchman, though, she would knife him in an instant.

The guests who were eating at the same table as the two travelers looked greedily both at the bag of gold from which the younger man took a louis to pay their four-franc bill and at the wallet his companion took from his coat to put in his pocket. The mayor of Velletri, walking back and forth among revelers, eyed the Frenchmen's money with as much greed as anyone; nonetheless, he still offered them a four-man escort, as had the stationmaster in Rome, to protect them as they crossed the Pontine Marshes.

Manhès pulled two pistols from his portmanteau and placed his hand on his sword, while his companion checked to be sure that both barrels of his rifle were primed. "This is our escort," Manhès said. "Weapons are the only escort Frenchmen need."

"A month ago," the mayor said mockingly, "a French aide-de-camp supped here as you are doing now. He too had lovely weapons. I can vouch for that, because I later saw them in the hands of his killers."

"And you did not have them arrested?" cried Manhès, jumping to his feet.

"My duty," said the mayor, "is to propose an escort to travelers, not to arrest those bandits who kill them when they refuse it. I stick to my duty."

Manhès let the matter drop. He motioned to his companion and together they left the hotel and returned to their cabriolet, which had fresh horses and a different postilion. They paid the postilion who was staying behind and galloped off toward the Pontine Marshes.

Everyone knows the reputation the Roman territory between Velletri and Terracina, that is, all the way to the border with the Kingdom of Naples, has sustained. The poisonous air you breathe there will kill you more surely than will any bandit: Do you recall the boat depicted by our great painter Hébert, with its skinny, haggard boatman, its feverish passengers, the girl dipping the tips of her fingers in the waters of the canal, while lush green plants hovering over them draw vegetable life from the pestilential waters?

During their meal, night had fallen. The road reflected silvery moonlight, mottled here and there by the trembling shadows of trees. From time to time a rock jutting out high above the roadside, as if about to topple down on them, would cast its mammoth shadow over their path. As they neared the Pontine Marshes, large streaks of vapor, more mists than clouds, rose intermittently toward the sky and passed over the face of the moon like a widow's black gauze veil. And the sky would take on strange, unhealthy, yellowish tones.

By the glow of the lanterns, their light dimmed by the heavy air, they could see enormous animals trolling in the pools of water. The night's eerie illumination made them seem even more monstrous when their heads came up out of the water, and their snorting came with a ghostly echo. They were wild buffaloes; the marshes were their safe havens, for even the most intrepid hunter would not dare to come hunting there. Now and then, frightened by the noise of the carriage, large birds as dark as dusk—gray herons and brownish bitterns—would fly off noiselessly, then with a mournful squawk and flap of the wing disappear into the night's shadows. The path that led Faust and Mephistopheles to their witches' Sabbaths cast up apparitions no more macabre than the road through the Pontine Marshes.

"Have you ever seen anything like this?" Manhès wondered.

"Yes, on the road from Pegu to Betel Land. But there it was not buffaloes bellowing that we heard; it was tigers roaring and alligators wailing. Nor was it herons or bitterns that were flying overhead, but rather huge bats, the ones called vampire bats because they can open the arteries of a sleeping man without him even realizing it, and then suck out his blood."

"I would have liked to see that," Manhès said. Then they both again fell silent.

Suddenly, the postilion pulled the copper posthorn that hung from his shoulder and blew it three times. Assuming it was a signal that might bring them to some harm, the young men went for their weapons. Within seconds, though, a similar trumpet responded. Soon, in the midst of the greenery in that cursed swamp, they could see the glow of a fire with figures that looked more like ghosts than men standing around it. They had reached a relay station.

The cabriolet stopped. Five or six of the ostlers hurriedly lit some torches, grabbed whips, and rushed off into the high grass. In a few seconds the postilion had meanwhile unharnessed the horses. "Pay me quickly," he said, "and I'm gone."

The travelers paid the postilion, who immediately leaped on one horse and galloped off with the other in tow. They disappeared in the darkness, the sound of their hoofbeats slowly fading.

In the meantime, the half wild ostlers were struggling with horses wilder by more than half. The men were swearing, the quadrupeds were whinnying. Their long, flowing hair blending in with their horses' manes, the men looked like animals out of some fable, like three-headed centaurs, as they approached the carriage. The horses had admitted defeat and stopped neighing, though they still complained. The ostlers got one horse between the shafts, then placed the other beside it. Two men on horseback took their positions on each side of the carriage, and the postilion leaped onto the back of the horse outside the shafts. The two horses were snorting and stamping their feet impatiently. The men holding them dropped their reins and leaped aside. Crazed with anger, the horses galloped off, nostrils smoking and eyes flashing fire. The horsemen shouted as they rode along on either side, their aim to keep the horses on their path and to prevent them from running into the canals bordering both sides of the road. The horsemen, the horses and carriage, and the two travelers disappeared in a whirlwind of their own making.

At the next three relay stations the same scene was repeated, with only one difference: The farther they went, the more fiery the horses became and the paler and more ragged the men grew.

At the final relay station, since the cabriolet's lanterns were no longer burning and neither the postilion nor the ostler had a candle to relight them, each traveler held a torch. They set off at the same frantic speed, with only two and half leagues between them and Terracina.

The land had been relatively flat until they reached a spot where the road began to climb among some rocks. The two travelers thought they saw shadows creep out of the ditch and onto the road.

"Faccia in terra!" a voice shouted.

Both men got to their feet, and suddenly a shot rang out. A bullet flew right between the travelers and went through the back of the cabriolet. Without even bringing his rifle to his shoulder, the traveler who'd given no name simply raised his gun and fired it as he would a pistol. He and his companion heard a shout, and then the sound of a body falling to the ground.

The two travelers tossed aside their torches, which now lit up more of the highway. They could see four or five men who appeared to be unsure whether or not to stop the carriage. Then one man grabbed the bridle of one of the horses.

"Let go, you rascal!" Manhès shouted, and at the same time raised his pistol. The man fell to the ground beside his companion.

Three shots rang out in response. One of them knocked off Manhès's calpac, another grazed his companion's shoulder. A third shot, this one from the nameless traveler's rifle, brought another bandit to the ground.

The two travelers leaped down on either side of the cabriolet, each holding a pistol, and the brigands had but one thought: to flee. Unfortunately for them, day was beginning to dawn and both young men could run to rival Atalanta.

Manhès fired his second pistol at one of the fleeing bandits. The man stumbled. He tried to pull his knife from his belt, but before he'd gotten it out of its sheath, the captain's sword was on his chest.

The last of the bandits, when he realized he was about to be overtaken by his pursuer, pulled a pistol from his belt, turned around, and fired point-blank. But the pistol misfired. And he felt first an iron hand gripping his throat, then the cold ring of a pistol barrel pressing against his temple.

"I could shoot you," the traveler said, "but I prefer taking you alive and showing you like a muzzled bear to those who still think that bandits are brave. Come on, my good man Manhès, prod all those face-to-the-ground men with your sword and have them come help us tie these rascals up."

For the postilion and the two horsemen accompanying the cabriolet had followed the bandits' order to the letter: they had dropped from their horse's backs and lay flat and facedown on the ground. Persuaded by the point of Manhès's sword, they got to their feet, saying, "What would the *signori* like?"

"Some ropes," Manhès replied. "And tie those rascals up tightly."

The men did as they were told. Afterward, they put the two bandits in the carriage and gathered up the pistols and guns that the travelers had tossed behind them as they fired. The two travelers reloaded them immediately in case there should be another attack.

"Well, by my faith, my dear comrade," said Manhès, taking some water in his hand and removing his companion's hat, "you asked me to be your godfather, and I believe the time has come to have the ceremony. In the name of Bayard, of D'Assas, and of the Tour d'Auvergne, I baptize you and name you Leo. It is a name you have come by honestly, if I say so myself. Comte Leo, embrace your godfather!"

Comte Leo laughed and the two men embraced. They then set out on foot toward Terracina, with two of the bandits tied up in the cabriolet. The three dead ones they left on the road. Trembling from fear, their escort, the two ostlers on horseback beside them, were even paler and more haggard than before.

CIV

Fra Diavolo

JUST OUTSIDE "WHITE ANXUR," as Virgil calls the town, or dusty Terracina, as we shall call it less poetically, a French post guarded the Roman border. There a small crowd quickly gathered around the two travelers, obviously fellow Frenchmen, not least out of curiosity at the sight of two young men escorting what appeared to be an empty cabriolet. Only when they looked into the cabriolet could they actually see the bandits, who had slipped down from the seats onto the floor. "Well," said the sergeant in command, "some gallows birds. Take them to Naples. There they can join others of their kind."

The two men entered Terracina. They stopped at the Post Hotel, where an officer stood on guard by the door. Manhès walked up to him. "Captain," he said, "I am Captain Manhès, aide-de-camp to the Grand-Duc de Berg, General Murat."

"How can I help you, my dear colleague?" the officer asked.

"A half league from here, we were just stopped by six brigands. We killed three of them. If you want to bury them before they breed plague, you can find them on the highway, dead or as good as dead. We also took two prisoners; they are in our carriage. Will you place a sentry near the cabriolet, with orders to put his bayonet into their stomachs if they make a move in any way to get away? In the meantime, we are in sore need of breakfast, and we invite you to join us. You can tell us how things are here, and we can tell you how things are back there."

"That," said the officer, "is an offer too good to refuse." He ordered two soldiers to take their guns and stand on either side of the carriage; he did not forget the advice about the bayonet.

"Now," the officer continued, "please do me the honor of introducing me to your companion, so that I can know him by name even though the name may not be well known. I am Captain Santis."

Together they went into the inn's kitchen. They found Leo by the spigot, washing his hands and face. "My dear count," said Manhès, "I would like to introduce Captain Santis, who has just put our two prisoners under guard. Captain Santis, this is Comte Leo."

"A lovely name, monsieur," said Captain Santis.

"And well deserved," said Manhès, "you can take my word for it. If only you could have seen him a few minutes ago: two shots, two men on the ground. As for the third, he didn't even take the trouble of firing his gun. He wanted to take the man alive, so he grabbed him around the neck with his small white hands until the man cried out for mercy. And that was it."

When the hotel keeper drew close to hear more easily the captain's tale, Manhès grabbed his cotton bonnet and swirled it around gaily, like a child playing with a toy. The hotel keeper reached out both his hands to grab it back, and Manhès said: "I would like to point out, my good man, that you neglected to greet us. Now that we have met, here is your cotton bonnet. Prepare us your best possible breakfast and give us two or three bottles of that famous Lacryma Christi that I have been dying to try."

The innkeeper sent his waiter down to the wine cellar, ordered his kitchen help to light the stoves, and had his chambermaids set the table. As he himself was walking back out of the kitchen, shaking his head and raising his arms to the heavens, he was saying under his breath: "*Questi Francesi!* Oh, those Frenchmen!"

Manhès began to laugh. "We are, and shall always be, an enigma for these good people. They do not understand how we can fight like lions and still play like children. They don't realize that that's what makes us so strong. Come now, waiter, show us to our room so we can taste your master's Lacryma Christi. I give you my word that if it is no good, I shall make you drink a whole bottle without pausing for breath." The waiter started up the stairs; the two officers and Leo followed.

By chance, the wine was good. "My good man," said Manhès when he had tasted it, "you will not sadden me by filling your stomach with the contents of this bottle, for I am reserving it for a different destination. But you would please me greatly by putting this crown in your pocket." He tossed the waiter a crown worth three pounds. The man caught it in his apron.

"Now," Manhès said to the captain, "tell us what has been happening here."

"I think that what has been happening where you came from is more interesting," the captain replied.

"The truth is," said Manhès, "that things happened slowly. Yet everything was over in a month. The campaign began on October 8, and Napoleon accepted Magdeburg's capitulation on November 8. In that one month, thirty thousand men were killed, one thousand a day—nice work, right? And one hundred thousand were taken prisoner. Of the remaining thirty-five thousand, not one man crossed back over the Oder. The Saxons went back to Saxony, and the Prussians threw down their weapons. They had an army of one hundred sixty thousand men; Napoleon blew on it, and it evaporated, leaving on the battlefield three hundred cannons and enough flags to wallpaper the Invalides. The King of Prussia is still King of Prussia; but now he has neither a kingdom nor his army."

"Well," said the officer, "although the Bourbons have withdrawn from Sicily, they are still richer than the King of Prussia, for they still possess Gaeta, which we are now bombarding, and they still have an army. While it is true that their army is made up mostly of condemned criminals, that only makes it all the easier for them to slit our throats one after the other. Oh, if only we had real battles! Real battles! That's what we need," said the officer. "Our war is just one long, bloody butchery, and I pity good officers like General Verdier and General Reynier who are forced to fight a war like that."

The innkeeper came in with breakfast, interrupting the captain's lament. "Soldiers are forbidden to drink when they are bearing arms," Comte Leo said to him, "but the prisoners must be dying of thirst. Take them a flask of wine to drink; it would be dangerous, though, to untie their hands. As for the soldiers, tell them not to worry! Once their sentry duty is over, they will have their turn. By the way, please tell the unwounded prisoner that the wine is from the traveler who spared his life. Also, please take breakfast and something to drink to our postilions from the Pontine Marshes, even if I find them a little too ready to obey when they hear the command '*Faccia in terra.*' Finally, have the carriage harnessed and get two good relay horses to ride along with us."

Once breakfast was over, the three men drank to France's honor, shook hands, and went back downstairs. Leo thanked the two guards, who, he said, had a good breakfast waiting for them inside the inn. He and Manhès mounted, and with a new postilion, who seemed excellent, the carriage started off on the road to Capua, where they would again change horses.

The young men passed near Gaeta just as General Vallongue's body was being carried away from the fire. A cannonball had taken off his head. Sixty artillery guns, mortars and twenty-four pounders, were meanwhile bombarding the citadel.

The postilion had promised speed, and he kept his word. At eight the next morning they were changing horses in Capua. At quarter after eleven they were entering Naples.

Naples, the sun city, always so noisy and lively that you can hear it buzzing with activity from a league away, seemed more boisterous than usual that day. There were flags sporting the city's new colors at every window. The streets were packed with people, not just those from the capital but villagers from the neighboring countryside as well.

Once the carriage and horsemen got caught up in that flood of humanity, they had no choice but flow with the current. It took them to the old market square, where an imposing gallows stood eighteen feet tall. The throng was humming with excitement; the execution was imminent, and the name Fra Diavolo fell from everyone's tongue. The two travelers wondered at the importance of the man to be hanged, for important he had to be if such an immense number of people had gathered to watch him die.

Just as the two travelers and their prisoners were entering the market square from the Piazza del Carmine, the cart carrying the condemned man was arriving through the Vico dei Sospiri dell'Abisso.

It is aptly named, the street of Sighs from the Abyss, because it gives the condemned man his first glance at the instrument of his punishment, be it gallows or scaffold. It was rare indeed for the damned not to utter a sigh when he first caught sight of his doom.

And when the crowd caught its first sight of Fra Diavolo, the bandit everyone thought was uncatchable, excitement and expectation rose to a fever pitch in the square. Even the two prisoners stood up to see what was happening, but Manhès and Comte Leo drew in closer and ordered them to sit back down. At that, the postilion, with that savage gaiety that is so typical of ordinary people, and especially of the people in Naples, advised, "Let 'em look, the poor devils. They can learn something from the spectacle." And he too tried to improve his view of the proceedings.

Let us see whether the man who'd put Naples in such an uproar measured up to his reputation.

CV

Pursuit

FRA DIAVOLO IS BETTER KNOWN in France through Scribe and Auber's comic opera than through the long correspondence about him between Emperor Napoleon and his brother King Joseph.

His name was Michele Pezza, and he was born in the little village of Itri. His family was poor, although they managed to eke out a living by using their mules to transport oil to neighboring villages. Michele was nicknamed Fra Diavolo by the Itrians: a name that was half sacred and half simple, like him, for he combined the trickery of a monk with the wickedness of the devil. Actually, he did at first seem to be destined for the church, but he left the priesthood and became an apprentice to a cartwright who made pack-saddles for horses and mules.

As it happened, he had a serious argument with the cartwright, and the day after, while the man was dining in his garden with three or four friends, the apprentice shot the master. That was in 1797; the killer was nineteen years old. He fled into the mountains.

By 1799, when the revolution came to Naples with Championnet's invasion of the Bourbons' territory, he had been a common brigand for two years. He soon became a brigand in the service of the Bourbons, for he'd had a sort of revelation that set him on the Royalist path. In expiation for his crimes, he joined the Sanfedisti of Cardinal Ruffo so that he might devote himself to the defense of divine right.

He was among the first to respond to King Ferdinand's appeal for warriors in the battle against the French. He began by recruiting his three brothers. He made them lieutenants, and he then tripled, quadrupled, quintupled, his band as volunteers streamed into his ranks. He immediately and continually proved his patriotism on the highway between Naples and Rome.

During Fra Diavolo's first campaign, he distinguished himself mostly by vicious murders. When General Championnet's aide-de-camp Major Claye, who was carrying a message to General Lemoine, unwisely hired an untrustworthy guide, he was led right to Fra Diavolo's band; they cut him to bits. Another brutish incident occurred after the attack on the Garigliano bridge. The aide-de-camp Gourdel, a light infantry major, and a dozen other officers and men remained alive on the battlefield until Fra Diavolo and his band gathered them up and tied them to trees, then piled branches around them and set them afire. The French soldiers were burned alive, while the villagers—men, women, and children alike—danced around them, shouting: "Long live Fra Diavolo!"

Championnet himself skirmished with Fra Diavolo on several occasions, and once he almost destroyed his band but was unable to capture him. He admitted that the brigand leader had been harder to fight than any general leading a regular army.

So Fra Diavolo was no unknown when he want to Sicily, where King Ferdinand and Queen Caroline had taken refuge to prepare a counterattack against the French. The king and queen welcomed him as a friend. He was royally entertained. The king made him a captain, and the queen gave him a magnificent ring with his initials in diamonds set between two emeralds. (Today that ring is guarded religiously by his son, the Chevalier Pezza, if he is still alive. When his father climbed to the scaffold, he bequeathed his title to his son, and by virtue of the treaty signed between the past king and the present one, the son continues to receive from Victor-Emmanuel the pension that Ferdinand bestowed upon his father.)

Fra Diavolo returned from Sicily to his native region, the Terra del Lavoro. He landed between Capua and Gaeta with four hundred men. Although he was serving the royal cause, Fra Diavolo had committed such atrocities in the Bourbons' names that Cardinal Ruffo refused to let him enter Gaeta. The cardinal did, however, inform the king that he had refused entry to one of his captains. The king responded in his own hand:

> I approve your decision not to let Fra Diavolo enter Gaeta as he expected. I agree with you that he is a brigand chief, but on the other hand I am forced to admit that he has served me well. So you must use him and not put him off. But at the same time you must find the appropriate words to convince him to put a brake on his passions. He must impose discipline on his men if he expects me to recognize any lasting merit.

If the excesses of Fra Diavolo earned him such a paternal reproach from Ferdinand, they did him no harm in Caroline's mind. After she regained possession of Naples, she deigned to write him in her own hand; her letter announcing his promotion to the rank of colonel was accompanied by a bracelet that had been woven with a curl from the queen's hair. At the same time he was named Duke of Casano, with an annuity of three thousand ducats (thirteen thousand two hundred francs). So he held both his title as duke and his rank of colonel when he was fighting the French in 1806 and 1807.

King Joseph's usurpation of the Bourbon throne gave Fra Diavolo still another occasion to prove his devotion to King Ferdinand and Queen Caroline. In Palermo, he was received and instructed by the queen, who dispatched him to the Abruzzi with her blessing. But she neglected, as did King Ferdinand, to remind him to pay special attention to his soldiers' discipline. Fra Diavolo wreaked such havoc on the French, ostensibly at Queen Caroline's instructions, that King Joseph decided it was absolutely necessary to get rid of him. As an enemy, he was perhaps less dangerous than Lord Stuart and his Englishmen, but he was certainly more unpleasant. So the king summoned Major Hugo.

The king had absolute confidence in Hugo's courage and devotion. He was a man out of Plutarch. He bore the weight of his loyalty. He had served under Moreau, whom he esteemed, loved, and admired. When Bonaparte came to the throne, Hugo did not hesitate to sign official notes of congratulation, but when he was asked to sign papers that made claims contrary to the truth about Moreau, papers that gave reason to incriminate the general, during Cadoudal's trial, Hugo simply refused. Bonaparte learned of Hugo's refusal, and Napoleon did not forget.

We all know that Napoleon famously held grudges. One morning Major Hugo was informed that he was being assigned to the Army of Naples, that is, he was being dispatched to a location far from the Emperor. We all know, too, that the Emperor favored and rewarded only those officers who fought within the circle that his eyes could embrace.

Major Hugo, however, could have taken as his motto the Spanish word that served for a time as his son's signature: *Hierro* (iron). Given that observation, it is no doubt unnecessary to add that Major Hugo was the father of our great poet Victor, who would later depict him as a true hero, a merciful as well as courageous man, in these lines from his collection *Le Légende des siècles:*

> My father, a hero with a gentle smile,
> Along with the faithful hussar he dearly loved
> For his courage and prowess,
> Was riding, one evening after battle,

Over a field covered by bodies as night was falling.
In the shadows he thought he heard a little sound.
It was a Spaniard from the routed army
Dragging himself along the highway,
Panting, broken, pale, and nearly dead,
And saying: "I'm thirsty! Have mercy on me!"
My father, much moved, held out to his faithful hussar
A flask of rum hanging from his saddle,
And said: "Here, let the poor man drink."
Suddenly, as the hussar bent down,
The man, a Moor,
Pulls out his pistol
And points it at my father's forehead, shouting: "Caramba!"
The bullet passed so near, his hat fell off,
And his horse leaped backward.
"All the same, let him drink," my father said.

CVI

Major Hugo

So, as I have said, King Joseph summoned Major Hugo to Portici. He
had known Hugo for a long time, and he admired him, but Napoleon inspired such fear, even in his brothers, that King Joseph dared do nothing
for any man who'd caused the Emperor displeasure. Perhaps he now hoped
to restore his friend's esteem in the Emperor's eyes by giving him the opportunity to capture a bandit against whom the bravest and most skillful
men in Napoleon's army had failed.

The king ordered Major Hugo to form a column of men from the various infantry regiments that made up the royal guard: the Royal African, the
Corsican Legion, and the First and Second Neapolitan. Then, with himself
at the head of the column, perhaps eight or nine hundred men, to which
some artillery pieces and fifty dragoons were attached, he was to pursue Fra
Diavolo relentlessly.

Fra Diavolo had become a veritable partisan leader with approximately
fifteen hundred men under his orders. He had chosen the mountains lying
between the sea, the Pontifical States, and the Garigliano River as the theater
of his operations.

Major Hugo's instructions were simply stated if not easily accomplished: cross the river, seek out the bandits, stay with them until they were destroyed. Strategic dispositions already contained the brigand in the area of his operations. General Duhesme, with his division, occupied the Roman States; General Goullus, with a brigade, was guarding the Sora Valley; troops patrolled the Garigliano, and General Valentin, commander of the Gaeta district, stood ready to take Fra Diavolo should he try to leave by boat. With three generals surrounding him and a brilliant major about to attack him, it is apparent that Fra Diavolo was being treated like a serious enemy.

Major Hugo dispensed with the artillery pieces and the dragoons, as he felt they would only be more hindrance than help in a mountain war, and in a mountain war he already had too few advantages over Fra Diavolo. Indeed, as soon as Fra Diavolo discerned the strategy to contain him, instead of simply waiting for the French to stage an attack, he himself took the initiative, taking San Guglielmo by surprise, destroying a battalion camped near Arce, and then heading for Cervaro.

Major Hugo set out behind him. He arrived in Cervaro an hour after Fra Diavolo. Reasoning that the enemy had encamped in the wild forests outside the village, he divided his troops into two parts. He sent one part around behind Cervaro onto the mountain, while he had the other search the village.

Hugo was not mistaken. Gunshots soon announced that the enemy had been discovered. The shooting was fierce, but it didn't last long. Fra Diavolo, by taking a shortcut, had traveled less than a third of the distance his adversaries had had to cover to get to Cervaro, so he figured that the French would be too tired to keep up with him. He headed back up into the mountains. Night fell, and Major Hugo determined it unwise to venture into unknown forests with only few supplies. He returned to Cervaro about ten that evening.

At three the next morning, however, the major and his men were up and marching in three columns. Fra Diavolo had left a rearguard in the Acquafondata gorges to protect the road against the French, but Major Hugo, marching at the head of the grenadiers from the Second Neapolitan, who were seeing fire for the first time, put the rearguard to flight. Unfortunately, nightfall was accompanied by a torrential downfall, and the French were forced to take shelter at a small, abandoned farm. They stayed there until daybreak the following day.

Fra Diavolo knew every road through the mountains, but he never used them. He preferred the little paths made by shepherds, and he ordered frequent and rapid countermarches. So, to stay on his trail, the French had to put their hope in shepherds, whom they paid well. The paths, though, were often no more than stream beds, yet the French soldiers followed every twist and turn, and sometimes even climbed down waterfalls. The beds were so strewn with rocks that most of the time the soldiers had to remove their shoes and walk barefoot.

Their dogged pursuit had now lasted a week. Still they had not been able to overtake their enemies, though they had been hard on their trail. The soldiers barely had time to rest; they ate on the run, they slept on their feet. Major Hugo flooded the province with spies provided by local police; he sent messengers to governors, prefects, and mayors. He knew where Fra Diavolo was each day, and he knew what he was doing, but he continued to be unable to press him and his band into battle.

As it turned out, a French battalion on its way to the Abruzzi received word that Fra Diavolo and his brigands were holed up in a woods near the village they happened to be passing through. They stopped, found a guide, took the brigands by surprise, and killed a hundred men.

The shooting brought Major Hugo and his grenadiers to the scene posthaste. Fra Diavolo, now almost completely surrounded, knew it was useless to fight, so he resorted to trickery.

The brigand gathered his men together. "Divide yourselves up into little groups of about twenty men," he instructed them. "Each group is then to tell whomever they pass that I am with them, and at the same time each group will take whatever path it chooses to reach the sea. We shall all meet in Sicily."

They immediately put the plan into action. In groups of twenty, they disappeared like smoke in ten different directions. Reports reached Major Hugo that Fra Diavolo had again given him the slip; that he was heading for the Abruzzi, that he had been spotted on either side of the Biferno, that he was trying to get to Puglia, that he was retreating toward Naples.

A few moments of thought led Major Hugo to realize Fra Diavolo's strategy, which had been used by Marshal de Rantzau. But in which group was Fra Diavolo traveling?

Since Major Hugo could not be certain, he had to have his troops force all ten of the bands to move in the same direction. To that end, he sent the Neapolitan detachments to the left bank of the Biferno, while he, with both the Corsican Legion he called back from Isernia and the Royal Africans, set off toward Cantalupo and the Bojano Valley.

CVII
At Bay

WHEN THE TROOPS ARRIVED in Molisse, the countryside looked as if it had been laid waste by a cataclysm, and indeed, not long before, an earthquake had struck the province. The inhabitants, all of whom had been forced to leave and some of whom had found refuge in hastily constructed shelters, were only now returning to their ruined houses. But Major Hugo had had frequent contact with them and knew them to be people of goodwill. He did not doubt for a moment that they would help him as best they could should he enlist them in his service. And they did. As couriers, they traveled courageously both night and day to deliver his requests and bring back answers. The national guards, no matter that their houses had been flattened, put aside thought of the disaster and served as guides or scouts. Their ready cooperation with Hugo alarmed Fra Diavolo, astonished as he was to see his countrymen becoming his enemies. The bandit found himself now forced to react to his adversary's plans rather than act upon his own. Pressed on all sides by Major Hugo's soldiers, he started moving with his band down through the Bojano Valley. So did Major Hugo.

The weather was horrible. Torrents were everywhere gushing down the mountainsides. Hugo's men seemed to be unable to take a step without having to cross a stream, the water sometimes waist-deep. Ordinarily, the Biferno ran only about two feet deep, but now it was so swollen that if the national guard had arrived from Vinchiaturo in time to defend the bridge, they'd have captured Fra Diavolo, because he would not have been able to cross the river. Finally, on a day when heaven's floodgates had opened, the rain pouring down, between Bojano and the village of Guardia, soldiers from the African Guard and Fra Diavolo's men met. The soldiers under Major Hugo's command were outnumbered four to one, but fortunately, other columns in pursuit of Fra Diavolo showed up to join in the battle. The rain was falling so heavily that the combatants could use only their daggers, gunstocks, and bayonets.

The combat was bloody, an immense duel in which each man either killed or was killed by his opponent. It lasted more than two hours, but finally the brigands were chased off. Just one hundred and fifty men, all that were left of Fra Diavolo's fifteen hundred, crossed the Vinchiaturo bridge and went down the Tammaro Valley as far as Benevento. Hugo's troops took about thirty prisoners; a thousand men died on the battlefield or drowned in the torrents. Had Major Hugo retained his dragoons, he might have wiped out the entire band and made Fra Diavolo his prisoner.

During the return march, one of the prisoners approached the major and offered, in exchange for his freedom, to lead him to the mountain cache where ten thousand ducats of the band's money, the equivalent of about forty-five thousand francs, were buried. Major Hugo refused the offer, for his duty was not to gather booty for his soldiers but to pursue Fra Diavolo.

When the column's vanguard reached the Calore, they discovered that the river had risen fifteen or sixteen feet above normal. They took the news back to the major at Benevento: another obstacle for the French, and another twenty-four hours for Fra Diavolo to gain on them.

They feared that if they lost Diavolo's trail, he'd be able to make his way to the beach and then, by boat, to Capri. So the major had dry shoes distributed to his men, and in spite of some murmuring, he ordered them to set out with him one hour after midnight. When they reached Montesarchio, he learned that Fra Diavolo had again slipped through the French columns and was already on Monte Vergine's opposite slope.

The village of Montesarchio sits on the road between Naples and Benevento, at the point where you encounter the famous Caudine Forks, beneath which the Roman army was forced to march during the Samnite wars. The Caudine Forks is a narrow passageway formed on one side by the Taburno and on the other by the Vergine, so named for a magnificent convent situated on the far side of the mountain. On the near side, the Benevento side, though, the mountain is so steep that no one but goatherds and their goats ever ventured there. By climbing that precipitous slope, however, Major Hugo figured he could make up the twenty-four hours he had lost and thus still have a chance to catch up with the elusive Diavolo. The guides tried vigorously to dissuade him, but to no avail. Major Hugo had decided. They would scale the mountain.

At daybreak, with the goatherds as guides, Major Hugo began the climb. His soldiers followed; they were muttering under their breaths, but at least they followed. As if their ascent were not already difficult enough, a fine snow started to fall. The rocks became more treacherous still. Fortunately, by then they had reached a part of the mountain where at least a few trees were growing, so they could use the branches for support or to pull themselves up. They also began to enjoy the challenge as well as the laughable sight of one another falling over themselves. After about three hours of strenuous effort, they arrived at a plateau, but it was veiled so densely in fog that they couldn't be sure where they were. Soaking wet, they had barely settled in when a mountain wind abruptly rose and dispersed the fog. It was as if a theater curtain had just risen; beyond them they could suddenly see the Gulf of Naples in all its glory. They were at the top of the mountain.

Quietly but joyously the column started down the other side, only to be greeted by a volley of musket fire as they headed toward Aletta. By chance they had landed right in the middle of the brigand's band, and though Fra Diavolo would have liked to have fled without fighting, in the circumstances that was impossible. The Corsican vanguard had surrounded his men, and there was fierce hand-to-hand combat. At the sounds of battle, other detachments hurried to the site and threw themselves into the fray.

Yet, on this occasion too, with about thirty of his men, Fra Diavolo managed to escape, perhaps because with two nights of sleep he was better rested than his pursuers. One hundred and twenty of his brigands were either captured or else threw down their weapons and slipped away. But the major gave them no more than a passing thought. He was interested only in their chief, for ultimately only he mattered. Once Fra Diavolo was taken, clearly the band could not re-form, for the men who served under him would never serve under any other.

Fra Diavolo had real hopes of escaping. He knew the region well, its every highway, trail, path, and road. He had only to reach the road to Puglia. He was soon on his way.

A precipice to the right of him forced Fra Diavolo to stay on the road, and suddenly, coming toward him on the same road, was a regiment of French cavalry on patrol. If he kept going, he would meet up with them, but if he turned back, he was bound to run into Hugo and the soldiers pursuing him.

The brigand's companions stopped in fear, their anxious looks telling him: "Nobody but you with one of your devilish tricks could ever get us out of this mess. That is how you earned the name Fra Diavolo."

Nor did Diavolo's genius betray him at that critical moment. "Tie my hands behind my back," he said, "and do the same to my lieutenant."

The brigands stood speechless, dumbfounded. "Hurry! Hurry!" Fra Diavolo shouted. "We have no time to waste."

Passive obedience won out. Since they had no ropes, they used their handkerchiefs and tied the two men's hands together. "And now," Fra Diavolo went on, "we shall start walking boldly down the road toward the cavalry. When they ask who we are, you will tell them that you have just captured two of Fra Diavolo's brigands and that you are taking them to Naples to claim the reward."

"And what if they want to claim the reward themselves?"

"Let them. You'll just withdraw, protesting the injustice."

"But you, Captain?"

"Bah! You can only die once."

Fra Diavolo and his lieutenant assumed a sullen, contrite look while their fake civil guards walked boldly toward the cavalry. They were stopped and questioned. Every Neapolitan knows how to improvise, and one of the brigands went into elaborate detail about how they had captured the two prisoners. The horsemen clapped at the end of the man's colorful account, and the little band of brigands found itself behind the regiment, which had continued moving in the opposite direction. They went their separate ways like good friends wishing each other well.

When the bandits got about three hundred yards away from the horsemen, they discovered a path that crossed the road and then ran parallel to it. They untied their supposed prisoners' hands, and Fra Diavolo gave orders to fire on the cavalry.

The cavalrymen knew they were being mocked by the band of men, but since they were on horseback and unfamiliar with the roads, they made no attempt to follow the men on foot who knew the territory so well. They did not realize how thoroughly they had been tricked until they met up with Major Hugo's soldiers, who identified the men they'd let slip through their fingers.

So the pursuit went on. That evening Major Hugo and his soldiers reached Lettere, a small village outside Castellammare. There villagers led them to some bivouac fires a short distance away, and they skirmished with a large group of the men still loyal to Fra Diavolo. In the fray, Diavolo himself was wounded, but he escaped with a few men and headed in the direction of La Cava. A boat was his last hope. Thinking it would be easier to continue alone, he sent away the last of his companions.

Now that he was almost alone, Fra Diavolo inspired little fear in the French, but the possibility that he might still get to Capri or Sicily and return with a new band of partisans remained a concern. The price on Fra Diavolo's head was six thousand ducats, or twenty-eight thousand francs. The national guardsmen and the French troops were alerted. In the Two Sicilies not only Diavolo's enemies were eager to collect six thousand ducats.

It was near the end of November. The night was cold, the ground was covered with snow. He found it unbearable to camp outdoors in the mountains. In another skirmish with the civil guards he had been wounded a second time; Fra Diavolo was beginning to lose strength. He had been on the run for twenty-nine days, and he was literally dying of hunger, as he'd not eaten anything since Aletta. In exchange for a safe place to hide, some bread, and a night of sleep, he would have been delighted to give the ten thousand ducats he'd hidden away on the mountain.

He walked aimlessly for an hour or two. He had wandered into a region completely unfamiliar to him. At about nine in the evening he stumbled upon a shepherd's hut. He peered through a crack and discovered there was only one man inside. He asked for hospitality, and while he was determined to take it by force if it was refused, the shepherd granted it willingly, the way the poor rarely hesitate to share with others what little God has given them.

Fra Diavolo asked if there were civil guards around. He learned there weren't. So he laid his weapons in a corner, sat down by the fire, and ate the rest of the shepherd's supper, a few potatoes cooked in the embers. Then he flopped onto a corn-husk bed and fell asleep.

Fra Diavolo had thought to inquire about the guards, but he had forgotten to ask about the bandits. At about midnight, four bandits from Ciliento happened by chance onto the shepherd's hut. The shepherd and his guest awakened to pistol barrels at their throats. Since Fra Diavolo did not know if they were some of his own companions or the civil guard, he did not reveal his identity. He put up no resistance. He was soon parted from his weapons and his money.

Once the bandits had left, Fra Diavolo hoped he had nothing more to fear but death. Since Major Hugo had begun to pursue him, all luck had deserted him. He had been beaten, he had been wounded, and now he had neither weapons nor money. What more could happen to him?

Well, the poor fellow had not yet suffered the last of his tribulations. Scarcely had the brigands gone a hundred yards than they realized they had left behind a man who might turn them in. So they went back to the hut and made Diavolo come with them.

He had little choice but to obey. However, he had been in flight for twenty-nine days, the last three days with no shoes, and the mountain paths, the thorns, the rocks, had made of his feet open wounds. He managed to hide his suffering, but he was unable to keep up with them. When he fell behind, they beat him with their gun stocks and poked him in the back with their bayonets.

"Kill me if you like," said Fra Diavolo finally, "but I can go no farther." And he collapsed to the ground.

CVIII

The Gallows

⁂

EITHER OUT OF COMPASSION or because Fra Diavolo now seemed so harmless, the bandits left him to die there on the path.

Why did Fra Diavolo not identify himself, one might ask. The answer would be the prize of six thousand ducats he carried on his head. Diavolo had no doubt that if the bandits knew who he was, they would turn him in immediately and each pocket fifteen hundred ducats.

When the bandits had gone, Diavolo struggled to his feet. Using a branch as a cane, he began to walk. He ended up in the village of Baronissi. He started down the first street he came to and soon found himself on the square. The ground was covered with snow. An apothecary had just opened his doors. He was surprised to see the man standing in the square and looking around nervously. He went out and asked what he was looking for.

"I'm waiting for a friend," the man said. "I'm from Calabria, and as soon as he gets here, I'll be on my way."

Unfortunately for Fra Diavolo, the apothecary was from Calabria, so he could tell the stranger's accent was not Calabrian. And he assumed the man must be a fugitive. He invited the stranger in; he offered him the warmth of his kitchen and a little brandy. While he pretended to take care of the man's needs so solicitously, he whispered to his young servant girl that she should run to the mayor's office and alert the national guard.

Within minutes, a private first class and four men had arrived at the shop. The private asked Fra Diavolo for his papers.

"What papers?" said Diavolo. "Can we no longer travel without a passport?"

"With so many brigands around," the soldier replied, "one cannot be too careful. So if you can't show us where you come from, we'll take you to Salerno." And they did.

They delivered him to Major Farina, who had just begun the interrogation in his office when Pavese, a sapper from Naples serving under Major Hugo, happened to come in. When he saw the prisoner, he cried out, "Fra Diavolo!"

We can understand everyone's surprise, especially the prisoner's. He tried to deny it, of course, but unfortunately, when the Bourbons were in power and Fra Diavolo, both a colonel and a duke, walked through the streets of Naples glorying in his uniform and title, the humble sapper had too often saluted him not to recognize him now, even though he was half-naked, dying, and covered with blood. The sapper's absolute certainty as to the man's identity eliminated even the faintest doubt. At last they had captured the fearsome Fra Diavolo.

It was Major Hugo who carried to King Joseph the news that they had arrested the dangerous partisan. Recognized his prisoner's courage and presence of mind, Hugo recommended clemency. Joseph pointed out, however, that in addition to his political crimes Fra Diavolo had committed civil crimes, and his civil crimes made clemency impossible. The king might easily have granted clemency to Fra Diavolo for being a Bourbon partisan, a colonel in King Ferdinand's army, and Duke of Cassano, but he could not extend his clemency to Fra Diavolo the assassin and Fra Diavolo the arsonist.

Fra Diavolo was very popular, and at his trial the seats were crammed with the curious. The defendant was present during the trial—prior to Joseph's kingship, judges had considered that particular defendant's right to be an unnecessary formality—and he was invited to speak in his own defense. He refused, although in prison he had kept repeating that he'd only been following orders. He calmly listened while his death sentence was being read, then cried out, "And I didn't even do half of what Sidney Smith had ordered me to do!"

The execution was set for noon the following day, which was the very hour and day that Manhès and Comte Leo came rolling into town. Thanks to the uniform Manhès was wearing, they were able to reach the Piazza del Mercato Vecchio along with their horses, their two prisoners, and the postilion.

At the same time, as we said earlier, Fra Diavolo was coming through the Vico dei Sospiri dell'Abisso. His face was pale, his countenance self-assured. His hair had been trimmed above his ears so as not to get in the way of the rope. Around his neck hung his commission as colonel in the king's army, affixed with Ferdinand's signature and the great wax seal. His coat was draped over his shoulders; it would be removed at the foot of the scaffold, to reveal on the wrist above one of his bound hands the bracelet woven from strands of Queen Caroline's blond hair and fastened by a diamond clasp.

Fra Diavolo was neither too insolent nor too humble. He was mostly calm, his demeanor demonstrating the power of mind over body and will over matter. Three quarters of the spectators knew him, but he did not respond when they called out greetings to him. A few women were rewarded with a smile from him, and he bowed to one or two of them. The French guards shoved people aside as the cart came forward, and they kept everyone at least thirty yards from the scaffold. At the base of the scaffold stood Master Donato, the executioner, and his two assistants.

The cart stopped. The assistants made a move to help Fra Diavolo down, but he leaped from the cart of his own accord and walked with one of the Brotherhood of Death toward the scaffold. The priest and the clerk of court followed.

The clerk read the sentence aloud. It contained all the complaints that society held against Fra Diavolo, from the murder of his master the saddle-maker all the way up to his killing of two French soldiers.

The entire Brotherhood of Death had followed the cart the entire distance from Castel Capuano to the scaffold, and the brother who'd sat beside Diavolo in the cart and then led him to the scaffold now stood with his hand on the condemned man's shoulder. Not until the brother removed his hand did condemned man belong to the executioner. After the sentence had been read, Fra Diavolo spoke in a whisper to the man in the white robe for several moments; the executioner waited patiently. Finally, with a strong voice, Fra Diavolo said to the brother standing with him by the ladder, "I have nothing more to say. Remove your hand, my brother. I am ready."

The executioner stepped behind Diavolo's back and started first up the ladder. He tried to help Fra Diavolo up by supporting him at the shoulders, but the brigand shrugged him off. "That is not necessary," he said, shaking his head. "I can manage by myself."

His hands were tied together and he had to climb backwards, yet at each rung he would stop to say *"Ave Maria, Ave Maria, Ave Maria,"* before moving up to the next. When Fra Diavolo reached the noose, the hangman slipped it around his neck, then waited for a moment in the event that the condemned might have something to say. And indeed, Fra Diavolo called aloud, "I ask both God and men forgiveness for the crimes I have committed, and I give myself over to the prayers of the Virgin Ma—"

He never finished; Master Donato had placed a kick between his shoulders and sent him off into eternity.

But Fra Diavolo, sensing that he was falling into the void, exerted so much energy that he snapped the ropes around his hands. The executioner quickly rushed up three or four rungs of the ladder and grabbed the swinging rope. He jumped onto the condemned man's shoulders, so that if Fra Diavolo's neck was still intact, the extra weight would surely break it. The bandit jerked two or three times, and the executioner began to slide down the bandit's body. He planned to hang from Diavolo's legs a moment and then drop safely to the ground, but either the noose was poorly made or the rope was too new to slide and hold properly, or perhaps Fra Diavolo's body was simply tougher than most, because just as the executioner slid down over his chest, the bandit grabbed him in a bear hug. Fra Diavolo had always been strong, only now, with the adrenaline and energy of a man fac-

ing death, he seemed to be superhuman in his strength—and to be squeezing the life out of his executioner.

The people cried out with one voice: "Bravo, Fra Diavolo! Bravo!" The
executioner, feeling he might be nearly as close to death as the man he was
trying to hang, was meanwhile bellowing with pain.

From out of the crowd shouts arose. Stones began to fly; the merchants
brandished their sticks and the *lazzaroni* their knives. They all rushed toward the scaffold, shouting, "Death to Donato! Death to his assistants!"

But the Naples populace was not as intractable as it had been back in the
days of Ferdinand, when it would demolish scaffolds and tear the executioner to bits if he failed to follow the rules of his game. The mob instead
yielded to the French troops who'd massed around the scaffold and crossed
their bayonets against the restive Neapolitans. Advancing in line, the soldiers then pushed everyone back to the far end of the market square and
kept them there.

Meanwhile, the officer in charge of the execution had noticed the strange
group of spectators composed of Manhès, the count, the carriage with its
two prisoners, and the postilion still on his horses. Politely, officer to officer, he had asked a few questions and received a few laconic answers. Manhès had briefly explained about the prisoners and asked what he could do
about them; the officer advised him to have them locked up in the Vicaria
prison.

Then the two young men had asked, "Which is the city's best hotel?"

"Go see the innkeeper Martin Zir, at La Vittoria," the officer answered
without hesitation.

"You heard the man," Manhès said to the postilion when he had thanked
the officer.

At the Vicaria prison Manhès and the count handed their prisoners over
to the jailer, who took their names and addresses. As they were leaving,
Leo realized that the poor devils surely did not have much money and must
be starving, so he slipped a louis into the hands of the man he had captured.

Ten minutes later, after paying off their postilion, the two men were
walking into La Vittoria and asking for a bath and lunch. They sorely
needed both after a night in the Pontine Marshes and the twelve leagues of
hard riding.

Before their baths, however, Manhès wrote a letter to Joseph Bonaparte's first chamberlain, while Comte Leo sent a card to Saliceti, Minister
of Police. Before they sat down at table, both men had received answers.
The first chamberlain at the royal palace sent word to Manhès that King
Joseph expected to see him as soon as possible, for he was eager to have
fresh news from the Emperor and from Murat. Comte Leo received word

from the minister's secretary that His Excellency would be pleased to receive him whenever he chose come to the palace.

Both men took note and set about getting dressed.

CIX

Christophe Saliceti, Minister of Police and Minister of War

FOR MEN WHO ARE NATURALLY ELEGANT, dressing is easy. Comte Leo, in whom our readers have already recognized René, stood among such men. Since his ranks as second in command under Surcouf and third lieutenant under Lucas had never been officially confirmed, it was inappropriate for him to dress in either the unconventional nauticals he wore as a corsair or the regulation uniform he wore as a sailor. So he donned what fashionable young people were wearing those days: a frock coat with a small cape and Brandenburg buttons, tight woolen pants, boots with turned-down tops, a tie and a white sweater, and a hat with a turned-up brim.

It was three in the afternoon when Comte Leo was announced to His Excellency the Minister of Police and War. Two or three other people were still waiting to see him, but the minister called for Comte Leo and sent word for the others to come back the next day.

Christophe Saliceti, the Minister of Police and War, was from Corsica. At the time he was about sixty years old. He had been a lawyer in Bastia when the Revolution broke out and was then named a deputy and a delegate to the Constituent Assembly, where he helped pass the decree giving Corsicans French citizenship. Later he became a member of the Convention and of the Council of Five Hundred. After the 18th Brumaire Napoleon had brushed him aside for a short time because he opposed the coup d'état, but eventually he returned to favor, and when Joseph assumed the throne in Naples, Saliceti was assigned the Police and War portfolios. He was handsome and quite refined. It was said that he had the complete support of Joseph Bonaparte within the Emperor's family.

He was seated at his desk when Comte Leo was announced. He rose from his seat and amiably offered Leo a chair. Leo thanked him for his kindness and prompt response.

"Monsieur," said Saliceti, "it is all the more surprising that I receive you, because I am racked by the fear that you have come to Naples to take my place."

"Oh, monsieur," the man whom we shall sometimes refer to as René and sometimes as Leo replied with a laugh. "Your position is much too ably filled for me to even dare think about the possibility."

"Are you not the man, monsieur," Saliceti continued, "who came with Captain Manhès from Rome?"

"Yes, Your Excellency, and you are giving me such proof of the quality of your police that I could never hope, or even desire, to replace you."

"You went to the Vicaria prison, where you had two bandits locked up. You had taken them prisoner, leaving three men dead as you did so."

"We do what we can in such circumstances," Comte Leo replied. "And that was the best we could do, monsieur."

"So might I now know, monsieur, what gives me the honor of your visit, and how I can help you?"

"Excellency, it is my great misfortune to be in disgrace with His Majesty Napoleon. On the other hand, I am—though I'm not sure why—in Monsieur Fouché's good graces."

"That is already substantial," said Saliceti. "Fouché, far from being the evil man people say he is, is not all bad. I met him during the Convention. We often were of the same opinion, and we have remained close. Did he not charge you with a commission for me?"

"No, monsieur. When I went to receive his orders and discover where I should go, he asked me, 'Did you find the earlier advice I gave you good?' 'Yes, indeed, my dear Duke,' I replied, and he said, 'Well then, go to Naples, see Saliceti, try to do something useful for the Emperor's brother, and then come back to see me.'"

"Did you not ask him for some particular references?"

"Yes, I did. But he said, 'My good man, I wouldn't dare. You are a man with luck. Go to Naples, and luck will find you.' With that I left. In Rome I met Captain Manhès at the relay station. That was the beginning of my good luck, just as Fouché had predicted. Then, in the Pontine Marshes, we ran into six bandits blocking our path. We killed three of them and took two prisoners, as you know. And finally, since luck was still with us, we arrived in Naples just in time to see Fra Diavolo being hanged."

"You are a good man, monsieur, as I already knew. Is there something you would like me to do for you?"

"Well, Excellency, I have begun to think like Monsieur Fouché. Set me on a path, and I shall follow it."

"You are neither a diplomat nor an intriguer, am I right?" asked Saliceti.

"Not at all," René replied. "I am a soldier or a sailor. Send me somewhere I can face death, on land or sea, I do not care which."

"Why face death?"

"Because I am ambitious. I want to achieve a high position that might help me recover the happiness I have lost."

"We have no navy, monsieur. We have ordered two ships, but they will not be finished for another two years, and that is too far off. Nor do we have any real wars. Gaeta is indeed under siege, but it should be surrendering in five or six days. I know that you have been a great tiger and panther hunter, and we have more of them here in the bush than there are in the Burmese jungles. But here our tigers have names like Torribio, Parafante, Benincasa, and Il Bizzarro. How about hunting that kind of tiger? There will be another promotion for each man you kill or capture alive."

"Fine," said René. "I would prefer real war, and I would rather be a soldier than a hunter, but Monsieur Fouché no doubt had good reasons to send me here."

"I believe I know what those reasons are, monsieur: He is looking out for you, and he sent you here so that I could look out for you as well. I will speak to the king about you, monsieur. Come back to see me again."

"When?"

"Tomorrow."

René got to his feet and bowed: "Will you permit me, monsieur," he said, "to tell Fouché how kind you have been to receive me?"

"Write back to France as little as possible. In your letters, never speak either of the people who have been helpful to you or of those with whom you might find fault. For at some time in the future, your own words might prevent your friends' recommendations from being of any use to you."

"Thank you for the counsel, monsieur. But how can it be that a man of Napoleon's stature—"

"Shhh!" Saliceti said. "Napoleon is a compatriot of mine, and I cannot allow anyone in my presence to compare him to anything, even the sun. The sun itself has spots, monsieur."

Comte Leo bowed once more, said good-bye, and withdrew. At the front door of La Vittoria he found Manhès, whose face radiated joy.

"I have something to tell you," announced the captain. "I spoke to the king about you, and he said he wants to see you."

"My dear friend," Comte Leo replied, "since I have been rubbing shoulders with ministers, as I have just done with Monsieur Saliceti, I have been learning something of proper protocol. Monsieur Saliceti was kind enough to say that he would speak to His Majesty about me, and I must let him proceed. I think he would hold it against me if I should follow a path other than the one he has proposed."

"Of course," said Manhès. "But whenever you go, I shall try to be there myself. And now, what are you planning for the rest of the day? How about dining in Pompeii?"

"With pleasure," said Leo. He rang for service: "My good man," he said, "we'd like a carriage and two good horses for the rest of the day."

Master Martin Zir provided his hotel's best carriage. For two guests like these, one of them summoned within an hour of their arrival by the king and the other by the minister, had to be looked after properly.

It was a lovely day. Although they were only halfway through January, they could already enjoy those warm, voluptuous breezes from Sicily that bring Paestum roses twice to flower before they die in the gulf. It was not yet springtime, but already winter was over.

The quay, so filthy and yet so exuberant with life, changed its name three times between Piliero and the Carmine gate. At one end of the breakwater they might have seen some thespian declaiming lines from Tasso, and at the other a Capuchin monk vaunting Christ's miracles. At every step they would have seen pigs, which in those days served the Neapolitans as street cleaners. Looking out over the sparkling waters of the gulf, with Cape Campanella on one side and Cape Misena on the other, off in the bluish distance they could see the Isle of Capri lying like a coffin on the surface of the water.

Girls walked through the crowds with flowers that in more northern climes were still buried under snowdrifts; their faces radiated the kind of youthful joy of which Metastasis wrote:

> O youth, life's springtime!
> O spring, the year's youth!

From the breakwater to Resina, almost two leagues away, everyone was laughing, singing, throwing flowers, swearing at each other.

In Resina, the spectacle added another element; for along with girls, monks, singers, and pigs, there were pasta makers. Almost every family in Portici made pasta, and they offered a strange picture: shirtless men rolling pasta on each others' backs until it reached the size dictated by the rules of gastronomy. Portici macaroni has the reputation of tasting better than the pasta anywhere else in Italy, no doubt because of the tables on which it is rolled.

As the two young men were approaching the Torre del Greco, they thought they were riding into a riot or a bandit attack. As the sounds of gunfire grew louder, they were regretting that they had not brought their weapons. They soon learned, though, that what they heard were blanks being shot in honor of Saint Anthony. They pointed out that the celebrations in honor of the famous theologian who was cast ashore by a storm when he was trying to go to Africa normally took place in June. And they found out that the celebration was not for Saint Anthony of Padua, the man who vanquished Vesuvius and tamed fire, but for the Saint Anthony being tempted in Callot's engraving. The esteem accorded Saint Anthony helped explain why there were so many pigs in the streets.

Eventually they reached Pompeii. The buried city was then still far from being excavated, but enough had been for visitors to get an idea of what marvels it would offer once an intelligent director led the excavations.

Comte Leo explained to his friend the architecture of a Roman house, from the atrium to the impluvium to the triclinium. Along the street of tombs, he pointed out the circular benches, still partially buried, that dead men who wanted companionship would place around their monuments. As if he had been alive when the freed slave Diomedes had built the most beautiful house in the neighborhood, Leo explained to his friend the function of each house and shop.

Night came before Manhès had gotten his fill of his friend's illuminating tales and lectures, but they had to get back. They had traveled eighteen centuries back in time and spent three hours with contemporaries of Pliny the Elder and Pliny the Younger.

Leaving the silent, gloomy necropolis, they again found themselves on the busy road back, which seemed even noisier at night than during the day. The moon was hanging just above the crater at the top of Vesuvius, like a giant mortar that might have just shot a colossal shell skyward. The sea resembled a film of silvery gauze; over it glided small boats, the bow of each lit by a lantern so that they could see, silhouetted in each, a man standing with a trident while watching for fish that the light would attract to the surface. The whole, long road from Pompeii to Naples was ablaze with a thousand lights; it looked like a street in Rome with all the *maccoletti* at the end of carnival.

In Portici, they stopped to rest their horses. Immediately a swarm of people, curious and not at all hostile, surrounded the carriage. They climbed up on the running boards, they studied the two men; some of them touched Manhès's silver braids, others grazed Leo's silk buttons. In the midst of the crowd, a beggar and a Capuchin monk suddenly appeared. The beggar elbowed his way up to the carriage while the monk humbly asked people to let him through.

The beggar, speaking in a horrendous Neapolitan dialect, sounded as if he was about to breathe his last: "A *grano*, Lord General! A coin! I'm dying of hunger. I haven't eaten for three days!"

The Franciscan meanwhile spoke with the nasal accent typical of Saint Francis's disciples; shaking a little money bag with a few coins in it already, he pled, "Lord Prince, give something for the souls of poor sinners who have been in purgatory for more than a thousand years. You would be able to hear them pleading, in spite of all the noise around us, if purgatory were not at the center of the earth."

The beggar kept saying, "Lord General! . . ." The monk kept repeating, "Lord Prince! . . ."

Manhès finally held up his hand to indicate he wanted to speak. The monk and beggar both went silent.

"My friend," Manhès said to the Capuchin, "if these sinners' souls have already been waiting in purgatory for a thousand years, they can wait a few more days, I'm sure. But if this poor man has had nothing to eat for seventy-two hours, there is not a moment to waste if we do not want him to die of hunger."

Manhès then took the money bag from the monk's hand, opened it, and poured its contents into the beggar's hand. He gave the empty bag back to the shocked Capuchin.

Turning to the postilion, he shouted, *"Avanti! Avanti!"* The postilion set out at a gallop and did not stop until they reached the hotel La Vittoria.

CX
King Joseph

AT NOON THE NEXT DAY, just as the two young men were finishing their lunch, a man on horseback arrived with a dispatch from the minister:

Monsieur le Comte,

I will expect you today at three o'clock to present you to His Majesty. Before I had a chance to make my request of an interview, he expressed the desire to see you. We shall have dinner after returning from the royal palace. I shall introduce you to my daughter the Duchess of Lavello, for she too would like to meet you.

I ask you to give the attached invitation to your friend Captain Manhès, as I do not have his address. The invitation will bring you and him both to my house, I trust, between five and six o'clock.

René handed the second letter to Manhès, who said he would of course be honored to accept the minister's invitation.

Promptly at three o'clock, Comte Leo arrived at Saliceti's house. He found the minister ready and his carriage harnessed.

Although King Joseph was the eldest of the Bonaparte brothers, he had recognized Napoleon's genius and ceded his birthright to him. He was now thirty-four years old. He had a kindly face, and in temperament was as calm as his younger brother was hotheaded. Napoleon loved him dearly; Joseph was the first member of the family to whom he considered giving a throne. We must add that, of his whole family, when he was on the throne as well as when he was a simple citizen, Joseph was the one most devoted and most obedient to his brother. It is interesting to note that in the eight or nine volumes of letters exchanged between the two brothers, Joseph always addresses Napoleon as "Sire" or "Your Majesty," whereas Napoleon invariably answers with "My brother."

Many of the letters contain advice; some are orders. They demonstrate that Napoleon, who has never been to Naples, knows the Kingdom of Naples, both topographically and politically, better than Joseph, who is actually living there. Napoleon says specifically that Joseph is too good-hearted, particularly in dealing with the partisans. He warns Joseph against any vacillating in their concerns, and he makes clear that he does not want Joseph to grant pardons to bandits or to priests.

If Joseph was inclined to leniency with the Marquis de Rodio, who had received his title from Ferdinand and Caroline, Napoleon was not. The marquis, who had continued the partisan war after Joseph became king, was caught in Puglia with arms in hand and was taken before the council. There he claimed he had surrendered as a prisoner of war, and so he was forgiven. After an *order from above*, however, a second council was assembled, and that council found the marquis guilty. The king was absent. Saliceti had the man shot.

On that occasion Joseph rued the fact that he had not been allowed to grant the partisan pardon. Napoleon wrote him a long letter in which appear the following paragraphs:

Since you are comparing Neapolitans to Corsicans, remember that when we went into the Niolo, we hanged forty rebels in trees. So great was everyone's terror that they ceased their activities. Piacenza had risen up when I came back from the Grand Army. I sent Junot, and he wrote back, claiming wittily that the countryside was peaceful. I sent orders to burn two villages and to shoot the leaders of the rebellion, including six priests. That is what happened, and the region was pacified and will so remain for a long time.

You can see the terror the queen inspires. Of course, I am not saying that you must imitate her, but nonetheless, she is powerful. If you act decisively and energetically, the people in Calabria and elsewhere will not rise up for thirty years.

I shall finish my letter as I began it. You will be King of Naples and Sicily, and you will have three or four years of peace. If you are a lazy king, if you do not hold the reins of power firmly, if you listen to the opinion of the population that does not really know what it wants, if you fail to wipe out abuse and the old usurpations so that you are not rich, if you fail to impose sufficient taxes to keep Frenchmen, Corsicans, Swiss, and Neopolitans in your service and to build ships, you will accomplish nothing at all. And in four years, instead of being useful to me, you will be a handicap, because you will limit my means. Remember what I am telling you. Your kingdom's fate depends on what you do when you get back to Calabria. Pardon nobody. Have at least six hundred rebels shot. They have slaughtered more of my soldiers than that. Burn the houses of at least thirty village leaders, and distribute their property to the army. Disarm all the inhabitants and ransack five or six large villages chosen from among those that have conducted themselves poorly.

Since Calabria has risen up, why would you not take half of its property and distribute it to the army? It would be a useful resource and at the same time a good example for the future. You cannot change or reform a State with weakness. You need extraordinary measures and great vigor. Since the people in Calabria are the ones who have killed my soldiers, I myself shall make a decree confiscating half of the province's income. But if you begin from the principle that they did not rise up and that they remain faithful to you, your kindness will be disastrous for France, for it is nothing but weakness.

You are too kind!

Joseph was indeed a kind and excellent man. He was King of Naples for only two years.

As soon as Saliceti sent in word that he had arrived at the royal palace, he and his protégé were invited in. Standing next to King Joseph was Manhès, who had said nothing of his plans to be there for the meeting.

"Monsieur," Joseph said to René after responding to Saliceti's compliments and René's own respectful bow, "yesterday I heard from your traveling companion Manhès, my brother-in-law Murat's aide-de-camp, about how you dealt with the six brigands who tried to stop you in the Pontine Marshes. For that, I offer nothing but compliments. But yesterday evening, Saliceti, to whom you were apparently recommended by one of his good friends, told me that you have come to take service in the army. For that, I owe you more than compliments. I also owe you thanks."

"Sire," Comte Leo replied, "His Excellency the minister surely told Your Majesty that I have no ambition. Whatever role you are willing to give me, however small, will be sufficient. Whether with a gun in my hands, if you make me an ordinary soldier, or with a sword, if you make me an officer, it will be up to me to prove that I merit your kindness. I shall do my best."

"Saliceti told me, monsieur," the king continued, "that you have served in the navy."

"I was a corsair, Sire, with one of our most famous seamen—Surcouf from Saint-Malo."

"I heard as well that you were at Trafalgar. How did it happen that you were at Trafalgar if you were on a pirate ship?"

"Knowing that a great battle was to take place the following day, I offered my services to the captain of the *Redoutable,* Captain Lucas. General Decaen, governor of Île de France, had given me such a strong recommendation, as had Surcouf, that Captain Lucas immediately proposed to me the place of third lieutenant, which had become vacant."

"And on board the *Redoutable,* Saliceti told me, not only did you fight like a lion, but also it was probably a bullet from your gun that killed Nelson."

"I have never taken credit for that, Majesty. First of all, there was no way of being certain, and secondly, Nelson was such a great combatant that it would be almost shameful to boast about being the cause of his death."

"And when you came back from the English prisons, did you not see Captain Lucas once more?"

"Yes, I did, Your Majesty."

"And did not Captain Lucas speak to my brother about you?"

"He did, Sire."

"Why did he not introduce you to him?"

"He did me that honor."

"And my brother neither granted you a reward nor confirmed you in your rank?"

"The only way I can respond, Sire, is by accusing myself, for otherwise I'd be accusing your brother. If you are ordering me to accuse myself. . . ."

"No! That is enough," said King Joseph, putting his hand on Comte Leo's shoulder. "You can talk later about all this with Saliceti. I have just made him Minister of War. In that capacity, he will do for you what you request." With a nod, he added, "And if you are not pleased with what he does, come complain to me."

"I never complain, Sire," René replied.

"By the way," Joseph said, stopping René in his preparation to leave the room, the audience apparently over, "I know that you are a great hunter. I cannot offer the tigers and panthers you found in India, but here in the Asproni forest we have many wild boars, and if you do not disdain game of that kind, Saliceti will make it possible for you to go hunting there as often as you like."

René bowed his thanks. As he was making his exit, Manhès indicated to him with a gesture and a glance that he would be out soon. For Manhès wanted the opporunity to judge the impression his companion had made on King Joseph. It was apparently excellent; the king's face was lit by joy.

The door had barely closed behind Manhès when King Joseph took from his pocket the little notebook in which he jotted down things he wanted to be sure to remember. With a pencil, he wrote: "Remember to recommend in my own hand, to Reynier or to Verdier, this young man, for he appears to be a model of courage and distinction."

CXI

Il Bizzarro

~·~

SALICETI TOOK HIS TWO GUESTS to the minister's palace. Saliceti had guessed that René would have a positive effect on Joseph, and Manhès had been reassured by Joseph's complimentary words about his friend during the few moments he remained behind. Indeed, Manhès had needed nothing more than the king's handshake to know René had made a splendid impression.

The Duchess of Lavello was waiting in the living room for her father and his two guests. Though still young, she was already quite a beautiful woman, and her father adored her. When the palace collapsed one year later, Saliceti almost died, not from the fall he himself had taken, but rather from worry over his daughter's injuries, as she was nearly crushed under the debris. A refined, elegant young woman herself, she was quick to appreciate similar qualities in René when they were introduced.

Saliceti had wanted the dinner private and small so that he could chat in a relaxed manner with his guests. He realized, too, that René, whether out of modesty or discretion, found it repugnant to talk about himself, and he was hoping that Manhès would supply details he'd not be able to draw from René. The sixth guest was the minister's first secretary, a Corsican like Saliceti. The conversation became lively as soon as they sat down to dinner.

"Monsieur," Saliceti said to his guest, "under what name do you wish to serve? In your place, I would choose the name your friend Manhès gave you. Leo is a lovely name, is it not, my daughter?"

"Especially if Leo means lion, as I think it does," the Duchess of Lavello replied.

"I do not choose that name, madame, because Leo means lion. I do so because it comes from a man I loved immediately and later esteemed. As His Excellency and you, madame, both love the name, that is one more reason for me to use it."

"And now, my good man," said Saliceti, "let us sort things out between us. Just as my friend Fouché explained that there were government ships and corsair ships, here we have regular troops on the one hand and on the other we have bandit hunters. Among the regular troops opportunities to distinguish oneself are few, but among bandit hunters, who run ten times more risks than the regulars, the opportunities to stand out are ten times as many. That is why Major Hugo, whom—and just between you and me, I can divulge this—a little grudge has kept from being promoted even after his heroic actions in Caldiero, will now be a colonel before the month is out. Because he has captured Fra Diavolo."

"What do you think, Manhès?" René asked.

"I think the minister's advice is sound, by God!—Ah, madame, I beg your pardon. I would be happy to stay here to go hunting with you, my friend."

"And all the more sound because I have a great brigand to propose," said the secretary. "Compared to him, men like Benincasa, Taccone, and Panzanera are little more than pickpockets."

"Have some dispatches come in today?" Saliceti asked.

"Yes. General Verdier's aide-de-camp wrote today."

"And who is your bandit?" the minister asked.

"He is still not widely known. But given the way he is starting out, he soon will be. His name is Il Bizzarro. He is still a young man, barely twenty-five years old, so we cannot expect too much from him."

"Tell us a little about him," said Manhès. "We can be judge of that."

"While still a child," Saliceti's secretary went on, "he entered into the service of a rich colonist whose daughter he seduced. When the two rashly allowed their love to be discovered, the girl's brothers felt dishonored, and they lay in wait to catch the lovers. They surprised them at a moment when there could be no doubt about their guilt—"

"Monsieur, monsieur," said the Duchess of Lavello. "Please be careful!"

"But, madame," the secretary said with a laugh, "I have to make myself clear."

"Go on, Robert," said Saliceti.

"With no doubt about their guilt," the secretary went on stubbornly, "they stabbed the boy full of holes and left him for dead on a pile of manure. Some kind passersby came upon the body and carried it to the village church. There, supposedly, after prayers for the dead were said, the body was to remain until the following morning.

"Lying there in the coffin, the fellow did not stir or interrupt the prayers. He simply waited until the priests tired of prayer and left the church for the night.

"They left thinking that all they'd have to do the next morning was nail down the lid of the coffin and put the poor fellow in one of the church's open crypts.

"Scarcely had the last priest left than the dead man opened first one eye, then the other. He raised his head. By candlelight he saw that the church was completely empty. At first he didn't know what had happened or where he was. But all the blood and the pain from his wounds brought back to him what had transpired. With great effort he climbed out of the coffin. He slipped out of the church and managed to drag himself off to the mountains, as had so many fugitives before him.

"That was the prologue to the tale I am going to tell. It took place in 1800, and my hero, Il Bizzarro, was then only nineteen years old.

"For the next four or five years, nobody heard anything about Il Bizzarro. However, when they found the coffin empty, they correctly surmised that he had escaped. He probably joined a band of thieves and killers who were infesting Soriano at the time. With the second French invasion, when Joseph was named King of Naples, they made the decision, brigands as they were, to become political partisans and fight under the Bourbon flag. And Il Bizzarro was certainly among them then, for his courage and sangfroid gained him their respect enough that they chose him as their leader. Once he held the band's autocratic power in his hands, he evidently believed the time had come for him to get revenge.

"One Sunday, about six or seven months ago, while the people of Varano—that was the village where he'd been left for dead—including the family of his former boss, were gathered to hear a mass in the same church where he'd lain in a coffin, Il Bizzarro, followed by his band, entered the church, walked to the sanctuary, turned around, and ordered everyone out. When the people, in shock and then in their terror, hesitated, Il Bizzarro revealed his identity and threatened to begin shooting. His reputation cured them of any reluctance; mute and in haste, they fled under his frightening gaze.

"To his band, Il Bizzarro pointed out two men in the crowd—his former boss's sons, his mistress's brothers, the two men who had stabbed him. Less fortunate than he had been, both men fell, never to rise again.

"But Il Bizzarro's account book was not yet balanced. There were three more men who had yet to pay, for his boss had five sons, his mistress five brothers. Il Bizzarro went back into the church with his men, and he found the other three, hiding behind the altar. He stabbed them himself, just as he had the first two, for he wanted the pleasure of vengeance to be entirely his.

"Still Il Bizzarro was not done. He had yet to attend to his mistress's father and his mistress herself. He found the old man in his house, in his bed, sick and nursed by his daughter. Recognizing her former lover, realizing that he had returned to exact some horrible vengeance, she rushed to place herself between him and her father. Il Bizzarro pushed her aside, then finished off his massacre of every male in the family.

"The daughter, the sister, the mistress fainted. He picked her up, laid her across his horse, and took her back with him to the mountains."

"What has become of her?" the Duchess of Lavello asked. "Has anyone heard?"

"Alas, madame, I have no choice but to speak to either the shame or dishonor of your sex, for in truth I am not sure which it is. Love proved to be stronger than blood. She had loved Il Bizzarro when he'd been the victim of her father and brothers, and she continued to love him after he became their murderer. From that day on, the brigand band began to organize itself as an army, and, dressed as a man, she would ride alongside Il Bizzarro, her courage and daring matching his own in that tumultuous brigand war."

"No one has ever been able to capture that wretch?" the duchess asked.

"Two thousand ducats have been put on his head, madame. But so far, not one single spy has ever betrayed him. He has always escaped from every trap set for him."

"Well, Comte Leo," said Manhès, "in your place, I give my word as a soldier, I would have his head or lose my good name."

"I shall keep my name, and I shall have his head," Leo said simply.

"When that happens," the Duchess of Lavello said, "I shall allow you to kiss my hand."

CXII

In Which the Two Young Men Part Ways, One to Return to Service under Murat, and the Other to Request Service under Reynier

≈∴≈

THE DAY AFTER THE DINNER, Manhès and Comte Leo accepted Joseph's invitation to hunt boars in Asproni, which they preferred to the smaller game available around Capodimonte. They killed a dozen and brought them back in a wagon so they could distribute them among the soldiers, who'd appreciate the meat.

Saliceti was proud of Naples, and he insisted that the two men stay for five or six days to take advantage of the pleasures the city had to offer. He himself accompanied them on some of their outings.

They visited Nisida, the villa that had belonged to Lucullus. They went to Pozzuoli, which had been the capital of Campania before Naples, and to the temple of Serapis, the remains of Caligula's bridge, and the Lucrine lake, which had been partially buried by the 1538 earthquake. They went to the Averno, on whose banks Aeneas picked the golden branch that would open the gates of hell for him. They visited the Acheron, where not flames but muddy waters flow for oysters and clams to find their habitat.

Taking a pleasant road lined with green trees and yellow heather, they reached the sea at Misena. It was there that the Romans were keeping their fleet when Pliny the Elder, the admiral, left by boat to get a closer look at Vesuvius and got suffocated by sand somewhere between Stabia and Pompeii. Later they visited Baiae, where Cicero had a villa, although he said it was in Cumae because the baths at Baiae had a bad reputation. Nearby was Bauli, with its earthenware bell tower glistening in the sun. There Nero pretended to make peace with his mother; as they parted, he kissed her breasts, which, according to Tacitus, is the greatest sign of respect and attention a son can give his mother. When Nero's plot to drown her went awry, Agrippina, without a cry, without a call for help, swam to her house in Baiae, where her slaves rescued her. An hour later Anicetus arrived to finish what had been begun, and these were her last words to her executioner and for her son: *"Feri ventrem"* ("Strike me in the womb!"). Thus would she be punished for giving birth to a parricide.

On the other horn of the crescent formed by the port of Naples, they went through Portici, Torre del Greco, and Castellammare, so named for its fort, which is falling into ruins in the middle of the Sorrento Bay. Then there was Cape Campanella, the point closest to Capri, where it was no longer possible to go because it had been in English hands for a year.

In spite of the risks to travelers going through the forests of La Cava to visit Salerno, the men could not resist their desire to see Paestum, where they wrote their names on monuments dating from ancient Greece, already in ruins during Augustus's day. In the middle of the thorns and giant grasses that protect those marvels of antiquity, René had all the trouble in the world finding just one of those roses that used to be sent to Naples by the basketful so that Lucullus and Apicius could have rose petals for the tables. As they came out of the thorn bushes, a serpent took fright, its golden coils slithering out over the dark paving stones in one of the temples and then disappearing over the cella. The serpent might have been the divinity protecting the ancient holy place.

They stopped in Salerno to visit the tomb of Pope Gregory VII, who, after persecuting the father of Henry IV of Germany, was himself persecuted by the king. Before dying, he ordered that the following impious epitaph be inscribed on his tomb: "I loved justice, I fled iniquity, and that is why I am dying in misery and exile."

Too soon, Manhès and the count had to thank Saliceti for his warm hospitality and leave the lovely city of Naples. Leo and Manhès had to leave each other as well; they swore eternal friendship as companions at arms and parted ways.

Saliceti had invited Leo to wait and travel with the first detachment going to Calabria, but the count was not a man to take precautions when it came to protecting his own life. He had been ordered to report to General Reynier, but all communication had been cut, so nobody knew exactly where the general was. However, he was almost certainly either in Amantea or Cotrone. René told the minister simply that wherever General Reynier was, he would find him.

"All you have to do is give your name," said Saliceti, "and he will realize he needs to discuss how best to use you."

The Duchess of Lavello tried to give René her hand to kiss, but he bowed to the charming woman instead: "Madame, such a favor must be a reward and not an encouragement," he noted.

René climbed on the excellent horse he found saddled and waiting for him outside Saliceti's house; Saliceti told him in confidence that the horse was a gift from King Joseph. Dressed in an officer's uniform, with his rifle at his saddle and his pistols in his belt, and with no concern for caution, René rode off by himself.

If René gave his horse a couple of hours rest during the heat of the day, they could travel ten hours a day. They reached Salerno on the first day,

Capaccio on the second. There, René learned that travel would become more difficult, and not only because the roads were more tortuous. Numerous bandit groups, *comitive* as they were called, had separated the French army from Naples, and they were the ones preventing all communication between the capital and the general. Furthermore, the English General Stuart had brought five or six thousand troops along with three or four hundred convicts into the Gulf of Sant'Eufemia.

It had been a long day. René needed to reach Lagonegro, and since he had seen no houses along the road, René thought it wise to put some chicken and bread in one of his saddlebags, and a bottle of wine in the other.

He set out at five in the morning, as day was breaking, and at eleven he found himself at a crossroads with three roads to choose from. That was the first complication he had been warned about, but René was counting on that lucky star Fouché liked to talk about to be his guide.

He dismounted. Within reach of his right hand he lay down his rifle, his pistols, and the bottle of wine; on his left he placed his chicken and bread. Then he sat down and began to eat; he was as placid as a picnicker in a park in Asproni or Capodimonte. Of course he was meanwhile hoping to meet some peasant either kind enough to show him which road to take or calculating enough to agree to guide him all the way to the French army.

He was not disappointed. He had barely cut into his chicken and drunk only a quarter of the wine when he heard a horse coming. The rider looked like a miller, as he appeared to be white with flour. He had a handkerchief over one eye, and his wide-brimmed hat hid half his face.

René called out to him. The miller stopped his horse and contemplated René with his one good eye.

"Comrade," said René, "are you thirsty?" He held up the bottle.

"Come have a drink. Are you hungry?" He pointed to the chicken.

"Come have something to eat." The man just looked at him.

"You don't know who I am," the man said, finally.

"But you know who I am," said René. "I'm a French soldier. If you can tell me which road I should take to get to the army, we are even. Or better yet, if you would like to earn two or three louis, you could guide me there."

"I am not hungry or thirsty," said the man. "But I will be your guide."

"Good."

The peasant stayed on his horse. René continued eating. When he had finished, he put the bottle, the bread, and what was left of the chicken together on the ground, for the first hungry traveler who might pass by. He put the pistols back in his belt, he tied the rifle back on his saddle. He climbed onto his horse. Holding out a coin to the peasant, he said, "Go on ahead. Here is a down payment."

"No, thank you," the man said. "If you are pleased with me, you can pay me all at once."

The peasant started off, and René followed. Although the man's horse didn't look like much, it began a rapid trot that pleased René, as he'd rather not be delayed by a slow guide. They reached Lagonegro without incident. Along the way, though, René had noticed that the guide had spoken occasionally with men who'd suddenly appear from the woods and disappear as quickly. No doubt his guide was native to the area, and the men in the woods were other peasants he knew; so René assumed.

René had worked up a good appetite, and he requested of the innkeeper an excellent supper both for himself and for his guide. He asked the guide to wake him up at daybreak; he wanted to spend the following night in Laino or Rotonda, and that would mean another long day to cover ten leagues.

The day passed like the one before. The miller's horse set a good, steady pace so they could cover two leagues an hour. Again the miller frequently met men he knew, usually as they approached a ravine or bluff or when they reached the middle of a woods. He would exchange a few words with the men, and then they'd disappear.

The next day, instead of taking the highway, if indeed there were any roads in Calabria in those days that could be called highways, René's guide went off to the right, and, leaving Cosenza to their left, they reached San Mango, where they would spend the night. They were now no more than a few leagues away from where the French army was camped, along the Gulf of Sant'Eufemia, René learned. He also noticed that his inquiuries were answered with some insolence. And his host's eyes were not very friendly.

René met his host's cold gaze in a way to remind him not to try anything foolish. The host respectfully handed him his key and a tallow candle, for there were no wax candles in that part of Calabria.

René went up to his room. The key was useless, as the door was held closed by nothing more than a string around a nail. The bed was mean. He lay down fully clothed, after he had carefully put his rifle and pistols within reach on the table.

He had been lying there for perhaps an hour when heard footsteps in the next room. Then the steps were coming closer to his door. Expecting it to open, René picked up one of his pistols and aimed it at the door. The door shook, but it didn't open.

With one hand René picked up his candle, and with his pistol in the other, he opened the door himself. There was a man lying against the door. He turned, and René recognized his guide.

"For the love of God," the guide said, "don't go out."

"Why not?" René asked.

"You would be killed before you could take ten steps."

"And what are you doing here?"

"I am protecting you," the guide replied.

René went back to bed. He was pensive, but he soon fell asleep. It suddenly occurred to him—after all the time he'd just spent with the man—that he'd heard that voice somewhere before.

CXIII

General Reynier

GENERAL REYNIER, whom René was seeking to join, had become part of General Dumouriez's staff in 1792 as an engineer. Soon an aide-de-camp, he had participated in the famous campaign in Holland when hussar regiments captured enemy ships by charging over the frozen Texel. He had been promoted to brigadier general, and then he had been named chief of staff in the Army of the Rhine led by Moreau.

In Egypt Bonaparte had entrusted a division to him: it was one of the square formations that were victorious at the Battle of the Pyramids. Once Cairo was taken, General Reynier was given the responsibility of pushing Ibrahim Bey back to Syria and taking command of Charki Province, during which time he won the esteem of the Arab people. When Bonaparte left Egypt, the command of the army went to Menou, as a favor, though by rights it should have gone to Reynier. The army grumbled.

Then, for no apparent right reason, Menou had Reynier arrested. He put the general on a frigate and sent him back to France; he gave no explanation. On his arrival in Paris, Reynier found himself out of favor with Bonaparte, who jailed him in the Nièvre.

Strong, proud personalities like Reynier's often did not sit well with Napoleon. However, he did restore Reynier to his former position during the 1805 campaign, and after the Battle of Austerlitz Napoleon put him in command of the army that was poised to invade the Kingdom of Naples in support of his brother Joseph.

King Joseph had been placed on the throne with absolutely no opposition, with much thanks to his brother and none to the Neapolitans. In his letters to the Emperor of the French, Joseph noted his pleasure with the way the Neapolitans had welcomed him, some of them with great enthusiasm, he said. Joseph was easily taken in by appearances. Opposition did come, and many troops were needed for the long siege of Gaeta, which had afforded former Bourbon supporters time to organize. It had also given bandits an opportunity to make their common banditry seem noble. They had formed bands and begun so-called political attacks that in reality were nothing more than excuses for pillaging and exacting personal revenge.

To aid Joseph, Reynier was sent to Calabria with a seven- or eight-thousand-man army. Not one town and not one band of brigands dared stand before him. He reached Scilla, he reached Reggio, and in both places he set up garrisons. By then, however, the refugees in Palermo, by whom we mean King Ferdinand and Queen Caroline, had had time to make contact with the English, eternally their allies against the French. The English began by sending money, powder, and guns to the rebels along the Calabrian coast, while organizing their fleet in Messina as a more effective means by which to intervene.

Not only was the threat of the English landing on the coast hanging over Reynier's head, then, but also every day rebel bands under leaders like Panedigrano, Benincasa, Parafante, and Il Bizzarro were overtaking his men, in ambushes, killings, and skirmishes. And for a month now English agents had been landing in Calabria and using every means possible to rouse people to insurrection. Without much success Regnier had sent out several columns to track down the English agents.

Then the English fleet sailed out of the Messina straits. Immediately Reynier wrote to General Compère, whom he had left with two battalions between Scilla and Reggio. Compère was to dispatch only enough soldiers to guard the castles and the hospital in Scilla and Reggio and then with the rest of his men join up with Reynier near the Angitola River. He also sent couriers to all the other regiments spread out here and there in the region with the same message: to come back to the Angitola.

When he got to Monteleone, Reynier learned that during the night the English had landed near Sant'Eufemia. Three Polish companies had tried to resist the landing but, suffering great losses, they had been pushed back across the Angitola. General Digonet had meanwhile stopped at the Lamato River with a company of Polish grenadiers and the ninth regiment of chasseurs.

With approximately four thousand five hundred men, Reynier set up camp above the Angitola. From the high plateau he was holding, he could look out over the Gulf of Sant'Eufemia. The enemy, numbering perhaps six or seven thousand, had not changed position since landing. On Reynier's right they had set up batteries near the base of the tower at the Malta bastion; on the left they established their presence in the village of

Sant'Eufemia. Reynier sent patrols to Sambiase and Nicastro, but when they saw the English, they rebelled and, holding up their red cockades, went down to join the enemy. Throughout the day, other reinforcements had been streaming down from the hills to Sant'Eufemia, brigand bands of twenty, thirty, forty men.

As Reynier watched all the activity in Sant'Eufemia from the plateau, he realized that the longer he waited the stronger the English would be. He decided, in spite of fewer numbers, to attack the English either on the following day or the day after.

Consequently, on the very day that René reached Amantea, Reynier came down from the heights above the Angitola to take up his position near the Lamato River, near Maida. From there he would be able to attack the enemy at its center, between the mountains and the sea, and at the same time be out of the range of fire from the guns of the bandits camped near the foot of the mountains as well as from the guns on the ships patrolling off the coast and extending the enemy lines out into the sea.

The evening before, René's guide had told him that the French army was only a few leagues away and that he would be able to join them the next day. So at daybreak he was up and armed. When he opened his door, he found his guide leaning against the wall, as ready as he was.

The guide motioned for him to keep quiet and follow him. He led René not to a door but to a window, where a ladder awaited. The guide went down first.

There were two saddled horses by a small gate in the back. The guide took his mount. "But," said René, seeing that the guide was getting ready to leave, "I believe we still need to pay for our lodging."

"That has already been done," the guide replied. "We must not waste any time." His horse set off at the same steady trot as before.

At about eight in the morning they reached the summit of Sant'Eufemia. From the mountaintop they could look out over the gulf; they could see the two armies and the fleet. Off on the horizon lay a long blue line, the coast of Sicily, and on the waters were five or six dark spots, with flames and smoke rising from a sugarloaf mountain on one of them—surely, Stromboli and its archipelago. René paused for a moment to take in the spectacle, in all its beauty and horror: mountains, forests, the sea, islands, a gulf with golden sand beaches, and, scarcely a league apart, two armies ready to massacre each other.

"Here we are," said the guide. "There are the French, and over here are the English, whose landing we heard about yesterday."

René reached into his pocket. "And here," he said, "are six louis instead of the three I promised you."

"No, thank you," said the guide. "I still have half of what you gave me when you left the Vicaria prison." René looked at the man in surprise.

The man took off his hat and loosened the cloth that covered half his face. Although he had cut off his beard and moustache, René recognized the bandit he had arrested in the Pontine Marshes. "What? It's you?" he asked.

"Yes," the bandit laughed.

"You managed to escape?"

"Yes," he replied. "The jailer was a friend of mine. Chance brought us together, and I remembered what you had done for me."

"What did I do for you?"

"You could have killed me, but you spared my life. I was dying of thirst, and even though I never asked, you gave me something to drink. I had no money, and, as you were leaving me by the prison doors, you slipped a louis into my hand. I might be a brigand, but I am also a man. I in turn have kept you from being killed several times these past few days. So now we are even."

The bandit set off not at his customary trot but at a gallop. He was out of sight before René recovered from his surprise. He shrugged, and said to himself, "You never know where in the devil gratitude might pop up." Then he looked back down at the beach where the battle would take place.

There was substantial movement toward the sea in the English ranks, and René thought for a moment that they might be returning to their ships. Then they separated into two columns but kept moving toward the river's mouth. One column waded across to the other side. A gunship, a frigate, and several launches with small cannons moved along beside them. The ships turned to the right toward the area above the Lamato River; it appeared that they intended to keep the French from using the Monteleone road. The column that had crossed the river meanwhile started back up the right bank, toward the French camp.

From where he was standing, René could almost count the men in both armies. The English must have had, counting their brigand allies, about eight thousand men. The French had only five thousand.

Nonetheless, General Reynier no doubt figured that it was a good time to attack. With the English troops now on both sides of the Lamato, it would be easier for him to crush their center with a vigorous charge. Once he had severed the chain of command between the two columns, the one deployed along the coast could probably escape by boat, but the column that was trying to outflank Reynier on his left would have to take refuge either in the swamps or in the forests around Sant'Eufemia.

If Reynier crossed the Lamato, there was nothing to prevent him from making a frontal attack with his infantry, light artillery, and cavalry, made up unfortunately of only those hundred and fifty men from the 9th Regiment of Chasseurs. If he allowed the English to cross the Lamato, however, he would lose all his advantages, for he would be forced to fight either in a ravine or a swamp, neither of which would allow him to maneuver his artillery and horses.

René, now only about a quarter of a league away, saw that General Reynier was sending two companies of light infantry as a skirmish contingent to slow down the English column that had waded through the river. At the same time he was sending two regiments totaling about twenty-five hundred men across the Lamato to prepare for battle there. They were being followed by the fourth Swiss battalion and twelve companies of the Polish regiment, another fifteen hundred men. Finally, the 23rd Light Infantry Regiment, under the orders of General Digonet, was being dispatched to the extreme right, and the four light infantry guns along with the hundred fifty chasseurs on horseback, to the center.

General Reynier ordered General Compère to place himself at the head of the first regiment and to march by echelons on the English; the Swiss and Polish would make up the second line. The 23rd Light Infantry Regiment, which had moved too far to the right, would come back closer to the Swiss and concentrate its efforts at the center of the English lines, just as General Compère was doing.

It was the first time René had watched a battle being launched and executed. He was so fascinated that he could scarcely move—and in any case, what difference would one man more or less make in such a fray?

The two attacks were carried out with efficiency and precision. When the English saw the French advancing, with General Compère at the head, they stopped within gunshot, arms at the ready but holding their fire. Then the first regiment sounded the charge and began to run toward the enemy; the 42nd regiment followed their example. General Compère, with his two aides-de-camp and his lieutenant, had placed himself between the two regiments.

When the French were only about fifteen yards away, both the first and second lines of the English army began to fire. But the French kept advancing, and when the English in the third line passed their loaded guns to the front, Compère's regiment met a second volley of fire point-blank. General Compère dropped to the ground; he'd been shot in the head and one arm.

At the sight of their fallen general, the soldiers in the first regiment turned and ran, an action that prompted the 42nd to stop advancing. René realized that panic might overtake the entire army. With no thought for any danger other than the steep slope, René turned loose of the reins. His horse's hooves seemed to skim over the ground, and he found himself in the midst of the fleeing men with a pistol in each hand.

His first efforts were directed toward stopping the rout, but when the retreating soldiers began to threaten him with their guns, he turned his attention to General Compère. His wounds had not been fatal, and the English were trying to carry him off the field of battle while his aides-de-camp were trying to protect him.

Two shots from René's pistols and rifle helped clear the path around the wounded general. Having no time to reload, René hung his rifle back on his saddle and put the pistols in the saddle holsters, then, without dismounting, picked up a cavalry saber and charged straight at the five or six Englishmen attempting to take the general. René could wield the saber as well as he could the sword, and in an instant three of the Englishmen were either dead or wounded. The other three fled, though one of them was killed by one of the general's aides-de-camp. René took advantage of the respite to reload his weapons.

Reynier too had rushed into the midst of the fleeing soldiers, mingled now with the general's hundred and fifty cavalrymen. From up where Reynier had been standing, he had seen René gallop to the battlefield and enter the fray. He had watched with astonishment. At first he could not determine by the uniform whether the horseman was in fact in the army, so he had hesitated. Then he'd decided that whatever the uniform, it surely covered a brave man's heart.

"Take command of these men," Reynier shouted without hesitation to René, "and give it your best effort."

"Do you accept me as your leader?" René called out to them.

"Yes," they responded with one voice.

René placed his hat on his saber and dashed forward into the midst of the English soldiers. He threw his hat down in their ranks and with his saber felled an Englishman. "Twenty louis to the man who brings me back my hat!" he shouted to his men.

Inspired both by courage, René's as well as their own, and by the hope of a reward, René's men tore through the first two English lines. But they were unable to advance any further.

His saber between his teeth, René pulled out his pistols and shot two men. He slid the pistols back into their saddle holsters and once more took up his saber. "Come on!" he shouted; then, sticking the saber point into the hat, he said, "It looks like I'm the one earning the twenty louis!"

The English had closed ranks behind him. Having already broken through the first two lines, he now burst through the third by knocking

down two men. He found, however, that he was the only Frenchman behind the English lines.

From a group of officers on horseback gathered around General Stuart,
two started riding over toward René. Clearly, they were challenging him to
a duel, but the duel would pit two against one. René pulled his horse to a
stop and raised his rifle. He shot one of the horsemen when he was fifty
yards away and the other at twenty. Both fell.

A third horseman left the group. Swinging his saber, he headed toward
René while René, his rifle reattached to his pommel, rode straight for him.
Like Homeric heroes or medieval knights in the early days of chivalry,
René and his adversary offered a spectacle in which both combatants displayed amazing courage and marvelous skill. After ten minutes of intense
fighting, the Englishman suffered a cut on his right hand, and with the
point of René's saber resting against his chest, he had no choice but to surrender.

"Monsieur," he said in excellent French, "will you allow me on my word
to go back to speak to the general?"

"Go ahead, monsieur."

René took advantage of the moment to reload his weapons and reholster
them before the English officer returned. His right arm in a sling, in his left
hand he was holding up a white cloth at the tip of his saber.

"What does the white handkerchief mean?" René asked with a laugh.
"Are you coming to talk me into surrendering?"

"I am coming to ask you to follow me, monsieur. And so nothing unfortunate will happen to you as you go back through the English lines to rejoin
your army, General Stuart has given me the charge of opening up our ranks
as you pass."

"Does General Stuart perchance think that I could not have opened
them up myself?"

"He has no doubt that you can, monsieur, but he so much wants to be
certain you pass through unharmed that if you refuse me as your guide, he
himself will come to guide you."

"Thank you all the same," said René. "I would not want to inconvenience him for so little. Proceed, monsieur, and I shall follow."

Meanwhile the battle had been decided. General Compère had been captured, the major leading the first regiment had been killed, the Swiss major
had been seriously wounded, as had the 23rd regiment's chief. All communication with Monteleone had been cut, and the French army was in open
retreat. The English army decided not to continue the pursuit through the
Lamato valley.

When the two men reached the English army, René's guide shouted out,

"By General Stuart's orders, stand and present arms!" The soldiers obeyed, and René rode between two lines of soldiers presenting arms.

They reached the point in the valley where the English vanguard had stopped. "Monsieur," René said to his guide, "no one but you can appropriately carry my thanks to General Stuart. I release you from your word, on the condition that you thank him warmly for me."

After bowing to the prisoner he had taken and just released, René galloped off and caught up with the French rearguard. They did not stop until they reached Catanzaro, six leagues away.

CXIV

In Which René Sees that Saliceti Was Not Mistaken

RENÉ HAD TAKEN UP his bivouac in the middle of what was left of the 9th Regiment of Chasseurs, with whom, under Reynier's orders, he had charged the English infantry. The good men who had followed him and seen how boldly he had penetrated the English ranks and then disappeared, had thought he was surely dead. So when he'd reappeared they had shouted with joy. They all shared their straw with him so that he could make a bed, and they gave him some of their food for his supper. He was grateful for the loaf of bread, of which he gave half to his horse. He spread his coat over a handful of straw he'd pulled together. Then he slept.

At daybreak the next day he was awakened by one of General Reynier's aides-de-camp, who had been sent to collect the young man wearing a navy lieutenant's uniform who had fought so valiantly the day before. He was not difficult to find as he was the only man wearing a naval uniform in the army camp. René got to his feet, stretched, mounted his horse, and followed the aide-de-camp to the town hall, where Reynier had set up his headquarters.

When René walked into the council room, now Reynier's office, the general was bent over a large map of Calabria on which every house, tree, swamp, and ravine were marked. Candles that had burned down to their rings and empty oil lamps were signs that he had worked all night.

René was announced as "the officer you have been looking for," and the general immediately turned toward René, straightened up, and raised his hand in greeting. "Monsieur," he said, "yesterday I saw you demonstrate such courage that I have little doubt you are the man recommended to me by Saliceti and by someone even higher up. You are Comte Leo, are you not?"

"Yes, monsieur."

"You told Saliceti that you wanted to speak with me about how you might serve in my army."

"And he assured me, General, that since what I am asking is bound to help our cause, you would grant it to me."

"You must be hungry," Reynier said. "For I presume that you found little to eat around Catanzaro. We shall have breakfast together. That will give us plenty of time to talk."

Two soldiers appeared with a table. On it were four cutlets, two chickens, one of those cheeses called *cacciocavallo* that hang from the ceilings of groceries in Calabria, and a bottle of Calabrian wine.

"I have spent the night," the general said, "writing to all my lieutenants that they should concentrate our forces on Catanzaro. When the news of yesterday's defeat spreads, all Calabria will rise up. When I got back here yesterday, somebody had already taken the initiative of replacing our national flag with a white one, and the tricolored cockade with a red one. During the night I had the mayor and his deputy arrested. They have probably already been interrogated, and if they had anything to do with such misprision, they will be shot this morning. Today I shall be writing to King Joseph. If you can see any resources that I fail to in our current predicament, please do not hesitate to tell me, and I shall do what I can to remedy the situation."

"General," said René, "you do me too great an honor, for I am neither a strategist nor an engineer. Besides, since I got cut off from the regiment and was caught in the middle of the English army yesterday, I was able to observe very little."

"Yes, I have heard that you brilliantly fought three English officers, killing two of them and taking the other prisoner. I've also learned that Sir James Stuart was so impressed by your courage that protected you from his own troops' fire and even ordered that you be escorted through an honor guard instead of running you through a gauntlet. So go ahead and eat, young man. Brave deeds can make a man hungry."

René did not wait to be asked twice; he turned to the food like a man who had spent an entire day in battle with barely a bit of bread to eat. Reynier continued: "Everything I myself saw and everything I've heard about your initiative and courage yesterday have convinced me to ask you seriously how you would like to work with me."

"If you really want to know what I've been thinking, General, I would like to lead a company that would be free to move as it needed to scout out the territory. I would be not only its leader but its master as well. For the company, I would select from among the best marksmen, and I believe we would be of great service. You were speaking about bandits who might rise up—well, would it not be wise to set some light troops up against those bandits who suddenly fall upon us and then quickly disappear? I have heard about two or three such bandits from Saliceti himself, and one of them I have vowed that I myself would capture."

"Tomorrow," Reynier said, "you can begin acting upon your vow. How many men do you need?"

"Neither too many nor too few," René replied. "Forty or forty-five men should be sufficient."

"Tomorrow, then, you yourself will select them from among our best marksmen. It will not hurt that news of your special company gets around. You must already have inspired terror among our enemy, and that will only be compounded when they hear about your men's exceptional skill at shooting. You will be free to attack whatever band you choose and to pursue it until you wipe it out, for a man like you with a company of forty-five soldiers will be able to go anywhere. You will also be my aide-de-camp, and when I have important orders to issue, I shall do so through you."

"So I shall be allowed to choose my men?"

"Whom will you choose?"

"Simply the best marksmen. And since I shall be running them relentlessly hard and exposing them to more danger than their comrades," René continued, "I would like to be permitted to increase their pay."

"I have no problem with that, except that it might create jealousies and even attract my entire army should you be rich enough to afford all my forces. In any case, we now have a good opportunity to attack the brigands, since our defeat will attract them like crows and jackals."

"Will you please order, General, that every report you receive about any famous brigands be sent to me as well?"

"You can be sure of that. Choose your men, have them practice their shooting skills, and may God be your guide! As for me, no reinforcements can reach us before two weeks are out, no matter how much they hurry. But with the five or six thousand men I can gather together, I can hold out against all of Calabria. And the English will never dare come inland to attack me."

"General, since we have come to an agreement, please announce a shooting exercise for tomorrow. Have each regiment send you its fifty best marksmen, each with three cartridges. The best shot will win a gold watch, the second a silver watch, and the third a silver chain with a pendant at the end. I shall choose my forty-five men from among all those marksmen. In addition to their regular pay, I shall add a daily bonus of one franc."

"Will you be able to bear the expense for a long time?"

"For as long as I am with you, General, and I would like that to be as long as possible."

The general had each regiment beat their drums and make the announcement that the following day each was to send fifty men to the practice field. The three prizes, which Comte Leo, as he was known by the officers and soldiers, had managed to find in Catanzaro, were incentive enough to make the sharpshooters eager to compete.

The shooting competition took place the next day. To demonstrate that he was not unworthy of leading skilled marksmen, Comte Leo first picked up a gun and put three bullets in the bull's-eye. Otherwise, four hundred marksmen had shown up. Fired at a distance of a hundred and fifty paces, fifty-three of their bullets hit the red circle surrounding the bull's-eye. The men who'd fired the closest shots were to be selected; but since three of the fifty-three shots in the red circle had in fact been René's, it turned out that there were exactly fifty men. All fifty were enrolled as chasseurs serving under Comte Leo. They came to be known as the Lion's Chasseurs.

The three prizes were distributed to the winners. The forty-seven others who had placed their shots in the red circle were given five francs each. And every man who participated in the competition received one franc.

When he got back to Catanzaro, Leo introduced the three winners to General Reynier, who promoted the first to sergeant and the two others to private first class. René then introduced the other forty-seven who would make up his company, as well as the men whom they'd competed against. So that they could consider the day truly a holiday, the general relieved them all of any duties and invited them to enjoy themselves as long as they maintained discipline.

Then he motioned to René that he had something to tell him. A peasant had just arrived bearing the news that the town of Cotrone had fallen into the hands of two bandit chiefs, Santoro and Gargaglio. General Reynier had the peasant repeat the news to René; then he turned and said, "You see, it's beginning."

Of course, retaking Cotrone did not fall in the sphere of René's responsibility, for he could not effectively undertake a siege with only fifty men. General Reynier instead sent some militia men under a major's command, and they gave the bandits no time to catch their breath. They were able to take the outskirts of the town easily enough, so the enemy was forced to hole up inside the walls. Still, the next day the bandits had the audacity to sally forth, but they were beaten back and suffered substantial losses.

On the third day the major hoped to be able to take back the town. Two English launches came near shore, however, and their presence encouraged the brigands. The French attempted two sorties, but both were repelled. It was when the English delivered four big cannons and helped the brigands hoist them up on the town's walls that the French realized they would actually have to besiege the town. The major sent word to General Reynier, who in turn sent General Camus and a company of soldiers to take charge of the siege.

That done, Reynier summoned Comte Leo. "How are things going with your company?" he asked.

"It is organized and working very well. All I need now are orders."

"Have a seat," the general said. "I have some orders for you."

CXV

The Village of Parenti

"I HAVE JUST RECEIVED some bad news, my friend. A company from the 29th Regiment, which was crossing the Scilla mountains from Cosenza to join us here in Catanzaro, had to go though the Scilla forest. That is where Parenti is located, and it is one of the most infamous bandit villages in the two Calabrias.

"The principal Bourbon supporters in the village, with a famous Basilicata bandit presiding, deliberated for a long time in trying to decide whether they should set up an ambush or whether they should trick the French into coming into town and then slit their throats when they least expected it. Attacking in broad daylight an armed detachment of eighty men, each of them with twenty-four cartridges in their pouches, was of course dangerous and gave them pause. So they decided to trick them.

"The bandit chief's name was Taccone, but because of the cruel horrors he had inflicted upon the French in 1799 as well as in 1806 and 1807, he had been given the nickname Il Boja, the executioner. He went out to meet the French regiment with three or four other townsmen. After introducing himself as a captain of the national guard and the townsmen as his lieutenants, he extended to the French soldiers an invitation, supposedly on behalf of the village, to enjoy the locals' food and hospitality.

"The captain had been told not to trust the local people, but he and his officers, with typical French trust, let themselves be taken in by the false offers of hospitality. They unwisely had their men lay down their weapons just outside the village hall where the refreshments were to be served. Inside, the French soldiers, giving little thought to their safety, had only begun to eat and drink when a pistol went off. It was a signal. Banditti began shooting everywhere.

"The captain and his two lieutenants, all in the same room, fell dead, and when the soldiers burst out of the building, the peasants were waiting for them, with the regiment's own guns trained on them. Most of them were shot from point-blank range.

"Only seven soldiers managed to escape. They arrived here in camp last night, and they are the ones who brought the horrible news."

"Ah!" said René. "That Taccone has to be taught a lesson."

"Yes, my friend, but first you need to hear more about the man you will be dealing with. Taccone is not, in spite of what the story I have just told you might suggest, a man of trickery and deception. He has often fought our bravest soldiers, and thanks to his advantageous positions, his knowledge of the terrain, and the protection of darkness, he has almost as often defeated them. Even when he's not been able to beat them outright, he has been able to trick them by some new strategy.

"In the middle of heavy shooting, if the terrain affords him enough cover, he sometimes signals his men to flee, and they scatter and flee in different directions. And when our own soldiers try to pursue the wily mountain men, it always turns out like that old story of the Horace and the Curiace brothers. The bandits suddenly turn around, each of them attacking one of our panting soldiers. They're barely over the surprise when they find they've already been struck by a bandit's bullet or blade. Then the bandits are again gone. Not even the devil can catch up with a man from Calabria once he has fled into the mountains.

"Taccone is the most valiant and the cruelest of the whole band, and those are the two qualities that give him authority over his men. Among such savage brigands a captain's title is never usurped; a man who rules in the mountains is worthy of ruling.

"What's more, of all the men in his band, none is faster afoot than he. You'd think that Homer's light-footed Achilles had bequeathed his golden cloak to him, or that Mercury had attached to the brigand's heels the very wings he used when he was carrying Jupiter's messages. He races like the wind, he leaps like lightning.

"One day, when our soldiers had mounted a fierce attack against him in a wood, it looked as if he would put up fierce resistance. Instead, taking advantage of the darkness, he suddenly disappeared like a ghost into the shadows. His men evaporated as quickly as he, and the next day they all reassembled just outside the walls of Potenza, having taken paths that everyone thought were impassable except by chamois and wild goats.

"Please note, my dear Comte, that Potenza is neither a village nor a town; it's truly a city, with eight or nine thousand inhabitants. When they saw Taccone's band, which appeared to have dropped from the sky, and when they heard Taccone's thunderous voice, all eight or nine thousand people hurried back into their houses and locked their windows and doors. They never even considered resistance.

"Then King Taccone, as he was called before he became Il Boja, sent a herald into the city. He ordered all the civil, religious, and military authorities, on pain of their death and the destruction of all their property by fire, to appear before him immediately. Not an hour later you would have seen a strange spectacle. The magistrates, preceded by the clergy and followed by all the populace, were coming forth in a procession to pay homage to a bandit chief. They got down on their knees and with clasped hands begged for mercy.

"Taccone let them wait for a moment in their humiliating positions, and then, with the magnanimity of Alexander raising back up Darius's family, he said, 'Get back to your feet, you miserable creatures. For my anger would be wasted on you. Woe to you if I had come at a less opportune moment, but today I defeated my enemies with the help of the Holy Virgin, so my heart is open to mercy. As this, then, is a day of celebration and joy for all the just, I do not want to besmirch myself with your blood, although your loathsome opinions could well encourage me to spill it. Don't think you're getting off scot-free, however. Because you rebelled against your king, because you renounced your God, within one hour you will pay the tax that my secretary will set for you. Now go; get back to your feet and send messengers into the city so that a celebration worthy of my victory can be planned. All of you here will join me; you will sing praises all the way to the cathedral, and there, Monsignor will chant a *Te Deum* to give thanks to the Most High for our feat of arms. Now stand up and get moving.'

"Holding olive branches in their hands, the people began singing sacred hymns along with the bandits. Taccone rode to the cathedral on a horse covered with bells, feathers, and silk caparisons. The monsignor chanted the *Te Deum*. The tax was paid. And when the brigands left, they took with them a treasure more precious than silver or gold.

"For as the victor entered the city, his head held high, he kept looking into the doors and windows as if he was searching for something hidden in the houses. The women, always eager to watch such spectacles, were especially keen to see this one because it was as unusual as it was unexpected, and a girl at one window timidly lifted the curtain, her face radiating youth and beauty. The bandit stopped his horse and stared at her. He had found what he was looking for.

"The girl, as if she realized that she was lost, took a step backward and covered her face with her hands. Taccone whispered something to two of his men. They went into the house.

"Taccone was leaving the church when he was approached by an old man. It was the girl's grandfather—her father was dead—and he had come to propose paying a ransom for the girl. He was willing to pay any price, he said. 'You miscomprehend, old man,' said Taccone. 'I do not trade on my heart. Your granddaughter is beautiful, and I love her. It's her I want, not your money.'

"The old man tried to stop Taccone, but the bandit struck him with his fist. He knelt down before the bandit, pleading, and Taccone kicked him over backwards. The bandit king climbed back on his horse and had the girl, in tears, laid across the saddle. At a walk, with nobody daring to oppose him, Taccone left the city, and with him left the young virgin who had never known a kiss other than her mother's. The girl has not been seen since in Potenza.

"When he left Potenza, Taccone headed for Baron Federici's castle. Federici was openly hostile to the Bourbons.

"Although the attack was a surprise, the baron had time to gather together some of his vassals and close the castle gates. He was attacked furiously, and he defended himself with rage. The combat lasted from morning till nightfall, and at the end of it a large number of enemy bodies lay at the foot of the baron's walls. Unfortunately, as Federici realized already that evening, if the combat were to continue at the same intensity the following day, the castle's defenders would run out of ammunition.

"The bandits greeted dawn with a terrifying salvo. After taking a city without firing a single shot, they found being thwarted by a simple fortress to be humiliating. They could see that resistance was going to be fierce, because the baron's courage was an inspiration for the peasants, who shot well and shot only when they were sure of their targets. The peasants posed a real danger to the bandits, except that their ammunition was beginning to get low.

"So the peasants were ready to listen to the bandits' proposals. They assumed the bandits would probably be satisfied by some money and would then withdraw without pillaging the castle and killing its defenders. 'Surrender, Lord Baron!' they cried to Federici. 'If we capitulate, we can set our own conditions, but if they overrun us, we are all lost, along with our wives and children.'

"'My dear children,' the baron replied, 'do you really think those brigands are honorable enough to respect a treaty? Unless we get help from the outside, we are lost.' But they could see, when they looked out of the highest windows, that the countryside was empty, and they knew that any help likely to appear would benefit only the attackers. For the peasants in the nearby countryside were the brigands' natural allies, and they were always attracted by the prospect of pillage.

"Taccone ordered a general attack. The occupants of the castle watched as ladders went up all around the walls. The brigands' gun barrels glistened; sunlight reflected off their ax blades. Their diabolical battle cries seemed to rise to the sky.

"When Baron Federici saw on the one hand his enemy's preparations for a deadly attack, and on the other his wife quaking, his daughters as pale as death, and his six-year-old son weeping in terror, he was filled with blind, desperate rage, especially when the women searched his eyes to see if any hope remained. Unquestionably, everyone wanted him to capitulate. So even though he did not trust the brigand's promises, Federici sent a messenger to Taccone.

"The bandits made the messenger wait a long time before allowing him to see the general, who was hidden away with the woman he had kidnapped in Potenza. When he did finally see Taccone and spoke of capitulation and a treaty, the brigand burst out laughing. 'Go back to your baron,' he said to the messenger. 'Tell him his castle now belongs to me. So there is no reason to sign a treaty. But the lives of the people in the castle will be spared.'

"The man left. Taccone's men complained that their leader was too generous, but he just smiled and shrugged: 'Who is to say,' he replied, 'that if we stayed here at the foot of the castle walls some outside help might not have come? Do you think that they would surrender if I did not promise to spare their lives? When we get in, then we can decide who will live and who must die.'

"Toward evening the castle gates were opened. Baron Federici handed the keys over to Taccone and then began to leave with his family. 'Where are you going, you scoundrel?' Taccone said, blocking his path. Then he turned toward his men: 'Keep him here while I go look around inside.'

"You can imagine, my dear Comte," said Reynier, "what happened when that horde of killers spread out through the castle's living quarters. All the cupboards were broken into, all the chests were smashed. What they considered to be debris they threw into the courtyard; they piled it up, and onto it they tossed paintings, furniture, anything the brigands could not use. The baron, who'd been tied up by the pillagers, was forced to watch the destruction while he waited to hear Taccone pronounce his sentence.

"Once they were done pillaging, the bandits began to shout, and they stumbled back into the courtyard, half drunk, carrying torches. When they all got back in the courtyard, where some of the bandits were guarding the baron, Taccone went up to his prisoner and put an old hat on his head, to mock him. Jeering, he begged the baron's forgiveness for leaving him in the shadows for so long and called for more light. His cohorts responded by lighting the pyre. Flames tore through the dry wood and leaped high toward the sky like a serpent's flickering tongue.

"'Good God,' shouted Taccone. 'It would be a shame if such a lovely fire burned for nothing! Come, come, my friends. Dance with these ladies. Lord Federici will not think it unseemly that his wife and daughters do the honors of the castle.' And he himself took the hand of one of the baron's daughters. His companions followed suit and grabbed the hands of the baron's other daughter, his wife, her chambermaid, servants, and soon every woman in the castle was dancing by force around the pyre.

"Unable to witness the scene before him any lonter, the baron tore himself from the hands of his captors and threw himself into the fire. In its flames he disappeared. 'Ah,' said Taccone to the baron's daughter at his side, 'what a bad father! He refuses to attend his daughters' weddings. Well, by God, I see no reason to keep the son. Let's have him join his father.' With that, he picked up the six-year-old by one of his legs and threw him on the pyre.

"All the women were raped and thrown in turn into the flames. The only member of the family to escape was the child. Miraculously, he had landed on the far side of the pyre, near an opening to the cellar. His fall cost him no more than a sprained ankle.

"After that barbarity, Taccone became bolder yet. One day he went so far as to send a challenge to a battalion chief who was about to leave from Cosenza with his men. He said he would meet him at a place called Lago, on the road from Cosenza to Rogliano. The officer merely laughed; his military pride would not let him take the threat seriously.

"The battalion received the order to set out, and when they reached a narrow gorge, huge granite boulders began to rain down on them from the cliffs above. The ground beneath them shook as if it were an earthquake, and at the same time the mountainsides began to burst with fire as bullets dispatched by invisible weapons in invisible hands whistled in on the soldiers.

"In less than an hour the battalion had spent its ammunition. Only twenty-three men survived, and two officers named Filangieri and Guarasci. Everyone else perished in the massacre. Taccone had the survivors brought before him.

"'Soldiers,' he said, 'truly your fate is sad, and I would gladly free you if I had not made a vow to Saint Anthony not to spare a single one of you. However, since you are at war, and are therefore fighting not of your own will but because you have been conscripted, I feel pity for you. To receive my forgiveness, though, you must show signs of repentance. And to do that, you must strike down your own officers. If you do so, I swear by the blessed Holy Virgin that I shall spare your lives. But if you refuse, you will all die, officers and soldiers alike.'

"When they heard this proposal, at first the soldiers did not move a muscle. None of them wanted to dip their hands in the blood of their officers. But the two officers realized that their own death was inevitable in any case and that their men might have a chance of escaping if they accepted Taccone's terms. So they begged and even ordered their men to shoot them. After much pleading, the soldiers finally agreed.

"The two martyrs were still in their death throes when, on a signal from Taccone, the brigands pounced upon the soldiers as well, tore off their clothing so it would not be bloodied, and stabbed them all while Taccone looked on.

"That is when people began to call Taccone the executioner." Reynier concluded, "That is the man we need to capture."

CXVI

The Iron Cage

A TOPOGRAPHICAL MAP WAS SPREAD out before the general. René pulled it closer. "I would like to study these roads," he said. "I prefer not using guides, because they might betray me."

The general pointed to the village of Parenti, lost in the middle of a dark area that signified a forest. Through the forest wound one much-traveled road, as well as an almost imperceptible path. "I should point out," the general said, "that there are nearly a thousand men in the village. So it would be impossible to succeed in an attack with only fifty. I shall provide you another hundred men and a captain. They will take the wider, easier road and advance to the village head-on. You will take the path, which leads to the hill above the village, and when you see the head of the column, you will fire into the air as a signal for the attack to begin."

"Am I free to change any of these arrangements?" René asked.

"Anything you like. I have simply laid out general instructions, not a rigid plan."

That very evening, as General Reynier was leaving to bring matters to a conclusion in Cotrone, René, with his hundred and fifty men, set off for

Parenti. When they reached the point, about five leagues from the village, where the path forked off from the road, René asked the captain if he would be willing to let him have his four drummers, as it appeared the captain did not really need them. The captain agreed, and the two groups separated. René asked the captain not to march too quickly, because he and his fifty men had a greater distance to cover on a path that was more difficult to travel than the road.

At four in the morning, just as the sky was beginning to pale in the east, René reached the highest point of the hill above the village. He sent one of his men down through the village to meet the captain; his orders were to shoot into the air when the detachment got within three or four hundred yards of the village. The messenger started down the path ahead of them, which ran dangerously close to the edge of a precipice. A short time later, they heard the signal shot.

Immediately René ordered his four drummers to beat the charge. His men began shouting, "Death! Death!" Together they swooped down on the village like an avalanche. They broke down doors with their gunstocks, although some of the doors were already open when they got there. Villagers were fleeing, among them Taccone himself. He was carrying a woman in his arms.

When René saw a huge man running with incredible speed, he had no doubt it was Taccone. If he aimed at his back, though, he was afraid the shot would go through the brigand's body and strike the woman he was carrying. So he shot the man in the legs. Taccone rolled to the ground, but as he lit he dropped the woman, whose momentum carried her to the edge of the precipice. With a terrible scream she fell to a terrible end.

Taccone got back to his feet, determined to sell his life dearly. It was the first time in his long career as a bandit that he had been wounded. He dragged himself over to a tree and leaned against it, rifle ready. His reputation was such that nobody dared to meet him in hand-to-hand combat. Still, René could easily have finished him off with his rifle, but he wanted to bring him back to Reynier alive.

"Take him alive! Take him alive!" he shouted as he ran toward Taccone at the risk of taking a bullet from the brigand's gun. But René's messenger was too quick to heed his words. He slipped through a thicket of trees and plunged his bayonet into Taccone's chest.

Taccone let out a scream as he fell; he dropped his rifle as if he were dead. The messenger was preparing to cut off his head, now worth a thousand ducats, when Taccone rose up like a striking serpent. He grabbed the man and planted a dagger in his back. The two men expired together; they might have been two brothers, but they embraced each other only in hate.

René let his men cut off Taccone's head and plunder the village of Parenti before burning it. He had no concern for such actions. His job had been to flush and kill the wild boar. He would let the others scramble for the spoils.

The next day he returned to Catanzaro. When Reynier, who had taken Cotrone, returned as well, he saw Taccone's head in an iron cage suspended above the Catanzaro gates. He summoned René.

"My dear Comte," he said. "I learned what happened when I got back to town; the head above the gate spoke on your behalf. As for me, I have received a letter from the king. He has not forgotten us. He will be sending two or three thousand men along with Marshal Masséna. Furthermore, Admiral Allemand and Vice-Admiral Cosmao have apparently left Toulon; they will land in Calabria and take up garrison in Corfu."

General Reynier's hopes for reinforcements were to be dashed, however. As Allemand and Cosmao were leaving Toulon, another English fleet was leaving Messina with the intention of taking Ischia in the same way they had taken Capri. So King Joseph chose to keep Masséna nearby, and all he sent to his general in Calabria were a brigade from his guard and two newly formed regiments, La Tour d'Auvergne and Hamburg, under General Saligny's command.

Thanks to the road that had just been opened between Lagonegro and the La Corona camp, there was now direct communication between Naples and General Reynier's troops. They were also able to move artillery and ammunition along that road.

The objective now was to take Scilla and Reggio, where the English had established garrisons composed partly of English troops and partly of insurgents. Napoleon was pressing his generals to get both cities under control of the French, because as long as they remained in English hands, it would be impossible for him to invade Sicily. Reynier began to move his troops toward Scilla.

René joined Reynier with his column of sharpshooters, as he had requested and been readily granted, since his fifty men had proven they could shoot sparingly yet never miss their targets. On their way to the heights above Scilla, they engaged in a few skirmishes with partisan bands prowling in the area. During one of them, an incident occurred that affected René directly.

Reynier's troops had taken a dozen prisoners, and since they were bandits, their fate had been decided immediately. A firing squad was already loading its guns to shoot them, when René, who was just passing by, heard someone from among the prisoners call out for Comte Leo. As he walked toward them in order to better see which man had called out to him, one of the bandits stepped forward. "Excuse me, Monsieur le Comte, but before dying I would like to bid you farewell."

The voice was not unfamiliar, and when René looked more closely, he recognized the bandit from the Pontine Marshes, still with a cloth over one eye and still dressed like a miller, who had guided him to the French army on the day of the battle at Sant'Eufemia. "Good heavens," he said, looking around and taking in the situation, "I think you were not unwise to call out to me."

René took aside the lieutenant in charge of the platoon. "My good man," he said, "can you grant me the favor of deciding the fate of this man who just spoke to me? Or must I make my request to General Reynier?"

"Well, Monsieur le Comte," the lieutenant said off-handedly, "one bandit more or less makes little difference to King Joseph. Besides, you no doubt have your own good reasons to ask for this man. In token of the admiration we all have for your courage and patriotism, you may take him."

René shook the lieutenant's hand in thanks. "Might I offer something to your men?" he asked.

"No," the lieutenant answered. "They would unanimously give the man over to you, but not one would agree to sell him."

"Indeed," said René, "you are fine men, my friends."

"Untie the man," the officer said to his soldiers.

The bandit stood mute in astonishment. "Come with me," René said.

"Wherever you go, I am your man." The bandit gladly followed René.

When René and his prisoner had gotten away from the firing squad, now ready to do its work, René said, "There's the mountain on one side, and there's the forest on the other. Choose, for you are free to go."

The bandit thought for a moment. Then he shook his head, and emphatically, with a stomp of his foot, he said, "No indeed! I prefer being your prisoner. I have seen the Grim Reaper a score of times. I've faced a pistol, the rope, and ten guns, and every time I've found the Reaper a cuss so ugly that I'd prefer having nothing more to do with him. Let me stay with you. Let me be your guide; you know how well I know the trails. Or you need a servant, I shall be that servant, and I'll take care of your weapons and horse. But I have had my fill of forests and mountains!"

"It's a deal," said René. "You can come with me, and if things work out as I expect them to, you will be rewarded instead of punished."

"I shall do my best," the bandit promised. "And if I do not give you everything you deserve, it will not be for my want of trying."

The French troops reached their destination. From the hilltop they could look out over Scilla, the coast of Sicily, Reggio, the Lipari Islands, and off on the horizon lay Capri's hazy outline.

In the hills, the roads had become impassable for the artillery because there were so many mountain streams cascading down from Aspromonte. They would be difficult to cross with heavy guns. General Reynier brought his staff together to discuss how they might deal with the situation. There were various proposals, none of them acceptable. And they needed to find a solution quickly as they were under fire from several Sicilian gunboats near the shore, some of which had come to anchor near Pampinello.

The gunboats were shooting with such accuracy and intensity that General Reynier finally had no choice but to set up some of his own artillery. Within a half hour, his twelve-pounders were able to rake the boats' decks and pound them into submission. Yet they were making no efforts to sail out to sea. So the general shouted the order for them to surrender—three times he shouted it—but to everyone's surprise, nobody appeared on deck to acknowledge it.

The general had just ordered his gunners to sink the boats when René walked over to him and whispered a few words in his ear. "Indeed," said the general, "you may be right." His artillery held fire.

And René, who had been talking with his bandit, threw down his coat and shirt and ran to the water, for he had realized why the English hadn't responded to General Reynier's orders. He swam out near the boats and called out for them to surrender—in English. Immediately they struck their colors. Each boat was carrying twenty men and a twenty-four-pound gun.

General Reynier came down to meet the young man, now dripping wet.

"You always give good advice, René," he said. "Go change your clothes, then come help us figure out a way to get our artillery within range of Reggio."

"General," said René, "I was in fact just thinking about that. If you give me leave for twelve to fifteen hours, I hope to come back to you with good news."

"Go ahead," said Reynier. "Experience has taught me that it is better to give you a free hand than simply to ask for your advice."

Ten minutes later, two peasants who seemed to be coming from Il Pizzo passed near the general and disappeared into the mountains. The general had thought they might be spies and had been about to order his soldiers to take them, when one of the peasants had doffed his hat to him. The general recognized René.

CXVII

In Which René Comes Upon Il Bizzarro's Trail When He Least Expects It

～:～

THE TWO MEN WERE INDEED René with his new servant as his guide. They had set out to see if it might be more effective to dam the mountain streams up at their source rather than trying to do so further down the mountainside. When they reached a point below Aspromonte, they discovered a road they could easily travel all the way down to Reggio; in fact, the road got even better as it descended. A week's work would surely enable them to transport their battery and set it up within cannon range of the city. Now all they needed to do was take the good news back to the general.

Night had meanwhile begun to fall. Alone, René would never have been able to find his way, but with his adept guide he had no concerns.

At some distance from the road, where they were hidden by underbrush, they sat down at the base of a tree and, relaxed, started in on their supper. As they were eating, René suddenly felt his companion's hand on his shoulder. The guide held his finger up to his mouth for silence.

René kept silent, and together they listened. They heard the tread of heavy steps, and it sounded as if something—or someone—cumbersome were being dragged along. They heard voices, harsh, and protests.

Then they saw five men, and two others who had been gagged and bound, and now were being dragged across the ground to a tree that was apparently strong enough to serve as a gallows. The bound men could not doubt that their captors intended to hang them. Their muffled cries of protest were proof enough.

René squeezed his guide's arm. "Don't worry," the guide said. "I know those men."

Once nooses had been slipped around the captives' necks, one of the five men, who appeared to be a muleteer, climbed up in the tree and tied the ropes to two branches. With the help of his comrades, who pushed while he pulled, in less than ten minutes he'd hanged the two men.

Not a breath had come out of René's mouth, though he'd had the utmost repugnance for the hideous scene.

When they had made certain the hanged men were no longer alive, the executioners parted ways. Four continued on toward Reggio; the fifth was about to start back the way he had come when René's new servant rushed out from the woods and called out to him: "Orlando?"

This Orlando had not actually participated in the hanging, but he had watched it with keen interest. He grabbed his dagger and turned toward the voice. "Ah," he said, "it's you, Tomeo. What in the devil are you doing here?"

"I'm not doing anything except watching what you're doing."

"I hope you have not gone honest," Orlando said with a laugh.

"Well, in that you hope in vain. Or at least I'm doing everything I can to change. But what did those two poor devils do to get their necks stretched like that?"

"They were two wretches who did not respect my signature. I had given a safe-conduct to those four muleteers, now on their way, as you see, toward Reggio. In spite of the promises Il Bizzarro and I had made to respect each other's signature, his men stopped the muleteers and robbed them. So the muleteers came back to me and asked for justice. 'Take me to Il Bizzarro,' I said. And they did. 'Brother,' I said to him, 'your men did not respect my signature. I need to set an example, a terrible example.' Il Bizzarro had me tell him the story while he kept drinking. 'Punish the guilty men, but do it quickly, my friend. You know I don't like to be bothered while I'm eating.' I called my muleteers who were waiting outside the door. They identified the thieves, and Il Bizzarro turned them over to me. You see what I did with them."

René had also come to the forest edge and had heard what Orlando had said. "Have a drink with us, comrade," René suggested.

Frightened or startled, Orlando turned around to see a man holding a bottle by the neck. He looked at his friend, who indicated that he could trust the new actor who had just appeared on the scene.

René held out the bottle after taking a few swallows himself so that Orlando would have no doubts about the bottle's contents. Then he asked for some details about his friend Il Bizzarro.

Orlando, who found the wine to be good, saw no reason not to share with his host what he knew about Il Bizzarro. Indeed, he gave René more information than he might have wished, and since the hour now was getting late, René reminded his companion that they had to get back to General Reynier. The three men finished off the bottle and, shaking hands, said good-bye. They left behind them the tree heavy with the cursed fruit that had appeared so suddenly on its branches.

Two hours later René was back in camp. At dawn the next morning he went to report to General Reynier. The general, already awake, was lying in bed worriedly studying a map of Calabria.

"General," René said with a laugh, "don't worry about those maps. I have found a path on which your cannons will be able to roll as easily as if they were on a billiard table. Within two weeks we can begin to bombard Reggio, and in eighteen days it will be taken."

The general leaped out of bed. "I don't doubt your word, my dear Comte," he said. "But things like that are worth seeing with my own eyes."

"Nothing simpler, General. Get dressed. I shall gather my fifty men, and if the place I lead you to is suitable, we can summon the rest of the army. Here we shall leave only as many men as are necessary to occupy Scilla."

"And what if only the three of us were to go?" Reynier wondered.

"Ah! As for that, General," the young man replied, "I don't want to take on such a responsibility. With my fifty men, I can guarantee your safety. But if I am only one man of three, while I can guarantee that I will die before you, that might not necessarily be of any help to you, so I think it is better to follow my original plan."

Fifteen minutes later, after General Reynier had dressed and left his quarters, he found Comte Leo's fifty men waiting with their rifles ready. He glanced over all the equipment. "My good man," he said to René, "you surely understand that with all this equipment there is no way to keep our expedition secret. So come have breakfast with me, and I shall have some wine distributed to your men."

Within half an hour they had set out. Tomeo took a different path than the one they had followed the day before; it was easier for the horses. At about nine in the morning they reached the top of Aspromonte. They calculated that once they'd managed to get the cannons to Maida, they could follow a road that led to the top of the mountain, and by descending from the mountain crest at Aspromonte they could then reach Reggio. General Reynier's experienced eye told him there was no other way to do it with their siege artillery. His young lieutenant had once again proven his invaluable inventiveness.

Back at camp, the general ordered part of the troops to bivouac on the heights; the others would remain near the coast to keep the English away. As soon as René saw that the engineers and the artillerymen were well at work, he asked General Reynier for permission to take a two-week leave.

"If it is a secret," General Reynier said, "I don't want to force you to tell me. But if it is something you can confide in a friend, I would like to know what you intend to do."

"Oh, heavens!" said René. "That is the simplest thing in the world. Imagine that I am dining with Saliceti, His Excellence the Minister of War, and the conversation turns to a brigand chief by the name of Il Bizzarro. Horrible stories are related about this monster of a man, and then imagine that the Duchess of Lavello, the minister's daughter, exacts from me the promise to send to her his head. I have been thinking constantly about that promise, but I'd not heard any real news about the man until yesterday. Since it appears he is a tricky rascal, I am requesting two weeks, though I cannot guarantee that even two weeks will be enough for me to capture the fellow."

"How may I help you during these two weeks?" Reynier asked.

"Well, General, you could be so kind as to have an elegant box made of olive wood and oak roots, then engraved with the Duchess of Lavello's initials, so that we can send her Il Bizzarro's head in a proper receptacle."

CXVIII

In Pursuit of Bandits

SINCE THE DAY René had sworn to send Il Bizzarro's head to the Duchess of Lavello, the bandit had been flushed out of Cosenza and had gone into the far reaches of Calabria, where the Scilla forest provided him refuge. He had wasted no time furnishing new proofs of his ferocity. Il Bizzarro dealt so harshly with townsfolk and the poor peasants that although they normally sympathized with the bandits and their cause, they began to turn against him.

Not only did he elicit the hatred of the local people, he also ensured the loyalty of his band. Not one of his bandits would ever dare to betray him to the law, for he made certain that they participated in his every crime so that they could not hope ever to be pardoned. For example, when a young shepherd who had been forced to help some soldiers track Il Bizzarro was captured and killed by the bandits, each one of them had to sink his knife in him. Even after the forty-ninth knife, the shepherd was still alive . The fiftieth knife thrust, Il Bizzarro's own, finished him off. Then the butcher had the boy cut up into as many pieces as there were members of his band; the flesh was barely dead when it was put into a huge cauldron. Every man was forced to partake of the shepherd soup and to swallow a chunk of the meat.

Il Bizzarro had two huge mastiffs. He starved them for three days and then threw to them two officers, naked and weaponless, from the Monteleone national guard. They offered a spectacle like those in ancient times when Christians were forced to combat ferocious beasts. At first the officers tried to flee, but when they saw it was impossible to escape their ravenous enemies, they turned and attacked. They tried to rip off the dogs' legs, they tried to trade bites for bites. But the dogs' fearsome teeth tore deeply into the poor fellows' flesh, while their own teeth could barely get through the animals' coarse hair.

Inhuman acts of cruelty like these had Il Bizzarro declared an outlaw. All Calabria swore to do what it could to bring him down.

Tomeo never had served under Il Bizzarro, or even met him. Tomeo, like many, was a bandit by profession, and he practiced his profession honorably with pride. He would steal, yes, and he might even kill if necessary, but he would never commit gratuitous crimes. So when René asked for his advice, Tomeo was quick to put himself at René's disposal to help capture Il Bizzarro.

First they needed to find out where exactly Il Bizzarro was hiding at the moment. Because he himself had worked in the Scilla forest for a time along with a famous bandit named Parafante, Tomeo expected to be able to locate Il Bizzarro in perhaps three days. But by the next evening Tomeo was already back.

He had come across an old woman weeping at the foot of a tree. When he spoke with her, he discovered she was the mother of the young shepherd Il Bizzarro had tortured and killed so hideously. On learning the reason for Tomeo's inquiries, the old woman vowed to give herself body and soul to help him and avenge her son. They arranged to meet two days later, at which time, she promised, she would bring more detailed information about the brigand's whereabouts.

On the appointed day René gathered his fifty men and confidently followed Tomeo. The old woman was waiting at the prescribed place. With great precision she explained for Tomeo and René the place where Il Bizzarro was planning to spend the following night. Once Tomeo was sure they had all the essential information, he and René withdrew.

René took up position with his fifty men. When night fell, they lit their torches and began to beat the bushes. They found no one, although they did manage to scare up some frightened birds and a few wild animals. They did, however, come upon the spot where Il Bizzarro had camped. Hot coals still glowed in the campfire. So Tomeo and René knew that their information had been correct. René's fifty men must have been too large a group not to have been detected by the bandits.

René made another attempt. This time, Il Bizzarro and his men were where they were supposed to be, only sentinels posted around his bivouac gave the alarm. There was some shooting, and one bandit was killed, but no further results. However, news of the hunt began to spread.

For some time, Il Bizzarro had been essentially the king of the region. When Reynier had been beaten at Sant'Eufemia and forced to withdraw back into the Basilicata, he had left that part of Calabria in the hands of the brigands. That is when Il Bizzarro had made his triumphal entry into Palmi—people still talk about it—and that is when he'd attained the height of his glory.

Walking at the head of a hundred men on horseback and a large number of bandits on foot, he'd been welcomed by the authorities and the clergy under a magnificent tent. They'd led him to the church amidst a great throng of people who had come from miles around. They'd sung a *Te Deum* in honor of his legitimacy. The celebration had ended with the shout: "Long live the king! Long live Marie-Caroline! Long live Il Bizzarro!"

The triple acclamation had made more than a few freethinkers smile.

⁂

[*This is where the serial ends. The final section was delivered on October 10, 1869. Claude Schopp, editor of this novel, proposes the following conclusion to the current episode:*]

His Tarpeian rock was not far from his Capitol. The man who had been king was now nothing more than a fugitive.

The bandit's outrages were now being answered by the people's hatred, for they had endured too long his cruel, violent acts. The civil guards had sworn never to lay down their arms until Il Bizzarro was dead.

René and Tomeo no longer had to go looking for information; it came to them. For five or six days they managed to stay on the bandit's trail, but always, at the last minute, he'd been able to slip away. Morning after morning they found the remains of his camp, sometimes warm coals—and sometimes the mutilated corpse of some brigand: Il Bizzarro, no doubt suspecting the man of treason, must have killed him and left the body to his dogs.

As they continued to follow Il Bizzarro's trail, they began to see, from the remains in his campsites, that his supplies were getting low. Like an Indian on the prairies, Tomeo would carefully examine what they'd left behind, whether it was a footprint or a stray scrap of food. He had concluded at one of the most recent campsites that only three people were left in Il Bizzarro's band, two of them a child and a woman. No doubt, as Taccone had done before him, Il Bizzarro had chosen to have his band scatter. Consequently, René decided to base his soldiers in Maida and to continue on alone with Tomeo; otherwise, surprise was impossible.

Some peasants had recognized Il Bizzarro on the road between Maida and

Vena. His meager band had likely taken refuge in one of the many caves along the mountain slopes. René and Tomeo reached a plateau near the crest and decided to spend the night there, in the shelter of some rocks bathed in the light of a bright moon as in a painting by Salvador Rosa. They planned to continue their search the following morning. After sleeping for an hour or two, René felt someone shaking him. Tomeo had his hand cupped to his ear. He motioned to René to listen carefully.

And indeed, René was soon able to distinguish some moaning sounds somewhere off in the distance, and then what sounded like growling. "Might that be an owl or some other nocturnal bird?" René whispered.

"No, it's a baby!" said Tomeo, and René remembered that the poor shepherd's mother had told them Il Bizzarro's young companion had recently given birth.

René quietly got to his feet. He and Tomeo started down toward the sounds, down through the rocky labyrinth. When the moaning stopped, they could only guess in which direction to go. Often, just when they thought they were no more than a stone's throw away from the bandit's hideout, they would hear a cry or growl again off in the distance. Suddenly, the sounds ended completely.

The following morning, no matter how hard they looked through the rugged terrain, they could find nothing. Yet they were sure the bandit was hiding somewhere in that rocky wilderness. They spent six nights there, and day after day they searched for the bandit's lair, but with no success.

On the seventh night René gave up. He decided they would go back to Maida the following day. But during the night he was awakened by the muffled sound of a shot that echoed in the distance off the rocky earth. René and Tomeo were on their feet immediately.

Heavy black clouds were rolling in, and soon they covered the moon. In the black night, René and Tomeo wandered around for about an hour; they slid over sharp stones, climbed rocks hanging out over chasms. A damp, hot wind blew up, and they were soon drenched with sweat. When they heard two more shots from about two or three hundred yards above them, they thought they were about to reach their goal. Struggling to find footholds in the rocky cliff, they began to inch their way up. Suddenly, the storm broke.

You have to have experienced a storm in southern climes to have any idea of how wind, rain, thunder, hail, and lightning can ravage nature. René and Tomeo were forced to give up their climb and drop back down to the base of the cliff. They tried to follow narrow paths that overlooked steep precipices, but soon they were themselves enveloped by scurrying clouds. Dazed by lightning, deafened by thunder, threatened by swollen mountain streams, they finally had no choice but to defer to the storm. In the raging winds and deep shadows they lost all hope of finding Il Bizzarro.

Resigned, they started back toward Maida under a driving rain that soaked them to the bone. The clouds, driven by the warm sirocco, left their faces and hands covered with sweat that quickly turned cold. They had to wade up to their knees through the raging torrents. Near morning they could hear people shouting; they saw some torches. Their men camping near Maida had begun to worry and come out looking for them.

They went inside the only inn in the village, a simple thatched-roof house that itself was shaking in the gusting wind. Through a large crack in one wall they could see the lightning flash. A fire was lit in the fireplace, where the innkeeper began roasting a skinny chicken on a hazel spit. He heated some towels for René and Tomeo to wrap themselves in. He spread the only available white tablecloth over the table and on it set two chipped plates.

Once René had warmed up a bit, he tore into a skinny chicken leg, only to be distracted by the soldier standing guard at the front door. He told René that a woman was asking to see him; she said that she had news of Il Bizzarro. "Bring her in," said René.

The woman came in, her long black hair and ragged clothes dripping wet. She was carrying something wrapped up in a large cloth with the four corners tied together. She stared at René, her gaze intense.

"Are you bringing me news about Il Bizzarro?" the young man asked.

"I've brought you something even better," she replied somberly.

She placed her bundle down on the floor, untied the four corners, reached in, and pulled out something that was difficult to identify in the room's dim light. She walked over to René, who was sitting at a table near the hearth. She was holding a head by its long hair. She placed it, still covered with blood, on the table near the plates.

René could not hold back a sensation of disgust. He stood up quickly.

"This head is worth a thousand ducats," the woman said. "Pay me."

René took two steps toward the fireplace where his uniform was drying over the back of a chair, and took some gold coins from his belt. He threw them down on the table beside the revolting head. The woman counted them one by one, placing them in an apron pocket as she did so. When she had finished, she started toward the door.

René called her back. "You are soaked and must be exhausted. Are you hungry?"

"Very hungry," she replied.

"Sit down here by the fire," René said.

He told the innkeeper to give her what was left of the chicken and sat down beside her. She fell upon the chicken he placed before her. Soon there was nothing left but the bones.

"Why did you kill him?" René asked.

Without a tear, her voice calm, she stared into the flames and related her tale of the bandit's death.

Surrounded as he was on all sides, Il Bizzarro thought he had found a safe refuge in a cave that only he knew about. The cave was indeed perfectly hidden from view, its entrance so small that you had to inch along on your stomach to get inside. And once you were inside, the opening could be concealed with moss, lichens, and briars.

The bandit had sent away his last two companions, so it was just him, his woman, and her child. But the baby had suffered a great deal in their wanderings. He was not well; he cried when he was awake and moaned even when he slept. "Woman! Woman!" the bandit kept repeating, "shut your child up. In truth, I believe it was given to us not by the Lord but by the devil to deliver me to my enemies." The woman would give her breast to the baby, but she had no more milk, and the poor child was always hungry, crying and complaining.

One evening the woman could not keep the child quiet, and the dogs were beginning to get nervous, as if they could sense men prowling about nearby. Il Bizzarro got to his feet. Without a word, he grabbed the child by one foot, tore him from his mother's arms, and smashed his head against the cave's rock wall.

"My first thought was to leap on that tiger and strangle him with my bare hands! I swore by the Madonna that I would get revenge," the woman said.

But she didn't say a word. She got to her feet, picked up the baby's body, wrapped it up in her apron, put it back in her lap, and mechanically began to rock it as if the baby were still alive, though her body was trembling and her eyes were burning.

The next morning, the bandit left the cave to scout around; he took the two dogs with him. With a knife, the woman then dug a small grave in the cave floor. She buried her child and placed her bed directly over the grave so the dogs would not be able to dig up the body and devour it, which they surely would have done if she had buried her child outside.

During her sleepless nights, the poor woman would converse in a whisper with her child, separated from it by only a layer of Scotch broom and a few inches of earth. She would promise the child vengeance, and then she would think about the poor parents she had left for a life of adventure with a killer, and she would tally all the suffering she had endured without complaining—her only reward being the murder of her baby. She realized, too, that she herself would soon be killed, when her own lack of strength endangered the killer.

So, the night before she appeared in the inn, while the brigand was sleeping, exhausted from his efforts to find some food that day, she as usual was watching over her baby's grave. She murmured a few words that sounded like a promise, kissed the ground, got to her feet, and walked like a ghost over to the bandit. She leaned over and listened to see if he was really asleep. His breathing was regu-

lar; he was still sleeping soundly. She straightened back up. She picked up the bandit's loaded rifle and checked to see that it was properly primed and the flint was in good condition. She put the barrel to the sleeping man's ear. Then she pulled the trigger.

Il Bizzarro did not even cry out. His body responded with a jerk, and he fell facedown onto the floor.

The woman picked up her knife and cut off his head. She wrapped it in her apron, which was still bloody from her baby's wounds. She took the bandit's two pistols and put them in her belt, then crawled out of the cave.

Before she had covered a hundred yards, the two guard dogs attacked, eyes bloodshot and hair bristling. They sensed that something had happened to their master and that it was the woman's fault. With two shots she killed them both.

"And afterward I came directly here. I stopped neither to eat nor to drink."

CXIX
The Duchess's Hand

That very day, under a sky cleansed by the storm, René and his sharpshooters left the village.

René had bought a mule from the innkeeper, and Tomeo had carefully tied a wicker basket to its back. In the basket was Il Bizzarro's head, again wrapped in the apron with the four corners tied together. Led by Tomeo, the mule walked ahead. The soldiers followed a hundred yards back, as if, in terror, they preferred staying as far away as possible from the head of the man who had committed so many odious crimes and caused such ill fortune.

René had asked Tomeo to lead them toward Reggio, as he wanted to learn if General Reynier had taken the city during their expedition. If he hadn't, they would perhaps get there in time to help retake Reggio. After their defeat in Maida, the Bourbon soldiers, with the support of the English, had massacred the small garrison in Reggio, shouting, "Long live King Ferdinand."

"You absolutely must take Reggio and Scilla. How shameful it is that the English are able to maintain a foothold on the continent. I cannot allow that to continue. So take the necessary steps," the Emperor had written to his brother Joseph. Reynier, in his eagerness to redeem himself for his defeat, had no doubt hurried his men, smoothed out the road that René had discovered, and transferred a battery so that it was within easy shot of the city. It was likely that the siege had already begun.

However, when they reached the slopes of the Aspromonte and René looked out over the Calabria coast, he could see no troop movements or any signs that the battle was under way. He noted only a few columns of smoke rising into the blue sky above Reggio. All the way down the mountain road, which now seemed to him as good as the road along the Averno, René kept wondering what was happening.

At an advance post, a sentinel answered his question. "When they heard the first shots from the cannons, all the brigands belonging to the so-called Holy Faith fled like a flock of sparrows. They piled into boats and are on their way to Sicily!"

"How about the English?"

"We never saw them. Milord Stuart and his ships disappeared over the horizon."

In the streets of Reggio the soldiers had stacked their weapons. Some, sitting in the shade on stone walls, had taken out their simple rations and were nibbling at them to make them last as long as possible. Others, at fountains, had taken off their uniforms and were standing nearly naked as they washed, laughing and splashing each other like children.

Five or six houses had caught fire during the bombardment and were still burning. In order to reach the old Aragon castle where, he was told, Reynier had set up his command, René and his men had to work their way through smoking ruins and step over half-burned bodies.

Corpses festooned a tree on the castle square. "They were brigands captured with weapons in hand," said a soldier who was guarding the sinister spectacle. "They are not going to massacre any more of us!"

Inside the castle some officers were sitting at a table finishing a meal that had been prepared for the former occupants, who had simply abandoned the meal and taken flight.

When René was announced, Reynier came to meet him, arms outstretched. "My dear René, you have arrived too late!" he said, embracing him.

"Must I hang myself as Crillon did?"

"No, I conquered without peril. To tell the truth, though you were not here, you are the real victor, for it was you who discovered the road for us to transport the guns for our siege."

"Keep the victory for yourself, General," René replied with a smile.

"You think I need it to get back in favor after my defeat?"

"If that were the case, it would please me to have done the favor for you."

"And how about you, my dear René? How did your own enterprise go?"

"I obtained Il Bizzarro's head without getting even a drop of his blood on my hands."

"Tell me about your bandit hunt, my friend."

So René told the general about his long, fruitless pursuit and about his decision to give it up just when bandit's woman brought him Il Bizzarro's head.

"I would not mind seeing this head, for it was the head that titled itself King of Palmi and made all of Calabria tremble."

Upon a signal from René, Tomeo brought over the wicker basket and pulled out the fearsome package. "So many heads have rolled over the past fifteen years!" Reynier murmured, turning away from Il Bizzarro's grimacing face, whose eyes no one had bothered to close.

"Yes, and by God, some heads that were dear to me," René answered dully. "During my years of forced solitude, I was able to give a great deal of thought to the meaning we might give to these human hecatombs that at first plunged me into despair."

"And what conclusions did you come up with?"

"That the scaffold has been used by some mysterious power you might call God or Providence to destroy any obstacles that people put up to oppose the march of freedom. . . ."

"So Dr. Guillotin would not be simply an accident of chance and his machine an accident of mechanics?"

"No, it arrived at its appointed hour, just like all absolute, fatal things. Guillotin needed to build a weapon for the Revolution. The flaming sword he invented, just like Jupiter's lightning, was made up of twelve rays: three of hate, three of vengeance, three of tears, and three of blood. Just as Saint-Just said: 'The man who, during a revolution, does not dig deep enough is digging his own tomb as well as the tomb of freedom!' General, we are living in revolution's troubled times, and atoms like us have a difficult time living through them."

"We need to forget, my dear René, that this brigand was a man, since through his actions he placed himself among bloodthirsty animals like those you fought in Burma. While you were pursuing him, I kept my promise. Go get Jean," the general said to an aide-de-camp. "Have him bring me what he made."

A few moments later, a soldier and erstwhile Parisian artisan entered the room. "Jean, show this gentleman the masterpiece you made for him," said the general.

The soldier placed before René a large olive-wood box with golden letters. It had been skillfully shaped and polished, and when René opened it, he saw that it was lined with red velvet.

"This is the case I had made for Il Bizzarro's head," said Reynier. "We shall ask the surgeon to prepare the head before you leave. For, my dear René, I am bidding you leave, or rather I am sending you on a mission to Naples. You will announce to King Joseph that we have retaken Reggio."

The next morning at daybreak, René and Tomeo left the castle and set out on the road to Naples. René was mounted on one of the general's finest horses. Tomeo rode the mule, of which he was beginning to grow quite fond; he'd named her Regina.

When they reached Maida, they took the same road they had traveled earlier. Once again they encountered sullen peasants who would suddenly appear from out of the forest, exchange a few hushed words with Tomeo, and then disappear quickly back into the shadowy woods. Every night, for René's protection at the inns, Tomeo would sleep outside his door.

Six days later, early in the morning, they were approaching Naples. As they drew near, they could hear the sounds of the city. Neapolitans are surely the nois-iest people in the world. Churches in Naples are filled with bells, little bells jan-gle on horses and mules, and its lazzaroni, its women, its children, all have throats that seem to have been cast in brass. There is noise everywhere: ringing, tinkling, braying, shouting.

On the Madeleine bridge, a dozen children came up to examine their bags, and Tomeo thought they had gotten a little too close. He shooed them away with the same stick he used to whip his beloved Regina.

René went to the hotel La Vittoria where he was warmly welcomed by Mas-ter Martin Zir. Zir had classified him among those generous travelers who, al-though they are not affluent businessmen, are certainly excellent clients. Scarcely had René cleaned up when an answer arrived to the letter he had sent to Saliceti, in which he had requested an audience as soon as possible with the king. Despite the early hour, he was expected posthaste at the royal palace.

He went immediately and was introduced by Saliceti. The king came forward to greet him: "Contrary to my brother, I would never ask to be awakened except for good news. And I believe that the news you bring is not bad."

"That is correct, Sire. Reggio has been retaken, and with very little shooting. A few cannonballs were enough to make the rascals flee."

"According to what Reynier has written, we have you to thank for finding a way to get the artillery to Reggio."

"If that is what the general says. . . . But I was absent when the city was taken."

"I know. He also wrote that you had gone looking for a brigand who was ter-rorizing Calabria in the name of the Bourbons."

"That particular brigand no longer exists in Calabria. Brigands, though, are a hardy race."

"Now it will be possible to think about invading Sicily," Joseph went on. "We could land seven or eight thousand men to occupy the land near Il Faro and set up our command on that point. We can set off from Reggio."

"Yes, Sire. But first we need to continue building ships in Naples so that we can transport as many men as possible to Sicily."

"You are right. Given the current situation in Europe, we shall have plenty of troops. The Emperor can see to that by sending as many as I request. I have here a letter from him." The king handed René a dispatch written in Napoleon's feverish hand:

> *In Naples, you must always be prepared to board your troops at Mortella with the purpose of taking Il Faro. And you must keep everything secret, for its easy for spies to carry news to Sicily, and indiscretion would expose us to the greatest dangers. Saliceti, a navy officer, and you must be the only people in on the secret, and even the officer you will be sending to Otranto and Brindisi must know nothing about it. You will give him a sealed letter which he is not to open until he learns something extraordinary in Otranto.*

"I need not tell you to keep the secret. . . ."

After they had taken leave of the king, the Minister of Police led René to the grand staircase. *"It is obvious, my dear René, that I must keep you with me for lunch. My daughter the duchess would never forgive me if I deprived her of your tale about Il Bizzarro's demise."*

When, three hours later, René walked into the drawing room at the Minister of War's residence, the Duchess of Lavello was waiting for him along with her father and his Corsican secretary. *"Ah! There you are!"* cried the duchess as soon as she saw him. *"We have been waiting impatiently. May I still call you Comte Leo?"*

René walked over to her and placed the olive-wood box at her feet. *"You may still call me by that name, for I have not lost it. And here you will find Il Bizzarro's head."*

"Here, then, as I promised, you find my hand, Comte Leo."

As René respectfully kissed the duchess's small aristocratic hand, color rose in her cheeks. Then, perhaps to hide her emotion as quickly as possible, the young woman knelt down beside the box and opened it.

She uttered a small cry and fainted the moment before René caught her in his arms.

APPENDIX

[The following three chapters, in Dumas's own handwriting, open a new episode in the novel.]

I

His Imperial Highness, Viceroy Eugene-Napoleon

We know that with the Treaty of Campoformio, all the territory belonging to the former Republic of Venice was given to Austria, and the territory on this side of the Adige was incorporated into the Cisalpine Republic.

The Cisalpine Republic would later become the Kingdom of Italy, to which in 1805 would be added the Venetian territory that the Treaty of Campoformio had granted to Austria.

That is when Prince Eugene de Beauharnais received the title of Prince of Venice, and the territory was divided into eight departments, each with an administrative seat.

Venice was the capital of the Adriatic, Padua of La Brenta, Vicenza of Bacchiglione, Treviso of the Tagliamento, Capo d'Istria of Istria, and Udine of the Passeriano.

Udine is a charming little city on the banks of the Roja River, in the center of a fertile plain. The inner city and the outer city are separated by walls and moats.

That was the city in which the Viceroy of Italy took up residence.

The court was appropriate for a prince twenty-eight years old. It was joyous, noisy, and flamboyant, and it was normal that youth should attract youth. The court was composed of lovely women and their handsome escorts. The men were intrepid, tender, and adventurous; the women were sentimental, in keeping with the times, and they would gather around the piano and sing romances written by Queen Hortense, Jadin the Elder, and Monsieur d'Alvimar.

They would spend their mornings taking walks in the country or hunting and fishing around the Murano lagoons.

They were at peace, everything was calm, and the viceroy's coffers were full. What else was there to do but enjoy themselves?

Since the morning of the preceding day, everyone at the court had been off fishing in the lagoons.

The date was April 8, 1809.

At nine in the morning, a dust-covered carriage drawn by three trotting horses rolled up the steep slope toward the Udine castle.

The castle, formerly the residence of the patriarch at the head of the government of Venice, was now the young viceroy's residence.

The carriage stopped for a moment in the market square. A young handsome officer stepped down to examine the Campoformio Column, erected in honor of the treaty. On it were engraved the treaty's date and praise of the

First Consul's grandeur and magnanimity for having taken territory from Venice. Then the carriage continued on its way and, as we have said, climbed up toward the castle.

When it reached the castle gates, the sentries motioned for it to stop.

"A letter from the Emperor!" two voices called out together.

One voice was that of the young officer inside the carriage. The other was from what looked like a servant from Calabria who was sitting on the coachman's seat.

"Summon the commanding officer!" said the young officer.

An old lieutenant appeared, grumbling.

He was a veteran of the Italian Wars.

"So," he said when he saw the officer, "another one of those young moustaches."

The officer overheard the old soldier's words.

"My good friend," he said with a laugh. "Not every moustache has had the honor of seeing Turkish sabers glisten near the Pyramids or cannons flame at Marengo. My young moustache is jealous of yours."

The lieutenant flushed, for he realized he had just offended a superior. The young officer was wearing the uniform and insignia of a light cavalry major.

"Excuse me, Commandant," the old soldier tried to explain, "as you know, or perhaps you are fortunate not to know, those among us who remain behind normally accuse our leaders of injustice rather than accusing our short legs. But in the end, when you have something like this," he added, slapping himself on the chest where a cross hung, "when you have something like this, you cannot complain."

"You are right, my good man. And you see," the officer said, showing his own undecorated chest, "that in that area I have not been as fortunate as you. But we are wasting precious time. I must speak immediately to His Imperial Majesty, the Viceroy. I am carrying dispatches from the Emperor."

"'I must,'" the old soldier repeated. "That's youth for you, thinking all it has to do is give an order and it will be obeyed. What if His Highness is not in Udine? What if he is hunting, fishing, or just enjoying himself at the lagoons? What about your 'I must' in that case?"

"He is not in Udine? Where is he? Wherever he is, I have to find him. I promised the Emperor that wherever he happened to be, I would find him by noon on April 8."

"In my country, Commandant, we say, 'Better lucky than in love.' I don't know if you have been in love, but I do know that you are in luck. Look over there on the road from Palanova, about a half league away. Do you see that dust rising? The court carriages are on the way back."

"Well then," the young officer said as he leaped down from the carriage, "for the time being my voyage is over. Tomeo, pay off the postilion."

Meanwhile, a large circle had gathered around the carriage, and a palace officer walked up to the major and invited him, in the name of the viceroy who was on his way home, to enter the castle.

The young man reached out and cordially shook the old soldier's hand.

"Thank you, my good man," he said. "I shall never forget the truth you have told me, and if the occasion arises to get a second stripe for your shoulder, I shall request permission to place it there myself."

The old soldier watched him walk away and shook his head.

"Greenhorn!" he muttered. "I think he has just promised to look after me."

And then, with a shrug, he went back to his men.

They took the major into one of the bedrooms and asked what he needed.

"Some water and my servant," he replied.

Five minutes later he had both.

Tomeo (we remember that is the name the traveler had used when calling to the Italian sitting on the coachman's seat), Tomeo opened an elegant silver traveling case and placed its contents on a shelf. From a hidden compartment he pulled out a lovely jewel made with pearls, diamonds, and heron feathers. Then he raised his head to consult his master.

"Yes indeed," his master replied with a smile.

Ten minutes later the young officer was dressed and looked totally different. He had been combed, brushed, and perfumed, as was befitting a true aide-de-camp in society.

He had just given one last twist to his moustache when the carriages rolled into the palace courtyard.

Scarcely had the prince entered his apartments when someone came to tell the traveler that His Highness was ready to receive him.

He put the Emperor's dispatch in his calpac and followed the aide-de-camp who was to introduce him.

Eugene de Beauharnais, whom we saw fourteen years earlier when he was taking fencing lessons in Strasbourg with Augereau, was now a handsome, elegant prince, about twenty-eight or twenty-nine years old.

The two men were about the same age.

They looked at each other with the admiration we feel when we see beauty. But Eugene quickly recognized in the young officer signs of resolve he himself did not have, signs indicating that the person who has received that fatal gift might perhaps be crushed by unexpected events yet will never bow his head.

Eugene greeted him with respect that neither the officer's age nor his rank commanded.

The officer bowed, then walked over to the prince and handed him the dispatch.

"A letter from His Majesty the Emperor of the French," he said, "to His Majesty the Viceroy of Italy, Prince of Venice."

"I'll take it, monsieur," said Eugene. And then he lifted the letter to his lips and opened it. "Paris!" he cried with astonishment. "The Emperor is not in Paris. The Emperor is in Valladolid!"

"Read it, Milord," said the officer.

The prince kept reading, and his astonishment turned to doubt.

"Impossible!" he murmured. "Impossible! The Emperor cannot have better information than I do about what is happening here." And then he turned to the messenger and asked, "Did the Emperor tell you the news you are bringing to me?"

"Yes, Milord. I have come with the invitation from His Majesty for you to prepare your defenses and to tell you that in three or four days you will be attacked by Archduke John."

"Just like that? Point-blank? Without even declaring war? It's impossible that I have not been alerted. He and his Austrians cannot simply be dropping from a hot-air balloon."

"Yes, but if he comes through Tolmezzo and Fella Torte, he can be on your outposts within two days."

"The Emperor says that he has asked King Murat to send a Neapolitan division and that it should arrive in Udine on the eigth or ninth under the command of General Lamarque."

The viceroy rang, and an aide-de-camp appeared.

"Summon General Sahuc right away," he ordered.

The aide-de-camp left immediately.

The two men continued their conversation, for the news the messenger had brought provided several matters of import to discuss.

"Did not the Emperor give you some orders to tell me directly?" the prince asked.

"He advises Your Highness to be particularly careful on all the highways. If your Highness's troops are ready and find themselves in an advantageous situation, they can, and indeed they must, attack. Your Highness must understand how important the first battle is. If it ends in victory, it will hearten the entire army. But if it ends in defeat. . . . We cannot tell what the consequences of a defeat would be."

Eugene wiped the sweat from his forehead with his handkerchief and paled visibly.

"And if my army is spread out, if it does not find itself in an advantageous position. . . ."

"Well then, Milord, the Emperor's opinion is that you should withdraw back over the Tagliamento and set your lines there."

"Begin a campaign by fleeing?"

"First of all, retreating is not fleeing. The reputation of one of the greatest generals of antiquity and of one of the greatest generals of modern times rests on retreating. Retreat for a week. Then stop and fight. Win your battle. And soon you will have regained all the territory you have lost during that week."

General Sahuc was announced.

"Bring him in," the viceroy called out.

"General," Eugene asked while he was still in the middle of his greetings, "do you have any patrols out on the roads?"

"Of course, Your Highness."

"Where?"

"Everywhere."

"Double them. Place a man who can speak Italian in every patrol so that he can question the peasants. The Emperor is warning me—and I am saying this for you alone, General—he warns that we will be attacked."

"Just as I was leaving to come here, I was told that a large group of people is coming from the direction of Venice," General Sahuc said, "but the three-colored flag they are flying indicates that they are French."

"That must be General Lamarque and his division," the prince whispered to the young officer.

"But who could possibly attack us?"

"Austria, of course."

"Without declaring war?"

"That would be just like Austria. In any case, General, the Emperor tells me that the fighting will likely begin between the thirteenth and the fifteenth. Let us not overlook any detail. Send out your patrols, and find out from headquarters where all your soldiers are stationed."

"I shall do so immediately, Your Highness."

"You may go now."

Scarcely had General Sahuc left the room than the maitre d'hotel entered and announced that lunch was ready.

"You will have lunch with us," Eugene said to the officer.

"The Emperor placed me at Your Highness's orders," the young man replied with a bow.

And he followed the viceroy.

II

At Lunch

The double doors swung open and the prince led the young man into a room where the whole court was gathered.

We have already explained what kind of people made up the court. The young officer was dazzled. Never had he seen so many beautiful women and elegant officers gathered in one place.

"Ladies and gentlemen," said the prince, "I would like to present Major René, whom the Emperor sent to me as a special courier. He is highly recommended by the Minister of War. He will be your rival, gentlemen, and your servant, ladies. Monsieur René, I authorize you to give your arm to the princess. Princess, please seat your escort next to you."

The dining room doors had just opened.

For a moment, all were busy finding their places. In the commotion, they all did their best not to get in each other's way. Once all the guests were seated, all eyes turned toward René.

When he had come into the dining room, they all had thought him handsome and elegant. But when they had observed the manner in which he offered his arm to the princess, escorted her to her chair, and bowed to her as he himself sat down, they had been forced to admit that he was also a man accustomed to the finest society.

"Monsieur René," the prince said, "I see that these ladies are eager to know where you come from and what you have done. Come now, tell them about yourself."

"Your Highness embarrasses me a great deal by asking me to so command the conversation. My life is the life of a prisoner, a sailor, a traveler, a soldier, and a bandit hunter. There is nothing very interesting in that."

"What?" said the princess. "You think that is not interesting? It all seems very interesting to me."

"Encourage him, Princess, encourage him!" the viceroy whispered to his wife.

"You were a prisoner?" the princess asked her neighbor.

"For more than three years, Princess."

"Where?"

"In the Temple."

"You were a state prisoner?"

"I had that honor," René said with a smile.

"And what did you expect when you were in the Temple?"

"That they would cut off my head or place me before a firing squad."

"Oh! Who?"

"His Majesty the Emperor Napoleon."

"But now here you are. . . ."

"He determined that I was not worth being guillotined or shot, apparently."

"So he pardoned you?"

"Yes."

"On what condition?" Eugene asked.

"On the condition that I would get myself killed by the enemy."

"It is good you did not fulfill that condition."

"It is not my fault that I did not," said René. He smiled, though it was impossible to see how bitter his smile was. "I did the best I could, I swear."

"But I hope you have made your peace with the Emperor."

"Hmm! We are still negotiating," laughed the officer. "But if I could get a nice wound while in the service of Your Highness, I think that would help my affairs."

The women were beginning to stare at René in astonishment. The men were unsure what to think of him.

"And then?" the princess asked. "Did you enroll as an ordinary soldier?"

"No, madame. As an ordinary corsair."

"Under whose orders?" Eugene asked.

"Under Surcouf's orders, Prince."

"Were you able to make some captures?"

"We took the *Standard*."

Among the prince's aides-de-camp there were officers of every rank and every branch.

"What?" one said. "You were among those bold pirates?"

"We were corsairs, monsieur," René replied proudly.

"Excuse me, monsieur," the naval officer continued, "You were one of those bold corsairs on a twelve-gun sloop with eighteen crew members who captured the forty-two-gun *Standard* with more than four hundred men aboard?"

"Yes, I was, monsieur. And that is when Surcouf, who had already given me the rank of a lieutenant, made me a captain and authorized me to take or buy a small ship and set off on my own."

"If I can believe what I have heard about your courage, it would have been easier for you to capture than to buy a ship."

"Both were equally easy for me, Prince, even if I needed to use my own resources, for my part of the take was five hundred thousand francs. Of course I always gave my share to my comrades, and that is what I did then. In any case, I planned to purchase an American ship and, since it flew a neutral flag, to take it to India. I was eager to hunt tigers, one of my fantasies. I bought a ship, took its name and papers from the captain who sold it to me, and left for the kingdom of Burma."

"And did you hunt tigers?" one of the officers asked.

"Yes, monsieur."

"Did you kill any?"

"Perhaps a dozen. . . ."

"But you must have undergone great dangers?" the princess asked.

"Oh, madame," René replied, "tiger hunting is dangerous only when your first shot wounds the tiger and it turns on you."

"And then?" the prince asked.

"I am going to sound like a braggart to Your Highness," René replied. "But. . . ."

"But. . . ?"

"I found an easy way to avoid the problem. I never wounded them with my first shot. I used my first shot to kill them instead."

"Where would you shoot them?"

"In one of their eyes."

"But then you must shoot like the famous Astor?" one of the guests asked with a doubtful smile.

"No, but I have excellent weapons made for me by Lepage."

"Please excuse my question if I am being indiscreet," said the officer who was questioning René, "but have you often fought in duels?"

"Twice, monsieur. The first with a shark about fifteen feet long, and I slit open its stomach from one end to the other."

"And the second time?"

"Using a boarding cutlass I fought a serpent that was crushing my two elephants."

"It must have been the serpent Python!" the officer said.

"I don't know what its name was, but I do know that it was fifty-two feet long."

René noticed that a doubtful smile was crossing every face, even among the women.

"Your Highness," René said, "ask your honored guests please to stop this inquiry, or else order me to lie. Nature in India is so unlike our own that it is difficult to believe what it can produce."

"But I find all this very interesting," said the princess. "Go on, please go on."

"Do go on, monsieur," the viceroy insisted.

"Yes, yes!" cried the women, always eager to hear about things they thought were impossible."

So René began to narrate his story, happy to avoid their painful questions. He told them about his return to Île de France, his combat with the two English ships shooting at Surcouf, his meetings with General Decaen, and his desire to participate in a great naval combat. He talked about how General Decaen gave him letters for the most famous ships' captains and how, when he reached Cadiz, he chose Lucas. He related how he went on board the *Redoutable* with a third lieutenant's rank, how he participated in the Battle of Trafalgar, how he was taken prisoner, escaped, went back to France, was sent to King Joseph, and remained with Murat.

He had reached that point in his tale when suddenly the announcement came to the viceroy that General Lamarque and his division had arrived. At the same time they could hear drums rolling, then martial music.

The martial music was so stirring that everyone turned toward the viceroy, to ask his permission to leave the table and go to the windows.

The windows were open wide and brilliant sunlight was pouring in. The division from Naples was marching up the ramp leading to the castle, their guns gleaming in the sunlight like the scales of an immense serpent. A long trail of light like that, reflecting the sun even through a cloud of dust and accompanied by the musical instruments and officers' shouts, will always be a magnificent concert and a splendid spectacle for French ears and eyes.

They reached the square in front of the castle, and then the musicians and officers, led by General Lamarque, entered through the court of honor.

When the prince saw so many good men who had crossed Italy to risk their lives for him, his heart, endowed with more goodness than strength, began to beat faster.

He went down to meet them with open arms. He embraced General Lamarque, whom he knew only by a reputation that had been enhanced by his victory on Capri.

For a moment they remained together in the courtyard to decide where the new arrivals would be billeted. The prince asked General Lamarque what he knew about their current situation, since he was coming to help.

But General Lamarque, near Rome, had simply received orders to march rapidly toward the Friuli and to put himself at Prince Eugene's orders.

He had obeyed.

The letter to Murat requesting help had come from Napoleon and had been sent from Valladolid.

That was all he knew.

As we have seen, Prince Eugene himself knew little more than that, except that on April 12 or April 14 the Austrians would attack.

The viceroy ordered the officers to be brought into a lower room where refreshments would be distributed.

As for General Lamarque, he would be introduced to the princess.

The women had moved to the drawing room for coffee. Their curiosity got the better of them, and with typical feminine eagerness and perhaps a touch of envy they examined the jewel with its pearls, diamonds, and heron feathers that decorated René's calpac. At a minimum, it had to be worth twenty thousand francs.

When the prince and General Lamarque came in, the princess herself was holding the calpac. Being a woman, she was just as curious as the others, and she wanted to see up close what the other women were admiring. She was much too used to diamonds and pearls to be dazzled by them, but she was impressed by the way they were set in the aigrette. She was so absorbed in studying the magnificent jewel that she did not see the prince as he came through the circle of women around her and walked up to her.

She gave a little cry of surprise.

"Madame," the prince said, "allow me to divert your eyes for a moment from that lovely jewel to introduce General Lamarque. His name, as you know, carries many meanings: courage, patriotism, and loyalty. His Majesty the Emperor Napoleon has sent him to help us, for you should know, Ladies, that the time for celebrating is past. We are under threat of attack any day now. We shall still have our ball this evening, but tomorrow or the next day there will be different music, music to which only men will be dancing."

General Lamarque bowed to the princess as both a military man and a man of society, for he incarnated the best qualities of the two.

The princess, a little dismayed, remained motionless, with the young officer's calpac in her hands.

"Oh, yes," the prince said, "that's the panache of our young messenger. It must be a gift from some princess, for I doubt that with his salary a cavalry major could afford such jewelry."

"Bah!" a woman said. "A man who can give five hundred thousand francs to his crew. . . !"

"Excuse me," the general said, reaching out his hand to examine the object that inspired such admiration. "I believe I recognize this aigrette."

He looked at it carefully for a moment.

"Of course," he went on. "It belongs to our friend René."

"Do you know the young man?" Prince Eugene asked.

"Quite well," Lamarque replied.

"And what about the aigrette?" the princess wondered.

"It's the one King Murat gave him to use as a talisman; it will open up the palace doors to him at any time, day or night. Is he here now?"

"Yes, indeed. The Emperor sent him here as a special courier. He arrived only two hours ago."

"And otherwise Your Highness does not know him?"

"No."

Just then, René, who had been talking with the aides-de-camp, came through the door into the drawing room.

"May I introduce him to you?"

"Yes."

"Oh," the princess cried. She was as curious as all the other women to find out more about the young cavalry major.

General Lamarque hurried over to René, who gave a cry of joy when he recognized him. Taking him by the hand, the general led him toward the prince and princess, saying:

"I have the honor of introducing to Your Highnesses the victor at Capri!"

"Capri!" the prince said. "But I thought you were the victor!"

"Indeed," said Lamarque, "I did take Capri, but it was this gentleman who gave it to me."

"Oh, Your Highness," said René. "Don't believe a word."

"Quiet, Major!" said Lamarque. "And I order you to remain silent while I am speaking. . . ." And then, with a laugh, he added, "About you, of course!"

"General," said the prince, "please come with me to my study. We have important things to talk about." And then, turning toward René with more deference than he would have shown ten minutes earlier, he added, "Please join us, monsieur."

III
Preparations

A large map of old Friuli was spread out on a table in the prince's study.

The prince walked over to the map and placed his finger on Udine.

"General," he said to Lamarque, "you are a true gift from the Emperor. I need to bring you up to date about the news this gentleman has brought us.

"It appears that Austria is determined to violate our peace treaty and to attack us on the twelfth. I received the warning only two hours ago, and already I have sent orders to our generals to bring as many troops as possible to Udine. But for those coming from Italy it will take more than five or six days to get here."

"Prince, may I ask you who the enemy is?" General Lamarque asked. "Do you know where his troops are concentrated and how many men there are under his orders?"

"My adversary is Archduke John."

"So much the better!" said General Lamarque.

"Why do you say that?"

"Because he is the most inexperienced of the three brothers and is quicker to take risks. He will make some error that Your Altesse can take advantage of."

"Unfortunately," the prince sighed, shrugging his shoulders, "I don't have a great deal of experience either, but we shall do our best. . . . But you asked three things. . . ."

"I asked where the Austrian troops were stationed."

"I thought we were in a time of peace, and consequently I have reduced our surveillance of the enemy. But I believe I am correct in saying that Archduke John is still near the Sava River and the Adriatic. As for the numbers, he must have from fifty to fifty-five thousand soldiers."

"And Your Highness, how many soldiers will you have in all?"

"When they all get here, we can count on forty-five thousand."

"The disproportion is not worrisome. Where do you think the attack will come from?"

"I have no idea."

"Excuse me, Your Highness," said René, joining the conversation for the first time, "but I believe the Emperor told you that he would probably come along the Fella River."

"How can you expect the Emperor, in spite of his genius," said the viceroy, "to guess from Paris what road Archduke John will take?"

"Please excuse me for insisting, but the map suggests the same thing."

"What do you mean?"

"For the Archduke to march straight toward Udine, he will have to cross the Isonzo and the Torre under fire from our soldiers. If he follows the Isonzo upstream, he will come to two bridges in his own territory that will allow him to cross easily. Then he can go through the mountains and reach the Pontebbena, come down into the Glaris Valley, follow the chain of mountains above the mines, and reach La Chiusa, your first outpost. Then he can take La Chiusa as well as Orpi and Osoppo, and his path will be clear all the way to Udine."

The prince looked over to Lamarque as if to see if he agreed.

"That is what I would do if I were in Archduke John's place," the general said.

"Prince," said René, "I have with me a very skillful man, a bandit whose life I saved. Would Your Highness like me to send him out as a scout?"

"He would risk being hanged," said the prince.

"Well, that was just about what was going to happen when I cut him down," said René, "and since that is how he is supposed to end up, little does it matter whether it will be today or tomorrow! But I trust he will manage fine."

"Go ahead."

"I shall give him a good horse. His instructions will be to cross the Chiarzo near Tolmezzo. That is where the enemy probably is, and they may attack sooner than we expect."

"How about money?" Eugene called out when René was already near the door.

"He accepts money from me alone," René replied. "You can rest easy on that score."

And he hurried out of the room.

Eugene looked at Lamarque.

"How about that!" he laughed. "Now that we are alone, tell me more about your René. If we were in the Middle Ages, I would think he must be the godson of some fairy."

"Or the bastard son of some magician. He is as handsome as Renaud de Montauban. He never hesitates, and he always throws himself into every battle, evidently in order to get himself killed, but never manages to do so. And yet he is strangely modest and never speaks about himself unless he is forced to, clearly unlike most of our young men today. The legend goes that he was the man who killed Nelson at Trafalgar. As I was telling you earlier, he is the man who threw himself into the breech with his fifty men and forced Hudson Lowe to surrender. As a corsair, his service was remarkable, and in the Indies he fought like Hercules against fabulous monsters."

"But then why does he have no decorations?" Eugene wondered.

"I don't know. It seems there was a problem between him and the Emperor. He had plotted, apparently, with Cadoudal, and then was saved by Fouché who took a liking for him. At least that is what I have heard from King Murat. Murat saw him in action and, amazed by his courage, wanted René to join his service. But René refused, saying that he would serve no other man but the Emperor and no other army but the French army. When Murat saw that, he sent him to his brother-in-law with the English flag he had captured in Capri, as well as with the news of his victory over the enemy his brother-in-law loved most to defeat—the English."

"And the Emperor never gave him anything, neither for the news he brought nor for his role in the marvelous victory? Normally the Emperor is so quick to recognize courage."

"No. At least there has been no sign of any special favor. He wears the uniform of a cavalry major, but he has always worn unusual uniforms. In Naples, he had fifty men fighting under him. The things he managed to do with fifty men were amazing.

"He surely must carry a talisman, because, although he is constantly trying to get himself killed, he never receives a scratch. It is fortunate that our ladies don't follow the army the way they did in Louis XIV's days. He is like the hero in a novel, and they would all fall madly in love with him."

"There must be a woman involved somewhere," Eugene said.

"Probably so," the general replied.

The door opened. The doorman requested permission for René to enter.

"That is the kind of request a true gentlemen would make," said Eugene.

René came back into the room. "Everything is set," he said. "By tomorrow evening or the following morning we shall have information or my messenger will be dead."

Just then the doorman announced General Sahuc.

The general was holding a handwritten note.

"Prince," he said, "I have just left staff headquarters. Here is a list of where our troops are located around Udine and of the generals in command."

"Tell me," said the prince.

And the prince, General Lamarque, and René leaned over the map as he read.

"'The first infantry division, under the command of General Seran, is in Palmanova, Cividale, and Udine.

"'The second, under the command of General Bouvier, is in Artegna, Gemona, Ospedaletto, Venzone, San Daniele, Maiano, and Osoppo. They are sending detachments into the Fella Valley as far as Pontebba on the Tarvisio road.

"'The third, under the command of General Grenier, is behind the first two, in Pordenone, Sacile, and Conegliano.

"'General Lamarque, with the fourth division, awaits orders concerning his destination from Your Highness.'"

The two generals bowed to each other, and then General Sahuc continued:

"'The fifth, under the command of General Barbou, is in Treviso, Cittadella, and Bassano. The sixth division, made up entirely of Italians and led by General Serteroli, is divided between Padua and Este and a few other points near those two cities.

"'The seventh, also made up of Italians and under the command of General Fontanelli, is gathering in the camp in Montechiaro. Part of the division is still on the way from the Kingdom of Naples.

"'Two divisions of dragoons under the orders of Generals Pally and Grouchy are waiting in Villa Franca, Rovigo, Isola della Scala, Roverbella, Castellaro, Sanguinetto, Mantua, and Ferrare.

"'The principal artillery park is in Verona, but we lack the necessary horses to bring the guns here.

"'The grenadiers of the Italian Royal Guard are in Padua, and in Milan or nearby are the carabinieri, the velites, the dragoons, the elite gendarmes, the horse artillery and the remainder of the Royal Guard.'

"And finally, I and my men," Saluc continued, bowing to the prince, "are ready to die for Your Highness. We are based here in Udine. Our first brigade, on the Torre, occupies a line running from Nogaretto to Vilesi; the second brigade has been sent to Ceneda, Pordenone, Conegliano, Vicenza, and Padua."

The two generals, after relating the information in General Sahuc's lists to the locations on the map, looked worriedly at each other. The thirty or thirty-five thousand men at Prince Eugene's disposal were spread out from the Tyrol to the Grado Lagoon and from the Piave to the Torre.

They sent couriers to every camp. The dispatches they carried warned the generals to be on their guard everywhere. They were expecting an attack, but since no one knew where it would come from, they should wait for the first cannon shots before setting out.

Dinnertime arrived. The viceroy invited General Lamarque and General Sahuc to stay for dinner, but nonetheless René remained the princess's escort. The ladies had paid special care to the way they dressed that evening.

Was it because of the ball and concert that were to finish the evening? Was it because of the handsome, mysterious stranger?

Everything General Lamarque had said about him had raised everyone's curiosity. The idea that an unfortunate love affair was the reason for his pallor and the melancholy cast of his face tugged at every lady's heart.

And indeed, what could possibly compel a man to seek death so obstinately if not an unfortunate love affair, especially when the young man is handsome, brave, and rich?

We know about court etiquette. Princesses choose the men who will have the honor of dancing with them. The princess told René that her husband had authorized her to grant him that favor, but René, with profound regret, explained that he had taken a vow long before never to dance. For anything else, however, he would place himself at her service.

"For anything else? What do you mean by that?"

"I mean, Princess," René replied with a smile, "that I am ready to let others dance, and then to accompany those ladies who will please us with their song."

"Accompany them?" the princess answered. "On what instrument?"

"On any and all instruments, madame."

"So you are a musician?"

"During the three years I was in captivity, music was my only distraction."

"And a poet?"

"Who has not tried his hand at poetry, for better or for worse?"

"After dinner I shall remind you of what you have just said."

"You will order, madame, and I shall obey."

Everyone joined in the following conversation. But René, who tried never to call attention to himself, said only a few words.

Since they were not part of the army, the ladies had been told that the following morning they would need to retreat to Venice, and the princess first of all.

The princess was the first to resist.

"What good will it do for us to get away from the army?" she said. "Are we not as safe among you as we would be in Venice?"

"Not completely," said René. "And for that reason I would encourage Your Highness not to resist the prince's orders."

He spoke quietly, but his words were solemn enough that they made a great impression on the princess.

"Is there something you are afraid of?" asked the princess worriedly.

"The troops are poorly placed," René answered. "And if Archduke John is not a total novice in the art of warfare, by attacking us separately, he will no doubt win."

"Have you told Eugene that?" she asked.

But he only bowed and said with modesty:

"I have no authority to predict bad news, madame."

"Do you share the opinion that we should leave for Venice?"

"I beg Your Highness to do so, and although my voice and opinion do not weigh heavily in your decision, I beseech you to obey your august husband."

They rose from the table, and the silence showed how great an effect the command to get ready to leave for Venice the next day was having on the women.

For a short while they vaguely listened to the same music that had been playing while they ate, and then they sent the musicians off for their own dinner.

The weather was magnificent, a typical April evening. So someone suggested a walk on the terrace and through the lovely castle gardens.

From the terrace they had a splendid view.

Through the clear evening air they could look out over the plain and see, in the midst of villages and country houses, the Isonzo and the Torre rivers winding like huge serpents whose scales reflected the setting sun. The Torre lay at the base of the city's ramparts, and the Isonzo curved along the Goritz Mountains. To the north and northwest they could see the Tyrol Mountains, and some of them, shrouded by clouds, looked as if they were capped with snow. And finally, in the shadows far to the west, the dark waters of the Tagliamento lay curved like a taut steel bow. Beyond the river flowed countless rushing streams, and whenever a ray of sunlight happened through a mountain pass, they sparkled like polished silver.

The air was so intoxicating, so pure, and so perfumed that they did not go back inside until it was completely dark, if one can ever say that nights get completely dark in Italy.

The drawing room was as bright as day, and as the women came back in they filled the air with perfume, as if they had gathered perfume from the flowers outside and now brought it with them back inside.

The windows were closed, and the piano was opened.

The princess ran her fingers over the keys and played a medley of notes that like magic brought silence to the room.

Everyone gathered around the piano.

"My friends," she said, "this is Monsieur René, who I have been assured is an excellent musician. During dinner he promised to do whatever I ordered. So now I am ordering him to come to the piano and to play and sing something of his own composition."

They all expected that the young officer would wait to be coaxed, like a typical virtuoso, but on the contrary, he went right over to the piano, sat down, and placed both hands on the keys.

And then everyone was able to remark how lovely his hands were. His fingernails were pink, his fingers pale and as slender as a woman's.

On the index finger of his right hand he wore a beautiful sapphire.

Never had greater interest or deeper silence set the stage for a virtuoso's success.

Suddenly from out of the silence rose a pure, mellifluous, and yet very masculine voice. It carried an ineffable note of melancholy, and the words were like lyrics Saint-Hubert would later make popular, although at the time they were completely unknown.

> The mountain drifts off to sleep 'neath the darkening sky;
> The valleys are mute and covered with dew;
> Dust begins to settle on the baked highway.
> Leaves hang motionless and the breeze is soft. . . .
> In a moment, you too will sleep!

It is impossible to describe the effect his short lamentation had on his audience. It was reinforced by his melancholic accompaniment, in which they seemed to hear the last murmurs of the leaves and the wind's final sigh. And then it ended with a cry from the instrument, just like the sound a human heart might make as it breaks, or like a harp string as it snaps.

When the last vibrations from the voice and piano had died away, it took several seconds for those listening to come back to the drawing room's reality. They exploded in applause and shouts of "bravo."

René rose and reached for his calpac.

"But," the princess asked, "you are not leaving already?"

"I promised, madame," said René, "to do what you would order me to. You ordered me to sing, to sing some words and music of my own composition, and I obeyed. But please allow me to say something. A soldier who sings, who accompanies others, or who plays an instrument in order to hear applause has always seemed laughable to me. But any man, soldier or not, who refuses a woman some favor, especially when the woman is a princess, is a coarse, impolite man. By obeying Your Highness, I escaped from the first category. I would prefer not being ridiculous in my own eyes by continuing to sing and play. When I sing or play an instrument, I do so for myself alone, to escape from my own thoughts. Please take pity on my weakness, for it is indeed a weakness, and allow me to withdraw."

And as he pronounced those words, René choked up and his eyes filled with tears. It seemed as if a whole world of painful memories were washing over his soul. The princess was deeply moved, and she stepped aside to let the young officer pass. And as René walked past them, all the ladies and gentlemen present in that brilliant society bowed respectfully.

A NOTE ABOUT PREPARING THE TEXT

It has already been pointed out, both in the Editor's Note and in my Introduction, that Dumas's newly-discovered text required a slow and careful reading. It has been scrupulously based on what was printed in the columns of *Le Moniteur universel*, but many errors, forgotten details, and lacunae demanded correction, strictly respecting Dumas's way of doing things. When he reworked his serials for book publication, he never felt compelled to follow his own text if as he reread he discovered egregious errors.

In a similar spirit, Dumas would often modify the punctuation of his first drafts, and sometimes he would ask someone else to do so. On this point as well, we proceeded as he himself would have done. We corrected mistakes and inconsistencies when they were obvious, and sometimes we adjusted the punctuation where it seemed appropriate to do so.

We also sometimes did not follow the original text when there were obvious misspellings of words and proper nouns.

We decided not to note every such modification. There would have been so many notes that our reading pleasure would have suffered, and Dumas never would have accepted that.